An Affair
of Honor

An Affair
of Honor

A NOVEL BY

Richard Marius

ALFRED A. KNOPF   NEW YORK   2001

THIS IS A BORZOI BOOK
PUBLISHED BY ALFRED A. KNOPF

www.aaknopf.com

Knopf, Borzoi Books, and the colophon
are registered trademarks of Random House, Inc.

Library of Congress Cataloging-in-Publication Data
Marius, Richard.
An affair of honor: a novel / by Richard Marius.
p. cm.
ISBN 0-375-41239-5
1. World War, 1939–1945—Veterans—Fiction.
2. Tennessee, East—Fiction.
3. Mountain life—Fiction. 4. Young men—Fiction. 5. Witnessess—
Fiction. 6. Adultery—Fiction. 7. Murder—Fiction. I. Title.
PS3563.A66 A67 2001
813'.54—dc21   2001032666
Manufactured in the United States of America
First Edition

For my friends
Jean and David Layzer

And the man that committeth adultery with another man's wife, even he that committeth adultery with his neighbour's wife, the adulterer and the adulteress shall surely be put to death.

—LEVITICUS 20:10

But I say unto you, That whosoever looketh on a woman to lust after her hath committed adultery with her already in his heart.

—MATTHEW 5:28

But the fearful, and unbelieving, and the abominable, and murderers, and whoremongers, and sorcerers, and idolaters, and all liars, shall have their part in the lake which burneth with fire and brimstone: which is the second death.

—REVELATION 21:8

An Affair
of Honor

*Y*EARS afterwards when an aging Charles Alexander held his new-born granddaughter in his arms and looked through the window of the hospital room towards distant trees along the Charles, he thought, *If Hope Kirby had not spared my life, this child would never have been born.*

He remembered the pistol pressed to his forehead, the resounding metallic click of the hammer cocked in the dark, the oddly compassionate words: "I'm sorry, boy. I've got to kill you, too."

Charles held his granddaughter—a bundle asleep, tiny and helpless and soft. His son put her in his arms. She breathed in a great sigh. Life. Her fingers and toes delicately sculpted by light. Charles almost cried, but he laughed instead. They all laughed while she slept.

"What is to be will be," the Primitive Baptists said.

And we know that all things work together for good to them that love God, to them who are the called according to his purpose. That was the belief of the Apostle Paul and of Eugenia Alexander, and until he met W. T. Stace and then Hope Kirby it was the gospel of Charles Alexander. Then something else replaced it. When he grew older he could remember himself, the passionate religious person he had been. But he couldn't understand it. All those foolish things piled together in his head! None of it made sense to the later Charles. But there it was in 1953.

All things are as they are for no reason at all, and if they were different, there would be no reason for that either. That was W. T. Stace and Charles Alexander. What was life? One damned thing after another, and if you had a lucky break or two you did something you liked, and so it passed. Charles's might have passed much more quickly than it did had he not had the mercy of Hope Kirby.

*S*ATURDAY night, August 8, 1953.

It had been miserably hot. The temperature broke slightly when the sun sank in the west, turning off the fire that baked the world. The round thermometer with the needle and the dial over the door of Kelly Parmalee's clothing store on the square showed ninety-four degrees at two-thirty in the afternoon. Bourbonvillians noted it. Kelly Parmalee stood outside, looking up, making conversation about his thermometer, laughing, clapping friends on the back. Everybody was Kelly Parmalee's friend. Pencil mustache like Errol Flynn's. Today he wore a canary-yellow blazer and a dark purple necktie and a pin-striped shirt with a button-down collar. Classy dresser, Kelly Parmalee—a walking model for the men's clothes he sold off the rack for the better classes in Bourbonville. You couldn't dislike him. He had a gift for believable flattery.

People wanted the temperature to go to a hundred. A hundred was something to brag about, something to recall proudly later on when anybody complained about the heat of this or that day. You didn't get a hundred every summer in East Tennessee. Lacking a hundred, people talked about hot days, hot places. "Hell, you don't know nothing about heat till you're in the Solomon Islands and the Japs are shooting at you. That's heat, boy."

When six o'clock came, the farmers headed home to milk, and the townspeople went home to eat supper, and sit on their porches afterwards and fan themselves, speaking in murmuring platitudes about this and that. Some of them sat inside and watched television now. Television was new in East Tennessee. Fuzzy, black-and-white, but free once you had put money down on a television set and started making the payments on the installment plan. People were proud of the big aluminum antennas on their roofs.

Red Eason, editor of the *Bourbon County News,* went home early after he wrote a little story about how hot it had been and what people said about the heat. He quoted six people. Names sold news. Put as many names in the paper as you could. Lloyd's wisdom, left behind when Lloyd died. Lloyd drowned in the lake last summer with that girl. She pulled him down, people said. Even with his gimpy leg from Cassino, Lloyd could swim like a shark, but not with the girl's panicky arms around him. Their bodies were pulled out of the lake four days later, puffed up and rotting, starkly white, and naked. People knew what they had been doing.

"I saved his goddamned life at Cassino, and that's how he died," Bones Spradlin said. "Dumb son of a bitch. I always told him his prick would kill him." Bones ran the Sinclair station across Broadway from the newspaper office. People called him Bones because he was obese. Bourbonvillians exercised irony in their nicknames. Bones had pulled Lloyd to safety at Cassino and risked his own life doing it. Now he spoke of it as wasted effort.

Lloyd Brickman—editor in chief, the *Bourbon County News.* Red said, "I keep waiting for Lloyd to walk in the door." That was over a year after Lloyd's death.

He wouldn't take Lloyd's desk. He gave it to Charles. It was in the corner behind the high counter. Myrtle Gillespie had a desk next to Lloyd's, and Red's desk was hidden behind the frosted-glass wall on your right as you walked through the door. When you stood at the counter, you could look down and see Charles and Myrtle at work, and one of them got up to wait on you. Lloyd always liked to greet people, his fedora on the back of his head, his double-breasted suitcoat open in front. Red bow tie. He must have had a hundred red bow ties. And the cigar. He always had a cigar in his mouth, sometimes lit, sometimes not. In movies editors smoked cigars and wore fedoras pushed back on their heads. Men in authority, men in a hurry. So Lloyd. When he was hauled up out of the waters of Fort Bourbon Lake, his naked body white and swollen, his tongue burst through his puffy lips like an insulting gesture against the world.

Myrtle went home after lunch that Saturday. She had a wedding to cover in the evening. Pat Goulding, age twenty-one, and Bettye (pronounced "Betty") Douce, age nineteen. "It's so sweet and such a fine wedding. The groom and the best man and all the groomsmen are going to be in tuxedos with white jackets. They went to Knoxville this morning to rent them from Squiz Green's." At Squiz Green's on Market Square it cost five dollars a night to rent a tux.

The groom was a telephone lineman, and the bride was a graduate of the Tennessee School for Beauty Culture. She worked with Abby Kirby down at the Triangle Beauty Shop on East Broadway. It had been a little hamburger joint, built in the shape of a triangle, but it failed, and Hope Kirby helped his wife buy it, and it became her beauty shop. Business was so good she had to hire Bettye Douce. The wedding was to be held at the white-frame Cumberland Presbyterian Church on A Street. Myrtle had to go home and freshen up before the wedding. Shower. Deodorant. Powder. A beastly hot day for a wedding, the church not air-conditioned.

Charles Alexander loved the newspaper office—reek of printer's ink, rattle of Mergenthalers when Turpin and Cooper clicked away at them during the week, loved the rhythmic crash and bang of the job presses, and loved the complicated reciprocal crashing of the Miehle Horizontal tabloid-sized press that put the paper out on Monday and Thursday afternoons. Now silence. Saturday afternoon and the office quiet and vacant except for him. He sat at Lloyd's desk amid the odorous ghosts of old cigars, using the upright Underwood standard typewriter that Lloyd had hunted-and-pecked on, now (like the '37 Ford) Charles's. Charles could type without looking at the keys.

On Saturday afternoons he wrote his own column for the Monday paper. This week it was about Agnes Ginn. Reminiscences of her father, an infantryman in the Confederate army. She was a neighbor. The week before, he spent an evening with her, drawing out of her faded eyes and wrinkled face the sound of bugles and the crash of musketry, the smell of blood on hot fields, long cooled. A little resentment: the Federal veterans in the neighborhood got pensions; her father did not. Charles wrote, restraining his imagination, feeling an occasional Miniver Cheevy pang that war was not as gallant as it once was. Korea not like the Civil War. Korea over a few days ago, the armistice on July 28. Charles turned twenty next day. No great joy about the end of this war. "Truman's War," people called it. "The Korean Conflict," they called it—not even a war. But people died.

About six he strolled up to the Rexall, greeting people, and bought a hamburger and a fountain Coke in a big paper cup and sat at one of the marble-topped little tables and talked with David Pleasant and Bob Saddler, who were having a bite to eat before going to a revival out at Varner's Cross Roads where the Pleasant Hill Baptist Church had a preacher from Valdosta, Georgia, blazing away with descriptions of the never-ending fires and thirst of hell. A full house every night and shouting and lots of people streaming down to the "altar" to receive the love of God.

Bob Saddler said, "Come on, Charles. Come and climb a spiritual mountain with us." Charles said, "Not tonight, Bob. I have so much work to do." Bob was disappointed. Bob was always climbing spiritual mountains, always disappointed when others were not. He went to revivals with the dedication of an addict. He wore a light-blue suit and a necktie and polished brown shoes, and he put oil on his thick black hair and combed it straight back. He went about wearing a radiant Christian smile, speaking of Jesus as if the two of them had just had a long, friendly talk. He did not have a car, but it did not matter. He walked from house to house knocking on doors and telling people that Jesus loved them.

Charles was an atheist. That is the most enigmatic thing about him throughout this story. His atheism was like black granite hidden deep under luxuriant fields. He could not confess it to anybody, not even to himself. A young preacher boy could not admit to anyone that he doubted the God he had vowed to preach for the rest of his life. He thought if he worked hard enough at it, his faith would come back and atheism would go away like a stray dog. Bob Saddler did not have a doubt in his head. Some people made twirling gestures with their index fingers against their heads when Bob Saddler's name came up. Hardly anyone in Bourbon County had escaped at least one of Bob's enthusiastic lectures on how beautiful heaven would be and how sweet it was to know that through all the starry universe the love of God ruled everything that was. Obviously in heaven birds would sing, Bob said, because the eye of God was on the sparrow, and every pain suffered by people and animals in this mortal world had some purifying purpose that was like the refiner's fire.

Charles came back to the office to edit a pile of reports from stringers scattered out over the county, women who wrote the news of their little communities. Names sell newspapers. The stringers wrote about who was sick and who visited at church and what the preacher preached about and who called on whom and what kids were doing at school and who made the dean's list at Tennessee Wesleyan or Carson-Newman or the University of Tennessee or Tennessee Polytechnic Institute or Middle Tennessee State College or wherever anybody in the neighborhood went to college. Their reports came in scrawled on cheap tablet paper and with uncertain grammar and syntax. Charles typed them up, deftly emending the language, and got them ready for the Mergenthaler operators on Monday morning.

He told his father he would be late. Paul Alexander said he would be missed at supper, but he had the other boys—Stephen and Guy—and he did not protest. Charles made thirty dollars a week. Money talked to Paul Alexander. He never stood in the way of jobs his sons did. Stingy, some people called him. Frugal, Juliet Ledbetter called him jokingly—before she had her stroke and stopped talking altogether.

Paul Alexander would be happy to have Stephen and Guy at home. Guy his father's pet. Guy, cross-eyed with his head sloped in back, a coarse beard that was like sandpaper to shave, and somebody had to shave him every morning because he could not shave himself. Guy the firstborn. Oldest in the family. Stephen was the great musician, younger than Charles. He would play for a square dance that evening at Farragut up in the country. He would eat and run. Charles thought that his mother, Eugenia, would object if she knew Stephen played for dances, even square dances. But she was dead since May. Cancer. The death she feared most. Sometimes when Charles thought of her, he wept, her absence an emptiness in his heart.

His mother thought he would marry Marlene Fieldston—the fine Christian girl who seemed everything Eugenia Alexander could want for the son destined to be a preacher. But Marlene had broken off with him before Eugenia's death. Another absence. Grief and jealousy devoured him in fits sometimes. Tonight in Chattanooga she was probably out with one of the nicely scented, curiously epicene boys in the Bible college she attended down there. She was right to break things off. He had sinned against her. Hormones against God, he thought much later in his life, not only forgiving himself with wry amusement, but mocking who he had been and wondering at his adolescent conviction that the Good Christian with discipline and willpower put aside every temptation to feel a beautiful girl's tits or to run his hands up her lovely legs to her moist and innocent crotch—even if the beautiful girl seemed at first to welcome his mouth and his hands. In August 1953 Charles felt an apathy, an inertia within that he could only fight off by working as hard as he could. Work was his cure. Guilt was his meat and drink. No one had as yet told him about Augustine and Jerome, those passionate warriors for the Almighty who spent their lives fighting sex as though it were Satan himself. Perhaps he would have sat in a tub of cold water and studied Hebrew, as Jerome had, to get his mind off his nether parts. He was twenty years old. That's some sort of excuse.

Tonight Charles had to read Balzac. He was enrolled in the summer school at the university—his last summer. He would graduate in June. This was the third consecutive summer he had gone to school. He intended to save a year of his life that way. Three years in college; three years in seminary. Then the pastorate. Maybe he would be a missionary. He would die a lonely martyr to the faith in some jungle, and Marlene would hear and grieve. He was disciplined, efficient, on his way to great deeds. "God has a special purpose for you, Charles," his mother said. "You're the answer to my prayers."

Unfortunately Charles had lost God along with everything else. The living God, the Almighty Creator of Heaven and Earth, Father of Jesus Christ our Lord, gone in a puff of smoke. All the fault of W. T. Stace. Everything is as it is for no reason at all, and if it were some other way there would be no reason for that either. The sky turned to cement in one moment, and his prayers fell back on him like the collapse of a ceiling. Charles couldn't tell anybody about his loss. Odd when he thought about it. You could go to the fire department for a lost dog or to the police for a lost child, but you couldn't go to anyone and say, "Oh please sir, I've lost my God. Will you help me get Him back?"

His mother and her sisters held that every word of the Bible was true. One error anywhere, and the faith on which they had staked life and death fell. His mother was afraid for him to go to the university. Godless professors will try to steal your faith, she said. Modernists rule the pulpits in the churches. The day of the Antichrist is at hand. The Rapture. The Great Tribulation. The return of Christ at Armageddon. Gabriel descending with a shout, the trumpet blowing its almighty blast across the universe. The millennium, a thousand years of peace when the lion would lie down with the lamb, and a little child would lead them. When his mother and her sisters talked about such things, the hairs on his arms rose up as if the air had been charged with electricity, the sky afire with divine light. He was born to preach that gospel. His mother said so. But then it all dissolved, and he felt himself dissolving with it.

He remembered his mother's hands on his shoulders when he knelt in front of the woman Pentecostal evangelist at Delanco in New Jersey (they were visiting Aunt Bess in Philadelphia at the time). She asked every young person who would be a missionary if God called to come down to the front and kneel, and all parents who would let their children go to come and put their hands on their children's shoulders to signal that they, the parents, would give them up to foreign parts and martyrdom. He went down; Eugenia came behind him. He remembered her hands gently resting on him.

He would still go to the mission field, he thought. Maybe he would get his faith back there.

Meanwhile he had to read Balzac because it was assigned in class. Dr. Stiefel would pose a question on Monday morning. The class would write an answer in French. At home Guy's radio, turned up loud to the Tennessee Barn Dance from WNOX in Knoxville, would blast through the house so that it was almost impossible to keep Homer and Jethro separate from la cousine Bette. His father said that Guy had few pleasures in life. Playing the radio at loud volume was one of them. Guy should have his pleasures. Charles could study at the library. Or at the newspaper office.

Beyond that, his mother's absence shouted at him when he came in the door. Colon cancer. No last words to him. He was in class at the university. It was a Tuesday morning. Paul Alexander insisted on bringing her home from the hospital to die. She lay in a bed by the window where she could watch the birds at her feeder and the birdbath, and she slipped away without a word. When Charles came home that afternoon, he found his father sitting in the kitchen weeping, the body gone, the bed empty with the blankets wadded, and a wet place in the sheet where her bladder had released itself. So death's vulgarity, with no tranquil last words, no angels singing, no skies opening. He dared to wonder if at the last his mother had believed. She had been terrified of cancer, and cancer was the cause of her death. God testing her faith, she said at first with a trembling voice. But what kind of God was this who hid himself and tested faith like a child playing hide-and-seek?

He unclipped his bow tie—the unofficial badge of his job. Crimson, like Lloyd's. "Goddamn little shit, you wear a long tie in here, and you'll get the fucking thing caught in the press, and you will be jerked into the works, and you will have the news of the day stamped on your bloody corpse, and you will ruin a pile of goddamned newsprint that I cannot afford anyway, and I will have to pay overtime to brush and hose your guts and your bones out of the machinery. At least with that burr cut of yours there won't be much hair to catch in the gears." Lloyd looked on Charles's plans for the ministry as a childhood fever. "You'll outgrow it," he said with a harsh laugh. No I won't,

Charles said—but he spoke the words silently in his head, thinking he had outgrown more than Lloyd could know. People like Charles did not talk with unbelievers about their faith. What was the use? You talked with other people who believed what you believed, and so you warmed each other. So Charles later, trying to work himself out, solved the puzzle that remained beyond him. Why had he been so afraid?

So Lloyd. Rotting speedily. Mr. Robinette said he could not embalm a bloated and rotting corpse. Lloyd buried with the coffin sealed. Funerals should be decorous, perfumed affairs; they should not stink of the dead. Was he in hell? Of course not. He was nowhere, and the body he had lived in decomposed in the coffin.

Tonight Charles took off the clip-on and stuck it into his shirt pocket. He sat at Lloyd's desk—his desk now. He edited the stringers quickly. Their reports were monotonously bland. The typewriter clattered like a machine gun under his fingers. By eight-thirty they were done, a stack of neatly typed social notes from Browder's, Salem, Paw Paw Plains, Providence, Varner's Cross Roads, Lee Heights, Martel, Silver Ridge, and other local communities lay beside the typewriter, and a quiet had settled over town. He took out his volume of Balzac, put his feet up on the desk, pushed himself back in the swivel chair, and read.

At midnight he would walk into the square behind the courthouse and drive the '37 Ford station wagon home. "Mother of shit," Bones Spradlin said. "That car gives ugly a bad name. Why in hell don't you put rings in the thing?"

He should put rings in it, Charles thought. A hundred-dollar job. He had a hundred dollars—more than that. He was frugal. But he hated to change things. Lloyd gave him the car as a joke. A used-car dealer unable to pay for advertising bartered the '37 Ford to Lloyd. Lloyd gave it to Charles. Now Charles drove it and felt faithful to Lloyd.

The '37 Ford left a plume of blue smoke behind. Charles usually parked it in the alley back of the newspaper office, but this afternoon there was a funeral at Robinette's Funeral Parlor around the corner, and when he got back from Knoxville, cars lined the streets, and some had pulled up into the alley. Charles parked behind the courthouse, near the railroad tracks. The hours slipped by.

The courthouse clock thundered its message of midnight—the clock Lloyd had campaigned to restore. "Move Bourbonville into Our Times": Lloyd's campaign, waged in the *Bourbon County News,* part of a twelve-point program Lloyd drew up to improve the town. And he got it done. A wiry-looking old man from Connecticut came down on the train carrying a tool-box and a scarred leather suitcase. He looked like one of Santa's elves too old for the North Pole, people said. For three weeks he toiled in the clock tower, taking machinery apart, cleaning, scraping off rust, oiling, taking inventory, telegraphing to some mysterious place up North for replacement parts. Charles climbed up there and watched him, talked to him about clocks, wrote a story. The clock dated from 1840, the old man said. When he finished, he pronounced the clock good as new. Sure enough, the clock, silent and still for forty years, now newly oiled and wound by the great weights that could be moved up and down, began to move again, its wheels and ratchets whirring in commanding regularity. Again it struck the hours with a solemn and reverberant crashing that flew on this night across the sleeping land and stirred Charles to lift his head and think of closing his book. Sunday began.

He kept the Sabbath. He had always kept the Sabbath. No work on Sunday. Country walks. They were all right because you would walk along praising God for the beauty of the earth. Now that his mother was dead, he kept it not only in God's honor but in hers. She was proud of him for doing it, for never going to movies on Sunday, for going to church morning and night. All the things you might expect from a boy who had been told since he was a child that he was destined to do something great for God. "He's a good boy," people in the county said. Not as kooky as Bob Saddler, who walked around with Bible verses printed on cards and tried to give the cards to people so they would memorize the verses. "When you memorize the Bible, you are thinking God's thoughts," Bob Saddler said.

With Marlene gone, Charles intensified (if anything) his religious rules. Redemption, he thought. Making up for his sins. He studied on Saturday nights until midnight, shut his books, and did not open them again until the next midnight, Monday morning. And he tried to think pure thoughts the whole time—a difficult task for a boy who thrilled to see a girl's panty line beneath her skirt.

He found purpose in Marlene's angry and weeping command for him to get out of her life. "You attacked me," Marlene cried, raising her bra over her breasts and pulling her blouse over her shoulders again, weeping wildly and looking at him in the dark with unspeakable horror.

"No I didn't," Charles cried. She was breathing hard, opening her mouth to him, moving her arms to give him access, and when he slipped his hand under her bra and over her beautiful breasts, she exploded in a sigh of pleasure, "Ahhhhhhhhh." He brought the bra down, and both breasts popped out, and he kissed them, and she took a deep, groaning breath and kissed him in the mouth, opening it, letting him slip his tongue in—something he had never done before to anybody, and it made him frantic with desire. He was beside himself. So was she. But when he started to slip his hand up the satiny firmness of her stockinged legs towards her crotch, she exploded suddenly in weeping and pushed him away and began hitting him. He felt covered in shame.

What purpose was there in that? God punished him for his lusts. God proved his own existence, playing hide-and-seek (as Charles later thought of it), and in the car that night crying out a divine "Gotcha!" Charles lost the one girl who was exactly what a minister or a missionary needed for a wife, a pure Christian girl who could sing with a voice so clear that some people said she might crack a crystal chandelier if she tried. He was proud to be seen with her, proud to be known as her boyfriend, proud to claim her, proud when she sang and felt people looking at him, Charles the lucky one, the chosen. He wondered if Marlene had told others. Did the town say: "There goes Charles Alexander. Hypocrite. He prates and prays and preaches about God, and Marlene Fieldston says he almost raped her"? Thank God no one had asked him to preach in months. He thought he would stand up before a congregation and find himself trembling with shame, the congregation staring at him with dagger eyes and contempt.

"I was a self-righteous little twit," he told himself in years to come, angry at what he had been because—because of everything. "And she was . . . She could not help what she was any more than I could help what I was."

On August 8, 1953, there he was with the day sliding over to August 9, to Sunday, the Sabbath, and the clock striking. Time to go home. Guy would be in bed, the house silent. His father might still be up, sitting forlornly at the kitchen table, reading maybe, or maybe staring out into the night, down the long slope and the field to Highway 70, beyond where the cars and trucks passed to and fro between Knoxville and Nashville. Stephen might have come in from playing at the square dance at Farragut. They would all sit and be sad together, and Paul Alexander would start talking about how he had met Eugenia, and the tears would come to his eyes. Maybe his father would want to play something with Stephen at that hour, something to cheer them up. Stephen would get out his guitar, and Paul Alexander would lift his mandolin, and they would play something mournful like "Amazing Grace," and Charles would be left out again because he could not play anything. Born unmusical, son of his father the magician with the mandolin, brother to the best young musician in East Tennessee, people said. Musician Charles was not. His father was disappointed in him but had long since given up trying to make Charles do something he thought he could not do, that he did not want to do. Like learning music.

The time zone is thirty miles west, he thought. It is only eleven o'clock in Crossville.

On the wall facing him the black hands of the electric clock swept beyond midnight, and the white face of the clock stared at him like an accusing eye.

The transom above the door was open, but the door was shut. The tall electric fan and its chrome grille rotated beneath the clock and swept the room with rhythmic gusts of pretended coolness, but his shirt was dark with sweat, and his arms glistened, and beads of sweat ran down his face. Air-conditioning still a novelty in 1953. In Knoxville you pushed through the revolving doors into Miller's Department Store on Gay Street, and the air-conditioning almost knocked you down. The *Bourbon County News* could not afford it. He read on. And then it was 12:45.

He shut the book and got up. First he thought he would not open the drawer where the photographs were. Then he could not help himself. He slid the drawer open and dug down through scattered cigars, all dry and brittle, that Lloyd had left behind. The open drawer exuded the faint ghost of their fading presence. He shifted old invoices, an out-of-date telephone book, an out-of-date city register for Bourbonville. The manila envelope on the bottom contained the photographs of the women.

How did Lloyd do it, get them to pose like that? Jane Whitaker. If the town knew what Charles knew . . . He didn't like to think about it. Shame overcame him as if his lusts had been projected on a huge screen in Cole's Drive-In south of town, and all Bourbon County could eat popcorn and laugh its head off while Charles Alexander, preacher boy, paraded before them as he really was. Charles masturbating before all those people who had heard him preach. He was ridiculous enough to believe with a fervor that seemed both humorous and mad years later that a good Christian boy never lusted for a voluptuous naked woman and that to masturbate was to commit adultery in his heart and so to prepare for himself a reserved spot in the dark fires of an eternal hell. Still he lusted, and still he yielded to the salvation that his hands allowed.

First, Jane Whitaker, laughing into the camera, eight different poses, all of them deliciously naked and to Charles seeming like the picture of water that might be shown to a man dying of thirst. Then the girl who had died with Lloyd in the lake—uncomfortable with her nakedness, looking almost reproachful at the camera even in her weak smile. Four pictures of her. She seemed shy and innocent and embarrassed. Probably why Lloyd liked her. She was not local; she lived in Knoxville, buried there now. Finally, a third woman, someone Charles had never seen, unsmiling and sultry, repudiating Lloyd even while she obeyed him, spreading her legs, lifting her naked breasts up with her hands, showing him how trivial he was. Perhaps a whore. They sat or knelt or lay on the imposing stone back in the print shop where the presses and the Mergenthalers stood cold and silent amid the reek of printer's ink and newsprint. They showed everything.

Earlier in the summer when he wrote the story about the barn bulldozed to make room for the mall, Jane Whitaker came into the office like a tiger raging to eat flesh and attacked him with all the considerable fury of her arsenal of insults. "What do you *mean* writing a ridiculous story like this! What are you *thinking* about, you tubercular little imitation of Mark Twain!" She had the paper with the story wadded in her hands as though it were Charles himself, and she had twisted the paper as if she was ready now to wrench the life out of it and Charles, too.

"Come on now, Jane," Red said, his face flaming almost as crimson as his hair. "What the hell is wrong with that story?"

"This little son of a bitch has written a wailing piece about our bulldozing a barn out at the mall. Why the hell do you give a rat's shit for a barn built in 1820 when we're bringing progress to this goddamned little town?"

Charles said nothing. He sat with his face blazing at her because she had called him a son of a bitch. He wanted Jane Whitaker to know that his dead mother had not been a bitch. He could have killed her. He was afraid to speak a syllable lest he start to cry, and to him crying was a shameful act that could damn a young man's reputation forever and ever.

"It's a beautiful piece," Myrtle yelled at Jane. "It's not about your mall. It's about time passing and losing our history."

"We've had ten or twelve people call up and say how much they liked it," Red said.

"Ten people! Red Eason, sometimes you make me want to throw myself down on the floor and laugh myself to death. Were you born that stupid, or have you worked your way down the ladder all your life?"

Before Red could give her an account of the development of his stupidity, she raged on. "You talk about ten people who like that piece of shit that boy put on the front page. The mall will employ hundreds of people when we're finished with it. Thousands of people will come to visit it every day. Who the hell will remember a goddamned barn built in 1820 that had a roof fallen in and walls that hadn't been whitewashed in a hundred years?"

Charles had been out to the new mall—a word he had never heard until Jane Whitaker and her Italian friend from New York started bandying it around. He had seen the huge yellow bulldozers at work. When one of them had knocked the tottering old barn down, one of the workmen showed him a name and a date carved in an enormous beam (cut from a tree of such unimaginable size that Charles marveled). The date was neatly incised by someone who cared about making things look good. "This barn was finished on June 14, in the year of our Lord 1820." The letters were on top of a beam at the end of the loft, and the roof above them had not decayed, and they looked clear and almost fresh, and Charles wrote a nostalgic piece.

Jane was not appeased by anything Red or Myrtle said. She raged on a good long time, flung the paper she had wadded up on the floor, and stalked out, hurling behind her a parting shot. "Just remember, Red Eason, that the bank can put this little shitty operation of yours out of business with a snap of our fingers. Why the hell does Bourbonville need a newspaper anyway? We get two goddamned papers from Knoxville, and most of the people in this town are too ignorant to read the telephone book."

Charles sat there furious and superior. In the drawer at his side were the photographs of Jane Whitaker naked. Charles, preacher boy bound for seminary and the pulpit, gleefully imagined taking one of those photos to Jane Whitaker, telling her he had dozens of them and that he was going to spread them all over the county if she did not fuck him. She would have to do it, he thought. She would have to accept him on his terms. The possibilities seemed so real that his mouth watered, and his heart beat fast and his ungovernable prick got as hard as wood. But he sat in outraged and furious silence while she stormed at him, and when she had slammed the door behind her, he lowered his head and continued working without a word.

Myrtle said in a tone of injury, "I thought it was a wonderful story, Charles."

He knew the photographs by heart. Every detail. He tried to resist. He opened the envelope, gateway to hell. He could not stop himself. He picked up the envelope and went back to the little shack of a room just off the press room—combination toilet and darkroom. His darkroom now that Lloyd had died, leaving the camera to the newspaper as a legacy. He put a photograph of Jane Whitaker carefully on the washbasin and unzipped his trousers over the toilet, and he was carried away into bliss.

In a few moments he came out, ashamed and sad. He should burn the photographs. Burn them all. He could not burn them. They were his friends, the only women he could be intimate with. He slipped back into the office and sat heavily down at the desk, feeling the wet in his shorts, and he heard the train blow up the line and, the faint, augmenting, rhythmic grumble of the diesel-electric engine rolling towards Bourbonville. It would be approaching the underpass beyond the cotton mill now. He had lost Marlene, and the pictures did not satisfy. He could not get through the thin emulsion that held the images of nakedness. The women were not there. He put them back in the envelope, carefully replaced the envelope in the drawer, snatched up his books as though in flight from the devil, and made nimbly for the door.

He locked the door behind him, and for a moment he stood unhappily in the street. The heat was thick and unyielding. In the trees the summer insects chorused on in their grand and immemorial monotony of courtship or possession or whatever it was. The town spread around him, restlessly asleep on its ridge and its plain, the heat pressing down and not a whisper of air moving. In front of him the courthouse rose amid its trees that made a canopy over the spacious square. Off in the dark to the east the river rolled with vast and silent power through the heat-stricken earth.

In the daytime when he drove back from Knoxville, back from the university, back from a world where God seemed lost beyond the range of prayer in a desert where miracles happened no more, the courthouse, ruby bricks fashioned by slaves long ago, rose before him to say that here, in this world, he was still safe, and God ruled, not to be denied, but how could God love a hypocritical preacher boy who masturbated over pictures of Lloyd's naked women? He thought of Jane Whitaker in her great house on the hill in the grove of trees at Martel. Desire flooded back. His prick, that insatiable organ, hardened again.

Beyond the courthouse to one side the depot stood. The semaphore signal cranked down to a forty-five-degree angle. A night telegrapher used to be on duty at the depot at this hour. No more. Everything done by radio now. Telegraphers phased out. Jack Mooney, the last night telegrapher, would have been comatose drunk by now anyway. Beyond, in the middle distance, the great muddy river below the dam flowed south amid its tree-lined banks. He imagined snakes coiled awaiting their prey, mice and chipmunks. Nature was a devouring beast. No, God's creation. This is my Father's world. An old hymn.

He heard the horn on the locomotive blowing for the crossing by the cotton mill. The steam engines were gone with their melodious and melancholy whistles flinging their ghostly tones across the night. The diesel horn made his spine vibrate. In a moment the lead diesel would come hurtling around the bend. He hurried towards the back of the courthouse to see it, the apparition of light and power bound magnificently to steel rails that like streaks of magical light guided all that immense force through the sleeping town. The grass smelled of dew. The heat surrounded him, ponderous and humid. The katydids in the trees roared out their rising and falling chorus of life in the summer dark.

Now no one can speak of the murders without remembering him.

*H*OPE KIRBY set a trap for the two of them, and his brothers helped him. He went fishing with Joye and Love Saturday nights when the season was warm and the weather good. They owned a little boat with a Johnson five-horse outboard, and they launched at twilight, set up somewhere in a cove, and fished until morning on Sunday. Two Saturday nights before the murders, they went on maneuvers. That's what Joye called it. They had all been in the war.

It was peaceful that time of evening in summer. The days were hot and sticky. At night the air cooled, and it was pleasant on the water, and the air was still. You could see the shine on the lake, smooth like dark glass on the windless evenings. Joye sat in back and steered; Love sat in the middle; Hope sat up front next to the coal-oil lantern. People at the dock saw them go out. Hope left Abby at home by herself. Just in the summer, he told himself. They did things together on Saturday nights in cold weather. He did anything she wanted, but in summer he fished with his brothers.

Daylight failed, and the stars shone hazily in the darkening sky. Just after midnight, they blew out the lantern and rowed ashore at a spit of land four miles up the lake from the dam. Love pulled at the oars, making not a sound. They had stuffed old shirts around the stems of the oar locks. Hope stepped out under overhanging trees where the darkness was profound, and he walked swiftly over to a dirt road. In a few minutes M.L. came along in his pickup and slowed for Hope to jump inside and crouch on the floorboards. M.L. drove out onto the old pike and down to Bourbonville three or four miles away, coming to the depot on a back street. The houses slept darkly except for an occasional naked bulb gleaming feebly alone by a door or a ramshackle garage. Behind a warehouse looming up like a mountainous shadow near the railroad tracks, Hope jumped out, and M.L. sped away.

Dim streetlights at the corners of the courthouse square shed faint illumination on the grass and the empty streets. The emptiness of a town asleep was spectral. Hope looked for any sign of life and saw none. He saw the faint white light gleaming beyond the square in the newspaper office—fluorescent tubes in a ceiling, never turned off. He could see the high wooden counter behind the plate-glass window fronting onto the square, but he could not see behind the counter, and he did not imagine that anyone was there. On that night, no one was.

Moving like a spirit, he slipped across the empty street to the courthouse and sat down behind the boxwoods against the wall on the side facing the railroad. The bricks were warm from the heat of the day, and he sweated, and the roughness of the bricks bit through his shirt. In the near distance beyond the cotton mill the night freight pounded down the tracks exactly on time. The horn on the diesel called harshly, vibrating the air and his bones, the train thundering down the straight from Martel. Hope missed the old steam whistles, the elongated hooting in the night, ghostly and sweetly sad.

At one o'clock the courthouse clock crashed overhead. While the reverberation of the single stroke died away, he heard the car coming and knew it was Abby's Plymouth. He could see her face when she parked. It was a white blur, and she was like a ghost in the car waiting for something, and he knew what it was, and he did not want it to come. The horn on the locomotive roared again, louder, at the crossing by the cotton mill now, and when the engine rounded the bend, the noise filled the night. The train raced exuberantly towards the depot and went by like an earthquake, hurling its noise, rising and falling, against the courthouse, which threw it back again. Just then a man slipped around the courthouse. He moved swiftly, looking from side to side.

Everybody knew Kelly Parmalee and his Errol Flynn mustache. He ran to the car and jumped in on the shotgun side and grabbed Hope's wife and began to kiss her. She kissed him back, her white arm showing in the window as she hugged his neck. In a moment Kelly Parmalee got out like a dog in heat and ran around the car and helped her out. She had already opened the door. She was in a hurry, too. He rushed ahead, leading her by the hand, over to his store on the side of the square. He was like a cowboy in the movies, looking this way and that, thinking nobody saw him, while the audience sat watching. He took a key out of his pocket and unlocked the door, and they went inside. He pushed her ahead of him. He ducked back and looked around the square, and he shut the door.

It was a long train. Boxcars, gondolas, flatcars, coal cars, tank cars, coming and coming. It went by, filling the night with noise, blowing for the crossing at the Car Works, and then the caboose whipped by, red lantern hanging off the back, and it was gone, and the noise faded towards Chattanooga, and Hope heard the horn shout at the crossing at Bucktown, and the night was left to heat and silence and the loud and monotonous carousing of the katydids in the oaks. He waited. Off towards the river, frogs faintly chorused in the marshy banks below the dam. Hope tried not to think of what was happening behind the closed door of Kelly Parmalee's store. The clock struck two. Still the door stayed shut.

Ten minutes after two Kelly stuck his head out first, looking around, and she came after him. She combed her long hair and looked cross. Her hair was honey blond, and at night when she sat by her mirror brushing it, the light gleamed softly in its folds. Kelly said something impatiently to her, trying to hurry her up. She followed him slowly, combing her hair, and when they passed Hope Kirby, she said in a peevish voice, "Can't you stay all night?"

"No, no. Of course not. What do you think this is?"

If they had looked, they could have seen Hope Kirby, watching them through the boxwood. They were so close that he could have said "Abby" and she would have heard him. They did not expect anybody hiding to watch them; Kelly worried about the accidental Bourbonvillian harmlessly abroad in the steaming night and likely to gossip in daylight. He did not think of someone inspecting the ground, preparing to kill him. She put her arms around Kelly and begged him softly not to go, so that he had to pull away from her, and he hurried off. She stood sulkily still, looking after him. Hope Kirby thought how pretty she was, her face now in a magical glow from the old street lamps. He started to say something, but he did not. She tossed her blond hair in a pout of anger and got in the car and drove away, gunning the engine, going home to sleep alone in her bed and to go to church tomorrow.

"*YOU GOT* to kill her," his father said. "It's a point of honor now."

They sat on Roy Kirby's front porch in the Sunday-afternoon shade, and beyond the grove of trees where his father's small house stood, the thick heat of July pressed itself on the earth, and below them the muddy river seemed still and glistened in the broiling sun. Heat waves roared silently up from the fields. The brothers listened to their father without looking at each other. Roy Kirby's face was like flint, his eyes blue tiles set in his head. For a while they didn't speak. Joye wiped his face with a bandanna and said in a low voice, "The dark of the moon. What does the almanac say about the dark of the moon?"

The almanac said the dark of the moon would be August 8.

Hope Kirby prayed that morning for rain. The brothers did not fish in the rain. It was a beautiful day, hot and clear. Abby kissed him warmly good-bye when he gathered up his things to go fishing in the evening. "You have a good time," she said. "Bring me a nice catfish for breakfast. I'll cook it real good. Why are you looking at me like that?"

He stared at her and almost told her. "I hain't looking at you no way," he said.

She laughed and squeezed him, and Joye drove up in the driveway with Love.

So at one in the morning Hope Kirby was sitting behind the boxwoods again. Only this time he had a .38 revolver in his hand. He saw the old car sitting behind the courthouse, the '37 Ford. It looked like a wreck, something that had quit, and the driver couldn't get it started again and left it for junk. The wooden sides were faded. Somebody would tow it off, and it would end in a junkyard covered with vines, rotting away, snakes coiled lazily on the seats in the spring sun pouring through bluish glass. Whose car was it? The Alexander boy's. The middle one. He must not have been able to get it started in the afternoon. No importance.

KELLY PARMALEE never meant any harm. He felt beloved in Bourbonville, and if he was unfaithful to his wife and made wives unfaithful to their husbands, he felt no guilt about any of it because the practice of adultery made him happy and gave him a feeling of accomplishment and success. The women loved it; he loved it. He was discreet. Nobody except the women knew. He did not intend to hurt them or shame their husbands. He liked their husbands. He persuaded himself that it was almost a tribute to the husband's good taste that he, Kelly Parmalee, appreciated the man's wife enough to fuck her. He did not imagine he would be killed for his pleasures. Women with their legs and bottoms and breasts and lips and tongues and all the rest of it, including the positions they could assume, their wetness, their groanings, were reality; death was an abstraction that became real to old people when they could not enjoy sex anymore. Everybody ought to have a sport, he thought. Keeps you fit.

You can see photographs of him still if you hunt them up in Bourbonville. He had relatives. And friends. Lots of friends with little box cameras. "Kodaks," people called the photos, black-and-white pictures with white borders, snapped with cameras that required the sun behind the back of the person who took the picture, and the person whose picture was taken had to be still. But you always posed when you had your picture taken in those days. You wanted to show who you really were. Who you wanted to be. You can see photos of Kelly Parmalee as a child in diapers, of Kelly Parmalee in a straw hat when he graduated from high school, Kelly Parmalee with his first mustache, drawn like a pencil line across his upper lip, photographs of him sitting behind the wheel of a convertible with this smart young woman or that. Kelly Parmalee at his wedding—grinning, grinning, grinning—often wearing a hat at a rakish angle. All the photographs were black-and-white. Color prints were too expensive then.

You can find photos of him presiding over the Civitan Club when he was president. He was chairman of the school board, although he had no children and had never been to college, but there he was, sitting with his big grin in the center of the table where the other members of the school board sat in suits and solemn expressions conveying to everyone the impression that they were serious men doing serious business—choosing textbooks, pure literature for the pure children of Bourbon County, setting salaries for teachers, deciding on the petty things that committees can always find to occupy their time and magnify their importance.

In the midst of them, Kelly Parmalee looked like a man having a good time—and he was. Several times the *Bourbon County News* ran photographs of Kelly Parmalee and Kenneth McNeil presenting a check on behalf of the

Civitan Club to Mackie Simms Robinson, comfortably potbellied, gravel-voiced, nonsmoking, virtuous Baptist superintendent of the Bourbon County school system. One of those checks was to buy new uniforms for the girls' basketball team at BCHS. Kelly Parmalee loved the smooth legs of those girls but he did not try to seduce any of them, not while they were still in high school. Afterwards? He managed to make it with a couple of them. They seemed grateful.

You might laugh at the photographs of Kelly Parmalee in blackface when he wore a zoot suit in the Civitan Minstrel Show. The Civitans did a minstrel every year. They thought it hilarious to dress up like "darkies" and make jokes, some of them even sexual, because everybody knew that Negroes were funny when they talked about sex, and they had sex like rabbits. One of the car dealers, Cas McDougal, put grapefruits in the bosom of the big flowered dress he wore in the shows, and when he bobbled the grapefruits with his hands, audiences went wild. Kelly was always Mr. Interlocutor, and people laughed and clapped when he asked questions and got from other black-faced Civitan members the wonderful dim-witted answers that Bourbon Countians expected from colored folk.

His wife? Ah well! Sophia—she pronounced it "Soph-EYE-a"—inherited her clothing store and her looks from her father. She was five years older than Kelly, and she did not take care of herself. She looked sixty. She refused to wear makeup, not even a trace of rouge, and sometimes Kelly thought she looked like a corpse. He was happy for her neglect of herself. It excused him. What was a virile man to do, married to a plain woman who did not care how she looked? "When you're old, you're old," she said with a self-righteous finality as if she had recognized a truth others refused to acknowledge. "God made us what we are, and if we don't accept it, we're saying He made a mistake."

Her hair turned chalky gray early, but she seemed proud of it as though it were, as the cliché held, her "crowning glory," a treasure to be preserved and protected and polished and exhibited as a badge of the essential thing she was. She washed it every Saturday night, and she brushed it every night before bed—one hundred strokes, rhythmically given. Every morning she coiled it like a crown in a hard braid around her head and stuck a steel pin in the back of it. Sometimes Kelly wondered if people thought he had married his aunt.

He hated Saturdays. They opened the store at half past seven. When he went to work at the store for Sophia's father, they opened early for farmers who came to town on Saturday as soon as they milked the cows. By 1953 the farmers were dying off, and their children were moving away, and their fields were going back to weeds and saplings and briars. The Saturday crowds thinned, but Bourbonvillians came downtown to talk with each other in good weather and sometimes to shop. Sophia was faithful to her father's ways. Early Saturday morning Kelly stood at the open door to their store smiling, smiling, smiling, shaking hands with the men, ducking his head to the women in a snappy little bow. Sophia said he smiled better than he did anything else. He smiled until he thought his face would crack. And he could talk about anything. His gift, eagerly given to anybody who wanted it and to anybody who didn't, for that matter. She took the money and rang it up with a great clang at the cash register.

To farmers they sold bib overalls and brogans with stiff soles and high tops, the unlined clodhopper shoe that would never know shine. He sold an occasional shirt for church and sometimes a coarse woolen suit or a cheap necktie for the ceremonial occasions of weddings and funerals. One suit to an adult life was the rule for most farmers, and for many not even that. Many of Kelly Parmalee's best sales lay rotting in coffins all over Bourbon County. More and more of their business was to people like themselves. Jackets and ties and dresses and shoes for men and women who did not walk in furrows. Kelly carried a stylish line for the Rotarians, the Civitans, and the Lions.

They stayed open until seven o'clock at night—just like in the 1930s. By six the streets were clearing. By seven the first picture show in the double feature of the Grand Theatre had started. The Gem down the street was showing its Saturday western in the stale air of the unventilated auditorium where a rat might crawl over your shoe in the dark looking for fallen popcorn. It cost a dime less to see a movie at the Gem than it did at the Grand. Sometimes the Gem showed dirty movies under the color of education. A great crowd turned out to see the classic of a girl gone wrong: *She Should Have Said No.* Except for the audiences in the movie houses and a few people hanging out at the Rexall drugstore opposite the courthouse on the square, people cleared out, and those who lived in town went home and listened to the radio. More and more of them were watching television. Knoxville had two stations now.

When the last customer left, Kelly locked the glass doors and let his face collapse. Sophia came out from behind the cash register with her envelopes, her records, and they got into the Buick and went home. They were childless. Sophia said the doctor told her she should never have children. She did not tell Kelly that until they were married. An unmarried lady did not speak about her nether parts or their functional possibilities to any male, not even to her future husband.

She cooked supper, and they ate. They had little to say to each other. All their conversations arrived from the outside, pecuniary subjects knocking cautiously at the front door, asking timidly to enter, and having entered and done their business, slipping away swiftly, hastening out the back, leaving a marriage possessed by silence. Kelly Parmalee used to see couples laughing together, and he'd think, *That must be nice.* He never laughed with Sophia. Since he saw other women only to take off their clothes and to have sex with them, he could not sit with them in public places and laugh and talk. He and Sophia did not look at each other while they ate. They perhaps did not have the courage to face the mistake that each of them had made. He told her once that they ought to drink a little wine with their meals to jolly them up. She said that if he ever brought wine into her house, she would divorce him.

After the meal, they washed and dried the dishes. He washed, shirtsleeves rolled above his elbows, necktie still in place, wearing a long apron, scrubbing away with a dish mop in a dishpan, suds to his elbows. Sophia dried, putting everything neatly away, the clinking of silver and the subdued ringing of crockery and the slosh of water, kitchen sounds, routine like a bell tolling a funeral. When they got married, he tried to make jovial talk with Sophia as though he had been at the Civitan Club with friends. Sophia was not the jovial kind. She answered in monosyllables, managing to convey that she thought Kelly was the most empty-headed man on earth. Now they washed and dried the dishes in silence, the radio playing bland music softly. By eight-thirty they sat down with the adding machine and counted up the receipts of the week and the expenses and calculated the sales tax and figured out the profits. Numbers were Sophia's passion. To her everything was definite. Worthwhile things could be counted. Saturday nights they counted her favorite thing—money.

When Abby Burdine had been married five years to Hope Kirby, Kelly Parmalee sold her a pair of shoes. He stroked her feet. He thought women's feet were beautiful. Abby had perfectly shaped feet and skin that glowed, and he stroked them almost absentmindedly, appreciating them. She gasped. He looked up, and she had a glazed expression in her eyes. It took him aback. She breathed fast and hard, eyes half shut, and when he responded by running his hands faster over her naked feet, she groaned, and he looked around in terror to see if anyone had heard. He sold her a lot of shoes after that.

He and Sophia finished their bookkeeping by ten-thirty or eleven. Sophia then went upstairs to take her weekly bath and brush her hair and to put on the nightgown that covered her from her neck to her toes, and she went to bed. They slept in single beds with a decent space between them as if they had regulated their sleeping arrangements to fit the Hollywood codes of the day. Not even Blondie and Dagwood slept in the same bed before the camera. Kelly sat downstairs with a magazine and a pack of cigarettes. Sophia's father had smoked; so she permitted Kelly to smoke, too. By midnight she was snoring like a water buffalo, and he could hear the harsh sound drifting down the stairwell. He continued to finger the magazines, to run his eyes down the pages, to look at the pictures without seeing them, and to smoke one cigarette after another until 12:45. Then he stood up, folded the magazine, and went to the front door. He held his breath and listened to Sophia's snoring upstairs. It came and went in mechanical regularity. He slipped out of the house and strolled down to the square smoking a Lucky Strike. If anybody came along, he could say he was out for a walk before bed.

Abby allowed him liberties that set him on fire. Sometimes she scared hell out of him. She loved risks. She was a member of the Church of God of the Union Assembly, and they beat even the Baptists in defining commonplace sins that would damn a soul in hell forever. Like many religious women, she did not go halfway into sin. She fell into it like a dolphin deciding to swim. If you were going to hell anyway, why hold anything back?

Abby told him once she'd be thrilled if they could have sex on the roof of his store under the stars. Kelly imagined passengers in airplanes looking down on them. He wouldn't do it. She said that if he could persuade Sophia to go on a trip without him, she'd do it with him in his own bed. The thought terrified Kelly. Sophia would never go on a trip because she had no one to visit, and if some accident or miracle took her away from home and if he brought Abby into the house, Sophia would return, sniff the air like an old hound, look at him, see everything that had happened as if it had been filmed in Technicolor as vivid as *Gone with the Wind*, and Sophia would start screaming, and the house would fall into splinters, and the world would dissolve in fire and ash.

Abby said they ought to slip into the window of Sullivan's Furniture Store on the corner of Kingston Street and do it on one of the big beds in the plate-glass window. "We could do it at three in the morning," she said. "Nobody would see us. Well, maybe a trucker driving through town half-asleep might see us, but he wouldn't believe his own eyes. He'd think, *I dreamed that. I was asleep at the wheel, and I dreamed I saw a naked man and a naked woman fucking in that shop window back there.* He'd probably turn the truck over making a U-turn down Broadway. The truck would block traffic, and the trucker would try to explain, and people would think he was crazy—until they looked at the bed and saw the wet spot on the sheet. We could read about it in the papers and laugh. Wouldn't that be fun?"

She laughed with her good, simple heart at the idea. Kelly grinned, but he shuddered within.

"I don't think that would be a wise idea," he said in an adjudicating voice as if he had given the matter serious thought.

"I don't see why not," Abby said. "I've always been good. Look where it's got me. I'm sick and tired of doing what I'm supposed to do. Let's run off to California, then. What can they do to stop us? We can both get a divorce in Nevada along the way. I've heard that getting a divorce in Nevada is as easy as getting your hair cut in Tennessee. Maybe we can get two for the price of one."

It was serious business. Kelly knew how serious it was after they'd gone through April and May and June, and he thought it might be time to wrap this one up. He would discover a bad conscience. He would say he couldn't bear to face Sophia knowing he was cheating on her. A love affair is an illusion, he thought. A man and a woman make a romance novel out of each other, and when it's over they shut the book and go on to something else. With religious women, a declaration of bad conscience did the trick. Religious women had consciences themselves.

But Abby talked about California, and he began to speculate. He speculated into July. And then into August. She was more passionate than any other woman he had known. On the rug in the shoe department when she lay on her naked back and drew up her knees and spread her thighs to him, he felt the purest joy. She told him she loved him. Her breath was warm and sweet. She was slender with voluptuous breasts and a warmth in her eyes that melted something inside him he did not even know was frozen, and he fell in love with her.

He was older—a good twenty years older than she was. But what did that matter? She turned back the calendar for him and brought out of his closet of memory old dreams that he had stacked out of sight, dreams so ridiculous that he would have been ashamed in his firm middle age to acknowledge that he had once cleaned and polished them with hope and believed that they were real. Abby spoke of California as though it were the promised land. It was as far away from Bourbonville as any place she could imagine.

This was the modern age, he thought. They could take a train to California, stop in Nevada, get their divorces, and leave everything else behind. In California you were a nobody unless you had been divorced two or three times. Abby could set herself up in the beauty line. He would find something to do—maybe clerk in a Sears, Roebuck store. He'd be free from Sophia, and when he thought of freedom and being with Abby, of being able to put his arm around her in broad daylight on the public street, any time he wanted, having her warm body, her immaculate skin next to him, of hearing her laughter—it took his breath away. He was willing to give up everything for her. He thought of palm trees. Palm trees and flowers and the ocean. He took *National Geographic*. Sometimes before Abby came along he sat down in his living room turning the pages of the magazine, and he imagined lying under palm trees on a beach somewhere with a beautiful naked woman who loved him and wanted him, and in the midst of looking at slick pictures in *National Geographic,* he almost cried with grief and loss and futility.

Perhaps he had never been in love at all before. Suddenly there it was, and he felt not only desire but affection and tenderness. Bourbonville, his safe and sure world, even the Civitan Club, became small and ugly. He began to dream, to see himself as something he had never imagined, something that dared to be real, and he accepted the fact of his love. He began to be happy. They began to make plans. He felt a resurrection coming. He even imagined himself standing up to Sophia, saying in a calm, measured voice, "I do not love you. I never loved you. You are a selfish, evil, grasping woman who knows nothing of life, and I am going to leave you because you are dead, and I am still alive."

On August 9, 1953, he walked down to the square at one o'clock in the morning, and he felt jaunty and bold, and he thought that if anybody saw him, he would not try to hide what he was doing but would boast of it, and he would be free forever.

THE TRAIN called again, an electrical howl in the night, mournful and warning at once, a rhythmic rumble and attenuated clangor, and Charles turned the corner of the courthouse in time to see the headlight of the locomotive blaze around the bend and the contained fury of it bearing down on him in a crescendo of sound. Hurrying towards the tracks, Charles thought he heard another noise, flat and quick, but he paid no attention. The train bore down on Bourbonville, its horn shouting at the crossing behind the square, the engineer amusing himself by trying to wake everybody in town, impressing his signature on the great and anonymous dark.

A long train. Four diesel electric locomotives coupled in series, the cars trailing behind. The thick foliage of the oaks hid the moon and cast an almost impenetrable darkness immediately around him. To his left he heard a car door slam. His eyes fixed on the train, he caught motion out of the corner of his eye, and he saw a shadow flying towards him. He turned. The shadow became a man. In the feeble light, Charles could tell with a terrifying intuition that the man was running for his life. A canary-yellow jacket. A necktie.

Behind him raced another shadow. The faint illumination falling from the clock face and the street lamps reflected on something in the second man's hand that Charles did not recognize as a pistol until it fired. The spurt of flame pierced the dark. An instant before the flame, Kelly Parmalee cried out. "Char—" he said.

The pistol spoke. Kelly Parmalee pitched forward, staggering, Charles's name stuck like mud in his open mouth—light gleaming on white teeth. The train rolled by, roaring like a cannonade, cars hurtling towards Chattanooga, rectangular shadows speeding through the night. Kelly Parmalee sank heavily to his knees. He seemed surprised. Not hurt, surprised. The shot from the revolver had hit him low in the back. He was feeling behind his back, looking up at Charles now from five feet away, and Charles's eyes had adjusted to the dark, and he could see dimly the expression of astonishment on Kelly Parmalee's narrow face, a shadowed, colorless face above his yellow jacket and necktie, dull in the dull light. In a shift of gray shapes, a transmogrification of light, Hope Philip Kirby was standing over Kelly Parmalee—Hope Kirby, tall, rawboned, muscular, wearing a black shirt and black trousers, hair cropped down close to his head in the military style he had worn since he came home from the war seven years before. Hope Kirby held the revolver in his right hand.

Kelly Parmalee looked up at him, mouth open, trying to speak, eyes bright in the murk of night. Hope Kirby put the muzzle of the pistol in Kelly Parmalee's mouth. "Do you know why I'm a-killing you?" he said. His accent was pure Sevier County, a mountain twang. Charles thought Kelly Parmalee nodded. It was hard to tell. Maybe he was trying to spit the pistol barrel out of his mouth. Whatever it was, his head moved. Hope Kirby fired—a flat crash, absorbed by the roar of the train. Ahead, the whistle of the locomotive hooted for the crossing at the Car Works. Kelly Parmalee's body flew back as though the shot had been a fist. Charles could see fire flash like a spark out the hole in the back of his head—a glimmer of indistinct light on colored liquids, life exploding, and the darkness came down over Kelly's eyes. Kelly Parmalee sprawled witless and crumpled on the ground, legs twisted under him, face up, dull eyes sightless and open towards the leafy cover of the oaks.

Hope Kirby turned on Charles Alexander, pistol lifted to his face, voice amazed. "What air you DOING here?" Hope Kirby had to shout above the sound of the train. Charles could not speak. Hope Kirby struck him angrily in the middle of his forehead with the muzzle of the pistol. "I said, what air you DOING here?"

"I was studying. Reading. In the newspaper office." Charles shook all over, and his voice quavered. He understood; this was the miracle he had been seeking; he did not think it would be like this. God's punishment was also God's miracle. Marlene. The photographs. The Sabbath. God had judged him. God lived.

"Studying at one o'clock in the morning? *Studying?*" Hope Kirby yelled at him, an amazed face pressed down, the pistol firm against Charles's forehead. Charles nodded, a speechless twitch of his head. "I didn't know ary a man was down here," Hope Kirby said, his voice dropping. Charles could scarcely make out the words above the sound of the train.

"Please," Charles said.

"You're the manager's boy. You brought John Sevier home oncet. Twicet, warn't hit?"

"Yes," Charles said.

"Yes."

"Your brother's the loony."

"Yes," Charles said.

"He's a loony. Like John Sevier." Hope Kirby was in his face, the pistol thrust at his forehead.

"Yes. No, he was born that way." Abruptly the train was gone; the caboose flashed by; they heard the roar dwindle, receding towards Chattanooga, sucking all sound out of Bourbonville. The whistle blew for the crossing at Bucktown beyond the city limits. Hope Kirby lowered the pistol. "You hain't supposed to be here. Lord! I didn't think nobody was going to be out here."

Hope Kirby's voice became a murmur. He looked around, perplexed and agitated. The streets and the empty tracks were spectral and silent. The train went farther away, sound diminishing.

He looked at Charles, took a deep, resigned breath. "Well, I got to kill you, too. I'm sorry, boy. But you seen me kill them two. You know who I am. I'm truly sorry. Hit won't hurt none. I'll make hit quick. Say your prayers." He raised the pistol to Charles's forehead and cocked it. It made a loud *tock* in the summer night, and Charles felt the hard, round thrust of the barrel against his skull.

THE MINISTER at First Baptist Church heard the shots. He was sitting at the kitchen table in the shabby old house at the corner of A Street and Second Avenue that the church used as a parsonage. He was trying to work out something eloquent and truthful to say to his congregation next morning. On that evening he was still trying to hide from himself his desperate conviction that he had made a catastrophic mistake. Bourbonville. Why had he thought this town could be a refuge?

He heard the train coming without listening to it, heard the single deep crash of the clock in the courthouse at one in the morning, and he heard the shots roll up the hill above the low rumble of the train passing in the night. His windows open, the curtains parted, and in the thick and miserable heat, not a breath stirred. He wanted a drink, but he had quit drinking, and he accepted the unremitting desire for a drink the way other veterans accepted chronic pain from wounds that would never fully heal.

It is an odd thing about sound: two things making a noise close to each other seem to meld together, one sound. You think the sound of machinery, for example, muffles the sound of a voice. It depends. If you stand next to a tractor with the engine running and you're talking to somebody, it's hard to hear what the other person is saying. You must shout above the sound of the engine. But sounds have different wavelengths. The sound of the engine has a different frequency from the sound of a voice. A voice in a field next to a tractor can be as distinct as a cry at midnight when you are at some distance, and the sound of the machine dies out, and the voice goes on. That's how it was with the pistol and the train. The train was one kind of sound, the pistol another, and the sharp crack of the pistol carried at a different pitch from the low and prolonged rumble of the train.

He sat by the open window and heard the shots—one, an interval, another, a longer interval, a third shot. He walked outside, curious, not alarmed. He looked down A Street towards the square, and in the humid misery of the night, he listened for something else, but he heard only the train, rolling through town and declining towards Chattanooga. *Some drunk shooting at the stars,* he thought. Still . . . He stood in the street. All around him the town slept. Bourbonville was his monastery. He had seen monasteries in France—museums now, guarded by the state as curious monuments to a remote age of faith. He thought of monks enclosed in their pious routines, rising at prime, singing and praying and meditating their way through the circular hours of the day, sleeping at night in the peace of God, complete in their obedience to God's vicar on earth, their abbot, harvesting grain in the golden fields under the sun, doing manual labor in perfect and serene obscurity, washing their temptations away in unending ritual, sleeping in the peace of knowing what they would do every day for the rest of their lives, dying to be buried in the anonymous earth. *How many of them were queers?*

He waited. The train passed into silence. The town slept on its sloping ridge under the hazy stars of a humid summer night, men and women avoiding each other atop the sweat-soaked sheets on their beds and haunted in their darkness with the hellish thoughts of what they might have been or else self-satisfied with accomplishments in their tiny world whose horizon was no wider than the brim of a cup. He stood in the empty street feeling the town in its placid dullness, like a sleeping cow, oblivious to pistol shots crackling up the hill to where he worked on a sermon that would disappoint his people on the morrow when he preached it. He listened. In a while he heard the starter of a car grind, heard the engine catch, and the car drive swiftly away.

"Ah well," he said. He went back into his kitchen and sat down at the kitchen table before the breezeless window and wrote again, dismissing curiosity. "Help me, God," he said. He was speaking about his sermon.

*H*UGH BEDFORD was dozing, neither asleep nor awake, and the shots brought him bolt upright in bed, his heart hammering behind his ribs so hard that the pale rectangle of his bedroom window shook in his vision. The heat was filthy, and he was fat. Obese. He began to shake. He couldn't stop shaking, and when he shook, the bed rattled. He *knew* he was in Bourbonville on a summer night in 1953. This was not 1945. This was not Italy. The Germans were not out in the streets. They were not shooting his men. The Germans were not about to climb the stairs to where he hid. There were not even any Italians in Bourbonville. The only foreigner in the county was Paul Alexander. He was out in the country. Not a man to kill anybody. And Dr. Goldstein, of course. But everybody knew he didn't even own a gun.

He got out of bed and found the whiskey in the dark. He drank from the bottle, pulling long and deep. The consoling warmth ran down his throat, widened in his gut. He did not turn on the light. He did not want a sniper to shoot him through the window. He could find all his bottles in the dark. He had them hidden throughout the house in case somebody broke in to steal something. He could not run out of whiskey. Running out of whiskey would be like losing your boat in the middle of an ocean at night, and you'd be there in the dark sea with the horizon a limitless circle around your head, and you'd thrash and kick and know you would drown as the lights of the boat receded in indifferent motion. That's what it was like not to have whiskey in the house. The world would not care, but he would die.

He sat on the side of the bed drinking whiskey in long pulls, and the shakes went away. The obscure shapes of his bedroom furniture asserted themselves. They were chairs and not monstrous signs of malice and danger. There was nothing to hurt him in Bourbonville. No Italians. No Colonel Sperling Winrod. The name pushing like a razor into his recollection made him drink more. *I almost killed the bastard. If they had given me ten more seconds, I would have broken his neck.* The fire of whiskey in his gullet was peace to his soul.

The house popped and creaked. He listened and heard nothing.

"Goddamn them!" he said aloud. "Goddamn them."

*A*T ABOUT the time that Hope Kirby put the muzzle of his revolver to Charles's forehead and cocked it, Jane Whitaker was slipping naked beneath the sheets in her house near the Martel Methodist Church and smiling to herself. Boxwood, the house was called, a glorious antebellum place built of brick and girded in front and down the eastern side with a gallery. Boxwood was two stories high, but it sat in such stately repose amid its thick grove of trees so luxuriously green that on coming upon the place along the Old Knoxville Pike, anyone was likely to see first only the trees and then like an afterthought the stately outline of the house built by Jane's great-grandfather as a monument to his place in the world.

Every spare penny she made went into keeping it glorious, from the magnificent carriage house in back to the wall of neatly trimmed boxwoods that rose high along each side of the curving driveway that ran down to the pike.

She had had a wonderful evening. Joseph Ignazio brought to her possibilities she had only dreamed of for years. When he spoke to her in his confident, swift sentences, she saw opening a future where she would be both free and rich and where at last she would be completely in charge of her destiny. She would drive a Lincoln, she thought. All rich people drove Cadillacs. She would drive a Lincoln. Black. She would fill Boxwood with antiques.

They met at the Highland Grill. It was Knoxville's best restaurant, but to Joseph it was not much. "It will all change," he said, looking around with energetic distaste as he drank his martini out of a coffee cup in the windowless restaurant on the basement level where the Highland Grill served customers carefully scrutinized to be certain that no law-enforcement men were among them. Joseph Ignazio had to show his New York driver's license to the colored doorman before he was admitted, and when he and Jane ordered drinks, he had to show it again.

"You recognize, sir, that it is against the law to serve drinks in Tennessee," the maître d' said in a confidential voice exuding the sentiment that by allowing Joseph Ignazio and Jane Whitaker to have drinks at all, he was granting them a privilege for which they should be passionately grateful and demonstrate their passion by their tip. When his martini was brought on the rocks in a nice china coffee cup rather than straight up in a real martini glass, Joseph Ignazio was nearly beside himself. But he recovered quickly.

"I am going to change this whole end of the state," he declared, not bothering to keep his voice down so only Jane could hear it. "In ten years you will have liquor by the drink here in Knoxville, and at long last you will have good restaurants. And it will all be because of me. Take a good look at Knoxville. What you see won't be here long."

At nearby tables other diners looked around in the staid atmosphere of a restaurant where polite people did not raise their voices, and they gazed with mild irritation on the source of this loud impertinence. But they were also curious. Ignazio's accent both annoyed and intimidated, and some diners ceased their own conversation so they could hear him better.

Ignazio was bland-looking with a soft, boyish face and a mouth that tended to hang slightly open in a grin that seemed fixed and automatic as if he had long ago decided that he knew far more than other people did and yet wanted to be considered one of them because he knew he needed them as much as they needed him. He was, without ever having read Machiavelli, fully in agreement with his illustrious countryman's understanding of human nature. The leader must see things clearly, and with theatrical ruthlessness grasp at fortune with such skill that his people would see him as their champion even as he used them for his own ends.

Joseph Ignazio's end at the moment was the mall. Already near Dixie Lee Junction the bulldozers were leveling a hundred-acre rectangle. "What we will have," Joseph Ignazio said, "is a rural, quiet shopping area that will create all around us some of the advantages of New York without the turmoil and the dirt."

Ignazio carried on enthusiastically. His two favorite subjects were the mall and himself. "Later on when journalists write about me, and when somebody writes my biography, they will all say my great revelation was born by an accident of military intelligence," Ignazio said. "My father came from Italy, you see. We spoke Italian at home.

"Now, I was in college at CCNY when the Japs attacked Pearl Harbor, and I went down to the recruiting station to volunteer on Monday morning. I'll tell you something about immigrants, about their children. They are the most patriotic Americans. We know what we have in this country. God bless America. That's what I say, God bless America. America gives us the chance to get rich. All we have to do is work for it."

Ignazio was smart. He did not think it immodest to recognize what was obvious, and he conveyed to Jane as he did to everyone whom he decided to take into his confidence the information of how high he had scored on the intelligence tests given to him when he enlisted. "They knew right away that I was officer material," he said. "And they knew that I spoke Italian fluently. So, when Eisenhower went into North Africa, I was in military intelligence. I interrogated Italian POWs. We had a portable radio station, and I did broadcasts on it, telling the Italians that the Germans were their real enemies, that I was Italian, that all Italians had relatives in the United States, that no Italian worth his mandolin would go to Germany. I was very creative. Lots and lots of Italians surrendered and told us they had done it because they heard my broadcasts. Then Italy jumped out of the war altogether and joined our side. I don't say I was responsible for that. But I helped it along. Yes indeed. I helped it along."

He nodded with tranquil pride over his drink, his grin widening because he was amused at winning a game. "I won't say I was the best translator in the army, but I was quick. I could catch the little innuendos, the tones. I could tell when somebody was lying to me. That's a very important gift, and I have it. I can tell by the tone of voice if you are lying to me—in Italian or in English."

"I promise not to lie to you in Italian," Jane said, laughing.

"You don't lie to anybody about anything," Ignazio said. He gave her a knowing smile. "I can tell. I'm a very good judge of people. That is why we are here."

"You say the nicest things," she said, feeling genuinely complimented. She hoped she seemed sophisticated enough for him. When she visited New York she went to plays and musicals and museums and ate alone in horribly expensive restaurants. She always asked waiters to advise her on what was good because she often had no idea what the menu meant, and of course she knew nothing about wines, and she was afraid of seeming like the hick she felt herself to be. She looked on waiters as mentors who could prepare her to go rich into the great world when the time came, and she was not embarrassed to question them. Often they gave her honest advice. In her three visits she thought that she was beginning to develop some sophistication, but she was not sure. Now as she listened to Ignazio's easy chronicle of his own deeds, she wanted with every particle of her being for him to think her worthy. These were not especially sexual thoughts, although with Jane sexual thoughts were close to the surface of most of her conversations with men. Ignazio was three years younger than she was, and she took it as a matter of course that women her age did not marry men three years younger than themselves. Men that age could find something prettier, sexier, more promising.

Jane knew her disadvantages. She was not fat, but she was somewhat Olympian, taller than Ignazio by a good two inches, and although in her most critical examinations of herself in the mirror she knew she was still attractive, she could also see that her skin had lost the blooming radiance and smoothness of real youth. No, she had no designs on Ignazio. But her most fervent desire was to think herself able to maneuver smoothly in his high-powered world, and for that, she yearned for him to certify her with his approval.

Ignazio seemed to approve of her very much. They had steak for dinner. Ignazio said he had already discovered that the only safe thing to order in Tennessee was steak. Here in the Highland Grill he ordered his steak very rare so it would not be cooked to death, and it actually arrived still pink in the middle. "This is not rare meat where I come from," he said, with a significant waving of his fork in the direction of his plate. But he ate it anyway, and Jane thought hers was good even if it was much less thoroughly cooked than she preferred it. She could not quite avoid associating red steak with blood, and she did not like the sight of blood, but she tried not to think of such things as she ate, keeping her focus instead on Joseph Ignazio's lively brown eyes.

"So then 1945 came, and the war was almost over, and everything was confused, and all of a sudden I got orders to go to Crete."

"Crete," Jane said.

"It's a long Greek island in the Mediterranean, south of the Greek mainland. It looks a lot like Sicily once you're on the shore. There's one small difference."

"What's that?" Jane said, intuitively knowing that Ignazio wanted her to ask the question.

He grinned broadly and leaned forward and spoke in a stage whisper as though uttering the punch line of a joke. "The difference is that Greeks live on Crete. Italians live on Sicily."

"Yes," she said, her puzzlement showing.

"Greeks speak Greek!" Ignazio said impatiently. "I don't speak Greek. I speak Italian."

"Oh yes! Yes! Of course." Jane felt her face redden. This man knew so much. She admired people who spoke foreign languages. The only people she knew who spoke a foreign language were Paul Alexander, manager of the car works, and Dr. Goldstein, the German Jew. They both spoke English with a heavy accent.

"So there I was with nothing to do. I had my orders to stay in Heraklion. That's the biggest city in Crete, and do you know what?"

"What?" Jane said.

Ignazio looked impatient again, and Jane understood that she should not have interrupted him after this rhetorical question. He went on eagerly. "Near Heraklion is one of the oldest cities in the Mediterranean—Knossos."

Jane felt desperate. She had never heard of Knossos and could not imagine why Ignazio was so excited about it, and yet he sat back now with that expectant grin, a morsel of (to Jane) shockingly red steak on his fork. "How interesting!" Jane said, feeling at once that she had failed miserably to say something a sophisticated New Yorker would have tossed off.

Ignazio put the morsel in his mouth and chewed and grinned triumphantly at the same time so that for a very fleeting moment he gave an impression of a predator animal pleased because he had just caught whatever it was he was eating.

"Knossos," he said, when he had swallowed, "is perhaps four thousand years old. An Englishman, an archaeologist, dug it up forty or fifty years ago. He reconstructed it the way he thinks it existed when it was in its prime, before it was destroyed by a volcano or an earthquake or something. And there it is. And do you know what is most important about Knossos?"

"No," Jane said, shaking her hands as if she had been accused of something and had to deny it although she knew she was guilty.

"It was the first mall."

"Oh," Jane said, looking at him in confused eagerness. "Really."

"I knew I would surprise you. Here's the thing. Knossos is all under one roof." He paused for effect, his mouth a huge expanse of teeth, and his coal-black hair seeming to tremble electrically over his unusually white complexion. He wore an elegant pin-striped suit, but he had tucked his napkin into his collar so that it hung down over his necktie like a bib. He was the only person in the restaurant who affixed his napkin that way, and Jane thought it showed remarkable good sense because it kept any food from dropping on his elegant silk necktie. But she also was embarrassed by it. She thought it kept people from understanding how intelligent and forward-looking Joseph was.

Very slowly Jane understood. Joseph Ignazio had already explained to her his concept of the mall. This he had done when he sat at her desk in January, the first time she ever saw him. He came in with a dream, and as he talked that day, a presence elegant in a beautiful suit and a sky-blue silk necktie, the dream swelled on her desk and in the bank. The mall of his vision was the future—a hundred or two hundred acres with free parking for thousands of cars, three or four dozen establishments all under one roof, greenery, fountains, walkways, theaters, department stores, small shops, restaurants that served liquor, but no bars. "You want people to come to the mall to buy things, to be entertained. You want them to walk, to look into shop windows, to feel safe, to be warm in winter, cool in summer. It's the future, Miss Whitaker. The future, and it is here. I'm talking about something bigger than the biggest cathedral in Europe. I'm talking about something with more structural steel in it than the Eiffel Tower. I'm talking about the new center of our civilization."

That Saturday night in the Highland Grill, Joseph Ignazio told Jane Whitaker of how his idea had grown in him. "I went to Knossos every day. I could never get enough of it. Sometimes I was there by myself, and I thought I could hear the voices of the Cretans from all those centuries ago. The sea is very close, and you can stand outside and hear the surf. It's a very quiet, whispering surf. It's the Mediterranean, not the Atlantic. But in that surf I could hear voices, and I knew they were telling me something. I couldn't understand it at first, but I knew they were telling me something important, something that would make me famous, something that might make me rich, too. And now, Miss Whitaker, I know it is going to make me both."

His father had friends in New York. Italian friends. They had connections. They were interested. Joseph Ignazio also knew they were dangerous. They were willing to make an investment, prime the pump, see what happened, take a quiet percentage. But they would not finance the whole thing. "Your father is a very loyal son of Sicily," one of them told him, a cigar-smoking gentleman who sat in an Italian restaurant with young Joseph Ignazio while two bodyguards with bulging coats stood nearby. "I think of your father when his son comes to me for help. But I think of myself and my own sons when I think of the future. I am willing to advance fifty grand at ten percent interest. If you are smart, you can use that investment of mine to get other money from down there. Do we understand each other?"

In the parking lot after the meal, Joseph kissed Jane on both cheeks. She wanted him to kiss her on the mouth. He did not oblige her that way. He tipped his beautiful Panama hat and helped her into her car, saying just as he was about to close the door, "I think this is the start of a beautiful friendship."

It was a line he had heard in a movie. At the moment he couldn't remember which one. But he knew it was romantic and conclusive, and Jane nodded her head quickly and said with unmistakable passion, "Yes. Yes."

She was not thinking of sex. She was thinking of money. She drove home along Northshore Drive, a quiet old road that led alongside the TVA lake backed up from the Fort Bourbon Dam at Bourbonville. It became the Old Knoxville Pike. The moon was down, but she wanted to look out at the water and see the stars and dream. She drove slowly, knowing she had had a lot to drink, but there was almost no other traffic. The world on its rolling hills slept soundly, and in the lake here and there the steady gleam of coal-oil lanterns showed where fishermen sat peacefully through the night, dangling their baited lines into the water.

Lloyd had drowned there, she thought. If he had not forsaken her, he would not have drowned. She stifled a sob. "It served the bastard right," she said sharply to no one. The tears rushed to her eyes, and she wiped them away with the back of a hand.

Then she thought of Joseph Ignazio and money again, and she was pacified. Boxwood loomed before her in the dark, stately on its low hill. A train came down, its pleasant thunder filling the night. Suddenly she felt very happy. Trains made her happy. They made her think of going places. She was going to go places nobody had ever dreamed she would see. You had to live for this world, she thought. In the end, you would be a name on a gravestone, and all your chances would be gone. She turned into her driveway, and the smell of the walls of boxwoods came in through the open windows. The night insects roared their chorus across the summer countryside. She parked in the carriage house where the light she had left on blazed against the quiet solitude. Some people told her they would not live alone out in the country. But this was Bourbon County, and nothing here had ever made her afraid. In her luxurious bedroom, she undressed quickly, felt her naked breasts tentatively, pulled the sheet over her, and by twenty minutes after one, she was fast asleep.

S *HERIFF* Coondog Myers stood on the edge of the square at a little after two in the morning with one hand on the big revolver in its holster at his hip. He stood behind one of the big oaks, peering around the trunk, surveying the courthouse lawn. The street lamps were dim; the moon was down; the oaks in the square entwined their branches above his head and deepened the gloom he tried to penetrate; and it was hot enough to make a snake sweat. He could make out a big, long-tailed dog, like a shadow, licking at something off under the trees. The sheriff took out his flashlight when he decided nobody was waiting to shoot him, and he found the bodies.

The dog was licking the blood out of Kelly Parmalee's mouth where Kelly had fallen back with his legs bent under him at the knees. He had been shot in the mouth, and the sheriff's light revealed the dark puddle of blood and brains in the grass under the back of Kelly's head, and he knew the bullet had gone all the way through. He drove the dog away and went looking for Abby. She sat still in her car, her head laid back amid her long blond hair and her eyes open, looking up at the bullet hole in the windshield, a hole surrounded by spidery cracks in the blue safety glass that caught the light. She seemed surprised at what she saw and could not stop looking at it, but she could not see anything. Flies buzzed around the hole in her forehead. The sheriff thought that flies didn't have respect for anybody. He had seen boys get their heads blown off on Omaha Beach. He thought his head would be blown away, too. He had seen boys die in the snow in the Ardennes, but by the night he found the bodies in the courthouse square, he had become unaccustomed to seeing people shot to hell. He felt like puking.

He was angry because he knew the Kirby boys had planned it all so slick that they were bound to get off, and part of the plan had been to trick him. He took it personally. Later he decided that had been his mistake, maybe the biggest mistake of his life. But that night he was mad about it. There he had been, sitting with his sock feet on his desk in his office at the new jail, when the telephone rang about twelve-thirty in the morning. His deputies had brought in three drunks, all regulars, and the sheriff locked them up, and he was listening to the radio, WSM out of Nashville, the Grand Ole Opry, and he was thinking it was amazing that a radio station could carry that far and be so clear, and the telephone rang.

He figured afterwards that whoever it was had a rag over the mouthpiece or did something else to disguise his voice. "Sheriff," the voice whispered, "there's a fight out at the Yellow Dog. You better come quick. It's bad. Real bad. Knives. Blood on the floor." A click, and the dial tone came back. One of the deputies was in the south end of the county near the river where there was a bunch of honky-tonks at the bridge. The other deputy was across the river in Greenback, where a barn caught fire that night. The Yellow Dog was over on Highway 70 beyond Varner's Cross Roads. So it was up to the sheriff to go see what was going on.

He took his dogs, Ugly and Duke, and loaded them into the car and drove out to the Yellow Dog. It wasn't more than a long shed covered over with tar paper and fitted out with siding so it looked like yellow brick if you didn't look too close and if it was dark. It had four or five neon beer signs in the windows in case somebody might mistake it for a schoolhouse or a church and wander in by mistake. Cars and pickups filled the gravel parking lot, and when he got out of his car, he could hear a hillbilly band thumping and shrilling inside, and somebody was singing in a nasal, whining voice.

The Yellow Dog was a blood bucket. Drunks got in fights there and stabbed and shot each other and sometimes cried and begged for forgiveness of the people they had tried to kill. When he went in, the air was smoky with cigarettes, and he could smell the stale beer of years that had soaked down into the wood. In a cleared space in front of the band, couples in blue jeans and plaid shirts were dancing the two-step, and the singer was wailing a Hank Williams song about jumping into a dry river. Nobody was lying in a puddle of blood. The sheriff leaned up against the bar and looked around. He was not happy. Nobody looked at him.

"You had a fight out here tonight, Hoot?" the sheriff said to the bartender.

"Hell no, Sheriff," Hoot said. "It's been like church."

"Nobody stabbed and laying on the floor?"

Hoot tried to look aghast. "Here? At my place? Ah, come on, Sheriff. I don't let stuff like that happen here. You know me."

"I know you. That's why I'm asking."

"Nothing, Sheriff. Nothing a-tall. See for yourself."

"Shit," the sheriff said. "Somebody—" He started to tell Hoot about the telephone call and decided it would be wasted breath. You wouldn't find Hoot Mullins calling the sheriff for a joke.

"Have a beer, Sheriff," Hoot said. "On the house."

"I don't drink on the job," the sheriff said. "If I did, I'd have some of that whiskey you got hid under the bar."

"Ah Sheriff," Hoot said. He went away, walking down the bar with a rag like he'd just seen a spot he had to wipe up before it burned a hole in his property.

The sheriff smoked a cigarette and felt mad and looked around for somebody to haul off to jail so the trip would not have been in vain. But, he reflected, people in bars vote too, and a sheriff can't go around arresting them for no reason. Besides, with the sheriff looking as mad as a wet tomcat, nobody was going to get out of line. They went on talking and dancing and drinking beer and whatever else they had in those glasses and cups, and they made out like the sheriff was a stuffed fish on the wall.

When he got back to the jail, it was getting on towards two in the morning, and the county seemed asleep. In the jail the telephone was ringing. He picked it up, and a woman's annoyed and high-strung voice screeched into his ear. "Sheriff, this is Hazel Moore. I heard shooting tonight. I know it was shooting. Just past one. It sounded like it was in the square." She went on like a pail of water dumped down a well. She repeated herself several times.

"All right, Miz Moore. All right. I'll go down and take a look." Hazel was a widow. The sheriff thought her husband, Harley, had died to get relief. Hazel had complaints. If you asked how she was, you didn't get a report, you got a whole medical education. She had to tell you how the doctor told her she had the worst case of whatever it was he'd ever seen. Now she said that lying awake on account of her bursitis, she'd heard gunshots in the middle of town.

"Miz Moore," the sheriff said as she was giving him an unabridged account of the history of her bursitis from the moment she'd had her first symptom three years before in church, "if you'll let me off this here telephone, I'll go on down there and see if anything's happened." When he hung up, she was in mid-sentence, and the silence was delicious. The courthouse clock struck two.

He left his dogs in the jail to look after things and walked down the blacktop road towards the square, moving carefully so as not to scare off anybody who might be hanging around there with a gun. He had his hand on his own pistol, but he left it in its holster. If you walk up on somebody with your gun out, he might see you first and shoot you dead. Everything was quiet. He crossed the railroad tracks into the back of the square, and he stood there a few minutes behind a tree, and he saw the mongrel licking something in the dark, and he found Kelly Parmalee. He spotted Abby's car over under the street lamp, and he said, "Damn!" She was a pretty little thing, or she had been. She didn't look pretty with a bullet hole in her forehead and the flies buzzing on it.

That damned cur began to creep back towards Kelly's body. The sheriff squatted on his heels and snicked the mutt over with his tongue. The sheriff said, "Good dog. Good dog." The dog came groveling up, belly low, flopping that long tail and looking stupid and hopeful as dogs do when they think they will get something to eat, and the sheriff took his billy club out of its loop on his belt and beat the dog's brains out with one lick. He was glad Ugly and Duke didn't see him do that. They might not have trusted him afterwards.

He went back to the jail and put out a call for his deputies on the radio. He took his cheap camera out of his desk and drove back down to the square and took flash photographs of the corpses. He pulled Abby's panties up before he made her picture. They were down around her knees. The sheriff thought Kelly might have been feeling her when Hope shot her. He didn't tell anybody that part. He felt awful, looking at the crotch of a dead woman. Thin brown hair. Not thick like some the sheriff had seen. Paris whores had big bushes. He pulled the panties up and pulled her skirt down before he took her picture. He figured out what had happened. Hope had shot Abby first. Kelly had jumped out of the car and tried to run away. Hope ran him down and shot him dead.

When his deputies rolled up, he'd taken three rolls of film, and he'd written down notes in his careful, methodical way. He sent one of the deputies over to wake Mr. Robinette up to tell him to come haul off the bodies. He put another on duty until Mr. Robinette came, and he drove up to tell Sophia Parmalee that her husband was dead. She howled with grief, uncomprehending, stricken, and old. He went next door and woke up the Clagets and got Mrs. Claget to come over and sit with Sophia. Then he went over to tell Abby's father and mother. That was awful, and he got away fast. By then the sky was pale in the east, and he could see the mountains running along the white of the coming day like black waves gone still. One of the deputies took the dead dog off and threw it in the river. The sheriff went back to the jail and made fresh coffee and sat down to think.

He knew that Hope Kirby had killed both of them. You can't keep secrets in a town like Bourbonville. If a man gets in the habit of walking down the street to the courthouse square every Saturday after midnight and taking somebody else's wife into his store while her husband's out fishing on the lake, somebody will see you after a while. Bourbonville had started to whisper. Whispering in a town like Bourbonville starts like a snake in dry grass, slithering along, making a little cracking sound, making the grass wave. The people that ought to know—in this case Hope Kirby and Sophia Parmalee—are the last to hear it. Hope had found out somehow, and he killed his wife and her boyfriend.

But how to prove it? He sat rared back in his chair listening to the drunks snore in their cells, and he drank coffee slowly and thought, and he got a hunch. The sun was turning the mountains red by then, and he was still angry because Hope and his brothers had tricked him. The telephone call. Making him run off to the Yellow Dog. Made him look like a fool to Hoot and the rest of them. His hunch was that he remembered Charles Alexander, studying in the newspaper office. Hope couldn't have seen him behind that tall counter. Yes, the sheriff knew Charles didn't study on Sunday. The boy's mother had died back in the spring. Cancer. She had been religious, even more religious than most people in Bourbon County, and that's saying a lot. It was one of the biggest funerals the sheriff could remember, and he remembered Paul Alexander and his three sons sitting by the grave under the green-striped awning. The idiot son was crying and beating a pencil against his knuckles. His name was Guy. Paul Alexander pronounced it "Ghee." Paul Alexander sat stone-silent, like a man who had been hit on the head with a club and didn't know where he was. Charles and Stephen didn't look much better.

Charles studied in the newspaper office on Saturday nights. Something he started doing after his mother died. Busted up with his girlfriend just before his mother died. Everybody expected them to get married. People said Charles and Marlene were made for each other. Yes, Marlene's father was off in the head, and mean, too. But the girl was sweet and religious and had a singing voice like nothing ever heard in Bourbonville except on the radio. A marriage made in heaven, people said. But now it wouldn't happen. A minor mystery. The sheriff puzzled it over and tossed it aside. He had other things to think about. Maybe Charles Alexander had seen something. At least talking to him gave the sheriff something to do.

So the sheriff decided he could use a cup of somebody else's coffee, and he drove up to Dixie Lee Junction with his dogs. The day was coming on strong by then. The sun was almost up behind the mountains, and the ridge tops flamed with the coming dawn. A breeze stirred, the freshet of air that tells a lie almost every summer morning in East Tennessee, the lie being that the day won't be too bad.

The sheriff was bone-tired, and even before the day turned hot, he was sweating. He needed to lose weight, but if you sit around in a patrol car or a jailhouse, and if you eat a lot of hamburgers and drink milkshakes because you don't have anything else to do, you get fat. His back hurt. He could feel the German bullet that the X-rays showed lying up against his thighbone just under his left hip so that sometimes when he sat down, the bullet smacked against the bone. Whenever he complained to Dr. Bulkely about the bullet, Old Buck said nobody could do anything about it because if a surgeon cut down that deep, the sheriff might die. Old Buck advised vitamins. He always advised vitamins. He had been on vitamins all his life, and he got old anyway.

Paul Alexander was in his garden, the garden that lay up the long slope behind the apple and peach orchard. He was standing out there holding a coffee cup. The sun was an orange disk rising over the woods that lay across the highway from the Alexander place, and the grassy slope where Paul Alexander stood sparkled suddenly with dew. Millions of drops of dew.

*A*LL *NIGHT* long Charles Alexander walked back and forth barefoot in his room. He shut the door so Stephen next door or his father downstairs could not hear him. There was a cross-breeze when the door was open, but with the door shut and his big eastern window open on the torrid night his room was like a furnace. He walked, and he sweated, and he stank, and he fought against the desire to vomit. He had vomited on the way home, once alongside the silent highway, again when he turned into the driveway.

His brain teemed with the events of the night and with images of death. Hope Kirby stood before him, the pistol cocked, and Charles knew that death was a second away. He was not a Christian going to meet God; he was a trembling gob of flesh shaking from head to toe. There was no God, and death was death. He wept for his life and shook with terror. Hope Kirby relented. "If you promise me never to tell, I will let you go."

Charles promised in floods of tears. God, he was ashamed of them! Now he would lie to cover up murder. He saw Kelly Parmalee die. He saw Abby's corpse. He would lie. He had left the newspaper office at midnight, driven a little while with the air blowing in the car window to ward off a dull headache. Charles had headaches. Sometimes they drove him to bed in pain. Doctors could not do anything about them. A good excuse now, cover for a lie that covered murder.

In the silence of the night he heard his mother's anguished voice. All liars will have their part in the lake of fire that burns forever and ever. A lie that covered up murder made the liar part of the crime. The last hope that Charles Alexander had to hold on to his mother's faith was gone. That was part of the thing, you see. In his crushing discovery of the truth taught by W. T. Stace, Charles still had hope. He would fend it off, bury it in forgetfulness. He would pray, preach, sing hymns, seek the company of devout Christians like Clifford Finewood and Bob Saddler, and finally he would get himself shelter in the seminary, where everybody believed, and he would be well again. If he lied now . . .

Maybe he would not have to lie. On an ordinary Saturday night, when he went home at midnight, he would have missed it all. Routine questioning perhaps. Then all over. Nothing left to tell. He would be silent, noncommittal, express conventional horror at the deed, write the story for the paper, and let his own story vanish into silence.

Back and forth he walked, exhausted beyond the telling but unable to sleep. Maybe he had it backwards. Maybe W. T. Stace was wrong. Maybe all this was God's purpose, a warning. Charles Alexander was born with normal intelligence after his mother's fervent prayers. When Guy was born, Dr. Youngblood had told her she should never have any more children. Any other child might also be a Mongoloid subnormal. That is what they called children like Guy in those days.

When Eugenia discovered she was pregnant with Charles, his coming unleashed an agony of prayer night and day. Eugenia and her sisters and her friends gathered on their knees to pray for the child's health. "If you were normal, I promised God you would belong to him. You have your brother's brain. It is to be used for the Lord." Someone told her that working crossword puzzles during pregnancy would ensure a bright child. Eugenia worked crossword puzzles whenever she was not sitting with her open Bible "claiming the promises," as she called it.

What could be clearer? All the events of this horrible night were God's doing, a warning. Get back on track. Be the child your mother promised to God. What God gives, God can take away. You can die so quickly.

It was the logic of divinity. It had to be like that. For all things work together for good for them that love God. Charles walked the floor. He had to keep his promise to Hope Kirby. Hope Kirby had now put his own life in Charles's hands. The day paled in the east, and as Charles stood wearily and almost comatose, the eastern horizon turned darkly red and then orange and then pink, and the sun rose, scattering a world of dew in the grass. He heard noises in the kitchen. His father and Jiggs came out of the house. Paul Alexander held a coffee cup and walked towards his garden. On the highway in the middle distance, a patrol car marked "Sheriff" slowed for the driveway and turned in. Charles threw himself on the bed in an agony of despair and exhaustion. What could he do?

*P*AUL ALEXANDER had the neatest garden the sheriff had ever seen. Every line seemed drawn by a ruler, and the dirt between his rows of vegetables was as clean as if the weeds had been plucked out of it by a troop of fairy gardeners.

He left his dogs in the car and walked over to Paul Alexander and told him what had happened. Paul Alexander listened thoughtfully and did not say anything for a little while. He was not known for talking a lot. "Terrible.

Terrible," he said finally. A quiet, accented voice. Still foreign after more than thirty years in America. "You're not from here," people said when they heard him for the first time, a mixture of surprise and accusation in their voices.

The sheriff said, "I remember your boy, Mr. Alexander. Was he down at the paper studying last night?"

"Charles," Paul Alexander said.

"I know he studies down there till midnight Saturdays," the sheriff said, uncomfortably.

"Yes," Paul Alexander said.

"Maybe Hope Kirby didn't know it," the sheriff said.

"The Kirby boys all work for me, you know," Paul Alexander said. "Except the unfortunate son."

"John Sevier," the sheriff said.

"Yes, the one the Japanese beat senseless."

"I'm glad we dropped the atom bomb on the little yellow rats," the sheriff said. "I wish we'd got it done in time to use on the Nazis."

"You want to speak to Charles."

"I don't reckon he saw nothing," the sheriff said. "The killings happened after twelve-thirty. That's when I got that telephone call about the Yellow Dog."

"What time do you think the murders occurred?"

"I reckon on about one o'clock. That's when Hazel Moore said she heard the shots. It was when the freight passed."

"It passes through Bourbonville at a little past one if it is on time," Paul Alexander said.

"You see, the old bitch was right," the sheriff said.

"My son did not come in until about quarter to two."

The sheriff's heart jumped. "Did he say anything to you about—"

"I did not speak to him," Paul Alexander said. "I was in bed. I suppose he thought I was asleep."

"Damn," the sheriff said. He took his hat off and looked into it as if trying to find something. He was not angry anymore. He thought that perhaps he did not want to find what he was seeking.

"Could I talk to him?" the sheriff said.

"Of course," Paul Alexander said. "Come in. I have fresh coffee."

"That's an offer I won't refuse," the sheriff said.

"He may not have seen anything."

"I hope he didn't," the sheriff said. "I reckon it's best if he didn't see nothing. I got to ask."

"Of course," Paul Alexander said.

The sheriff thought all of a sudden that he should say, "Hell, Mr. Alexander. I'm sure he didn't see nothing." He could have got back into his car, and that might have been the end of it. That's what he thought later on when it was too late. Afterwards he thought that was the moment when it all began to go wrong, and it kept on going wrong until the end.

*H*OPE KIRBY knew the end of the story while he watched the red taillights of the '37 Ford disappear around the courthouse. *There hain't nothing I can do about hit,* he thought. He stood a moment feeling death and hearing the katydids and the barking of a dog far up the ridge where Bourbonville slept fitfully in the humid dark. He moved quietly towards the river. His shirt was soaked with sweat. He thought of going back to the car and looking one last time at Abby, but he did not. In the instant when he slapped the pistol to the windshield, he had seen where Kelly Parmalee's hand was, and he did not want to remember that, and he did not want to see his wife's shattered face.

He did not take the blacktop road by the jailhouse, but went east along the railroad tracks, and when he was safely out of town, he set off across lots, passing in swift silence over the low hills that rose between the railroad and the lake. He had to roll under a couple of fences, and he went carefully, holding to the line of woods as much as he could, not worrying much about being seen because the moon was down. Even the stars seemed hazy in the hot night air. Now and then a dog barked from one of the houses built against the hills, but he kept moving. He knew how to be quiet. It was a lesson he learned in the Philippines. He had the pistol in his belt under his shirt. Even if some unlikely soul should see him at this hour of the morning, the pistol would be hidden.

He hadn't done me no harm. He could not kill somebody who had done him no harm. He went over the hill where Doc Bulkely's house with the high columns loomed against the dark sky. A bare lightbulb burned over the front door and another over his garage, and out in the gloom he could see the barn where Doc Bulkely kept horses. The doctor had children who loved to ride. They were grown now and gone, but still Doc Bulkely kept horses and coaxed other children to ride them as if he might reclaim time. Hope descended to the edge of the lake a mile above the dam, and in the distance he could see a line of lights shining over the dam to mark its place in the dark water. Behind him he heard the courthouse clock toll two. It was a distant sound, muffled by the hill he had crossed between it and the lake.

Upstream he could see a few coal-oil lanterns glittering on the dark water. He knew they were on the bows of boats where men fished, but he could not see the boats. The water was black, and in it floated the reflections of the stars, and for a moment Hope paused to take in the still beauty of the world. He wished he could stop things then, sit there for the rest of his life in the dark, hidden like that, looking at the stars in the water, not having to think about what he had done or what would happen now. At home in the mountains when he was a child, he loved to look at the stars shining in the pond at night, when it was a mirror, and he thought he could put his hand down and catch the stars and bring them up and take them home and sprinkle them around the house like Christmas candles.

He walked back along a spit of land jutting out into the lake with trees bending over the water, and it was so black that he could see the small rowboat only as an indefinite smudge. Joye and Love sat so still that they seemed to be shadows with no flesh and blood to them, like spirits, and for a moment Hope wondered if they might be dark angels come to judge him for what he had done. He shook off the feeling and removed his shoes, rolled up his trousers, and waded out to the boat and stepped up into it.

Nobody said anything. They shook hands silently, and Joye at the oars pulled them out into the lake. He was so deft that Hope could hardly hear the bite of the oars in the water, the suck and gurgle as the oars pulled through it. The little outboard motor was pulled up, and on they went like ghosts, the boat a phantom, and out in the middle of the lake where the old river channel ran deep, Hope dropped the revolver overboard. Joye kept rowing, and soon they were out of sight of the lights on the dam, sitting in a cove, fishing. They fired the coal-oil lamp so no one would run over them in the dark, and they dropped their lines and fished in the almost perfect silence of a hot August night.

*T*HE SHERIFF was standing in the kitchen drinking coffee when Paul Alexander went upstairs and knocked on the door of his son's room. Paul Alexander came back, and the two men drank their coffee in silence. They heard water running in the bathroom. Charles finally came walking into the kitchen tacked onto the end of the house. *Everything is so neat,* the sheriff thought, looking around at the house in a kind of subdued awe. It was like a French hotel where he had stayed one night after the war, when he had been released from the hospital. You would think a woman had cleaned and straightened it, but the sheriff knew there was no woman in this house. Paul Alexander and his sons had done it all, because Eugenia Alexander was dead and lying in the graveyard at the Midway Baptist Church atop the hill.

Charles forced a grin. "Hi, Sheriff! What brings you around this early in the morning?" Charles always grinned at people. He was popular in town. The sheriff thought he grinned too much. Something anxious about people who grinned too much, he thought. Now he realized Charles was pretending. *He ain't slept a wink. His eyes are red like a drunk's.*

"What have you done to your head?" the sheriff asked.

Charles lifted his hand to his forehead as if he had forgotten about the bruise. "Oh, that! Last night, down at the office, I went back to use the bathroom before I came home, and I walked into the door."

"Which door was that?" the sheriff said.

"The door to the bathroom. The toilet, I mean. It's back in the press room."

"You didn't turn on the light back there?"

"Oh, I can usually find my way back without doing that. But I didn't see the door."

"I thought Red left a light on there all night long."

"Oh, he usually does, but last night it was turned off. I guess because it was Saturday."

The sheriff did not say anything for a while. "You ought to be more careful."

He's scared, the sheriff thought. Paul Alexander filled his own coffee cup and sat down. His dark eyes turned onto his son. "Do you want some coffee, Charles?" Paul Alexander said.

"Oh yes. Yes. Thanks." *Too eager,* the sheriff thought. The boy sat down, and his father filled a cup and handed it to him. When Charles took the cup, his hands trembled and the coffee sloshed over the side and splashed down on the checkered oilcloth that covered the table.

"Is something wrong, Charles?" the sheriff asked.

"Oh no, no," Charles said. "I didn't sleep well last night." He hesitated. "The heat, you know. My room was terribly hot, and I had a headache."

"From hitting the door," the sheriff said.

"Yes. Well, no. Not exactly. I mean, I had the headache before that. Hitting the door made it worse."

"Charles has headaches from time to time," Paul Alexander said in his careful, accented voice.

"That's too bad," the sheriff said. The silence sat at the table with them. "Go ahead and drink your coffee, Charles," the sheriff said.

"Yes, well . . ." Charles picked up the cup with both hands, but his hands still trembled, and he drank with difficulty.

"What time did you leave the office last night?" the sheriff said.

"Oh, a little before midnight," Charles said. He set the cup down. He had barely managed to take a sip of the coffee.

"But your daddy says you didn't get home until nearly quarter to two," the sheriff said.

"Yes, well, I had a headache, and I drove up towards Knoxville with the windows open on the car. I wasn't sleepy. What's wrong, Sheriff? Why are you asking me these questions?" The voice had a nervous edge to it.

He's scared, like a trapped dog, the sheriff thought, but he said, "Something happened in town last night."

"In town?" Charles said. His face was pale.

"Two people were killed, Charles. Shot to death on the back side of the courthouse. Along about one in the morning." The sheriff told the story— an abbreviated and censored version. He spoke slowly and deliberately and came to the end. "I figure Hope Kirby's the only man that had any reason to kill them. But I can't prove it. I thought maybe you'd seen something—anything. Did you see anything, Charles?"

The boy's face reddened. "I told you, I left before midnight."

"Do you know Hope Kirby, Charles?"

"He did some work on our house," Paul Alexander said. "He helped me remodel this kitchen. Yes, Charles knows him."

"The war hero," Charles said, trying to look as if he remembered Hope Kirby from some vaguely recalled encounter.

"Yes, the war hero," the sheriff said. "One of them at least. You'd recognize him if you saw him?"

"I guess I would," Charles said.

"Did you see him in town last night?"

"No," Charles said. "No, I didn't see anybody last night."

"I see," the sheriff said, sipping his coffee slowly, probing with a tone of mild curiosity. He waited for Charles to say something. But Charles was silent, looking down miserably at the coffee. "Just when did you leave the paper office, Charles?" the sheriff said.

"Leave? What time?" He looked baffled. "I told you. Oh, I don't know. A little after midnight."

"A little after midnight."

"Yes, about then. I don't know. The clock had struck. I remembered that the clock had struck."

"They's a big electric clock on the wall of your office," the sheriff said. "You didn't look at it when you went out?"

"I—I don't think I did. My head—my head hurt so much, you know. I don't think I did look at the clock."

"If you know something, you ought to tell the sheriff," Paul Alexander said, his voice quiet and level, somehow tentative.

"I told you. I don't know anything."

The sheriff looked down at the floor again. The silence came back. The sheriff sipped his coffee.

"I drove out towards Varner's Cross Roads about twelve-thirty. I could swear I seen your old station wagon. Maybe I'm wrong. But I'd swear I seen your '37 Ford parked against the curb in back of the courthouse."

It was a hunch. The sheriff hadn't seen the Ford. He hadn't looked in that direction. The hunch paid off. All at once Charles started shaking all over.

The sheriff spoke gently. "You can tell the truth, and nothing will happen to you. We won't let nothing happen to you. It's all right."

Charles started to cry then.

The sheriff drank the rest of his coffee and put the cup down. He pulled out a chair and sat down in it, and Paul Alexander silently filled his cup again. Charles sobbed, his head down, his body shaking. The sheriff thought, *A rabbit will shake like that when he's caught in a box trap and can't get out.*

The idiot boy came into the kitchen then. Most people in the county called him "G," the letter of the alphabet. He had a rasping voice, and now he looked perplexed. "Why is Charlie Boy crying? Why is Charlie Boy crying?" Paul Alexander put his arm around him. Guy's eyes were crossed, and the back of his head sloped. He was twenty-eight years old.

"It's all right," Paul Alexander said, soothing Guy. "It's all right."

The younger boy, Stephen, came in then. He was thin and good-looking, and he stood there for a moment startled from sleep and looking with amazed sympathy at his brother. "Charles, what happened?"

"I'm trying to keep a promise," Charles whispered. "I promised him. He said he had to kill me because I saw it. He put the gun up against my head. Right between my eyes. He hit me with it. He was mad at me for being there. He didn't know where I'd come from. He cocked it. He said he'd make it quick, and I begged him to let me go. I promised him I wouldn't tell."

"Who?" Stephen said.

"Hope Kirby. I promised him." Between sobs and gasps, it all came out, full of repetitions and garbled sentences and fear. All spoken in a voice creaking with exhaustion, slow, worn out.

*T*HE SHERIFF took out a little notebook with a slick cover and found a yellow wood pencil in his shirt pocket and began to write everything down, slowly and carefully. When he wasn't clear on something, he made Charles back up and tell it again. Slowly Charles stopped trembling. He spoke in a comatose state. Hope Kirby turned on him, hit him in the forehead with the muzzle of the pistol, probably frustrated nearly out of his mind to find Charles there, his own plans ruined.

The sheriff summarized it all in his notes—Charles begging for his life, Hope Kirby on the point of squeezing the trigger, blowing Charles to kingdom come. If he'd killed Charles, he never would have been caught, the sheriff thought.

"If you promise you won't never tell, I'll let you go free," Hope Kirby said, lowering the pistol slowly, reluctantly, inevitably.

"I'll never tell. I swear I will never tell. Wild horses couldn't drag it out of me," Charles cried. He repeated himself in a torrent of relief and supplication.

The sheriff had been afraid in the war, and he had been shot, and he had almost died, and before he was wounded he had seen the bodies the Germans left when they shot down American prisoners at Malmédy. He was not one to condemn people for what they did in danger of death.

Finally it was all down. Charles looked pale and exhausted and sat staring at the linoleum-covered floor with his hands folded in his lap as if he'd given up on the world. "I'll get all this typed up, and I'll have to come back and ask you to sign it, Charles. I'll have to ask you to sign it, too, Mr. Alexander. I'll get it notarized then."

The sheriff cleared his throat. "Let me give you a piece of advice," he said. "The Kirby men are mountain folks. They ain't going to take kindly to what you've told me, Charles. You'll have to testify in court."

"Oh God," Charles said dully. It was more prayer than curse.

"And what I mean is, if you ain't there to testify, the state ain't got no case." Charles looked at him blankly. *He still don't get it*, the sheriff thought. "Look, Charles. Any one of them boys except the loony might kill you." The sheriff looked sharply at Guy. "I'm sorry," he said, flustered and red-faced. "It's what folks—I'm sorry."

Paul Alexander said with cool detachment, "It is all right, Sheriff. We understand."

Guy was drinking coffee, slurping it noisily out of the cup and sitting at the kitchen table having his breakfast, indifferent to everything but his food, which he shoveled into his mouth as if he were starving.

Nobody said anything for a moment, and the sheriff stood up. "Listen, Charles," he said. "Any of them Kirby boys might kill you before the trial to keep you from testifying. You be careful, you hear? If you see anything you don't like, hear any noises around here at night, anything—you call me, you hear?"

"I do not believe they will hurt my son," Paul Alexander said.

The sheriff stood, looking at Paul Alexander with a hint of impatience. "Well, they all work for you. I reckon you got a right to your opinion, Mr. Alexander. Still, I'd be careful if I was Charles. I'd be real careful."

"They will not harm him. None of this is Charles's fault."

"Do you know their daddy, Mr. Alexander?"

"I know him to speak to him. We both have afflicted sons. I believe he is a man of honor."

"If you say so, Mr. Alexander," the sheriff said. He thought of saying more to Paul Alexander, thought of shouting at him that men of honor were more likely to commit murder than anybody else, but he controlled the impulse. "If it was up to me, I'd go on a trip. Between now and the trial, I'd go somewhere and not tell nobody where I'm going."

"I have a job," Charles said quietly. "I can't leave it."

The sheriff started to say something else, but he changed his mind. He picked his hat off the table where he had set it. "It's your life," he said. The sheriff felt the absence of a woman in the house. It was an odd business, a sudden comparison of this house and his own where his sturdy wife presided with the unflinching sense that she was in charge of him and their four children and everything that moved across the threshold of front or back doors. He left with Charles sitting there, the coffee pot in the middle of the table, Stephen staring at his brother, and Paul Alexander already at the stove making a breakfast which the sheriff declined to share. "I've got to get down to the docks at the lake," he said.

He drove off full of regret, all his anger at Hope Kirby dissolved.

*T*HEY had a pretty good night. It was cooler on the lake than it was on land. They caught some medium-sized catfish on the bottom and some crappie and a few bluegills, and when he pulled a catfish into the boat Hope remembered what Abby had said about bringing one home for breakfast. He felt a surge of pleasure when he thought of giving her the fish, how happy she would be, then he remembered that she was dead, and all pleasure left him, and a heaviness fell over him. They caught some carp, too, but they threw them back. Three fishermen in a boat. They bothered no one, and no one bothered them, and the world off the lake was distant and soft.

His brothers thought he had done what he went to do. He said nothing about the Alexander boy. They watched the day come on slow and quiet and felt the surprise that never grows old for people who stay up all night, the earth suddenly visible at a distance, colorless but shaped and familiar, and then the color came, dully at first but deepening, and first light made the east pale and turn white and then the color of violets, and the sky reddened like fire, and the stars went out like candles, and Joye blew out the lantern.

It's going to be hot, Hope thought. He almost said it, but he thought he did not need to speak since they could all tell it would be hot, and the Kirby men were not the kind to throw around unnecessary speech. These were the dog days, when dogs lay under houses in the dust and panted with red tongues hanging out. Now, on the water, the day smelled sweet and new, and a breath of air made ripples in the lake.

Off in the middle distance a cabin cruiser sat in the water near the shore. A man in a blue swimsuit came out on the deck, holding a coffee cup. He waved at them, and they waved back in the minimal way country people waved. They wanted people to see them. They wanted to come to the dock with a crowd of witnesses to remember them. A little after eight when the sun was high up the eastern sky, Joye said, "I reckon hit's time," and he hauled up the little lard pail filled with cement that served them as an anchor. Joye pulled the starter cord on the Johnson. The motor fired quickly, giving off a burst of blue smoke, and they slipped out into the channel and turned downstream towards the dam and the dock, leaving a white wake streaming in a V behind them. The sun gleamed on the wake, and the light made a foamy path in the lake, and they could not look at the brightness in the water.

I can imagine that Abby is at home, waiting for me, Hope thought. He thought of how pretty she was. He remembered the first time he saw her—the Fourth of July celebration in 1946 when he had come home with John Sevier, and there were stories in the papers about him and his decoration from General MacArthur. The Distinguished Service Cross—pinned on his military blouse by MacArthur himself. He hated MacArthur. He remembered the promises of hundreds of ships and thousands of airplanes that never came. He didn't want any part of the celebration. He was not from Bourbon County, but his aunt Hattie Toliver, his mother's aunt really, told his father that he had to get all his soldier boys up there on that platform, and Pappy Kirby did what Aunt Hattie told him out of respect for his dead wife. Hope's mother was dead by then.

Every veteran from the county who had come home was up there and in uniform, and the Bourbon County High School band in its orange-and-black uniforms blasted away at patriotic songs. Hope sat with his brothers, including John Sevier, who didn't know where he was and did not recognize the neat uniform he wore. *Hit was nice,* Hope thought. *Real nice. All them folks being proud of us. And we was new in the county, and they didn't even know us.*

Preacher Ruskus from the Pentecostal Church was supposed to give the invocation and let the mayor speak, but Preacher Ruskus got happy and started jumping up and down and hollering about how God had given the victory to America. The mayor had to wrestle the microphone away from him, and when he did, Preacher Ruskus did cartwheels across the platform, shouting, "Praise God! Praise God!" People in the audience started to laugh, and the microphone was screeching and howling, and it was turmoil compounded.

Hope sat on the back edge of the platform feeling bashful and thinking it wasn't right for people to be laughing at Preacher Ruskus. At the same time he wished Preacher Ruskus would sit down and hush. That's when he looked down just behind him and saw Abby. She smiled up at him, a girl with large breasts discreetly hidden under a virginal white blouse with the front buttoned up to her neck the way Church of God women wore their blouses, and it had long sleeves, but somehow her clothes made her all the more provocative and pretty, and that smile! Hope's heart turned warm and watery. He smiled back, and he felt his face burn from embarrassment because he had never done such an intimate thing with a woman before. He had been through the war, and he was not only a virgin, he had never kissed a woman.

"Would you drink a Co' Cola with me afterwards?" she whispered shyly. She told Hope it was the boldest thing she'd ever said to a man. "I never would have dreamed of asking a man for a date," she said. He thought even yet that she told him the truth. It was cool in the shade, and he sat on the platform and felt happy. Preacher Ruskus finally went cartwheeling off the platform and running around the square, stopping now and then to cup his hands to his face and hoarsely shout "Praise Jesus!" before he turned another cartwheel. People were laughing, and Hope started laughing, too, not at Preacher Ruskus but at the day, at his happiness.

He'd been in the jungle almost three years in the Philippines, and afterwards he stayed in San Francisco while the doctors tried to do something for John Sevier, and when they failed at everything, he brought John Sevier to Bourbon County, where Pappy had settled after he was driven out of the Smoky Mountains. In the Philippines he used to dream about a girl who came to him and started saying to him in his dreams, "Do you want to do this today?" Or she'd say, "Let's do this." Now here was Abby, inviting him to have a Coca-Cola with him as if she had been his dream girl, and he said to himself, "Why not?" She was so clean. She smelled like soap, and the smell of her rose to him while he sat on the platform. He went two years without washing with soap. He thought it was funny afterwards that he thought so much about soap when the Japs were looking for him, trying to kill him. One of the best things about coming home was to see how clean everybody was, and Abby was the cleanest of all because she was young and beautiful, and she liked him.

He had a Coke with her, and she said, "I felt like hugging myself all over when you said you'd have a Co' Cola with me." He laughed. That was later on when they sat in the drugstore and all the praying and singing and speaking were finished, and people milled around, and lots of people Hope didn't know came up and introduced themselves and told him they were glad he and his family had decided to settle in Bourbon County. He did not know what to say. Abby teased him because he turned red every time somebody spoke to him. He thought she was the dream woman who came to him in the Philippines.

They came ashore at the boat dock a little after nine. They could hear church bells ringing off in town, distant and holy and out of tune. Bourbonville had fourteen churches, seven of them Baptist.

They moved slowly, deliberately, and took their fish out of the water on the lines, and people at the boat dock saw them and came over and bragged on their catch and asked where they had been for the night. Joye laughed and said, "That's for us to know and you to find out," and they laughed, too. Fishermen didn't tell their secrets.

Hope looked up the hill where the road came down to the dock, and he saw the sheriff sitting there with his two dogs in the car marked "Sheriff" on the door. The sheriff had the windows in the car rolled down, and his bare, beefy arm was hanging out the window on his side, and he sat looking calmly down the hill, a man who seemed in no hurry at all. The car was black and white and dusty, and Hope stood looking at him, and after a while the sheriff started the engine and came rolling down, still without haste. Joye saw Hope looking up and whispered to him, "Don't stare at him. You don't know nothing about what's happened. You hain't got nary reason to be scairt of ary sheriff. You been with us all night. You don't know she's dead."

Hope had already supposed the sheriff would come to tell him that Abby was dead. *I will have to act all tore up,* he thought. But something grabbed him inside. He knew. He was not surprised when the sheriff got out of his car very slowly, a man with all the time in the world, looked him directly in the eye, and said, "Hope Kirby, your wife was shot to death last night while she was sitting in her car on the square. Mr. Kelly Parmalee was shot, too. They're both dead. I'm arresting you for her murder. And for his. You don't have to say nothing until you get a lawyer. But anything you do say can be used against you in court."

"What time was she shot, Sheriff?" Joye asked. He was red with anger.

"It was about one in the morning, I reckon," the sheriff said.

"Then you got to do better than that, Sheriff," Joye said. "Hope and us was out on the lake fishing all night long. Folks here at the dock seen us go out with him, and they seen us come back."

"But they didn't see you all night long, Mr. Kirby," the sheriff said affably. "And sometime between the time they seen you go out in your boat and now, your brother got out of the boat, come back into the square, and shot his wife to death and killed the man who was with her. I'd be careful what I say, if I was you. If you helped him in any way, I might have to arrest you, too."

Joye's voice was like fire. "You're spinning moonshine, Sheriff. You hain't doing nothing but blowing smoke."

"I've got a witness," the sheriff said without raising his voice.

"And just who might that be?" Joye said with a sneer.

"Charles Alexander," the sheriff said. "I reckon you know the name, Hope. He says you put a pistol up to his head and made him promise not to tell. He tried to keep his promise, Hope. I swear to God he did. He couldn't do it. I had a hunch. When I went up to see him, he tried to lie for you, but he couldn't do it. He broke down, and it all come out. His daddy heard it all. I'm placing you under arrest, Hope. You better come along."

Joye and Love turned on their brother, speechless and incredulous. Hope looked at them and gave a little shrug, throwing his hands out a little. "I better go with him," he said.

"Hope . . ." Joye couldn't say anything else. Love couldn't say anything at all. People stared, and the sound of the lake gently slapping at the boat dock was audible, and the church bells rang on and on over the hills in the distance. Joye was scared. He wouldn't have admitted it to anybody in the world at the time, not if you pulled his teeth one by one, but he was scared.

Hope followed the sheriff to the car, and the sheriff opened the back door, and Hope got in. The back windows were rolled up, and a heavy mesh steel screen stood between the backseat and the front. The insides of the doors in back had no handles.

I hain't got no place to run, Hope thought. He settled back in the seat and watched the familiar country go by. "I'm sure sorry about this, Hope," the sheriff said.

"Don't pay hit no mind, Sheriff," Hope said. "I'm sorry about hit, too."

"The Alexander boy done his best to lie for you, Hope."

"I knowed he would," Hope said.

"He couldn't do it," the sheriff said sadly. "He broke down. But he tried."

"I knowed he would," Hope said.

They drove in silence the rest of the way to the jail. *What is to be will be.* The thought ran through Hope Kirby's mind like a consoling psalm.

MOST of the population of Bourbonville went to church that morning, and the news of the murders spread through the congregations like a fire in a hayfield. The congregation at the Church of God of the Union Assembly felt itself beaten in the face by a blow from nowhere, incomprehensible and horrifying. Abby was so sweet, such a good Christian girl. She sang so pretty. She looked like an angel.

Sunday after Sunday Abby sat in the center of the choir ranged in semi-circular ranks behind the preacher and facing the congregation, her beautiful eyes following in rapt piety her father's hands as he stood before the singers directing the hymns with sweeping gestures of musical command.

Today her seat in the choir was empty.

At First Baptist, Larry Arceneaux heard the news from his secretary, Louise Renfrow, as soon as he walked into the church offices in the back of the building a half hour before Sunday school. Mrs. Renfrow was breathless with excitement. Part of the excitement was her good luck at being able to deliver astonishing news to someone who had not heard it. She was a gushy and insincere woman, and Arceneaux hated her, but he listened gravely. He had seen Abby and noted in a thoroughly dispassionate way her healthy skin and lively eyes. Kelly Parmalee was an oily man, he thought. But ordinary people often turned oily around preachers. Most people talked to preachers much as they talked to babies.

Arceneaux was not succeeding in Bourbonville, and he knew it. Kelly had grown up in First Baptist because his family had always gone there. He moved to Central Methodist because his wife refused to leave her own church when they married.

Kelly Parmalee always had a good word for Arceneaux. "Don't let folks bother you," he said once when the two of them lingered to talk under the awning of the clothing store. "There're lots of folks in this town who like you a lot, and I'm one of them." Arceneaux warmed to him after that.

Kelly was effusively complimentary to everybody. He studied ways of agreeing with anything anybody said so that he seemed to have reflected mightily on the subject for years and arrived at the same opinion. Arceneaux took Kelly to be a lightweight. Still, given the current of discontent he could feel running against him, he appreciated Kelly's greetings and his warmth, insincere though it may have been, and he recognized that despite everything, Kelly Parmalee was good-hearted and hungry himself for approval and affection. Arceneaux heard from others that Kelly complimented and defended him every time his name came up at the Civitan Club.

Now he had been murdered. Abby was dead, too. Arceneaux knew they were guilty of adultery, but he offered not even an internal whisper of condemnation against either of them. He found the murders horrible and sad, and adultery an indifferent matter. In their adultery, he thought, they were better than he was.

He did not tell Mrs. Renfrow that he had heard the shots. He found some conventional expression of horror and surprise to trade with her loud and excited voice, and as soon as he could he gained the quiet safety of his office and shut the door, leaving Mrs. Renfrow frustrated in her part of the space, where she ruled as queen of the typewriter and the telephone and her jungle of potted plants. Time and again Arceneaux had told Mrs. Renfrow that he did not need her on Sunday mornings and that she should stay at home enjoying her coffee and newspaper until time to come to services with everyone else. But Mrs. Renfrow assured him that her main interest in life was to look after him and that she would not think of letting him be in the office without her. "Someday you may need me. It may be life or death. And if it is life or death, Louise Renfrow will be there. You can count on me, Preacher Arceneaux." These bubbling eruptions from the hot spring of her insincerity sometimes aroused in Arceneaux fantasies of importing a few of his old OSS buddies to strangle Mrs. Renfrow quietly in her sleep and dump her body in the mountains for the crows and the bears to eat. He restrained these thoughts, and besides he knew that his closest comrades would have nothing to do with him now. Nine years! He supposed that the reproachful dog would be dead.

Louise Renfrow had done him one major service. She had spread the word—discreetly, of course, a woman delivering inside information only to those in whom she had complete confidence—that Arceneaux had been a clerk-typist during the war. Since Louise was in ceaseless courtship of the world, part of her art of seduction was to reveal confidences. She considered revelations of private knowledge the surest proof of goodwill and the most certain road to being beloved by all. Her closest friends included every human being who spoke to her more than three minutes, and she would tell somebody any secret she knew within ten minutes of learning it. She was better than a radio station.

She thought Arceneaux's great secret was that he had served as a clerk-typist in a safe place during the war while other young men fought in actual combat and suffered wounds and death. Her misinformation made people assume that an able-bodied guy like himself was embarrassed to speak of hunching over a typewriter doing woman's work while millions of brave men risked life and limb in battle. So Arceneaux was relieved of having to hide from people what he had really done in the war, things he yearned to forget and could not. He did not have to protect himself from confessing unwittingly through some slip of the tongue in a careless moment that he had murdered a child for reasons of "military necessity."

Arceneaux made Mrs. Renfrow feel shut out of his life. He typed his own letters. "He types so fast the typewriter sounds like a machine gun," she said. (When this remark was carried to Arceneaux by someone else as a form of praise, he could not stop himself from imagining Louise before a real machine gun, wondering how fast the middle-aged busybody could run once she set her mind to it.) "I've always typed all the letters for the ministers I have worked for," she said to Arceneaux in tones of utmost injury.

"Well, you can be thankful you don't have to type mine," Arceneaux said with cool and unsmiling finality.

"But I *want* to type them," she said peevishly.

"But you see, Mrs. Renfrow, since I compose them at the typewriter, you don't need to type them," he said.

"But don't you want me to type them over so you can be sure you haven't made any mistakes?"

"No," he said. "I don't make mistakes in my typing."

The logic was implacable, but she mourned over it anyway, and she protested quietly to others that she thought Arceneaux wrote some letters he did not want her to see. The remark seemed freighted with suspicion. It added to the store of gossip about Arceneaux that floated around the town, but it was not as interesting as the whirring curiosity about why a young man like Arceneaux, in the prime of life, had not yet taken to himself a wife.

"I think some woman broke his heart," Louise said confidentially. That rumor, too, flew through the county, causing a great many eligible young women, some of them not even Baptists, to consider ways of demonstrating to Arceneaux that they could mend his broken heart and fill the void left by a lost love. The most obvious way for such a demonstration was to invite the preacher to dinner. Arceneaux became the most dined-out minister in the history of Bourbon County. For him it was bliss to be able to stay at home in the church's ramshackle parsonage in the evening, to read his books, to listen to his records, and to drink tea and cook his own meals. He was proud of his ability as a chef, as a man from New Orleans should be.

He made a rule. He would accept no invitations for Saturday night. He had to work on his sermons for the following day, and he needed, he said, to have some quiet meditation time to ponder what he should say. This was a white lie, but it sufficed. Bourbonvillians acceded to it almost reverently. They understood that a sermon was special business to be conjured up by mysterious mental and spiritual gymnastics between the preacher and God. So Saturday was Arceneaux's favorite night of the week. He could count on being at home alone.

Arceneaux did not mention the murders in the sermon he preached that morning. (He spoke on Saul and Samuel, Samuel's cutting Agag of the Amalekites in pieces when Saul had spared his life, and he pondered ideas of justice and seemed to many in his congregation, including the ever-watchful Tommy Fieldston, to be suggesting that Saul was a better man than Samuel.) Afterwards he had to go to Sunday dinner with the Pettibone family, where yet another unwed daughter was supposed by her mother, her father, and herself to be exactly the woman a bachelor preacher in need of a wife would find irresistible. Oh yes. It should also be said that Arceneaux's wealth put an extra glow on his candidacy to be the husband of any unmarried woman he might fancy. No other preacher anybody in Bourbon County knew drove a white Jaguar, and when Arceneaux accepted the "call" of the people of First Baptist to become their pastor, he asked them to set aside the money they would have given him as a salary to devote to charitable causes he would designate. His favorite cause was a Baptist orphanage near Sevierville. Later on he decided that this act of generosity had been yet another of his many mistakes, but he thought at the time that since he already had more money than he could ever spend, it would only complicate his income tax forms to take a salary from First Baptist. He did not understand then that generosity from the rich may earn gratitude from the poor but from the middle classes it gains only resentment and a heightened desire to find something wrong with the benefactor.

Henry and Gracie Pettibone, Lucille's parents, were full of the story of the murders and of opinions about it. When they were not begging Arceneaux to eat more of their greasy food, they spoke ceaselessly about the horror of it all, and naturally they reported observations they had made over the previous months that should have tipped them off to what was happening. "Kelly always had his hair cut by old Tom Foster in the barbershop on Broadway," Henry said. "Well, old Tom's eyes got so bad that he'd just as soon cut your ear off with his scissors as trim your hair, and I wouldn't let him get less than ten feet away from me if he had a razor in his hand. I think Kelly went to him as long as he did out of the kindness of his heart, and I'll tell you this, Preacher. No matter what he did, Kelly was a good-hearted man."

"Yes he was," Arceneaux said.

"So, I was surprised when he started going to Abby's beauty shop to get his hair cut. He said a woman can cut hair better than a man because a woman has more of it. Still, him and old Judge Yancy were the only men brave enough to go down there and sit amongst all them women to have their hair cut."

"I saw him there many a time," Gracie Pettibone said. "That poor little thing. She always cut my hair so good. She cut it just Friday afternoon. I can still feel her fingers on my head. I don't know who I'll get to cut it now."

"Everybody knew Judge Yancy was crazy about her. Not that you ever figured he had an immoral thought about her. But Kelly! I would have thought he was too old for her. You know, Preacher, I've never had a thought about another woman in the world but my Gracie here, and I don't ever suspect another man of having bad thoughts. That's what an innocent mind will do for you."

"Henry says the sweetest things," Gracie said.

Arceneaux resisted the desire to say, "Damn, Henry, that's awful." Instead he managed a weak smile and gave his attention to his plate so he would not have to look at Henry Pettibone's smug and self-righteous smile.

Henry and Gracie explored the love affair and the murders from every angle, and Arceneaux listened politely, eating as little as he could without offense, and uttering an occasional and noncommittal "It's too bad, really too bad." He spoke with just enough force to seem to agree with what everybody else at the table might be thinking.

"I can't understand how a woman can be unfaithful to her husband," Lucille said. "If I was married, I'd be so happy I couldn't even dream of doing anything but making my husband happy."

Her remarks made Arceneaux wonder if by some mad trick of time and space he had been whisked into the midst of a Molière play, but he couldn't remember a scene precisely like this one in Molière, and he assumed he was still in commonplace reality. He was embarrassed because Lucille seemed to demand some response, gazing hungrily at him with her soft brown eyes. Her implicit demand was seconded by her adoring parents who turned glowing faces towards him as if to say, "See what a fine, pure daughter we have raised. Why don't you propose marriage right this minute?"

Lucille was not bad-looking. She might even be intelligent, Arceneaux thought. He had reached the stage in his life where he considered finding a sexually undemanding woman and settling down with her. Having children. He was sure he could manage that. Everything would be all right then. Or would it? He was struck by a fit of pondering. It might work. But it might not. The thought drove him to desperate fear, far too much fear to allow him to settle on a woman to court. Too dangerous by far, he thought. At least now. He looked at Lucille and smiled vaguely at her, contemplating. If he married, his wife had to be one of two extremes. She had to be dumb like Lucille and therefore easy to deceive, or she had to be bright and understanding and indifferent to sex. Or maybe he could marry a lesbian. A perfect contract. The queer and the lesbian, and maybe they could compromise enough to have a child. All these things ran through his mind with the speed of lightning. Lucille smiled warmly back at him, and he cut his smile off lest she leap across the table and jump into his lap and shout, "I do."

In an effort to sound measured and grave, Arceneaux heard himself saying quietly, "I think we cannot judge people until we know the complete stories of their lives. But since those stories are always hidden from the rest of us, even when we think we know the people involved, we do not know them, and we cannot judge. That is why Jesus tells us to judge not that we be not judged."

"How true! How true!" Gracie murmured with a deep and theatrical sigh.

"I do think the Alexander boy might have kept his word to Hope Kirby," Henry Pettibone said reflectively. "Not that I'm for telling lies, you understand. I'm against lying. You know, Preacher, a businessman has to live according to Christian principles, or he won't stay in business long, and I'm one hundred and ten percent against lying for any reason. Still, Hope could have killed the boy, but he let him off because the boy promised not to tell, and he did tell. If Hope had killed him, the state wouldn't have a case against him. No evidence at all."

Henry Pettibone's garbled remark was Arceneaux's introduction to the story of the promise Charles had made to save his life. He was suddenly fully alert. He drew the tale out one detail at a time so far as Henry Pettibone had learned it on his trip down to the Rexall drugstore to get the Knoxville papers just before Sunday school. Henry could not tell the story without reflecting on it. His reflections seemed less certain than he usually was about everything. "If he tells the same story in court that he told the sheriff early this morning, he might send Hope Kirby to the electric chair. Premeditated murder, you see. No doubt about it. And the whole Kirby family was involved in it up to their necks if you ask me. Maybe the whole bunch of them will go to prison."

Arceneaux was aghast. The memories of his own nightmare rained down on him like the sulfurous fire onto Sodom and Gomorrah. He stayed at the table as long as minimal courtesy dictated. Outside, the sun pressed on the earth. Finally, when he had consumed his last cup of the revolting coffee the Pettibones drank, he rose and excused himself. "So soon?" Mrs. Pettibone said, sounding miffed.

"Preacher, you need to relax," Henry Pettibone said. "If you eat and run, you won't digest your food."

"It's such a nice day that you two young people ought to take a drive over by the lake," Mrs. Pettibone said hopefully.

"I'd just love to," Lucille said as if Arceneaux had extended the invitation. She opened her eyes wide. She had seen all the Doris Day movies and practiced Doris Day expressions in front of the mirror. Arceneaux rejected this opportunity with an excuse whose weakness hung in the room like the embarrassment of a loud fart.

"Oh I'm sorry," he said. "I have to preach again tonight, you know. I have to get ready for it." Baptists demanded two preaching services on Sunday, one in the morning, the other at night. Only about a quarter of the

Sunday-morning congregation turned up for the evening service, but that quarter expected a sermon, and every Baptist preacher in the South contracted to give it to them, just as every preacher was required to deliver another homily at Wednesday-night prayer meetings.

"Just trust the spirit," Henry Pettibone said in a demanding tone. "Just stand up there and let fly. Get inspired this afternoon by taking a drive along the lake with Lucille here."

"No, I'm sorry," Arceneaux said. "Maybe another time. No, I really must go and do some work."

At last he was free, leaving the Pettibones disappointed and, he thought, annoyed with him, even perhaps angry. They had given him a good dinner of fried chicken, mashed potatoes, green beans, Jell-O, and ice cream and angel food cake at the end, and the least he could do was marry their daughter.

*A*RCENEAUX sped up the highway towards Dixie Lee Junction, his white Jaguar flying across the route of the two-lane blacktop like a streak of light.

The woodlands on each side of the road were a brooding and heavy green in the furnace of the August afternoon, and the world was so still that it seemed dead. He thought of afternoons at the sugar plantation in Louisiana on Sundays, sitting on the screened veranda, drinking gin over cracked ice and feeling the pleasant enveloping of the damp heat and looking out at the saturated green of the landscape in the company of his mother and father. They loved him. Arceneaux sometimes marveled that never in his life had he ever had the slightest doubt that his parents loved him. His father and his mother worshipped him with eyes that had never lost the wonder of a child born to them when they had almost given up hope, a child who had grown up strong and healthy and popular and smart, a child who had gone to the war, done dangerous and daring deeds, been decorated for gallantry, and come safely home in honor, unmaimed. It was a miracle, a blessing from God. When they looked at him, their love nearly suffocated him, and every time he thought of them, his heart darkened. He could hear his father clearing his throat, see the aging man look at him in pained hesitancy, saying, "Lawrence, you will have to think of marriage someday. All this is here, waiting for your wife and your children."

*H*OPE KIRBY spent Sunday afternoon in jail feeling more peaceful than he had felt since he had learned about Abby and Kelly Parmalee.

Maybe he was more peaceful than he had been since he and John Sevier had worked the wheat harvest in North Dakota in the summer of 1939. Everything was flat and golden in the wheat fields, and the sky was immense, there seemed to be no end of the land, and nobody could find them there. Yes, he thought, he had not felt this much peace since then.

His father and his brothers came to see him. The boys called their father Pappy. Hope thought his father was the best man he had ever known. He never raised his voice. But he could be angry. The anger was there, so powerful it was scary, and Hope could see it boiling inside. "You should of kilt him," Pappy said with steely quiet. "Now look what you done."

"Hit warn't his fault," Hope said, looking at the floor, not looking at Pappy, not wanting to look at him because something had changed in him. Pappy was getting old, for one thing. You could see it in his eyes and his neck. Worse than that, he was bitter. *He never got over it,* Hope thought. *Losing his land. I hain't never got over hit neither. Mr. Hamilton. And then the sheriff of Sevier County showing up, telling Pappy he had to sell out now, take what the government wanted to pay him, and because it was not Mr. Hamilton dealing anymore, Pappy got only three thousand dollars for the place. Five thousand dollars lost. A fortune. The sheriff told him if he didn't take it, Pappy and all his older boys might end up in state's prison. Maybe the electric chair. It broke him.*

After a while they left. Hope settled back on his bunk and looked out the window. It had steel bars, but the window was thrown back, and a breath of air moved through the cell, and he could see the white clouds drifting aimlessly across the hazy blue sky. It felt peaceful.

The sheriff came up after a while. "Hope, you doing all right?"

"I'm just fine, Sheriff."

"I'm sorry about this, Hope. I truly am sorry."

"Hit's all right."

"You want a cup of coffee?"

"Wouldn't mind one."

"I can get you a Coke if you want it."

"Naw, I never did like Coke. But coffee."

"They say coffee cools you off more in hot weather than iced drinks," the sheriff said.

"Aw, this hain't so hot. Hain't like the Philippines."

"Well, it's a damned sight hotter than the Ardennes," the sheriff said. "Do you want something in your coffee?"

"You got ary molasses?"

"Molasses. You drink molasses in your coffee."

"That's what we done when I was a little 'un. Pappy made molasses, and we put them in our coffee."

"I'll get you some," the sheriff said.

"I'd be much obliged. We used to make molasses. Pappy used to let us suck on the cane when we was making them. I sure like the smell of molasses. Pappy, he used to walk the mule round and round while we punched the molasses cane through the mill the mule made turn while he walked with that pole strapped to his back."

"Yeah, we do that in Bourbon County, too, Hope. I mean we used to. You don't see many mules no more. Everything's changing."

"Yep, everthing's changing."

Hope thought of Pappy, the way Pappy used to be before Mr. Hamilton came, Pappy, the best man that ever was and the most patient.

*A*S ARCENEAUX drove towards Dixie Lee Junction, he told himself that he had a chance with Charles Alexander. They were friends, he thought. *No slip-ups,* Arceneaux told himself. *No intimacy with a young man who might—* Arceneaux blocked the rest of the thought when Charles Alexander came to mind. A skinny, good-looking kid who grinned too much. *A little shy,* Arceneaux thought. *He hides it by grinning.*

But Arceneaux liked what Charles Alexander wrote. "It's just to fill up space," Charles told him. "We have to have something to go around the ads." Self-deprecating wit. Arceneaux liked it. And Charles introduced Arceneaux to Bourbon County. Summer 1952. Arceneaux the new minister at the church and Charles Alexander about to be nineteen years old, writing a column for the semiweekly newspaper that gave Bourbon County its news and its verbal definition of itself. Most things in the paper were booster stuff. Pretty dreadful, most of it. Endless announcements of meetings tricked out to seem like news, ending always, "All members are urged to attend." Or if it was a report of a meeting, a social event, a speaker at Rotary or Civitan or Lions or the Garden Club or the Clionian Club, the story inevitably ended, "A good time was had by all."

Charles went about the county talking to old people, people with stories of the past. He pored over old letters, scrapbooks, diaries, and he talked to anyone who had a yarn to spin. Arceneaux picked up the paper with scorn when he settled down in Bourbonville. It was a scruffy-looking sheet, tabloid size, photographs made from halftones in which the image dissolved into dots, and he turned through it with the idle contempt that was a signal of his own disaffection from Bourbon County before he had begun his "ministry" there. But then he hit on Charles's column—a story about an old woman in town, daughter of a Confederate veteran, a surgeon in the Army of Northern Virginia, his recollections preserved in the letters that Charles summarized, and quoted and wove into a narrative thread that lived on the page.

The county had been divided during the war, some going north to fight for the Union, some joining up with various Confederate armies. Charles wrote a story about the last public hanging in the county, an affair on the courthouse lawn in the summer of 1885, a man named Simson who had beaten his wife to death one morning while she slept. Hub Delaney, sheriff at the time, had kept a diary. Nobody knew about it, but on Hub's death the diary passed to the Ledbetter family, and Charles read it and wrote about Hub Delaney and even quoted Jim Ed Ledbetter and Charles's father, who had known Hub before he died of cancer.

Then there was the portrait of the Confederate soldier in the home of Jim Ed Ledbetter, a life-sized image staring into the camera but now, after nearly a century, staring into the large room from its place over the fireplace and fixing its eyes on you no matter where you stood. That portrait, too, came with a story. A son who disappeared. A mother who went crazy and died in the asylum in Knoxville, restrained by a straitjacket to keep her from harming herself. The house sold for taxes to Moreland Pinkerton so that his story became mixed up with the story of the solemn face of the soldier who left no trace but this and a gravestone in the Methodist cemetery by the river. Charles wrote it all down, and Arceneaux read it and looked up from the page wanting to know what happened. Why did the boy run away? It was the day after the hanging. Was there some connection? It was like a crossword puzzle with blanks staring him in the face, but the words that might fill them remained hidden and in mystery. The day after the story appeared about the portrait, Arceneaux went down to the newspaper office one afternoon, introduced himself, and asked Charles to take him on a tour of the county.

"You know more about this place than anybody else here," the minister said with genuine admiration. "I'd like you to show it to me."

Don't go too far, Arceneaux warned himself. *The boy . . . that other boy in France. What would he be now? Probably a waiter in one of the little bars in the town. He wouldn't have amounted to much. On the other hand, he was the mayor's son. He might have gone to university. But the mayor was a collaborator. Hard on him after the war.* He was beaten, Arceneaux heard. The mayor, that is. But he did not hear the end of the tale. Jean-François would not let him stay long enough. *I did what I had to do,* Arceneaux thought. *No,* he thought. He was lying to himself. *It was—a mistake.* The word was too bland. *The boy might have become . . . not a priest or a minister.* Arceneaux laughed bitterly at the thought. *Maybe a great historian or novelist or philosopher. The boy seemed smart. Who knows what he would have become? Who knows what I might have become?* Arceneaux thought. *He is dead. No going back.* At least he would not kill Charles Alexander. He could comfort himself about that. The war was over. No sex with boys, ever again.

"Sure," Charles said. He was flattered. He even blushed. "There's more here than anybody thinks," Charles said.

"You really love this place, don't you?" Arceneaux said, the amazement a little too strong in his voice.

"Well, yes, I do," Charles said.

"And you are going to be a minister."

"Yes, I am."

"Would you be happy here, perhaps having my job? Pastor of First Baptist Church?"

Charles laughed, embarrassed. "Well . . ."

Arceneaux understood and laughed. "I won't stay forever, you know. You wouldn't have to run me off to get the job."

"Oh, well. Yes—yes, I would love to be pastor here. I'd love to spend my life here. I don't think I could have anything better." He spoke in a rush of almost dreamy enthusiasm. Arceneaux was disappointed in him. He had already decided that Bourbonville was a dreary colony of God's empire, perhaps a good place to do penance for murder and to prove capable of the discipline that might shape a career, but after only a few weeks in the town he awoke every day with a heaviness in his heart that he could only describe as homesickness. He let the subject drop and gave his attention to what Charles could tell him, for he supposed that if he learned more about Bourbon County he might find something to make his time here pass faster.

So on several Saturday afternoons Charles drove Arceneaux around the county in the '37 Ford. "Let's go in my car," Arceneaux said. The white Jaguar.

"Oh no," Charles said definitely, with a touch of incredulity. "Not on some of these roads."

"Look, a car is made to be driven."

"I couldn't stand it if your paint job got scarred up," Charles said. He was adamant. He could be stubborn. Arceneaux argued but in vain. They went in Charles's car, the car Lloyd had given him, and Lloyd was alive then. He limped about town with his cane, hat pushed back on his head, cigar in his mouth, sometimes lit, sometimes not, the man who got the clock fixed, the man dedicated to getting Bourbonville moving again, waking it up from its slumbers. A poseur, Arceneaux thought. He cursed like an Irish atheist and mocked the preacher with his eyes. He had been hit in the legs with machine-gun fire at Monte Cassino. Arceneaux could tell that when he walked, Lloyd was in pain, but he did not complain. Too bad, his death, Arceneaux thought. He died trying to save the girl he was screwing in the middle of the lake. After Lloyd's death, Arceneaux wished he had talked with him more.

Charles drove the '37 Ford station wagon, trailing foul blue smoke. When they hit a gravel road, the old station wagon shook and banged enough to rattle the wooden sides off, Arceneaux thought. But they held on.

"You could get that engine fixed for a hundred dollars," Arceneaux said.

"A hundred dollars is a lot of money," Charles said.

Arceneaux wanted to say, "Jesus Christ, I'd give you the money to get away from that stink." But that was not preacher's language.

"I'm doing a story about a grave down at Salem Baptist Church," Charles said.

"A grave?"

"Well, it's a tomb really. I reckon you'd call it a tomb. You know, it's a vault above the ground."

"You call that a mausoleum," Arceneaux said. "You have one here?"

"I'm going to show it to you."

"We bury above ground in New Orleans," Arceneaux said. "The water table's so high we dig a grave, and we have a well. Hard on a family to drop a coffin down into a well."

"I guess it is," Charles said. He laughed easily.

They came to a spidery iron bridge across the Tennessee River, very narrow, with a filling station on the north side, and on the other side a scattering of houses and fields rising on rolling slopes fringed here and there with forests. The river was broad and brown, and Arceneaux knew already that it was considered a lake here, one of the TVA system. "Don't fill your bathtub too full, Preacher," somebody told him. "TVA will come and build a dam across the middle of it."

"That's Motlow across the river," Charles said. "Should have been a town, but the Talliaferros got a grant for all the land over there, and they didn't want a settlement to spoil their view. They had a general store there to go with their ferry, but they wouldn't let anybody else build on that land as long as they owned it. And they owned it until twenty years ago. Motlow's not incorporated."

"Who were the Talliaferros?" Arceneaux asked.

"They were the people who built the tomb, the mausoleum," Charles said.

With that Arceneaux had to be content.

Just before the river Charles turned west onto a broad gravel road that followed the riverbank. Now they left a storm of white dust behind them, and Arceneaux heard the rocks flung up by the tires rattling against the bottom and the back of the station wagon. He was glad he had not driven his Jag.

Salem Church came in sight, a large, white frame building roughly in the shape of a cross and more gracefully proportioned than any of the other old churches in the county. Its steeple rose grandly skyward to a weather vane, and in its plainness lay its beauty. Its casements were painted black, and as a congregation, it was the oldest Baptist church in the county. Charles had written a story about Salem Church for the paper, and he had consulted the leather-bound minute book that recorded the church's beginnings in 1803 as a big log cabin, and the raising of this present building in 1855, perhaps the only church in Bourbon County designed by a real architect, a man who had constructed churches in places like New York and Boston and came down to Bourbon County through God knows what expense and hardship, saw the land and the river with its sweeping bend below, and designed a church to fit here as though God had intended it from the foundation of creation.

Arceneaux was impressed. "It's beautiful," he said. "It looks like a church in New England. Have you ever been to Connecticut?"

"No," Charles said. "I've never been much of anywhere. I've been to Philadelphia. I have a couple of aunts up there. People say the Talliaferros built the church to be worthy of their tomb. It's just a story. I've looked at the minutes of the church. They tell when this meeting house was built—1855. And they record the gift of two thousand dollars from the Talliaferro family. But they don't tell why the family gave the money. I'm just guessing. General Longstreet held a meeting with his staff there when he was marching on Knoxville in 1863. He stopped again in Bourbonville and held a meeting in the courthouse. We have photographs of both meetings."

Arceneaux did not say anything, for suddenly he took note of a thick grove of darkly green European cypress trees pointing towards the sky, and within the deeply shaded grove he saw the mausoleum. It was set apart from the church. The church faced south, and the river, visible over a large and treeless graveled parking lot, was scooped out like a great cup with a flat bottom in the rolling land. The parking lot had hitching posts, waist-high cast-iron columns set in the ground, each topped with an iron ring, all painted black. Arceneaux could imagine buggies and wagons drawn up there, the animals patiently steaming in the summer sun. Cruel to the animals, he thought.

The mausoleum within its grove crowned a rise of ground that Arceneaux knew instinctively was artificial. It faced the east whence they had come. He could imagine men—slaves perhaps—with wheelbarrows pushing their loads of earth higher and higher along their rising mound with the patient and ceaseless persistence of the Egyptian labor gangs that built the pyramids, waiting without eagerness or despair for the taskmaster to declare, "It is enough." Then the leveling of the high base that now commanded the parking lot, the road, and the river itself at a splendid distance from the church so that neither seemed to partake of the other, as if the Talliaferros had not wished to have thoughts of God's presence in the county detract from admiration for their own presence here. "Whoever surveyed that hill must have been an artilleryman," Arceneaux said.

Charles looked at him in surprise. "Why do you say that?"

"You can put a field piece up there and block the river and the road with your fire."

"Were you in the war?"

Arceneaux backed away quickly. "I was in the service," he said. "I was not in the artillery. I just—I'm just talking."

"But you're right, you know. Luciano Talliaferro was an artillery officer for Napoleon. He wrote the story of his life. It's in manuscript in the Lawson-McGee Library up in Knoxville. Written before he died in 1874. I've read it."

"You've read it. Is it in Italian?"

Charles blushed again. "Well, yes."

"You read Italian."

"My father taught me French. So I read French. If you know French it's not hard to read Italian."

"Mais vraiment, vous parlez Français bien?"

"Oh, assez bien. Mon père me dit que j'ai un accent américain."

"Mais certainement, mais enfin, vous êtes Américain." Arceneaux laughed, admiring and somehow grateful. French in this place!

"Oui," Charles said with an embarrassed laugh. "We'd better speak English. My father says we should never speak French out in public. Not here in Bourbon County."

"But why? Why?"

"Well, he says people fundamentally don't like foreigners here. They can turn against you very fast."

"I would hate to believe that," Arceneaux said.

"I don't really believe it, but my father does. He says to me all the time, 'Do you not think I sound as if I were born here?' " Charles mimicked his father's accent with this last sentence.

"If he uses the subjunctive like that, nobody could imagine he was born here," Arceneaux said.

"Yes, well, it's not just the subjunctive. He also thinks his accent is completely American."

"I'd like to meet him," Arceneaux said. "People talk about him, you know. He's Belgian, is he?"

"That's where he grew up," Charles said noncommittally. "What do you think of it?" Only much later on in recalling this conversation did Arceneaux realize that Charles had deftly changed the subject. For the moment he was captivated by the mausoleum.

"I think it's one of the most beautiful things I've ever seen in my life." Charles had lowered his voice and spoke in a quietly reverent tone.

Arceneaux stared at the tomb. It was a perfectly proportioned building made of mottled marble where pink and dark-green lines ran rhythmically against each other, aged and weathered so that it gave off a quiet and dignified radiance, a glow of settlement in time, somehow unpretentious and unself-consciously grand. In the dense, cool shade of the cypresses it conveyed an otherworldly mystery so that for one brief moment of surreal expectation Arceneaux thought he would not be surprised to see nymphs and bacchae come dancing out of the sacred gloom in diaphanous garments and circle the two of them, carrying them off to some forest haunt where the lyre of Orpheus would lift them to a timeless peace. He was amazed. The building was hypnotic, as if it had some power to cast a spell out of its mute stone, to take life in the stillness. Abruptly, for no reason that he could fathom, Arceneaux felt himself on the verge of tears.

"I think it is the most beautiful thing in Bourbon County," Charles tried again. He was embarrassed. He sensed Arceneaux's emotion, was puzzled by it.

"It's just amazing. Amazing," Arceneaux said. It was familiar somehow, and then he recognized it. "It's built to resemble the treasure of the Athenians in Delphi," he said suddenly.

Charles looked at him, uncomprehending. "Delphi, in Greece," Arceneaux said. "On the Sacred Way, there's a small marble building where the people of Athens stored their gifts to the oracle at Delphi. The French have reconstructed it. But this tomb was built before the French did their work. How did this family, these Italians—how did they know to do this?"

Charles shrugged. "They owned the ferry down there. It used to be there, before the iron bridge. "

"It's larger," Arceneaux said, paying no attention to what Charles said. "It's not exactly like the Athenian treasure. But it's close."

"They were Waldensians," Charles said. "See? You can see it on the stuff up there."

"The stuff up there is called a frieze," Arceneaux said with a trace of irritation. The frieze was white marble, and it ran just under the black sloping marble of the roof. At each corner of the frieze, a chaste female statue, modestly dressed in chiton and delicately carved in solemn grief, head bowed, looked down. He stepped closer. The ground beneath his feet was thick with fallen needles from the trees. FAMIGLIA TALLIAFERRO, the frieze said. And next to that, PIETRO WALDO DISCEPOLI FEDELI.

How strange that they should come here, he thought. *How strange that I should come here. Everybody has to be somewhere.*

"In Luciano's memoir he attacks the Pope for being opposed to Napoleon. He was very proud that his family was not Catholic. When they came here, I suppose, the Baptists seemed to hate the Catholics more than anybody else. So they became Baptists."

"Like mine," Arceneaux mused aloud. "My ancestors were French Huguenots. They thought all good people should hate the Catholic Church."

"I've gone back in the courthouse records," Charles said. "I found a deed to land bought by Luciano Talliaferro along both banks of the river back in 1819 for seventy-five gold dollars. After the Battle of Waterloo he had to leave Europe, and somehow he landed here. The deed gives boundaries. Creeks. They're still there. A grove of trees. It's long gone. And a large white boulder on the corner of a field. You can still see the boulder. It's just over that hill, east of the church. It's about a square mile of land overall. On both sides of the river. So they had a ferry landing. The main wagon road from Knoxville to Chattanooga ran through it. It must have been pretty wretched. That's Highway 11 now. Anyway, it went into the water where the bridge is now and came out the other side, and the Talliaferro ferry was the only way to get across the river since the Talliaferros owned the land on both sides."

Charles knew the whole story, and he recited it while Arceneaux listened admiringly. The kid was a scholar and didn't know it. Something innocent about that. Arceneaux blocked his own thoughts.

Modest fees add up. The ferry made the Talliaferros rich. They built a mansion in Greek Revival style overlooking the river on the south side where from their great veranda they could look down through its high columns onto the source of their wealth. Sometime before 1850 Luciano went back to Europe, taking his family on the grand tour. He went back to Piedmont and to Florence, but he proudly recalled that he did not visit Rome, the seat of the papal Antichrist. Yes, he went to Greece, too, Charles said. Yes, he went to Delphi. All that was in his memoir. But he did not say anything about where he took the inspiration for the tomb. In fact in his memoir he said little about the tomb at all—as if he felt reluctant to entertain the thought that he would ever use it.

It was said that he employed an Italian architect, brought him to this country, gave him an unlimited budget, and paid for imported blocks of pink and black marble from Italy, transported to the site by ship and then by railroad, draped with Italian flags. But, said Charles, since Italy was not yet a united country, it must have been the flag of Sardinia-Piedmont. Then there was the problem of transporting the stones from the railroad to the site of the Salem Baptist Church a mile away, commanding a great bend in the river.

"The last burial in the tomb was 1937," Charles said. "I don't think anybody in the family has been back here since. I looked the name up in the New York telephone directory, but there were so many Talliaferros that I didn't try to call anybody. This family may have all died out."

"Maybe so," Arceneaux said. He looked at the marble door. It had a brass wheel in it, like the wheels he had seen on the hatches of ships. The brass had turned green. "Can we go in?" he said.

"I don't know," Charles said. "I've never tried." He was obviously reluctant.

"Let's see," Arceneaux said. He took the wheel in both hands and wrenched it experimentally, gradually increasing the force he applied. For a moment the wheel resisted. Then, as if it had been oiled for decades, it turned smoothly and silently, and when Arceneaux had turned it all the way counterclockwise, he gave it a pull, and the door, perfectly balanced, swung quickly open, and looming ahead in the dry, mysterious dark were the tombs of the Talliaferro family, arranged in ranks on each side of a corridor.

They stepped into the corridor. "They say it's completely watertight," Charles murmured. "They say you could drop this building in the river out there and it might float."

On the tomb nearest the door was an inscription:

LUCIANO TALLIAFERRO
Born in Turin, Italy, October 2, 1783
Died in Bourbon County, Tennessee
November 28, 1874
Sempre in luce

Always in light, Arceneaux thought. *A nice idea.* He thought of his own soul held up to the sun, to God's light, and himself purged, all the darkness made to vanish in eternal light. And song. There would have to be song.

"There is no inside wheel to work the lock," Arceneaux said.

"I suppose they didn't want the spirits to get out," Charles said.

They laughed.

*W*HEN Pappy settled with Mammy in the valley up from Gatlinburg back in 1925, the forest had been logged, and great stumps of the poplars and maples and birches and ashes and chestnuts stood scattered amid the second growth so that you could look out on a sunny day and see the light streaming through the foliage showing the round, flat stump tops, and you could think you were looking at tables made for the biggest all-day-preaching-and-dinner-on-the-grounds you'd ever seen in your life. Only it was sad, too—the forest ruined, devastated with all those stumps, wasted and desolate even with the second growth coming up. Hope Kirby was eight years old then, and Mammy was pregnant with M.L., the last son.

They lived in a lean-to at first, and Mammy cooked on a fire in the open, and when it rained at night, the water trickled through the roof Pappy had made, and you were likely to get a drop or two smack in the middle of your face. But it was amazing when Hope Kirby thought about it later that they stayed as dry as they did. Pappy knew how to weave vines to make a mat over the lean-to that kept most of the water at bay, even in a violent storm. He had patience.

The first thing Pappy did—even before he built a cabin—was to construct a snake-rail fence, firmly anchored with upright chestnut posts he had cut from saplings. The chestnuts were dying, but saplings still grew up through the moist mountain earth, and they made good posts to anchor a rail fence. You could sink a chestnut post in the ground, and it would not rot for a hundred years. The same with a chestnut casket. Mammy was buried in a chestnut casket at the Red Bank Baptist Church, and Pappy said sometimes that he thought that chestnut casket still held the water out. That was a comfort.

Pappy fenced in thirty acres of his new hundred-acre domain—including the fifty acres of lumbered-out forest that you wouldn't think was worth ten cents or wouldn't be until another fifty years had passed and the trees had a chance to grow back. He turned razorback hogs into his lot—twenty-five razorbacks for thirty acres. He spent his last dime for those pigs.

"That much land could take more hogs, but I hain't got no money to buy more, and besides, we want fat ones," Pappy said. When they put the hogs in the lot, Pappy turned to building his cabin, and Hope and John Sevier and Mammy worked, and the other boys helped out however they could, and the cabin took shape—one big room with a stone fireplace on one end, the roof shingled with thick white birch and so watertight that you could have a storm big enough to break down trees in the woods, and you wouldn't have a drop of water inside. You could lie there in your bed and listen to the storm howl and beat, and you were safe. Hope Kirby never forgot that feeling; it was the best feeling he ever had—being safe in a storm because Pappy had built the cabin right.

It was hard work. The pigs ate acorns that first year and stayed lean, and all his life Hope Kirby could remember when Pappy and Mammy and the boys sat down to a meal of boiled acorns with just a little salt to season them. They drank sassafras tea and ate groundnut turnips and a wealth of other things Mammy knew how to dig for in the woods. Sometimes Mammy caught a rabbit in a box trap, and they had rabbit stew, and in November when the leaves fell off the trees, Pappy killed squirrels now and then, and they had squirrel dumplings, and they were never hungry. When he was in the Philippines, he remembered how to live off the land, and he did it for himself and for his men, and he felt that what Pappy had taught him kept him alive.

Pappy saved all the salt he could, and in January of that year he found a cave where a black bear was sleeping, and he put the shotgun up against the bear's eye and pulled the trigger, and they had salt bear meat the rest of the winter.

Pappy kept the pigs through that first year and into the late summer of the next, and he sold the pigs in Sevierville—drove them down with his boys and sold them at auction. He sold them live because he did not have enough salt to slaughter them and cure them himself, and Hope was secretly glad because he liked the pigs, and they nuzzled him when he scratched their ears, and he couldn't bear to think how the pigs would look at him when they knew Pappy was going to kill them. So the first year, he got to pretend that the pigs were not going to die, that they were going on a trip where they would see things and be happy.

Pappy kept back a few piglets and a few sows and a boar when he sold off the hogs, and the next year they had fifty pigs, and he had plenty of salt by then, and they had all the pork they could eat, and they sold pork down in Sevierville that went out to Knoxville and God knows where else. Pappy did what he had to do every day, and they prospered. They had pork to eat and in the spring poke salat and dandelions and peas, and when the mountain summer came on, hot in the days, cool at night and very still, Mammy had a garden, and they had tomatoes and pole beans, and she canned tomatoes and beans and blackberry preserves in jars, and Pappy raised more pigs and sold them and cleared more land and built onto his cabin and added a veranda and bought a secondhand wood stove and built more fences and tore stumps out of the ground.

Oh, that man could be patient! He had to root out chestnut stumps five feet across, black oaks and elms three or four feet thick, and how did he do that? First he burned the stump in a fire, piling the brush on it until it got so hot you couldn't stand ten feet away from it. But you ran up and threw on brush and ran back again before your face burned, and the fire blazed at that stump, turning the wood to smoke that the wind blew away.

Finally, when you got it burned down so far, you had to attack it with an axe, with mauls and wedges, and you went down and down, and finally you cut up the bottom of it and used long iron levers and worked it loose in the ground like it was a giant tooth wrenched from the jaws of Mother Earth, and finally you hitched the mules up, you sweated over the levers, and they pulled, bowing their strong backs and pushing with their strong legs, and with a big heaving noise the stump came out of the ground, sucking earth behind it. Sometimes it took a week of working daylight to dark to get one stump out, and every day Pappy was out there with his boys, and although he did most of the work, they took turns. And when at last the stump came out, Pappy didn't pause more than to take off his old black hat, wipe his face with his bandana, look at the hole where the stump had been, and say, "Good!" before he moved on to the next one.

Pure patience! That's what it was. "Us Kirbys know how to work and to wait," Pappy said. And there it was—the enduring, steady, unfaltering patience that built the pyramids of Egypt, those peculiar, black spiked shapes with yellow camels in front of them that appeared in a brightly colored picture in the only book in the house, a Bible that Pappy had bought in a dime store somewhere but that, he said, had all the words in it that the big, costly, leather-bound Bibles had in them, and Mammy read out of it, and they learned maps and geography by the maps of the Holy Land that were stuck in the back of it.

In the worst times of his life, Hope looked back on those days with a pleasure that was like sleep on a rainy summer morning, one of those sweet mornings when the rain drummed down on a shingle roof, shifting sometimes with the wind, augmenting and diminishing, and he lay on his bed upstairs in the loft of the new part of the house, lying on the corn-shuck mattress with its sweet, familiar crackle and smell, and he was content.

The rain meant peace. They did chores, and they came home and sat in the house while the rain fell, and Mammy read out of the Bible, or Pappy talked in a slow, steady voice about his pappy and life back up in Virginia near the Cumberland Gap when Pappy was a boy, and about his grand-daddy and lots of other granddaddies Pappy had never known personally, but whose stories he had heard, and he told them to his boys, all the way back to places that came shining out of some distant bright place in memory before multitudes of the dead were born, names like Brandywine and York-town and Kings Mountain—and before that the green hills of Ireland. Pappy could start in talking, and it was like it was all written down in his head or maybe carved in stone that his mind could see when they couldn't.

John Sevier had the gift that Pappy had, even when John Sevier wasn't more than ten years old. He could hear the stories, and out working a fence row or putting up hay or chopping corn John Sevier would tell them, half under his breath, sometimes out loud, and the other boys laughed at him at first, but Pappy said no, don't laugh at John Sevier because he had the gift, and Pappy said that was the way the stories were passed on. And if the stories weren't passed on, you forgot who you were. When he got stuck on something, couldn't remember, John Sevier asked Pappy, and Pappy told him, and John Sevier would go on, like a boy memorizing a poem in school, only this was a lot more than a poem; it was history.

Marching out of Bataan with the Jap soldiers guarding them with their guns, grinning and mocking them and using their rifle butts to club American soldiers in the head and their swords to cut heads off, John Sevier and Hope walked along together, and John Sevier—so tired he could hardly put one foot in front of the other—was telling those stories, gasping them out in a worn, singsong voice like old ballads memorized in childhood, something to hold on to in the killing heat and with the murderous Japs on each side of the road. "Hit makes the time pass," he said. Hope Kirby said yes it did. It made the time pass.

Now that John Sevier had been clubbed senseless by the Japs, now that he stared out at the world with those steady, vacant, ice-blue eyes, Hope Kirby had to wonder if anything was back there. Did John Sevier remember any of the stories? Did they move through his head like shadows on a wall in a house where maybe one candle flickered in a room, and its light was thrown from wall to wall in diminishing and mystic glowing and all the shapes of life became suggestions of darkness moving against a pale reflection on a surface no one could quite define? Hope wondered.

In jail in Bourbonville he thought back to those good days, the summer rain falling on the roof, and he was snug and dry because Pappy had cut every one of those shingles and fitted them and nailed them, and they were going to keep the water out and every bad thing at bay.

He remembered when the family started going to church. Pappy wasn't a religious man. He didn't care for crowds, and he didn't like near neighbors. Hope never heard him say a prayer, never saw him praying, never heard him say anything about God. Pappy didn't cuss or smoke or drink, and people said to him sometimes, "Your father is one of the best Christians I've ever knowed in my life." But Hope was not sure that was true. The best man he had ever known. He could agree with all his brothers on that. But Hope never was sure about the Christian part, and sometimes he wondered about it and could come to no conclusive answer. People said you had to have an experience to be a Christian, and it didn't look to Hope like Pappy had ever had an experience.

But then Pappy never was one to talk much about his feelings. Mammy was a Toliver, and sometimes she'd tell them all about her feelings, how pretty she thought something was—the sky at night in spring when the moon was down, for example, or the wildflowers that grew in the woods or the clouds standing white and mysterious over Mount LeConte above their heads sometimes in the summer when the whole world was still as if God had breathed on it and made it stop for a minute so He could look at it. Then Mammy would say, "Ain't it pretty!" That's the way the Tolivers were. Talkative about their feelings and suchlike.

Anyway, religious or not, with feelings or not, Pappy decided they would go to church. That was all right with everybody. None of the boys cussed or smoked or drank, and they didn't figure that they were going to run into anything in church they couldn't handle. They knew the Bible stories if anybody wanted to ask questions about them. Hope still remembered them—Adam and Eve and Jacob and Joseph and Pharaoh and Moses and Joshua and Gideon and Samson and Ruth and Saul and King David and on and on. At night Mammy read the Bible to them by the light of the fire in the big stone fireplace in winter or by the steady yellow light of a coal-oil lamp in warm weather. Mammy gathered her children around her and read to them, and they all listened, Pappy sitting in his rocking chair and rocking just a little bit, just enough so you could barely hear the rockers making little thumps on the plank floor, and he held his hands folded in his lap, and he looked into the fireplace whether it had a fire in it or not, and he listened in the solemn, expressionless way he listened to everything, and his boys sat on the floor, and they tried unconsciously to imitate just the way he was listening to Mammy.

Even then Hope Kirby didn't think the Bible was for religion. It was for entertainment. Nobody in the house prayed, not even Mammy although she was a Toliver, and there were some Tolivers that had been known to pray out loud. When he thought about people praying out loud to God, Hope was always a little embarrassed. It seemed ridiculous, silly—grown-up people talking to the air, acting like there was somebody standing up above them to hear them and to grant what they asked for. It never did get over seeming, well, odd to him, even when he got to be fifteen years old and Pappy decided that they were going to go to church, and all of them got used to hearing people stand up in the church house and pray every Sunday morning.

Pappy didn't explain anything. He just said one morning after milking time, "I want all of you to get clean Saturday night because we're all a-going to church come Sunday morning." Mammy looked at him maybe with her eyebrows raised just a little bit in an expression of inquiry and even surprise and maybe with a hint of approval and pleasure. But she did not express happiness or sorrow or gratitude or anything at all beyond that slight and swiftly passing, silent question that perhaps was not even that. Saturday night came, and she said, "You heard what your pappy said. Get cleaned up." So one by one the boys took baths in the number-two galvanized iron washtub, heating the water on the wood stove, walking around naked without shame or without even thinking about being naked because they had always been naked before Mammy and Pappy and each other. Next morning they put on clean overalls and clean shirts, and they harnessed up the mules and hitched them to the flatbed wagon.

There was a flatbed wagon by this time. Pappy bought the wheels and other metal parts from the hardware store down in Sevierville, and he built the wagon himself from white ash and hickory, and it was as tight and solid as the house. And in the wagon—built without springs because springs put an undue strain on the mules that pulled them—they banged and bounced and clattered down to Gatlinburg, a village with three or four houses and a hotel for summer people and a little Baptist church at one end of it, and they went to church.

After that they went to church every Sunday morning, even when it rained. Yes, it was still a mystery to Hope, and the thought of it bounced around his mind during the nights he spent in jail. He tried to solve the mystery with the same idle indifference that some people worked crossword puzzles on the ship bearing him to San Francisco from Manila so many years before.

It was commonplace when you thought about it—Pappy decided to go to church, and he went to church in every imaginable kind of weather with the slow, steady application he brought to rooting out stumps or to extending the snake-rail fences on his property or to killing pigs in November or to milking the cows in the morning. Hope supposed Pappy went to the church for the pride of it.

And why not? Pappy had a right to be proud. By God he did!

He had come into the mountains with nothing to his name except sixteen good mules, the clothes on his back, Mammy in tow, four young boys of whom Hope was the oldest and only eight years old, and Mammy pregnant with another one. Pappy owned a single-shot twelve-gauge shotgun and a box of shells, and he had a good knife. He swapped twelve of his fine mules for a hundred acres of lumbered-out hills and a coldwater creek that ran down the mountain and through his land and out over one overgrown and worn-out red-clay field choked with blackberry briars and sedge grass and sassafras and with so many rattlesnakes lurking about that you didn't dare walk through it without a big stick in your hand to club them when you heard the dry-bones rattle they gave a moment before they struck.

People laughed up their sleeves at Pappy when he made his bargain with a man named Stokes—twelve good brown mules, most of his life's capital, for a worn-out, lumbered-out piece of ground. But he had fooled them all. Nobody thought a man could have that much patience or maybe the dogged stubbornness and endurance to do what Pappy did. Seven years passed, and fields were cleared and fenced, and most of the rattlesnakes were gone because the pigs found them delicious, and the pigs fertilized the land, and now it was in hay and brought in two cuttings every summer, and part of it was pasture with four milch cows on it, and Pappy sold a can of raw milk a day to the dairy in Sevierville, which sent a truck chugging out to get it, and he had pigs running in the fields that were clear of stumps and running up the hills behind the house, all of it neat and the fences clean and the buildings firm.

The Depression hit, and they didn't feel it much. Sometimes they couldn't sell their milk, and Mammy would make butter and cottage cheese, and they swapped butter sometimes for things they needed in town, but they didn't need much of anything they didn't make for themselves. Roy Kirby was a man of property, and it was his right, Hope thought, to go down to church, to the meetinghouse of the community and display himself and his family and to say merely by his being there, "I have made something of my land, my boys, my woman, my livestock, and myself."

You had these parables that Jesus told about the men whose boss gave them talents, the boss expected them to do something with them, and some of them did, but in every group there was one man who was timid or just plain lazy, and he buried his in the ground where it would be safe. The boss gave him hell at the end of the story—hell and outer darkness to boot.

That fate would not have been Pappy's. He could show what he had done in just seven years—seven years of working six days a week from sunup to sundown, seven years of doing something all the time, the little things and the big things, orderly, as if he kept a notebook in his head, and he ticked off the items on the list as they were done, and like a man moving to the next stump to be rooted out of the ground, he kept going.

Hope was proud of Pappy. Pappy was patient with them just like he was with the stumps or with the invisible list he ticked off in memory. He never lost his temper when they did something wrong. He just told them to do it over again, and if one of the boys fretted, Pappy told him to go off and cool down awhile, and Pappy kept on working, and pretty soon the boy in a fret came back, a little embarrassed not to be working, and they all went on without mentioning that anybody had been in a fret about anything.

In church and standing around outside afterwards when men talked, Pappy stood with the rest while Mammy visited with the women. But he never had much to say outside the family. There were men who talked a lot, who told stories in crowds, who vaunted themselves. But Pappy never did. He told his stories to his family, but he did not tell them to strangers. He was not timid. He was just proud, or maybe it was only that he was so sure of himself that he never had to put on any airs, to make a display. Sometimes men asked him questions—respectful men with respectful questions. Not much of anybody ever tried to joke with Pappy. You looked at him and decided he wasn't the joking kind. But they asked him what he thought about this year's market for pigs. What did he think about the weather? What did he think was a good poultice on a bad bruise? And he would answer, not haughtily, not with many words, but enough, and if people disagreed with him about something, he said indifferently, "Well, that's the way I see hit," and that was the end of it.

He wasn't angry or sullen or snappy. He could say "Well, that's the way I see hit" with the simplicity of a man looking out the window in the morning and saying to nobody in particular, "Hit's a pretty day," and you believed him because he was standing there looking out the window, and you figured he didn't have any reason to lie to you about what he saw. That was Pappy's way. He seemed to look through his own private window onto the world, and he told you what he saw. If other people saw something else, well, that was their affair, and maybe their window was on the other side of the house, and it might be storming over there. You never could tell.

Hope watched Pappy, and he was proud of him without even knowing until years and years later that the emotion he felt was pride. He simply saw Pappy standing there with the other men, most of them playing to each other, and there was his father, calm and quiet with his hands in his pockets, and Hope knew that Pappy was the best one of the bunch. It was as simple as that. It was all so much of life that Hope took it all for granted.

Then the man in the black car showed up one day and took it all away. His name was Hamilton. He wore a gray suit and a felt hat bought in the kind of store that existed in Knoxville or towns larger than Sevierville—towns Hope and his brothers had never seen. He drove a Ford car—not the old split-windshield Model T that you could see chugging around the mountains, the hand-me-down cars with three pedals on the floor that mountain people could barely afford to buy when flatlanders had already worn them out, and that the mountain people drove then until the cars collapsed into rust and oil and were pushed off to the back of a farm somewhere to sit and to be overgrown with weeds and vines.

Mr. Hamilton drove one of those new streamlined Fords, painted black and shining under the dust of the mountain roads that Mr. Hamilton had to traverse. Hope and his pappy were building a new chicken house out back and up a hill a ways when they heard the car drive up to the house and stop. Pappy and John Sevier were working with the shingles on the outside, and Hope was inside fixing up a roosting bar that would be just high enough for chickens to fly up onto at dark but just out of the reach of any fox or possum that might happen to work his way into the chicken house at night in search of supper. Love and Joye had gone down to the sawmill with the wagon to bring out some more planks, and there was the sudden, unexpected, unnatural sound of a car pulling up to their house and stopping. It was on the downhill side from where they worked, and they could not see it for the house.

They all stopped working, and they listened. "Hit might be the preacher," Pappy said. He had a new car—not a completely new car, of course, but one new to him, and he was driving around his church field, as he called it, visiting his people and praying over them if they were sick or shut-in and if they wanted him to pray, and he was showing off his car and showing all the tricks it would do.

In another minute or two they heard a horn blowing—sharp, quick, impatient, harshly musical blasts that echoed up the mountain, and they heard Mammy come around and start calling up at them.

With Mammy's call they all with one unspoken accord threw down their tools and headed down the hill almost on the run, and in a minute M.L. met them, all out of breath from running. He was not more than eight years old at the time, and he looked scared as only an eight-year-old who has seen something unimaginable can be scared. "Pappy, they's a city feller down there in a car, and he says he's got to see you right now." All the while the car horn kept blowing in intense, spasmodic blasts that sounded like the meaning of impatience, haste, anger all rolled up together.

M.L. stood in the middle of the path so frightened that they all stopped a minute to see what the matter was. He looked ready to cry. "He says we're going to have to move. We have to give up our land and move away."

ON THIS Sunday afternoon Arceneaux found Charles sitting alone except for the dog in the yard of the Alexander place. Paul, Stephen, and Guy had made their weekly departure for the home of Jim Ed and Juliet Ledbetter, a habit so ingrained in Paul Alexander that he apparently did not think once that on a day when Charles had witnessed murder, walked the floor all night, tried to lie, failed, and sunk into a silent lethargy, some break in years of routine might have been worthwhile. Paul Alexander was a creature of habit and order, and Sunday after Sunday in fair weather and foul, he, Jim Ed, Stephen, and other musicians gathered at one house or another to play music. Another year they might have come to the Alexander place, and on a steaming summer day such as this one, they might have assembled in the front yard under the flourishing maples, and in the warm shade they would have made their melodies, and Charles would not have been left alone.

But a year before, Juliet had had a stroke. Jim Ed had wakened in the night feeling that something was wrong, terribly wrong, with his wife, who lay still beside him, breathing in the shallow gasps that had roused him. Paul Ledbetter, the younger son, was practicing medicine in Bourbonville by then, and he came flying in response to his father's frantic summons by telephone. But a stroke is a stroke, one of the mysteries of the human brain and the dispassionate collision of atoms that creates chance. Juliet recovered enough to sit up and to take the food offered to her and to try with all her might to speak, but no words would come that anyone could understand, and she could not write even by pecking out messages with one finger on the typewriter that Paul Ledbetter set before her.

She seemed to know people. When Jim Ed or one of her children came into the room and spoke to her, she responded with a gargle of confused and chaotic sounds that no one could decipher. When her older son, the one everyone called Blackie, came home from hospital duty in the Korean War shortly after her stroke, her welcome was a hurricane of noise, and when Paul Alexander entered the room, she always greeted him with a similar outcry. But no one could make sense of what she said.

So now every Sunday the group of musicians appeared at Jim Ed's house, and they tuned up their instruments and played. Both the Ledbetter sons were musical. Dr. Goldstein, in Bourbonville since three years before the war when he arrived with his family from Germany, came with his violin that, after his long association with the county, had become a fiddle. A couple of Jim Ed's friends joined them, and Sunday afternoons swelled with music until everyone was tired, and then the silence and languid talk came and twilight and dark, and the group reluctantly folded instruments away and went home.

Years before, Charles had stopped attending these sessions, and his father had given up his efforts to persuade him otherwise. Charles believed that his father believed that he, Charles, could learn to play an instrument if he only applied himself. But an iron certainty in Charles's head told him that for him music was impossible, and his failures as a child to master simple things that his father tried to teach him confirmed his defiant conviction.

Perhaps there was stubbornness on both sides. Whatever the cause, the effect was that between Paul Alexander and his second son was an invisible barrier. It made them both uncomfortable. When on this afternoon Paul Alexander tried to coax Charles to come along to Jim Ed's place, Charles refused, and perhaps with too easy an acquiescence Paul Alexander took his other sons away, and Charles was left alone. So it was when Larry Arceneaux drove up the driveway and saw Charles sitting in the shade of the maples.

The dog came charging across the yard barking, and Charles got up slowly, as though utterly spent, and called the dog off, a command the dog seemed happy to obey. Then, in the way of dogs, it came sniffing cautiously to Arceneaux who scratched the beast behind the ears and so gained more of its friendship than he wanted. At least Jiggs, the Alexander bulldog, was a real dog and not one of those ratlike creatures that women in New Orleans held in their laps like a live fur ornament.

Charles invited Arceneaux to sit down on one of the shabby and weathered pieces of wooden lawn furniture that Paul Alexander had set in the yard years ago. Paul Alexander was frugal. He never spent money unless he must, and the chairs were still sturdy enough to hold the weight of a human body, and it never occurred to him to buy something more shapely and modern to replace them.

When Charles called off the dog and invited Arceneaux to sit down, explaining that his father and his brothers had gone to play music at Jim Ed Ledbetter's house below town, Arceneaux felt a surge of confidence. He could explain himself. Well, not everything. Of course not everything. But he could talk to the boy in peace, make his case, make Charles see what had to be done.

Sympathy. "Charles, I'm so sorry about what happened. It must have been awful."

The boy sat there looking exhausted and blank. Arceneaux didn't understand the blankness. He thought it meant acquiescence, and he began to talk eagerly, with animation, gesturing, sometimes with both hands, his words gushing out in a confused flood. He was sure he was right; he was sure Charles would see that he was right. Later Arceneaux remembered it painfully, heard his own words tumbling over one another as if he had recorded them and played them back to himself. The stillness of the Sunday afternoon was deep. The heat put the birds to sleep, and not a breath stirred. Arceneaux sweated in his white linen suit. He laid his Panama hat on the bench beside him, and he talked on. And on and on. "I am asking you not to do something that you will regret the rest of your life." Charles stared at him.

Arceneaux talked harder, obfuscating, philosophizing, calling up Greek drama Charles had never heard of to speak of the Eumenides and the end of a cycle of violence and the evils of revenge and the problems Hamlet had brought upon Denmark by his efforts to obey the command of the ghost for vengeance. "Don't you see?" Arceneaux said, his eyes burning with his own kind of truth. "The ghost may have been a demon after all. Hamlet should have tested it, measured consequences. What happened? The ghost wanted revenge against Claudius, but in the end Polonius is dead, Ophelia is dead, Laertes is dead, Claudius is dead, Gertrude is dead, Hamlet is dead, and Denmark is in the hands of the invader. Don't you see, Charles? The moment the ghost cried out for vengeance, Hamlet should have said, 'Get thee behind me, Satan.' "

Finally he got to the point. "You will have another chance at the trial," Arceneaux said.

"The trial," Charles said dully.

"You will be asked what you saw. You can say a simple thing. You can say you are not sure what you saw."

Charles stared at him.

"You will be asked, you see. The prosecuting attorney—whatever he is called. I don't know what he is called in Tennessee. I'm not even sure what he's called in Louisiana. They are called different things in different states. Is it 'district attorney' here? Whatever. He will ask you, 'What did you see?' Or something like that. You will be asked, 'Are you sure what you saw?' You see? The impossible question. How can any of us answer it? Are you sure I'm sitting here, talking to you now? No, you're not sure. I may be a figment of your imagination. A hallucination. We never know what reality is, do we? Or we never know what happened in the past. One person remembers an event one way; another, another. Don't you agree?"

Charles stared blankly at him, eyes like eggs.

"You can begin right now, telling people. Have you seen any reporters? The newspapers?"

Charles shook his head.

"You will see them. And you can start telling them that you are not sure now what you saw, that it might have been Hope Kirby but you can't be sure. At the trial, that's all you have to say. You can't be sure it was Hope Kirby. That's all."

"You are asking me to lie?"

The direct question made Arceneaux feel an electric flash of anger. "I'm asking you to save a man's life. Would you have told the truth if you were hiding Jews in your basement in the war and the Nazis came to ask you if you were hiding Jews? Would you have said, 'Oh yes, I'm hiding Jews.

They're downstairs in the basement scared out of their wits that you will take them to the gas chambers. Go ahead and drag them upstairs. I am like George Washington. I cannot tell a lie.' "

Charles gaped at him, his mouth partly open, looking as if he had been struck in the head. He *had* been struck in the head. Arceneaux saw the bruise on his forehead. He didn't ask about it. Only later did he learn that the bruise was there because Hope Kirby had hit Charles in the forehead with his pistol.

"You have to lie to keep your conscience clean," Arceneaux said. He was almost yelling.

Lord God! What a fool I was, Arceneaux thought in the years of his wisdom.

And Charles? He thought of trembling, of breaking down, of weeping before his father, his brothers, the sheriff. He was covered with the shame of it.

*B*Y EIGHT o'clock Monday morning Roy Kirby's red Dodge pickup sat slantwise on the square by the Rexall drugstore across from the courthouse. Roy Kirby sat behind the wheel. John Sevier sat beside him staring blankly into an unfocused space. When the word spread that the two of them were sitting out there, people came out of the drugstores and the cafes and stared at them, but nobody came over and spoke. It was going to be a hot day, and everybody moved slowly.

Some people came from the back side of the courthouse where the brown stains left by Kelly Parmalee's blood and brains were still evident on the grass. They had been staring at the blood, speaking to one another in low voices as if expecting the stains to tell them something, but the stains remained silent—just as the Parmalee store across the way remained shut and silent, yielding nothing to the amalgamated curiosity of multitudes who felt vaguely that they had been robbed of a spectacle because Hope Kirby had shot his wife and her lover while Bourbonville had been asleep.

You could not tell that anything was wrong with John Sevier when you first looked at him. He was slender with coarse coal-black hair, high cheekbones, and the sharp blue eyes of all the other Kirby men. Scotch-Irish to the core, you'd say if you knew about such things. But then you noticed that his eyes were blank and stared straight ahead, never moving no matter what walked in front of him. John Sevier could stare straight through you as if you had been the Invisible Man. Roy Kirby was wiry, brown with the sun, his skin like soft leather well tanned, and he had the clean-shaven dignity of a country man who worked hard, took baths, minded his own business and expected you to mind yours. People called the Kirby men hillbillies behind their backs. Their accents, you see. But you didn't say anything like that to Roy Kirby. Not to his face. Not that he had ever made even so much as a threatening gesture or raised his voice to anybody in Bourbon County. You just knew he was not a man to fool around with.

When Hugh Bedford pulled up fifteen minutes later in his 1940 Ford coupe, he muttered to himself, "Well, there they are." While Hugh parked, Roy Kirby got out of his pickup like an unhurried cat with a purpose, and by the time Hugh flipped off his ignition, Roy Kirby stood by the open car window, a straw hat pulled down over his forehead, looking in with blue eyes like steel drills. "My oldest boy's in trouble, Mr. Bedford," he said softly.

"He's in a shitload of trouble," Hugh said with the world-weariness of his nature. "Come on up. I was expecting you." He labored out of his car, pulling his clothes away from his body, sweaty and foul from the thick heat of an August morning although he had stood almost an hour in his shower when he got up. He felt like shit. That was the funny thing about drinking as much as he did. Even a habitual drunk like himself felt like shit after a night of drinking whiskey, but he kept on drinking, and he didn't think he could ever stop. He thought that as much as he drank he might arrive at immunity from being hung over. But not yet.

"Come along, John Sevier," Roy Kirby said in the gentle tone grown-ups use with little kids. He opened the pickup door for his son, and John Sevier got out. They were both scrubbed and clean. Hugh Bedford wondered briefly if Roy Kirby washed his son the way you wash a dog in a tub.

They climbed the dark and narrow interior stairwell to Hugh's office. The air inside was stale and thick and reeked of varnish sweated out of the wood by the heat. It was like going up a steep tunnel sided with wood in stale air, and every morning when he labored up there, he thought he would die. Old Doc Bulkely told him once he thought climbing the stairway kept him alive. "It's the only exercise you get," Doc Bulkely said disapprovingly. "As much as you drink and smoke, I'm surprised you've lived as long as you have."

Doc Bulkely had come to Bourbonville years ago armed with vitamins and diets and charts showing what you needed to do every day to keep healthy. He became a propagandist for health, and people listened to him. But even when they took vitamins and went on diets and brushed their teeth morning and night and drank a glass of warm water when they got up in the morning and chewed their food fifty times a bite, they finally sickened and died, some young, some not so young, and some old. It was discouraging. Dr. Bulkely persisted in giving his good advice, but it was more habit now than hope. Sometimes Hugh thought Dr. Bulkely was irritated with him for continuing to live even when he drank so much.

Hugh puffed like an old leather bellows by the time they got to the top. Roy Kirby said in mild alarm, "You all right, Mr. Bedford?" Hugh said, "Hell yes, I'm all right." The heat in this confined space was miserable, and when Hugh found his key and unlocked the padlock on the door, it didn't get better. He didn't know why he locked the office. Nothing was there to steal, but sometimes he made notes and doodles about foes and judges and cases and all the rest of it. He did not want somebody to put on Judge Shirley K. Yancy's desk a paper that would show in Hugh's own handwriting that he thought the old judge was a homicidal maniac who ought to be hanged after he had been beaten at the public whipping post that Hugh Bedford would have installed on the courthouse lawn if it had been up to him. Hugh was good at drawing—something most people didn't know—and sometimes in court while Judge Yancy was hearing one of his cases, Hugh would doodle a finely recognizable Judge Yancy being strangled with a hangman's noose on a gallows or being raped in the rear end by a jackass. The image of the gallows was out of date because the state of Tennessee did not use the noose anymore. It executed its murderers and rapists with the supposedly instantaneous and therefore merciful device of the electric chair. Hugh Bedford thought Judge Yancy embodied the malice of Lucifer, and he ranked Judge Yancy close to Colonel Winrod in his pantheon of hatred.

When Hugh brought somebody new into his office, he felt a pang of shame. He was not proud of how he lived. The filthy windows were pulled down. The air was thick and foul, haunted by the myriad ghosts of dead cigarettes. He raised the windows and turned on the fan and had a Camel lit by the time he fell into his worn leather swivel chair, the one object in the office that seemed comfortable. He sucked hard on the cigarette. He had not had one in ten minutes.

Roy Kirby stood with his straw hat in his hand. It looked new, one of the dressy kind with a short brim and a crease in the top, shaped like a felt hat, not one of the big floppy straw hats farmers wore when they went out in the fields. John Sevier stood beside him, eyes blue like china and vacant as a doll's. *Put him on his back and his eyes would shut,* Hugh thought. "Sit down," he said. He had hard chairs for his clients. He didn't want them to get comfortable. They'd take up too much time if they sat in easy chairs.

"Sit down, John Sevier," Roy Kirby said, raising his voice just a little, the way you give commands to a dog.

"He can understand you," Hugh Bedford said, mildly surprised.

"Some things," Mr. Kirby said.

"I wish we'd dropped atom bombs on Japan from one end to the other," Hugh said.

Roy Kirby shrugged slightly. "I am proud we dropped the ones we did," he said.

"Does cigarette smoke bother you?" Hugh said.

"Hit's your house," he said.

Hugh laughed. "You're a polite man, Mr. Kirby. Cigarette smoke bothers the hell out of me. I smoke four packs a day. What do you think of that?"

"Hit's your life," he said.

"My death, too," Hugh said. "I started in the army. I didn't smoke before I went to the army. I try to quit, but I can't. I swear to God I can't."

"Never smoked myself," he said. "Never chewed neither." He spoke without an inflection of pride.

"And you don't drink," Hugh said.

"No sir, I don't," he said.

"And none of your boys smokes or drinks."

"No sir, they don't."

"And one of your boys is in jail this minute, and he will soon be indicted by a grand jury for murder in the first degree with malice aforethought, which carries a punishment in this state of death in the electric chair, and you have come to me to get him off." He took a deep pull on his cigarette.

"If anybody can do it, you can," he said.

"I can't work miracles," Hugh said.

"You got the Peabody girl off," he said.

Hugh laughed. "Ernestine Peabody! She was a wronged woman."

"I reckon she kilt that other woman," he said.

"Damned right. Shot her dead. Loretta Oaks. You know what Loretta said to Ernestine? 'Ya ya ya, you had him once, but I've got him now.' "

"She shouldn't of done that," Roy Kirby said.

"Damned right. Ernestine borrowed her daddy's pistol and shot her dead."

"You got her off," he said.

"I did pretty good if I do say so myself. But she was a woman. A mother. President of the PTA, too. She was protecting her home and her family."

"My boy was a soldier, and he's got a medal to prove it."

"It's not the same as being a mother." Hugh turned slightly in his chair and stared out the open window and smoked. His office looked directly at the front of the courthouse. The World War I monument showed a doughboy cast in metal with his fist in the air in an attitude of running towards the Rexall drugstore across the street under Hugh's office. The names of the World War I dead from the county were incised in the stone pedestal of the statue. Hugh had an affection for that statue. He knew that behind Doughboy some cowardly pissant of an officer like Sperling Winrod was safe in headquarters, playing Doughboy like a pawn on a chessboard.

Sometimes Hugh thought it would be great if Doughboy charged into the Rexall and said, "I want a Coke, damn it, and I want it now." But Doughboy remained in endless stillness, and at the base of the monument, the county had affixed a marble plaque with the names of those who had died in World War II. One monument for two wars. *My name could be there,* Hugh thought. The Germans who killed his men were in Germany telling people how they had always been against Hitler.

"I was going to volunteer my services," he said to Roy Kirby.

"You got a lot of business here," Roy Kirby said. "Can you keep up with all of hit?" He looked at the desk. It was piled high with papers, not only documents from probate and trials and depositions but also yellowing old newspapers and magazines, law books and other books, all heedlessly set down at one time or another and forgotten, a thousand interrupted moments, suspended conversations, unfinished fragments of a life. The walls were lined with books, most of them law books in buckram bindings, and there were papers—some yellowing—stuffed between the books and laid across their tops and strewn over small and nondescript tables. On most surfaces and even on the parts of the desk that protruded from beneath the stacks, a thick patina of dust covered everything. Hugh knew Roy Kirby was doubting, wanting to know if he—Hugh Bedford—was competent enough to take responsibility for his boy's life.

"I keep up with everything I need to keep up with, Mr. Kirby. I'll keep up with your son's case till the end."

"Just wondering," Roy Kirby said. He fixed Hugh Bedford with his pale blue eyes.

"You have the right to wonder." Hugh laughed without humor. The electric fan rotated on a thin stalk of yellow metal, turning like the blank face of a robot back and forth, stirring the air like syrup and making a humming sound. Hugh wiped his face with a red bandana handkerchief. Roy Kirby's face was dry. He looked almost cool. His body was thin and wiry and relaxed, and he sat in unastonished and serene repose beyond this garbage dump of a desk, his straw hat on his lap, denim shirt and denim trousers much washed, spotless and pressed, a lean face, and a voice commanding, yes, commanding, "What do you think the chances are?"

Hugh took a deep breath. "Looks to me like he killed those two after making a careful plan of it. It will look that way to judge and jury, too. That is premeditated murder, Mr. Kirby. You admit that yourself."

"He done what a man has got to do when his woman is stepping out on him."

"That may be true, but in this instance what he did happens to be against the laws of the state of Tennessee and the common law of the United States and England."

"They is law, and they is law."

Hugh sighed and leaned back in the swivel chair and rocked a little and smoked and studied the ceiling where the ancient brass fixture for an electric light stood vacant and crusted with corrosion and dirt. "I suppose that is true, but with Charlie Alexander's testimony, it is going to be hard to get your boy off. I don't think he'll go to the chair. But he may do time. A crime of passion. Maybe that's enough to get a charge of manslaughter rather than murder."

"You heard all about hit, then," he said. "About the boy who broke his word."

"I have not heard about anything else since yesterday morning at ten o'clock. I came down here to get a newspaper at the drugstore, and I heard about it." He did not say he had heard the shots.

"The boy promised Hope he wouldn't say anything if Hope didn't kill him."

"So I hear."

"He didn't keep his word."

"It is not a promise the law would recognize, Mr. Kirby."

"A promise is a promise, Mr. Bedford."

Hugh started to argue, started to be a lawyer and explain to this lean, quiet man that a promise extracted by a pistol would not be considered binding in any court in America. His thought fell to powder at the calm certainty of Roy Kirby's face. "You think it's an affair of honor, don't you?" he said at last.

"That's right," Roy Kirby said.

"Tell me, Mr. Kirby, what will you do if I fail? What will you do if Charlie Alexander holds to his story and puts your boy in the electric chair?"

"I will kill him dead."

"Just like that. You will kill him."

"Hope give him his life. If he breaks his word in court, and if Hope dies for hit, hit will be my bounden duty to kill him."

"For your honor," Hugh said.

"The honor of my people," Roy Kirby said, looking Hugh Bedford dead in the eye.

Hugh Bedford said, "Mr. Kirby, have you ever killed anybody?" They sat looking at each other for a moment, and Hugh understood two things. He should not have asked the question, and if Roy Kirby had answered it, he would have said yes. "Forget I asked that," Hugh said. "I don't want to know."

Hugh looked at Roy Kirby and spoke carefully. "Just for argument—I'm not saying you're right, and I'm not saying you're wrong. Just suppose you do kill him after the trial—if your son goes to the chair. Why not kill Charlie Alexander now? He's already broken his word. If you kill him now, he won't be able to testify in court. If you do it yourself—and do it carefully enough—you won't have any witnesses, and the whole lot of you will get off." Hugh was careful not to urge murder on a client; he merely raised the question. But the question interested him. It represented a solution.

Roy Kirby gave him a long and level look. "I hear they's bad blood between you and Mr. Alexander."

"Paul Alexander was responsible for my father's death," Hugh Bedford said.

"Then why don't you kill him yourself?"

For a minute Hugh Bedford felt rebuked and angry, as if this wiry old man had accused him of cowardice. The anger came up in him like vomit, and he felt his pulse pound in his temples, and his face turned hot. He supposed his face stayed red enough from drink that people could not tell when he blushed. He considered telling Roy Kirby to get out of his office. Almost immediately he gave it up. *I am a coward*, he thought.

"The Alexander boy made a promise," Roy Kirby continued in his neutral tone. "He has put Hope in jail, but he might come to hisself between now and then and do the right thing."

"Reverse himself? Tell the jury he doesn't know who was out there?"

"It's only his word that has got my boy in jail."

"And only after he gives up that chance to keep his promise will you kill him."

"That's about the size of hit."

"Code of honor," Hugh Bedford said.

"Code of the hills," Roy Kirby said.

"I might point out—just for the sake of argument, you understand—that we are not in the mountains here in Bourbon County."

"I come from the mountains, Mr. Bedford. I lived in the hills all my life till I come down here. I brung my code with me when I come. If everbody had a code, we'd have a lot less trouble in the world."

"I have a code here," Hugh Bedford said, sweeping his plump hand in a theatrical gesture around at the ranks of dusty and disused law books that rose imperially on his shelves ascending from floor to ceiling. "It is called the *Tennessee Code Annotated*. It's the code of the whole goddamned mother-fucking, ass-licking, ass-kicking, snot-sucking, Jesus-mad state of Tennessee. It tells me that the state of Tennessee puts people convicted of murder to death in the electric chair. If you kill Charles Alexander, you may very well follow your son to the electric chair—if I don't get him off."

"That don't make me no mind," Roy Kirby said, speaking with a maddening patience, unblinking and inhesitant. "If you do what you're supposed to do in this old world, you hain't got no call to worry about what comes to you after."

They looked at each other across the wreck of a desk, and a silence fell, broken by the quiet, electric rush of the fan and the faint, rhythmic crackle of pages blown by the mechanically stirred air.

Hugh Bedford snubbed out a cigarette in his ash tray and lit another. "All right now, Mr. Kirby, I can only give you my advice. My main job is to get your boy off. That's going to be hard. You can help out by not scaring people. I don't want you or your boys to talk about this case to anybody but me. Do you understand that?"

"We hain't the kind that talks to folks," he said.

"You stay that way, you hear? Don't talk to your neighbors. Don't talk to reporters. Don't talk to people who ask you questions on the street. You can't trust anybody in this town. I've lived here all my life except when I was in the army. You can't trust any of them."

They sat still again. Hugh Bedford felt that Roy Kirby found him tiresome.

"So, air you going to defend my boy?"

"You're damn right, I'll defend him. I wouldn't miss it for the world."

"I'll pay what it takes."

"Don't worry about that."

"You just send me the bill when hit's done." The old man abruptly stood up and put out his hand. Hugh Bedford heaved himself out of his chair and took the hand. Roy Kirby's fingers felt like steel, and when he squeezed, Hugh Bedford almost cried out. Then with a tenderness no one might have suspected, Roy Kirby turned and laid his hand on John Sevier's shoulder. John Sevier seemed to waken from one trance and pass into another. He got up.

Afterwards Hugh Bedford stood in his window smoking and watched Roy Kirby put John Sevier into the pickup and get up into it himself. They had a farm down on the river, not far from the Salem Baptist Church. They appeared there in 1940, bought a chunk of the land that had belonged to the Talliaferros. Somebody said there was something peculiar about the sale, some obscure family connection to the Talliaferro family. How could that be?

It did not concern Hugh then. Not now either. Roy Kirby lived down there with John Sevier, and the two of them farmed the place and lived off what they raised and kept to themselves.

How old was he? He was the sort who gets to fifty and seems to stop growing older—leathery, lean, and ageless. What did he feel? Whatever it was, Hugh Bedford knew that his actions corresponded to some code of chivalry that made no sense to anybody but the man who held it, something distant ancestors had brought unblemished and unembellished across the water to nourish in this unkempt and strange land.

He should be in Shakespeare. Hotspur, perhaps. Or maybe Hal. Jesus Christ, there are not many people like that left in the world. It's unreal. His world is dead. Why do I have to get mixed up with him?

But he knew he was in it to the end. He lit another cigarette and put his hand down to the big drawer in his desk. He slipped it open and took out a bottle of bourbon and held it towards the light. A full bottle of bourbon. A man felt secure holding a full bottle of bourbon in his hand. It provided bravery. But he put the bottle back without drinking from it. He knew he had work to do.

*J*ANE WHITAKER came charging into the newspaper office holding a handful of checks. Red sat at his desk behind the frosted glass. Jane stood at the counter glaring over it at Myrtle Gillespie, who got up like a woman called forth to battle and ready to kill the enemy.

"Goddammit, Myrtle, where is he?!"

"I'll have you know this is a decent place, Jane Whitaker. You can't come in here and cuss like that. If you want to go somewhere and cuss, you climb up to the Smoke House Pool Room and sit down with one of those dirty books they sell up there, and you can cuss all day long. But you can't cuss in here."

"Listen, Myrtle, I don't have any quarrel with you. You don't write these goddamned bad checks."

Red came around the corner and stood behind the counter looking abashed. "Look, Jane. I'm picking up some ad money this morning. If you wait till this afternoon, I promise I'll have the money in the bank."

"Red, I can't cover bad checks for you every week! It is criminal to write bad checks. I could put you in jail for writing bad checks."

"We're coming up to fall, Jane," Red said. "We're going to have lots of ads. And the print business is going up. People owe me money. I just have to collect it."

"Cash and carry, Red. That's the secret. Make these goddamned sons of bitches pay you before you let them take the job out of your shop."

"Jane, give me two hours. That's all I need. Two hours. I'll get the money. Ford and Chevy both owe me big bucks for ads we ran on Thursday. And we've got another ad for the '54 Ford in today's paper. Look, I can show you. They are just late in paying."

"Two hours. I'll give you two hours," Jane said. "Where's Charlie Alexander?"

"He's up at the university. He's always there in the morning," Myrtle said.

"You mean he went to the university after what happened to him? How is he?" Jane seemed to soften.

"He's all right," Red said. "I called him yesterday afternoon late. He answered the phone."

"And he's gone to class?" Jane seemed startled.

"What else do you want him to do?" Myrtle said indignantly. "The poor boy had a gun put up to his head, and he was almost killed. What do you expect him to do? Stay home and brood about it?"

"It must have been awful," Jane said. "Tell him I asked about him. Tell him he did the right thing. Those hillbillies. They give us all a bad name."

"Well, his wife did him wrong," Myrtle said. "She got what she deserved if you ask me."

"Did him wrong!" Jane said contemptuously. "Got what she deserved! What do you expect when he leaves her at home alone on Saturday nights and goes fishing?"

"She could have gone and sat with his brothers' wives," Myrtle said. "She didn't have to be—" Myrtle caught herself before she said a bad word. "She didn't have to do what she done with Kelly Parmalee."

"Do you really know what she was doing with Kelly Parmalee, Myrtle?" Jane looked at her hatefully. "You tell Charles he did the right thing by telling the truth," she said. "For Charles's sake I'll give you two hours, Red. Those damned hillbillies! They didn't have any business moving to Bourbon County. My God. I'm trying to bring progress to this hick town, and it's like I was trying to outlaw guns in a cowboy movie."

She went out and slammed the door.

"That bitch," Myrtle said. "Excuse me for using that word, Red, but she is a bitch."

"She wasn't so bad when she was Lloyd's girlfriend," Red said, musing. "She changed when they broke up."

"Well, if you ask me, Lloyd saw right through her. He saw what kind of a woman she was, and he broke off the engagement. You know what I bet? I bet she cussed Lloyd out once, and he knew right away that a woman who'd say words like that was not a woman to be trusted. A woman that uses language like that would do anything."

"I don't know," Red said. "I thought Lloyd loved her. I thought, 'This time he's really in love.' He told me he was going to marry her. And then it was all over. He wouldn't talk about it."

"Well, poor boy. He'll never talk about anything anymore. Poor boy."

"That damned fool. In a rowboat. Why couldn't he—"

"He died trying to save her," Myrtle said. The tears came up in her eyes, and she dabbed at them. "And Charlie—if he'd died, it would be almost like there was a spell on us. A jinx."

"Ah, hell, Myrtle. I don't believe in things like that." But Red was not sure. He *was* sure that he wasn't the businessman Lloyd was. Not the writer either. Well, he had Charles, and he had Ted DeFord writing sports. Thank God for the two of them. Red picked up his hat. "I'd better get out there and raise some money," he said.

*B*Y *NINE* o'clock that Monday, Charles was sitting in his French class at the university, and the chimes rang softly, three melodious tones. Dr. Stiefel walked in jauntily, a dapper man in a hard European suit even in August, in an old building, Ayres Hall, that had no air conditioning. How did he do it? He was Swiss. He had five people in the class. The university let him teach such a small group only if he took on another elementary French grammar class with twenty people in it, but to teach Balzac it was worth it. He looked back at Charles, and he was startled to see him. The story was in the morning *Journal.* Charles's picture was on the front page.

DOUBLE MURDER IN BOURBONVILLE
Eye-Witness Fingers Army Vet

But if Dr. Stiefel thought of speaking to Charles, he reconsidered. He sat down at his desk, smiling benignly. A polite man. Reserved.

"Alors, mes amis," he said, as though to a group of beloved children, *"ce matin il nous faut écrire de la cousine Bette. Son caractère. Trois pages."*

And so the five of them, three young men, one not so young, and the girl, bent forward and wrote, an eager soft whirring of pens on paper, inked words flowing, and Charles thought, *I could have been killed because of Cousine Bette, dead all these years, a construct of the imagination.*

The bells chimed, and the girl walked over to him. "McKinley and I want you to have a cup of coffee with us. We think you need friends."

McKinley stood behind her, a big man with a large jaw and a long, friendly face. He was losing his hair prematurely. Charles supposed he must be nearly thirty. Maybe beyond. They had spoken casually.

"Well?" she said. Charles laughed nervously, but it was a laugh. She was a slender girl with brown eyes and brown hair and a face that seemed precisely shaped as though an artist had carved it so that every line was clear and sharp. She smiled at him with shy eagerness and with a tincture of doubt, as if she expected him to refuse. Her front teeth were slightly recessed, showing when she smiled, and that was one of the first things he had noticed about her. McKinley said, "We're not going to let you say no."

From the time he entered the university Charles made no effort to make friends with other students. The university was like a cafeteria. Charles approached it in the morning to collect what he needed and took it home with him in the afternoon. He did not want to talk to other students. He lived in his religious hothouse, closely guarded from friendships that might distract him from his resolve to believe his mother's religion. He knew the girl's name. Temperance Barker. Tempe, she was called. They had spoken after class before. Charles supposed Tempe and McKinley were a couple, McKinley a big, friendly sort who assumed a protective air towards her. They walked down the sunlit campus to Cumberland Avenue and to the Ellis and Ernest drugstore. A soda fountain with three tall hydrants, one for carbonated water, one for fountain Coke, one for plain water. Seats along the counter. Smell of fried things. Orange-and-white pennants. Rise and fall of conversation. Companionable laughter. The Ellis and Ernest drugstore a hangout for football players, but it was still summer and the season hadn't started yet. Tables reposed in rows on the floor, and McKinley marched with a commanding stride to the back and took an empty one near the glass cases rising to the ceiling and holding patent medicines for age, the liver, female complaints, the stomach, and the bowels.

"Well, you've been through hell since we saw you last," McKinley said with a sympathetic frown.

"It was not something I'd want to do again," Charles said softly.

"He put the gun to your head, the paper says."

"Yes," Charles said softly.

"I was shot at in the war, but nobody ever put a gun to my head," McKinley said, looking down at the marble top. He shook his large head reflectively.

"You were in the war?" Charles said.

"Yes. Three years of it."

"It must have been awful," the girl said, speaking to Charles.

"But he didn't kill you," McKinley said, the words hanging tentatively in the noisy air. McKinley looked reflective. "Have you dreamed about it?"

"Yes," Charles said.

"You will for a long time. But you'll get over it."

"McKinley," the girl said. "Let's not talk about it. I don't think Charles wants to talk any more about it. Do you, Charles?"

"No," Charles said gratefully. "I wish I could forget about it."

"People are different," McKinley said. "I know people who went through the war and can't stop talking about it. They're already old men, because the most important thing in their lives is already gone, and they will never have anything else to talk about."

"And you don't talk about it, McKinley?" the girl said, smiling slightly, joking with him, Charles saw.

McKinley laughed. "I don't *have* to talk about it. That's the thing," he said.

"Where were you in the war?" Charles asked.

"Europe."

"He's just come home from the army," Tempe said.

"Really?" Charles said.

A young woman waited on them. "Hey," she said. "I know you. Your picture's in the paper this morning."

"He doesn't want to talk about it," McKinley said.

"Lord, I don't blame you," the waitress said. "What can I do for you?"

Charles wanted to say, "You can take me home with you. Take all your clothes off, or let me take them off, and hold me all day long, and let me fondle your breasts." But he said, "Coffee, please. Cream and sugar."

"Care for toast?" the waitress said. She was chewing gum.

"No," Charles said.

"You ought to eat something," McKinley said. "When somebody shot at me, I didn't want to eat anything. But you have to eat."

"All right," Charles said. "Bring me some toast."

The others ordered coffee and toast, too, and the waitress flounced away, flipping her apron with a hand. She had firm breasts under the white shirt she wore. The apron went around her waist, and her bottom was nice, too. She looked willing, Charles thought. He had never been out with a girl who was willing, but he thought such girls must exist. Obviously they would lead him to hell. But if there were no God, there was no hell either. Why not feel as many breasts as possible before the darkness? He was exhausted, and his thoughts were crazy, one after another without his willing them.

"Why did you quit the army?" Charles asked.

"I liked the army too much," McKinley said. "I was in ten years, and all of a sudden I could see myself doing the same thing for another twenty years, saluting and being saluted, and I thought I wanted more out of life than that. So I quit."

"What did you do in the army?" Charles asked.

"Army intelligence. You know what I did most of the time? I read French and German newspapers to see what people said about America, about NATO, about communism. I wrote reports. I classified writers. Pro-American. Anti-American. Pro-Communist. Anti-Communist. In between. It was like measuring the water in the ocean with a cup."

"It sounds exciting," Charles said dully.

"It wasn't. You see, you don't think in the army. You get orders. You obey orders. Writers don't hide their ideas no matter what that creep Joe McCarthy says. Telling whether a writer's pro-American or anti-American is about as hard as telling the difference between an elephant and a cow. But I tell you the real bitch. That's telling the army that a writer is neither pro-American nor anti-American, that you have an honest man here trying to make sense of us. The army doesn't believe stuff like that. Nobody's honest. Everybody has an angle. So I quit. Just in time, too. I was about to be promoted to major."

"McKinley is doing an M.A. in French," Tempe said.

"I thought I'd see if my brain had gone to cantaloupe in the ten years I was in the service," he said. "If I like the M.A., maybe I'll go somewhere to take a doctorate. It's a good life, teaching French. I mean, don't you think?"

"I don't know," Charles said. He was secretly amused. McKinley's accent in speaking French was as elegant as a load of bricks tumbling down concrete stairs.

"You get to read good books, and you know something? Balzac didn't give a damn about the American army, he scarcely mentions America at all. What a relief."

They laughed. McKinley seemed at ease with the world. He talked amiably, and he made them both laugh.

Tempe said, "I read in the paper this morning—I don't want to talk about what happened, the murders—but I read that you plan to be a minister."

"Yes," Charles said.

She looked troubled. "But why?"

"I have always wanted to do it," he said. He wanted to tell her that he wanted to be a minister now so he would learn to believe in God again and know that death was not the end and that he would live forever and ever. But no one said such things.

"Really?" she said, clearly perturbed. "But why? Do you believe in God?" The question was like a blade made of ice.

No, the voice inside Charles shouted. *Not since W. T. Stace. When I pray, nothing happens. Do you know what it is not to be able to pray?* But he said, "Yes, I believe in God."

"Well, I don't," she said. "I don't see how anybody can."

"Oh well, 'Everybody to his own taste,' said the man as he kissed the cow," McKinley said. "Anyway, you shouldn't criticize people for their religion."

"I'm not criticizing him," Tempe said. "I'm just saying how can anybody believe in God these days? How can anybody as smart as Charles is believe in God? That's all I'm asking." She looked at him and smiled. Charles thought that was the way Eve must have smiled when naked in Eden she handed Adam the forbidden fruit and said, "This is the best thing I've ever tasted." Except that he knew there had been no Adam and there had been no Eve, and humankind had evolved out of a slime pit.

*B*Y TEN o'clock that Monday morning Hugh Bedford was sitting on a cot in Hope Kirby's cell. Outside the sun blasted the earth in still fury, but here the thick walls and a faint stirring of air through the open windows gave an illusion of coolness. Hope Kirby leaned against the wall next to the barred window, gazing at him in sad and somber stubbornness, a stony recalcitrance that bordered on resentment and that Hugh Bedford felt as soon as he walked in.

"I want to put you on the stand in your own defense," Hugh said.

"What good would that do?" Hope said.

Hugh Bedford smoked, puffing nervously at a cigarette, and when it burned down to his yellow fingers, he flicked it almost angrily out the barred window and lit another one.

"I'll tell you what good it will do. The jury will hear your story out of your own mouth. You tell it exactly like it happened—your wife cavorting around with a married man, what you did in the Philippines, how you met her, how much you loved her. Now listen. You are hurt to the bone. Your heart's broken, and you were mad as hell because she had done you wrong, but now you're sorry. You were out of your head. But you loved her, and you love her still. The jury will be men. Judge Yancy will think a case like this is not fit for a lady's delicate ears. Every man jack on the jury would kill his wife if she screwed around on him—if he thought he could get away with it. Now, truth to tell, some of those men might die of shock and disbelief if they thought anybody in the world wanted to screw their wives. But they'd still do exactly what you did—if they thought they could get away with it."

"You think they'll take my part," he said.

"Damned right they will take your part," Hugh said. "They will admire you for going man to man with them, looking them dead in the eye, telling the truth. I drag the story out of you. You don't seem boastful about it. Hell no. It's something you don't want to talk about, but when I ask you the questions, you answer them. And you know something? When you get through we won't have a dry eye in the house, and the jury will not only find you not guilty, but they'll give you a medal for putting that wife-snatching son of a bitch in hell where he belongs."

"Do you believe in hell?" Hope asked. The question came in the neutral, inquiring tone of a man asking if a certain store might be open tonight.

The question startled Hugh Bedford just because it was so serious, as if a grown man had asked about belief in Santa Claus. He looked at his client and for a moment lost the glittering train of his thought.

"Believe in . . . ? Hell no, I don't believe in hell. Listen, Hope, this is not Sunday school. This is a plan, and it will work. Trust me. It will work."

"So hit works this way," Hope said. "You get me on the stand and ask me a lot of questions, and I tell you the truth, and the other lawyer, the district attorney, gets to ask me questions." He looked through Hugh Bedford.

Damn, he's got eyes like ice picks, Hugh thought.

"That's right. It's called cross-examination."

"And I have to answer all the questions they ask."

"Yes, you have to answer the questions to the best of your ability. But listen, Hope, Ken McNeil's brain is like an adding machine. He can put two and two together and get four. But give him something more complicated, give him a little human algebra, and he's as helpless as a sixth-grader trying to read Egyptian."

"I reckon some sixth-graders can read Egyptian right good—if they happen to be Egyptians, I mean."

"Listen, Hope. I've known Ken McNeil all my life. He's no Egyptian. He's a methodical, Church of Christ, boring son of a bitch, the kind of man who knows his way from one to two and from two to three, but put him in a woods where he has to make his own path, and he's as lost as a dog in the stars." Hugh was sweating now, sweating profusely, and he was nervous and uncomfortable. He was not helped by the calm, faintly amused expression on Hope Kirby's face.

"Hope, get this into your head. We are talking about life and death. Your life. Your death. You get on the stand, tell the truth. The men on that jury will admire you because you are being honest with them. And they will let you off. Oh hell, suppose they give you a year and a day for involuntary manslaughter. It'll pass fast, and you'll come home to the biggest damned party the town's ever seen, and we'll invite Ken McNeil so he can look every man and woman at the party in the face and know they will all vote against him in the next election."

"You want me to say I done hit," Hope said.

"Well, I don't want you to say it like that, like you're ordering a hamburger at the grill. No, I want you to be shook up, maybe cry a little. Can you cry, Hope?"

"I hain't never cried in my life," Hope said.

"All right. Don't cry, but duck your head and look like you feel real bad about it. This is a crime of passion. You killed the woman you loved because she betrayed you. You lost your head. And if you had it to do all over again, you'd forgive her and take her back."

"I didn't lose my head," Hope said morosely. "We planned hit all out."

Hugh wanted a drink. "Details, Hope. Details. Let's agree right now you'll take the stand, tell the truth. At least tell as much of it as you need. Tell the truth, and you'll pull Ken McNeil's teeth. You'll make Judge Yancy pee in his robes. The senile old son of a bitch."

"Judge Yancy thought a right smart of Abby," Hope said. His voice was neutral.

Hugh took a deep draw on his cigarette. Time was when a Camel hit him like a cyclone. No more. Now he had to hold the smoke in his lungs awhile before he got anything out of it. "People say the old fool was in love with her," he said.

"I loved her, too," Hope said, his face changing the way light will change on water when a cloud passes over the sun.

Hugh Bedford's hopes came up like a fountain. *If I can get him to show that face on the witness stand, the jury wouldn't have to exit the courtroom to give its verdict. They'd start to cry. Somebody would shout, "Not guilty," and we'd have time for a couple of drinks before supper to celebrate.*

"Yes, you loved her, too," Hugh said eagerly. "That's exactly what I want you to say to the jury. You've got to speak to Judge Yancy, too, Hope. He thinks she was an angel. You have to show Judge Yancy she was a slut."

Hope grabbed Hugh by the shoulders and for a moment seemed ready to pull him off the cot and strike him, but Hugh was too heavy, and the two men fell into a futile wrestling match that ended in stalemate, and Hugh pushed Hope away with a violent shove.

"What the hell got into you?" he gasped.

"I don't like you talking about Abby like that," Hope said.

Hugh stumbled to his feet. He was as tall as Hope, and he had once been muscular, and now he was angry too. "Listen, damn it, do you want me to be your lawyer or not? If you don't want me to be your lawyer, just say the word, and I'll walk out that door, and you can go to hell in a handbasket carried by Ken McNeil. Your daddy wants me to be your lawyer, but if you don't listen to anything I say, you're a dead man, and this is hopeless shit, and I'm wasting my time."

For a moment a tense, hard silence ruled in the cell, and Hugh thought, *He is going to tell me to get the hell out of here.* A wave of regret swept over him. He wanted this case.

Hope backed off. He went to the window and looked out. "All right," he said in a voice so low it was almost inaudible. "If Pappy wants you to be my lawyer, you can be my lawyer. Whatever Pappy wants."

Hugh sat down again. "Look," he said in a placating tone. "We've got a jury and a judge to worry about. I'm going to make a motion for a change of venue, a different judge, another town. I'm going to tell Judge Yancy that he's too much involved in the case, that he ought to recuse himself, but how far do you think I'll get?"

"I don't know," Hope said.

"I won't get anywhere. The old buzzard will turn me down, but then I've got grounds for an appeal for a new trial. He will want to fry you, Hope. So will Ken McNeil. Mark my words. We have to cover all the bases."

"With what?" Hope said.

Hugh looked at him without comprehension for a moment. "Didn't you ever play baseball?" he said.

"I hain't never had no time for games," Hope said.

Hugh took a deep, impatient breath. "All right, let me spell this out. The old buzzard loved her. Like a daughter? Like a sweetheart? God knows. But he loved her. Everybody knows that."

"He married us," Hope said. "He performed the ceremony. Her preacher prayed, but hit was the judge that done the ceremony."

"And he's the judge that will hear your case because he will not recuse himself. Right now we've got to prove to him that Abby wasn't what he thought she was."

"Don't go saying nothing bad about Abby," Hope said. The fire blazed up in him again.

"Oh fine. We won't say anything bad about her. We won't do anything but tell judge and jury what you knew, what you saw, and you don't have to say anything about her character." He lit another cigarette. *My lungs must be like tissue paper. One day they will catch fire from a cigarette, and I'll explode and burn like that character in* Bleak House.

Hope looked out the window of his cell. He could see the trees by the river, but the river itself was out of sight. Beyond lay the mountains. He recognized Mount LeConte's three heads, and he remembered what it was like up there. Jack and Pauline Huff in their inn on top. He thought about the coolness at night on the mountains. You needed a fire sometimes up there even in July. He liked the Huffs. They got to stay when the park came. They were still there.

"Judge Yancy offered to send her to college," Hope said.

"He was an old fool," Hugh said.

"Still—he meant hit."

"He was trying to buy her," Hugh said. "He was an old fool who was trying to buy her love by giving her things."

The town laughed at Judge Yancy, the lonely old bachelor with his bald head and dewlapped neck fixated on a devout young girl who wore her clothes with innocent sensuality. She seemed to wait with eager and guileless joy to jump out of dress, bra, and panties and come naked like Venus on the water to anybody who invited her, including a fond, foolish old man who was doubtless a virgin at age seventy. Who could tell what maddening fancy tormented the old idiot at night when he lay in bed alone with his flaccid dick? Hugh Bedford trusted no man's disinterested benevolence. Everybody had a motive. Sending her to college would have been for him like fucking her with money—the only manhood he had.

Abby refused him. He pressed. She refused again. Judge Yancy begged her to reconsider. He called on her parents. He extolled her mind, her personality, her character, and they heard him out in the abject and profound embarrassment of peons bowed and afraid before the bald majesty of the Lord of Law. Like peons of all ages, they plodded on in the stubborn inertia of what seemed fitting to their doomed place in the world. Abby went to beauty school in Knoxville.

"She used to laugh about him, about the judge—not meaning no harm, you know," Hope said in a nostalgic and yearning murmur that floated on the hot summer air. "She'd laugh at herself, thinking about being a coed. That's what you call a woman student in college. A coed."

"I know," Hugh said. "I went to college. I even went to motherfucking law school."

"She didn't know how pretty she was," Hope said. "She didn't know why he wanted to do so much for her."

Hugh started to say what he thought but decided against it. Hope Kirby had no suspicions of anybody. Why try to plant the truth in him now?

"When are they going to bury her?" Hope said.

"Tomorrow afternoon."

"I wish I could go."

"She couldn't hear you or see you, Hope. They can't open the casket."

"I reckon not," he said. The silence poured back. A dove called in the distance, towards the river, a soft, crooning sound making the morning sleepy and peaceful. Hugh sweated, and the sweat soaked his cheap summer suit. *I want a cold shower and a toddy. Lemon in it and ice and sugar and a shade tree somewhere. I want anything but this, but I want this.*

"What about it, Hope? Can I put you on the stand? Will you tell the truth?"

Hope stared out the window again. He did not look at Hugh when he spoke. "Look here, Lawyer," he said with resignation and regret. "I can't tell the truth, and I can't lie. If you was to put me on the stand, I'd say I kilt her, and I'd say I was sorry I had to kill her, but then I'd say if hit was all to do over again, and hit was Monday a week ago instead of today and Abby was flitting around the house and fixing me supper and humming while she worked and I knowed why she was happy and hit warn't because of me but because of him, I'd think hit was all out there for me to do, and come Saturday night I'd kill her again."

"You'd say all that if you were asked?" Hugh said.

"I'd say it."

Hugh took another deep breath. This was harder than he imagined it would be, and a thought ate at him like acid on his skin. *This man is not afraid to die. He does not care if he dies or lives.* Most of the time his clients did what he told them to do, obeying him in the obsequious, frightened tremor of children who have done something bad and now must face punishment and humiliation. They would tell any lie to get out of being punished. That's how he got them off. "Look," he said, taking another deep, impatient breath and letting it out again. But the breath made him cough violently, and he turned red enough to die, and Hope Kirby came over and began pounding him on the back as if Hugh had something stuck in his throat. Hugh shook him off, weeping with his coughing, and after a time he recovered himself.

"You ought to quit smoking them cigarettes, Lawyer," Hope said. "They is coffin nails."

"I can't quit," Hugh said. He took out his handkerchief and wiped his eyes. His heart was pounding in his ears. It sounded like a jazz drum gone wild. *One of these days I am going to die in a fit like that.* The thought frightened him. His mind tracked back to the subject at hand.

"McNeil has got to ask you questions before you can say anything in cross-examination. You don't get on the witness stand and make a speech."

"I reckon that's so," Hope said. He went back to the window, his hands stuck down in the hip pockets of his jeans. He stared at Mount LeConte in the distance. *Hit were Mr. Hamilton's fault,* he thought.

"McNeil," Hugh said, "is all show. Pants ironed with a crease sharp enough to cut your balls off if he brushes up against you. Wears that stupid grin. Somebody told him he'd be more popular if he smiled all the time, and he grins like a damned schoolboy asking a pretty girl for a dance."

"I know who he is," Hope said.

"But you don't know *what* he is. His mind's too neat for him to think of asking you what you'd do if you had the chance. You get on the stand. You answer the questions. You say yes or no when you can get away with just that. You don't say a word you don't have to say. Don't volunteer a word, not one word. You got that?"

"No, I hain't got that," Hope said with impatient and resolute irritation. "You've had your say, Lawyer. Now you listen to me. Before I done hit, we talked hit all over—me and Pappy and the boys. Pappy told me what I had to do, and he told the boys they had to help me do hit."

"Just like that," Hugh said. He shook his head, not in perplexity, not even in surprise, but merely at the rock-hard strangeness of codes of honor. *I would have been Falstaff if I had the chance all over again. What is honor? 'Tis but a word.*

Hope Kirby plowed on, stubborn and resolute, explaining something as a mountain man might point out to a lowlander a path in the woods that led to a gap in the peaks, all carefully spelled out to a blundering novice who had never been in these mountains before, had never been in any mountains at all. Hugh thought, *I know all about honor, Hope Kirby. I had honor once. It's not good for anything at all. Hope would have stared me in the face and said, "But you don't know nothing about family, Lawyer. Your daddy was a loudmouth fool who got hisself shot dead by being where he had no business being in a strike at the Car Works when you were a snot-nosed kid, and your mammy was a lazy cow who couldn't do anything but moo and rant about Paul Alexander all her life and never had a good thing to say about anybody and died when she choked on a piece of meat. How could a slob like you, from a family like that, know anything about real family or real honor?"* The thoughts rattled like rocks in a can through Hugh's brain, giving him a headache, and it was no defense to say that Hope Kirby did not know any of these things, could have said none of them, because he thought that if Hope Kirby knew the facts, he would say all these things, and Hugh could do nothing but admit to them.

What Hope Kirby did say was this: "Here's the way hit was. We worked hit all out. M.L. was the one that called the sheriff and told him they was a stabbing out at the Yellow Dog. Love and Joye taken me out in the boat and to the riverbank later on in the night, and hit was M.L. picked me up on the road and brung me back into town. Joye and Love come down the lake then and met me at the point above the dam, and if Pappy could of left John Sevier all by hisself, Pappy would of been in on hit, too, maybe waiting in the square to see that I done hit, maybe shooting Mr. Parmalee hisself with his own gun."

Hugh shut his eyes, smoking with tasteless displeasure. "You are saying that if I put you on the stand, your whole family, your clan, including the wives who doubtless knew everything you planned—"

"No," Hope interrupted. "We didn't tell the wives nothing. They would of told Abby."

Hugh got up and indulged himself in a rare feat of exercise: he paced the floor. "So the wives didn't know, but the rest of you not only knew but you all worked on it together. And you think you may be asked about all that on the stand, and you will have to tell the truth, and they may be hauled into court as accessories before and after the fact. Oh, excuse me for once again burdening this discussion with incomprehensible legal jargon. You are telling me that if I put you on the stand, you might not get off of it again until you've got every man in your family except the poor loony lined up to go to prison and maybe some of your brothers to the electric chair with you. Shit. Shit. Shit."

"You better sit down, Lawyer. You don't look too good," Hope said.

Hugh felt dizzy and sick. That was a fact. He went back to the bunk and sat heavily upon it. "You're making it damned hard," he said wearily. "Damned hard."

"I hain't going to say nothing to get my folks in trouble," Hope said. "If I give Judge Yancy a chance, he's going to go after all of them. All my brothers has got wives and kids. I don't got no kids. But they got kids."

Hugh ground one cigarette out on the floor and lit another. There it was, all laid out like a sign in letters twenty feet tall on the side of a brick building. Judge Shirley K. Yancy. Hope had read the character of that mean old man. "He's been mad all his life because his daddy named him Shirley," Hugh said.

"If my daddy would of called me Shirley, I wouldn't of been mad at hit. I was his boy, and he had a right. But I hain't Judge Yancy."

"Damn right," Hugh said, shutting his eyes again so he could see something. "So, you will not take the stand, and it's put to me to plant reasonable doubt in the minds of the jury that Charlie Alexander didn't see what he claims to have seen that night when those two unfortunate people were shot to death out there by person or persons unknown. I have to do it on my own."

"Lawyer," he said in patient resignation, "let me tell you what's God's own truth. I don't care what happens to me now. With Abby dead, I don't care if I live or die. You do what you can, but hit don't matter to me."

"I am going to get you off," Hugh whispered. "Just don't you do anything to hurt my case. I swear to God, I'm going to get you off."

Hope Kirby stared bleakly out the window. A billowing white cloud lay piled over the mountains, a tower of cumulus with folds and caverns and shades and rounded edges and vaguely defined blotches of gray and pink and violet. "I reckon if I die, I can float up there and fly around that cloud and look over the mountains where I was raised and be a boy again."

"You are not going to die," Hugh said fiercely. "Not in the electric chair. Not if I have anything to do about it."

"What is to be will be."

"You don't believe that Baptist crap."

"Yes I do."

"All right," Hugh said, getting up. "Now listen. Don't you talk to anybody, you hear? You tell your daddy and your brothers and their wives and their children to sew their mouths up like a feed sack, and don't say anything. Tell them not to speak your name."

"They hain't going to say nothing. And I hain't talked to nobody but the preacher."

"The *what?*" Hugh Bedford was aghast. "What preacher?"

"The feller at First Baptist. Mr. Arceneaux. He come down here late last night and talked to me."

"Jesus H. Christ. What the hell was that son of a bitch doing coming to talk with you? What did you tell him?"

"I didn't tell him nothing. We just talked. He had stuff to tell me."

"What in God's name did Arceneaux have to tell you?"

"Hit hain't none of your business, Lawyer."

"None of my—"

"Well, hit was a private conversation. He was in the service, too, you know."

"He was a clerk-typist," Hugh said, raising his voice so that the scorn dripping from it would have farther to fall through the still air. "Everybody knows that. He was a damned clerk-typist and didn't do shit in the war but sit on his ass and type papers for officers and stay out of danger."

Hope shrugged. "We just had a talk. That's all."

"Well, don't do it again!" Hugh shouted. "You let me handle this."

Hugh would have been worried if it had been anybody else. But it was Lawrence Arceneaux, a queer duck, people in Bourbonville said. He preached sermons full of poetry and eloquence, and everybody said he had a voice like music. But nobody knew what he was talking about, and a wave of dissatisfaction was growing in his congregation. He was unmarried. It was said that every woman of marriageable age and status in Bourbonville was after him, but he went on with his vaguely distracted air as if he did not even see them. The one good thing people said about him was that he was quick to visit the sick and the dying. If you developed a high fever, Larry Arceneaux was likely to come knocking on your door. People expected their pastor to give them attention. Still, he was odd. Too much book learning, people said. His house was filled with books, some in foreign languages. Hugh Bedford had nothing to do with preachers himself. To his mind they were all frauds.

"From now on, you don't talk to anybody," he commanded Hope Kirby again. Hope Kirby looked at him with an expression of faint amusement.

Hugh Bedford waddled down to his old car and drove the few hundred yards back to the square below his office. He picked up the afternoon newspaper that had come down from Knoxville. It had photographs of Abby and Kelly Parmalee and Charles Alexander on the front page and a long story written by a reporter named Joe Marks. The story of the murders made the banner headline across the front page. Hugh Bedford climbed the stairway to his office through the fetid summer air, and he sat down and read the story. Finally he tossed the paper into his trash can. Things looked bad. Very bad. His father had died because of Paul Alexander. Now Charles Alexander could put Hope Kirby in the electric chair. Hugh Bedford took it personally.

He swallowed a gulp of whiskey from a bottle and felt better. He lit a Camel and felt better still. Bourbon and cigarettes, the elixirs of life. He had one hope. If Charles Alexander had an attack of honor, he might change his story. If he said on the witness stand he couldn't be sure who he'd seen out there, Ken McNeil would be left up shit's creek without a paddle, and the state's case would collapse. There was still hope.

*W*HEN Hope Kirby had been in the army for a while, he understood Mr. Hamilton better, and he ceased to blame him for what had happened. He knew that all the world existed in a chain of command, that people at the top gave orders, and the orders rippled down the chain, link by link, rattling and banging, and making the links at the bottom fall into their assigned place by laws that worked as irresistibly as the laws of physics. Mr. Hamilton was almost on the bottom.

Had he known more about Mr. Hamilton, Hope Kirby would doubtless have felt even greater sympathy for him. In some fantasy world of another dimension, some different reality where all the dead are provided with grandstand seats to observe their own lives flashed on a giant screen as big as the sky, they might have watched the lives of one another in prodigious detail. But in that other dimension, time would be limitless, and the years of a life would amount to an interlude, and afterwards Mr. Hamilton and Hope Kirby might have repaired to a substantial cloud in cool remove from the hurry, noise, and limitations of the lives they had known, and who can tell?

Given a few decades of conversation and review, they might have seen that all human beings were spots of dust blown by a cosmic wind whose invisible and impalpable force propelled them through illusions of choice to a destiny set down as far back as the big bang—which, of course, Hope Kirby and Mr. Hamilton never heard of in all their lives.

Mr. Hamilton came on the Kirby men like the avatar of city arrogance and scorn. He did not like mountain people, and he did not like his job. He considered both beneath him—far beneath him, although his superiors told him that it was a promotion, and he wanted to believe them. Still, it was no job for a craftsman who considered himself—who was considered—a genius at drafting and making blueprints. During the boom years of the 1920s he had been the president and general manager of a small blueprint company in Charlotte, North Carolina.

He had had so much work that he sometimes did not go home before midnight, but he slept soundly, and he was back in his shop whistling over his drafting tables and his vellum by seven in the morning, and he never took off for lunch. "I live on cigarettes and sardines," he said with a proud grin when his workmen commented admiringly on the unbelievable hours he put in on the job. He was bone-thin and young, still in his twenties, investing carefully in the stock market and looking forward to marriage to his sweetheart, who waited patiently for him to get rich.

"I won't get married until I can take my bride straight home from the church and carry her across the threshold of her own little bungalow," he said in the big-hearted confident way he spoke about his plans. His plans were special plans because he thought himself a special person who had life figured out.

Mr. Hamilton knew he wasn't as smart as some people, and he knew he couldn't mix in high society because he lacked an education. He had not finished high school. He was not interested in art or books, and he had no hobbies, and he did not waste time talking about politics or anything else over which he had no control. "My great strength is that I know my limitations," he told his sweetheart. He made this pronouncement with the pride and authority with which an explorer might have described journeys along fever-ridden coasts of Central America or Africa or other exotic lands. And indeed Mr. Hamilton considered his self-knowledge a dangerous exploration that others lacked the courage to make.

"There are not many men, Ida, who have had the intestinal fortitude—I hope my language does not offend your delicate ears, my dear—but I say it plain, the intestinal fortitude to look into their own personalities and see their limitations." "Personality" was a new word tossed around in those days by people who considered themselves "in the know," which was another new expression being tossed around.

Ida listened to Mr. Hamilton's estimate of his superiority and admired it as she admired everything he said and did. She did not trouble herself with the paradox that Mr. Hamilton's superiority consisted (as he saw it) in his willingness to face boldly his inferiority.

In fact, Ida was one of Mr. Hamilton's calculated bows to his limitations. She was a plain woman with a long face and large teeth. Mr. Hamilton had without embarrassment or hesitation described her to his mother in Danville, Virginia, as "horse-faced." She wore her hair flaring out unattractively on each side of her head in artificial curls that she painfully renewed every morning with a hot curling iron. Her large teeth had a certain protuberance, so she tried to keep her mouth shut at all times, and yet she had read somewhere that a smile made a woman attractive no matter what nature had done to her. She tried, therefore, to smile as much as she could but with her lips shut tightly to hide her bulging teeth. The result was mechanical, even strained, so that more than one person thought she might be suffering grievous pains in the abdomen, gas perhaps, and some described her without malice as constipated.

Mr. Hamilton was comfortable with all this. "A plain woman is happy to have a plain man like me to be her husband," he said. "She's not going to embarrass him by flirting with other men or humiliate him by running off with a sailor and asking for a divorce. Ida is just my speed, and that's why I'm going to marry her."

If anyone had asked Mr. Hamilton if he loved her, he would have replied with a vigorous and somewhat perplexed affirmative. "Love her! Of course I love her. I'm going to marry her, aren't I?" (Mr. Hamilton was always careful not to say "ain't.") But it has to be said that "love" was not the first word Mr. Hamilton mentioned when he spoke of his sweetheart to others or even when he talked with her about their deferred future life together.

Ida accepted all of this. She admired Mr. Hamilton for the reasons he thought he should be admired. She lived with her mother and father in a nice old house they had inherited, and they thought she was far luckier in Mr. Hamilton than they had dreamed she could be in a prospective husband. Being honest, unaffected people, they frequently told her how low their estimate of her prospects had been. While the years slipped by and she waited for Mr. Hamilton, she gave piano lessons to children and played the piano for a Presbyterian church and collected sheets and towels and glassware and various ornamental knickknacks for her hope chest, and—like Mr. Hamilton—kept a placid expectation of good things for the future that one of these days would become the present.

Mr. Hamilton's consideration of his limitations kept him from dreaming of making a killing in the stock market. People with less self-knowledge might use such sanguinary metaphors with abandon, but they were not for him. He invested cautiously, wisely, with great diversity according to the best advice he could get from the architects and contractors and bankers with whom he did business. He felt happy when in his daily consultations of the business pages in the newspapers he saw that other stocks were enjoying spectacular growth while most of his were climbing steadily at a modest and *limited* gait. "Slow but sure," he told his banker in the satisfied tone of a man who knew exactly what he was doing. The banker nodded his head of thick white hair and looked through his gold-rimmed glasses with conservative enthusiasm and congratulated Mr. Hamilton on his conservative good sense and his business acumen. The same banker performed precisely the same gestures and said exactly the same words to his other customers—the plungers and the gamblers—but no matter about that.

Mr. Hamilton planned to get out of the market in the spring of 1930, for by that moment he calculated he would have enough to pay cash to buy a nice little bungalow in a developing part of Charlotte and have enough left over for a new Buick automobile—not the highest-priced house and not the highest-priced car, but both well within the carefully modulated means Mr. Hamilton had at his disposal.

Besides, in May 1930 he would be thirty-five years old, and he told people that he thought thirty-five was just the age for a man to settle down and start raising a family. But Black Friday came in October 1929, and careful Mr. Hamilton lost exactly as much as the plungers and the gamblers and all those unwise or cowardly people who had never dared to face up to their limitations. That is, he lost everything.

He did not lose his little blueprint business immediately, and he did not go bankrupt. He had been far too prudent for that. No, his little business failed because nobody built anything. Contractors went bankrupt, and architects started selling brushes and Bibles door to door, and carpenters sold apples, and banks shut down, and the banker who had advised Mr. Hamilton and congratulated him for his business acumen committed a messy suicide with a shotgun in his empty bank vault. There was no business for a draftsman and a maker of blueprints. None at all.

First Mr. Hamilton let his employees go. Then he stopped smoking to economize. Day after day he sat in his empty shop and waited for business to come. None did. Then he put a For Sale sign on his shop. When he had no buyers, he locked his doors in the fall of 1930 and set out to find a job. He could find nothing in Charlotte. He was so desperate that he was willing to do manual labor. But so were hundreds of men much stronger than he.

Finally, in the greatest humiliation imaginable, he moved out of his furnished room, vowing to pay his landlady the back rent he owed her as soon as he could lay hands on any money at all. (It was a promise he kept.) He packed an imitation-leather suitcase and walked and hitchhiked—wearing a clean but unpressed white shirt and a little leather bow tie he had worn in his shop—to Danville, Virginia, and moved back in with his mother, and the two of them lived on her meager pension from the railroad for which her late husband had worked for forty years. Miracle of miracles, the Dixie Railroad did not go bankrupt.

And Ida? Mr. Hamilton wrote her hopeful letters, telling her that the best-laid plans sometimes were interrupted by chance but that he was on the trail of this job or that and that he was sure that the Depression would end soon and then he would start all over again. She wrote that they could get married and live with her mother and father, but he said that would be a humiliation he could not accept. One day in 1932 she wrote him that she was going to marry a brakeman on the Dixie Railroad whose wife had died and who had young children to raise and who also had a job. Mr. Hamilton burned all her letters and never spoke her name again.

When the New Deal came along, he landed a minor administrative position with the Works Progress Administration, the WPA. (Mr. Hamilton voted for Hoover in 1932; it seemed too much a condescension to vulgarity for him to vote Democratic.) He could type a little, and he had a clear, precise handwriting and a sense of order, and so he was the ideal low-level functionary.

But he was not the same. All his plans had been careful, fully in keeping with his keen-eyed estimate of his own limitations, and he had assumed in the old days that he probably erred on the conservative side—as a good planner did. That is, he thought that he was probably a little better than he told himself he was. Now he was an abject failure along with all the rest. He had lost his business and his sweetheart. He had lost years of careful savings so that he was just as broke as people who had gone to Florida every winter and loitered on the beach and eaten in fancy restaurants at two dollars a meal, drinks included.

He was therefore invaded by dark feelings of pessimism. Perhaps he was no better; perhaps he was worse than those people he had hitherto scorned because in his careful estimates of his own worth and the worth of others, he had assumed that they were far beneath him. With his precise blueprints, he never had to worry about offending a superior. He was the boss.

Now he knew that he was doing a job that any man willing to wear a suit and a necktie and punch a typewriter and fill out forms could do with no more than two hours of training and perhaps two days on the job. He was as interchangeable as a cigarette in a pack and just as disposable. He knew that if he gave the slightest cause for dissatisfaction, he could be out on the street again in a day with no prospects, no job, no references, no hope. Every day he walked into the main office in Knoxville like a man entering a cavern where torrents of water roared somewhere faintly in the distance beyond the hearing of anyone but himself, suggesting a nearby abyss where he might with one misstep tumble down and down, arms flailing helplessly, to ignoble and anonymous destruction with no one to help and no one to care. He crept before his superiors in subdued terror, and they hated him as hunters will hate a cowed dog.

He took his isolation for granted. He spent so much time absorbed in calculations about himself that he was seldom cognizant of a world existing beyond himself—although like all such men, Mr. Hamilton was sure that his understanding of a cruel world could hardly be equaled by anyone else, even if that person were endowed with an IQ of 180. ("IQ" was another term people talked much about in those days.)

The contempt that his superiors felt towards him propelled him out of the WPA and into the job that led him to the Kirby farm, that made him get out of the car and look around in distaste at the tedious and squalid life this house implied with its privy and the barn and the corn crib and the rank smells and the isolated fields. He spoke harshly to the bewildered woman who came to inquire with polite terror as to the purpose of his visit, and then he leaned upon the horn in a harsh announcement of the time he felt he was wasting until he could talk to the object of his journey, the man of the house. He had so little authority that he had to use all of it whenever he had an occasion or an excuse.

Mr. Hamilton made himself see the vision. He thought that if Ida could see him, she would swoon in envy and despise her cloddish husband the brakeman who doubtless never wore a suit. He thought of the national park, spreading over these great mountains with their secret valleys and their singing streams, their misty hollows, and their brooding peaks, a park that would become again the haunt of the black bear and the bobcat, the lynx, the deer, the red fox, the beaver, the wild boar, the howling wolf, and even the mountain lion and every other fierce and glorious animal he could think of. They would roam through the thick forests and bask in the sun of rocky outcrops older than time, and the ghosts of the Cherokees would whisper in the trees, and phantom drums would thunder magical tattoos from ridge to ridge. Mr. Hamilton's troubles in the present were such that he tended to become romantic about the past, especially about the wilderness where he had had no disillusioning experiences.

He thought of tubercular, ashen city people withering in the fetid air of soot and crowds now expending their last energy to journey from the motley streets of their accursed and unnatural homes and come here, to the fresh vistas of the wild mountains, and by seeing and smelling the forested land and by hearing the pure sounds of nature, they would be lifted up and restored to vigor in body and mind, and the country would sweep out of the Great Depression and shine as a paragon to all the world.

All this was a dim and imperfect vision to Mr. Hamilton because he could not express it very well, especially to the obstreperous hillbillies who happened to live on that land which he saw as the source for the regeneration of the American people. The hillbillies stood in the way of his new-found dream. They were selfish, narrow, ignorant, and uncouth, and they wore clothes you saw in photographs intended to show how terrible the Depression was for the poor. Just being with them made Mr. Hamilton feel poor, despite his certainty that he was not poor but only temporarily inconvenienced by hard times.

Even before he pulled up in front of the little shotgun cabin Roy Kirby had built back up in one of the mountain valleys, he had already met enough of these people to be revolted by them and to know what to expect. He assumed as forbidding a pose as he could muster, and he impatiently honked his horn as part of a deliberate strategy of intimidation. By the time most of these people came to see what the matter was, they were prepared to submit.

"Mr. Kirby," he said when Pappy walked around the corner of the house, "I represent the United States government."

He did not offer to shake hands with Pappy. Pappy did not extend a hand to him. They stood there looking at each other, unsmiling.

"My name's Kirby, and that's a fact," Pappy said. "But I don't know yourn."

"Mine's not important," Mr. Hamilton said. "What is important is that I represent the United States government."

"You've said that, but so does the mailman," Pappy said in perfect tranquillity. "And I know his name. Hit's Mr. Duff. So if I'm going to talk to you, I'll have to know your name, or else you can get off my place."

Mr. Hamilton was insulted and exasperated. He was always astonished that these slow-moving hillbillies never seemed to understand how valuable his time was, the number of calls he had to make, the irritation he felt at having to explain his obvious authority so many times a day to yokels who should see what kind of car he was driving and that he was wearing a necktie.

"It's Hamilton, if you want to know," he said, making every effort to show how impertinent he found the question. "You can call me Mr. Hamilton. But like I say, that doesn't matter. What matters is that I represent Washington.

I'm here because in another year or two, there's going to be a national park right here where we're standing. I'm sure you've heard about it."

"I hain't interested in no national park," Pappy said. "Hit don't have nothing to do with me."

"Oh, but that's where you're wrong, Mr. Kirby. The national park has everything to do with you, because it is going to include your farm. I've seen the maps. Like I say, it's going to include the very ground where we're standing right this minute. The blacktop highway over the mountains will run right through this place, and the park headquarters will be right there, where that little shack of yours is now standing." Mr. Hamilton loved to give startling bad news to people. He liked to see the expression on their faces when they slowly understood it.

Pappy's expression didn't change. "Well, Mr. Hamilton, you can say that if'n you want because this here is a free country. But hit hain't going to happen, and right now you are wasting my time because my boys and me has got a new chicken house to build."

"Now, Mr. Kirby, let's not be difficult, shall we? All your land is going to be federal property when we get through with it. Maybe we'll keep your little cabin here on the side of the road to show city people how mountaineers lived once upon a time. If you got a still back there hid someplace, I know we'll keep that." Mr. Hamilton made what he thought was a gesture of friendship, laughing a little as if he and Pappy shared some manly and guilty secret about whiskey.

"I don't have no still back here," Pappy said. "I don't drink, and hit's agin' the law to make whiskey even if I wanted to make it, which I don't."

"You don't have to lie to me, Mr. Kirby. I don't care if you make forty gallons of moonshine whiskey every day. That's not my department in the government. I'm telling you that when this park gets started, there's not going to be room to have you folks here on this place."

"Well, if'n you ask me, there hain't going to be no room for the park, because this here is home and we hain't leaving," Pappy said. He was being patient. All his boys could tell that, and they thought it was almost funny that the stranger sweating under his city hat couldn't understand the plain words Pappy was speaking to him but that Pappy was polite enough to keep on trying to explain.

"Mr. Kirby, this *was* your home, but now the federal government is going to buy it from you, and it won't be yours any more. That's why I'm here. That is why I have taken all this trouble to come up here, to let you know what the government is going to do."

"Well, I'm much obliged to anybody that takes the trouble to tell me something I don't know," Pappy said. "But I hain't much obliged to folks that wants to tell me something that hain't so. I hain't planning to sell my land to the federal gov'mint or nobody else, Mr. Hamilton. This here's my home, and hit's going to stay my home."

Mr. Hamilton made a great effort to look patient, but he did not have patience in him, and what came out sounded like a grown-up talking to an idiot child.

"Mr. Kirby, let me explain. You have no choice in this matter. Your land has already been condemned by an act of Congress that has been certified by the federal courts. We are obligated to give you the fair market value, and you are obligated to accept what we say that is. Then you are obligated to move away. That is the way it is. That is the way it will be."

"This here is my propity," Pappy said in confident equanimity. "I don't have to sell hit lessen I want to, and I don't. That's the code of the hills." Pappy said this last with a subtly increased confidence, as though reference to the code of the hills would stop this nonsense once and for all. But on a moment's reflection, he added, "I am an American, and hain't no American that has got to sell his home when he don't want to sell hit."

Mr. Hamilton repeated his own infinitely tired and superior sigh to show the burden he accepted, talking generations of imbeciles into civilization. "Mr. Kirby, let's get down to brass tacks. I am authorized to offer you thirty dollars the acre for your little place. That comes to a total of three thousand dollars. Now if I was as poor as you are, I'd take that money and run before you could say Jack Robinson."

For an instant, Hope Kirby—not nineteen years old—thought that for the first time in his life he was going to see Pappy lose his patience. There was a little steely wrinkle around each corner of Pappy's mouth where you might think it was a smile if you didn't know better, and there was a blaze of fire in Pappy's blue eyes. It made Hope hold his breath.

But then, just like a little dark cloud blowing out of the way of the sun, Pappy's face relaxed, and he resumed his patient expression and looked Mr. Hamilton in the eye. It was the word "poor" that did it, that made the fire leap up in his eyes. But Pappy seemed to recollect that this sweating man in the felt hat and the suit that fit him like a feed sack didn't know any better, and the patience came back.

"I got three things to say to you," Pappy said carefully, as if he conveyed a piece of information Mr. Hamilton would sincerely want to have. "First of all, I don't know nobody name of Jack Robinson. Second, I hain't poor. And third, I hain't going to sell my land for no thirty dollars the acre or for no three thousand dollars the foot. I made this farm what hit is, and I hain't going to sell hit for nothing to nobody. Hit's mine till God calls me home."

Mr. Hamilton resorted to aggrieved patience. "Mr. Kirby, I am not a fool. I have been down to the Sevier County courthouse. I know that you bought one hundred acres of land ten years ago for twelve mules. That is precisely what your deed said. I swear, I can't believe some of the things you hillbillies put in your deeds, but there it is in plain black and white. Twelve mules for one hundred acres of ground. Now any fool that can add two plus two knows that a man who buys one hundred acres of land for twelve mules and turns around ten years later and can sell that land for three thousand dollars is making himself one hell of a deal. But that is the generosity of the United States government and our great president, Franklin Delano Roosevelt."

Pappy looked at him and did not show a flicker of emotion. "I'd appreciate it if you'd not cuss here in front of my boys," Pappy said. "If you was to be cussing down in town or out there on the public road, I wouldn't say nothing 'bout hit. But being as how you're on my propity, I reckon I can ask you please not to cuss on hit, not in front of my children."

Mr. Hamilton was just about at the end of his ability to pretend courtesy. He took his hat off and rolled it around in his hands and put it back on his head and took a big white handkerchief soggy and stained with sweat and grime out of his pocket and ineffectually wiped his pink face with it. He took a deep breath as if in final witness to the world of how patient and long-suffering he was, and he threw his eyes skyward as if to implore divine grace to deal with this simpleton. Pappy stood there calm all the while, his hands clasped against his chest inside the bib of his overalls, and he waited for Mr. Hamilton to get through with his performance.

"All right," Mr. Hamilton said at last. "Let's talk turkey. I'll give you thirty-five dollars the acre. That's as far as I can go. I swear it on my mother's honor. The president of the United States, Mr. Franklin Delano Roosevelt himself, could not offer you more than thirty-five dollars the acre for this land, because the Congress of the United States that looks after the taxpayers' money would not let him."

He swept a smooth hand vaguely around as if to encompass all the land in question and gave an impression of encompassing all the world. "At thirty-five dollars the acre, you will have thirty-five hundred dollars in a lump sum. That is three times as much as a schoolteacher in this state makes in a whole year. I'd be willing to bet it's six times as much cash as you've ever held in your hand before."

"Begging your pardon, but I hain't no betting man," Pappy said. "And I hain't no schoolteacher, and I hain't selling you my land for no price that you can name."

"Mr. Kirby," Mr. Hamilton said, changing his tone just a little. "I want to share a vision with you—all these mountains as part of a great national park, the land restored like God made it, the hills echoing with the sound of bears and the growling of the bobcat and the lynx, and lines and lines of automobiles coming to drive through the mountains and see everything God intended them to see out the windows of their cars. And they are going to be on a highway that will run up there to the top of the mountains right across this piece of dirt where we are standing this very minute."

Mr. Hamilton faltered. Like many other people, he was capable of having soaring fantasies of a golden age about to dawn. But when he tried to communicate this grand vision to others—particularly to inferiors—his words failed, and the vision turned the color of rusty leaves. He tried to go on against the flinty indifference and patience Pappy threw up in his face, but in a moment the spiraling words about the national park became garbled and died into babbling and fell, taking the vision to earth with a soft plop like a cow relieving herself, leaving Pappy standing there unmoved, his hands serenely clasped inside his overalls.

The calm, the indomitable calm, was what did Mr. Hamilton in. He had had a long and dusty day, and he was thirsty, but he did not like to drink out of cisterns, and he supposed (erroneously) that the Kirby family took its water from a cistern. He had talked with a lot of mountaineers. Most of them had been unwilling to consider moving off their land—until he told them how much the government was willing to pay. Then they faltered and looked down at their scarred and dirty clodhopper shoes and lifted their eyes to the sky and turned red and said they would have to think about it, and he knew he had them. He loved to use words like "lump sum" and "fortune." Even the hardiest among the men he talked to looked a little anxious behind the eyes when he paraded before them the power of the United States government that he faithfully represented. For Mr. Hamilton, hesitation in their eyes was the beginning of the end, sufficient for the time being because he knew he would come back and that they would sign or make their illiterate marks on the dotted line.

He had a cheerful formula. "Well, you folks can think about it for a week, and the federal government and I will be happy to wait for you that long. But I'm here to tell you that you don't have any choice. Once the government of Mr. Franklin Delano Roosevelt decides to do something for the good of the whole country, nobody can stand in the way. It's up to every one of us to do our bit, and if that means you have to give up your home and move someplace else, well, you better get used to it." With those words, Mr. Hamilton tipped his hat, shook hands all the way around, patted two or three barefoot urchins on the head, and drove on to his next stop feeling completely satisfied with himself.

Nobody had resisted him like this man Kirby. It was not anything in particular that Pappy said. Oh, he said sufficient to upset Mr. Hamilton. But much more unnerving than the words was the unvarying calm, the serene conviction that Mr. Hamilton was irrelevant to anything that was a part of Pappy's life, past, present, or future.

So Mr. Hamilton lost his temper. "You just don't understand, do you, you ignorant hillbilly? You don't understand that I represent the full power of the United States government—the army, the navy and the marines and the FBI and the House and the Senate and the Supreme Court and Mr. Franklin Delano Roosevelt himself and his wife, too. I speak for every man jack of them. And I am standing right here to tell you that we are going to have your miserable little piece of dirt, and the national park is going to sit right here, and millions and millions of honest Americans are going to walk and drive right over this property, and they are going to see nature like God meant for them to see it, and they are not even going to know your name. And if you try to stand in the way of the United States government and me, I personally am going to bring the army up here, and I am going to lock you up and lock up every one of these feeble-minded boys of yours in the jailhouse, and you are going to sit there until hell freezes over and you rot. No, I take it back. You are going to stand at the window of your cell looking through the bars, and you are going to see millions and millions of automobiles driving by to visit the greatest national park in the world. And you can put that in your pipe and smoke it."

The moment of silence that came after this outburst was like all the ice in the world piled up in one small place in the dark. Then Pappy said, "I don't smoke."

"You don't smoke." For just a second, Mr. Hamilton seemed perplexed. He did not understand. Then he did understand, and he thought Pappy was mocking him, and in complete loss of control he shouted, "You may not smoke, you hillbilly, but you will burn in hell before you stand in the way of the United States government!"

Hope Kirby had never seen anybody talk to Pappy like that. He had never dreamed in his wildest nightmares that anybody *could* talk to Pappy like that. But Mr. Hamilton did it, even though his face looked red enough to explode and his voice became so loud and uncontrolled that it threatened to dissolve in a screech of rage, the way a circle saw will sometimes catch in a knothole in an oak log and nearly tear your ears out with the unbearable howl of metal against resisting wood too hard for it to cut.

Pappy stood there, his hands folded, his blue eyes not betraying a hint of emotion, nothing there but that *patience,* and when Mr. Hamilton finally ran down and looked deflated and ashen after his face had been so red, Pappy spoke quietly to him. "You are not making your manners to me or my boys, Mr. Hamilton. If you can't be more polite than that, I'm going to have to ask you to get off my place."

"Damn you!" Mr. Hamilton said, his voice not loud now but low and ugly, almost a whisper, and filled with meanness. "Damn you. I will come back here in one week. One week! And if you are not ready to sign on the dotted line, I guarantee that I will do exactly what I have promised to do. I will put you all in jail, and I will throw away the key."

With that he glared around at all of them, and M.L. started to cry. Pappy looked at M.L. "Don't cry, boy," he said. M.L. stopped crying as if he'd been a spigot turned off. The crying unnerved Mr. Hamilton. He got back into his dusty black Ford and tore off down the hill, throwing up dust and gravel behind him.

Almost as soon as Mr. Hamilton got away from the Kirby farm, he was filled with remorse. He had not meant to lose his temper. He thought of himself as a man of self-control and moderation. It was not that he felt compassion for the Kirby family. It was that he had allowed white trash like Roy Kirby to make him lower himself. "Why did I do that?" he asked himself aloud. "I have all the horses on my side. When the time comes, I will bring that ignorant sheriff up here and jerk those hillbillies off that place, and yes indeed, if they put up a fuss, I can put them in jail just like I said I would. Why did I have to let that old goat get to me like that? I could do it all with a smile on my face." His remorse faded into the conviction that he next time he ran into somebody like Roy Kirby, he'd take it easy. "I'll laugh and tell jokes," he told himself again aloud. "I'll not raise my voice, and I'll let him be the one who gets mad. I'll be in perfect control." Taking his resolution for the finest kind of reality, he drove back into Sevierville. He would eat supper in one of the greasy spoons the little burg had to offer, and he would listen to the radio a little while in his hotel, and he would go to bed.

He drove along humming a little song. It was a fine September afternoon. White clouds hung over the hills against a blue sky. This was a great place for a national park, he thought. The government that he represented had done *very* well. Mr. Hamilton was very happy and pleased with himself. He hummed as he drove down the gravel highway. He did not know that within a week he would be dead.

WHY DID one essay by W. T. Stace bring Charles's faith crashing down around him like the temple of the Philistines? Because he read it and knew it was true. Because his mother was so afraid that faith was something that could be lost. Because the whole stirring world around Charles Alexander lived as if W. T. Stace were right. Fundamentalists like himself were isolated holdouts from what everybody else knew was true. Fundamentalists manufactured a world of their own and had to keep patching it up all the time, or the secular rain would tumble down on it and wash it completely away as if it had never been.

FOR A long time after Mr. Hamilton left that afternoon, Roy Kirby sat on the steps of his house and thought. "You boys take care of the milking," he said in an absent-minded way, and they sprang to obey and left him sitting there.

When they came back into the house from the barn, bearing their milk pails, he was still sitting there. The sun sank in the west and almost touched the tops of the trees. It was dark red, the color of fire deep down in wood. Some leaves were beginning to turn. Early in the morning up here you could feel the bite of autumn. To the west the mountains smoothed away towards Knoxville, the mysterious city.

Mammy came to the door. "Air you going to eat your supper?" she said.

Her voice stirred Pappy out of his reverie. "I hain't hungry tonight," he said. "I got to go see somebody."

With that he went out to the barn and put a bridle on his stoutest mule and threw a gunnysack over the mule's back and rode down towards the villages of Gatlinburg and Sevierville on beyond. By then the shadows of the mountains had thrown the valley into twilight, but the sky overhead was still blue.

Mammy put supper on the table for the boys. It was the first time Hope Kirby remembered sitting down at the supper table when Pappy was not there. He asked Pappy about it later on, when he came home from the army and the mountains of the Philippines. Yes, it was true, Pappy said, it was the first time that Pappy and Mammy had been separated at suppertime since they got married.

Where did Pappy go? To Sevierville to find Sheriff Harvey Ambrose Cate. Sevierville was almost ten miles away, and Pappy rode slow because he didn't see any sense in tiring out the mule, and he wanted to think about Mr. Hamilton and the national park and the United States government. When he got to the jailhouse it was already eight o'clock. The sky was clear and dark, and the stars were coming out. The moon was not yet up. The deputy on duty was sitting in the office listening to the radio and more than half asleep in front of a cup of cold coffee, and when Roy Kirby walked in, making no more noise than a panther, and spoke to him, the man started up. "Lord, you scared the tar out of me," the deputy said.

Roy asked him where the sheriff was, and the deputy said he'd gone home for the day, and Roy asked him where the sheriff lived, and the deputy told him, and the sheriff's place turned out to be four miles back towards Gatlinburg in Wears Valley. So Roy rode out there and got to the sheriff's house just as Sheriff Cate had put his false teeth in a glass of water and had taken off his trousers and his shirt and had put on his nightshirt and was getting ready to join his fat and comfortable wife in bed.

By then it was almost nine o'clock—Roy's bedtime, too, but with what was on his mind, he couldn't wait. He did what manners in the country required. That is, he didn't walk up onto the front porch of the sheriff's house and knock so that the man who came to the door wouldn't be more than two feet away when he saw you and didn't have any warning about what your intentions might be. No, Roy reined up his mule and sat there and hollered, "Shurf Cate! Shurf Cate! It's Roy Kirby, Shurf Cate. I'm from up t'other side of Gatlinburg and I got to talk to you about something." In the meantime the sheriff's hound dogs penned out back set up the most god-awful howling and barking, and a mean old mongrel the sheriff kept around because he, the sheriff, was softhearted, set up some serious growling and barking from underneath the front porch and sounded as if he'd like nothing better than to take Pappy's foot off at the ankle. It was one more reason Pappy never did like dogs. They were unsociable animals to strangers.

Sheriff Cate heard the racket and knew what it meant when he heard Roy Kirby say where he was from. The sheriff didn't know the name of every man in Sevier County, although when he ran in elections he acted as if he did and called them all "Bub" or "Bo" or "my friend," or "sir," or "buddy." But the mention of where Roy Kirby was from was enough to let him know just exactly what Roy Kirby was even if he didn't know exactly who he was, and he could guess with a fair degree of certainty why he had come down here and what he was doing out there in the road at this time of night.

"Hold on! I'll be right out!" Sheriff Cate hollered out the window, and sighing with fatigue and misery, he pulled his trousers back on and put in his teeth, but he did not take his nightshirt off, and he did not put his shoes on. He went out with the nightshirt hanging down over his trousers to the knees, his belly pushed out like a loaded feed sack, and his naked feet making a padding noise on the cool plank floor of his house.

He went through the country ritual of hollering at his dogs until they stopped. He kicked the mean old mongrel gently back, telling Roy Kirby to watch out, this one bites, and cursing the dog softly until the mongrel crept back under the porch and lay there growling in the dark with apparent sincerity. Roy got down off the mule and tied the end of the bridle to a sapling and came up on the porch, and the sheriff said, "That dog ain't good for nothing but barking. I don't know why I keep that dog."

Roy said, "A man's got a right to a dog, I reckon. I never did like dogs myself."

"I love my hunting dogs," the sheriff said. "I tell you, them hounds back there can tree a bear quicker than lightning strikes."

"I just lay up in the woods with my shotgun and wait for Mr. Bear to come to me," Roy said. "That keeps me from having the trouble of dogs."

"You hunt bears with a shotgun? Lord, you are a braver man than I am," the sheriff said. "I use a Springfield 1903 rifle I bought after the war. I wouldn't feel safe with no shotgun."

"If you hit him in the face with a twelve-gauge close up, he hain't going to do nothing to you," Roy said. "Not 'less'n you miss."

"Have a seat," the sheriff said with a big sigh. "Take that rocker there." The sheriff did not think this was going to be a very agreeable talk.

"I'm much obliged," Roy said.

The sheriff took the rocking chair next to it. The sheriff rocked back and forth. The rockers went thump-thump on the planks. Roy sat still with his old black hat in his lap. "I reckon I'll have me a chaw," the sheriff said. "Kin I offer you one?"

"No sir," Roy said. "I don't use no tobacco, but hit's your place, and hit don't matter to me if you want a chaw."

"You don't use no tobacco? Don't you even dip?"

"No sir, I don't dip neither."

"Well, sir, you're a good man if you don't chew or smoke or dip, I reckon. Tell you what, though, I started chewing when I wasn't more than twelve year old, and now it's a habit, and I can't break it, and that's a fact. You sure you don't mind if I have me a chaw?"

"What a man does in his own house is his own business," Roy said.

The sheriff took a big bite out of a twist of tobacco that he'd laid in the windowsill for such an occasion as this, and he said that if there were more people like Roy Kirby that minded their own business and let other folks mind their business, the world would be a whole lot better place. The two of them sat there for a little while, the sheriff rocking back and forth, thump-thump, thump-thump, in the rocking chair and Roy sitting there with his hat in his hands and not moving, almost like he was not sure he had the right to rock on the sheriff's porch and in the sheriff's chair when the two of them really didn't know each other all that well. The sheriff's porch faced the southeast, and before them the mute bulk of Mount LeConte rose against the stars.

The sheriff talked about the weather, about the heat of the summer just past, about the Depression and how he hoped that Franklin Delano Roosevelt was a better man than Woodrow Wilson, the last Democrat they'd had in the White House, and he said he sure was glad we weren't in the League of Nations and hoped Roosevelt wouldn't try to put us in it when Wilson had failed. He said he never could trust a Democrat, even when one was the president of the United States.

The sheriff talked on and on, pausing now and then to lean forward and spit copiously into the grass, and Roy with his infinite patience sat there, polite and silent, and listened and waited for the sheriff to run down. After a while the sheriff did run down, and when the insect-warbling silence of a mild September night finally engulfed both of them, Roy said, without preliminaries, "This feller Hamilton. Who is he? He claims he can make me sell my place, don't matter if'n I want to sell hit or not. Who is he?"

The sheriff groaned silently in that part of his uncertain spirit where he kept his most worrisome thoughts, one of the most worrisome and most secret his abiding hatred of being high sheriff, that indeed he was afraid to be high sheriff because of men like this polite, leather-faced, humble, and patient man sitting next to him in his rocking chair at this very minute. Sheriff Harvey Ambrose Cate had survived twelve years as high sheriff of Sevier County in part because he had developed a trustworthy intuition about the kind of man who might kill him and the kind of man who would not. Roy Kirby was the kind of man who might kill him.

"Well, Mr. Kirby," the sheriff began in a mournful tone, taking the opportunity to lean forward and shoot another jet of tobacco over his porch railing and into his yard, "I'll tell you all I know about that sneaky, no-good white trash Mr. Hamilton. It ain't much. I swear to God, I don't know much about him. But he is the kind of feller that ought to make his own mama ashamed because she carried a man like that nine months in her belly, the kind of low-down, two-faced son of a bitch that would make his own daddy feel good if a rattlesnake bit him."

"Then how can a man like that tell me he can make me sell him my land?"

"Well sir, that's the misery of it. He can make you sell your land because he has got behind him the whole army and navy and police of the United States government. I can't do nothing about it, and Mr. Kirby, you can't do nothing about it. The United States government is a ornery mule, and that feller is riding him."

"But how can he just walk in here and tell me I have to move off my land?"

"Mr. Kirby," the sheriff said, "I am a legal man. The law is my business. Now I hain't no lawyer. God no. I thank the good Lord that I hain't sunk that low. But I know something about the law because I have been high sheriff of this county for twelve year. It is called 'eminent domain.' That is what this jackass Hamilton is talking about. Eminent domain. It means that whenever you get a Democrat in the White House up there in Washington City, he sets out to make all the labor unions and the Communists and the niggers and all the other trash we got in this country as happy as flies on shit on a hot day. He has decided that—"

"Mr. Hamilton? Is he the one that has decided?"

"Why no, bless your heart. It ain't Mr. Hamilton that has decided nothing. It is Mr. Franklin Delano Roosevelt. He has decided that he is going to give all them folks a national park. He give them legal whiskey, and that warn't enough to make 'em happy. Now he is going to give them a national park."

"Mr. Hamilton told me about the national park, but I do not understand what hit is," Roy said.

"Why bless your heart, there ain't no reason for you to understand what a national park is because, Mr. Kirby, you are a downright sensible feller. You know what's what. But all them folks that votes for Roosevelt, they think a national park is just like a picture show with bears and bobcats. That feller Hamilton told me that in five years' time, maybe less, they's going to be a paved road over the mountains from here to North Carolina, and you are going to have a line of cars miles and miles long driving along that road day and night and looking at the bears and the bobcats and the deer without ever getting out of their cars. He told me this. He said that it's going to be the greatest thing it ever was for fat city ladies and cripples and anybody else that can't walk. All they have to do is get somebody to drive them up that road, and they can see more bears in a day than Daniel Boone seen in a month."

"He wants to run me and my folks off my farm so fat city ladies can look at bears out their car windows?" Roy Kirby did not seem exercised by this amazing information that confirmed what Mr. Hamilton had told him more or less. It was just something he turned over in his head and spoke aloud about as he turned it over.

"That's about the size of it," the sheriff said with a hopeless sigh, leaning forward to spit again and falling back in a gloomy lethargy, a silence broken only by the rhythmic, nervous thumping of the rocking chair.

"Don't we have a congressman to do something to stop hit?" Roy asked at last.

"Why bless your heart, Mr. Kirby, our congressman is a Republican. This is a Democrat government we got up there in Washington City, Mr. Kirby. Republicans are as scarce up there as legs on a snake. They got us outnumbered, Mr. Kirby. There ain't nothing I can do about it, and there ain't nothing you can do about it."

The sheriff spat yet again and wished with all his heart that Mr. Kirby would get back on his mule and go back home. The moon was rising just over the mountains as they talked. Heat lightning was flickering off in the distance.

"What about that?" Roy said in a musing way, his voice toneless, strange for its lack of feeling, its flat, metallic slap against the quiet night.

"How much money has he offered you for your place? Thirty dollars the acre?"

"He started with thirty. He upped hit to thirty-five," Roy said.

"Thirty-five!" the sheriff said, shaking his head admiringly in the dark. "Well, that ain't bad," he said. "Maybe you ought to think it over."

"I hain't going to sell my land," Roy said. "I made that place out of nothing, and hain't nobody going to take hit away from me just so's fat city ladies can look at bears."

The sheriff took another deep breath, spat, and sighed mournfully. "Everbody else is selling out," he said in a low, amazed voice as if he and Roy were two of a kind, lamenting the decline of morals in the country. "Some of them folks is awful mad about it. I'll grant you that. And they's lots that feels terrible about it. But what can a man do?"

"He don't have to sell out the land he's made his own," Roy said.

They sat there for a long time, and Roy thought, and the sheriff prayed that Roy Kirby would go away. But then the sheriff had an inspiration. "How much land did you say you had? A hundert acres?" He stopped rocking and looked out into the dark. "Say, you know what I'd do if somebody was to give me that much cash money?"

"No," Roy said without interest.

"Why, I'd buy me a filling station. Let's put it this way, Mr. Kirby. This Hamilton feller, he's probably right. Five, ten years from now, you're going to have cars driving up and down that there mountain packed to the doors with fat ladies with money to spend because the Democrats have give it to them. They got to buy gas for their cars. They're going to need air for their tires. They got to buy candy bars for their fat children."

"Candy rots teeth," Roy said.

"Sure it does, but they don't know that, do they, or if they know it, they don't care. They buy candy bars and pay a nickel apiece for them, and that's three cents for the people that makes the bar and two cents for the feller in the filling station that sells it along with the gasoline. Now look, you could put you up a filling station right here in Sevierville or maybe over at Pigeon Forge, and you could rake in the cash."

"Selling gas to fat ladies?" Roy said.

"Gas and candy bars. Them fat ladies eats lots of candy bars. Somebody's got to sell them what they want."

"Hit hain't going to be me," Roy said. He sat for a while longer, looking out into the moonlit dark and thinking. Everything looked magical in the moonlight. It was a sight Roy Kirby loved. It was clear to him that the sheriff was not going to help him.

"Well, hit's time I was getting back home," Roy said finally. "I'm much obliged for your time, Sheriff."

The two men got up from their chairs and walked down into the yard where Roy had tied his mule. The stars were glittering across the clear sky, and the moon cast shadows before it, but towards the west they could see a blackness where clouds were piled. The lightning flickered there. "Well, now you listen to me, Mr. Kirby. You think about all this. Don't be making no trouble before you think about it. If you was my brother, I'd tell you the exact same thing. Don't be rash. Think about it." The sheriff rubbed his bare feet in the grass; the grass was moist and felt good.

"I've thought about hit," Roy said.

"Maybe you ought to think about it some more, Mr. Kirby," the sheriff said. "Who can tell? Maybe the national park will do us some good. You got children, Mr. Kirby? Five boys, you say. Where they going to get jobs when they all grow up? You can't keep them all on that place of your'n. Even with one hundred acres, they's a limit to how many boys you can raise and keep fed for a lifetime. You got to think about it."

Roy didn't say anything. He did not believe in wasting words. He put his shapeless hat back on his head and got back on his mule, flinging himself up quick and catlike, his legs dangling on each side. Without another word, he rode off into the night towards home, and the sheriff stood there and listened to the mule's hoofs click on the road and die away so that he was left with the September night around him.

"I knowed right then," the sheriff said later to people he trusted, "that Mr. Hamilton's life wasn't worth a plugged nickel. I knowed right then that he was a dead man and didn't even know it."

O*N MONDAY* evening after the paper was out, Charles walked through the woods to see Preacher Finewood. Preacher Finewood was an event, a miracle, and his coming to Midway Baptist Church seemed to be one of those acts of God akin to thunderstorms and hurricanes, although as far as his congregation was concerned, his effects were entirely benign. He brought the kind of success that seemed possible only if God were in it, the power that let Solomon build the Temple or that raised again the walls of Jerusalem when they had been torn down.

He had driven up into the driveway of the Alexander home one bright morning in early summer about the time that Lawrence Arceneaux arrived at First Baptist. But he was an entirely different kind of man. Eugenia Alexander, thin already with cancer, was working in her garden, and he introduced himself to her humbly enough but with blazing confidence. Rosy, his plump daughter, sat timidly in the car looking shy and uncomfortable. She was about eleven or twelve then, and in describing her later Eugenia said, "That girl needs to go on a diet."

Rosy probably inherited her size in part from Mr. Finewood. (Her mother was dead and was therefore not available for comparison.) He was a large man, tending to fat but not obese. Rather he looked a little like the image of prosperity in eighteenth-century British portraits where successful men put on a little flesh almost in token of their having made their way in the world. He had an almost psychological gift for converting his size to a radiation of power when he spoke.

All this he turned on Eugenia when he introduced himself and declared, "Sister Alexander, I hope I do not offend you, but my daughter and I were driving through this beautiful community, and I felt the voice of God telling me to stop. That church up on the hill there needs a pastor. I believe God has called me to be that man."

Midway Baptist did indeed need a pastor. Its last preacher had been a pleasant, elderly man named Johnson who had a penchant for preaching the same sermons again and again. His patient congregation took him to be what he was, a good man without either the memory or the talent to deliver new sermons. He lived in Knoxville, where he had another job, elevator operator in one of the large banks up there, and the pittance the church paid him was a welcome supplement to his meager income. Only a few weeks before Mr. Finewood appeared so miraculously on the scene, Mr. Johnson collapsed and died over his elevator crank. Since then Midway Baptist had been conducting services with whatever preacher it could pick up from the gang of bricklayers, carpenters, farmers, and others in the county who like Mr. Johnson had jobs and preached on the side.

None of them was what the congregation wanted to listen to every Sunday. And some bold souls in the congregation looked at the neighborhood, full of new houses and new people, and suggested that it was time Midway had a full-time pastor. The neighborhood was growing; the church was not.

And here was Mr. Finewood. He proved to be a spellbinding preacher. He said he thought his work at the Valley View Baptist Church in Charlotte, North Carolina, was done, and with Eugenia's influence he got a chance to preach at Midway Baptist, and after that he was elected almost unanimously.

It should be said that before she presented him to the church, Eugenia conducted her own careful inquisition. That first day, she led Mr. Finewood and Rosy to the front porch, poured them iced tea, and gave Mr. Finewood a thorough examination. Did he accept every word of the Bible as the literal word of God? Did he believe that Jesus was coming soon? Was he a premillennialist? Did he believe in the Rapture? Did he believe in the Virgin Birth? Did he believe that Jesus was the Son of God, the redeemer of humankind? Brother Finewood not only believed all these doctrines, but as Eugenia advanced them, he expounded on them at great length and lamented the pastors of the "modernist" churches who had let these precious doctrines come to nothing because they had been seduced by liberalism and other evils, including communism itself. Mr. Finewood would have nothing to do with the social gospel. The job of the church was to preach Jesus Christ and Him crucified and the fast-approaching end of the world. Eugenia was ecstatic. For a while they lived together the near-at-hand moment when the damned would be cast hopeless into hell and the righteous in Christ would live for a thousand years in a redeemed and peaceable earth. Eugenia felt that she had listened to the Lord's anointed.

Mr. Finewood had a powerful voice in conversation, and he carried it into the pulpit. The church installed him and Rosy in a shabby house that had been standing vacant next door, and men turned out to scrape and paint and repair so that when everything was done, it was not a bad arrangement. Mr. Finewood set out to visit every house in the sprawling neighborhood.

The results of his preaching and his visiting quickly made the little white frame box of a church obsolete. It literally was ready to burst at the seams. Within months it was decided to raise a large new building, and now in the summer of 1953, a great block of pseudo-Georgian architecture with no particular distinction except its size towered on the crest of the hill next to the Alexander place. The little frame church was no more, and the auditorium that held four hundred souls was filled every Sunday, and some were saying that they had not planned boldly enough. Mr. Finewood became a paragon in the county, the pastor whom members of First Baptist used as a comparison for Arceneaux. They appreciated Arceneaux's class and his education, but some of them slipped away and heard Mr. Finewood, and although they felt something a little too fervent about the man, they did wish they could understand Arceneaux's sermons as well as they understood Finewood's.

Charles listened spellbound to Mr. Finewood. The man *meant* it. He was on fire for God with a certainty that was like a flame blazing on a hearth. When Mr. Finewood preached, Charles believed with a certainty and a passion that made W. T. Stace shrink to a cloud no larger than a man's hand in Charles's religious sky. When the two of them talked, Charles felt that he was in the presence of a man who had a hand firmly gripped on the Rock of Ages.

Mr. Finewood had not gone to college. "I started preaching in high school," he said, "and I saw that the Lord gave me power, and I didn't see any sense of losing that power by going to college to sit at the feet of a crowd of godless professors. Don't let them steal your faith, Charles. They are like the serpent in Eden. They promise you knowledge and lead you to death and destruction."

Charles did not tell Mr. Finewood about W. T. Stace. He could not confess to anyone that he had lost the faith, lost it utterly, and was struggling with all his might to get it back. He could not bear the emotional scene that such a confession might have created.

On his way to Mr. Finewood's house that night, his heart was as heavy as bricks. He picked a little bouquet of flowers for Rosy out of his mother's garden before he went up the hill. His mother had planted the garden so something was blooming from spring into the first frosts of fall. This time last week, none of this had happened, he thought. He could not make anything of the thought except to wish none of it had happened still. He walked up the path beaten down by years of footsteps. His. Stephen's. Guy's. Eugenia's. He could walk in the total darkness without a flashlight. He came up the western side of the cemetery. The city of the dead. His mother was buried in a corner, on the eastern side, under a large red cedar tree. Would the roots grow into her coffin? No. Paul Alexander had put her coffin in a concrete vault. Dry forever and ever. Was her spirit there? No, in heaven, people said. What then was the resurrection? What was she in heaven without a body? Did bodies rise to join souls? The dust reassembling itself into bodies. And the sea gave up the dead which were in it. Or were they all just—

She might see his thoughts now, his lusts for women's breasts and bottoms, his imaginings of the garden of delights in a woman's nakedness. Sometimes he saw a pretty woman and crossed the street to pass her without speaking so he could see the line of her bra beneath her blouse. Sometimes the panty line. And in swimming pools. Charles did not like to swim. The chlorine in the water burned his eyes. Still he went with friends swimming at Concord and Alcoa sometimes to see the girls in bathing suits, which sometimes worked up the backs of their hips so he could see that fold of flesh where the hip began against the thigh, and he could imagine the rest, driving his soul to lust and perdition.

He crossed the church parking lot under prodigious oak trees. To the southeast he could see the dark shapes of the mountains blotting out the lower stars in the moonless night. Above the mountains the stars gleamed. He walked in front of the church to the Old Stage Road, gravel still, and the gravel crunched softly under his feet. He stood in the road and looked back at the church, looming up in the starry dark. No cross on the tall steeple. Baptists did not believe in crosses. Idolatry. Something Catholics put on their churches. A big auditorium, now silent and dark. A good piano. Stephen said it was good. He played for all the services, his fingers dancing like magic over the black and white keys. God still does miracles, Mr. Finewood said in every sermon. Our God is the God of the Bible, the God of Abraham, Isaac, and Jacob. He still works with those who have faith. This church a testimony to God's miracles. No abstract argument here. God at work—through His instrument, Clifford Finewood.

The preacher was sitting on his front porch in his shirtsleeves and without a necktie. He wore suspenders like people of the old time. It didn't matter. In fact, compared with Mr. Arceneaux, Mr. Finewood seemed honestly primitive, the man with no pretensions who preached the straight gospel as Jesus would have preached it. As Jesus did preach it.

His wife died young of cancer. He had suffered. Character, Eugenia said. He came to see her when she lay dying, and she put out her hands to him as though for help, his hands to pull her out of the cancer as though from a bottomless lake where she was sinking. But she died anyway.

Rosy was now about thirteen, on her way to becoming a large, plain woman with flat cheekbones and a broad face. She had few friends, said little, watched the world with an expression of watchful anxiety. Pale skin. A white rose, people said. Mr. Finewood was kind to her, spoke lovingly to her, a quiet voice. People spoke of him as a good father to a girl whose mother was dead. Why didn't he marry again? Somehow his marital case did not seem as urgent as Mr. Arceneaux's at First Baptist, perhaps because any wife would have to take care of Rosy, and that would be a hard job. General acknowledgment of that. Charles felt sorry for Rosy.

Rosy sat a little way off on one of those metal gliders that swung on a stationary base so that you could rock yourself back and forth without moving the chair. An improvement over a rocking chair, people said. The glider creaked unpleasantly, making metallic sounds. The preacher stood up when he saw Charles's vague form advancing on the driveway, feet crunching softly on the coarse stones.

"Charles!" he said warmly. He came down the stairs. "I called last night. Your father said you were asleep. I feel like I let you down. I didn't know about—about all that happened until after church yesterday. Nobody told me, and we're so far out in the country here."

"Yes," Charles said.

Rosy stood, her hands folded in front of her, looking at him with a longing Charles could feel in the dark.

"Princess Rosy," Charles said, handing her the bouquet with a bow. "I brought you some flowers."

Even in the dark, Rosy seemed to bound with joy. "Oh thank you, Charles. Thank you. I'll put them in water."

"You're so kind to Rosy, Charles. She appreciates it. I appreciate it."

"I'm so happy that you are all right," Rosy said in a meek voice.

"Thank you," Charles said.

He sat in a rickety wicker chair. Rosy went in to put his flowers in water. The preacher sat in a big wooden chair. No one piece of furniture in the parsonage matched anything else. Nobody said anything for a while. They heard a chuck-will's-widow off somewhere in the woods. The trees were alive with the chorus of katydids. Not a breath stirred, but the heat was not as thick as it had been before sunset. Rosy came out again. "Your mother said she was going to teach me to grow flowers," Rosy said.

"I wish she had lived long enough," Charles said.

"It must have been a terrible thing to see," the preacher said at last.

Charles could think of nothing to say.

"God spared you," the preacher said in a ruminative voice.

"I know," Charles said with more fervor than he felt. He knew he should talk like this with Preacher Finewood. You could not talk this way to everybody. When he was with Preacher Finewood he felt surrounded by warmth, by goodness, and above all with belief. They could talk the language of faith.

"The Lord's ways are mysterious," the preacher said quietly. "During the war when I was preaching at the Valley View Baptist Church in Charlotte, North Carolina, one of our young men was in the navy in the Pacific. His name was Joel Davidson, a fine young Christian boy. His mother called me once in the middle of the night and said she had been overcome by a terror that her son was in mortal danger at that moment. I put my trousers on over my pajamas, and I went over right that minute to pray with her. She, her husband, and I got down on our knees and sought the Lord for His help. Do you know something? Two days later a telegram came that he had been wounded in action but that he would recover. And three weeks later she got a letter from him. He was in a hospital in San Francisco. He said that a Japanese torpedo had hit the engine room of his cruiser just as he was going up a ladder to the next deck. The explosion blew him out through the open door above him. The hatch, I think he called it. Every other boy in that engine room was killed, but he was spared, and he is alive today."

They sat for a moment in the reverent silence. It was as Mr. Finewood had said to him time and again: "The atheist has his arguments, but God has His deeds."

Mr. Finewood spoke again in a while, his voice still solemn. "I don't know why those other boys were killed and Joel was spared. Was he better than they were? We are all sinners in the eyes of God. Was it because we prayed for him? I think so. But why did others not pray for their children? We know God does things; but we can't know why He does them."

"Yes," Charles said.

The leaves in the huge oak trees before the parsonage shook with a faint breeze that stirred from the west across the dark. It was a minor motion, but something in the stirring of the wind seemed to Charles like the still, small voice which the prophet Elijah heard in the wilderness when he thought God had forsaken him and when he alone had not bowed to Baal. God was not in the mighty wind that shattered stones, and He was not in the earthquake and the fire, but He was in the still, small voice. Charles felt abruptly like weeping again.

Instead he told of Mr. Arceneaux's visit.

It was not meant to be a betrayal. It was release, steam escaping, a safety valve. It was a plea for agreement, maybe for vindication, for comfort, for sympathy. For pity? Perhaps for that, too. Receiving pity was like being excused. It was a mistake. I should stop, Charles thought in the back, upstairs room of his mind above the area where words were formed which gushed out, telling his story. I should keep this to myself. But he kept talking. He could not stop talking once he had begun.

Mr. Finewood listened in appalled shock. Charles could not see his face. He saw the glimmer of sourceless light on something that he knew was a face, but he could read no expression. Mr. Finewood's emotion came out in his words. His voice trembled with incredulity. "A man calling himself a preacher of the gospel of our Lord Jesus Christ told you to lie! I knew that man was—" He did not finish the sentence. The awful things that defined Lawrence Arceneaux rose mute in the night air, a horror of darkness. Perhaps Mr. Finewood himself did not know how much of his indignation rose from honest righteousness and how much came from the lower cellars of his heart where he brooded that preachers like Larry Arceneaux had advantages—like wealth and education—that for reasons hidden in the mystery of God had been denied to Clifford Finewood.

"Please don't say anything about this," Charles stammered after a long silence. "I told you because—because I had to tell somebody."

"Charles," Preacher Finewood said earnestly, learning forward at him in the dark. "You have to tell the truth. When you go to court, and when you sit in that witness chair, your mother's spirit will be watching you, Charles. You have to tell the truth. You will be holding your mother's hopes and your very own soul in your hand."

Mr. Finewood made him no promises. Instead he gave him a command. Tell the truth. Always tell the truth. Eugenia Alexander in the graveyard not far away murmured in the silent language of the dead, fuller than words and sound, "Yes . . . yes."

*W*HEN Clifford Finewood became privy to the information that Charles Alexander gave him about Lawrence Arceneaux, it was bound to be shared with those souls at First Baptist Church who might be sympathetic to the indignation that swept through Mr. Finewood's heart. The first of these was Tommy Fieldston, who had found Mr. Finewood in the way that fundamentalist Christians have always found each other, by a grapevine that throbs and shakes with the news of where true believers may be.

Tommy Fieldston was not the sort of person to hide such information under a bushel. He went down to First Baptist as soon as he could to have it out with Arceneaux, and he supposed in his journey that its end would be Arceneaux's resignation from his position. This would have been a triumph of the first order. It would demonstrate to a congregation that didn't like him very much that Tommy Fieldston had been right all along about Arceneaux, and the next time First Baptist set out to find a minister, it would listen to Tommy because of the proof of his judgment rendered in the Arceneaux affair.

But Arceneaux was not an easy nut to crack. Their conversation, held partly on the sidewalk and partly in Arceneaux's office with Louise Renfrow listening avidly outside, was loud and stormy.

"I do not share with anyone what I say to somebody when I am doing pastoral counseling," Arceneaux said with some heat.

"But what you call pastoral counseling is telling a boy to lie. You're telling him to lie so a murderer can go free and murder somebody else."

"You do not know what I said to Charles Alexander because you were not there," Arceneaux said.

"So you deny it? You're saying that the boy lied to Brother Finewood?"

"I am not saying anything. I told you, Tommy, whatever I said to Charles Alexander is none of your business. It's something between Charles and me." Privately Arceneaux fumed and felt an unspeakable sense of betrayal.

"Oh, I get it. It's like the secrets of the confessional in the papist church. Your Catholic priest can't breathe a word if somebody confesses that he's about to commit murder."

"You can't go to a priest and confess sins you're about to commit, Tommy."

"You seem to know a lot about it."

"I'm from New Orleans. Remember? But yes, it's the same principle. A minister doesn't tell other people what he's told a third party."

"You're talking like a lawyer, Preacher. Do you know why you're talking like a lawyer? I've got you dead to rights. Now you're the one trying to lie. That's why you have a lawyer. So you can get away with lying."

"I don't have a lawyer. I'm telling you that it's none of your business what I said to Charles Alexander."

"I'm saying it's everybody's business if you told Charles Alexander to lie. A Baptist church has the right to know if its preacher believes in lies."

The conversation became more circular after this, going back and forth over the same ground until Arceneaux and Tommy Fieldston were about equally angry with each other. It went on for the better part of an hour, and Arceneaux finally stood up and said, "Tommy, we're not getting anywhere. I have work to do. I'd appreciate it if you'd leave."

"I am going to sit right here until you tell the truth," Tommy Fieldston said, slumping down a little in the big overstuffed chair where he sat opposite Arceneaux, glaring at him across the polished desk.

Arceneaux surprised himself then. He stood up. He said, "No, Tommy, you are not going to sit right there. You are going to get out of my office."

"It's not your office. It's the church's office," Tommy said. But then he looked at Arceneaux. Arceneaux was in his shirtsleeves, and Tommy saw something he hadn't noticed before. Arceneaux was a strong-looking man. Furthermore, Arceneaux looked angry enough to kill him.

"I want you to get out of here," Arceneaux said in a dangerously level voice.

Tommy stood up then, too. He got behind the chair, feeling safer to have it between him and Arceneaux. It was too heavy for him to lift in self-defense, but he might have done that if he could. He told Clifford Finewood later on, "I thought the man was going to attack me. I truly did."

Finewood shook his head sadly. "It's modernism, Brother Fieldston. Modernism and communism, and they're right here in Bourbonville. Why does that man not take a salary? I say it's because the Communists are paying him to corrupt this community. They have agents everywhere."

That morning Tommy went out the door, yelling at Arceneaux and saying to Mrs. Renfrow, "We have a liar for a preacher, Louise. A liar and a coward. He's told a lie, and he won't admit it."

Arceneaux came to the door of his office and stood there, looking as hard as a railroad track. Louise looked frightened. "I thought they were going to fight," she told her closest friends, who included everybody she saw in the next week.

Tommy left. "What happened?" Louise said to her employer in an emotional tone that for once was not contrived. She was truly scared.

"Nothing," Arceneaux said. He almost added, "that is any of your damned business." But he thought that would be going too far. He desperately wanted a drink. If he had had a bottle of gin in his desk drawer, he might have broken all his vows right then. Instead he went back into his office, slammed the door, and collapsed in his chair, staring across the desk at the photograph of Mack, Jean-François, and himself sitting at the table in the cafe when the beachhead had been established and their mission was over. In one corner of the photograph he could see a scrap of the Mediterranean. The photograph was black-and-white. It did not do justice to the blue of the sea. Mack and he were in their uniforms then. Jean-François had not yet found out about the boy.

Arceneaux took a deep breath. "Life is a bitch," he muttered to himself. He bowed his head and shut his eyes and took another deep, careful breath. "God forgive me," he whispered.

*H*OPE KIRBY gained weight in jail. "Jesus, Hope, you look good," the sheriff said.

"I hain't doing no work," Hope said. "I do push-ups and jumping jacks in here like we done in the army, but I don't do nothing else."

"I reckon you'd be better off in prison," the sheriff said. "They've got exercise yards in prison where the prisoners can walk ever day."

"I hain't complaining," Hope said. "I just wish I could walk around some. But hit don't matter." He was standing by the window looking out.

The grand jury brought in a true bill. The sheriff felt miserable. He had to testify, to look at those ranks of solemn men and tell them what he had done, what Charles Alexander had said. He was not the man to admit his misery to anybody or to say he was sorry for something he had done. Ken McNeil grinned triumphantly. The man had the most obnoxious grin the sheriff had ever seen. Bland and self-righteous.

"Lord God, Coondog," Bones Spradlin at the Sinclair filling station said. "The man was screwing Hope's wife. What would you do if you was to come home and find your wife in bed with another man?"

"I'd figure he was crazy," Coondog said. He knew he was lying. He knew he'd kill the son of a bitch.

It was getting on towards October. The days were warm, the nights cool, and the leaves were turning. The sheriff was in the cell with Hope. He did not bother to lock the cell door behind him.

"Look, Hope," he said. "I'll do something if you'll make me a promise."

Hope looked at him.

"If you'll promise not to try to get away, I'll take you for a walk late at night."

"I hain't going to try to get away," Hope said.

That's how the sheriff started loading Hope into the patrol car late at night and driving him far out into the country and walking with him on the dark, unpaved roads under the stars. At first the sheriff thought he'd hand-cuff Hope's wrists. *Hell, he's given me his word*, the sheriff thought. *It would be an insult if I put the cuffs on him. He'd think I didn't believe him.* So the two men got in the habit of going out to tiny country churches in groves on back roads, parking the patrol car behind the church, and walking together in the dark. *What the hell do I care if he makes a run for it*, the sheriff thought. It would be hard to explain. No, it would be easy to explain if he told the truth, but it would be hard on the sheriff afterwards.

They went to see Abby's grave. It was in the Methodist cemetery down by the river below town. Her folks used to be Methodists, and all their people were buried there. Hope stood in the dark and said nothing at all. Her folks had put up a new gravestone. He bent and kissed it, and he and the sheriff went away. Many of the graves here were older than the county.

Hope never made a run for it. The cool September nights brought back a world of memories. He did not share these with the sheriff. The two men walked along, exchanging bits and pieces of sentences, and sometimes making noncommittal remarks about the weather or else telling a brief anecdote about the war. Otherwise they plodded along in quiet contempla-tion of the night, the waning summer, the stars and the moon, and the peacefulness of a country evening. Sometimes a dog barked from a house shut up with sleep. The nearest sound was the slow tread of their feet on the gravel or a dirt road. Sometimes the sheriff sat on a big rock or a stump or the steps of a dark church and smoked a cigarette in silence, and Hope sat down with him, and they said hardly a word. Once Hope said, "Hit would be a good night to jacklight a deer if'n they was any deer in the hereabout."

"It would," the sheriff said. "You know something? I still think about how good it is to be able to light up a cigarette and not be scared that some Kraut sniper is going to shoot at the light."

Hope said languidly, "I can't never sit out in the dark without thinking about Japs sneaking up on me."

"I don't know which was worse, the Japs or the Germans," the sheriff said. "They was both as bad as they could be."

"My boys didn't take no prisoners," Hope said contentedly. "Hit was like killing rats."

"Well, they was human beings," the sheriff said. "Sometimes we went through their pockets, you know. When they was dead. Looking for souvenirs or cigarettes. I remember pictures of wives, I reckon, or girlfriends. And children. I never did care for no souvenirs myself."

"Missionary liked souvenirs," Hope said.

"Who the hell was Missionary?"

"He was a guy that fought in my group. He'd been a missionary. He was a teacher in some kind of church school. He was off in the mountains when the Japs taken Manila, and they chopped the heads off all his teachers. He joined up with us then to kill Japs. He was something."

"Lord God," the sheriff said.

Hope did not like to think about Missionary. He knew Missionary was the only member of his band who hated him. Maybe he had got over it by now, wherever he was.

"We'd best be getting back," the sheriff said, looking at the luminous dial of his watch. "It's almost three in the morning."

Hope got up. "I'm grateful for this, Sheriff. I sure am grateful."

"Aw, shit," the sheriff said.

*H*OPE KIRBY thought: *Maybe Pappy was wrong.* But how did a man ever know when his father was wrong? You had to believe in some things. Didn't you?

The morning after Pappy came home in the middle of the night from seeing the sheriff down in Sevierville, he sat at the breakfast table after milking time and was silent. The storm broke before he got home, and his clothes were soaked. Mammy waited up for him, and in the morning she hung his wet overalls and his shirt and his socks out on the clothesline in the sunshine, and Pappy sat silently in fresh, dry clothes on the front porch and thought. His eyes were red, and Hope knew that Pappy had not slept. Nobody asked him a question. Everybody knew that Pappy was thinking and that when the time came, he would do something. After he drank his second cup of coffee, he stood up and said, "I'm going to see how winter wheat will do in the field that lays up hard agin the woods."

That was the field on a slope back off on one end of the place—ground Pappy had cleared with the help of his boys. They used it for summer pasture, and sometimes Pappy grew beans back up there because he said a man could always live on beans, and Mammy canned dozens of quarts of green beans and shelly beans.

He and the boys went up and looked at the field, and Pappy said, "I reckon hit will do." He hitched two mules up to a plow, and he and Hope and John Sevier plowed it in a day, and next day they harrowed it, the mules working patiently in the radiant September air that seemed to surround every line of leaf and tree and rock and grass and the mountains rising above them with an invisible power that made everything sharper and more real than it usually was. Hope thought that the day they harrowed the field was the most beautiful day he had ever seen.

Pappy said, "I want you boys to come out here and help me dig a hole tonight, after dark."

Hope and John Sevier looked at each other, and Hope thought John Sevier might be on the point of asking a question—not an impertinent or querulous question but one that sought information, to respond to the natural curiosity that rose in a boy's head when his Pappy told him that he was going to help dig a hole after dark. But John Sevier thought better of it.

Pappy said that a lot of life was like hunting bears. You could go looking for a bear, and you might find one after you'd walked all over the mountains with a bunch of dogs and got your face clawed by blackberry vines and swatted by limbs and your feet skinned raw by climbing over rocks and your ears annoyed by trying to hear your dogs. But while you were looking high and low for the bear, wearing your body down, ole Mr. Bear was on the move, too, and you'd likely walk around each other, dogs or no dogs.

But if you sat down in the woods with your twelve-gauge near a path alongside a creek or near a big beech tree where the bears came to drink or to eat the beechnuts, you were more than likely to hear Mr. Bear crashing along through the underbrush after a day or two, and you could pick your minute and your angle, and you could blow his brains out with one shot or maybe two, and you wouldn't have to drag the carcass all over kingdom come to get the meat home to your smokehouse, and you didn't have to fool with dogs.

That was the way it was with most of the questions you might ask about the future. You could wear yourself out asking questions. Best thing to do was wait to see what the future might bring, and then you didn't ask questions; no, you saw what was right, and you did it—quick, without thinking about it. Then you weren't all worn out by thinking about questions you could have asked when you couldn't answer a one of them.

So John Sevier shut his mouth, and Hope, who had never thought about asking a question, kept his shut, too. They milked and poured the milk up, and the early September twilight fell like dark velvet over the world, and

Love went up to the old chicken house where all the chickens and the cock were already up on the roost, and the chickens were cooing and clucking very low the way chickens do at night, and he shut the door and turned the latch down so the foxes couldn't get inside.

When he got back, Mammy had supper on the trestle table, and they ate by the light of the coal-oil lamp. It was a soft light that made everything in the room look gentle. They ate rabbit that Mammy had caught in one of her wooden box traps. Mammy had fixed dumplings to go with the rabbit, and they had green beans boiled in pork fat and good lard biscuits made with buttermilk, and they had sweet milk to drink, and Mammy said, "I've got blackberry cobbler for dessert." Her announcement was met with a soft murmur of appreciation around the table, and Pappy said, "I think black-berry cobbler is one of the bestest things on earth." For him this was a con-siderable statement, and Mammy looked pleased.

They all had so much to eat that Hope thought it would be pleasant if they forgot about digging the hole and went on to bed. But he knew Pappy would not forget, and Pappy didn't. When they had taken care of the black-berry cobbler, Pappy wiped his mouth with his bandana handkerchief, and he said, "Me and Hope and John Sevier has got some work to do before we go to bed."

Mammy looked at him, and even in the lamplight, which was not bright, you could see a flash of worry dart across her face, the way a spark will sometimes jump from your fingers when you have built up electricity in your body. "You got work to do this hour of the night?"

"That's what I said," Pappy said, his voice mild, unhurried, almost tone-less.

"Outside?"

"That's what I said."

"If you have got work to do outside, why don't you wait till daylight?"

Pappy just looked at her. He did not say a word for a minute. He stood and looked at her, and she looked both anxious and guilty. "That was a mighty good meal," Pappy said. "Come along, boys."

The boys got up without a word. "You hain't going to take ary lantern?" Mammy said.

"Won't be needing one," Pappy said. He went out, and Hope and John Sevier followed him.

It was a moonless night. The stars were shining by the thousand and seemed so near that you could imagine climbing Mount LeConte and reach-ing a foot over your head and pulling down a dozen stars like grapes hanging on a bunch in the sky. They would probably burn your hand, Hope thought.

Pappy led the way up to the barn. It was sweet with hay piled in the loft. New hay, cured in the sun, forked up there, ready for winter. Pappy was a substantial shadow moving with unfaltering certainty to one of the empty stables. He brought out two long-handled spades and a pickaxe. He handed a spade to each of his sons and took the pickaxe himself.

He went ahead wordlessly, and they followed him, back up around the cow lot and out onto the new-plowed ground. The night was cool, and the infinite choir of insects sang in the woods, an unvarying and primordial rhythm in time to the swinging of the earth in the cradle of the deep. Hope knew that just a little way up the mountains the forest would be still. He had been up there sometimes with his father hunting the annual bear. One bear a year: that was Pappy's rule. Kill the bear when cool weather set in, cut him up on the spot, and bring the parts back down to cure in the smokehouse along with the hams and the venison. You had another kind of meat for variety to go with everything else they had to eat. "We take one bear and one deer a year" Pappy said. "That's our share. Hit lets stay enough for other folks, and hit makes sure we got a bear awaiting for us to shoot him next year."

Up there, sitting wrapped up in quilts and layers of clothes, they sat still through the night and watched, not saying a word, waiting, listening to the silence. No insects called up there. It was quiet like an empty church, but when you heard something, it sounded loud, and you could tell the sound of a bear tramping through the woods—lurching, irregular and heavy. And in the morning, when Mr. Bear came along, he was dead before he knew to be afraid.

Deer were different. You put a coal-oil lantern in the path or in a clearing, and the deer came to look at it. Deer were drawn to light like flying bugs. You sat just outside the small circle of light shed by the lantern, and Mr. Deer came—walking so soft that you could not even hear his steps, those little brass-colored hoofs coming along like they were in moccasins. You saw his eyes, gleaming like green fire out of the dark, and around the eyes you saw a shape, darker against the great darkness of the forest. Those eyes, those green-glowing jewels, came on and on, hesitant, looking for danger, smelling something maybe if the wind was right, but fixed on that lantern, the deer wondering what it was, entranced and made helpless by the divine magic of light. And very slowly and silently you brought the twelve-gauge up, and you put the bead sight on those green eyes, and you pulled the trigger. You loaded your twelve-gauge with lead slugs, and at no more than twenty or thirty feet it was as good as one of those high-priced rifles. It did the job. Then you had yet another kind of meat to put on the table for winter.

Hope took great satisfaction in those nights with Pappy, and he remembered how he got his first bear, the slug going true to the head, right at the eye where the bear's thick skull was vulnerable. "You done good," his pappy said in that low, level, unperturbed voice of his, but it was enough for Hope.

"A man has to know how to make his own life," Pappy said sometimes. "You got one thing you can depend on in this old world—your own head. You got to know what to do with it." And as Hope grew and learned, he had the sure confidence that he could walk out in the mountains with his own two hands and maybe a sharp knife and know how to live, not just survive but live like a king. The confidence made him feel grown-up.

When he was in the Philippines, living off the land in the jungle with the rest of them, the crazy American missionary and the privates and the corporals and the sergeants in the American army who had escaped the Japs, the confidence kept him and them alive. He could always find food—even if it meant eating snake. Hope Kirby learned early how to survive.

Now as he and Pappy and John Sevier walked back up to the new-plowed and new-harrowed wheatfield-to-be, he felt satisfied and peaceful because he knew Pappy was going to teach him something else about how to live in the open, where you had to get along on your own.

It was a perfect night—just enough sharpness in the air to portend autumn when the mountains would flame with cool fire. Above them, against the starry sky, stood the unmoving shoulder of the mountain, black and mysterious and filled with benign secrets. To the north the Big Dipper stood on its side, pouring whatever blessing it held down on earth. They moved quietly over the ground with the sure footsteps of mountain men, almost unconsciously feeling the earth before they put their full weight upon it.

"Right cheer," Pappy said finally. He had come to a corner of the plowed ground, up near the dark woods far away from the house across a hummock of ground that shut them in as if it were its own place. "We want a hole about six foot long, about two foot wide," Pappy said.

He set to work with the pick. He worked like a machine. Their eyes were adjusted to the dark now. They could see Pappy's wiry form bending, flinging the pick high over his head, bringing it down with a big, soft thump in the earth already prepared by the plowing. The pick bit down into the stony subsoil, and then the pick started hitting small rocks. He worked awhile and stepped back. "All right," he said softly, breathing a little harder than usual but not much. "You boys spade it out."

John Sevier and Hope leaped to comply. Far off on a rise of ground a couple of miles away a dim suggestion of light in the dark. That would be the Henderson place. The Hendersons were the nearest neighbors. Mr. Henderson beat his wife. Pappy and the neighbors went to see him about it, and Mr. Henderson cried and said he wouldn't do it anymore. But he did, and the neighbors were talking now about taking him out to whip him.

You want to whip him without shaming him, Pappy said. If you shame him in public, he might go home and kill her. But if two or three men grab him and stuff something in his mouth in his barn and tell him what they are a-doing and whip him hard with his shirt on his back so he won't bleed too much, maybe he'll get the point. That was Pappy's advice, given at church a week ago when some men stood off in a corner of the graveyard talking about Mr. Henderson, and somebody asked Pappy's opinion, and that was what everybody said was the thing to do. Hope Kirby was old enough to be included in the group then, and he was proud when the men turned to Pappy and asked him and when Pappy told them what he thought and when the men nodded slowly and said, yes, that's the way to do it.

All that seemed distant now as the three of them dug in the dark. The rest of the earth was dark. Hope knew that no matter how good somebody's eyes might be, no wanderer could see them from more than fifty or sixty feet away.

The night had a profundity to it that Hope could not have talked about. He felt it. As they worked, the solemnity, the mystery seemed to grow as the hole deepened in the ground, their spades sometimes making a ringing noise against rocks as big as a man's fist. As they worked and the hole took shape, Hope realized what it was. John Sevier knew it too. The two brothers could communicate without saying a word. It was a grave. They were digging a grave, and they knew whose grave it was going to be.

It was past midnight, and a lopsided moon was rising when Pappy climbed out of the grave, breathing just a little hard, and said, "Shovel what's in there out, and we're done with the digging."

John Sevier and Hope jumped down into the grave and shoveled fast and efficiently. The new-earth smell was all around them, stronger than the night smells. The grave was as deep as their heads, and when they climbed out, they had to hold on to Pappy's down-reached hand to make it.

"All right," Pappy said, "they's a bresh pile over there. Let's move hit here. Mind the snakes. Copperheads like bresh. They be sluggish now, but they can still bite."

The idea of being bitten by a copperhead was not as bad to Hope as the thought of wrapping his hands around the fat body of a snake in the dark. Pappy waded right into the brush pile and started hauling out felled little trees and all the other stuff that ends up in a brush pile that you heaped up to burn in the fall or winter, just after a heavy rain, when there wasn't any danger of having the fire get out to set the mountain ablaze.

By the time they had wrestled most of the brush pile over the grave and the pile of earth next to it, the Big Dipper was lying over the North Star, and Hope was tired in every muscle and bone of his body. Pappy stood straight, a shadow against the velvet sky, and he looked around at what they had done. "Hit'll do," he said. They gathered up their tools, and they went home.

Mammy was waiting up for them when they got back. She sat in the rocking chair with the Bible on her lap. "You air going to kill that man in that air car," she said.

Pappy just looked at her.

"You air going to kill him, hain't you?"

Pappy looked at her a long time, but she looked back at him. "Hit hain't nothing to talk about," he said. With that he went to bed.

Next day, if you walked back up towards the new-plowed field, you could see a big brush pile in a corner of it, and if you had been taking a shortcut cross-country, you might have seen the brush, and you might have deduced that it had been moved there recently, after the ground had been plowed. And then, if you had nothing better to do, you might have asked yourself why somebody had plowed ground and then piled brush on top of part of it. But most people walking cross-country where there were fields and two or three brush piles on every farm had much better things to do than to waste time pondering the relation of a snaky-looking pile of felled and dry cedar trees and birch saplings to plowed ground.

Those people would have paid a lot less attention to a trash pile than they might have paid to an oblong hole in the ground, especially when that hole had the neatly squared-off proportions of a grave when there was not a churchyard in three miles.

The next day was a Sunday, and just as regular as the calendar, Pappy supervised the milking and told everybody to dress up, and he hitched the two brown mules up to the flatbed wagon, and he and Mammy sat up front on the seat, and the boys sat sprawled over the back, and they went down to the Gatlinburg Baptist Church for Sunday school and preaching.

Somebody said to Hope, "Didn't see you folks in town yestiday." Hope said, "We don't go to town much," and that was true. The other young man laughed and said the Kirby men worked too hard, but that was all there was to it. Hope stood there friendly enough, but not saying anything else. If you wanted to make small talk with a Kirby, you had to work at it.

Pappy was more silent than usual that day and next morning. Mammy was even quieter. She didn't say anything. She looked at Pappy, and he looked at her, and they looked away from each other.

They milked, and Pappy came back to the house and puttered around. Hope had never seen him fooling around, doing nothing, and he knew that he was waiting for Mr. Hamilton to show up.

Mr. Hamilton had vowed to come back in a week, but "a week" in the country meant only that it would be sometime after the next Sunday. You might have expected a man like Mr. Hamilton to put off dealing with a stubborn mountaineer like Roy Kirby. You might have expected him to pick on somebody more malleable, more intimidated, more "reasonable," as Mr. Hamilton would have put it, using one of his favorite words.

A reasonable man saw how the world turned and turned with it as best he could, for as Mr. Hamilton was fond of saying, the world was going to turn anyway, whether you turned with it or not, and if you tried to turn in a different direction, you were going to get all heated up for no good purpose. Mr. Hamilton might have waited for the reason inherent in the universe like gravity to force itself into Pappy's hard skull, and that might have meant that he would have delayed until Friday or even Saturday.

But Mr. Hamilton was not a man to wait. He wanted his victory as soon as he could get it, and besides that he liked to give bad news to inferiors. Maybe it was because he had had so much bad news himself. He was also irritated when people were unreasonable. He believed that unreasonable people thought they were better than he was, that they were possessed by a peculiar arrogance, and he took a solid satisfaction in knocking the arrogance out of them, in making them understand that they were only one of a great mass, that the same hard rules applied to them that applied to him and everyone else, and that in Mr. Hamilton's fair-minded and uncompromising world, no exceptions were made.

So Mr. Hamilton could hardly wait to go back to show Mr. Kirby exactly how low the Kirby family was to the ground and how unreasonable it was to turn up their noses at thirty-five hundred dollars in a day when for some people—Mr. Hamilton, to name one—that sum represented a fortune.

Around nine-thirty in the morning by the mid-September sun on Monday, they heard Mr. Hamilton's Ford speeding up the road towards them, throwing gravel every which way. In a minute, there he was, the mild sunshine pouring down on the dusty black Ford as it shot out of the trees growing each side of the rutted dirt road, flinging up a cloud of reddish dust and white gravel that gave his entry a certain imposing authority. The car was a clattering intrusion on a luminously perfect day.

Mammy saw him, wrapped her hands in her apron, and went back into the house and shut the door, commanding the younger boys to come with her. She left Pappy and Hope and John Sevier in the yard to greet Mr. Hamilton.

Mr. Hamilton brought his Ford to a stop, and the dust boiled up around it as if the earth had just given birth to the car that stood there like a throne with Mr. Hamilton sitting in it, holding his steering wheel like a scepter and looking as sleek as a town dog.

For a second Mr. Hamilton sat there, looking at three silent men in faded denim shirts and bib overalls and clodhopper shoes who had unselfconsciously formed a line in front of the car. All three had their thumbs hooked in the bibs of their overalls. Even somebody as confident and as eager as Mr. Hamilton had to pause just a second and to look at these men with a faint tremor of anxiety struggling down inside him to leap out, to express itself, to shout a warning. They say that a mean dog can smell it in the air when you resolve to hurt him and that he will back away, even as he barks. That is something of the feeling that rose in Mr. Hamilton, but he put it down. He got out of the car and adjusted his felt hat so that it came down an inch lower over his forehead. He might have been unconsciously trying to look a little like George Raft or one of those other movie stars playing tough, big-time gangsters in the picture shows that had become for Mr. Hamilton his one indulgence and the anodyne for loneliness now that his business was gone and Ida had forsaken him forever.

In keeping with his pulled-down hat brim, he spoke in his best imitation of a movie gangster. "All right, Mr. Kirby, what's it going to be, thirty-five hundred dollars or the sheriff and a bunch of pistol-packing deputies up here to throw you people off the government's land?" You might not have been able to believe that a man whose face had grown as soft and round as Mr. Hamilton's could have growled like that, but they all heard it. Had they ever seen a horse opera at the movies, they would have recognized the tone, but none of the Kirby men had ever seen a movie.

Pappy looked at him a minute without saying anything—just long enough to make Mr. Hamilton's face redden as he started to boil over with yet more unanswerable declarations of fact. And then, as Mr. Hamilton was opening his mouth to shout at them, Pappy got there first.

"I've thought and thought, Mr. Hamilton, and I figure you got me between a rock and a hard place. But I tell you something else, if'n you don't mind. My woman in there, she's awful upset that I've decided to do what I really don't want to do, but hit's just there to be done, and there hain't no cure for hit."

"Well," Mr. Hamilton said, a little confused and even disappointed because he was sure he would have a quarrel with Pappy. "Well," he said again, uncertain about how to proceed. Pappy seemed to be saying all the right words, but he didn't seem much affected by them. He seemed too calm, too *unbowed*. "Does this mean you've decided to be reasonable?"

"Well, yessir, I reckon hit does," Pappy said, swallowing, making his Adam's apple jump a little and giving the impression that he might have been more nervous than Mr. Hamilton first supposed. "I mean, you might could say that. Reasonable. That's hit."

"Well, I'm sure glad to hear it," Mr. Hamilton said. He was not speaking the entire truth.

"That's hit perxactly," Pappy said, recovering his perfect calm, all slow and easy and patient like he had all the time in the world. He looked around, looked at Mr. Hamilton, and cast a significant look towards the shut door of the house. "If'n you don't mind, could we move off from the house so we won't get my woman all shook up? I'd sure be much obliged if we could go up back out of her hearing."

Pappy seemed to shrink into something pathetically polite, humble all of a sudden, and Mr. Hamilton's confidence filled again. "I can understand that," he said, gushing a little with the superiority males shared. "A man has to take care of his wife's nerves. Never have been married myself. Almost made it to the altar once, but . . . Well, I reckon I'm just not the marrying kind." He faltered, and his world turned dark, and he felt a rush of horrible depression. He had got his adrenaline up to be as nasty as he could be to this stubborn dirt farmer, and now the adrenaline left him, and without it, he could scarcely bear to think of Ida and her betrayal and his nice little business, all lost and gone. He cleared his throat.

"Well now, I'm sure glad you folks have decided not to make trouble. I tell you flat out, Mr. Kirby, this national park is going to be a great thing for the country. A new day is dawning. No sense starting it with a storm." He seemed pleased with this unexpectedly poetic utterance. It came to him suddenly, without strain, and he thought he would write it down when he finished up here so he could use it again another day.

"That's sholey so," Pappy said.

All the while they were talking, Pappy was walking slowly, in languid, irregular paces. Mr. Hamilton followed in an almost unself-conscious expectation that they would stop with the next step. Pappy moved up the slope behind the house, idling thoughtfully along with his hands folded behind the bib of his overalls, and to look at him anybody would have thought him lackadaisical.

"I reckon we're causing you a little trouble by making you walk back up here, but you might as well take a look at the farm you want to buy. I tell you, hit's a nice little place."

Mr. Hamilton looked around with great distaste. "Yes," he said without any conviction. "How much farther do you want to go?" Mr. Hamilton was breathing hard because the walk tended uphill, and he was not as fit as he once was.

"Well, I want to get far away from Mammy so she won't be bothered by nothing," Pappy said. "Lord, I promise you this, Mr. Hamilton, after this morning you hain't never going to have trouble with me again."

"Good! Good!" Mr. Hamilton said. He felt expansive. He had conquered these people so easily, and this man Kirby seemed so meek and cooperative that Mr. Hamilton felt as magnanimous as the victor in a game with a child. "I always appreciate it when folks see the light," he said. "It's the best for all concerned."

They were abreast of the smokehouse. As if the idea had just occurred to him, Pappy said, "This here is our smokehouse. We got some good hams hanging up inside. Reckon maybe you'd like to look at them?"

"Oh I don't think so," Mr. Hamilton said. "I reckon once you've seen one ham, you've seen them all." He made an effort to laugh.

"Maybe you can pick you one out you'd like to take home with you?" Pappy said in a tone so soft it seemed almost timid. "Kind of a handshake on our deal, the deal you and me is going to make?"

Mr. Hamilton stopped. The smokehouse was a square made of logs, closely notched and plastered with thick mud that had hardened into a tight seal. It was covered over with a big mound of yellowing pine sawdust for insulation. Out of the top rose an iron-pipe chimney so the hickory smoke had a place to go after it passed over the meat hanging in bundles from the ceiling. You built a fire of almost green hickory under the meat after hog-killing time, and the fire gave off thick clouds of smoke that swirled around the top and escaped through the little chimney, keeping the circulation up and the smoke rising so that it imparted its savor to the meat while it cured it.

"Well," Mr. Hamilton said. "I'm living in a hotel room down in Sevierville right now, and I don't have anywhere to keep a ham."

"Why, that don't make no mind, Mr. Hamilton," he said in a slight excess of joviality that Hope could not have imagined in his father unless he heard it. "This here ham will *keep*. A man can wrap hit up in newspapers and put hit in his hotel room, and hit hain't going to spoil. Nosiree, a man fixing to go back home could just take hit home with him and hit'd be just fine. And hit will make his room smell awful good for the time it's there."

Mr. Hamilton was swayed. Part of it was the simple triumph of getting something valuable for nothing. Then, too, a gift like this would make a good story back in the office in Knoxville, where functionaries with their jackets off and neckties loose and sleeves rolled up were making plans for the new national park. Not many field agents moving hillbillies off the land were smart enough to make a man quit his farm and give the agent a country ham as a gift. Yes, he thought, the ham would boost his reputation among people who, he suspected, were sometimes not as enthusiastic about his work as he thought they should be or even as they said they were.

But more than anything else, it was the simple friendship offered to him—a friendship more warmly received because it came from such improbable people and in such an improbable place. Since the onset of the Depression and his troubles, Mr. Hamilton had become a desperately lonely man. The people most friendly to him were the waitresses with bad teeth and stringy hair and lumpy bodies who served him in the greasy spoons where he took his meals or stopped for an occasional cup of coffee. He knew that they were friendly out of a contrived ambition to exact from him a nickel or a dime to be left beside his plate as a tip. Now he was offered a gesture of friendship that could have no selfish motive. He wanted to cultivate it, to be friends with these good country people.

He thought that he would not lose interest in them. He would not forget them. No, he would help them get settled somewhere else, and he would call on them from time to time and sit with them on the front porch wherever it was and watch those boys get married and raise families, and all the rest. He had a warm vision of spending Christmas day with them far in the future, when he was old, when they would thank him for opening doorways that took them away from this remote and godforsaken place and introduced them to culture and civilization.

It was mad, to be sure, but a madness that can burst on a lonely man beyond all rationality, a vision as huge and beguiling as the sight of palm trees swaying against a horizon on an oasis where water springs out of the earth and he was the traveler, thirsty in the desert that had stretched around him for years as far as he could see. He clapped Pappy on the back, trying with the friendliness of that touch to call back and apologize for his previous harshness, to begin that recovery of the past that is also a reformation, a reinterpretation of what has been said so that it comes out gentle and benign. "Well," said Mr. Hamilton, "that is a *peachy* idea, Mr. Kirby. An act of generosity on your part. I do confess that I like country ham and fried eggs. Let's see those hams."

"You air going to like them. You hain't never in your life going to taste a ham as good as mine," Pappy said. He unlatched the smokehouse door and in splendid confidence walked down into the gloom that lay behind it.

The smokehouse was dug out under its mounded roof, and the earthen floor at the bottom of the stairway was carpeted with thick sawdust. It was so cool inside that it was almost cold after the sunlight in the open September air.

Mr. Hamilton stood at the top of the stairway but did not move. "I can't see anything," he said, some of his joy gone.

Pappy was already down inside. "Just put one foot down in front of the other. Your eyes gets used to it fast." The fragrances that rushed out of the interior overpowered Mr. Hamilton. They were like a narcotic—a thickness that almost drove him mad with the desire for food and this after he had eaten a heavy breakfast of bacon and eggs and grits and biscuits. There is not much of anything on earth that smells better than a smokehouse with hickory-smoked hams hanging from hooks all over the ceiling. It is a combination of fragrances—the cured meat itself, its fats, its smoked rinds, the salt, the residue of hickory fires left to smolder under the hams so that the smoke gets into the meat, helping preserve it, giving it a taste that nothing else can duplicate. Mr. Hamilton looked up, and his mouth watered so suddenly and vigorously that it almost hurt.

Added to his vision of friendship now was another, more carnal fantasy of himself sitting at a table with a plate of that ham and three fried eggs and hot biscuits and sweet butter and honey and grits with redeye gravy poured over them. His stomach unexpectedly growled in anticipation, and he felt weak with desire.

He came down the stairs slowly, cautiously, feeling his way with his feet and his narrow, uncomfortable shoes, and Hope and John Sevier came down after him, silent, their feet making no sound on the solid wood steps Pappy had built as carefully as he had built everything on the place. Mr. Hamilton's eyes slowly adjusted to the cool and fragrant obscurity. By the time he stepped into the sawdust on the floor, he could see hanging overhead hams wrapped in cheesecloth, and he salivated so copiously that he had to swallow repeatedly, and he was already trying to figure out which was the biggest ham up there so he could choose it.

Pappy never was one to hesitate when it came to killing a hog. You did it, fast and slick. He said to John Sevier, "Let's put him up against the wall." Mr. Hamilton had time only to hear the words, not to register what they meant before he felt himself slammed against the wall of the smokehouse so hard that he almost had the breath knocked out of him, and his head struck one of the wooden logs so that he saw stars. Pappy had him by one arm, and John Sevier had him by the other, and Mr. Hamilton was as astonished by their strength as by the speed by which they acted. These lightning thoughts protected him for a moment from understanding what was happening to him.

"Stop this!" he cried, an incoherent mixture of scream, of anger, of indignation, of unbelief. "Let go of me! Let go of me!" He struggled with all his might, and the first premonition of terror struck him in the vitals when he felt how firmly his arms were pinned by the two strong men, one on each side, who flung his elbows and his hands high on the wall. He fought, kicked, squirmed, exclaimed, cursed, and cried for help, and he understood all at once how shut in the dark interior of the smokehouse was and how removed he was from all other human beings.

All this happened in seconds. "Get down to his belly," Pappy said to Hope. "Pull them clothes off of him." Hope tore open Mr. Hamilton's nice white shirt so that the cotton ripped and buttons popped off. "Get his pants down so you can find his belly," Pappy said, and Hope jerked at Mr. Hamilton's belt, not loosening it but yanking it and the top of the trousers down until Mr. Hamilton's stomach and his pubic hair and his dangling white penis were exposed.

Mr. Hamilton had a powerful, instinctive urge to protect his private parts, and he bucked and twisted and bent and kicked, trying to get his hands free to pull his trousers up and to protect his modesty and his manhood—showing just how a man in terror can mistake the intentions of adversaries. Mr. Hamilton was unable to change anything. The arms held him as though they had nailed him to the wall at his back. He was ashamed of his predicament—his shirt in tatters, his trousers down below his privates, his suit filthy now, and the naked flesh of his bulging belly surprisingly white in the dimness of this chamber illuminated only by the light pouring in an oblong shape on the floor from the September morning beyond the open door. He was also enraged.

"Git the butcher knife off that air table," Pappy said to Hope. Mr. Hamilton heard these words as sounds, and then, as the mind does, converted them to meaning by replaying them in his mind, and his terror leaped so that his vision swam. "Jest like a hog," Pappy said.

Mr. Hamilton could not put any meaning at all to these words, but Hope understood them, and he took the long-bladed butcher knife and held it edge-up and put the point at a spot just above Mr. Hamilton's black pubic hair and gave a quick little thrust so that the knife broke the skin and entered the abdominal wall maybe a half-inch, just enough to set the blade above the pelvic bone. At this little thrust, done as expertly as Hope had set the blade in many a hog hanging from a rack in November, Mr. Hamilton screamed. The pain was awful, and the scream, muffled somewhat by the hanging hams and other meat and by all the sawdust on the floor, was still enough to hurt the ears of all three of the men concentrating on doing what they had to do to Mr. Hamilton.

Mr. Hamilton's mind during all this time—measured in fractions of seconds if one were measuring—was racing like a locomotive that has lost its brakes careening down a mountain. A brain can only with difficulty imagine its nonbeing, and to the last Mr. Hamilton was constructing a drama in which these men, human beings like himself, would scare him within an inch of his life, even do damage to him, cut him, make him bleed, but then release him, fling him to the ground in a flood of profanity and obscenity and further threat, and order him to get out of the country and never come back. He would bawl, weep, promise them anything—and afterwards go to the sheriff and see them all in prison and come to visit them every week so he could mock them forever. He may not have had time to think the words to all these thoughts; they flashed before his eyes in images as quick as light. But they were the essence of the turmoil that swept through his brain, and even after Hope had made that small incision in his lower abdomen, Mr. Hamilton expected to be released, the knife withdrawn. But then Hope made his second thrust, hard, steady, and the knife went all the way through Mr. Hamilton's guts and struck his backbone from the inside, and almost in the same motion Hope brought the knife up, cutting through guts and organs and drawing the knife out just under the heart as one did in killing a pig so that the heart could pump a few beats and do its part to drain the carcass of blood. Mr. Hamilton's blood gushed out along with his gray guts and yellow fat, and Mr. Hamilton himself was amazed at how much blood there was in him, and the fetid stench of blood and warm guts filled the smokehouse along with the fragrance of the cured hams. Mr. Hamilton uttered a deep sigh, as if the breath had been knocked out of him, and he was looking down astonished at his guts pouring out like a bucket of slop from his slit belly all the way to the sawdust on the floor, and he saw and smelled what was happening to him, and he had perhaps fifteen seconds to realize that no doctor could put all this back together again, that indeed he was going to die, and then he died.

John Sevier and Pappy threw the corpse forward, and it fell into the saw-dust facedown in the muck of its own guts, quivered reflexively, and lay still. Hope was wearing a long-sleeved shirt, and the sleeve that held the knife was soaked with Mr. Hamilton's blood. A dark pool of blood darkened the saw-dust around Mr. Hamilton.

"Hope," Pappy said. "Take off your shirt. Mammy will be right broke up if she sees the blood. Go wash it out in the creek. We'll leave him here till night. We got to get rid of that car."

John Sevier and Hope did not reply. Hope looked down at the prostrate form of Mr. Hamilton, sprawled as if he had been awkwardly asleep, over-come by such fatigue that he was aware of nothing around him. Mr. Hamilton was the first man Hope killed. Hope dreamed about him time and again. Later on, when others followed, he sometimes thought back on Mr. Hamilton as if maybe this proud, foolish man from the city had cursed him and had won some strange battle of which Hope was only dimly aware. After Mr. Hamilton everything was easier, until Hope came to kill Abby.

*W*HEN he was older and the intensity of memory faded in him like bright colors painted on a beachside building will fade through decades of sun, Charles could remember how frightened he had been of Tempe. It was another of those foolish things. Imagine a devout Muslim, orthodox in all his ways, who forms a passionate attachment for a girl who mocks Mohammed and refuses to wear a veil. That was how he imagined himself when he thought of his tentative look into another world. She represented a world that seemed natural and easy, and he did not want to enter it. In his mad world of religion and doubt, Tempe was Eve. She represented death and the cherubim placed before Eden so that its exiled inhabitants could never enter it again. If he fell in love with her he would be saying goodbye forever to something dear to him, the essence of life. *I was a coward in that as I was in other things,* he thought bitterly to himself when these oppressive memories came in on him. Tempe was different.

Marlene was glamorous in the spectacular manner of movie stars for whom the world is a camera trained on them to record a beauty that belonged in magazines and on posters. People turned almost involuntarily to look at her when she passed on the street because they thought they were seeing someone extraordinary, someone who had to be well known because such beauty was so commanding. No one would ever have put Tempe's photograph in a magazine, but to Charles she was beautiful, and even her uneven teeth were that flaw that some classical philosophers suggested was necessary if beauty was to be human. Or perhaps the beauty he saw was only an attitude that made her different. When he talked with her, he realized that she had no pretense and that everything she said came out of a wrestling within to say something she meant and that she never thought of trying to make an impression on anyone and that she was even a little shy and had no desire to create for herself an exalted status among those who knew her.

He was afraid of her because he knew from the beginning that she possessed an honesty that he did not have, that perhaps he could never have. He was a practiced deceiver. He could not tell his mother as she lay dying that he did not believe in her God. He could not tell himself that it was hopeless, that he could never believe in that God again. He could not give up on that warm, fertile world of belief where every leaf in the sunny forest radiated the glory of God and the stars in the night sky spoke not only order but benevolence. He could not throw away the woman preacher at the camp meeting in Delanco who put out her hands toward him and said, "Lord, call this boy to the mission field," and he felt almost an electric charge surge through his body so that he imagined himself already a martyr with his soul speeding in triumph toward the eternal skies. His mother's hands on his shoulders—that seemed a seal of some kind. He could not admit that when he saw a long-legged woman walk down the street he sometimes followed her, drinking in the music of her thighs swishing together under her dress and lifting her skirts with his eyes and having a freedom with her body that intoxicated him with its fantasy. No, he was a deceiver. Deceit came as natural to him, he thought, as the banded browns of the copperhead came to the snake by birth so that it could lie in the leaves of the forest floor or in the piled timbers of a brush pile and be unseen by its victims.

Except that he did not want to make anyone his victim. He did not. He did not. He did not want Hope Kirby to die. He thought of him every day, the jail. Perhaps he should go to see him, he thought. But no, that would be impossible. What would they say to each other? Charles thought that he might cry. Such futility! Years later he looked at his aging face in the mirror and said forlornly, "I never wanted to hurt anybody."

Balzac ended with the summer term. McKinley disappeared. He did not say where he was going. Tempe went home to her mother and father in Memphis, not to return until late in September when the fall term began. She wrote him occasional cheerful notes, sometimes saying funny things that made Charles smile in spite of himself. He did not write her back, but he kept her letters in a drawer in his room and reflected against his will that they were much more interesting than the few letters Marlene had sent him from the Bible college in Chattanooga.

Marlene was like everyone else in the Bible college, and she was like Eugenia Alexander and her sisters. Conversation was a contest to see who could find the most reasons to mention "the Lord." It was not carefully timed and regulated like the life of monasteries Charles had read about. It was a haphazard effort to squeeze everything out of life that could distract from the coziness with God that people in the Bible college wore as their symbol of Christian perfection. Marlene's major subjects were the Lord and His will and the latest concert where the Lord had allowed her to be a star once again. Even with Marlene it was hard to talk about the Lord because the Lord seldom had anything new to say, and the boys and girls at the Bible college seemed locked on a treadmill of repeating themselves about the Bible and the Holy Spirit and Jesus the Redeemer and His will for our lives and all the rest.

When Marlene asked him to give her back her letters when they broke up, Charles offered her only a meager pile, and although his heart was administered another crack, as the months passed and now as Tempe wrote him, he recognized with yet another pang of disloyalty that he didn't miss

Marlene's letters at all. He was beginning to think he would get over his broken heart, but he did not want to fall in love with Tempe. He had no desire to fall in love with anybody. Trouble lay in that direction. He wanted his life to be as simple as an empty plate.

September came on with a rush of golden light, and classes began again, and faithful Dr. Stiefel made his five faithful students pledge to him that they would not abandon Proust before the year was over. What could they say? It was daunting, but it could be done, and Charles knew that his father read Proust, but for the moment he did not tell his father that he was taking the course. He did not want to face the embarrassment of his father's pleasure.

It became a habit to drink coffee with Tempe and McKinley after the Proust class, and they talked by silent agreement about every subject under the sun except the murders in Bourbonville and the impending trial.

Tempe's father was a cotton factor in Memphis. "He lives for cotton and the football team at Ole Miss," she said. "He wanted me to be a boy," she said. "He wanted lots of boys, and he had only me. He loves me, but he was disappointed. He's told me how brokenhearted he was when the doctors told him that my mother could not have any more children. He doesn't mean any harm by it, but it's painful to look at him and to see that he imagines having a son who might return a kickoff a hundred yards and beat Tennessee."

"You went to Ole Miss a couple of years," McKinley said, almost as though prodding her.

"Yes, I went to Ole Miss, and I dated football players. My father was so happy when a tailback I was dating came up to Memphis and had dinner with us one Thanksgiving. The team was playing in Oxford that weekend, and so the tailback could come, and my father was in heaven. It was awful. The boy's name was Chuckie Henderson. Oh my, he was dumb! Dumber than a doorknob. He belonged to a group of football players who read the Bible and prayed together, and he was convinced that God let him score touchdowns. When he made a touchdown, he got down on his knees a second in the end zone and thanked God for it."

McKinley laughed out loud. Charles felt the foolishness of the gesture, but he thought of his mother, and he thought of Preacher Finewood, his good friend, and he knew that both of them would look frowningly on Tempe and tell her that she was being disrespectful of religion and that a young man who prayed in public like that was a manly Christian and that if all young men were like that young man, the world would be a better place. Charles knew that both of them, his dead mother and the live preacher, would expect him to speak up in defense of Chuckie Henderson. But he could not do it. He thought it was silly to pray after touchdowns.

"I'm not as complete an atheist as you are," McKinley said, shaking his head and showing such amusement on his broad, open face that he might have just heard the funniest joke in the world. "But think of it! All heaven gathered to watch Ole Miss play football and God sitting there in his box seat waving an Ole Miss Rebels pennant and inspiring Chuckie Henderson to score touchdowns. Now, I ask you this. What does that do to the other side? Does anybody in the heavenly grandstand dare cheer for Tennessee when God is cheering for Ole Miss?"

"My father hoped I would marry Chuckie," Tempe said. She shook her head, and her expression abruptly changed to something Charles could not fathom. She took a deep breath, and for a moment she did not say anything, and McKinley looked down into his coffee and seemed sober himself. Then Tempe laughed again. "Why do so many football players have infantile names? Do you know what I thought when Chuckie asked me to marry him? I thought of being called by a baby's name all my life. Mrs. Chuckie Henderson, and people would say to me, 'Oh, I remember when Chuckie played football for Ole Miss,' and I would have to listen to them talk the way my father talked to Chuckie at Thanksgiving, as if being a football player were the most glorious thing that could happen to a human being and that talking to a football player was like talking to a god."

"I suspect that Achilles was a big dumb clodhopper until Homer got ahold of him," McKinley said with his broad grin.

"You didn't stay at Ole Miss," Charles said.

Again Tempe's face changed, and she furrowed her brow. "No," she said. "I was there two years, and I couldn't stand it anymore. I dropped out for a while." She looked up at him. "I went down to New Orleans and lived there for a year. Then I decided to transfer up here."

"I'm going there to seminary," Charles said.

"You're going to that seminary in New Orleans?" Tempe threw back her head and laughed again, all her good humor restored. "Charles, you are not serious."

"Yes I am," he said doggedly. He felt his face turn red.

"But why?"

"Well, I've heard it's a good place." He was otherwise noncommittal. Fundamentalists did not argue with atheists. It was a kind of rule. He had heard that at the New Orleans seminary no modernistic professors were allowed. In the New Orleans Baptist Theological Seminary everyone believed in the Virgin Birth of Jesus and the miracles and the resurrection and the infallible word of the Bible, and nobody believed in evolution, and the preacher boys went out and preached the gospel every Sunday, and every class began with prayer, and in a school like that he would get his faith back, and everything would be as it had been before he discovered W. T. Stace.

"Charles, it's an *awful* place," Tempe said. "Those fanatics. They will have you out on the street corners preaching to sailors. Listen, the New Orleans seminary has a new campus out on Gentilly Boulevard at the edge of New Orleans. Do you know what kind of trees grow there?"

"No," Charles said. He looked at her desperately. He did not want her to laugh at him.

"Nut trees. The seminary is located in an old pecan orchard."

"Oh, leave him alone, Tempe," McKinley said. "Maybe we can make him change his mind. He's got a year before he goes."

"We'll do our best," Tempe said cheerfully. "We will not let you go to such an awful place."

"That's what the preacher at First Baptist in Bourbonville says," Charles said, and he smiled, pleased to be able to make some concession. For no good reason he did not go on to say that the preacher at First Baptist was named Lawrence Arceneaux and that he came from New Orleans. At the time it did not seem like a piece of information that belonged in the conversation. And besides, after his experience with Arceneaux and Preacher Finewood, Charles did not want to bring up Arceneaux's name again. He still felt ashamed about all that. And he was sick and tired and fatigued almost to death with being ashamed. Shame ought to be like the flu—debilitating for a while, but then you got over it. Charles could not get over his. He hated it in the Ellis & Ernest when people stared at him.

*F*ROM the beginning, Jane Whitaker felt the murders as a personal affront. Without taking note of the absurdity of her fantasies, she had believed that Joseph Ignazio's vision of what would come in Bourbonville was not a dream to be deferred for ten years or twenty years but that it should appear almost overnight because it was all so sensible. In her visits to New York City when she mixed with the swirl of people moving in their private orbits through the metropolis, she felt always a quiet triumph that she was one of them, that no well-dressed New Yorker looked at her with contemptuous authority and said, "You are a hick, lady. You don't belong here."

Now, in the slow, rural tranquility of Bourbonville, she felt an almost angry impatience that the people on the street lacked something. They did not measure up to what they could be if they tried even a little harder. The businessmen wore suits nice enough to get them into restaurants that required ties and jackets, but they wallowed happily in the small-town muck of being happy as long as they could greet each other with guffaws and clap each other on the back and believe that everyone important in the town liked them and gather in their civic clubs like a crowd of oversized children whose summit of pleasure was to know they would not be excluded from games at recess.

As for the lesser beings who peopled the town, Jane tolerated them fretfully, because she had looked out of train windows on the approach to New York, and she recognized that even the great city wore its necklace of slovenly houses and decayed buildings and dirty streets where a cluttered aimlessness ruled. Yet these people did not customarily walk along Fifth Avenue or Forty-second Street. She supposed that some innate sense of propriety kept them away, as serfs in the Middle Ages had remained distant and respectful to their lords unless these masters directly addressed them.

And the murders made her furious. Grieved more than she could tell anybody because Kelly Parmalee had been shot down with a merciless cruelty that made her run a fantasy of his death through her mind again and again and again so that it became like a film seen over and over but, because it was visible only to her, becoming more horrifying every time. After the murders, she did not sleep well at night. It was not that she was afraid of some danger to herself. Far from it. She was not that kind. No, she watched the green hands of her clock register the passing minutes and then the hours, heard its relentless ticking, and lay in her bed naked and sweating and sometimes breaking into uncontrollable weeping that she could hear echoing through her cavernous house, and she realized how empty it was, how alone she was in the great universe, and how everything in her life depended now on the success of the mall.

All these emotions contributed to her hatred of the Kirby clan. They were hillbillies, murderous mountaineers, an infection descended on Bourbonville, carrying it backward when she wanted to make it soar into a future that fitted Joseph Ignazio's vision. "When we succeed," he said in his glowing confidence, "people will be coming from all over the country, all over the world to see what we have done. We will be the model for something. We will be in the encyclopedias. We will go down in history." When he talked like that, Jane was mesmerized, and she could see it all rise before her as though the mall were a limitless expanse of crystal towers gleaming in the sun and visible for miles and miles in every direction.

Joseph Ignazio worried about the murders. "It's bad publicity," he said gloomily. "Very bad publicity, and bad publicity can do lots of damage." Jane had never thought of publicity the way Joseph Ignazio talked about it. It was something else he taught her, explaining with his exuberant air of superiority Pavlov's dog and the art of conditioning people to think good thoughts whenever they heard the words "shopping mall." Joseph Ignazio had explained enough about this magic "publicity" to make Jane Whitaker explode when Charles Alexander wrote his nostalgic piece about the bull-dozed barn when the grading began in July. Now the murders made Jane Whitaker conceive a hatred for the Kirby men, especially for Hope Kirby, that she flung about the town in a rage of insult.

"I'm tired of talking about those murders," Jane Whitaker said to any-body who spoke to her about them. "It's not good for business. It's not good for Bourbon County. I wish people would shut up about them. Let the trial begin. Condemn the hillbilly to death and get him out of here."

Her demand for Hope Kirby's death surprised people. It was not that they thought Hope Kirby should get off scot-free. But he had killed his wife and her lover almost in the very act, and almost any man in the county would understand that this was a special kind of crime. Prison? Yes, for a while. But the electric chair? That seemed extreme.

She tossed her long hair—still naturally brown, a brunette, people said—and looked so impatient and cross that people shut up. "Here I am, doing all I can to bring progress to this county, and a damned hillbilly who should be off feuding in the mountains kills a couple of people in cold blood. I wish he was dead."

Daily she stormed through the bank in such a rage that no one dared say even that things might not be as bad as she thought. Everyone knew that she was preoccupied with the "shopping mall." Nobody in Bourbonville had ever heard of a shopping mall before Jane Whitaker and her New York Italian friend began talking about it every third breath. But now the idea was beginning to percolate through the county, provoking everywhere incredulity and amusement. A few bold people expressed these sentiments to Jane Whitaker and received for their trouble a tongue-lashing that made them feel lucky to have escaped with their lives.

And she remained firm about Hope Kirby. "You can't get capital into a town where murderers can get off for killing people in the streets." Most people thought she exaggerated, and they did not understand why, but many who knew her recalled quietly to one another that she had changed when Lloyd Brickman broke off their romance. She had become harder, more outspoken, more querulous, more bitter than the pretty girl whom people remembered from her growing up in the country. That girl, come to the city, had been almost meek.

She had a private reason for wanting Hope Kirby dead. She loved Kelly Parmalee. It was a retrospective affection. Perhaps it made no more sense than her love affair with the mall. But there it was, coming down on her with his death with the force of irrevocable loss and all the things that might have been if only she had done this or that differently and been daring when she had been meek. And so long ago! It was like standing by the gravestone of someone dead many years and feeling all at once an unexpected onslaught of grief, time, loss, and the fragility of all things and with all those uncontrollable feelings a sense that her own life had been lost already although she might expect to live for decades more.

We should have run off together, she thought. It seemed so evident now, but at the time, in the mad whirl of their passionate affair, they had agreed that they both had too much to lose. She was rising in the bank, taking more and more lines into her hands, and wavy-haired Mr. Oliver—weak, incompetent, impotent, endowed only with a craggily thoughtful expression that seemed always to be giving serious issues the serious attention they deserved—seemed happy to let her do everything as long as he kept his title and played golf and had the freedom to feel her up when and where he wanted, the feeling never involving "penetration," as he called it, and therefore never being truly adultery, though his fingers got wet stroking her pussy over the thin cloth of her panties.

She did not tell Kelly Parmalee about Mr. Oliver. She would have been humiliated to tell him anything so personal. He took with him to his violent death the trophy represented by her virginity. When he understood what he had done, he almost wept. "Oh Jane! The gift! What you've given to me! I'm not worthy of it."

Men like Kelly Parmalee said such things when they realized they had robbed a girl of her virginity and did not intend to marry her. So she thought. She did love Kelly Parmalee at the time. Not in the wildly passionate way she loved Lloyd later on. No, she thought she owed it to the man who took her virginity to love him. Kelly Parmalee became an incident. So she thought. She turned out to be wrong about that, too. Kelly Parmalee was weak. She could feel the weakness. That is why everyone liked him. He was harmless. Lloyd was not harmless. With his gallant limp, his steely eyes, his hard hands, he was a man.

Kelly was available first. Mr. Oliver excited her. When he ran his spotted hands up her thigh and stroked her, she gasped with her eyes closed and her thoughts in the heaven of love. Not for him. She wanted someone in her, even Mr. Oliver. But he could not get hard. She thought no one else would come along, and there was Kelly. Yes, if she had not done it with him, Lloyd might still be alive. They might be living together with their kids in the house he talked about building—picture window overlooking the lake. Everybody talked about picture windows after the war. The boys came home from fighting in Europe or in Asia, and they wanted to look through picture windows onto an unthreatening nature, neatly framed in perpetual place. Or maybe they wanted to look through the picture windows to see if something might be sneaking up on them. Whatever it was, they wanted picture windows.

"But who knows?" she said aloud sometimes to herself. She talked to herself more and more now that her mother had died. The sound of her own voice broke the silence in the great palace of a house. Her father had loved it. He called it "the estate." It came down to him from a grandfather who made a fortune in tobacco before the Civil War, invested the money in the North, and built the house just before catastrophe overwhelmed the South. The grandfather was tubercular. He took no sides in the war, although his money did. The war in turn passed him by and let him will the house on to his son—who began to lose money and sell off the land. Jane's father managed to stop the decay and hold on to the estate and twenty-five good acres of land.

It was his refuge when he came home from the First War, and she kept it beautifully painted and clean, with its sprawling carriage house where no horses had been housed since her father died. She could afford to fix anything that went bad, to install new plumbing, reinforce the beams in the ceiling, shingle the roof with slate, pave the driveway, and she insisted on a tile bathroom. The contractors were delighted.

She loved the thick screen of trees that grew between her and the Old Knoxville Pike. She cherished her privacy. Protected by her trees, she sat out on her hardwood porch and smoked and drank bonded whiskey in the evening—never too much. The Martel Methodist Church stood by its graves amid the brooding cedars only a few hundred yards from her house. But Sunday after Sunday she drove into Bourbonville to the Central Methodist Church so she could be seen by the better sort in town. People felt encouraged when they saw a banker in church. A lady banker like Jane Whitaker had to take care to give the right impression everywhere she went. Women in such positions made men nervous, and it was men who deposited money and took out loans. Sometimes when it was very dark and she was completely sure no one could see her, she sat on her porch with a couple of drinks inside her and slipped her hands under her panties and masturbated herself with her eyes shut, imagining some man who loved her, until she exploded in a quaking passion that left her able to get a good night's sleep.

She had a knack, an intuition, a talent. She didn't know what to call it. Mr. Oliver said she was a genius. Maybe the times were simply good, and anybody else would have done as well. Mr. Oliver gave her the credit; she took it gladly. She studied the stock market, read the *Wall Street Journal*, read every financial publication she could find, traveled to New York now and then to glean what she could from talking with people in banks and on Wall

Street. One room in her house was piled with company reports. But more capacious was her memory, which held graphs and charts, profits, loss, futures, inflation rates, averages, interest rates, mortgages, long-term loans. She never forgot anything. And she succeeded brilliantly.

When her mother died, she briefly considered leaving Bourbonville. But the thought of leaving the estate was more than she could bear. Besides, who would place a woman in the position of power that she had here? No, she thought, she had to do something grand, something that would establish her reputation so she could walk into any bank or brokerage house and introduce herself and see the red carpet rolled out, champagne poured in glasses, men bowing her to posh leather chairs. She had a staunch and unquenchable faith that she could make it in Bourbonville. Joseph Ignazio seemed to come along in the fullness of time.

Joseph Ignazio came home from the war to his father's olive oil business in New York and settled down as a dutiful son in his father's business. A couple of years passed. His future began to look like one of those monotonous grassy plains that turned up in western movies where people got excited about cows and fences and horses and square dances. His father ordered him about like a slave. Olives, cheese, almonds, pasta excited his father with passions that were all-consuming. A son like Joseph Ignazio who assumed that when all was said and done, an olive was an olive, seemed like a blasphemer who ought to be treated like a potential patricide.

Joseph Ignazio noticed his father's rage in a detachment that was almost absentmindedness. He made mistakes because he was thinking of other things, and when his father raged at him, he only looked at the old man with an air of surprise, as if he had been suddenly wakened from sleep. He had a vision. Other people bubbled about this and that, as effervescent and as ephemeral as a bottle of Coke with the cap off left in the sun. Joseph Ignazio's vision came on him like a broadening day, illuminated by one great sun. Wealth lay in predicting what the country would become.

Where would America be in ten years, in twenty years? Joseph Ignazio went to the New York Public Library and read all he could about regions of the country where he thought people might begin to move. California, of course. But there were no bargains in California for people with as little money as he could command. Florida. Perhaps. He would give it a try. He was patient and methodical. He got on the train, paid for a Pullman, and went to Florida. His father almost had a stroke. "I'm going to Florida," Joseph said. "On business."

"Florida! You are going to Florida to be filthy stinking lazy on a beach while I must stay here and work my fingers to the bone to keep this business alive, to have something to leave to you. Ingrate! That's what you are! A lazy and worthless ingrate." The old man turned so red Joseph Ignazio thought blood might spurt out of his eyes. It made no difference. Joseph Ignazio had saved his money in the army, and he went by Pullman to Florida.

The trip was gorgeous. The food in the diner was delicious. He slept soundly to the rocking of the heavy Pullman car on the steel rails cutting through the varied and surprising land. The train was air-conditioned. It was July. He got out of the train in Fort Lauderdale, and the heat was like a hammer driving him into the ground. He had a moment of absolute panic when he thought the air would smother him. The hotel where he stayed was not air-conditioned. It had a double door in each room. One door was solid. The outer door was built like a Venetian blind with slats across it arranged so that no one could see through it but with openings between the slats that would let air through. An electric fan in the window pulled hot and sticky air through the room. Joseph Ignazio lay naked atop the sheets and booked a Pullman the next evening back to New York. Air-conditioning would come to Florida. He knew that at once. He took a taxi around Fort Lauderdale, and the cab driver showed him dinky little houses with air conditioners in the windows. The coming thing, the cab driver said. Some stores were air-conditioned. But walking out of the air-conditioning into the streets in summer was like going from an icebox into a furnace. He imagined doing that change twenty-five times a day. No, he decided, Florida would always be a place for old people with poor circulation. Decades afterwards Jane Whitaker would remember that enthusiastic conversation of his—no, it was more than a conversation; it was a sermon—and she would say, "He was right about that. He was right about everything."

He believed in efficiency. "I don't believe in reading the same book twice. I never see the same movie twice. I don't believe in going the same place twice unless there's money to be made there." So he made a logical decision. Instead of returning to New York by the Atlantic seaboard as he had come, he would take another way home. He would see some other southern states. So he booked from Florida to Atlanta, thence to Birmingham, and thence to Knoxville and back through Virginia to New York. He talked to business-men in club cars and in diners. He walked around in the intense heat of rail-road stations large and small, and he felt the sweat break out on him as though pumped through his skin. Birmingham looked like hell, the great steel mills pumping smoke into the air, the furnaces blazing with fire along-side the great railyard.

He came through Chattanooga in mid-morning and saw the mountains looming above him, above the bend in the river, and he was taken by them. On the way into Knoxville the enormous bulk of the Appalachians rose to the east, and he was entranced. The train moved slowly and seemed to stop at every village. That was fine with Joseph Ignazio. He could not get enough of the mountains, not because he thought them beautiful but because he knew that mountains meant tourists. Tourists meant money. He sat in the lurching diner across from a Knoxvillian who gushed at him like a president of a chamber of commerce. In Joseph Ignazio's mind such people were bores because they thought enthusiasm was everything. They usually knew nothing and could imagine nothing. But this man had an interesting piece of information. More people visited the Great Smoky Mountains National Park every year than all the other national parks combined.

In Knoxville he accompanied his newfound friend off the train. This was 1951, and the steam locomotive had to take on water and coal, and so the train was in the station a half hour. Joseph Ignazio walked up onto the Gay Street Viaduct for a few minutes and looked up into the heart of Knoxville. A dreary town. No doubt about that. It reeked of smoke and dirt, although from somewhere he smelled the fragrance of coffee. But although it was July, the temperature was bearable, and the train coming into the city had chugged along a lake. The land beyond the windows looked cool and green. Here was something important.

He came back to New York with Knoxville on his mind. In the library he studied road maps. He called the chamber of commerce in Knoxville. Yes, the town was growing. He went back and checked into the Farragut Hotel on Gay Street. Gay Street was crowded with people, and some of the stores were interesting, especially a big jewelry store next to a large clock set in the sidewalk. Some people in Knoxville had money to buy expensive things. But Joseph Ignazio saw at once that Gay Street was moribund and that hardly anybody realized its coming death. Another decade, he thought. He walked around and with considerable satisfaction saw that parking downtown was completely inadequate. Sears, Roebuck had moved out to a large store a couple of miles away from the center of town. It was an ugly, flat building with an enormous parking lot. Ignazio had already determined that a huge parking lot was the key. He had seen lots of old masters in the museums of Europe. But beauty was in the eye of the beholder. For him nothing was as beautiful as a huge and crowded parking lot.

He looked in the telephone book for artisans with Italian names— stoneworkers, tile men, house painters. And he found a tile man. Joseph Ignazio went to talk with him. His name was Giuseppe Noce, and he was first-generation, but yes, he spoke Italian, and so Joseph Ignazio wooed him in their mother tongue. What was happening in Knoxville? Much work for Giuseppe Noce? Yes, people were building new houses all over the place. Most of it junk, but some of it—*mamma mia*. Some houses were going up that cost forty, fifty, even sixty thousand dollars. Imagine that!

In which direction? West. Everything was going west. You had to go west out of Knoxville to get to both Chattanooga and Nashville. That's where the traffic was. That's where people looked out their car windows and decided they wanted to build a house—there, in those trees, there on that rolling hillside, there by that little stream of water. Be near the highway but far enough away to have quiet and a lawn. No matter what they said, Americans liked to live near highways.

And the weather? A little snow in the winters. Sometimes no snow at all. It melted fast, within a day or two or three at most. Flowers bloomed in February. Yes, a few seething days in summer, and now and then a summer could roar with heat. At night it nearly always cooled off, and some summers were so mild that you thought spring lasted from March to September. The autumns? Nothing more beautiful.

Joseph Ignazio took the train back to New York, his mind humming. The automobile. Air-conditioning. People moving in from the north. He would return. He would visit banks. He needed only one. Then others would follow.

In the spring of 1953 when he walked into First Bourbon County Bank at Bourbonville, invited Jane Whitaker to lunch, and sat down with her in the mirrored restaurant of the King Bourbon Hotel, he opened his vision to her. "Pretty soon, you are going to see something new right here in Tennessee, my friend. You are going to see shopping malls. Do you know what a shopping mall is? Well, of course not, because you've never seen one. But let me tell you."

He had to explain what a mall would be. She could think only of the diabolical ugliness of the Sears building on its plaza in Knoxville. He explained his vision, and she saw it. He said the time would come soon when the farmland between Bourbonville and Knoxville would be paved with one mall after another. Jane listened entranced. She had seen the houses growing up, Knoxville creeping outward year by year, but she had not put it all together. Here was a man with a decided New York accent and a deep intensity who touched a random pile of pieces from a jigsaw puzzle heaped on a table, and magically they all came together, and a picture unfolded before her eyes as beautiful as anything she had ever seen in her life. Automobiles parked in rank after rank in spacious parking lots. Thousands on thousands of people streaming inside to buy, to buy, to buy. He wanted a gigantic mall, all under one roof, climate controlled, greenery inside, a stream flowing through it, a world apart except that it was attached by golden and silver commerce to the world outside where people lusted to buy.

Where to locate the mall?

Joseph Ignazio loved running water. It was something he discovered in Frank Lloyd Wright at the New York Public Library. He had to explain who

Frank Lloyd Wright was. Not that he knew a lot about Wright. Joseph Ignazio never tried to learn everything about any subject. He picked out what struck him as important, and in the big black-and-white architecture books about Frank Lloyd Wright, he discovered running water. He looked at photographs in picture books, and even in black-and-white he heard the water run and sing across the pages. Running water soothed people. A water-fall made music that could relax a multitude. When people were soothed and relaxed, they tended not to worry about paychecks and budgets and other such mundane things. They spent money more freely.

Ignazio employed an engineer. He felt a great satisfaction in using a pro-fessional because, as he told Jane, one of his gifts was to recognize that in this new age of expansion and prosperity, no one person could manage everything. "Engineers spend their whole lives learning things other people don't know, but what they learn is essentially boring to most people. Why fill my mind with boring details when I can hire somebody for whom these bor-ing details are the center of life?" The question seemed invincible, carrying its answer with it with the inevitability of a tail on a dog. He and the engi-neer found a great plain of beautiful land ten miles west of Knoxville, a fine creek running through it. "But that is almost ten miles from Knoxville," Jane said in exasperation, as if Joseph Ignazio didn't quite understand geog-raphy.

"What's ten miles when you have a car and the prices in the mall are less than anything you find downtown?" he said. The engineer agreed. This land would take little grading, and paving would be easy, and the creek that ran through it could be easily managed.

Everything was perfect except that the farm couple who owned this beau-tiful land refused to talk to him. They refused to let him in the door. They threatened him with the sheriff if he did not quit trespassing on their land. He mentioned fantastic sums of money, money he could not possibly raise. Once he got started upping the bid, he could not stop himself. It was exas-perating, and he could not understand the hostility of these people not only to progress but to a comfortable life of their own where they would never again have to do any hard labor. All to no avail. They turned him away with an almost brutal contempt. For days he was depressed. But the cure to depression was to work harder, and he went west along the highway beyond Dixie Lee Junction to a stretch of land along Highway 70. Suddenly he was taken with it, a grand intuition. The land was hilly and forested and had a splendid distant view towards mountains that the engineer told him were the Cumberlands, more gentle than the Smokies and somehow giving an impression of a nature that was more manageable. Most important, at a place where two low hills rolled together a powerful and cold spring came gushing out of the earth. The water came out with such force that it represented to Joseph Ignazio the biggest fountain he had ever seen. He imagined his mall built all around this natural wonder, the water pouring out of a carefully laid concrete bed with trees and shrubs planted along the side, and high overhead the glass roof of the atrium he envisaged reaching as high as a three-story building. He found the whole scene enchanting, and it is just possible that Joseph Ignazio, proud to hold suspended in his head many ideas at once, imagined that when the bulldozers had worked their magic and the mall went up, the scene that he looked at would retain the beauty he saw before the work began.

The engineer was skeptical. More than skeptical. Anxiously incredulous. "You will have a hell of a lot of grading to do here to level those hills, and I don't like the look of that spring. I've never seen water coming out of the ground with force like that."

Ignazio saw this unguarded apprehension as both an annoyance and an opportunity for instruction in his vision. From the first he had taken for granted that the person with vision had to persuade the dull clods of earth without it that the vision could be made reality. So Andrew Carnegie. So John D. Rockefeller. So Leland Stanford. So all those who had made America and the world a better place and themselves fabulously wealthy at the same time. Joseph Ignazio was already thinking of his future, huge enclosed malls spread across America, himself in the company of presidents and senators and sudden silence when he walked into a restaurant and heads turned at every table to look at him while he pretended not to notice.

"Listen, my friend," he said grandly to the engineer, a man named Donovan, "let me explain how things work. I get the ideas. It's up to you as an engineer to work out the practical method of putting those ideas to work. Look at the Empire State Building. Look at the Panama Canal. Those great monuments started as ideas in a head just like mine. Once they had the ideas, the engineers found a way to do it. That's what you will do, my man. And when you see your name on a granite plaque at the entry to our mall, you will be the proudest man on earth."

"It's going to cost one hell of a lot of money," the engineer growled, knowing he was being condescended to and as a Tennessean feeling a natural resentment towards a Yankee who pretended to know everything. But in the end he put away his hesitation. For the moment money was there to be made, and a man was a fool to run away from honest cash offered in honest enterprise, even if he thought Joseph Ignazio was ten times a fool. Like many others, the engineer wondered if Joseph Ignazio had got into Jane Whitaker's underpants, but he assumed that that was none of his business except that he did feel a slight and fantasy-laden envy at the prospect.

Jane Whitaker objected that the land Joseph Ignazio wanted was more than twenty miles from Knoxville.

He smiled at her naive innocence, delighting in revealing a wisdom that would make them both rich. "What's twenty miles when the mall has stores with things to sell that people in Knoxville have to buy? What happens when you turn shopping into an art form? We're going to construct an indoor park. People will drive not just twenty miles but a hundred miles to see it. In my concept the mall will draw people like one of the seven wonders of the world, and when they are here, they will buy."

Neither he nor Jane Whitaker could have named any of the seven wonders of the world except the Great Pyramids of Egypt, but the idea had a ring to it, and Jane bought into it. Literally so.

He needed money to begin, money to show other investors that the mall was underway, that they could contribute their money knowing that others had contributed before them. Jane rolled a loan of a hundred thousand dollars through the bank. It was the largest single loan First Bourbon County Bank had ever made. The land was acquired. Yes, the price was higher than it might have been had the owners of these unproductive hills and woods been selling to their neighbors. But Joseph Ignazio accepted all that, knowing in his proud, professional way that it was natural for people to make a profit when they could and pleased at having the obvious goodwill of those to whom he handed over the money.

In July the grading began, the big yellow bulldozers scraping flat over a hundred acres of land. Every day they worked. Every day Jane Whitaker drove out to see the behemoth machines with their great caterpillar treads pushing the red earth in front of them, moving back and forth, slowly, slowly reducing the hills towards Joseph Ignazio's goal of making them level. Meanwhile Joseph Ignazio circulated through East Tennessee, fetching other bankers to the site, showing them his vision, promising to make them a return on an investment that would give them not only wealth but everlasting glory.

Joseph Ignazio came about a year after Jane broke up with Lloyd. Or rather after Lloyd broke up with her. Joseph Ignazio took her mind off her heartbreak. Yes, Jane Whitaker had a broken heart for a while. She loved Lloyd. That was over. The bitterness stayed. When she looked back through Lloyd, she saw poor, ineffectual Kelly Parmalee, and she loved him, too, in a nonsensical way. He was sweet and kind, and he was what he was, weakness and all. The weakness made him vulnerable and good, she thought. Now he was dead. She grieved for him with a force that she had not dreamed she possessed. She believed that he had loved her. Yes, he was so tender with her. He must have loved her. He had loved her as she was. She had given him something that seemed casual at the time but now seemed precious. Everything could have been different. She was taunted by that thought. Everything could have been different.

*W*HEN Mr. Hamilton disappeared, Sheriff Cate was not surprised. He had known maybe six or seven federal revenue agents to disappear in the mountains. They went back up there where they had no business fooling around, and they meddled with hard-working men making a little whiskey to sell for an honest price and not doing anybody any harm, making good whiskey, not the stuff that could turn you sick or blind or that could kill you deader than a chopped-up snake, and the revenue men went back up there with their dogs and their pistols, and nobody heard of them again except that now and then a mountain man came down to Sevierville for supplies on a Saturday, and he'd be wearing new boots and twill trousers a little small for him, and he'd have a dog with him that he hadn't had before, and that dog might look powerful like one of the dogs the last revenue agent had with him when he disappeared with his fancy leather boots and his big pistol and maybe a federal marshal or two back up in the mountains.

But people in Sevier County, Tennessee, were polite. They did not go around asking questions they didn't have any business asking, and people said, "Fine dog," and the mountain man said, "Thankee," and he bought a few items—sometimes a hundred pounds of sugar to take care of his sweet tooth or something like that, paying cash, asking the storekeeper to write down "supplies" instead of "sugar," the storekeeper obliging with alacrity, loading the sugar onto a wagon and covering it with canvas so it wouldn't get wet in case a cloudburst came along—which can happen any time in the mountains—and the mountain man took his new dog back with him, disappearing into the somber haunts of the Great Smokies, the mist and the quiet, and that was the end of it.

The trouble with the disappearance of Mr. Hamilton was that his Ford car did not disappear. It was found off in a ravine, its nice new front end smashed up from where it had gone through the trees when somebody pushed it off the road up above. Somebody saw it because it made a right smart path through the trees, taking down the saplings and the sassafras and the other little stuff left over from the logging, and the shiny black paint caught the sun, and people thought somebody might have been killed in it. But it was empty, no blood, and Mr. Hamilton was gone.

The boss of the new park office in Knoxville was upset. His name was McCloud, Scotch-Irish, tall, thin, with craggy eyebrows and a shock of brown hair flecked with gray, and blue eyes that had steel in them, with a streak of anger across his liver that he had often unloaded on poor Mr. Hamilton because he thought Mr. Hamilton a blundering and arrogant imbecile.

"Now look here, Sheriff," McCloud said, "somebody has done something to my man, and I want him found. I want fingerprints off that car, goddammit. I want to find out who has touched it, who put it there."

"If you ask me," Sheriff Cate said in his slow, unhurried way, "nobody put it there but your Mr. Hamilton. He was drunk and drove it off the road, and it went rolling down that air ridge, and he hit hisself in the head, and he got the sense knocked out of him. He probably wandered off in the mountains and got lost. Happens ever' year. Folks get lost in them there hills, and they don't never come out again."

"That dumb son of a bitch did not have any sense to be knocked out of him," McCloud said. "He has worked for me six months, and if he had any sense, I'd be the first one to know about it. He didn't drink either. If he had taken a drink now and then, he might have been bearable. I want fingerprints. I want Hamilton found, dead or alive."

"Well, truth to tell, Mr. McCloud, I hain't got the fixings to do fingerprints. I don't know nothing about fingerprints."

"Goddammit, then call in the FBI. Ask for their help. Hamilton was on federal business. Get them to dust that damned car until we can tell everybody who has touched it for the last two weeks, and you haul every man jack of them into jail, and you question them until you find who saw Hamilton last and you discover what happened to him. I tell you what I think. I think the son of a bitch is dead. I think one of those yokels up in the mountains has killed him. I want to know which one of them did it."

"Well, I wouldn't be jumping the gun," Sheriff Cate said. "I still say you're going to find Hamilton wandering around someplace with a knot on his head. Or maybe you won't find him. Like I say, somebody disappears up there every year. They don't never even find the bones. Bears eat them and scatter them, and the ants does the rest."

"You get those damned fingerprints," McCloud said. "And in the meantime, you get a deputy up there and keep people from touching the damned car."

Sheriff Cate did as he was ordered to do—slowly. He thought that he had no choice. He called the FBI, hollering into a telephone that crackled and roared in his ear, making contact with the faint voice on the other end. The FBI chief in Knoxville was not sure he had authority, but since Mr. Hamilton had been working for the federal government, maybe the Bureau could at least lend its services. He dispatched an agent. He would arrive after lunch, and he had men with him able to do fingerprints.

Sheriff Cate took his only deputy, Leonard Butterfield, who was tall and gangly and not the smartest man who ever wore a star. He drove Leonard up to the car and he gave him a towel and told him to rub the towel over the car every place he could. "Even the glass, Leonard. And on both sides! You got that? On both sides! When you get done, stick the towel in a stump somewheres." Leonard began to complain because he didn't have any cigarettes and he hadn't had lunch, and Sheriff Cate told him that he ate too much and smoked too much anyway, and it would be good for him to miss a meal and that if he didn't polish that car good, the sheriff would fire his ass. Since Leonard knew he could not get another job as soft as this one, he grumbled and complained and talked about the way everybody was against him, but he stayed put and rubbed the car down as best he could, and when he'd rubbed everywhere he could think of and hidden the towel in a stump, he crawled into the backseat and went to sleep.

Sheriff Cate knew the FBI agent would be in Sevierville within two or three hours. He went to see Roy Kirby. He drove up to the Kirby house. He had never been there before, but he stopped along the way and asked directions. He was not surprised that the Kirby family lived not more than three miles from where the car was found, and he was not surprised to find Roy back up in a field broadcasting winter wheat and a tribe of boys weeding out fences.

He walked back out into the field where Roy Kirby was working. The sheriff's brogan shoes crunched over the newly plowed ground, and he had to watch himself to keep from spraining an ankle. The sheriff was a big man, not precisely balanced, and if there was anything he hated, it was to walk on newly plowed ground. The dirt got into his shoes, and always he had to stop and take his shoes off and shake out the dirt.

"Howdy, Sheriff," Roy Kirby said, looking as mild as spring, not upset, not afraid. "What brings you up here?"

"I got a hunch you know what brings me up here," Sheriff Cate growled. He was in no mood to fool around. "I am looking for that dumb-ass feller Hamilton that's been trying to push you off your land."

"Well, you can see he hain't here," Roy Kirby said.

"But he's been here, ain't he?" the sheriff said.

"Sure he's been here. I told you that."

"Well, I want to know where he is now."

"I can't rightly say, Sheriff. I don't know."

"You don't know if he's in heaven or hell," the sheriff said. He was feeling impatient with Roy Kirby.

"Or in the earth or in the clouds," Roy Kirby said, not giving an inch.

The sheriff looked around. "You got a big place here. I reckon you could hide a body all sorts of places."

Now Roy Kirby didn't say anything. He just looked at the sheriff, and Sheriff Cate felt a chill in those eyes. Roy Kirby had eyes like ice picks. The sheriff knew he was on the right track; Roy Kirby and his boys had killed Mr. Hamilton. That was the way it had to be. The sheriff took a deep breath.

"Look here, Mr. Kirby," the sheriff said. "I want you to know something. I don't give a piece of chickenshit about that feller Hamilton. He never was nothing but chickenshit. I didn't like him, and I don't care what happened to him. But a big-shot gov'mint feller named McCloud down in Knoxville cares a big hoot about what happened to him. And so does the FBI."

"Who is this feller McCloud, and what is the FBI?" Pappy's voice was level, just a hint of calculation in it. And the sheriff thought to himself, *This man is going to make a list, and he is going to kill everybody he has to kill to protect his land. I will tell him who McCloud is, and Roy Kirby will figure out a way to kill him. And if I told him that the FBI was a big barn down in Knoxville filled up with men who are going to come with machine guns and rifles and tanks and airplanes to drive him off his land, he would set about figuring out a way to go to Knoxville and burn that barn down.*

It was hopeless, the sheriff thought. He explained about Mr. McCloud. He explained about the FBI. He explained about fingerprints. "I got Leonard down in the woods polishing that damned car, Mr. Kirby. But Leonard ain't much in the brains department, and he ain't much in the work department. He misses one fingerprint, and there may be the devil to pay. Like it is, I figure this Mr. McCloud ain't going to be happy when he comes on the onliest automobile in Sevier County that has been polished in the last six months, and it just happens to be down in a ravine and just happens to belong to a feller that is just probably deader than a cold rock and that there car just happens to be less than three miles from your house."

Roy Kirby had never heard of fingerprints. He did not know what fingerprints were. The sheriff held out his own hand, showed him the whorls in his fingers. "There hain't two pairs just alike in the whole world," the sheriff said. "Looky here. Your fingerprints and my fingerprints is different. You can see that, can't you?" Roy Kirby could see it. He stood looking down in amazement at his own fingers and at the sheriff's while the sheriff talked to him, talked *at* him.

"What about that!" Roy Kirby said in mild curiosity.

"Now I do not know how that car got down in that ravine, and frankly, Mr. Kirby, I figure it ain't none of my business what happened to that Hamilton feller. He ain't from Sevier County, and if he ain't from Sevier County, he don't make me no mind because he don't vote. But I got to tell you something. If that there car got down there by a bunch of boys pushing it, if they was anybody around here that laid hands on that there car after, say, getting rid of Mr. Hamilton in some way that ain't nobody's business, maybe putting him on the train and buying him a ticket to New Orleans where he can visit whorehouses and get clap and the pox and God knows what else and dying in the gutter somewhere—I say that if anybody put his hands on that car and Leonard don't wipe it off, the FBI is likely to know about it by dark, and if they come around here asking questions and taking fingerprints off folks, you may have a whole lot more than the sheriff of Sevier County to fool with. If I was you, and if it was any of mine that had left their fingerprints on that car, I would advise them to take a long trip. I'd advise them to go join the army or ship out on a freight train to California or go somewhere else. But I'd go far away. And I'd go fast. That's all I got to say to you, Mr. Kirby. That's all on earth I got to say to you. The FBI is going to be here in a couple of hours. Maybe less than that. That's about all the time you got if you are going to protect some boys and maybe even their daddy from the electric chair."

With that the sheriff pulled his hat down over his forehead, hitched his big pistol belt with its load of revolver down lower on his belly, and he stomped back across the plowed field, cussing as he felt the dirt jump up into his brogans, and after he had taken them off and shaken the dirt out, he got back into his car, and started driving to Sevierville, cussing some more.

Roy Kirby called after him. "Much obliged, Sheriff. Much obliged." The sheriff did not turn around.

Pappy was not slow, and he was not dumb. He called Hope and John Sevier, and they went up to the barn, and they sat around on milk stools and they talked. The barn was full of hay, all for winter, and it smelled strong and good, the way a barn ought to smell in September. It had an air of permanence about it, of endless tomorrows. Pappy explained to them about fingerprints.

They looked at their fingers, and Hope and John Sevier looked at each other. They had known they had fingerprints; they did not know their fingerprints were different from everybody else's fingerprints. They could not understand how the police could tell such things, but in their minds the police had a mythic power. The police could do anything they said they could.

Hope and John Sevier had taken off Mr. Hamilton's car. Hope knew something about cars, and he got Mr. Hamilton's to running, and very, very slowly, after dark and without any lights, they drove it down the empty road away from their farm. John Sevier went with him, and when they found a steep place, they got out, and they pushed the car off down the ravine. They walked home. Nobody saw them. No car came along the road after dark. If a car had come along they would have seen the lights and heard the engine a long way off, and they would have jumped off into the woods to hide. But no car came, and no one else was abroad. They heard no sounds but the gentle wind crooning in the trees and the last insects of summer and the spooky cry of an owl and the cool loneliness of the mountains after dark in September.

They thought that they had finished with Mr. Hamilton. They knew now they had left fingerprints all over the back of the car. Pappy looked at them.

"Go see if you can join the army. Go to Knoxville. Don't stop down to Sevierville."

It was not a debating point. It was a command. Hope and John Sevier looked at each other, their thin, angular faces showing no emotion, no thought even, not even the puzzlement they felt at the words "join the army." They did not know what it meant. They knew there were soldiers, wars, guns, wounded, dead in the same way that they knew there were oceans and steamboats on bigger rivers than they had seen, and cities where there were so many cars that people had to have red lights and green lights to know when to stop and start and keep from hitting each other. Neither of them had seen a picture show, but they had stood almost transfixed outside the one little building grandly called the Smoky Mountain Theatre in Sevierville, and they had seen the big photographs, usually luridly tinted, of posed scenes that they might have seen if they had possessed the ten cents each necessary to enter those dark and sacred precincts to see a movie projected on its screen. They had talked with people who had been to Knoxville and even once to a fruit-tree salesman who told them about being in London and in Paris during the World War, and their imaginations reached out to this strange, distant world and stumbled against the reality of it. But they did not know how to enter it.

When Pappy spoke, they knew he was right because he was right about everything. They knew something about prisons—more than they knew about cities. There were old men and young men all over the hills who had been in prison—for moonshining, for bank robbery, for murder, for God knows what all. The Kirby boys had heard talk about high stone walls and guards and barbed wire and working in chain gangs while guards sat smoking at each end of the gang, holding a double-barreled shotgun over their knees, as happy as they could be to shoot anybody who got smart or threatened to run away.

They threw a few things in a couple of paper pokes. Pappy told Mammy to take the coffee can of money out from under the bed, to dole out thirty-five carefully smoothed-out one-dollar bills. Pappy hitched up the wagon, and they rode off down towards Sevierville less than an hour after Pappy spoke his incantation "Join the army."

They were on the road below Gatlinburg, bouncing slowly over the gravel and the ruts and raising gritty dust when the sheriff came back in the other direction in his old car, and behind him was another car, much newer, bigger, filled up with four tough-looking men in suits and neckties and looking straight ahead. Sheriff Cate ignored the Kirbys. Neither he nor they lifted a hand, gave a gesture of recognition, even glanced at each other. They were strangers on a strange road, unacquainted, and by four in the afternoon Hope and John Sevier sat in the caboose of the one train a day that went back to Knoxville after it had come up in the morning, and the dinky coal-burning engine was blowing its way out of Sevierville, hauling its three boxcars and the caboose, and the brakeman was chewing tobacco and spitting out the open window, and not saying much of anything because it was clear to him that the Kirby boys, whom he did not know, did not want to talk. He knew enough not to force talk on mountain men because he was a mountain man himself, now displaced, removed to Knoxville, which he hated, and he paid no attention to them, and if a stranger later asked a question about them, he would not say a word because it was nobody's business.

It was a fine afternoon. The leaves were starting to turn. Some trees were crimson, and some were yellow, and many were on the verge between green and yellow or red. It would be a pretty autumn in the Great Smoky Mountains, and Hope and John Sevier were on their way to Knoxville to join the army. Pappy said as they left home, "Don't write! They might find out where you are."

It was 1935. Pappy, Hope, and John Sevier did not see each other again until the spring of 1940, when the two brothers got a furlough to come home after basic training before they were sent off to the Philippines. They found Pappy just in time to go to Mammy's funeral at the Red Bank Baptist Church. By that time Pappy and Mammy had moved down to Bourbon County, where Mammy had a Toliver cousin, and somehow because of Mammy they had the right to more land than they had in the mountains, and it was better land. But something in Pappy's spirit had broken. He had been beaten. He was quieter, much quieter than he had ever been, and Hope thought he was angry, too, not in a manner to shout at people and lose his temper at the slightest thing, but still angry. He was different. Mr. Hamilton had been right in the end. Not even Pappy could stand against the authority of the United States government.

It was not as easy to join the army as Pappy thought. In 1935 the country was in the bottom of the Depression. The army was not taking recruits, and Americans were resolved never again to get themselves into a foreign war. They looked back on the World War as a great mistake. They had been duped into it by the imperialist British and French and munitions makers. It was not that the wrong side had won; it was that there was no right side. Americans should have hugged their invincible shores and let the Old World go to hell as it would. No one wanted an army. Woeful looks from a sergeant in the post office. "Get a job, fellers." Where? No answer to that. A new post office building in Knoxville, but no more labor needed.

When the army turned them down, Hope and John Sevier were on their own. The mysteries of fingerprinting stayed on their minds. If the government could tell their fingerprints from every other fingerprint in the world, they had better be careful. They assumed that they had left fingerprints on everything they had ever touched and that if the government had any inkling of where they were, police would fall on them with clubs swinging and guns drawn. For a time government and especially the FBI became as mythologically present and all-seeing to them as the eye of God blazing down from on high. The fantasy of government was stronger than their fantasies of God because they had never seen God's angels or demons at work. But they had seen the FBI men chugging toward the Ford once owned by Mr. Hamilton, and Pappy had told them of the urgency in Sheriff Cate's voice when he explained about fingerprints and about what might happen if they didn't leave Sevier County.

Once they discovered they could not join the army, they hit upon the idea of riding a train out of Tennessee. Freight trains lumbered by slowly, empty boxcars with open doors beckoning for the wanderer to run alongside, to leap, to throw himself inside, and to go where the train went. Wherever the train went had to be better than here, and Hope and John Sevier flung themselves into a boxcar looking for something vague, a job, a place in the world, something they could not define because everything that they could define in their lives had been left behind in Sevier County, with Mammy and Pappy and Love and Joye and M.L. and the everlasting hills.

Hope Kirby never sorted out where he and John Sevier went. He recognized with pride that he had done nothing more dishonest in those years than steal apples or peaches out of an occasional orchard. There were plenty of orchards in summer and fall, and the woods had nut trees in them, and sometimes they gorged themselves with black walnuts, breaking off the husks with their strong hands, staining their skin brown with the juice, breaking with stones the hard shells, and devouring the sweet nutmeat inside. A walnut grove was a banquet.

They wandered into Kansas and Nebraska, and in wheat harvest they got jobs because they worked hard, stayed sober, showed up on time, and kept going as long as there was light. When they heard there was work somewhere, they found a train going there or near there, and they went looking, and sometimes they found something. Sometimes they did not. They never begged.

Hope fell into desperate melancholy sometimes. He kept these dark and bitter thoughts to himself because he thought it would be unmanly to share them with a younger brother who depended on him, a younger brother too silent and too obedient. Slowly as the days and the weeks and the years slipped by, Hope understood that John Sevier would never again be what he had been. They never spoke once of Mr. Hamilton. Hope thought about him, of the thrust of the knife, the sound of the blade point striking Mr. Hamilton's spine, just like killing a pig, all done so fast that Hope had no time even to think of anything but obedience. Often at night Hope dreamed that Mr. Hamilton was crawling slowly in the dark trying to hold in his guts, and he woke up with a start of horror, looking around, happy to find himself in a quiet barn loft, in a field, in a bunkhouse, on the floor of an abandoned house with the prairie wind making the doors slap against the walls, even in a swaying boxcar rolling comfortably behind a great locomotive commanding the night. He wished they had clubbed Mr. Hamilton over the head or strangled him or held him under water—anything but what they had done.

Sometimes Hope commanded John Sevier to tell some of Pappy's stories, and John Sevier did, word for word as Pappy had told them, and Hope sat listening, remembering the stories as John Sevier talked, and the memory almost broke Hope's heart. It made Pappy seem nearby, ready to tell them what to do next, but as soon as the story was done, Pappy was a million miles away, and the two brothers were lost in the vast openness of Depression America and on their own. Nearby John Sevier would be rolled up in his blanket asleep, and Hope lay there awake, and so lonesome that he thought he might cry. He refused to cry. John Sevier depended on him, and Hope refused to cry.

In long passages in trains, Hope daydreamed of Tennessee, of the blue mountains rising above their farm, of the thick birches showing their white trunks and branches in the forest, of the streams splashing and roaring down channels that exposed the rocky ribs of the mountains, of the quiet of the forest at night above the line where the chirping insects could not live, of the thin white mist in early morning standing above the creek that ran through their place, of Mammy's voice reading the Bible, and of Pappy's rocking chair thumping, thumping on the floor planks that he had chosen from middling timber and hauled down to the sawmill and seen cut himself. On cold nights he dreamed of being warm in the cabin.

Then things started getting bad in Europe in 1936, and in 1937 the army started growing just a little, and in December 1939 John Sevier and Hope went to a recruiting office in Sacramento, California, and they were taken

into the United States Army as privates. It was a miracle, the greatest of
Christmas gifts, they thought. Hope again almost cried with relief. Bad teeth
almost kept him out. An army dentist took care of that in one fifteen-minute
stretch of blinding pain. Three teeth out of the back of his mouth, and the
army pronounced him fit to serve and told him to brush two times a day.
"Last thing you want when some son of a bitch is shooting at you is a
toothache," a sergeant said. The sergeant was plump and rubicund and
smelled of drink, but he had the air of a man who had been shot at
thousands of times and knew all the advantages and disadvantages for every
fix a man could be in while he was killing or when somebody was seeking to
kill him.

It wasn't bad, the army. Hope and John Sevier could shoot like wizards.
With a 1903 Springfield they could lay five .30-caliber bullets in the middle of
a bull's-eye at one hundred yards in the prone position so that all five bullet
holes made one hole you could just about cover with a silver dollar. They
amazed their sergeants, their officers. When their turns came on the rifle
range, officers came to stand behind them, holding field glasses, looking at
the targets, looking at the marker flag waved by the man down in the trench
below the target to show that there had been a hit on the bull's-eye. The officers spoke to each other in low voices and murmured their respectful compli-
ments to the brothers and bragged about Hope and John Sevier to other
officers in the officers' club. John Sevier and Hope made Expert and each
wore a little rifleman's badge with three little bars hanging under it.

When they got through with basic training, Hope Kirby decided they
would go home. They had a furlough coming. They could go back to Tennessee for thirty days, courtesy of the United States government, Hope Kirby
making up his mind for the first time in his life to do something without
Pappy's advice, maybe even against Pappy's word since Pappy had told them
to join the army, ordered them not to write, and commanded them to stay
away. It was spring when they arrived on the train in Sevierville. They wore
their uniforms and sat in the red caboose on the single train pulled by the one
locomotive owned by the Smoky Mountain Railroad, and they could hardly
keep from getting down from the train and running ahead of it to home.
Once in Sevierville, they set off walking as hard as they could, and they
walked out to their farm along the old road, and they saw quickly that there
were yellow earthmoving machines tearing a road out of the mountains, and
when they got to their land they discovered that all Pappy had built had been
torn down and that the road was going right through their place on its way
up to Newfound Gap—which did not exist when they had lived at home.

Hope Kirby had kept a map of the farm in his head. The map was his
collection of memories that laid everything out in order and kept them

straight and kept himself located in that place and in life. Now it was all gone. The yellow bulldozers had seen to that. He and John Sevier stood there, watching men working impassively with their mammoth machines, the earth pushed aside like flour before a baker's hands, and only slowly could they get things in order, make out how their old and now vanished world corresponded at the corners at least with this new world being built in front of their eyes.

Hope thought of Mr. Hamilton. That would be something—the yellow bulldozer plowing through the ground and suddenly a skeleton clothed in rotted fabric, what was left of Mr. Hamilton's suit, erupting out of the ground like Hope Kirby had seen a snake come to the surface before the driving of a plow behind one of the patient mules. But no, that would not happen, because as they slowly adjusted to the new order of things, they saw that the field where Mr. Hamilton lay buried was already scraped, and a building was going up there, and one of the workingmen told them that this was the spot where the main headquarters for the new national park would be, and out there would be a parking lot. Mr. Hamilton would be under there until the national park was no more, and that would be a long time, and if anybody found him, it would not matter then who killed him. They had buried him deep, very deep. Pappy did things right, even when he was digging a grave.

They walked back into Gatlinburg and hitched a ride in the back of a pickup truck going down to Sevierville, and they found Sheriff Cate. He was older now and had lumbago and creaked around when he walked, but he knew who they were right away, just as soon as they walked into his office at the jailhouse. They exchanged greetings, the sheriff in his slightly effusive, electioneering way, welcoming them home, telling them how good they looked, how proud the county ought to be of them, and passing along the information as if it had been an afterthought that nobody had inquired about "that Hamilton feller" in a couple of years now, that the government people down in Knoxville had other things to think about, and that it looked as if nobody ever would know what happened to him. "If you ask me," Sheriff Cate said, "I think he must of been drinking and runned that car down the mountain and got scairt and run off so's he wouldn't have to pay for the Ford car he tore up. That's what I told the gents from the FBI. That's what I told the folks from the Park Service, too. Feller had that weasely look about him, don't you know. Looks like the kind that blinks his eyes to the light and couldn't stand up and face his boss and say, 'I wrecked that new Ford car because I was drunk.' I still think he may have got lost in the mountains and starved to death. I figure he's been eat by bars long ago." The sheriff chewed and spat a brown jet of tobacco juice into the brass cuspidor.

Hope Kirby looked at the sheriff carefully. Sheriff Cate's broad and grizzled face was so amiable, so unrevealing, that Hope thought, *He believes hit. He's told hisself that story so long he believes hit's true.* But that didn't matter. Mr. Hamilton didn't matter anymore. Mammy and Pappy mattered. What had happened to them?

"Well," Sheriff Cate said, spitting stolidly into his brass cuspidor and looking with solemn meditation after the long brown jet of saliva and tobacco, "it's like this. I told your Pappy that he couldn't hold out against the United States gov'mint. I told him he was like to get his whole family put in jail and him with them and maybe worse than that. You know the gov'mint. If they want to put a whole family in the electric chair, ain't much to stop them. He missed you boys right powerful. 'Deed he did. He didn't seem like himself after you boys went away. I mean, I knowed why you left—no jobs around here, boys restless, got to see the world, put a few miles under your feet, and now look at you. You done the right thing. 'Deed you did. But it like to of broke your daddy's heart when you two taken off like you done. He wasn't the same no more. Wasn't the same."

The sheriff went on in a meditative monologue, and Hope and John Sevier waited him out, knowing that a mountain man got around to things in his own way, and it usually wasn't the straightest way. No, the way a mountain man told a story was not like a bee going from a flower to his tree cross-country like he was following a line drawn by a straight-edge ruler through the air. A mountain man told a story like a hound dog running in circles through the woods, nose to the ground, waiting for the smell of bear to jump up his snout, and then he'd take off.

The story did come out after a while. Pappy had taken the government's money. Thirty dollars the acre. Mammy had a cousin down in Bourbon County. The Kirbys went down there, to a spot on the Tennessee River where it bent west south of Bourbonville. Got some kind of deal on the land because of Mammy's kin. The Tolivers. The sheriff guessed the boys had been so busy they hadn't had time to write.

But then, Sheriff Cate said, nobody in Sevier County had known the Kirby family very well. "It was something," he said. "When them FBI folks was poking around, swearing in front of the ladies and doing suchlike, why, folks forgot all about you boys. That's the way it is sometime. Folks forget. Them FBI folks thought they was three Kirby boys. Nobody told them they was five of you. Hell, wasn't none of their business if you ask me. Don't you figure it that way? Wasn't none of their damned business. Funny thing, too. Them FBI folks never did say they even got any fingerprints off that car. I had me a deputy back then. You remember old Leonard Butterfield? Well, Leonard was watching Mr. Hamilton's car, and he figured he'd polish it up just to have something to do." Sheriff Cate laughed. "That FBI feller, he was mad as hell, but tell you the truth, I don't figure they found nothing on that car."

Hope thought about that detail sometimes—nothing found on the car. They could have come home anytime. Nothing would have happened to them. It was a puzzle he could not solve except to say to himself, "What is to be will be," and that was enough. It had to be enough because it was all there was.

They went to Bourbon County, and Mammy was dead. She looked asleep when they came in. Roy Kirby sat all hunched over, his head down and his hands clasped before him. He looked up when they came in, and the expression on his face was worth ten thousand miles of wandering to get home. But he didn't cry. He never cried. They buried her back up in Sevier County, and Sheriff Cate came to the funeral, and they all stood around and felt sad. They put her on the little hill in the graveyard of the Red Bank Baptist Church in Richardson's Cove. That's where some of her folks, the McCarthys, were buried. Her mama had been a McCarthy.

By the summer of 1940, Hope and John Sevier sailed off to the Philippines on a troopship. It was an awful voyage, the ship rising and falling in the sea, men getting sick, vomiting all over the decks and over the sides and even in the big mess hall where the enlisted men sat on long benches and ate in a room that smelled of puke and iodine and chlorine. The ship stopped at Hawaii, at Pearl Harbor, and men got off and got into fights with the sailors in the bars at night, and they came back to the ship bloody, bruised, and happy, and the ship started off again, and the men started puking again, and they puked until the ship stopped at Wake Island, and then the soldiers fought with marines before they got back onto the ship and sailed on, puking and puking until it seemed to John Sevier and to Hope that there must be a wake of green and yellow puke running across the ocean and all the way back to San Francisco, and almost four weeks after they left San Francisco, they landed in the Philippines. Hope and John Sevier had not puked once. But they had seen enough of boats.

They were in the Philippines, stationed at a base outside of Manila. It was not a bad life. They did not drink or smoke or chase Philippine whores. They did not get in fights, although one night in a bar when a marine was fighting with a sailor and spun around and hit John Sevier, Hope came down on his head with a fist and fractured his skull and put him in the hospital. Hope was cleared of any wrongdoing. "I was sitting there drinking a Co' Cola, and this man suddenly hit my brother," he said. It was enough. The officers who heard him were army men. He had hit a marine. He was not court-martialed. They stuck together, quickly promoted to corporal both of them. They were not made sergeants, not offered admission to OCS. They were not conscious of being passed over, and their superiors might have had a hard time saying why they were passed over, might indeed have denied that these two perfect soldiers, obedient, trustworthy, sober men, were unfit to be in command of other men. If any excuse had been offered, it would have been that both of them were too silent, too withdrawn, to command. They never spoke unless they were spoken to. The quality of silence did not lend itself to praise by their superiors or to yelling commands at troops.

They appeared to belong exactly where they were, sleeping in bunks one bunk atop the other, side by side in drill, side by side in the bars and the streets of Manila when they were on leave, complacent, silent, dutiful—so dutiful that their officers and their sergeants took them to be what they were and never assumed that they could or should be anything else.

Then the Japanese came, December 1941, first in planes flying low over Clark Field, strafing and bombing, American fighter planes and bombers parked in lines in the middle of the runways, the American aircraft exploding on the ground in balls of orange fire laced with incandescent white and swirling with smoke, and Hope and John Sevier were lying out on the parade ground shooting at the Japs with rifles, and Hope always thought that he hit one, that he led the fighter plane as he might have led a partridge flying up from a field and fired his rifle with a sure hunter's instinct, and the plane he had sighted bucked up as if it had been jerked by an invisible cable, and then dipped and fell and exploded.

Later on when they were penned up, the Japanese advancing from the sea, shooting at them, killing men, Hope said to John Sevier, "I think I shot one of them Jap planes down. I'm sure I got one of them," and John Sevier said, "If you think you hit one, you did," because John Sevier believed his older brother, always had believed him, because Hope Kirby had never told an untruth, never had a fantasy, said only those things that he knew he had seen. But a sergeant—his name was McCulley—said, "Bullshit. You shot a Jap Zero down with a Springfield rifle? Bullshit. You're dreaming, soldier. Dreaming or drunk."

"My brother does not tell lies, and he hain't never been drunk in his life," John Sevier said, looking quietly at the sergeant. Sergeant McCulley was a big, swag-bellied man, veteran of hundreds of gallons of beer, thirty or forty barroom fights, a scar over his left cheek where a limey sailor in Hong Kong had taken a broken beer bottle to him in a brawl, and in the end Sergeant McCulley, with a cascade of blood like Niagara falling down his cheek, had put the Brit in the hospital with a broken neck.

That was the man John Sevier spoke to, the man who doubted his brother's word, in the dark, with the Japs creeping closer and shouting at them from the forest and sometimes opening up with machine guns, firing them in long, raking bursts, stopping, going to silence, and then you could hear the shriek of Jap laughter, mockery, and a voice, hollering at them in English, "We gon to fly your plicks in hot grease, Yank."

"All right," Sergeant McCulley said. "I didn't mean nothing. Sure, if you say your brother shot down a Zero with a 1903 fucking Springfield, hell, you need one hundred fucking Springfields, and we're going to drive them Japs back into the sea and make boiled fish out of them."

It was not exactly that Sergeant McCulley was afraid. It was just that he knew John Sevier was serious, would fight with him, would try to kill him; perhaps in the close quarters in the dark where they all lay awaiting the Japanese, straining their eyes to see, sweating, Sergeant McCulley might get killed by a Yank, by one of his own. He backed down. He grumbled, looked off to the side, and said nothing else. Out in the dark, the Japs crept closer.

Later Sergeant McCulley fought beside Hope in the mountains. Hope commanded, and the sergeant obeyed. One night after a firefight with a Jap patrol when they had killed the Japs to the last man, Sergeant McCulley said to Hope, "I want to thank you for my life. You could of kilt me for doubting you about shooting down that Jap plane. I want to tell you I appreciate you not shooting me. Lord God."

Then there was all the rest of it. And it was a lot.

*T*OMMY FIELDSTON was from Ohio, and he ran a hardware store that fronted on the square. He and his wife and daughter lived in a little house on Seventh Avenue, in a shabby part of town, west of the principal ridge on which Bourbonville was built, but the street had trees on it, and the house was cheaper than the house they had owned in Toledo.

Like Mr. Finewood, Tommy Fieldston believed every word in the King James Bible was literally true, and his whole life was an angry crusade against infidels who hid their own unbelief under a pile of honey-roasted words. He read *The Sword of the Lord,* the *Christian Beacon,* and the *Sunday-School Times* in the full conviction of these journals that American pulpits were filled with "modernists" whose only goal in life was to show how superior they were by tearing down the Bible and making it nothing but a watered-down vehicle for the social gospel, which meant salvation in this world but not in the next. Tommy Fieldston had only one ethical principle, and that was to obey the Ten Commandments, and they had nothing to say about the social gospel and liberal religion and all that stuff.

Why didn't Tommy Fieldston drive five miles to Dixie Lee Junction and go to church at Midway Baptist? He didn't look like a member of First Baptist. His clothes were decidedly third-rate, cheap stuff he bought from cheap stores, too gaudy, especially his neckties, and since the cheap stores didn't do alterations, he bought things straight off the rack, and they didn't fit. He always looked as if he had to gather his pants around his skinny waist so they would not fall down around his ankles.

Mr. Finewood preached every week on the Bible, told people they had to believe every word of it or no salvation was possible, and warned against all the evil people in the world trying to make the Bible seem full of mistakes so they could seduce the young. Mr. Finewood believed in a Communist conspiracy to take over the churches, and he thought that if somebody didn't believe in the Virgin Birth of Jesus Christ (which Mr. Finewood sometimes called the Immaculate Conception because he didn't really know the difference between Virgin Birth and the other doctrine), that person was damned as a blasphemer to hell forever and ever. Mr. Finewood told stories about miracles God had done, many that Mr. Finewood had seen with his own eyes, and when he preached you felt the spirit so full in the church that the building seemed almost ready to fly apart. That big new building, put up under the impulse of all the people Mr. Finewood had brought into the church during the couple of years while he had been its pastor. Why didn't Tommy Fieldston go there? Why did he insist on taking his wife and daughter to First Baptist?

For one thing, he believed he was just as good as anybody. That's what he told his wife and his daughter, Marlene. "We are just as good as anybody on earth. This is America." He made pronouncements like this in a vicious tone, as if somebody had told him that he wasn't as good as anybody else, indeed as if a billboard had been set up at the edge of Bourbonville declaring, TOMMY FIELDSTON IS THE MOST INFERIOR PERSON IN BOURBON COUNTY.

Nobody had ever said such a thing to his face. But Tommy Fieldston knew the world was filled with snobs and stuck-up people. He hated all people who thought they were better because they happened to be rich or educated or well known. And more than he hated almost anyone else he hated movie stars, because movie stars lived immoral lives, drinking and dancing, the women smoking cigarettes, the lot of them divorcing and fornicating and cursing, and millions of stupid people paid good money to see them act out stupid and unbelievable stories. Movie stars were the new gods, with never a thought about money, living grossly immoral lives before the world, and here was Tommy Fieldston struggling to make a go of his Christian hardware store. Lots of people at First Baptist went to movies. He saw them going and coming from the Grand Theatre just up the street from his store. Some of them smoked cigarettes, too. Even some of the women.

He thought the snobs at First Baptist didn't believe the gospel the way Baptists were supposed to believe it. He was not a great student of the Bible. Some parts of it were utterly mysterious, no matter how hard he tried to crack the hidden codes that would reveal their divine message. Some of the prophetic preachers could make sense out of Obadiah or Zephaniah or Zachariah or Haggai, but Tommy Fieldston was more likely to take their word for what they found rather than to follow their lead and study the sacred text until it became as clear to him as it was to them. Still, he read enough in the New Testament to be sure that he understood the essentials, and he knew what was what. He also knew that snobs never wanted true religion. They wanted something comfortable that would not upset them at bridge parties and their clubs. (Tommy Fieldston hated all the clubs in Bourbonville. He thought true Christians ought to leave all those worldly things like Rotary and Civitan and the rest to infidels.)

People at First Baptist didn't want to hear about real sin. They wanted poetry when they needed the fiery, crushing Word of a wrathful God. Often Tommy Fieldston chortled in pleasure when he thought of their surprise when they arrived before the great white throne and found themselves condemned to everlasting fire. What good will your poetry be then? Are you washed in the blood of the Lamb? There is power, power, wonder-working power in the precious blood of the Lamb. There is a fountain filled with blood, drawn from Emmanuel's veins. Snobs didn't like a bloody religion. They wanted everything laundered, bleached, ironed, and folded. They thought blood was a topic that should not be introduced into the pulpit. It made him mad. He was never a person to back away from a righteous quarrel. He went to First Baptist so he could show those people up on the hill what a true Christian was—and naturally to show them that they were not true Christians. He came south to get away from Catholics in Toledo, but he came south also because he thought there were more true Christians down there than anywhere else in the country. He was disappointed.

He had arrived in Bourbonville in January 1951. Marlene, his only child, was about to enroll in the Bible college in Chattanooga. Nobody could teach on the faculty there who did not sign a contract saying that he believed every word of the Bible and that if the time ever came when he doubted any part of Scripture, he would resign immediately. If the president and the board of trustees suspected that a faculty member didn't believe every word in the Bible, he was fired forthwith no matter what he said in his defense. That was the way a school should be run, Tommy Fieldston thought. He thought that his beloved only daughter would be safe there.

Tommy was proud of Marlene. He thanked God for such a daughter, and he felt for her the tenderest emotions he knew. The only child God had seen fit to let survive. There had been a son. He was born dead. Tommy and his wife could not understand it. Had God punished them for some sin? Or was it a test of their faith? They decided it was a test of faith, and so they thanked God that he had taken little Alfred away because it gave them a chance to show God that they still loved Him. Marlene came as a reward for their faith. When she was thirteen years old she had a singing voice that could make chills run down your spine. By the time she was eighteen, she could make people gasp with the full, thrilling beauty of a voice like nothing they had ever heard before. She would be a singer for God. Everybody knew that from the moment she opened her mouth to sing the first time. At the Bible college she was the lead soloist in the choir, and when she sang whole congregations wept with joy. A single spotlight came down on her, leaving the rest of the choir in dimness, and she seemed like an angel ready to rise towards God, carrying everyone within earshot with her.

Tommy bought the hardware store Douglas Kinlaw had run for years. Douglas Kinlaw was one of Paul Alexander's best friends. He was quietly deferential, balding, nervous, polite, with a surprising laugh and pleasure in simple things. He loved music and good company, though he seldom had anything to say himself. When Paul Alexander and Jim Ed Ledbetter played music together with friends on Sunday afternoons, Doug was always there. He did not play an instrument. But he was one of the best-read men in Bourbon County. He subscribed to lots of magazines, and he took the *New York Times* by mail, and any time he found something interesting about music, he clipped it out and sent it to Paul or to Jim Ed. He clipped articles about religion and sent them to Charles.

The hardware store was a little like a reading room. Magazines lay about everywhere, and Douglas did not mind if you came in and sat in one of the many chairs scattered about and read to your heart's content. If he had an enemy, nobody knew about it, and his business thrived because he told people when cheaper tools were just as good as the more expensive ones, and he knew everything about anything he sold, from the quality of steel in a pocket knife blade to the torque that a wrench would take without breaking. Paul Alexander said he was an encyclopedia of "the simple and beautiful world of fact" that Paul considered the basis of all truth.

Douglas died in December 1950 when during a light snow he walked into his kitchen and slipped on ice he had tracked in and hit his head on an open drawer of a cabinet. His funeral was one of the biggest in memory. Everybody puzzled over his death. It came from nowhere. No reason for it. The only consolation people took from it was that it was such an odd accident it could not happen to any of them.

Douglas Kinlaw's wife held on to the store for a month or two and then put it up for sale. As though by magic, Tommy Fieldston appeared to buy it. Tommy worked in a glass factory in Toledo. He yearned to go into business for himself, and he wanted also to escape Toledo, where the idolatry of the Catholic Church affronted him on nearly every street. His brother Oswald was in the hardware business in Cincinnati and very successful, and religious only in that he thought it good business to be seen in church. Oswald drove through Bourbonville en route to his annual winter vacation in Florida, saw the "For Sale" sign on Kinlaw Hardware in the square, got out of his car, looked the place over, and telephoned his brother on the spot. "I've found a happy life for you," he said. In fact Oswald didn't like his brother very much, and he was not sure Tommy could ever have a happy life, but he thought it was worth a try. A boost for the wife and daughter, he thought. They deserved a boost. But then it is not entirely certain that Oswald did not coax Tommy to buy the store knowing that Tommy would fail, thus humiliating the arrogant bastard once and for all.

Tommy took one look at the store and decided it was old-fashioned and beneath his dignity. He set out to change things. It took a little time, but in June 1951 Tommy Fieldston welcomed Bourbonville to a remodeled hardware store "under new management." The first thing people saw was that the Fieldstons were serious about religion. You walked into their hardware store and on a neat little table just inside, you saw a stack of religious tracts and an open Bible. A banner sign over the cash register said, IN THIS PLACE JESUS CHRIST IS LORD. Above the words was a cross with red glow marks all around to indicate that it shone.

You couldn't buy a bag of fertilizer without Tommy taking your money and ringing it up and looking you in the face with his pale blue eyes and asking, "Do you know the Lord Jesus Christ as your Lord and Savior?" It was unnerving, even to Bourbonville, which was as impregnated with Christianity as the Vatican. But, like the Vatican, Bourbonville did not take religion seriously enough to spoil the pleasures of this life.

When Doug Kinlaw ran the hardware store, it had a dark, old-fashioned look, and it smelled of oiled leather and aged wood and something indefinable that could only be described as comfortable. Paul Alexander sometimes sat in there and smoked a cigar and listened to men talk—retired farmers and others who gathered in the pleasant dimness as if it were a club of some sort. Doug Kinlaw kept horse collars and leather harnesses and hame strings hanging on the high, dark walls long after nearly every working horse and mule had been retired or sent to the slaughterhouse to be converted into canned dog food. In Doug's book, a hardware store sold gear for horses and mules, and he followed the book. It was cool in the summer, even without air-conditioning, because the walls were brick and the high ceiling let the heat rise, and a big, quiet exhaust fan high on the back wall blew the heat out.

The hardware store reposed on the east side of the square, facing the courthouse, not far from the railroad tracks, and when trains passed conversation stopped, and somebody looked at a watch and said, "That's forty-two. He's twenty minutes late." In winter Doug put up a potbellied stove and built a coal fire in it. Men sat around it on chairs and benches of disparate origins, some spitting tobacco juice into a box of sand conveniently provided. Some read magazines. Sometimes on rainy Saturday afternoons Paul Alexander and his third son, Stephen, Jim Ed and Jim Ed's sons, and one or two others played music in there, and people crowded in to listen, and Doug Kinlaw stood by with a pleased look on his face, and Guy the idiot boy beat time with his pencil, and Doug sometimes patted Guy affectionately on the back.

Tommy Fieldston didn't know anything about the hardware business except that his brother had done well in it. He was envious of his brother— an envy he would never confess even to himself. He thought it would be great to show Oswald that anybody could make a success in hardware, and he was annoyed because although his brother was a Christian, he did not demonstrate his Christian faith with the ardor Tommy thought fitting to the true believer.

"Toledo is filled with Catholics," Tommy said. "I hated for Marlene to grow up surrounded with idolatry." No smug superiority here. Tommy was afraid of Catholics. He thought they were conspiring with the Communists to take over the world. The pope was the Antichrist. Clear in the Book of Revelation. All the prophecy preachers were certain of that.

"Yes," his wife said, "you never know if Marlene might fall in love with a Catholic. We're so relieved to be in a Christian town." She was a nervously energetic woman named Muriel. She adored her husband. She thought women ought to obey their husbands. She was known to stand up in prayer meeting now and then in First Baptist and give her testimony, often with a voice breaking in love and obedience to her husband. Arceneaux at these times was embarrassed, and he was sure he dealt with a crazy woman, so he tried not to provoke her.

Tommy Fieldston's hardware store reopened after remodeling with fluorescent lights, a new paint job, electric heat, air-conditioning, and an appliance department that sold automatic washing machines, driers, and steam irons. He did not sell television sets, because he thought they brought the abominations of Hollywood into the home. Gone were the harnesses and the horse collars and the fragrances. Everything now smelled vaguely of new boxes and new paint.

Paul Alexander, creature of habit that he was, went in to buy something after the store reopened for business. By that time Tommy Fieldston had picked up a lot of information about Paul Alexander, his curiosity piqued by the appearance of a short olive-skinned man with a Roman nose, a large mustache, and wavy hair, both mustache and hair going white when Tommy Fieldston came to town. Tommy Fieldston could tell a foreigner or a Jew when he saw one. He thought Paul Alexander might be both, but that was all right as long as such people took Jesus as their personal Savior and agreed with Tommy in all things.

People in Bourbonville were accustomed to Paul Alexander after he had lived among them more than thirty years. And he played the mandolin like a magician.

Some people thought Paul Alexander was a nigger lover, but they didn't say such things in public. Some could remember when he was almost lynched years before when a black man had been hanged and his body burned below town. Something nobody talked about out loud. Paul Alexander had been the black man's friend, and that was recalled sometimes in lowered voices and half-sentences. Altogether it was one of the dark stories of the county, one remembered among the other dark stories that had faded to gray. Paul Alexander never went to church except for the ritual occasions of weddings and funerals, and they knew that on leaving after these rites, he departed swiftly and seldom talked to preachers. Yet his second son was going to be a preacher. Well, that was his mother's influence. Everybody understood that. And by the time Tommy Fieldston moved to town, she was dying.

Tommy Fieldston got it into his head that God wanted him to lead Paul Alexander to Christ. That's the way fundamentalists talked about their missionary work. They led people to Christ. Tommy supposed that if Paul Alexander met a *real* Christian, he would be converted. Tommy was a real Christian. On the day Paul Alexander walked into the hardware store, Tommy Fieldston settled on him with a hard smile and a sugary voice. "I have heard so much about you, Paul," Tommy said with that iron grin of his. "I'm delighted to make your acquaintance at last. You have quite a reputation in this town. Everybody tells me how smart you are, and I hear you're a great musician, too. Well, my daughter is a great singer. I hear your son is going to be a preacher."

"My second son," Paul Alexander said as though making an important and not altogether happy correction.

"A fine young man," Tommy Fieldston said. "Paul, I understand you are a Catholic."

Paul Alexander looked at him with the expression of someone who has come upon a cockroach swimming in his coffee. "I do not discuss religion," he said curtly.

"Oh, I don't talk about religion either," Tommy said. "I hate religion. Religion is not going to take us to heaven. Only the Lord Jesus Christ can do that. The Lord Jesus Christ is not a religion, Paul. He is our blessed Savior, the son of the living God." Tommy Fieldston rushed on, caught up in the great fundamentalist fantasy. If the mark lets you keep talking, keep telling him about Jesus, and conversion is inevitable. Tommy Fieldston bored in.

"Paul, Jesus is big enough for your sins. If you could know my Savior, you'd have happiness greater than anything you've had in all the years of your life. I'd be glad to pray with you right now, right here." His freckled, stupid face beamed with benevolence.

Paul Alexander looked at him in thunderous and outraged silence. His beloved wife was dying, and this maniac was trying to convert him. In the self-delusion of the fanatic, Tommy Fieldston thought Paul Alexander's expression meant warm interest. He rushed on. "If this place out here is too public, we can go into the back room and get down on our knees there, and you can walk out of my store with a song in your heart and your heart right with God. It will give you peace, Paul. A peace the Catholic Church with its idols and superstitions can never give."

He put his hand on Paul Alexander's arm, only to have it rudely shaken off. Paul Alexander looked at him as if Tommy Fieldston were a piece of chickenshit. "He scorned me. He thought he was better than I was." The revelation to Tommy Fieldston was instantaneous—and he repeated it in outraged self-pity to all the Christians he knew. It was confirmation of his suspicion that Paul Alexander was a foreigner settled like a parasite here in Bourbonville, a Jew among good Americans, sucking their honest blood. All Jews, Tommy Fieldston thought, belonged to a worldwide conspiracy that would continue until the last days, when the Jews would be converted and have all their disbelief washed away in the blood of the Lamb. Paul Alexander stalked out of the hardware store and took his business else-where.

*J*ANE WHITAKER had learned to live with death. First her father, then her mother, then Lloyd, then Kelly Parmalee. Jane's mother did not come into the kitchen one morning for breakfast. Wearily Jane went up to her bedroom and found her lying there, more peaceful-looking than Jane had ever seen her before and stone-dead. For just a moment Jane felt regret, the kind of regret that anybody feels before the death of somebody familiar, whose departure from this life demonstrates that we all have our departing time marked down in the future, and that it will come sooner than we want or think. The feeling passed quickly.

She called the new undertaker in town, a blond young man free of the pomposity of old Mr. Robinette. Mr. Robinette thought he wasn't giving good value unless he appeared to be the most profoundly affected mourner at the funeral. He could call up tears on command, and he usually broke down when he expressed his "deepest sympathy for your great loss" to the bereaved family. Strangers and sometimes even the bereaved family comforted him. The new undertaker was not like that. "Glenn," she said crisply into the telephone, "come and get Mama. She's dead."

"Violent or natural?" Glenn said easily.

"Natural. I didn't have to kill her myself," she said.

"Good. My brother and I will be right out. Do you have any coffee?" She hung up the telephone laughing and put on the coffee pot. Glen was funny. He passed out little notebooks with the name of his mortuary on the front. "Keep one of these in your car," he told people. "If you get killed in a wreck, I'd like the business."

Jane's mother was never happy with anything, complained about how people did not appreciate her, and tried continually to instill in Jane dark feelings of guilt for not loving her enough. Jane wanted to say to her sometimes, "Look, Mama, the railroad is a half-mile over there. I'll drive you over, and you can jump in front of a train." No more of that. "I'm free," Jane said to herself aloud.

Jane loved her father. She thought her mother had killed him as surely as if she had poisoned him slowly. Her father waited on his wife hand and foot, fixed her breakfast in the morning, lunch at noon, and supper at night, and listened in patient silence while she bitched about what a lousy cook he was. When she took to her bed with unexplained illnesses, he helped her in and out of the tub, lifting her up when she refused to help herself and became dead weight in his arms. He died when Jane was a freshman in high school, one year after she started having her period and growing hair in her crotch that scared her to death because she didn't know grown women had hair down there; nobody had told her. It was amazing what a girl didn't get told in a small rural town, especially if you were prettier than other girls so that they didn't take you into their groups and none of them tells you what it means when you start to bleed into your panties, and your mother's a silly old bitch who wouldn't tell you anything if you asked her because she could not bear to say words like "vagina" or "period."

Jane's mother lay in bed with a damp cloth over her eyes on hot afternoons because she claimed she couldn't bear the light, even with the shades drawn. Her husband read to her at night, cheap romances out of pulp magazines and *True Confessions* and movie magazines, trash a lady wasn't supposed to know anything about, but in the secrecy of their home in the country, Jane's father read the pornography of the lower classes out loud, and his wife mocked him and smirked and said, "It's a good thing I never knew a man like that. I never would have married you." She always believed—and said to anybody who would listen or to Jane who had to listen—that she had missed her fate when some handsome cavalier or rich banker didn't carry her off on horseback. "Daddy stayed with her because of me," Jane told herself defiantly, knowing that her father had loved her and deciding that he had put up with her mother only because of her—Jane, his child.

When her father died, Jane began to have murderous fantasies about her mother. She thought that if she had engineered some plan to kill her, she might have prolonged her father's life. Pushed her down the stairs, maybe. Smothered her with a pillow. He might have lived.

Her father had come home shell-shocked after the World War, and he'd been gassed. The gas left him with bad lungs. He coughed up blood when he had coughing fits. His wife was the one who claimed to be sick all the time. He loved her and petted her and killed himself taking care of her.

He had written his fiancée steadily during the war and while he was in the hospital in France after he was gassed. Jane still had his letters, the sad, passionate ones he wrote from the front when he was fighting and the happy ones he wrote in the hospital when he knew he would come home alive. Sometimes he wrote in the open field in France, and several of the letters had rain spots on them. Jane read them soon after he died. Her mother was not interested in them. When she was a senior in high school, Jane read them for the last time and cried for three days. Afterwards she didn't look at them again, but it would have killed her to throw them away.

Her father made her mother up, constructed in those letters a fantasy of the faithful girl back home waiting for him, and he couldn't tell the difference—or maybe he refused to tell the difference—between what he made up and the mean bitch she was.

She did wait for him—Avery Taylor waited for her sweetheart, the wounded hero, and people in Bourbonville praised her because she was true to her man. The old photographs show how beautiful she was as a young girl. Yet Jane could look into that stylish face, the inflexible smile in the photos, and see a face as empty as a clean plate. It was a pretty emptiness, the cold, china prettiness of a Dresden figurine, stiff and posed and slick and hard. Jane thought her mother liked the drama of it, the town cooing over her when her fiancé came home wounded and gassed and so feeble he had to live on a government pension the rest of his life because he was too frail to hold any job except teaching English part-time at the high school. With his disability pension from the army he saved Boxwood. *Poor, foolish sweetheart,* Jane thought. He was sentenced to hard labor taking care of Jane's mother as soon as Jane was born. *She had an excuse to be in bed then,* Jane thought. *I guess she never let him fuck her again.*

Why did she marry him at all? The question would insert itself. Jane thought her mother was nothing at all except the fiancée of a war hero, and when she got her name and engagement picture in the paper and an editorial written by Ted Devlin, who edited the paper back then, there wasn't anything to do except marry the man she had waited for because otherwise she would be scorned by the town. *Lord God,* Jane thought. *They had me ten months after they tied the knot. He had to be the passionate one. I don't think she ever felt passion for anybody but herself, not in her whole greedy life. I wanted to ask her sometimes, "Mama, did you like to fuck Daddy?" That would have been a way to kill her. If I'd asked her a question like that, she would have had a stroke on the spot. Or maybe she would have gained strength by telling all her friends how ungrateful I was, how she had failed in raising her daughter, the filthy language I used.*

The only friends Avery Whitaker had were the members of Miss Ethyl's Bible class, women who gathered once a week to hear Miss Ethyl, graduate of the Moody Bible Institute in Chicago, Illinois, lead them through the Scofield Reference Bible and explain prophecy to them. Anybody could be a member of that group who looked up in the sky every morning expecting Jesus to descend with a shout and the trumpet of the archangel. *I don't ever expect to die, Jane. I think Jesus will come before I die and take me off to heaven with him. Oh Jane, I hope you keep yourself pure so you can go with me.*

When her mother suggested spending eternity with her, Jane thought that she would beg a merciful God to send her to hell.

Maybe Avery's treatment of her husband was revenge. Jane read books. She couldn't work *all* the time, and she shut herself off in her room upstairs in the back of her house and read books she bought at Matheny's bookstore in Knoxville or at Miller's Department Store, the only other place you could buy books in Knoxville when she was a girl. She read some books in the Bourbon County Library, but none of them had anything in them about Freud or sex or other dangerous topics. The library board was careful what it allowed into Bourbonville. She read enough to think that her mother felt herself forced into marriage and driven to take revenge on her father for shattering her fantasy that she might have married a rich, handsome man who would have taken her to Europe and introduced her to kings. Instead she lived in a ghostly mansion her husband had inherited from his family four miles out in the country from Bourbonville, and she was stuck there because she had given her beauty and her body to him and could not escape a decision she made without due consideration.

Jane never remembered anybody saying, "Your father is a handsome man." She remembered his frail arms when he held her in the rocking chair and sang to her when she was a little girl. He had to sing quietly because if he didn't, his wife would yell out of her bedroom, "Claud, I can't sleep when you make so much noise."

He was the sick one. He was the one who needed somebody to take care of him. When he died, her mother, dry-eyed and angry, said to her, "You're a silly girl for grieving so for him. People die. My father died. His father died, and so did his mother, and their father and mother before them. I will die. Then you'll be all alone. The way I feel, I'll die someday soon. Then where will you be, you naughty girl?"

Jane wanted to scream at her: "Die then. Please God, die, you old bitch. Die." But Avery Whitaker primped and went to church with her daughter in town and thought some rich and gallant man with a fine black mustache and an ivory-headed walking cane and a house on the Mediterranean coast would look at her ruby-red lips (painted with the brightest lipstick in a little cupid's mouth that did not match her own) and her dyed hair and her rouged cheeks and carry her off to the romance she had missed by the sacrifice of marrying her frail, heroic husband.

Jane could not go to college. Oh, she thought later, maybe she could have gone—waited on tables, worked afternoons in an office. She could type. But her mother was aghast at the idea. "If you go to college, who will take care of *me*?" They had the government pension. Jane finished high school, and she was pretty, and she had learned enough about the world to be hard and to take care of herself. She was good at figures, could do complicated arithmetic in her head. And it didn't hurt that her father was a war hero who had left a sickly widow who had to be taken care of. She got a job at the bank. The town thought she was owed a job at the bank—respectable work, clean surroundings, good hours, in touch with the leading citizens of Bourbonville, Tennessee, good Christian people. She worked as a teller for slave wages, and she worked as hard as any black man loading 850-pound iron wheels on boxcars at the Car Works.

Then there was J. Pauley Oliver, the wavy-haired president of the bank, over sixty years old, a craggy-faced, jovial man who wore three-piece suits nine months out of the year and in summer wore seersucker or pongee and smoked cheap cigars and wore gold-rimmed glasses and grabbed her one day in his office and gave her a slobbery kiss. It wasn't a kiss like any of the kisses she'd seen in the movies, dry and passionate and loving and coming at the climax of a long love affair where it seemed every moment that the lovers would be parted forever and ever, and when they kissed the first time, the movie was almost over, and you knew they would live happily ever after as soon as "The End" flashed on the screen and the music swelled. No, it was simple assault. Mr. Oliver grabbed her without preamble, without a word, and pulled her onto his lap and nearly choked her by sticking his cigar-reeking tongue down her throat.

She was startled and revolted. Here was the dirty old man of obscene jokes. But her mind worked like lightning. She didn't have any other chance of being something or getting something in life, and she wanted it all. Oliver was a fool, ugly with bad breath and yellow teeth from his cigars and the boisterous insincerity typical of businessmen in small towns who felt the weight of enforced joviality. People would not do business with a sourpuss. Oliver had lips that looked like sausages spoiled from being left too long in the sun. What did she care? She had something he wanted—a nubile young body. He had something she wanted—money, power, the ladder with a rung she could step on and climb. So she kissed the old fool back and even groaned a little to make him feel good. She went to the toilet afterwards and gargled with mouthwash she kept in her purse.

Why didn't he do more than kiss her? He was too old, she thought, his dick as wilted as a dandelion after the first frost. Maybe he was too modest to take his pants off. Maybe he was afraid she would give him a social disease. Maybe he thought that his wife would find out. He asked her once if she was a virgin, and she said she was. He braced himself and looked her in the eye for once. "My dear," he said in his hoarse old voice, "you need have no fear. I would never, never violate a virgin."

Jane thought he was relieved that he had an excuse to do nothing but kiss her and slip his brown-spotted hands under her bra and feel her tits, or run his hand up her stockinged thighs to the top. Always when she sat on his lap she was careful to spread her thighs in as large a welcome as she could muster.

He called her his "little doll" and "darlin' " and "Sweetie Pie." The old fool got all his terms of endearment out of *Collier's* and the *Saturday Evening Post* and the movies. Within six months Jane could twist him around her fingers—or her nipples—as if he'd been a chunk of yellow modeling clay. Jane had good tits, not a mole on them and nipples that stood up like rocks when Oliver put his fingers on them. She became the real boss in the bank, and people knew it. Oliver was almost relieved. He was tired of banking. He liked to walk up the street to the drugstore and smoke a cigar and talk to people. Did other people in the bank think she was Oliver's mistress? They made jokes. Men will always make jokes. But it was hard to see how such a thing could be possible—Jane so young, so pretty, and Oliver an old bag of a man with those gold-rimmed glasses and the soft look of a grandfather in cheap prints. Before the Depression, several banks had done business in Bourbonville. During the Depression only First Bourbon County survived. Mr. Oliver steered it safely through, and people respected him for it. He seemed the soul of integrity. "See Miss Whitaker," he said to people when they asked him a question. People could believe at first that he was doing a favor to the daughter of a war hero; then they could believe—and this was true—that Jane Whitaker was supremely confident, that she had a head like an adding machine, and that they could depend on her judgment and her word. She shared his reputation. "Pure granite," people called him. *His head may be granite, but his prick is wax,* Jane thought.

Then Kelly Parmalee entered the play. When the war came along, and all the young men went away, Kelly Parmalee was left, and he was not old. Just a little too old to go to war. He was good-looking, too. Everybody was busy. Motion everywhere. The war was almost thrilling when you thought back on it—although you couldn't admit such a thing without saying out loud with fervor that the war was terrible, too. All those boys killed. The attendance on the news. The fear. The telegrams. "We regret to inform you that . . ." Still, amid terrible times, there was excitement. Oak Ridge went up in what had been a lonely and isolated valley beyond the Clinch River, and when the shifts changed, the cars ran for miles along the two-lane highways and the gravel roads leading into the "project," the Clinton Engineering Works. Engineering for what? No one knew. The Car Works in Bourbonville put out iron and steel for the war effort and ran three shifts, sometimes seven days a week, and the cotton mill made cloth for khaki uniforms, and the post office was plastered with colored posters that shouted alarming messages: LOOSE LIPS SINK SHIPS. Men sat in uncomfortable chairs waiting a couple of hours on Saturdays to get a haircut, and the barbers worked until almost midnight.

A spirit of daring ran through the county, the kind of daring that comes when people feel all the old ties loosened before the prospect that life can be destroyed in a moment, not only that somebody you love may be killed in some distant place but that life was being reconstructed according to new patterns that nobody understood yet, and with everything uncertain and mysterious and the fragility of life visible in every news broadcast and every newspaper, why not break loose in every way you could?

Kelly Parmalee was attractive in his slick magazine-model style—and he was married to a woman who looked like the Wicked Witch in *Snow White.* The upshot was that a woman could look at Kelly Parmalee and read him to the bone—the feckless expression, the bondage to a wife who had inherited a store, the desperate look a vigorous man had when everything had gone wrong. He was nice to women, gallant in a slightly exaggerated way, and Jane felt sorry for him.

Kelly Parmalee was standing in front of his store one weekday morning smoking a cigarette when Jane walked by on an errand for the bank. He greeted her, spoke about the weather, inquired about her mother's health—which was of course bad. He commiserated with her. "It's a shame for a pretty thing like you to be locked up with an invalid mother, but I admire you for your loving care." He sounded completely sincere. Jane supposed he meant what he said while at the same time she knew it was a line thrown out, and if she took it, he'd try to reel her in. Why not? What did she have to lose? She paused, lit a cigarette, and smiled. "Oh, I can get out late at night when she's in bed asleep. She sleeps like a stone. She never knows when I'm gone. Sometimes I just get out and drive."

Kelly Parmalee glanced furtively behind himself to see if Sophia might be lurking behind the door, ready to pounce. When he spoke, he lowered his voice. "Well, my wife is a sound sleeper, too. You ought to stop by my house some night late and have a cup of tea. Or something stronger." He laughed, almost a ritual. If she put the cold shoulder on him, Kelly could say he was just kidding.

Mr. Oliver had felt her up this morning, and she was tired of being felt up and aroused and having nothing happen. So she said, "What time?"

Kelly Parmalee took a hard draw on his cigarette and looked at her sharply. "Are you serious?" he said.

"I am if you are," she said.

"What time would be convenient?" His voice was husky, and she smiled.

"Mama is dead to the world by ten," she said.

"Isn't that a coincidence," he said with a nervous, explosive laugh. "Mrs. Parmalee is also dead by ten o'clock. The only night she stays up late is Saturday."

"Shall we say ten-thirty?" Jane said, exhaling her smoke as she had seen Claudette Colbert do it.

"We shall say ten-thirty," he said with a laugh of triumph. He looked around, finishing his cigarette. "Are you serious about this?" he said.

"Yes," she said. "I am serious about this. Are you?"

"You come by and see," he said with a big grin. "I've always wanted to get to know you better."

"You can know me as much as you want," she said. That shook him up, and again he looked around with a birdlike fright, ready to fly away at any sign of the cat, as if he thought old men might be overhearing from the park benches where they sat in the sun, old men rushing to the pay telephone in the bus terminal to put in their nickel and call Sophia and say, "Kelly's getting ready to fuck somebody."

"Well, well," he said, and he spoke in a husky, confidential voice as if the sidewalk might have a microphone embedded in it. "Come around to the back door, will you? We wouldn't want the neighbors to get the wrong idea."

"The wrong idea," she said with as flirtatious a grin as she could muster. "Yes, they might think we were going to drink tea."

It was easy and sweet, too. Yes, Jane had a sweet memory of the whole affair. By ten-thirty at night Second Avenue was as dead as a tombstone, all the lights out except on a few porches, and Jane drove up in front of Kelly's house quietly, turned off the engine, got out quickly, and walked up the Parmalee driveway and around to the back of the house. Before she could tap on the back door, it opened, and there he was, and he took her into his arms and kissed her with his mouth open and passionate, and she opened her mouth to him, and when he pressed himself against her, she pressed back, and when he ran his hand up under her dress, up the backs of her thighs and over her bottom over her tight panties, she gasped. This was going to be "it," she knew—whatever "it" was. It was all over in five minutes. He used a rubber, and they did it on the kitchen floor, and she could smell the linoleum. She was wearing a skirt. He whipped it up as he laid her gently on the floor and pulled down her panties with her lifting up her bottom to let him ease them off, and he pulled his pants down and fumbled the rubber onto his prick, and bang! It was over, and to Jane it burned like hell.

They lay there for a few minutes, and he said, gasping, "God, that was good. God, God, God." Jane was still breathing hard, but she said, "It wasn't very good for me. Can you do it again?"

"Do it again?" he said. "Oh yes, yes! Just give me a minute."

She was sopping wet. He was as good as his word. In a minute or two he took off the rest of her clothes. She had to help him with the bra, and she said, "It's not fair if you keep all your clothes on." He laughed. He undressed clumsily. All their conversation went on in whispers, and the laugh was a whisper, too. The lights were out in the kitchen, but she could see his body dimly in the reflection of the yellow street lamps that glimmered outside. She could make out his white shape, and maybe, she thought afterwards, it was better that she had an impression of him and felt him rather than saw him in bright light because she didn't think she could bear those furtive eyes of his. He put on another rubber, and he did it again slower, and she came in a blast of excitement and joy and hugged him tight and had to fight with all her force against the desire to cry out. Upstairs Sophia snored like a water buffalo.

She liked it, despite the pain. Kelly had good hands, and after he had done it the second time, he used his hands on her, and she nearly went crazy with pleasure, and that heated him up again so that he did it a third time, and her body exploded. She did not know she could do anything like that. Her head jerked as if it might fly off her body, and she could not control it. He said, "Shhhh! Shhhh! Shhhh!" She lay there spent, breathing like a bellows, whispering, "My God! My God! My God!" He kept saying, "Shhhh! Shhhh! Shhhh!"

"How did you learn to do that?" she whispered. Without thinking he said, "Practice." He laughed, and she laughed, too.

"You'll have to teach me so I can do it to myself," she said.

"I'll give you all the practice you want," he said.

They lay there for a while, and they heard the great quiet of the town spread out all around them, not a silence exactly because a dog barked somewhere a long way off, and Sophia's snoring came to them from a distance, and down on the highway an occasional truck ground its way through Bourbonville, the engine low and sonorous and passing into emptiness. Behind it all, a deep and tranquil stillness.

"I've never done this before," she whispered. "I didn't know what I was missing."

That was when Kelly Parmalee grabbed her and hugged her and almost cried. "You mean you gave me your virginity?" It sounded funny to her when he said that, as if she had wrapped something up in a Christmas package and given it to him so that she did not have it anymore. All she could think of was that she had something now she had never dreamed she possessed, something more thrilling than her expectations, which, given her mother, had been so confused and even chaotic that they were scarcely expectations at all. Rather they were something vague hidden behind a mass of ignorance.

That was the way they began. It did not last long. Jane thought that was the way it was with men, with most of them. They want to sow their seed like dandelions and hope thousands of their kind will populate the world. Years later Jane saw a bumper sticker: GROW DOPE; PLANT A MAN. She laughed out loud. Kelly began to get nervous, and one night after they had done it on the kitchen floor four times, he told her that he thought they ought to lay off for a while. "I'm afraid somebody's going to notice your car parked out there night after night. People will recognize your car, you know. It wouldn't be good for either one of us. People might put two and two together," he said.

Putting two and two together was approximately the extent of Kelly's ability at arithmetic, Jane thought. She knew he was right. It would not do him any good to have rumors fly about a love affair with her. It would be catastrophic for her. You could do anything you wanted in Bourbonville in 1943, but if you got caught doing it and it became public, you might as well leave town or hang a red light over your front door and start charging a fee.

So she did not complain to Kelly Parmalee. If anybody had told Mr. Oliver that Jane was slipping over to Kelly Parmalee's home to be fucked on his kitchen floor while Mrs. Parmalee slept like an overripe watermelon upstairs in the connubial bed, her job would have been out the window like dishwater. Kelly always spoke gallantly to her afterwards on the street, stopped, lifted his hat, chatted in his warm and charming way about the weather or about harmless town gossip and how pretty she looked, and Jane played along and thought good thoughts when she saw him. *He is weak,* she said to herself. That was consolation enough for any loss she might have felt when he did not make love to her anymore.

Then Lloyd came home from the war with all the rest of them. It was 1946. Lloyd and Jane had gone to high school together, BCHS class of '39, and they worked on the school yearbook together and went to a couple of movies, and once Lloyd had given her a quick peck on the mouth when he walked her home after dark. He was shy with girls. Yes, actually shy. Walking a girl home in the 1930s was a big thing, an important first step in courtship. But nothing came of Lloyd's walking her home except that he did remember her, and when he was in the hospital in Italy, he wrote to her once, and she wrote him back. He did not write again. He was busy, he said later, busy trying to walk without a limp and busy then getting used to the idea that he would limp for the rest of his life.

He'd been such a good dancer. The Baptists didn't let the high school have dances, but there was a little country club at Martel, at a wretched little nine-hole golf course built in a rolling pasture up there, and Lloyd managed to get himself invited to parties where swing bands played, and when he went to the university after high school, he joined a fraternity. He danced like a professional, people said, bending and twirling to the music with an almost comic grace given his muscular size.

He was wounded by machine-gun fire in Italy in 1943, and after that he had to wear a brace on his knee, and he limped and sometimes walked with a cane. He needed the cane, but he also thought it made him look genteel and English, and it was very stylish. Once his wound healed, he started writing for *Stars and Stripes.* That was the army newspaper. He went crazy about writing. He and Red Eason had been friends in high school, and when they got home to Bourbonville and Ted Devlin was ready to retire, they bought the paper from him.

The first thing Lloyd did was to put eight hundred dollars into a Speed Graphic camera. He didn't need a Speed Graphic. He bought it because, like the cane, it made him look like someone uncommon in Bourbonville, someone apart, and by that time Lloyd thought he was something special, that he had outgrown the town but that he would use it as a runway whence to take to the air. It was almost funny to see Lloyd limping around town with that camera, taking pictures of people while he looked so serious and important, as if the town depended on him for the essential commodity of news and image that only he could deliver. People admired a lot of things about Lloyd, and he wrote well, a lot better than Red, and you had the feeling that Lloyd himself didn't know what he wanted, but whatever it was, it was something he didn't yet have. Once he said to Jane, "I have a future. I'm marked for greatness. Maybe I'm going to write the great American novel. Maybe something big is going to happen somewhere, and I'll be working for *Time* and I'll cover a war. Any time they think of the story from then on, they'll have to think of my story."

He could be so enthusiastic that she believed him. They got to going out together. Lloyd learned to drink in the army. That, too, was part of his image. He liked to drink, and he took her to clubs in Knoxville where they could drink and dance. They could not dance long, and he could not dance gracefully because of his leg. No grace to him, but a ton of grit. He insisted on dancing until the pain became unbearable.

The camera obsessed him more and more, and he bought photography magazines and studied the pictures, and he studied *Life* magazine as though it were the Bible. The photography magazines had pictures of naked women in them, and that's how he got Jane to pose for him. That and the booze. Lloyd gave her her first drink, another milestone in her life.

He was still living with his mother and father and his brother Ben and a sister named Candy. He and Red put every dime they had into the newspaper, and he couldn't afford a house. But he had the building where the newspaper was, and he and Jane would go to a picture show and walk back there and sit in the back on stacks of newsprint next to the presses, and they drank bourbon, and one thing led to another.

He showed her the photographs of nude women, and he said, "I need a model." She loved him by then; she wanted to help out. Besides, she liked it. She supposed she was perverse for liking it, but no matter. She liked it, posing for him, putting herself in positions she had never dreamed of, letting the camera stroke her with its single eye, feeling she had nothing to hide, hearing Lloyd's praise.

In Bourbonville, to talk about sex might be scandalous, and even if women mentioned it to one another, told about their husbands, asked advice, they had to lower their voices, giggle a little, look around to see if anybody was listening, and get through with the conversation as quickly as possible because it was about sex, and ladies didn't talk about sex for prolonged periods of time. When Jane had a chance to display herself, it was like cracking all the windows in the universe with a rock and letting the fresh air in, and she loved it.

After Lloyd photographed her, she looked at other women and thought how odd it was that they considered sex outrageous and dirty and covered it with clothes so that they might as well have been veiled Muslim females walking around one of those dirt-colored cities whose pictures you saw in *National Geographic,* exotic-looking places where you could almost feel the sun blast off the page and the women must be roasting under all those robes, covering their sex as if it were the Garden of Eden with angels standing on each side of the gate with flaming swords to keep men out. It was just sex, and it was great, Jane thought, and dogs did it in the public streets, and flies did it on windows, and she didn't know why people were so ashamed of it.

Lloyd was the romantic. Nobody quite understood that about him as well as Jane did. He loved romantic poetry, and sometimes he and Jane would sit back there on the newsprint under the bare bulbs on the end of wires dangling from the barnlike beams of the high ceiling of the pressroom, and Lloyd would read poetry to her—stuff she had never heard before in a county where the high school had never progressed beyond Longfellow and Tennyson and a little Poe and the general population believed Edgar Guest was the most perfect poet in the world. Lloyd read to her from Swinburne and Aiken and Wilde and Housman. He read with great feeling, almost too much feeling sometimes. His voice warbled, and she was tempted to laugh at his affectations, but she knew that wouldn't do.

It was not until the second round of photographs that Lloyd made love to her. He did not want to rush into things. That was part of the romance he wanted—a slow, loving introduction to sex that would be fitting in a romantic novel to be made into a movie where the music swelled to a crescendo of sweetness and, more than that, rightness, not righteousness, but the satisfaction of everything turning out exactly the way it should with the true lovers joining forever and ever after they had slowly and inevitably come to adore each other.

He had a little rubber pad that he slept on sometimes when he couldn't stand being cooped up in the house with his family anymore. He said he sometimes took the pad out to a field with a blanket and slept under the stars. They put the pad on the imposing stone and made love on it, with Lloyd absorbed in her as if she had been a blotter and he had been ink so they became one, and if they had been a big Rorschach test, anybody looking at it would have seen the most complete and blissful sexual passion that two human beings could have together. When they made love it was like dynamite blowing up a dam and afterwards like the sun on still water.

Lloyd told her they would have to make their own rules, that if they were going to be free people, convention had to be tossed out the window. That was one of his favorite expressions: "tossed out the window." His litany. All the Old World restrictions, customs, religion, lies, hypocrisy, deceits, posturing would be tossed out the window, and when he said the words, it was as though he had done it all single-handedly, changed the world, brought in a revolution in everything, and they were king and queen of a glorious kingdom of liberty.

Jane believed him when they made love, when her whole body bucked and humped and she cried out in uncontrollable pleasure that Lloyd made her have again and again so that he was always exhausted before she was completely satisfied, and she begged him to do her with his hands, and he did, and he said proudly, "I hope I can make you do that all your life."

Sometimes Lloyd wrote poetry for the paper. He signed his news stories, but he didn't sign the poetry. He told Jane it was his, some of it written for her, he said. It was mournful and sad, about lost love and people in old age remembering when they were young and strong and beautiful, and sometimes it was incomprehensible, and too often it rhymed. Jane knew that some people read it aloud and laughed at it, but they didn't dare laugh at Lloyd to his face even when the word got out around town that the poetry was his. He was a big man, tough and, since the war, unpredictable, and there was the example of Junior Millbank.

That's what Lloyd called him: Junior. His full name was Leonard Bulwer Millbank Jr., and his father, Leonard Bulwer Millbank Sr., owned the King Bourbon Hotel during the war, and early in 1952 he was convicted of income-tax evasion and sent off to Atlanta to serve a year and a day in the federal penitentiary down there. Lloyd wrote a scathing editorial about him. "Leonard Bulwer Millbank and his greed in time of war pose a problem for the editorial writer who would discuss his case objectively," Lloyd wrote:

Do these ponderous and pretentious names drag Leonard Bulwer Millbank down into a bottomless pit of ignominy whence he shall never rise except on that final day when he shall be summoned to appear before the Great Judge of the Universe and cast into the depths of hell that his heartless and cowardly greed so richly deserves? Or is this name merely the infallible manifestation of something rotten that, like all rotten things, eventually rises like scum to the top of the pool of humanity where it gives off a foul odor of decay until at last nature takes pity on the rest of us and dissolves it into dust that the wind blows away? Perhaps the high and mighty Mr. Millbank illustrates an astounding deviation in the laws of physics themselves, for it may be that he is both as heavy as the most traitorous villainy that has ever been perpetrated in our fair town and that he is also light-weight, stinking scum whose removal to the federal penitentiary in Atlanta will cleanse our nostrils of his presence. While some of the brave men who fought a war so Mr. Millbank could profit from their valor are dead in combat and are represented by gold stars in the windows of grieving homes and will never return, Mr. Millbank can expect to be back with us within a year and a day. Be it known, Mr. Millbank, that we shall be waiting for you with a welcome worthy of your infamous deeds.

While the rest of Bourbonville was reading Lloyd's editorial and laughing and nodding over it, maybe not understanding all the words but knowing full well the sense, Junior came storming down to the newspaper office to find Lloyd and, as he said, "to thrash him within an inch of his life." Lloyd was not there, and he was not to be found at his home, so Junior returned the next morning when the newspaper office was open and Lloyd sat at his desk smoking a cigar with his feet on the table, reading his own editorial and admiring it. He had his hat pushed back on his head, and he was wearing his double-breasted suit. In stormed Junior, a big man, as big as Lloyd, and looking in pretty good shape, although he had been 4-F during the war. He raged and demanded that Lloyd step outside. "We'll settle this thing before the whole town," Junior hollered.

"Aw, go on, Junior, I don't want to hurt you," Lloyd said. "Besides, I'm not mad at you. I feel sorry for you for being kept out of the army on account of your flat head."

"I didn't have a flat head. I had flat feet!" Junior shouted. He was very red-faced.

"Flat feet, flat head. One end of you was flat, and I'm sorry for that. Is your prick flat, too? Now run along and be a nice boy and don't be picking fights when it's not your style."

Junior hopped up and down, screaming that he wasn't going to go away until Lloyd gave him "satisfaction." A crowd gathered outside. Lloyd sat there, his feet propped up, puffing in unperturbed tranquillity at his cigar, and Junior was making so much noise that the men came out of the pressroom to see what was going on. Myrtle said, "Let me call the sheriff, Lloyd." Lloyd said, "Oh hell, I reckon I have to take care of it."

He swung his legs down and got up, looking a little weary and bored with the whole thing. He retained the lit cigar in his mouth, and he did not take off his hat. He did not even unbutton the coat of his double-breasted suit. Junior ran out the door ahead of him and threw his own coat onto the sidewalk and whirled around and put his fists up in the position of a boxer coming out of his corner to fight for the world's heavyweight championship. Lloyd limped out, puffing at the cigar, belted Junior in the mouth with a crushing right fist, and Junior went flying backwards and fell unconscious on the sidewalk and lay there still as a rock. Lloyd looked at him with an expression of faint curiosity, and he said to somebody, "Did I kill the son of a bitch?"

Just at that time Junior released a heavy groan, and people assured Lloyd that everything was all right. Lloyd spat and went back into the office and sat down and put his feet on the desk and kept reading the paper. "I found three typos on page three," he said to nobody in particular. "I'm going to give the little shit the job of reading proof. He's better at it than I am." The "little shit" was Charles Alexander, already working for Lloyd then—and adoring him.

That was Lloyd the poet, and people didn't think they should mock him for his verse. Jane did not understand some of it, but she didn't think she had to understand it to love Lloyd. She took it for granted that he was smarter than she was, and because she was a rural southern girl, she thought that was how she was supposed to feel about the man she loved. She was glad she felt that way because it seemed that now her life was going to be what a woman's life ought to be, and at the same time she and Lloyd were going to be free of all previous restraints—whatever that meant. She could not tell yet what it meant. She knew it would be good.

It occurred to her later that writers—even writers like Lloyd—think that because they write something or because they say something fervently, it is true or it will be true. "We make our own rules," Lloyd said when he photographed her on the imposing stone, and they were both naked, and he got her to put her body into all sorts of crazy positions, and they were laughing.

He talked, and Jane listened, and it was like listening to somebody dreaming or maybe trying to make sense out of the dreams you had last night when you can recall only a hum of words and people saying important things, but once day comes and you wake up, even with the dream a second ago in time, you can't quite make sense of it, and the thing dissolves like it was sugar, and the daylight clear water, so that the sugar makes it all sweet, but you can't distinguish the separate grains. When he talked to her, she could not distinguish the separate parts of meaning in what he was saying, but she'd lie back against him, both of them naked, sharing the bottle, passing it back and forth, sitting on the pad, and he would ramble on, and to her it was beautiful because it was uplifting. Not moral. No, she did not think it was moral, but it lifted her out of Bourbonville, out of Bourbon County, out of the bank and

Old Man Oliver and his pawing hands and his tongue that tasted like cheap cigars, and she thought Lloyd and she were something different, like birds who fly in the clouds and look far down at the hills and the rivers and the valleys wheeling below and feel in their quiet and rising and swooping naturally superior to the lazy, dull people who spend their lives keeping their feet on the ground.

Lloyd loved her, too. She was sure of that. She supposed he loved her for her body and because she listened to him read poetry and spin out his dreams. He said once, "I read Shakespeare, and I think, *I could do that*. It's in my power."

"Why don't you, then?" she said.

He said, "The time's not ripe. I'm still teaching myself." He was serious. He didn't laugh. She thought he believed that someday tourists would visit Bourbonville so they could see the place where Lloyd Brickman had been born, the place where he had edited a newspaper, the place where fame hit him like a blazing star falling to earth.

One night he said, "I think we ought to get married."

She said, "I think that's a good idea. Then we can fuck in bed."

"No," he said. "Then we can go out in the woods and fuck in the leaves, and if somebody sees us, it will be all right."

"As long as you don't make me lie down in poison ivy," she said.

They decided on it. Lloyd said he would run a brief story in the paper and that he would write a fulsome story of the engagement, emphasizing their churchgoing and their contribution to good works and their desire to bring up good Christian children who would be preachers and missionaries and never smoke or drink or use dirty language and to have all their children by having Lloyd beat his meat and Jane would use an eyedropper to pick up the sperm from a cup after he'd left the room and she would insert the eyedropper into her pussy so she could conceive children without the impurity sex caused even in married couples. "I'll write it all out like a medical story in the *Reader's Digest*," Lloyd said, howling with laughter, and Jane laughed, too, and they made love again, and Jane loved him, loved the taste of him, loved his smell, loved the laughter.

She thought she could tell him everything. He had caught her up in all his romantic fantasies. She was caught up in her fantasies about him. They had broken all the rules. They were Bohemians in Bourbonville. She thought she owed it to the kind of people they were to tell him about Kelly Parmalee. Maybe she was testing him, testing themselves, testing the myth they constructed naked in the pressroom late at night, drinking whiskey and fucking and talking about poetry with the smell of bourbon and newsprint and printer's ink and sperm in their nostrils like the scents of paradise, and all around them Bourbonville slept, rooted in the ordinary, walled in by convention, and peopled by men and women whose every waking moment seemed devoted to loud assurances that they would surrender life and property before they could admit that Bourbonville was less than perfection or that to be loved by all its upstanding, rules-keeping, unspeakably boring inhabitants was anything less than the summit of human aspiration. Maybe she wanted to confess, to get something off her chest, as people said.

She lay back against him one night, her long, naked legs outstretched and, as it happened, the bourbon bottle on the floor between her thighs, and she said, "Lloyd, if we're going to get married, I have to tell you something. You may not like it, but I owe it to you."

It was her fancy that Lloyd would take her in his arms, laugh, sympathize with her, even pity her because she was bored in the war, trapped in life by her mother and her incessant complaining. She hoped he would hold her and tell her that they would never mention the subject again, that it was all over and done with, buried in the sea of time, that it didn't matter because they loved each other, and he would probably tell her about women he had had in Italy, and that would hurt her a little, but he was choosing to marry her, not them, and it would be all right. They had each other now. Nothing else counted.

Lloyd did not see it that way.

She sat, leaning comfortably against him, her back against his bare chest, his hairy legs around her, with the brace and the awful scar on his shattered knee, the bourbon bottle between her legs, and she could feel him turn cold, worse than ice, because ice is dead and he was alive, flesh and blood and bone, turning cold. He didn't say a word. She could tell it was not going well, that his silence was like a sudden settling of still arctic air, as if the world were dying all around them and rigor mortis was setting in. As if to pump life back into her world, she talked faster and faster, trying to explain everything, bringing in her mother and father and in a colossal miscalculation bringing even Old Man Oliver in. When she mentioned Old Man Oliver, Lloyd finally spoke. He said, "Oliver? That old fool? You let him do those things to you?"

"What was I to do?" she said. She would not let herself cry. She knew things were going badly. She knew everything had changed.

"You could have said no," Lloyd said. "You could have slapped his stupid old face. You could have told his wife."

She could have done all those things. And she could have lost her job. And she could have been talked about all over town because Mr. Oliver would have told his wife what he wanted her to hear, and she would have told everybody in the beauty shop, and everybody would have believed her, and Jane would be out of a job with no one to help her in a town where gossip ran like a viper in a closet and bit when someone reached for something ordinary in the dark. She thought Lloyd would understand what she said, but when he barked at her, he made it all sound simple, and she could not say anything in reply.

She sat feeling like a prisoner in front of the judge, waiting for the sentence of death, knowing she could do nothing about it, that her case was ended, her fate decided, that it was a matter of waiting, letting time pass, and somebody else—Lloyd—would do everything to be done, and she had no choice. None at all.

Finally Lloyd pushed her aside. He started putting on his clothes. She was still lying there naked, and she said, "Lloyd?"

He didn't say anything. He put on his drawers and his undershirt. He put on his shirt. She felt him slipping away. She said, "Lloyd?"

"Get your clothes on," he said.

"Lloyd," she said, "I'm sorry. You and I didn't have . . . It was before . . ." She wanted to tell him that it was like she had been married and her husband had died, and now she was ready to marry again.

"Kelly Parmalee," Lloyd said in disgust. "Kelly Parmalee. While the rest of us were off at the war, you were rutting with Kelly Parmalee."

She was angry with him then. Her anger was the only thing that got her out of there. She was angry because he couldn't understand what it had been like. She was angry for what he had said, as if what she had done made her a slut and a whore, somebody who would have done it with the postman or a dog.

He had a roadster, and he drove her home. It had suicide doors, doors that opened into the wind. She thought she could open the door on her side and hurl herself onto the blacktop, and the door would hit her and kill her as she fell. But she was too angry for suicide. He drove fast up into her driveway and dropped her off without looking at her, without getting out of the car to open the door for her. While she sat there, waiting for him to be polite, he reached across her lap and wrenched the door handle down so the door opened, and she got out and slammed the door, and he sped down her driveway and out the gravel road to the blacktop, and she heard in the distance his tires screeching on the pavement.

A couple of months passed before he sent the photographs back. It was spring, 1952. Charles Alexander came into the bank one day with a thick manila envelope. "Lloyd asked me to give this to you and to nobody else," he said. Charles laughed. The boy had a nice, engaging laugh. "The way he swore me to give this to you made me think it must be money or something. He said I wasn't to let anybody else touch it. Pretty secret stuff." He laughed again. Jane said, "Oh yes, the accounts. I was expecting them."

"Well, good to see you," Charles said. He grinned again, open and innocent, and without warning Jane felt a rush of affection for him, or perhaps
not for him but for the more abstract quality of his innocence, an unspoiled
boy who had never been betrayed, and she wished she could go far back into
her memories to the time when she did not feel betrayed either and be as
sunny and kind as Charles Alexander was.

She knew Lloyd had sent her the photographs. She trusted him. She did
not open them. She took them home and burned them to ashes in her fireplace after looking to see that the negatives were there. The negatives burned
slowly. It was late at night, and her mother was asleep.

Afterwards Lloyd passed her on the street, limping, but moving rapidly.
He tipped his hat to her, said not a word, and hurried on. She hurried on,
too. They did not speak again. Later on Lloyd was drowned with the girl on
the lake. Jane resolved never to speak another private word about him. Since
her mother had died, she lived alone. In her mind Kelly Parmalee loomed up
as a sweet and gentle man who had never deceived her. Sometimes she
thought of speaking to him, telling him that she could love him, and that he
could come out to her place in the country and make love to her in a bed and
stay through the night and get back in plenty of time to be there when
Sophia woke up. But she did not. She could not be so forward. Then in
August he died.

Now she had Joseph Ignazio and the prospect of the mall. The more
Joseph Ignazio talked, the more she believed. She saw money pouring in on
her. She would drive a Cadillac, she thought. She would tell people what she
really thought of them. She would be free. For the first time in her life, she
would be truly free. It was all a matter of money.

She did not know that Lloyd had betrayed her even in death, that he had
not returned all the photographs, and that Charles Alexander knew that she
had a mole just above her pubic triangle or that her pubic hair was not as
dark and thick as that of the other women in Lloyd's pictures.

W_HEN_ Charles sat with Mr. Finewood, he felt surrounded by a protecting armor of epic deeds, the undeniable miracles that God did for those
who had faith in Him and lived their faith out every moment. Charles felt
uneasy talking like Bob Saddler, mentioning the Lord in every breath, wit-
nessing to strangers, telling the story of his own experiences with God,
assuring people that despite their cozy lives and happy days, they were
doomed to hell's everlasting fires unless they took Jesus as their "personal
savior." Here he was, Charles told himself, a hypocrite because he said he
believed in God and was going into the ministry, and he not only had dis-

graced himself with Marlene, he also did not trust God enough to identify himself in every moment as the devoted Christian he wanted to be. That is why God does not bless me, he thought. That is why I live in fear that none of it is true. And then his mother died. When she was gone, the house strangely and irrevocably empty of her presence, he held to God not only to assure himself of his own salvation but to trust in a world where he would see his mother again, and he would tell her the torments of all his doubts, and they would laugh together and never be divided again as long as eternity should endure.

Mr. Finewood was his salvation when Eugenia Alexander died. "God moves in mysterious ways," the preacher said in his solemn, weighty, and perplexed voice. "Believe me, Charles, I have agonized over God's purposes. Sometimes He does miracles. Just when we think He has abandoned the world and left it to the devil, He does something to let us know He is still here. My beloved wife died of cancer; so did your dear mother. I thought until the very end that God might heal both of them, bring them back from the brink of death and give them testimony to move the souls of multitudes. He chose not to do it. I don't know why. I know He had a purpose. But I don't know what it is.

"Just as I don't know why He saved a woman over in North Carolina, at my church over there. Her name was Dora Hammond. A beautiful woman. She was married to a wonderful Christian man named Jeremiah Hammond. A Christian couple with a house full of young children, all of the children under ten years old, and Dora was stricken with cancer. I'll never forget— Jerry weeping and Dora so peaceful when she got the news and trying to comfort her husband. She said she accepted the will of God, and she was ready to go.

"She wanted to die at home, just like your mother, Charles. But Jerry wanted to try one more treatment, one more operation. The doctors said it was hopeless, but he insisted. So she went to the hospital for surgery. I remember it well. She was to have the operation on a Monday morning at seven o'clock. So that Sunday night I spoke to my congregation, and I said, 'I want us to stay here tonight and pray for Dora Hammond. I want us to pray until we get the assurance one way or another that God has heard our prayers. It may be God's will that Dora die; but God can do miracles, and He has promised us that anything we ask in His name will be granted.'

"Oh, Charles, we prayed! How we prayed. We got down on our knees in that church, and we implored God for His mercy. We pleaded with Him to give us a sign as He gave Gideon the sign of the fleece. Hour after hour we prayed, one at a time, taking turns until we came all the way back to me. I began the prayers, you know, and I prayed again, and we went around the whole church once more, and it came back to me the third time. It happened that just when I started to pray for my third time, the clocks out in the town began to strike three. I was on my knees, and I heard them, and Charles, suddenly I had assurance. O blessed assurance! I started to pray, and my mouth was stopped. I stood up. I said, 'Brothers and sisters, she is going to be all right. We can go home. Dora Hammond is going to be all right.'

"Well, people got up. Some of them were really tired, and all of them looked doubtful. Why shouldn't they have been doubtful? I'd just announced that a miracle would take place, and they looked at me like I was crazy. That's the strange thing about us Christians, Charles. Sometimes we pray our hearts out, but we don't really believe that God will answer our prayers, do a miracle. Rosy remembers, don't you, Rosy? It was such a moment. I'll never forget it."

"What happened?" Charles said.

"What happened?" Mr. Finewood said, laughing in wonder and shaking his head as if the wonder had risen again before them out of the sweet haze of the moment when the world was suspended between daylight and dark.

"What happened?" the preacher said again. "I'll tell you what happened, Charles. I went home and went to bed. I was worn out. You know, it was as if something had been all balled up inside me, some power that God had put there, and it was gone, and I was like a car battery that has held the lights on all night long, and when daylight came, I was discharged and dead, and I wanted to sleep.

"Well, I was asleep as soon as my head hit the pillow, one of those deep and dreamless sleeps like the Christmas carol talks about. I was dead to the world, caught up in heaven, I guess. I think sometimes that happens to us; we sleep, and what we think are dreams is the soul caught up into heaven, and when we don't dream our bodies are gathering the heavenly energy that God has up there to give us. Anyway, I heard a knocking at my door. A real pounding. Enough to wake the dead. I heard a voice shouting at me from what seemed a long way off 'Preacher! Preacher!' the voice shouted. It took me a minute or two or maybe more to wake up and realize that was Jerry Hammond shouting at me to wake up.

"I went to the door. It was just after seven-thirty in the morning. Jerry's face was lighted up like those pictures I've seen of Times Square in New York City. And do you know what he told me?"

"What?" Charles was so rapt he could hardly breathe.

"He told me he had been sitting up with Dora, sitting by her bed, and she was doped up, and she was sleeping and breathing real shallow, you know, so weak she couldn't breathe deep. Just little breaths, like panting. Jerry said he dropped off to sleep himself. Poor soul, sitting up with Dora night after night. He was exhausted. Well, he said he didn't know how long he slept, but he woke up, and he sat there in the dark, you know, and he said he noticed something was different. He sat there wondering what it was, and then it hit him like a ton of bricks. Dora wasn't panting for breath. She wasn't gasping. She was breathing deep, healthy breaths like she was in no pain at all, and he spoke to her. He said, 'Dora?'

"And she said, 'Darling, I woke up at three o'clock. I heard the clocks striking. And, I feel better, darling. I feel that something has happened.'

"Well, Jerry turned on the lights in the room, and he looked at her, and Charles, the color was back in her skin. She was still terribly thin, but she looked different. She looked not well, but she looked *better.* Jerry, he told me it almost scared him. It was something he didn't expect, didn't dream about, and he didn't know how to act or what to do. So he went running down the hall to the nurses' station and asked the nurse on duty to come back with him, and she did, and she was amazed. So amazed she was scared, too. She took Dora's pulse and her blood pressure and her temperature and all those things, and she didn't say a word. She went flying back to the telephone down at her desk, and she called Dora's doctor. Got him out of bed, and Jerry could hear her yelling at him into the telephone, telling the doctor he had to get right over there to see Mrs. Hammond. The doctor was giving her an argument, telling her, he said later on, that if she was dying it might be the best thing and he sure couldn't come running across town to see a dying woman when there was nothing he could do and probably nothing that he should do but let her die.

"But then Jerry heard the nurse yell, 'Doctor, you don't *understand.* She's *well.* She looks *wonderful.* I think she's *cured.*' Well, that brought the doctor driving through the town like a fire truck. He had pulled his pants on over his pajamas, and he didn't have any shirt on except his pajama top, and he was wearing shoes without socks when he came into the room and started examining Dora Hammond. What more can I say, Charles? She was cured. The cancer was gone. They examined her and examined her and examined her, and they couldn't find even a spot of cancer anywhere. She started gaining weight again, and you can go right over to Charlotte, North Carolina, today and find her walking around and praising the Lord."

Why didn't God save his mother? Why did He not do a miracle for the best human being Charles had ever known?

Mr. Finewood did not wait for the question to be asked. "Someday, Charles, when we all get to heaven, God will show us everything that has ever happened to us, everything He has ever done. We see a thread here, a thread there, and we don't understand, but when we get to heaven, we'll understand why God has spoken, and we will understand why He has been silent."

Charles imagined himself becoming a missionary or a preacher like Billy Graham, moving thousands of people to the gospel that he would believe with all his heart, and because he believed, his voice would cut like a blade of fire through the ice of resistance that people threw up against God. People would flock to him, certifying his faith by their adhesion to it, and he would tell in sermons, "When I was young, my mother died of cancer, and I was in the university in Knoxville, and I ran into the usual intellectual doubts that young Christians sometimes have. I was tempted to doubt that God even existed. But we had a wonderful minister at the Midway Baptist Church. His name was Clifford Finewood, and he taught me a lesson I've never forgotten. It was a lesson that kept me in the ministry, that made me a preacher. The lesson is that God is not what we say about Him or what we think about Him; God is what He does for us. God is an unmistakable presence in our lives." Perhaps there would be one miracle for Charles like the miracle done for Dora Hammond. One miracle, he thought, and he would never doubt again.

In the peaceful assurance of Mr. Finewood's deep pool of warm and comforting words, Charles's mind flew to Palestine, to Jerusalem within the Judean hills, and Jesus in a robe walking with disciples gathered from hither and yon through fields of grain, a gentle presence, speaking quietly, looking on the people with love, doing miracles that startled the whole region but then dying naked in the hot sun with the flies swarming in the wounds of his hands and his feet and worst of all the shit and the piss running down the wooden stem of the cross, the victim of crucifixion unable to control his bowels or his bladder even in the public gaze directed on him by the curious and jeering multitude. INRI.

How could any of those men and women who had followed him believe that this tortured and dying and finally dead body, reduced by its suffering, could ever live again? He had read W. T. Stace, and his faith collapsed like a castle made of dust. Those people saw a bloody and stinking crucifixion, and they drifted back to their homes or to the open fields where some of them slept, and they lay down in despair. Everything exists for no reason, and if everything were different there would be no reason for that either.

But then . . .

In Matheny's bookstore in Knoxville he found the Modern Library edition of Pascal's *Thoughts*. Pascal asked how the disciples of Jesus could have done what they did, carried the gospel, unless they had seen the resurrection.

But what happened to the disciples? Most of them disappeared. Paul never saw Jesus. Peter kept on. He was a fisherman. He had a wife. A better living being a prophet of a risen god than a fisherman. Peter's brother was

Andrew. What happened to him? He was bringing people to Jesus every time he was mentioned in the Bible. Then he vanished. The Book of Acts does not mention him. Why? Maybe he discovered his brother Peter was a liar, that Jesus stayed dead, did not rise from the dead. Charles chased names through the Bible, using *Strong's Exhaustive Concordance*. He felt foolish while he was doing it—looking for God the way a physicist searched for a missing element or as astronomers had sought the dark planet Pluto, noting the eccentric motions of Neptune and Uranus. Yet for all its foolishness, it was a desperate silent quest, and Charles drove himself to it and did not admit it to a soul. What would he have said? "Yes, I preach anytime anyone invites me, and I'm going to seminary, and I'm going to be a pastor, an evangelist, or a missionary, and I swear that I will die for Jesus in a savage land if that's what God wants me to do. But before I get really started on my divine mission, I want to be sure there's a divinity around to make it all worthwhile. Besides that, I am terrified of death, and when a man put a pistol to my head and cocked it so that I believed I was on the point of death, I did not say, 'Lord Jesus, receive my spirit,' but I wept and begged for my life. He gave it to me; I should have lied for him. I should have by that lie renounced God and hope, all hope." No, he could not have said any of those things, not in Bourbon County, not in 1953.

*A*RCENEAUX was furious with Charles Alexander for telling Mr. Finewood about their conversation. He did not seek Charles, and Charles did not seek him out either. All Arceneaux knew was that Charles had betrayed him.

"Well," Arceneaux said to himself, "I couldn't tell the little bastard not to tell what I had said. That would have seemed cowardly, unmanly."

Arceneaux cared about manliness. Manliness had been the chief aim of his life once he discovered he was queer and began to hate himself. If he could be manly enough, nobody would suspect. You didn't sit with your legs close together as though someone were about to look up your dress. You didn't make mincing, head-tossing gestures with your eyes shut like a silly woman. You didn't do anything effeminate. You made broad, brusque gestures. You sprawled when you sat. You hid what you were.

He dreamed at night of Charles—chaotic, erotic dreams that woke him up in a sweat even after the hot weather broke and the cool nights of early autumn came on. He lay abed disgusted with himself and wanted a drink. He could not start drinking. Not again. That would be death to everything, and he could not do it. He prayed. "Why did you make me like this?" Saint Jerome studied Hebrew to put down sexual desire. Always pictured in the desert near a peaceful lion, with a book open in front of him. The lion was a symbol of stilled and dangerous passions. The book calmed them. Jerome with his anachronistic cardinal's hat. Dead a long time, Arceneaux thought. Centuries gone. No more lust in the grave or in paradise. In paradise our bodies and all their impurities disappeared, Arceneaux thought. Our souls were absorbed into pure light.

Arceneaux sat at his large kitchen table late at night, under the bright ceiling light, his Brown, Driver, and Briggs lexicon spread out next to his open Torah, edited by Rudolph Kittel. And sometimes he used the *Analytical Hebrew and Chaldee Lexicon* done by A. B. Davidson. He felt that was cheating, but it helped to go right to a difficult form. Hebrew did take his mind off sex. He studied Greek, too, but Greek was easier than any other language he had studied. He preached many sermons about words, explaining the Bible to his congregation like a teacher preparing them for an examination, and his people listened patiently and even sometimes with interest when he told them things they had never dreamed of finding in a text. But they were becoming more and more discontented. "Why doesn't he preach the good old Baptist gospel?" They noticed that he rarely preached against specific sins.

How good gin on cracked ice would taste on a warm night! The thought came to him like the memory of shade trees to an explorer in Antarctica.

Maybe if he pitched a good drunk the church would fire him, and he could admit to himself that his decision to become a preacher was crazy from the beginning and get on with his life. Getting on with his life would mean going back to the sugar plantation in Louisiana. He could imagine the shout of joy his father would deliver at that decision.

His father's letters of dignified pleading piled up on Arceneaux's desk in his study—the almost European handwriting, the beautiful paper, the coal-black ink. He seldom read one of them all the way through. They all said the same thing. The ministry was a fine vocation, but it was not for him. God had given the family land to husband and people to work on the land who needed the care of a strong and just proprietor, and the Arceneaux family needed an heir. He should think of getting married. Many fine girls about. True, Karen de Vitry had grown tired of waiting for him, and she had married someone the elder Arceneaux didn't like very much, but Arceneaux could almost see the yearning and the envy glow in the words his father wrote to inform him that Karen had given birth to a fine healthy son.

Arceneaux had become a minister for so many reasons that his head buzzed when he tried to work them out and decide which was the most important. One was to court God's favor. If he could not stop being a queer, he could at least be a martyr, denying himself like a medieval monk or Saint Jerome himself to carry the message of God's enduring love to the world and hoping that in his preaching he could convince himself that God loved him for renouncing what he was. He wanted to help people, too. If you helped enough people, God would forgive you for being a queer—especially if you didn't murder anybody else and never, never, never practiced sex.

The ministry was perhaps the only profession that would not strike his father as betrayal pure and simple. The Arceneauxs were an old French Huguenot family, driven out of France by the revocation of the Edict of Nantes, keeping their lineage defined through a period of exile in England and then in their settlement in Louisiana after Jefferson had bought it for the United States. Besides the pursuit of wealth and land, the Arceneauxs generation by generation were ruled by a fierce, vengeful anger towards the Roman Catholic Church which had dispossessed them and been responsible for the horrible deaths of both male and female members of the family. One Arceneaux had been broken on the wheel. Such was the black legend preserved and recounted whenever Arceneauxs retailed their family history, the anger rekindling itself with each telling of the tale.

They established themselves with authority in Louisiana, and the family tombs in the sprawling cemetery in Metairie testified in statuary and in epitaph the weight of a tradition that made the dead partners with the living over generations of time. A statue of Admiral Coligny, replica of the one on the rue de Rivoli, and an inscription commemorating the Saint Bartholomew's Day Massacre stood gallantly at the entry to the Arceneaux vault, the vault itself enclosed with a delicately wrought iron fence whose fleur-de-lis ornamentation was pictured in many of the guidebooks to the city. Arceneaux himself reflected from time to time on the contradictions here—the family memory of a France with one king, one law, one faith, and the memory, also, of how that France had massacred the Huguenots whence the Arceneauxs had sprung. No accounting for the accidents of history, he supposed, and besides that, his ancestry was of little interest to him.

They became Baptists in Louisiana for the simple reason that Baptists, of all the American sects, were the most furiously anti-Catholic, the most likely to tell lurid tales about Catholics from the pulpit, and the most aggressive in a missionary enterprise that sought to win Catholics away from their old and idolatrous faith. Besides that, the First Baptist Church of New Orleans was similar to the First Baptist churches in most large Southern towns—except that it was in New Orleans, and everything merely exaggerated in other Southern cities was hyperbole in New Orleans. It was a stylish church, built in the generally gloomy Gothic of the nineteenth century and attended by ladies and gentlemen who dressed up to go to services and who expected from their minister both erudition and decorum. The pews were ornately carved and comfortably cushioned with red plush.

At the First Baptist Church of New Orleans preachers did not rant and did not deliver embarrassing "altar calls" in which sinners were exhorted to come forward and repent of their sins before they were overcome by the raging fires and eternal thirst of hell. Indeed, hell was seldom mentioned at any First Baptist church, except during an occasional "revival" when some young and enthusiastic evangelist preached on hell with the fervor expected in schoolboys but also with a bit of nostalgia, as if an old photo album had been taken out of a trunk to be studied as a reminder of a family's heritage and then put back again when the revival was over.

Southern Baptists who attended the "First Baptist Church" in a city like New Orleans loved nostalgia, especially in the rollicking hymns congregations belted out with an enthusiasm that might almost make you think they believed them until you considered that no congregation of carefully tailored and perfumed middle-class people could take very literally words such as "There is power, power, wonder-working power in the blood of the Lamb; there is power, power, wonder-working power in the precious blood of the Lamb." If anybody had sacrificed a lamb in the carefully engineered American Gothic confines of First Baptist in New Orleans, he would not have been invited back. All First Baptists would have refused invitations to a crucifixion. They would have gagged at the newsreel, too.

That was the church where the Arceneauxs went when they were in town. In the summer they were more likely to be down on the plantation. A small Baptist church reposed on one corner of the place, and the elder Arceneaux financed a young minister there, and they dutifully attended. It was a good place to start a preaching career, and Lawrence Castillon Arceneaux Sr. exercised a careful veto power over the congregation's right to choose their own minister. No fanatics. No ranters. No one who preached gory sermons about hell and judgment. No vulgar displays of emotion.

When the Arceneaux family attended this little church during plantation season, both Arceneaux and his father wore linen suits with neckties, often the only neckties in the little frame building except the one worn by the preacher. "They expect us to dress up," the elder Arceneaux said. "We cannot disappoint them." He was not above inviting the minister over to Sunday dinner to give him a searching critique of everything the poor man had said and the way he had said it. True to his Huguenot forebears, Arceneaux's father beamed whenever the minister spoke in reasoned disgust about any practice of the Catholic Church or any pronouncement from the bishop of New Orleans.

Arceneaux recalled, from when he was a teenager, an especially vigorous sermon of shame and condemnation of the pope blessing Italian soldiers on their way to kill Ethiopians in Mussolini's only successful war. The elder

Arceneaux gave the young minister a raise afterwards, although it was during the Great Depression when the plantation was going through hard times.

The Arceneauxs had a certain place in the world, and when Larry graduated with highest honors from Tulane and went off to war and joined military intelligence and thence was taken into the OSS by Allen Dulles, it continued a family tradition. Military valor—an ancestor had been with Beauregard all the way through "the War." Civic leadership. Ethical probity. Religious devotion. No doubt about it. The Arceneauxs were aristocrats in an American democratic tradition, and Larry Arceneaux was to the manner born, and people nodded approvingly whenever his name came up, and they approved especially his becoming modesty, his refusal to give newspaper interviews, and his near-disdain for the medals that, according to the papers, he had won for his service.

Larry Arceneaux's major problem was that he was queer. He had other problems as well, including a belief that he had committed murder. But since he had committed the murder because he was a queer, the larger problem subsumed the smaller ones into itself.

So he came home from the war, and memory obsessed him like a motion picture he was condemned to sit through again and again and again, unable to get out of the stale, dark air of the theatre, the reek of smoke and the stench of other human bodies and the misery of his condition, condemned to see himself committing murder again and again and again until it seemed that he had committed a thousand murders and that the universe was an accusing finger pointing at him and screaming his shame to every soul in creation.

Arceneaux never disbelieved in God. He marveled when he ran into the hard, bleak atheism of others. He supposed that some people were religious and some not, and that there was no fathoming the difference. His God was far from the thunderer of the Old Testament, and he did not take the miracles of the New Testament literally, not even the Resurrection of Jesus. In Arceneaux's mind the Jesus of the Gospels was a sort of human lens through which all the divinity of the universe was concentrated as a very bright light that to be seen in all its clarity was to be adored. The light had the power to purify, and Arceneaux craved purity more than he desired anything else on earth. He didn't think much about God raising the dead in general or him in particular. He supposed there was something after death, a timeless light, a dreamy contemplation of something beyond things. In that state he would have no body, and he would not be a queer. To be a queer, you had to have a body.

When he considered the matter, he thought that his conviction that God existed might have come from his equal conviction that he himself was wicked almost beyond redemption and that God's searching eye had judged him with an intense and immaculate light that, though cool and impalpable, was enough to burn every cell in his body to ashes.

But Arceneaux had a body, and it tormented him. When he came home from the war, he had no energy and no desire. He sat hour after hour sipping gin on cracked ice in their house in the Garden District of New Orleans. His father frowned on spirits, although he accepted with alacrity Paul's counsel that it was fine to take a little wine for the stomach's sake. That meant wine with every meal except breakfast. Arceneaux discovered spirits in the war, and he found that he had a taste for them. Now he indulged his taste, and his father made glum, oblique comments about "your health" and "exercise." In the war Arceneaux's body had been as hard as a marble statue and yet as flexible as string. From the first obstacle course he ran in basic training all the way through to Nuremberg, Arceneaux excelled in the physical. Now he grew flabby, and his complexion went white.

To his mother he could do no wrong. When his father commented with acerbic discretion that spirits had been the ruin of many a man, Marie-Therese Arceneaux said that wars were always hard on young men and that if the gin helped him relax, it was a good thing. She had never drunk anything stronger than wine herself, never tasted gin, and had been shielded from drunks all her life, and Arceneaux thought that she lived in never-never land. But he was grateful for her love and her tolerance, and he sat in a hammock in the garden under two great live oak trees dripping with Spanish moss, and he felt spring surge through New Orleans. It was March 1947. He had been home from the war a month, after finishing his last job—interrogating Germans at Nuremberg. He had seen Goering's bloated body after this fat colossus, once able to fly an airplane weighing hardly more than paper, had cheated the gallows with cyanide.

His mother prattled on about the people asking about him and the parties she would have when he felt like having parties, and his father asked regularly if he was ready to go with him out to the sugar plantation and saddle a horse and ride the land, survey the crop. Arceneaux usually begged off. Now and then he did ride with his father, drinking in the green land, smelling the marshy air, following with his eyes the herons and the seagulls and the pileated woodpeckers and absorbing the dense and familiar woodlands bordering the cane fields and the river. The senior Arceneaux engaged his son in a man-to-man talk, told him it was time to marry, time to have children, time to prepare heirs to take over the land in days to come. Larry was almost rude to his father. "No, no, not yet. Not yet," he said impatiently, and his father nodded in grave and correct blankness and could not understand.

His father and mother had already picked out a prospective wife—Karen de Vitry. She was a tallish, blond woman, pretty enough, her face a little too long, her jaw a bit too broad, but not unattractive at all. She inherited her hair and perhaps her mechanical voice and her fixed smile from her mother, Nancy, the daughter of a Rhode Island merchant and factor. Nancy had met Beau de Vitry when she came to Sophie Newcombe to go to college, having heard that it was a great place to meet rich Southern men. Sure enough, she met Beau, who took his father's fortune and added to it and inherited one of the largest houses in the Garden District with its prodigious live oaks and its beautiful fences and splendid verandahs. Karen went to Sophie Newcombe, too, and since Larry went to Tulane and had to invite somebody to dances, he invited her, and a certain expectation thickened. The war was a relief. When Larry went off to it he supposed that Karen would meet someone else and write him a Dear John which, in whatever danger he found himself, would cause him infinite rejoicing.

Her heart, however, was unfortunately true. She, or more properly her father and mother, saw how the Arceneaux plantation prospered during the war, and there she was when Arceneaux came home, still in the full flower of such beauty as she possessed and waiting romantically for him. She had now taken an M.A. in English literature and emerged certain of her ability to conduct superior conversations and sure also that she would become the greatest New Orleans woman writer since Kate Chopin. The de Vitrys called to welcome him home. Karen set in on telling him about the collection of short stories she was writing, and Arceneaux drank himself almost coma-tose as an anesthetic against what he now saw as her monotonous artificiality and criminal innocence.

He had grown up in the Southern gentleman's tradition of making small talk with women on almost any subject, civility as much a part of him as the calcium in his bones. He listened with elaborately feigned interest to her mechanical voice, scarcely hearing what she said. His muttering of assent to her discourses on writing were such that everyone, especially Karen, seemed to think that as soon as Larry got over the war he would ask her to marry him, the engagement would be announced, and a wheel of social events would start turning that would be remembered as the juggernaut of all wed-dings in the century.

Perhaps that was all the more reason Larry Arceneaux sat in his garden and sipped gin on cracked ice and looked up into the live oaks, and the live oaks and the Spanish moss hanging in the branches seemed to possess some meaning, some writing in a foreign script drawn against the scroll of the sky, arcane and mysterious, that he might translate if he contemplated it long enough and sipped enough gin on cracked ice.

He woke up with headaches and nausea. Sometimes the nausea struck him in the middle of the night, and he rushed to the bathroom adjoining his bedroom and vomited, and sometimes he had diarrhea so that it was as if somebody had put a high-pressure hose down his gullet, the hose attached to a pump in a sewer, and turned it on so that the foul liquid stuff gushed out his rear end in a stream. Sick in the head and the guts and too dizzy to stand, he resolved never to take another drink, but by mid-morning he would crave not alcohol but the state of nonthinking that alcohol induced. He went out into the garden with a pitcher of gin poured over cracked ice, and sat sipping, wrapped in a pleasant lethargy as though floating on his back in a warm and supporting sea, comforted by the assurance that now that he was in New Orleans among civilized people again he could never run out of gin.

He thought that he might marry Karen, hire somebody to fuck her, and listen to her talk about literature and her writing for the rest of his life, happy in the conviction that he never had to make any response. He could imagine a worse life. Maybe he could do it. There was that girl back in 1938, his first trip to Europe on the *Ile de France*. He had managed to relieve her of her virginity and himself of his own, and it hadn't killed him. It had given him no pleasure other than the chivalrous sense of duty accomplished that he felt in consummating her shipboard romance, giving her something to remember as she journeyed to England to marry a fiancé waiting for her. Yes, it was possible. Imagine you had a man in bed with you, and you could fuck a woman. All cats look gray in the dark. So Sancho Panza.

Even his mother gradually became alarmed. She and his father conferred. In the quiet, reserved alarm of upper-class people, they were unwilling to admit that their only child had returned from the war a drunkard. They coaxed him to go to church, saying that their friends all wanted to greet him but secretly thinking that if they could get him back into old habits, all the panoply of his life before the war would return, including the sobriety and discipline that had been much admired by others. "Larry is going places," people used to say. They did not anticipate that one of the places would be the war, and no one knew he was queer, and some now thought that he might go to one of the hospitals for drunks like the one up at Byhalia, Mississippi. You called a place like that a "sanitarium." They were always far enough away to avert the worst kinds of gossip.

Arceneaux wanted to please his parents. He loved them and he put himself in their place, imagined what it was to have hope shipwrecked on a drunken son, imagined the humiliation they would feel to know that he liked men better than he liked women, imagined the horror and grief that would overcome them, and he made himself so miserable that the only thing he could do was drink the misery away. They wanted him to go to church. Their pleading eyes! A soft, heartfelt desire, full of love and bafflement.

So one Sunday morning he got up early and sipped vodka instead of gin over cracked ice and dressed up in a seersucker suit, poured another tumblerful of vodka, drank it hastily, and went with his mother and father to church. Just like Norman Rockwell, he thought. He had fought a whole goddamned war for Norman Rockwell, and he might as well pay his debts.

Clean, immaculately dressed people pushed to shake hands with him before the service, to welcome him, to tell him how good he looked, to ask how it felt to be home, and he told them it felt good to be home, and he told them they looked good too. In truth, they all looked as if they'd scanned the latest fashion magazines, bought the latest styles to blend in with all the other respectable people in church and among those same respectable people at lunch afterwards at the country club. Everybody smelled aggressively nice. People reeked of soap and toilet water and hair pomade and cleanliness, the women of perfume, the men of shaving lotion. Once on a beach in southern France Arceneaux had shaved in the sea. Like sandpapering his face.

The Arceneauxs sat in the pew directly behind the de Vitrys, Beau and Nancy and Karen and Karen's sister, Katherine, and they all turned and greeted him as if he were the visiting ambassador from the Court of St. James. Beau's handshake was in the manly Southern style that includes an effort to fuse the knuckles of the other man unless that man grips as hard as he is gripped. The women did not shake hands. Women were not supposed to shake hands with men other than their preachers and the business associates of their husbands. They merely greeted Arceneaux with gasps and exclamations of joy at the surprise and pleasure of seeing him, and Nancy de Vitry, whose hair gleamed chemically blond, seemed so rapt that she might have passed into a mystical trance on the spot had any of these emotions been real.

When the service began, the choir director welcomed Lawrence Castillon Arceneaux Jr. by all his names from the platform and announced that in his honor and in honor of all the other veterans in the congregation, the hymn would be "Onward, Christian Soldiers." The organ roared. Bodies rumbled as people stood up and opened their hymnals. Men and women and little children seemed to outdo themselves in singing as loud as they could as if to honor him by enthusiastic volume. They looked at him admiringly to see how he was taking this overflow of honor and joy. Their voices and their glances came on him in waves, almost like waves of heat, although by that time the church was air-conditioned, and it was like a department store inside, cool and relaxing so the customers could come in to linger over God and choose whatever divine bauble they wanted to take home. He felt dizzy and wanted to sit down again, but his mother gave him a desperately plead-ing look, and he kept standing and singing, and the building swayed danger-ously, up and down, up and down, side to side, and Arceneaux began to sway slightly to keep his balance, so that when the building swayed left, he bent right, and his mother whispered in anguish, "Larry! What are you doing?" And when they got to the chorus where the music rose tremendously on the phrase "with the cross of Jesus going on before," his stomach rose with the crescendo of song, and he vomited all over the sky-blue summer dress of Mrs. Beau de Vitry, who stood, delicately scented, directly in front of him, holding her hymnal with both hands, her head uplifted in noble piety, singing the hymn with a fervor that showed clearly in her carefully managed face.

The worst of it was that Arceneaux started to laugh. He could not help himself. Mrs. Beau de Vitry did not understand for a moment that she had been vomited upon; she felt a jet of warm liquid explode on her back, imme-diately followed by a stench so alien to church—especially First Baptist of New Orleans—that her mind rejected immediately, imperially, and pro-foundly its impulse to define this odious smell for what it was. Yet even as her mind rejected its first temptation, her senses—especially those of smell and touch—counterattacked all the conventions of her experience, battering them down with the perception that something truly new and original had happened in church and to her, and her brain had to yield, and she turned with her mouth still wide open as though rounding and holding a long note but now mute and in shock, and she looked down at him, heroic veteran Lawrence Arceneaux collapsed in laughter on the elongated red plush that cushioned the Arceneaux pew, and he sprawled on his back, looking up at her, looking up at Karen, at Katherine, their blank and aghast faces, and at a chivalrously outraged Beau de Vitry himself, Arceneaux laughing and laugh-ing and laughing, unable to stop. He thought afterwards that it was the first time in his life that he had seen Karen look completely natural, her fixed smile wiped away from her doll's face in a horror that was full and genuine and almost attractive.

For a while the congregation sang doggedly on like Christian soldiers heroically advancing against heavy artillery and a gas attack, finishing the chorus, beginning the second verse. "Like a mighty army, Satan's host doth flee—" But around the vast auditorium a ghastly pool of silence widened, and in the middle of it Arceneaux howled with laughter, looking up at Mrs. Beau de Vitry with a hilarity that grew in proportion to her amazement and wrath, and the congregation stumbled to a ragged halt in its march on Satan except for a couple of deaf old gentlemen who bellowed away even after the choir had followed the congregation into a collapsed and appalled silence and the organist had given up her frantic efforts to raise a wall of music against chaos, and finally every other sound in the church stopped, even the bellowing of the deaf old gentlemen, and Arceneaux laughed until he was crying amid that appalled and awful and profound silence, and he said to Mrs. Beau de Vitry, "I could have broken your neck. So easy. You're lucky. I only vomited on you, but I could have broken your neck."

*C*HARLES was summoned to talk with Ken McNeil. They sat in the district attorney's office in the courthouse with a bailiff and a young woman on McNeil's staff. Her name was Myra Crawford, and she wore a dark outfit, a suit top and a discreet skirt. She had big tits barely contained by the suit top though it was discreetly fastened with leather-covered buttons that, standing in their wide buttonholes, suggested that they could be undone easily though they were now held in tension by the forward surge of those mighty breasts. She smiled at Charles and dipped her head over her notepad as she crossed her legs, showing a flash of hose-covered knees, looking up as though to see if he had noticed, and, smiling covertly, settled to take down shorthand notes.

McNeil sat behind a government-issue, tax-bought desk, scarred and mottled, old cigarette and cigar burns, and an empty cuspidor at the side, not used in years because even in Bourbon County men did not chew tobacco as they had done once. McNeil did not smoke or chew or drink. Never had done any of those things. His life had been solid rectitude. Full of hymns hummed in the bath and on his walks. He looked blandly at Charles and half-smiled, McNeil's peculiar tic, a half-smile in improbable circumstances.

"Now, Charles, I have heard rumors. Solely rumors, sometimes by unsavory characters, and sometimes by men of good standing in this community. Yes, I have heard rumors that people are trying to influence you to—well, not exactly to lie, but to say that you did not see what you have said, told me, the sheriff, you saw that unfortunate night."

Charles shrugged, resigned and tired. His legs ached with fatigue. He slept fitfully and felt tormented by bad dreams, and he awoke before dawn, unable to sleep again, lying in bed with the window open, too tired to get up and read, impatient for the sun. His mother's face swam before him. Sometimes even when he was awake, he was so tired that he could close his eyes a moment, and his mind drifted, and she was there. Her face was in pain. In heaven she could see all he was. Not the golden boy.

"Now Charles, you and I know that murder has been committed. Cold-blooded, premeditated murder. The man you saw kill those two—"

"I saw him kill just Mr. Parmalee," Charles interrupted.

"Ah yes, yes. But you infer that he killed Mrs. Kirby, his wife, too. You have no evidence to suggest that another killer was abroad on that fatal night, do you?"

"No, of course not," Charles said in a low, weary voice, thinking that McNeil must draw his words on an imaginary blackboard to make them as pompous as possible before he spoke them, and thinking as though it were revelation that he did not like McNeil, that he, Charles C. Alexander, twenty years old, was still old enough to judge that some older people were fatuous and uninteresting and disagreeable, Charles, whose mother had taught him, "Judge not that you be not judged," and said in his hearing, proudly, "Charles never criticizes anyone. It's so nice to have a son who never sees anything but the good in people."

He saw less and less good in Ken McNeil.

"I understand that even a minister of the gospel—for reasons no one, least of all myself, can comprehend—has counseled that you lie to save the life of a cold-blooded killer."

It was not quite a question, but it had an inflection that might have become a question in a breath, and McNeil's coldly soft eyes played over him speculatively. Charles started to speak but shut his mouth without offering a word and looked beyond McNeil's shoulder out the window where the autumn leaves of October showed in the square in a haze of gold, crimson, and brown.

"I simply want to warn you, Charles, that there is a felony called perjury. If you take an oath on the Bible, the sacred Word of God, and if you swear to tell the truth, the whole truth, and nothing but the truth so help you God, you incur not only the future wrath of God if you lie, but you incur the immediate wrath of the state. You can be jailed for lying under oath, Charles. I hope you understand that. Do you understand that?"

"Yes, yes, I understand," Charles said impatiently.

"Twenty-seven years. You can serve that long for perjury, Charles. You would be almost an old man when you came out of prison."

"I know," Charles whispered.

"Good," McNeil said, smiling again his insincere and inappropriate smile and nodding in satisfaction and with a tic of triumph. He savored his victory already, Charles knew. Tasted it and rejoiced.

McNeil got up. "I will ask the questions, and you answer them truthfully. Hugh Bedford will defend the murderer."

"I know," Charles said. His voice was hardly more than a murmur.

"Don't let him rattle you," McNeil said expansively. "He will probably be drunk. The man is a disgrace to the legal profession. I think he should be disbarred. He's a charlatan. No question about it. That hillbilly family of Hope Kirby's is just dumb enough to get a man like Hugh Bedford to defend him. Well, they don't have a chance. Not with you in the witness stand, Charles. And remember. No perjury. No matter what anybody says."

Charles looked at him and felt a heaviness that left him unable to say anything. He turned and walked out of the office, feeling McNeil's bland smile on him.

*H*E *TOLD* Tempe and McKinley what McNeil had said. McKinley said, "This man Arceneaux, he is from New Orleans. His father owns a sugar plantation. Isn't that right?"

"I think so," Charles said.

"I believe I know him," McKinley said.

"How could you know him?" Tempe said.

"Don't look so surprised. Everybody has to be someplace. He and I happened to be the same place in France. We blew up a tunnel."

"You blew up a tunnel! Like *For Whom the Bell Tolls*," Tempe said ironically.

"That was a bridge," McKinley said. "This was a tunnel."

"Are you sure it's the same one?" Charles asked. "People say he was a clerk-typist."

McKinley shook his head. He seemed more solemn than usual. "He wasn't a clerk-typist. What kind of car does he drive?"

"A Jaguar," Charles said. "People don't like it. They think he ought to drive a Chevy."

"A Chevy! Arceneaux?" McKinley put back his head and laughed. "He talked a lot about cars. The man loved cars. He thinks Chevies are made by imbeciles to be sold to morons."

"It's a beautiful car," Charles said wistfully.

"So he's a preacher! Well, life is funny as hell. Lawrence Arceneaux preaching in a Baptist church." McKinley shook his head, amused and thoughtful at once. He looked off to something undefined in the distance.

"You ought to go see him," Tempe said.

"We don't have anything to talk about," McKinley said.

"But you were in the war together," Tempe said.

"Just like I say. We don't have anything to talk about," McKinley said.

"He told you to lie," Tempe said, turning her large brown eyes upon Charles. "A minister?"

"I bet Ice isn't an ordinary minister," McKinley said.

"Ice?" Tempe said.

"We called him Ice. He didn't have blood inside him. He was all ice."

"Are you sure you have the right person?" Charles said.

"There are not two Larry Arceneauxs from New Orleans who would be driving a Jaguar."

Charles took a deep breath and looked around. The Ellis and Ernest was filled with orange and white. People were happy. Football players were proud of themselves. They had beaten Louisville 59–6. It was good to beat up on somebody. Even a dinky little football team like Louisville. That's what football teams did, especially when they had lost as many games as Tennessee had lost this year. No bowl for them, but they had one rout to their credit.

"He told me I could save a life. And he said if I could save a life, a lie didn't matter."

McKinley lifted his eyebrows. "He told you that? It doesn't sound like the Arceneaux I knew. The Arceneaux I knew was not interested in saving lives."

"What do you mean by that?" Tempe said.

"I mean . . . 1 don't mean anything." He heaved a great, impatient sigh. "We were in the war together. It was kill or be killed. I hate talking about the war. I don't want to talk about Arceneaux." He picked up his coffee cup and sipped at it.

No one said anything for a while. The buzz, whir, murmur, laughter, and clatter of the Ellis and Ernest was like a world taking place on a stage they were not watching.

"And now that DA is threatening you with prison if you back off your testimony when the trial comes up," McKinley said.

"Yes," Charles said.

McKinley grunted contemptuously. "Don't let him scare you. He's trying to bluff you. You can say anything you want on the stand, and he can't do a thing about it. You're in charge."

"But Charles can't lie," Tempe said.

"Why not?" McKinley said. "Ice is right. If he lies, he saves a life."

"It's too much trouble to lie," she said softly. Now she took a deep breath. "Listen, what happens happens. If you lie about it, you have to keep on lying about it. You have to apologize, explain, tell more lies, apologize some more, lie some more. Pretty soon your whole life is wrapped up in lies and explanations and apologies, and you are nothing but your words and your evasions and your lies."

"Yes, but if Charles tells the truth, this poor guy who did the killings may end up by being fried," McKinley said. He paused for a moment and spoke in a soft, careful voice. "He did spare Charles's life. He could have killed him."

"You don't thank a murderer because he could have killed you and didn't. He's still a murderer. Charles still saw what he saw."

"Lots of times I thought I saw things in the war I didn't." McKinley laughed with a touch of bitterness. "You're up in the hills, in the dark, and you hear the snap of a limb or the trees creaking in the wind, and you put a whole German division with it, and you see it for a minute. You see your death."

"If Charles lies," Tempe said, "he will spend the rest of his life lying and lying and lying some more." She looked sharply at Charles. "I'm not saying any of this because I believe in God. I don't want anybody to think that."

McKinley gave an abrupt and good-natured laugh. "No one would accuse you of that. Would you accuse Tempe of believing in God, Charles?"

Charles tried to smile and failed. He knew McKinley was not mocking him. He knew also that he should make some response, something brave and believing, but he could not. He was again caught up in the great puzzle of his life, that within his heart he yearned with all his might to believe things that seemed ridiculous when he spoke them to people he liked in the normal world, people who seemed oblivious to the importance of these questions. McKinley looked across the table in serene amusement, his craggy face beaming with good humor and, more than that, with goodwill. Charles could not meet his glance and instead concentrated on his coffee as if McKinley's wry indifference to the great eternal questions had no effect at all. The result was to leave Charles slightly disoriented as he had felt once when he rode a roller coaster through dives and whirls with gut-wrenching speed and then stepped out on solid ground and felt uncertain about how to keep his balance when he walked.

Tempe was the one who took the questions seriously. But it was not the side of seriousness that Charles wanted—or thought he wanted. He was twenty years old, he thought later. He did not know anything. Everything was falling on him too fast, far too fast. At the time when Tempe spoke, a wall came up in him, slick as ice, impenetrable as lead, high as Mount Everest.

Tempe said in a level voice, "In fact, just because I don't believe in God I'm telling Charles he can't lie." She turned her eyes urgently on Charles. McKinley looked serious, too. His face was naturally thoughtful. No one would ever have called him handsome. He gave an impression always of reflecting on things, or perhaps of recalling memories that added a commentary in his head to whatever was going on in front of his eyes.

She finished her thought. "I don't think there's anything out there."

"We don't know whether there is anything out there or not," McKinley said mildly.

"Yes we do," Tempe said. "I think we come from nothing and we go to nothing, and all we have in the midst of billions and billions of years of time is this little moment we have the luck to live. I don't believe in life after death; I believe in life before death. It's our one chance in eternity to be whatever it is we are. If we get in the habit of lying, we lose it. All we have. We go on and on and on in life, and we're not living the life that chance gives us to live. We're just more of the nothing that gave us birth and that will give us death."

"Do you look at an ugly baby and tell the mother that the father must have been a chimpanzee?" McKinley said. He did not smile.

"I don't say anything about ugly babies," Tempe said. "I'm talking about something important."

"I wish I could live like that," McKinley said.

Tempe was the one who laughed. "Oh McKinley, you do live like that. You're too big to pretend. If you were short, you could be a liar. But a big guy like you has to be what you are."

McKinley smiled slightly. "I don't believe that is true," he said. "I have lied by silence." He turned towards Charles. "And Ice told you to lie."

"Ice? Mr. Arceneaux? Yes, he said I could save a life. He said it would be important to me later, the rest of my life. He said the worst things we do don't go away. They come back to us and haunt us like ghosts we can't touch and we can't flee."

"He said all that?" McKinley said.

"Yes, he said a lot more."

"Well, well," McKinley said.

"What would you do?" Charles said.

McKinley shook his head. "I can't tell you that. I really can't."

"Well, I can," Tempe said.

"I don't think I can lie," Charles said. "I tried my best—" He started to say that he tried his best with the sheriff, and he could not. When he remembered, his voice broke, and he thought he might disgrace himself by crying here in the Ellis and Ernest with all those football players standing around in their orange-and-white sweaters. He took a deep breath.

"Hell," McKinley said, "look at it this way. Even if the jury convicts the poor slob, he won't be in prison more than a year. My God! He caught them almost in the very act. He went crazy. That's his defense—temporary insanity. If the jury is all male, they'll probably let him go."

"I don't know," Charles said. "He doesn't seem crazy. People say Judge Yancy was in love with her."

"In love with her! The dead woman?" Tempe was aghast. "An old man like that?"

Charles told the story of Judge Yancy and Abby. The more he talked about it, the more it was like talking about the symptoms of a disease, something like cancer, that he could not discuss abstractly. He had seen the foolish old judge, his round face as stern as an executioner's, striding down Broadway to the Triangle Beauty Shop with an air that said he would kill anyone who laughed at him. He had heard people laugh at Judge Yancy—behind the judge's back, of course. He told about the gossip, the offer to send Abby to college, all of it.

McKinley said, "Then he ought to recuse himself. He should not try the case. It's a simple as that."

"But he won't," Charles murmured. "I know he won't."

"All right. Let's take the worst case. Take my word for it," McKinley said, "he's found guilty and he serves a year and a day for involuntary manslaughter. That's what it will be. He's not going to get the electric chair for what he did. Not in Tennessee."

"Maybe," Charles said. He felt the darkness around him like a velvet hood. He did not feel like walking or talking. He could sit here in the Ellis and Ernest all day long, all night long, all day tomorrow, forever, withering into the sleep of death, rotting, falling to a dry puddle of dust on the imitation-leather cover of the chair. His arms and his legs felt like stone. Years later he could recall his fear like something he had read one time in a book. He could not recapture the intensity of it. He could remember only that it had pressed on him and filled him with melancholy and weakness. At night, he slept badly. Every night.

THE TRIAL was something to remember, and those who witnessed it never forgot it. You can go back to the transcript and read the bare bones of it, and not long ago a theatre group at the university in Knoxville successfully staged it as a play. But some things cannot be recaptured—the winey smell of an Indian-summer October day drifting through the wide-open windows and the occasional twirling fall of a dusky leaf releasing itself early from the branch. The crowd was tense and quiet before the glory of the law and full of fear before the bald little gnome who would preside, Judge Shirley K. Yancy. Above all was a thrill of expectancy of great things, as before a football game between undefeateds when spectators gather afraid that they might miss something that they will want to tell about for years.

People there and alive to this day recall District Attorney Kenneth McNeil sitting there prim and blandly smiling at the table reserved for the prosecution, and on the other side of the open space before the bench sat

Hugh Bedford. He hunched over his elbows frowning through his reading glasses at a legal tablet of cheap yellow paper. The yellow pad was thick with penciled notes. His pale blue suit had been to the dry cleaner's, but there were stains on it that no chemical would ever remove short of burning the fabric away.

Judge Yancy allowed no smoking in his court. Poor Hugh throughout the trial grabbed at the shirt pocket where he kept his cigarettes, felt the comforting bulge of the pack, and then remembered Judge Yancy's cold reptilian eyes glaring down at him, and his hand fell back, and his anger swelled.

Hope Kirby sat next to him. He looked good—lean, calm, and as indifferent as a model in a magazine ad for clothes. He wore a new suit, off the rack at Penney's, but since he was almost a perfect 40 long, the suit looked tailor-made for him. He was clean-shaven, his hair neatly trimmed in the short military cut he had worn in the army and as a guerrilla fighter in the Philippines. Any stranger walking into the courtroom that day might have been forgiven for supposing the dapper-looking young man was the lawyer and the disreputable-looking older man in the disgrace of a worn suit the defendant, and that he was surely guilty of many more crimes than whatever was on the docket for this day.

The first task was jury selection, and that went on scrappily for most of the day. It brought a surprise. Kenneth McNeil asked each juror if he objected to the death penalty, and he challenged all those who said they did. Hugh Bedford trembled with anger at this indecency. It was, he thought, Kenneth McNeil bringing his friendship for Kelly Parmalee into the courtroom and seeking personal vengeance. He pointed this out to Judge Yancy, but Judge Yancy dismissed the objection. Thereupon Hugh Bedford asked every prospective juror if he had known Kelly Parmalee or Hope Kirby or Abby or Sophia or the sheriff or Charles Alexander. To one poor dirt farmer he said, "Do you like to see people die horrible deaths?"—for which he drew an instant rebuke from the judge.

Jury selection was done at three. All the jurors were farmers, many dressed in bib overalls, some thin, some fat, some eager and others sour and one or two with a blankness that could have been read as stupidity or watchfulness. At one time or another they all had voted. Someone said they looked like men standing under a shed while a cloudburst roared down, the downpour too loud to let them talk but too heavy to let them leave. In fact they represented a typical American jury—ignorant of almost everything as a guarantee that they would be ignorant of the facts of the case.

Judge Yancy was in a hurry. He thought enough time was left in the day to make the opening statements, and so after a fifteen-minute recess with women standing forlornly in a long hopeless line before the one-toilet ladies' room in the courthouse and with men piled into their rest room where there was a long trough of a urinal, the trial began.

McNeil presented the prosecution's case. He did so with as much fervor as anybody had ever seen in him in a courtroom, and it was a particularly bloody business. He announced at the beginning that he would ask for the death penalty. He declared that no one knew whether Abby and Kelly were having an illicit affair. Mrs. Parmalee would testify that she knew all about her husband's meetings with Abby, and she approved of them because the girl needed some fatherly shoulder to pour out the brutality and the contempt she suffered at her husband's hands. At this a gasp went through the courtroom, and Judge Yancy pounded his gavel.

McNeil announced with heavy emphasis that he would present a young man of impeccable credentials to provide an eyewitness account of the murders, and he called the name of Charles Alexander. Along the way Abby and Kelly rose ghostly in McNeil's praise of their virtues and the cruel violence of their deaths.

Hugh Bedford had a great time with McNeil's claim that Sophia Parmalee had known of the connection between Kelly and Abby. He ridiculed the notion that these two people would be reduced to discussing Hope Kirby's alleged cruelty at one o'clock in the morning in the town square, and he promised to get from Sheriff Myers testimony that Sophia was shocked and devastated by the news of her husband's death. Time and again while he spoke, Judge Yancy had to bang his gavel to silence a titter of laughter that ran wavelike through the courtroom. It's all there—Hugh Bedford's roaring and eloquent defense of his client, not admitting the crime. "I shall prove beyond any shadow of reasonable doubt that the deceased Kelly Parmalee had seduced and abandoned many women in this county and in other places." A gasp in the audience, and Judge Yancy pounding, pounding, Hugh Bedford looking on the assembly like an angel of wrath ready to descend.

"This court will not allow you to defame the names of innocent women," Judge Yancy squeaked.

"I promise that not one innocent woman's name shall pass my lips," Hugh Bedford said.

It is said that a number of women in the audience turned pale at this exchange.

"Reasonable doubt!" Hugh shouted. "Reasonable doubt. That is all that the defense must produce to gain acquittal, gentlemen of the jury. Reasonable doubt. I shall present reasonable doubt by the truckload."

So the first day ended in turmoil.

*C*HARLES had spent the day waiting in the witness chamber. He sat reading Proust. He could not concentrate. When the bailiff came back and told him he could leave, he waited until the empty silence beyond the walls of the room told him that the courtroom was empty. He came out then and started down the quiet corridor to the small back stairway. He descended, and there was Tempe. She was wrapped up in a stylish leather jacket and wore a red scarf and a little wool cap. She smiled shyly at him.

He was surprised. "What are you doing here?" he said.

"I think that must be the most ridiculous question you could have asked," she said. She laughed. But she also seemed uneasy, as if she feared that he might tell her to go away. He was glad to see her. He had not slept in several nights, and he was weary beyond the telling, but he also knew that if he lay down to sleep, he would simply lie awake. He had discovered that this kind of insomnia was a rack on which his body lay in torture.

"Well, I didn't expect you."

"Here I am."

"Where's McKinley?"

"I don't know where McKinley is," she said. "We don't see each other much except in Proust class. We don't date, you know."

"You don't?" he said.

"Do you think he's my boyfriend?" She laughed again, genuinely amused.

"Well, you're always together."

"We're not always together. We're always together when you see us. But that's because you don't see much of us."

They fell in beside each other walking across the courthouse lawn. The air was crisp but not cold. "Is this where it happened?" she said.

"Right over there," he said.

"It must have been awful."

"It was."

"Are you going to eat supper?"

"I'm not hungry. I thought—I didn't know you were coming down. I was thinking of driving up to Gatlinburg, to the mountains." He shook his head and shrugged helplessly. "This is not the best time in my life."

"And when it's not the best time in your life, you go up to the mountains."

"It's quiet up there. You can think."

"Fine," she said. "I'll drive my car back to Knoxville, and you can follow me. I'll go with you."

He considered what she was saying, and he thought that she should not go with him, and he had many other thoughts, but mostly he felt a deadness inside that was absent of all thoughts. He said, "Do you really want to do that?" He hoped she did not.

"That's the second stupid question you've asked in five minutes." She smiled again, more confident now.

He drove behind her to Knoxville. She drove a new Buick. It was a big car. He supposed her father had bought it for her. She parked on a leafy street near the university. When she got out, he could see in the illumination of a street lamp how slender and pretty she was and an energy that seemed to charge her body. "Can't we go in my car?" she said.

"I'd rather go in mine," he said.

"But your car stinks."

"You get used to it." He got out and fetched a big jerry can of oil from the back.

"What are you doing?" she said.

"I have to pour oil into the engine every fifty miles or so."

"Good God," she said. He did not reply. He opened the hood and took off the oil cap and, without measuring, he poured oil into the engine.

"Why do you drive a car like this?" she said.

"I hate to have money in cars. Besides, my boss gave me this one."

"I think I'd ask him for a better one," she said.

"I can't ask him anything," he said. "He's dead."

"Oh, I'm so sorry. How did he die?"

"He was drowned." He told her about the girl, Lloyd, the rowboat, their naked bodies. He spoke in the dry, dead tones of someone repeating an old story told too many times.

"He must have died trying to save her life," Tempe said, suddenly very sad.

They got into the '37 Ford, and he drove back onto Cumberland Avenue, passed by the gate that led up to the hill where the main part of the university stood with the Ayres Hall tower rising through the dark autumn leaves and illuminated by floodlights, and then onto Main Street and up the hill, where he turned right and crossed the Henley Street Bridge onto the Chapman Highway. They drove in silence for a long time, Tempe absorbed by Lloyd's story. Charles did not tell her about the photographs.

"He died being what he was," she said at last.

The comment irritated Charles. He could not pinpoint the reason for his irritation. Lloyd should not have died. He could have been what he was without dying like that, without being fished up out of the lake with a boat hook. He told her about Lloyd's tongue swollen through his rotting lips.

They were rolling through a forested land with the hills rising around them and an occasional gleam of light from a farmhouse or a store or a filling station beside the road. The foothills rose dark on each side of them against a sky sprinkled with stars, and the oil smoke funneled out from behind the car.

"Do you think he loved the girl?" Tempe said.

"I don't know," Charles said. "Lloyd wrote poetry. He didn't sign it. He put it in the paper, and we didn't say anything to him about it. I think he wanted to be in love."

"Was it good poetry?"

"Well, I don't know. It was all right."

"A bad poet dead romantically in a lake with a woman he wanted to love. I've heard drowning is an easy death. You should write his story."

"Red wrote it for the newspaper. Red's my boss now. He cried when he wrote about Lloyd. We didn't even know Lloyd was going out with this girl. He'd just broken up with somebody else."

"They both died, and he might not have loved her, and she might not have loved him. You see. Life is absurd."

Charles felt so tired that he almost hallucinated. Objects beside the road became unfamiliar. He had planned to drive and let his mind slip into neutral and be as passive as a rock on a hill. Now with Tempe sounding like W. T. Stace, it was as if some terrible, pursuing presence had climbed into the comfortable old car against his will and forced him into thoughts that wore him down. When he stole a look at her, she sat with her eyes fixed on the road ahead, seemingly lost in thought. Her profile was sharp, and her uneven teeth gave her something, a uniqueness, something you noticed and remembered and perhaps thought about years and years later. He did not want her with him. He did not want to think. Most especially he did not want to think the thoughts she forced upon him.

"I think there's a purpose in things," he said defiantly.

"What purpose could there possibly be in a man and a woman drowning in a lake?" Her voice was quiet and wondering, like gentle fingers stroking a wound.

"We don't know what it is, but there is one."

"Oh Charles," she said. "You don't believe that." Again the voice was mild and not argumentative.

Charles did not turn his head. He drove carefully, keeping his eyes fixed on the dim yellow wash of the headlights of the '37 Ford, the blacktop highway rolling beneath the wheels and only occasionally meeting another vehicle as a solitary pair of lights sweeping towards them and quickly gone. "I heard some people say that it was God's punishment for—for what they were doing. Adultery."

"Oh God!" she said, her voice filled with disgust. "I can't believe you even repeat trash like that. Do you think that everybody who commits adultery dies?"

"I saw Kelly Parmalee die," he said softly.

"So God—" She started to say something vehement, but she broke her words in mid-sentence. "I'm sorry," she said, and she was gentle again and laid a hand on his arm as he held the wheel. "It must have been awful. Just awful." She paused. "But God didn't have anything to do with it."

For a long time they did not say anything. All at once he wanted to tell her what he had not said to anyone, that yes, it had been awful, that he had been terrified, that he dreamed about Hope Kirby and the pistol, that sometimes when he was driving alone, he thought of the whole episode again and cried out, and he wanted to tell her about W. T. Stace, and he wanted to shout at her that if we gave up purpose, if we thought the world was absurd, our lives were all absurd, and nothing mattered, and we would breathe a little while and be dead for billions of years. He wanted to tell her that if she was right, his mother had been deceived all her life, and that the roseate divinity he had felt in the woods and in the clouds and in the fields had all been a hoax. But he said nothing about such things. She would think him mad if he erupted in such talk. Even in his hard-core fundamentalist longings, he thought with amusement later on, he could not take up such dire thoughts as the end of civilization and all human life and meaning when the earth tumbles into the sun some billions of years from now. He never knew anybody to feel pain over such things.

Yes, he could see well enough later on that his timidity at being thought mad was a sign of some sort, a clear prophecy of what was to come for him, although he could not believe it then. Appointment in Samarra. The tale of Oedipus. People don't accept fate; they do their best to escape it, and their effort to escape brings their fate upon them.

So they drove, and Tempe took her hand away. They passed through Sevierville, the streets almost empty, the one movie house about to begin its evening feature, people lined up outside, some eating popcorn. The ugly courthouse with its dome-shaped tower stood up in the midst of the town. Then he thought that the courthouse in Bourbonville was not pretty either. It was something he was used to, a sign of home and safety. When he got home from the university, the sight of the ruby-brick courthouse gave him the assurance that all was right with the world and that his beliefs were not absurd. People in Bourbonville believed what he believed. The courthouse stood to confirm that what people had believed in the past was also believable in the present.

They ate at the Mountain View Inn at the edge of Gatlinburg. It was intentionally rustic, with tables and floors of polished knotty pine and a big stone fireplace at one end of the long, high-ceilinged dining hall. Off-season. Only a couple of tables occupied when they went in. Smell of wood smoke, and the fire blazing cheerily around big hickory logs. Fragrance of hickory in the air. They sat to one side of the fireplace, not too close, and outside the night covered the mountains. Gatlinburg lay in a narrow valley, a stream rushing swiftly and noisily through it. Above it towered Mount LeConte. The air tonight outside was chilly.

"I grew up in flatland," Tempe said while they ate. "Down in the Mississippi Delta, and even around Memphis, it's as though the land was scraped by a knife. Mountains are always a wonder to me."

"I don't think I would like flatland," Charles said.

"Don't live in Memphis, then. At least it's better than New Orleans."

"Didn't you like New Orleans?"

"I hated it. And I don't want you to go there to seminary."

"Maybe I'll like it better than you did."

"If I had been in the seminary, I would have really gone crazy. Charles, they are dumber than dirt. They revel in being dumb. Listen, there is a church near the seminary. It has a big sign painted across the front in Gothic letters: 'God Said It; I Believe It; That Settles It.'"

"Well, it's a way of saying something," he said vaguely.

"Yes, it's a way of saying we're stupid and dumb and determined to hold on to a bouquet of lies even if they rotted long ago and stink to high heaven."

Charles made no reply. He was so worn out that his bones ached. At night he slept in fits of exhaustion and vague nightmarish dreams. He awoke early in the morning and rolled from his side to his stomach to his back, trying every position to induce sleep to come again, but it came only as dozing, and he rose early, before the sun, and walked back and forth in his room.

Now in his immense fatigue, his mind could not work before Tempe's onslaught. He felt baffled and hurt by the intensity with which she berated him, and he was resentful in a dull, tired way that went beyond thought. He thought that he would be at peace with the world if he could only retreat into an enclosed garden where God walked in the cool of the day and he had not eaten of the tree of knowledge of good and evil. Sex and knowledge! If he could have been relieved of both of them in exchange for peace of mind, he would have gladly subscribed to the motto "God says it; I believe it; that settles it." But he could not say such things to Tempe, who sat across the table from him looking incomprehensibly irate and intense. Polite people did not berate others about religion. Religion was a subject people did not discuss when they disagreed.

"I don't think you will ever believe the way I do," he said softly.

She started to say something, but she looked at him, and very abruptly the tears came to her eyes. "Oh Charles," she said in a rush, "you look awful." She dabbed at her eyes with a napkin. "I'm sorry," she said. "You're so thin. How much do you weigh?"

"I weigh a hundred and thirty-eight pounds on the penny scale in front of the Western Auto in Bourbonville."

"With your clothes on!"

"Yes, well, I don't weigh myself naked on the streets in Bourbonville."

Suddenly they both laughed in a burst of pent-up emotion. People in the large and almost empty restaurant looked at them. Tempe sat stifling her laughter, but she couldn't stop, finally putting her face in her hands and laughing wildly while Charles laughed, too, but more circumspectly, looking around at the curious and somewhat disapproving faces that had turned their way. Tempe took a deep breath and got control of herself, but she looked ready to break out into laughter again.

He changed the subject. "Why did you go to New Orleans if you didn't like it? Why did you stay there for a year if you hated it? Did you have a job there?"

She did not answer him for a long time, and he had a premonition, an unexpected understanding, that he had intruded. She looked into her plate where she had scarcely touched her meal, holding a knife and a fork in clenched fists, and for just a moment he thought she was going to cry. He was confounded.

"What's wrong?" he said.

She laid the knife and fork aside, picked up the red napkin out of her lap, wiped her mouth, and looked out over the restaurant where now no one paid any attention to them.

"What was I doing in New Orleans?" she said.

"It's all right," he said, perplexed and alarmed at the bleakness of her expression.

She took a deep breath and turned her eyes directly on him. "I didn't stay a whole year," she said.

"Well, it doesn't matter," he said. "I thought—"

"I was there nine months," she said. "Less than nine months really. Only eight months."

"Well," he said blankly.

"I was at a Florence Crittenden Home."

"A what?"

"Don't you know what a Florence Crittenden Home is?"

"No," he said. He was completely bewildered.

"It's a home where unwed mothers can go to have their babies."

The significance of what she said broke in his brain like ice cracking on a lake. He felt a surge of pain. He did not speak, but he saw her bleak face turned on him, an expression of profound inquiry.

"Well?" she said. "What do you think of that?"

"I don't think anything of it," he said. "I mean—" He faltered stupidly.

"You don't think I'm a whore?"

"No," he said. "No."

"Will you have something for dessert?" The maternal-looking waitress stood over them abruptly, and her cheerful voice came down on them both like icewater poured out of a pail.

"What?" Charles said. He looked up, startled.

"Oh, I'm sorry," the waitress said. "I didn't mean to scare you." She laughed, big and benign.

"No, well, we're not through yet," Charles said.

"Take your time then," the waitress said. "As you can see, we're not busy tonight." She went away smiling, an emissary from another world where people lived ordinary lives.

"My father said I was a whore," she said. Her voice was like a steel file.

"Well, he—" He stopped again, his words like glue in his throat.

"Don't you want to know all about it?" she said, almost accusingly.

Charles reached into his armory of Christian convention and courtesy, a response almost mechanical and designed to cover up the turmoil he felt inside. "No," he said. "Not unless you want to tell me."

"I don't want to tell you anything if you don't want to hear it," she said sharply.

"I'm sorry," he said. "I don't know what to say."

"Then you don't want to hear."

"I do," he said. "Yes, please tell me."

She laughed again, not humorously. "I'm sorry. It's perfectly all right not to know what to say. Everybody else seemed to know exactly what to say," she said. "Poor Chuckie! He knew what to say."

"Chuckie?"

"The football player from Ole Miss. He was the father of my child. My father went down to Oxford and called him out. He told Chuckie if he didn't marry me, he would regret the day he was born."

"But he refused?"

"Oh no, he didn't refuse. Chuckie was a good Christian, you know. He believed that God helped him score touchdowns. He agreed to marry me on the spot. My father came home and told me that Chuckie had cried and said that he was sorry and that he would marry me, and he told my mother to pick out the invitations and the wedding dress because the wedding was going to be in two weeks. He actually seemed happy. He liked Chuckie. He was proud of him for being willing to do the right thing. Boys will be boys, you know."

"But he didn't marry you."

"I refused to marry the dumb jerk. I didn't want to be Mrs. Chuckie Henderson the rest of my life. I didn't want to sit around and talk about old football games when I was forty years old and Chuckie was fat and boring. Football players always get fat when they get middle-aged. Haven't you noticed?"

"I haven't paid much attention," he said.

"You haven't paid much attention," she said, laughing again. She reached across the table and laid a cool and slender hand on his. "You're so innocent."

He felt vaguely insulted.

"I'm sorry," she said, squeezing his hand and taking hers away. "I said I absolutely would not marry Chuckie Henderson. I told him to his face that he was a fool and a bore and that if I had to marry him I would screw all his friends just to let him know the contempt I had for him, and I said I'd wear a bright red wedding dress to show I wasn't a virgin, and when the baby was born, I'd tell everyone it was not premature." She sat for a moment, a hard smile of recollection breaking across her face. Charles felt almost afraid of her, as if she were on a dangerous edge and might stand up and tell the whole restaurant what she was telling him.

"That's when my father called me a whore," she said, her voice low and solemn. "He thought any Memphis girl ought to wet her pants if she could marry a tailback from Ole Miss." She looked at him, and he returned her gaze in complete perplexity, feeling mute and foolish.

"Don't you want to know the rest of it?" she said.

"If you want to tell it."

"Oh Charles, you're so damned polite. You must have been brought up on a manners book and the Bible."

"I'm sorry," he said, shaking his head and taking a breath and wishing they could leave. He caught the eye of the maternal waitress without meaning to look at her, and she came hurrying over, smiling broadly.

"Have you finished?" she said. "Oh my, honey," she said to Tempe, "you've not eaten enough to keep a bird alive. Was something wrong with it?"

"No," Tempe said. "I wasn't hungry."

"Then will you want dessert?" The waitress's face became sad.

"Oh yes, I'll have dessert," Tempe said. "Do you have any cherry pie?"

"Why yes, we do," the waitress said, smiling again. "They're not fresh cherries, you know. We have to get them in cans this time of year, but the pie is delicious. We make it right here. We make a butter crust."

"Then I'll have cherry pie," Tempe said.

"Oh good!" the waitress said with such enthusiasm that she might have just sold an expensive car. "And you, sir. Will you have the same?"

"Yes, thank you," Charles said, not wanting the pie but wanting to do anything to get the waitress to go away. She departed, looking pleased with herself.

"Poor Charles," Tempe said. "You have to get your cherries out of cans."

He looked at her blankly, and she laughed again.

"I'm sorry to tease you," she said. "I'm not as vulgar as I sound. I don't know why I said that. I suppose—I don't know what I suppose. I'm damaged goods now. You know how the South is. Once you're damaged goods, you may as well be a whore, and you can be as vulgar as you want and people won't think any less of you, because they can't." She laughed nervously and looked away with a distracted expression across the large restaurant. By some sort of mute accord they did not speak again until the waitress brought their pie back. Each piece had a big scoop of vanilla ice cream on it.

Tempe looked down at her pie and lifted her face towards Charles, filled with anguish. "I don't know why I ordered this," she said. "I can't eat it. I'm not hungry."

"I'm not hungry either," Charles said.

"I'm going to the ladies' room," she said. She got up abruptly and left, clutching a little purse she carried.

Charles went over to the maternal waitress. "We've decided to leave," he said. "I'm sorry. We're not so hungry after all."

"Oh, but why? What's wrong? Oh dear, I hope it's not a lover's quarrel."

"We're not lovers," Charles said quickly. "She's just a friend."

He put down a five-dollar bill. It was at least a dollar more than enough. The maternal waitress was still protesting when he hurried away. The vanilla ice cream was melting into the cherry pie. The ice cream was staining red as it melted into the cherry juice. Suddenly he was hungry again. He liked cherry pie. But he did not stop. He went to the men's room and leaned his head against the tile wall while he peed. Not only was everything the way it was for no reason at all, but nothing was what it seemed to be. He thought he could go to sleep leaning there with his head on the wall.

Tempe was waiting for him at the door. She stood with her arms wrapped around herself.

"I shouldn't have told you," she said.

"No, it is all right. I'm glad you told me. I'm glad you trust me." Charles was saying what he thought he ought to say. The words came out forced and unnatural. She did not seem to notice.

"I guess we should be going back," she said, looking up at the clear and starry sky as they walked across the parking lot.

"We could go up to Newfound Gap," he said. "It is beautiful up there."

"I've never been in the mountains," she said. "I came to the university this summer, and I could see them from Knoxville, but I never drove over. McKinley is always talking about coming up here, but he never does."

"How do you know McKinley?" Charles said.

"I met him in class. We had some beers together. I trust him. He has his own story to tell."

"What is it?"

She looked up at him without smiling. "He will have to tell it himself." He felt the rebuke, and he heard her heels making noise on the asphalt pavement. "It's so quiet here," she said.

"In summer it's filled with tourists," he said. The chill air worked its way under the dark corduroy jacket he was wearing and through his shirt. "Hope Kirby is from up here somewhere. He worked on our kitchen a few months ago. Father hired him. I asked him where he was from, and he said up towards Gatlinburg. His family was driven out when they built the park."

"Let's drive up to Newfound Gap," she said. "Will this jalopy make it?"

"As long as I put oil in it," he said. He took the jerry can out of the rear of the station wagon, lifted the hood, removed the oil cap, and poured in oil.

He opened the door for her. He eased the car out of the parking lot and turned left, through Gatlinburg. A few people were on the streets, but most stores were closed. In moments they were gliding along the two-lane blacktop, and the mountains rose steep and dark on each side, and the highway climbed steadily in curves. Only an occasional car passed. He turned on the heater, and the amber light from the heater knob on the dash reflected dimly in her face. She looked straight ahead.

"Well, aren't you going to ask me any questions?" she said.

"Well, did you have the baby?"

"Yes, I had the baby," she said. "I got pregnant September a year ago, and I had the baby in May. May 17. A fine, healthy baby girl."

"What did you name it?"

"I named her Mary. I hoped she would remain a virgin all her life."

Charles could think of nothing to say.

"I nursed her for five days. The doctors said it was healthful for her to have her mother's milk at first. Then they took her away."

"For adoption," Charles said.

"Yes, for adoption. I'll never see her again."

There was no moon, and as they climbed through the dark, the stars glittered innumerable over the dark shapes of the mountains. Charles knew Tempe was crying, and he expected her voice to break. But it did not.

"I think about her all the time, every day. When you hold a baby in your arms, and it's your baby, and it nurses from your breast, you can never forget it." She made a cradle with her arms. "When I hold my arms like this, I can feel her."

"I'm very sorry," he said at last, his voice husky. He reached out and took her hand for a moment, and she unfolded her arms. He put his hand back on the wheel. Some of the curves were sharp, and he had to keep shifting gears.

"Oh well, I brought life into the world. Some people never bring another life into the world. I made two people happy who could not have children of their own. I wonder if they will ever tell her about me. I wonder if they will even call her Mary."

"Were you drunk, when—" He stopped, wishing he had not asked the question. She turned sharply to look at him.

"You sound like the women at the Florence Crittenden home. No, I wasn't drunk. Chuckie took me up to his room in the frat house after a party, and he started kissing me, and I kissed him back, and I knew he wanted it. He had a pleading look in his eyes. He looked like a puppy begging for a bone. I decided to let him have it. What good is virginity anyway?"

Charles had no answer to that question. He felt a terrible hurt, and he was not old enough or wise enough or perhaps foolish enough to know why he felt the pain or why anything in Tempe's life should mean anything to him.

"The women in the Florence Crittenden home wanted me to say I was sorry. They wanted me to pray to God for forgiveness. We had to go to chapel every Sunday, and a sappy little preacher with slick hair and fat cheeks came in and preached nervously to us. He always wore the same black suit. He had one of those unctuous voices, the kind that say "God" in three syllables—'Gaaa-awwwww-ddddd.' You know the sort. He almost talked baby talk. I think he did it because it was his way of masturbating himself. He looked at all of us, and he imagined us doing what we'd done to get pregnant, and he had his own fantasies."

"You don't know that," Charles said.

"Yes I do," she said firmly. "I never repented. I never said I was sorry."

Much later on he thought of himself that night and laughed—all those things dumped on top of him, and he was like a baby without any experience in the world and about to be a witness in a murder trial the next morning, and it was too much. He felt giddy—seriously giddy. The blood came up in his head, and he was glad to pull the '37 Ford over at Newfound Gap, and he cut the engine, and they sat there gazing out into the dark, seeing the mountains almost as suggestions rather than real, their great mass translated into dim and uncertain light that might with a slight shift of his own consciousness vanish utterly away as if he had created them and as easily destroyed them. They ran in dark waves to the east. Above them the stars glittered across a clear autumn sky.

Nothing that night felt real to him. He heard Tempe's story out, and he could not get his brain around it. Oh yes, in time he would ridicule himself, and like so many other things in the year 1953, the end of the second decade in his life, the person he had been would stand in his memory like a stranger as insubstantial as the mountains appeared to him that night from Newfound Gap, a dreamlike figure hidden in darkness whom Charles could not see clearly and whose mind and heart were as mysterious as those of an annoying alien speaking a strange tongue and making demands on him in an airport, asking directions or delivering imprecations, saying something that the later Charles could not penetrate or comprehend.

He remembered the pain—the strange and unexpected pain.

They got out and sat on a low stone wall on the edge of the parking lot, and they looked out onto the North Carolina side. "Put your arm around me. I'm cold," Tempe said. She was shivering.

Charles obeyed. She put her head on his shoulder, and they sat in silence. She felt soft and passive and sad. He knew he could have kissed her. But he did not. She did not try to kiss him. He felt her hair on his neck. He remembered all the simple fantasies of his growing up—a little church somewhere in the country with a parsonage and a garden and children and a wife who would pray with him and love him and without ever being told that he had lost his faith would bring him back to it, bring him back to the eternal sunrise where all the loose ends of life were tied up, and God was a bright presence in the multicolored silence where mystery verged on the visible and made everything complete. The child who worshipped Zeus or Athena, he wondered, did he come to a place where he decided these gods did not exist except in effigies of marble and granite in temples now shattered and left to be museums?

He thought of Tempe's child. The child and the invisible and unmeasurable space between a little girl and a young mother who would never see each other again.

He had been sitting with one arm clumsily around Tempe, uncomfortably gazing into the indistinct nightscape with the orderly stars spangled overhead. Suddenly he put both his arms around her and held her tight against himself. "I'm so sorry," he said. "I'm so sorry for—" He started to cry.

She put both her arms around him, and she cried too. The two of them held each other wordlessly and wept.

*H*E DID not know how he got home that night. He drove like a drunken man, the cars approaching him bright suns in the tremendous dark, and houses and cars alike flashing by him so that when they were gone their transit seemed to be a dream. Once somebody blew at him, and he was aware of a metallic mass hurtling by, the horn on full. In the backyard he urinated under the stars and saw the woods beyond as a veil of darkness where mysterious flashes of light came and went.

His father was waiting up for him. "Dad, I'm so tired," he said.

"Go to bed," Paul Alexander said. "I have been so anxious about you."

"I was out with a friend."

Without another word Charles staggered for the stairway. He threw off clothes in his room, letting them go where they would. When he at last lay down, sleep would not come again. He prayed for sleep to come, angry with God for not letting it come, rethinking himself about what it was to be angry with God and rebuking his arrogant spirit.

He drifted. He lay in the dark in Palestine and heard a German soldier have his way with Mary, the pretty young girl he had seduced in the village. Jesus came down in tradition as blond. Why not a German soldier as father? They lay near the hibiscus and made sweet love under the stars, and Charles felt it as though he had been lying nearby and could smell all the fragrance. Jesus blond! No wonder he would attract a crowd. The sun shining on that golden hair. One of the liberal theologians had said yes, why not? Why not have his real father be a German mercenary in the Roman army? *The Sword of the Lord* and the *Christian Beacon* raged against this man for months. This was what young people got when they went to liberal seminaries, seminaries that had been founded to propagate the word of God. Charles read what they said, and he thought, *This may be so.*

And Joseph? An older man, happy to have a tarnished young girl to keep his bed warm at night in his great age. Old men like Judge Yancy made foolish by voluptuous youth. Why not? Why not? Judge Yancy would have been the perfect Joseph, leaving his wife in perpetual virginity afterwards. One time might not count. He thought he could smell the hibiscus.

It was a hallucination, camping in the room with him. He got sick, staggered out of bed, and went downstairs and out into the front yard, and there he vomited up his supper. His father came out behind him in the dark. "You may have eaten something that disagreed with you."

"I went up to Gatlinburg, with a friend. We went to the Mountain View. The food was good, but I am so tired."

"Charles, a shot of brandy might help you." Two men standing barefoot in the grass talking about brandy, and Charles wanted to ask his father, "Do you think Jesus was the son of a German soldier?"

"No, I'll be all right." He went inside and washed his mouth out at the sink and went to bed again. Stephen was up now, the younger brother helping his brother up the stairs. "I'm so tired," Charles said.

"I'll call the judge. You can't testify like this," Stephen said.

"No, no, no. I want to get it over with. I want to testify and get it over."

He went back to bed, and it rocked gently on the still floor, the room swaying slightly, but he did not vomit again. He lay awake thinking of Jesus and of Tempe and the little girl somewhere and a soldier perhaps dead on some desert battleground not knowing, not dreaming that he was the earthly father of the Savior of the world.

Except that he was not the Savior of the world. Charles's mind throbbed. In all the stories about salvation that his mother told, the sinner began by doubt and indifference, and the tale ended in lugubrious tears and thanksgiving and gratitude for a heart washed clean. Charles's story was not ending like those. What if that same German soldier were called upon to be in the detail that carried out the Crucifixion? Neither of them knew, father nor son. A job for the soldier, one of many. Crucifixion was not uncommon. Soldiers did crucifixions with the routine and practiced ability of doctors taking out an appendix. So father and son came together at the cross. Neither of them knew, and Jesus the son died while the German mercenary cast lots for his robe. *I hope he won,* Charles thought wearily.

He tried breathing deeply, and he dozed. He heard his mother's voice, but he could not tell what she said. She was very near. He knew she disapproved.

*H*E CONSENTED to ride in with his father the next day. As a witness he sat in a little room apart, and he did not hear the almost routine questioning that went on through the morning. The sheriff first. Late in the morning in the isolation of his room Charles heard the muffled sound of voices raised in anger. It was Hugh Bedford drilling the sheriff, when he got to tell of another instance when he had found Kelly Parmalee in the very act with a woman. The woman and her husband had left town. The sheriff named them, because Hugh Bedford browbeat him into doing it. The judge allowed the testimony. That fact has amazed recent students of the case. How could he have allowed it? The answer is simply that in any court at a given time, the judge is the law. Yes, he can be reversed on appeal. But in his court before appeal, he is commander in chief. And on that fact everything was to turn in the case of *State of Tennessee* v. *Hope Philip Kirby*.

After the sheriff, Dr. Cameron Bulkely testified about the fatal shots. It was all routine except that people with long memories observed that despite drinking warm water every morning and taking multiple vitamins and eating fruit and chewing each bite fifty times before he swallowed it, age had still crept up on Cameron Bulkely like a thief in the night.

Then it was Charles's turn.

He had not been inside the courtroom since the trial began, and he was unprepared for the great, unsteady lake of faces that rocked back and forth in his vision when he made his way to the witness stand. He could not look at them because they seemed all in motion, and he got dizzy trying to focus on them; so he kept his eyes on the floor, and people noted that he seemed thin and pale. The bailiff thrust a Bible under his nose, and he laid his hand upon it, and he heard the bailiff rattle off a question, and he heard himself answering, "I do."

Then Ken McNeil stood before him, asking questions that seemed to come from a great distance as though out of an echo chamber, and it took every particle of Charles's energy to answer him. Charles wanted to lie down somewhere, and he thought that if he lay down now, he might be able to sleep. He yearned for sleep.

McNeil was slow and methodical, like a man hammering nails into a coffin, Charles thought afterwards. Detail by detail, McNeil re-created that hot August night, and Charles answered most of his questions with a yes or a no, not lifting his eyes. He spoke in such a subdued voice that several times McNeil had to prompt him to speak louder, and he tried to do so, but as he was forced to relive the murders he seemed to withdraw all the more into himself. And finally the climax:

"Did you recognize the assailant, Charles?" The silence after the question was like a million years set in stone, and the crowd bent forward as if the floor had tilted. McNeil had to repeat the question, and he added, "Charles, can you tell us who the man was?"

Charles looked up, and the floor swayed dangerously, and at the back of his throat he tasted the bile of vomit. He was afraid of vomiting. He was afraid of weeping.

"Yes," Charles said in barely a whisper.

McNeil spoke up in an irritated voice. "Is your answer yes?"

Charles nodded and spoke minutely louder. "Yes." He looked back at the floor.

"You can identify him?"

"Yes."

"You have no doubt who he was?"

"No"

"You could see him clearly in the night under the oak trees?"

"Yes."

Charles held on to what he knew, the simple facts as he remembered them, and McNeil seemed to make them more simple, more possible to affirm without vomiting or collapsing on the floor or, worst of all, beginning to weep hysterically before all this crowd that he had somehow not been prepared to see.

"Charles, is the man you saw that night here in the courtroom now?"

A shuffle of bodies, the amalgamation of sounds rising in the old building as if the courthouse itself had shifted ever so slightly and come to rest again with a subtly prolonged settling the way a four-legged animal will lie down in a narrow space. Charles stared at the floor. His head began almost suddenly to ache as though he had been struck on the top of it and his brain had swollen inside his skull and throbbed with every heartbeat.

McNeil's voice became more insistent. He bent now to Charles so that Charles could smell his cologne. It was a sickening odor, and Charles backed away from him and raised his head. Then a strange thing happened. His entire vision went blank, not black but rather a smoky gray. It was the kind of thing that came on him sometimes when he crouched in a library examining the books on a lower shelf and stood up suddenly. But this time things stayed blank for a very long time, and he sat in a quiet panic thinking he might have gone blind forever, and when his vision did slowly float back to him, he was staring at Hope Kirby, and Hope Kirby was staring back at him with a grave expression that revealed nothing of threat or rancor. They were two men, or rather a boy and a man, staring at each other across a room as if seeking recognition, all alone, and some voice was asking Charles for verification of a well-known fact, and he said, "Yes. There."

"Charles, speak up. What did you say?"

"I said yes. Mr. Kirby. He was the man I saw that night. He's sitting there." He did not point at Hope Kirby, but he looked at him, and it was enough.

McNeil repeated the question amid a release of collective breath in the courtroom, a sigh, an inarticulate murmur. Judge Yancy lifted his gavel, his gnomelike face hawkish and predatory, as if seeking a head close enough to pound. The tense, charged silence returned, and Judge Yancy let the gavel drop. Charles shut his eyes again. McNeil drew out the rest of it—Charles's terror, his pleading with Hope Kirby, his weeping, the promise he made, and then his drive home through the night, his life intact.

When McNeil was done, Judge Yancy looked down at Charles and said, "Are you sick?"

Charles answered this question as he had all the rest, with simple truth because the truth was the easiest thing he could say. Judge Yancy, in probably the only act of kindness the old man had been guilty of in years, ordered a fifteen-minute recess, and Charles was led back to his room where he walked into the adjoining toilet and bent over it and felt his whole body racked by dry heaves from which only a little string of green vomit emerged to swirl around the flushing toilet waters. But he did feel better after the heaves had run their course, and lacking a cot, he lay down on the floor in the little room, and he went to sleep—a genuine sound sleep whence he was wakened by the bailiff at the end of the fifteen-minute period and hurried back into the courtroom.

Hugh Bedford came at him then like a tiger. Hugh had been taught since childhood to hate Paul Alexander, and now he turned all that hatred on Paul Alexander's son. Hugh Bedford's father died in the exchange of gunfire between strikers and National Guard that had taken place during a strike at the Car Works when, as Hugh Bedford's mother saw it, Paul Alexander was showing off by leading a group that included the woman reporter whom he would marry across the railroad tracks where angry men confronted each other with guns. The Guard fired on the strikers. It was a massacre. Hugh's father was among the dead.

Now it seemed that all the hatred of his family was distilled and concentrated in Hugh Bedford's fury. He was an obese drunk now, and his words rumbled out in bibulous flow as though they came pouring out of his full guts. He stank of alcohol. But many could recall a Hugh Bedford who was not obese and who was not known to drink. He had always had a bulldog quality, grim and ready to bite, unpredictable of temper, and when roused to anger putting every atom of his being into winning the conflict that caused the anger in the first place.

When he was in high school in the thirties, he was a strong, muscular young man who played fullback for the high-school football team. He ran off the single wing and crashed into opposing teams like a bull with his head down, running hard with his knees pumping high to hurt those who tried to tackle him and often succeeding. He scored touchdowns with a grim, joyless explosion of precisely directed energy, and high, churning knees, and when fans screamed his name, he kept his head averted, refusing to acknowledge their cheers. He tackled with manic ferocity and slammed opposing backs to the ground as if they had been made of sticks. He wanted to hurt people, and he did, and the newspapers praised him for it, and crowds came out to cheer him.

When he graduated from high school Bob Neyland recruited him to play for the Tennessee Volunteers, and Hugh Bedford refused. He went to college with the South's best-known football coach begging him to play on a team that now went to bowls every year, and Hugh Bedford refused. He thought the reasons were simple, but no one else ever understood them. Bourbonville was proud of him, gloried in his exploits, felt good about itself because of him. But he despised the town, despised the people who had let him and his mother live in penury, despised a town that kowtowed to the foreigner Paul Alexander and accepted the dictatorship that the Dixie Railroad exercised over too many, laying off men when it would, bringing them back when it would, giving some young people opportunity and rejecting others, sending them to the lint and danger of the cotton mill, a hypocritical town sick with religion and greed, filled with hollow people with no life but football, and Hugh Bedford gloried in dashing their hopes, depriving them of their enthusiasms. When Tennessee haplessly lost 0–14 to Southern California in the 1940 Rose Bowl and was upset 13–19 in the 1941 Sugar Bowl by Boston College, people in Bourbonville spoke to him almost with tears in their eyes and said, "Hugh, if you had been on the team, we could have won." *We could have won.* As if these fat, slovenly, vacant-faced people could have run one hundred yards on a football field without collapsing and dying from oxygen deprivation. His stock reply: "I decided it was a damned stupid game, and I didn't want to play it anymore." So he insulted those who tried to flatter him, and he did not care.

He kept himself in tiptop shape. Put Hugh Bedford up before Charles Atlas and "dynamic tension," and Hugh Bedford would knock Charles Atlas down and kick sand in his face. A few months before the war began in 1941, a shabby little traveling circus came through Bourbonville and set up its tents on a vacant lot near the railroad tracks on the eastern edge of town. One of the acts was a wrestling bear, and the ringmaster introduced the bear's trainer, who came out with the bear waddling upright beside him. The trainer was some kind of foreigner. He wore a thick mustache oiled to points, and he spoke with a heavy accent into the screeching microphone.

His bear was trained to throw a man to the ground. Anybody who could last five minutes with the bear and not get thrown would win five dollars. The only requirement was that the human contestant had to grapple with the bear, who was safely muzzled so he could not bite, and declawed so he could not tear the flesh of anything. Five dollars! A lot of money in 1941, and Hugh Bedford was working his way through UT by doing heavy manual labor, and he was as hard as granite. He was dressed in blue jeans and an old plaid shirt. He jumped into the ring while other men were still thinking about it, and the bear trainer waved his arms around expansively and bellowed to the crowd about the "bravery of this fine young citizen" and assured everyone that the act was completely safe. People laughed. Somebody hollered out, "What about Hugh? You going to put a muzzle on him to protect the bear?"

Jim Ed Ledbetter was there with his boys, and Paul Alexander had his boys there, too, and Jim Ed said you could see a little surge of doubt run across the trainer's face when he looked at Hugh.

But it was too late now. The ringmaster led Hugh to the center of the ring; the trainer brought the bear out and took off the big leather leash. The ringmaster held up a big silver watch and held it in one hand looking at it while he raised the other hand in the air. He made a swift, downward gesture with the upraised hand and shouted, "Go!" The bear shuffled forward on his hind feet, and Hugh Bedford jumped like a cat and did a little acrobatic shift, and next thing you knew, he was on the bear's back with his strong arms wrapped around the bear's neck in a death grip. The poor bear roared, but he could not shake Hugh off, and Hugh choked the animal to death while the spectators watched, cheering at first and then in awed silence when they saw that Hugh would not let go and the bear couldn't breathe, and the trainer was on Hugh's hard, muscular back crying and beating him on the head and trying to force him to release his grip, but Hugh held on, and the bear's neck cracked so the silent crowd heard it, and the bear died.

The trainer threw himself over the furry corpse of his pet and wept with wild grief. Jim Ed stood up with a dark look, nodded to Paul Alexander and his three sons, Guy babbling, "Is the bear dead?" Jim Ed said, "I don't know about you, but I've had enough." They all got up then and went home, and Jim Ed said, "That was cruel and deliberate." But he was awed, too. It pretty well ruined the circus.

Then Hugh Bedford came home from the war as thin as a bone, and drinking heavily, smoking cigarettes, and he became obese, and his teeth turned yellow from nicotine, and nobody knew what happened except they knew he had been in combat, and he had received a medical discharge. He would not wrestle a bear again. Still, when he loomed up in front of Charles, who sat thin and worn on the witness stand, Hugh looked dangerous, and Blackie Ledbetter said later that he, too, remembered the wrestling with the bear and that he was prepared to rush headlong to the front of the courtroom and do his best to keep Hugh from strangling Charles to death.

Hugh bored in on Charles with questions, pounding them home quickly like a jackhammer eating into concrete. Charles seemed to be somewhere else—not in a daze, simply not present. Hugh's questions were insulting, and McNeil leapt to his feet time and again to object, and most of the time Judge Yancy sustained him, but Hugh succeeded in humiliating Charles, and that seemed to be his main object. The boy had begged for his life. His pleading had been granted—according to Charles's own story, which Hugh was not prepared to acknowledge as true. Charles had broken his promise, and he had proved himself a coward and a liar. All this took a lot of weaving and knitting, but Hugh was up to the job, and at the end of the day when Charles was released, the boy was sick and in tatters and went back to the witness room and sank down on the floor on his back and begged the bailiff to let him rest there for a half hour until all the reporters had gone and the crowd had thinned away.

That was where Tempe found him. She sniffed her way around the courthouse, and she came up the stairs looking in rooms until she found him lying on his back asleep. He awoke gathered in her arms.

"I've spoken to your father. You are coming with me," she said. "Don't argue." And so he did.

She hurried him beyond the remnant of people still gathered in the October gloaming, and against his weak protests she pushed him into her Buick. She opened the door, and she pushed him inside.

Abruptly a voice spoke from the gloom, tentative and only slightly raised. "Charles."

It was Rosy. She stood with her old bicycle, something that looked as if it ought to be in a junkyard somewhere.

"Rosy, what are you doing here?"

"I sneaked into the back of the courtroom," she said.

"And you came on your bicycle?"

"Yes. It's just five miles."

"What on earth will your father say?"

"I didn't tell him I was going."

"He'll be worried sick," Charles said.

"I had to come," Rosy said. She hesitated again, looking at Tempe, who smiled at her. "Charles, I'm glad you told the truth."

There she stood, overweight, shabby, her face round and her hair blown by the wind, and she looked at him with a fervor that was anything but childish and with something else that Charles could not fathom except that he knew that somewhere in it was affection for him. After holding himself intact by a combination of inertia and force of will all day long, he felt tears coming, and he did not trust himself to speak.

Tempe stepped in. "Where do you live?" she said.

"Just across the woods from Charles," Rosy said. "I'd better be getting back."

"On your bicycle?" Tempe said. "You don't have a light."

"It's all right. I'm careful. I get off the road when a car comes."

"I'll put your bike in the trunk of my car," Tempe said.

"Oh no, it'll get your beautiful car dirty."

But Tempe was already putting her key into the lock, and the trunk of the Buick popped open. "Bring your bike here," Tempe said.

Full of wonder, Rosy pushed the bike over, and with a surprising dexterity Tempe picked it up and put it back wheel first into the trunk, which didn't quite close, and said, "We'll drive up the road with the trunk open, and if the police stop us, we'll sing them a song, and they will let us go. Get in the car, Rosy. I'm Tempe Barker."

"I've never heard a name like that," Rosy said.

"I never have either," Tempe said.

Rosy sat in the backseat silent and enthralled, except that once she asked, "Are you rich?"

"I'm not," Tempe said with a laugh, "but my father is."

At the place where the unpaved Old Stage Road crossed Highway 11 Charles had Tempe pull over, and he got out and lifted the bike out of the trunk. Rosy got timidly out of the car. It was full dark now, and the stars glittered overhead, and Tempe waited with the engine idling and her window rolled down.

Rosy looked up at Charles. "I'm so thankful you told the truth," she said. While Charles was still thinking of something to say, she threw herself on her bike and sped away up the gravel road in the direction of the church and the parsonage, and disappeared in the dark.

"What a sweet girl," Tempe said. "You didn't tell me who she was."

"She's the daughter of the preacher at Midway Baptist. Her mother's dead."

"Poor thing," Tempe said. "She loves you."

"She's thirteen years old," Charles said, weary and irritated.

"Her age doesn't have anything to do with it," Tempe said. "She loves you."

Charles could not respond. He put his head back on the seat, and he slept. He knew when Tempe pulled up in front of her place, and he was aware of McKinley helping him out of the car, and the two of them went ahead to the elevator in the apartment house, and he was in her place, and McKinley was making him lie down in a bed, and Tempe was taking his shoes off.

"You're going to sleep a little while, and when you wake up, we'll have a supper the like of which you've never eaten before, because I cooked it," McKinley said.

Charles felt his exhaustion, and blessed sleep came over him like a powerful narcotic. When he awoke it was almost noon the next day, and he was in his underwear in the bed, and except for himself the apartment was empty.

A note rested on the table in Tempe's little dining nook. "I called your father to say you were all right," she had written.

For a moment all Charles could do was to lie back down in the bed and sleep some more.

*M*EANWHILE the trial went on, although Charles had contributed all he had to say on the subject. Then a great surprise.

Old Dr. Bulkely was called to the stand once again. He, too, had not attended the trial except to give his testimony, and he was deeply troubled by something that Ken McNeil had asked him, and he did not know whether it was moral for him to testify or not. Ken McNeil told him he had no choice. He would place him under subpoena and under oath, and since the information he had to give was about a third party, there was no way that the old man could claim self-incrimination.

Had Dr. Bulkely consulted a lawyer of his own, he might have found some way to release himself from an ordeal that he said morosely to a few friends was the worst thing he had been called upon to do in his medical career. But he was a simple man, accustomed to trusting authority because he had lived a simple life well within the boundaries of what authority told him he could do, whether that was the Constitution of the United States or the code of ethics of the American Medical Association. He thought that McNeil had authority, and although he protested the client-patient relation, McNeil assured him that such a relation had no status in the courts and that in a murder case it had no standing whatsoever. So Dr. Bulkely testified and created a sensation.

The story was this. Dr. Bulkely had examined Abby a few months before her death. She wanted to know if she was capable of having children. With great reluctance and under intense, unremitting questioning from McNeil, Dr. Bulkely testified that she was in perfect shape to have children. But he also discovered that her hymen was intact. Six years and more after her marriage, Abby was still a virgin. Some people in the courtroom did not know what a hymen was, and one resounding whisper was heard in the back— "It's her cherry, you asshole."

Hugh Bedford was furious and cried out his objections, but Judge Yancy rejected them. The judge seemed mesmerized by this testimony. McNeil turned condescendingly towards Hugh and purred, "I want to establish the facts, Your Honor. That is all I intend to do. I want to establish that the late Mrs. Kirby was married to a perverted man who kept her as his wife but did not use her as his wife. What perversion motivated him I do not know. I am not skilled in the psychology of abnormal sexual behavior. I intend only to establish the fact that this unnatural man was the person she sought to escape when she did whatever she did with Kelly Parmalee—if she did anything at all. This man killed her because she sought help."

He pointed grandly to Hope Kirby when he made this last statement, one of those theatrical gestures reminiscent of movies in the 1930s. McNeil smiled in his inappropriate way and handed poor old Dr. Bulkely over to Hugh Bedford, and for once Hugh seemed baffled. He had known that Dr. Bulkely was to give this testimony, the law requiring that the prosecution present the witnesses it would call. He had not known how to question his own client about the charge, except that he could tell by what questioning he did that Dr. Bulkely was telling the truth. "I just never could do it," Hope said, looking for the first time as if he were caught up in a storm of emotion that he could not control. He would not tell his lawyer any more, and now in open court Hugh Bedford could only ask Dr. Bulkely if he had had enough experience in these matters to be a competent judge. Without the slightest humor, the old doctor responded that often in his practice women who had had the hymen broken before marriage consulted him on the subject, wondering if the men they intended to marry could tell the difference. This innocent response brought a laughter through the courtroom that even Judge Yancy had trouble controlling, and without more ado Hugh allowed Dr. Bulkely to step down.

*H*UGH BEDFORD went back to his house that night and sat down with a bottle. He was puzzled and deeply troubled, and he ached for a drink. He picked the bottle up and started to drink, but he hesitated, thought for a moment, corked the bottle, and got into his car. He went up by the lake and looked out. *Sperling Winrod*, he thought. A damned silly name. The night darkened, and the water in the lake was black. Lloyd Brickman had died out there. Now Hugh Bedford could not look at the lake without thinking of Lloyd. His head ached. Lloyd came back from the war with a limp. A hero. *Lucky bastard*. Medical discharge. Lloyd had one. But he had a Purple Heart and a Bronze Star, too. Hugh Bedford had a medical discharge and was lucky not to be in prison or the nuthouse. He had no medals for bravery.

He sat looking out at the dark water, and every cell in his body ached for a drink. *All right*, he said. *All right*. He drove back to his house and uncorked the bottle. He did not bother to pour the whiskey into a glass. He drank in great gulps. The warmth soothed him. It would be all right, he thought. He drank again, more deeply. It would be all right.

*J*UDGE Yancy stayed in the King Bourbon Hotel on the square, rising in brick grandeur three floors high directly across from the courthouse. He ate alone at one of the small tables in the back of the hotel coffee shop and restaurant. He had long ago spread the word that he did not want anyone to join him when he ate. "I want nothing to distract me from the business at hand," he declared. No one wanted to talk to him. Perhaps his command was a way of saving face.

Tonight he sat at his usual seat in a corner. He looked wasted and unwell. On the two windowless sides of the restaurant, plate-glass mirrors without frames extended the length of the walls. Judge Yancy sat before the corner where the two mirrors came together. If you sat at a certain angle, you could see a quartet or a half-dozen look-alike judges taking their solitary meals. Not a pretty sight. They moved in identical gestures like a gathering of mute phantoms. He had a light supper and ate it quickly, had a cup of black coffee, and retired to his room without meeting the eyes of a soul. When he had gone through the door, those left behind took a collective breath akin to the gasp a diver makes on coming up for air from a plunge into the depths. "If that old bastard was up to his neck in quicksand, I'd step on his head." Laughter, uneasy and sputtering quickly out.

*A*T THE jail the sheriff brought Hope Kirby his supper. "I'd bring you a slug of whiskey or a beer if you wanted it," the sheriff said.

"I don't drink," Hope said. "I hain't even hungry."

"Hugh's doing a pretty good job," the sheriff said tentatively. "I reckon he's a good lawyer."

"He drinks a heap," Hope said without emphasis. He stood looking out the barred window at the thickening dusk. He had not wanted a lawyer. It was something Pappy forced on him.

Did you ever fuck your wife, Hope? The sheriff looked mutely at him for a moment, looking for something to say. "I don't reckon we can go for a walk tonight. All them reporters here—folks looking to make a lot out of nothing."

"Hit's all right. I don't much feel like walking."

"Well, you holler if you need anything, Hope."

"I won't need nothing, Sheriff. You go home and go to bed."

"No, I reckon I'll stay here tonight," the sheriff said. "You want to listen to the radio? I can bring it up here if you want."

"Nah, I never did like the radio if you want to know the truth."

"All right," the sheriff said. He turned and went downstairs.

*H*OPE stared at the black shapes of the distant mountains folded and stacked against the horizon. He remembered when he was a boy and here and there at points different from one another faint glimmerings of firelight and oil lamps showed in the dark to signal that here someone lived, existing on a perch of solitude surrounded by the great, whispering forest, with sometimes a treeless bald spot covered with grass where the trees had been cut decades ago so cattle could pasture. With the national park, the habitations were gone, and at night total darkness settled down on the ridges. Hope knew that at this distance, a good twenty or twenty-five miles, he could not see any lights that might be there. But he knew also that there were none, except over in Cade's Cove. The loneliness of the mountains now was a dead loneliness with only a few human beings to feel it and to know its immensity and the mystery that it cast on the soul.

I should of kilt Missionary. Missionary messed up so many things.

It was Missionary's idea to raid the Jap "comfort station," the whorehouse. Hope didn't want any part of it. Missionary wanted to be boss. Maybe that came from being educated and having all those diplomas and talking like somebody saying the news on the radio. He was a man used to getting his way. The men were afraid of him. Some of them whispered, "We ought to knock him off, Hope. The man's crazy. He's going to get us all killed." But he cast a spell on them, too, like a snake moving its head back and forth in front of a bird, and some liked the lessons he gave them in cruelty.

Missionary was one ace of a fighter. Brave or crazy, it didn't matter. He scared people. He loved to take chances as long as at the end of the chance he could kill Japs. Hope thought sometimes that Missionary considered himself bulletproof.

"That crazy priest is going to get us killed, Hope."

"Don't you worry none. I'm boss. We hain't going to do nothing that I don't think is good." Yet he worried. *Missionary don't care for nothing but killing Japs. That means he don't care if we get killed trying to kill them.*

Missionary spoke Spanish and Tagalog and just about every kind of dialect you heard in the Philippines. He found out from a Filipino that the Japs had a whorehouse for officers up in the green hills above Manila. "Comfort ladies," the Japs called them. Korean women, people said. The whorehouse was for officers. Jap officers went up there to rest up from beating American prisoners to death and cutting heads off sick people and slaughtering Filipinos for the sadistic pleasure of murder. Nice view. Fuck a few women and drink sake and take hot baths and get back to work. The Japs brought in Korean women to service the officers. Missionary thought it would be "a coup," he said, to raid the whorehouse and kill everybody in it, letting the Japs know they weren't safe anywhere. "It will demoralize them as nothing else can." "Demoralize" was one of Missionary's favorite words. It gave him an excuse to do lots of things.

"Hit will be too dangerous," Hope said.

"That's just it," Missionary said, his face aglow. "The Japs don't dream we can get that close. We hit that whorehouse, and they will know they are not safe anywhere. You need to think about psychological warfare, Tennessee boy. You mess up their minds, and it's that much easier to kill them."

Hope slipped down through the forest from the mountainside and looked the place over. The Japs were not supermen. In fact the Japs left to occupy the Philippines were not smart or brave or even young. The young ones and the brave ones and the smart ones were off in places like the Solomon Islands or New Guinea or China or Burma. The Japs in the Philippines were older. They made stupid mistakes, and when they made mistakes Hope and his men killed them.

The mistake they made with the whorehouse was to locate it in an old stucco mansion from the Spanish time, a gingerbread building with a couple of high fancy towers on the front of it and tall windows and high ceilings and nothing that looked real. It was painted yellow and sat on a terrace of land with a commanding view over a valley that was filled with mist in the morning and evening. The sun burned the mist off during the day, but at morning and evening twilight it was ghostly and quiet, and in the quick tropical rains it seemed almost to dissolve. Every day in the rainy season the sky went black in the afternoon and a torrent of rain fell. It didn't last long, and the wind blew the clouds away fast, but then the world steamed with the recent rain, and in the evening the mists were thick.

Missionary said it looked like a Chinese painting, except that in Chinese paintings philosophers sat under the mystical trees and debated the good life by lanterns. Missionary knew a lot about art and such stuff. Hope saw only that the mist came up to the edge of the old mansion and that it offered cover for his men to move into place and that it had no fence around it, and when the rain fell it might be easy pickings. The place was guarded by Japs in guard shacks, and when it rained the guards stayed inside their little shacks, gripping the illusion of safety. The terrace of land that gave the mansion its view also made it hard to get reinforcements up there.

Hope said all right. They would do it. As it turned out, they killed the guards so easily that Missionary said it wasn't even much fun. Then Hope and his men roared into the mansion and killed everybody in it. Jap officers died naked or with their pants halfway up their knees. Missionary carried a BAR cradled in his arms. He fired it as though it were part of his body. One

Jap officer was soaking himself in a big marble bathtub, and when Missionary got through, the Jap was shot half in two, and he was sitting dead in blood and hot water with his eyes and his mouth open.

The whores screamed and ran around like chickens when a fox gets into the coop. Hope could see their beseeching eyes and hear the terror in their voices, knowing they wanted to live. But killing was drunkenness. When guerrillas overran a bunch of Japs, it was kill or be killed. Hope learned early that you set your head and did it, and you went on killing like a machine, your mind mesmerized by overcoming all those restraints raised by the sympathy of one human being for another, that tell you to do no harm to others because they are like you, and you felt what they felt. You killed by gathering your interior forces like you decide to dive into a cold pool of water in the mountains on a summer day when you have pieces of hay stuck to your skin and you are sweating like a squeezed dishrag, and you make yourself go headfirst into the pool. Once you start killing, you don't stop. Hesitate to think about it, and you give somebody permission to kill you.

Hope fired with his bolt-action 1903 Springfield. The other men fired in a frenzy that was not consciously savage but it was merciless, and the whores fell in heaps of blood.

Hope shot one of them in the belly. He didn't mean to shoot her there. She was plump, and her skin was almost pink. She came running out of the room naked, her arms lifted towards him, and he saw the motion and shot at it, and the bullet hit her a few inches below her navel. She fell stumbling forward, putting her hands over the hole with the stuff coming out, blood pouring out of her mouth suddenly. When they were all dead and Hope looked at her again, he saw that blood and shit had oozed out of her body. Lots of the whores shit on themselves when they died. The brown shit mixed with red blood ran in semiliquid streaks down their dead, naked thighs. He felt awful.

The men looked around when they had done killing and sobered up fast. It was the biggest kill Hope's men made during the entire war. Thirty-eight bodies, twelve of them whores. Most of the Japs and most of the whores naked. Something unforgiving about the sight of bullet holes in naked bodies unmasked by clothes. Even bloody clothes kept you from seeing how soft and flimsy human flesh was.

Missionary seemed filled with rapture. He was like people Hope had seen at church when they got religion, hopping about and shouting. "That was glorious! Glorious! They were begging for their lives."

"I reckon they was," Hope said, staring at the plump woman he had shot. "We shouldn't of kilt the women."

"They shouldn't have been here," Missionary said.

"Maybe they couldn't help hit," Hope said.

"You're getting soft, General," Missionary crowed.

"Maybe so," Hope said, staring down at the woman he had killed.

"War is war," Missionary said. "In war you don't think about anything but killing the enemy. Otherwise you go crazy."

Hope did think about it. He did learn after the war that the whores had not wanted to be there. The Japs picked them up in Korea and forced them to be whores. He thought about that often. They were sex slaves, and they died as if they were war criminals.

When he gathered Abby into his arms on their wedding night, she came to him naked and breathing so hard she couldn't talk. He ran his hands over her, and she cried out with pleasure. She was soft, but not weakly soft. Firm with being young and pretty, and all his. "I've waited for you," she gasped. "I didn't know I was waiting for you, but I have waited for you. All my life." Coming to her wedding night a virgin was like winning a race. She had won. But he kept thinking that under the surface of her beautiful body was a skeleton, blood, guts, shit, and bile, and a bullet could tear through it all in less time than it took to wink, and putrefaction would set in, and her body would stink. It was like hugging death, and when he tried to enter her and produce life, his poor prick went soft as the empty finger of a rubber glove. *This is what we are.*

She wept with frustration. Night after night she wept with frustration.

I should of let her go, he thought to himself, thinking of her in her coffin, her sweet body rotting down there as he had seen it rotting in his mind when he tried to make love to her.

He could not tell her what it was. He couldn't tell anybody. He buried it in himself. Finally she stopped crying at night. *Pappy didn't know.*

At night he lay with his arm around her, feeling her naked body close to his, hearing her soft, regular breath as she slept, and he told himself that this was enough. *I will get over this,* he thought. *Hit will be like a sickness, and you get well from hit, and life goes on like hit did before you got sick.* They would mutually take virginity from each other and have children as all his brothers except John Sevier had married and had children. The brothers did not tell each other what they had done in the war. They never talked about it. *If they got over hit, I will get over hit, too,* he thought. Then everything would be all right, and he would be proud of his children as he was proud of Abby when they went to church together and when she sang in the choir on Sunday mornings and when she sat laughing with the wives of his brothers and even with Pappy when the family got together for things. He liked to look at her. He took her to the picture show in Knoxville. They could not go to the picture show in Bourbonville because lots of people of the Church of God of the Union

Assembly thought picture shows were as bad as dancing, but she liked to go to the picture show, and Hope loved to do anything she liked to do. He was amazed at what they could do in the picture shows to make pretend things seem real. He never saw any girl up there on the big screen at the Tennessee Theatre on Gay Street that looked as pretty as Abby.

It would pass, he thought. The way the war passed. And in the meantime she was his peace and his safety.

But it did not pass.

Hope Kirby's supper went cold and uneaten. He stood at the window looking out at the distant darkness of the sleeping mountains, and he wanted with all his heart to die.

*B*Y GOD, *I am going to win this case.* Hugh Bedford did not open another bottle when he finished that one. He threw himself onto his bed in his clothes and slept three hours. When he woke up, it was still dark. He took off his clothes and took a cold shower. His head hurt like hell. *I should have drunk another bottle.* Instead he took a handful of aspirin.

When the trial resumed, he called Joye and Love to the stand. "Tell us what you did in the war."

McNeil rose. "Your Honor, I'm sure these boys did great things in the war, but what they did has nothing to do with this case or their testimony."

"It may not mean anything to a man who stayed here at home while these men were at war, Your Honor, but what they did tells you what kind of people they are."

Judge Yancy let him continue. Joye had been at D-Day in Normandy. He was in the third wave at Omaha Beach. Late that night he helped stack American bodies. Like cordwood, he said later. He never liked to talk about the war. Love had been at Iwo Jima. They had medals. They had done their duty. First Joye, then Love. Hugh Bedford drew out all the details from each of them. They seemed embarrassed at their heroism. They made a good impression.

Each one had the same story to tell about Hope. "He couldn't of done hit," Joye said in his high-pitched mountain accent. "He was with us all night long." He talked like a man who believed every word he said because he had been there. So did Love.

In cross-examination, McNeil bored in on them. He threatened them with charges of perjury. And he brought up a more serious subject. To Joye he said, "A dozen or more witnesses saw you and your brother go out into the lake with the accused on the night of the murders. Two dozen or more saw you return to the dock the next morning with the accused in the boat. Now it stands to reason that if the accused is judged guilty of murder, the two of you let him off somewhere during the night to give him the chance to get to the courthouse and to do the deed. And after the deed, you picked him up again, and you came into the dock in the morning to provide an alibi. If that happened, you are accessories before the fact of murder."

Hugh Bedford was on his feet to object in a whiplash. But Judge Yancy overruled him and made him sit down. "The district attorney," the judge said ominously in his squeaky little voice, "is informing the witnesses about the facts of the law. There is nothing objectionable about that."

"An accessory before the fact of murder is also in part guilty of the murder even if he did not pull the trigger on the murder weapon. Is that clear to you, Mr. Kirby?" Joye, and then later on Love, answered in the affirmative. But a cloud passed over Joye's face. With that solemn announcement hanging in the air, McNeil repeated his questions. Joye did not change his testimony one jot. He repeated his answers, laconic, firm, eyes fixed on McNeil as if he were a cur they had kicked into a corner. The whole scene was repeated with Love. Love seemed thoughtful when McNeil threatened him. But he did not waver either. Everybody in the courtroom knew they were lying. Nearly everybody admired them for it. They never recanted their story. Joye told it all over again four or five years ago, just before he died. It was in the newspapers, a resurrection of mysteries unsolved. Maybe in the end they believed it.

Then a surprise witness. Billy McKenzie from Hazard, Kentucky.

"I had the honor of serving with Hope Kirby in an irregular band of guerrillas in the Philippine Islands during the Second World War."

Hope remembered that McKenzie was from Kentucky, and Kentucky was close. Hugh Bedford called every William McKenzie in six Kentucky telephone books before he got the right one. A good witness, too. A schoolteacher no less, teaching agriculture and sponsoring the Future Farmers of America in a Kentucky high school. His belly bulged over his belt. Hope remembered how skinny he had been in the war. You could almost see his backbone through his stomach then. He spoke with a quiet voice full of authority, a little bit of a hillbilly accent, but that was all to the good since under it he sounded confident and educated. "This man," he said firmly, "got us all through the war without losing a one of us to the Japs."

As he spoke, a quietness settled over the courtroom. People listened rapt. Hugh got out of him a calm description of what it had been like to ambush Japanese patrols and run away, to hide at night in the mountains of the Philippines, listening always for the furtive approach of a cruel enemy, fearful always of betrayal, battling sickness. "We won because we had a good cause, and we had a great leader in Hope Kirby. That's why I'm alive here today. MacArthur ran out on us; Hope Kirby stayed and fought."

It was the stuff of the movies or the *Reader's Digest,* and in the silent courtroom Billy McKenzie's testimony became one of those memorable moments when for no good reason the spectators imagined that they could be proud of something somebody else had done.

McNeil saw an opening, and in his cross-examination he made for it, only to discover that he had impaled himself. "Tell me this, Mr. McKenzie. You say you killed Japs. Killed a great many of them, you say. Would you also say that the defendant enjoyed the killing? Is it possible that he acquired a taste for killing that he brought back with him here to this country?"

McKenzie gave Ken McNeil the kind of look a dignified man might give to a worm he found twisting in his chocolate ice-cream sundae. "In war," he said quietly, "you fight the enemy because he is there. You kill him because he has killed your kind, and he will kill you if he can. The Japs had no mercy on our prisoners of war. They beat Hope Kirby's brother senseless, and when Hope escaped, he killed a couple of them and hauled his brother John Sevier away on his back and kept John Sevier alive during the war while he kept us alive, too. We stayed alive because we killed Japs. We killed them like you slaughter pigs or cows. It was our job. We came home to live the lives we earned by killing them. But all a soldier wants when he comes home, Mr. McNeil, is never to kill again. Maybe folks like you who stayed home during the war can't understand that, but that's how it is."

Blackie Ledbetter said it was the kind of speech that ought to go in the schoolbooks and be memorized by kids a hundred years hence. People looked at one another and nodded as if they had all understood something in a lightning flash, solved a puzzle, felt the pleasure of seeing complicated things fit together so close you couldn't see the lines, indeed saw a kind of beauty in the fitting, the kind of beauty that comes on you unawares when you were not expecting beauty to be there, and then, there it is! They saw McNeil squashed like a cockroach.

"I have no more questions, Your Honor." McNeil could not even flash his bland little grin. He sat down and shuffled some papers as if he had important things to think about.

Billy McKenzie walked over to where Hope sat at the defendant's table. Hope stood up, and they shook hands. "Hello, General," Billy said. The two men embraced. It was heartfelt, and it made an impression. Some said later that it made the biggest impression on Judge Yancy. He saw something slipping away.

*J*UDGE Yancy recessed the court for lunch. People gathered around the tables in the cafes or ate their lunches seated on the grass or the park benches around the courthouse or stood in little knots under the great, crimson-leafed oaks. A subdued anticipation hung over all the conversations.

Dr. Bulkely's testimony stayed in people's minds. It was for some men the opportunity for delicious obscenities. But there was something more troubling in the air than smut. If Abby had lived a virgin for all those years, her husband was responsible. If he would not use her as a wife, what was the poor girl to do? It was a matter of intense discussion, and the consequence was that the town brooded in uncertainty, and opinions were less fixed than they had been. If the testimony had come from anybody else but Dr. Bulkely, it might have been dismissed. But Dr. Bulkely was a man of great integrity, and if people laughed at him for his vitamins and his prescriptions for chewing their food, they still respected him as a doctor.

Opinions about Charles wavered, too. Those in the courtroom who knew him otherwise saw at once that he was not himself. Judge Yancy's surprising recess so that Charles could rest confirmed what many had surmised, that Charles was sick during his testimony and that he seemed to be someone else. But Charles and his testimony took second place to Dr. Bulkely's revelations.

Lawrence Arceneaux, sitting near the front of the courtroom, could observe the cold and expressionless face of Roy Kirby. He read into that face a future of horror. He sat thinking of the boy in France and wondering if it were ever possible in this world to atone for evil. *Well, that's why we have to have a God*, Arceneaux thought. *When we can't forgive ourselves, we can believe that God forgives us.*

The afternoon was given up to summations. McNeil spoke for the state, standing stiffly before the jury holding his notes in one hand, reciting the facts of the case in his careful, pedantic voice. He was like a schoolmaster reciting well-known truths without emotion, as though emotion might color and distort the crystalline clarity of his beloved facts. McNeil was a reasonable man. The law was clear and reasonable. Crime was unreasonable. Sexual crimes were the most unreasonable of all.

McNeil's father had preached against women who cut their hair and wore slacks and went swimming in public swimming pools and danced and played cards. The elder McNeil screamed his sermons. McNeil was not so emotional. He believed in rectitude. Reasonable men on a jury should be able to see their duty without requiring a torrent of rhetoric intended to make them do the right thing when the right thing was evident. Hope Philip Kirby had committed cold-blooded murder. An unimpeachable eyewitness had been there. That witness had identified the murderer. Nothing remained but for the jury to do its duty and find him guilty of murder in the first degree.

He went on for a very long time and repeated himself often, being sure that every fact was clear. One of the reporters from Knoxville wrote that McNeil's summation "was so boring that one might have supposed he was explaining how to wash a car to an audience that lived on a dirt road and found washing cars a waste of time." Several people went to sleep. The jurymen listened with stolid faces. Judge Yancy fidgeted on the bench and from time to time looked up at the clock, and even with the electric lights on, the courtroom darkened.

McNeil defended himself later on. Judge Yancy had allowed the sheriff under badgering from Hugh Bedford to tell of finding Kelly Parmalee *in flagrante* with another woman, since moved away from the county, and McNeil thought the judge had finally lost his mind. He thought that Judge Yancy had already made so many errors that the trial would be thrown out by an appeals court, he said, and he was tired and disgusted. He felt that he was dealing with a crazy judge and a lunatic defense attorney who was also malicious and diabolical. Everything that McNeil might have said, he claimed, would have been futile because this trial was not going to count, and he knew it. It was all to be done over again.

Hugh Bedford seemed to absorb energy from the trial as though he had been a battery charged by lightning. It was almost four-thirty when he stood up to make his summation. He was fierce. While McNeil had stood still, speaking in almost a monotone, Hugh stalked the jury, moving back and forth like some predator animal ready to leap over the wall of the jury box and feast on all the jurymen. He built an argument that moved step by prodigious step so that many who heard it recall it all these years afterwards, and some of them believe it with the same conviction that they believe in visitations from space aliens in UFOs or in Oliver Stone's movie about the Kennedy assassination.

Any number of people had reason to have killed Kelly Parmalee, Hugh Bedford said. Angry husbands. Adulterous wives used and abandoned. Children defending the honor of a mother. A father avenging a daughter's lost honor. He would not name names, but he could name enough of them to fill a good-sized telephone book. And what, he asked, would any member of the jury do in such a circumstance? Kelly Parmalee, he said, was like a snake who could charm helpless birds so that they could only stare at him as he opened his mouth to devour them. Abby Kirby had been only one of those poor birds, and husbands and fathers throughout the county might have done a chivalrous deed had they banded together long before now and whipped Kelly

Parmalee within an inch of his life to show him that women in Bourbon County stood on a pedestal of purity protected by their valiant men. Yes, shouted Hugh Bedford, it was a collective failure of manhood that had allowed Kelly Parmalee to have slithered through the county as long as he had.

It was melodramatic and corny. Inviting lynch law? In 1953 maybe. But what mob of Southern white men ever hanged another white man for screwing women? People reading the transcript over recently have expressed amazement that the audience did not burst out in laughter as Hugh Bedford marched through his rhetorical flourishes. A difference in time and perception. Then and now. These are people nourished on television's cool medium where conversational banalities ooze from automatons.

Hugh Bedford was one of the last great courtroom orators. His words rolled forth like an invincible river sawing a canyon through sandstone as hard as iron. In his mood of fiery indignation he could have read the label from a Campbell soup can and left the contents hot enough to eat.

Hugh Bedford believed that nearly every man on that jury believed he had the right to kill his wife if he found her screwing somebody else. His eloquence lay in his ability to say that without saying it directly, to say it by implication and innuendo and metaphor. A good lawyer could lift a dull audience to art without their being aware of it or embarrassed by it. Later he had a refrain: "If that cowardly little son of a bitch hadn't got in the way, everybody in this shithole of a town would have known Hope did what a man has to do, and they would have patted him on the back and winked." He could not say to the jury, "Hope did it, and that's it." But he did say, "Let's suppose that a war hero who adored his wife and did everything he could for her found out that she had been committing adultery with a rich citizen of this town. Suppose you were that man. Suppose the sudden revelation of betrayal drove you completely out of your mind. Would you be justified if you killed the man and the woman who broke up your home and destroyed your dreams?"

Reasonable doubt! That was the test. Two good men and true had testified that Hope Kirby was with them all night long. "To my mind their testimony under oath is enough to plant reasonable doubt in your minds as you weigh the evidence in this case. Let me say this to all of you. And listen carefully, gentlemen. There are laws written in books. There are laws in the minds of judges. But there is also the law written on your hearts. In this case, gentlemen, you are the law. You have it in your power to let my client, Hope Philip Kirby, go free. Ask what you would have done. Consult the law written on your hearts. You can, and you must, decide according to that law."

Hugh looked at them all and paused a very long time. People thought he might sit down then, a dramatic period to the silence that hung in the expectant air like the instant after lightning has flamed brilliantly across the sky and you wait for thunder to crash.

"Gentlemen, the man who sits here accused of murder is a hero from the greatest war America has ever fought, a war against the cruelest enemy we have faced. He led a guerrilla band in the Philippines against the Japs, Japs who cut the heads off our boys, Japs who sent our boys on the Bataan death march. Some of you proudly wore the uniform the defendant wore. Some of you were fired on by a savage foe. Some of you know what it is to have your friends die. Some of you know—" And here Hugh Bedford's voice broke.

It was for everyone who saw it the most confounding part of the trial. Hugh Bedford's hard voice fractured into a sob, and for a moment he could not continue. He stood with his head bowed. Judge Yancy looked down at him in astonishment. "Counselor," he growled, "are you ill?" The real question was: "Hugh Bedford, are you drunk?"

Hugh Bedford shook, then got control of himself. He lifted his big, round head to look out on his dumbfounded audience. Then he turned to stare out a window, and tears glistened in his eyes and rolled down his cheeks. He resumed, his voice hoarse. "Gentlemen, perhaps some of you know what it is to lose comrades to the enemy, to lose men you knew and cared for as you can only care for those who day by day shared with you the possibility that at any moment you can die a violent and painful death. Some of you know what it is to see the bodies of your friends stacked up like wood on a battlefield when the shooting has stopped."

He stopped. The courtroom was as still as the moon on the desert. He took a deep breath. "My client, my friend here, knew that danger night after night, day after day, for almost three years. He brought all his men and a wounded brother home to their families. If other men had been like my client, if our generals had had the spirit of my client, his wisdom and his courage, we would have won that war faster, we would have had fewer dead, and we would have killed more of the enemy." Another pause, a struggle against himself, the voice coming at last hoarse and low. "If I had had commanders like this man, gentlemen, some of my own men would still be alive."

People looked at one another. People in Bourbonville did not know what their men in the war had done. The men came home and did not talk about it. Hugh Bedford never told what he had done. He had a medical discharge. A few people knew that. They did not know what it meant or how it came about. Some thought he had been wounded. They did not know that Hugh Bedford had commanded men in battle.

"This is the man you judge, gentlemen. This is the man whose life you hold in your hands. This is the man you can send to his death. This is also the man you can free to take his rightful place in the world of light and breath and friendship and family. In that terrible war, Hope Philip Kirby gave us an example. We owe him something. But what we give him, gentlemen, is up to you. That's all I have to say."

He stumbled to his seat looking exhausted—a Hugh Bedford abruptly strange to Bourbonville. Silent spectators stared at him. The jury seemed mesmerized. When he sat down, the jurymen seemed to come out of their trance, and some of them looked at one another and nodded silently.

Judge Yancy broke the spell with a bang of his gavel. "Court will be adjourned until tomorrow morning." He seemed unusually perturbed. People in the courtroom noticed that instead of the usual scowl, he had a different expression, troubled and impatient, a bit like a man who (some said) had a sudden and urgent summons by his bowels to get to the toilet as soon as possible. He stood up abruptly as the bailiff cried, "All rise." When he strode into his chamber at the rear, the judge slammed the door behind him, and everyone knew that Hugh Bedford had scored big.

*A*NOTHER cool October night. Passionate arguments in subdued murmuring. Families talking over the supper table. Hugh Bedford had scored big with one audience—the town. And yet Dr. Bulkely's testimony remained like a rock in a shoe. Where did it fit? What kind of man was Hope Kirby? If Abby was a virgin six years after her marriage, shouldn't Hope have divorced her? And maybe . . . Some things were whispered but were not spoken.

When court resumed next morning, there were some empty places in the courtroom. People had errands to do, lives to live, ordinary obligations, and no one expected much from Judge Yancy beyond a dry, mechanical instruction to the jurymen. It was up to the jury now, and people could wait until the jurors were ready to deliver their verdict. In the meantime life could not stop for a trial.

Judge Yancy surprised everybody. The charge, lifted out of the inerrant transcript, has been resurrected by the newspapers, has been studied by reporters and TV people like some Talmudic document releasing secrets from the past, and on one of the television stations a couple of lawyers sat before the cameras pontificating grandly on events in this antediluvian period, neither of them yet born in the autumn of 1953. They agreed with a show of anger and disgust that Judge Yancy's charge to the jury was an outrage impossible to imagine in a modern courtroom. "The judge must have gone crazy," one of the lawyers said, showing considerable indignation and shaking his head incredulously enough to demonstrate his wisdom to every viewer in the land. "He would be removed from the bench if he did such a thing now. Any court of appeals in the country today would declare a mistrial for such a travesty of justice."

Why did the old judge explode like that? It has become a resurrected mystery to Bourbonville, but it will never be solved because it all happened too long ago. Maybe the judge could not have told why himself. He was all spite and bile and rancor. What did Judge Yancy believe about Abby? The old fool's mother died when he was eight years old. He was an only child. His father ran a livery stable, and some old-timers said he used to whip his son with the leather strap that attached to the bridle of a horse. When cars came along, the father, Wayne Tobias Yancy, went out of business. That was about 1915, when Henry started making the Model T Ford, the one with the brass radiator. By then the son, Shirley Yancy, or S. K. (for Shirley Kimbrough), had worked his way through the university in Knoxville washing dishes in the cafeteria and carrying newspapers, and he was reading law, and making his way without friends or family.

He did well in the law. He cultivated a rhetoric of meanness. Maybe he didn't have to cultivate it. It seemed to come naturally to him to break opposition witnesses like dry sticks, reducing them to confusion and shame. In 1925 he represented the state in the Scopes "Monkey Trial." He called in brass-mouth William Jennings Bryan to help the state against Clarence Darrow. He said he didn't give a damn if human beings descended from monkeys or jackasses, John T. Scopes violated the laws of the state of Tennessee by teaching evolution in his classroom at Dayton, Tennessee. That's why Shirley K. Yancy argued against him, and that's why John T. Scopes was found guilty, and that's why he was fined one hundred dollars.

He said to a reporter once, "Everybody wants to ask me about that Scopes trial. Why doesn't somebody notice the most important part of my life? I have sent more felons to the electric chair than any other judge in the history of Tennessee."

It was a short history. The electric chair was introduced only about the turn of the century. Before that, Tennessee hanged its felons, often in public before audiences of families who brought picnic lunches.

Wayne Tobias Yancy died in 1926. Lawyer S. K. Yancy did not go to his funeral. Shortly afterwards he was appointed judge in the Fourth Circuit. There he stayed. If Judge Yancy ever had a lover, nobody ever knew about it. He loved Abby. She was embarrassed by him. He looked at her like a big dog and took his hat off his bald head when he spoke to her. But it is a rule in small southern towns among white people who wanted to be considered ladies and gentlemen not to make a scene, and Abby was not about to tell the old goat off when he took an interest in her. The occasion was a visit by her high-school class to talk to the judge about the law. She was the class secretary, and she wore modest clothes and no makeup because girls in the Church of God of the Union Assembly didn't wear makeup. She was pretty enough without it, and she smiled with her pretty mouth, and she seemed to hang on every word the judge said, and, more important, she wrote it all down.

He told them that he had put more felons in the electric chair than any other sitting judge in the history of Tennessee. Abby asked him to explain what the electric chair was. She thought it was a chair with electric lights. Yes, she was that sheltered, that naive. When he told her that it was a chair that fried felons so they could not murder anybody else, she cried. He took it on himself to explain, to justify himself. He was touched by her innocence. Maybe she became his Virgin Mary.

So here was the question: Did Judge Yancy believe that Abby had defiled herself by fornication? Was he so angry with her that he transferred his anger to Hope Kirby, not only for killing her but for breaking down the last illusions that the poor old man had? Or, to the contrary, did he refuse to believe everything he heard in the courtroom? What was the difference between believing in Abby Kirby and believing in the Virgin Mary? People believe in the Virgin so intensely that she appears to them in visions. Their world may be a mess, but they believe in her. Why could not Judge Yancy have continued to believe in Abby no matter what evidence rose up to the contrary?

Whatever his motive, his charge to the jury was like hitting them collectively in the head with an axe.

He started quietly. After the pyrotechnics of Hugh Bedford, Judge Yancy seemed almost subdued, perhaps weary, even exhausted. The jurymen leaned forward to hear him. Some of them cupped their ears. As he continued, his voice gathered strength. Blackie Ledbetter, a veteran of battlefield surgery in Korea, knew how men expressed themselves in pain. They might try to hide it, but the pain rose beneath their pretensions like a ridge of bone under broken skin. He wondered if Judge Yancy might be on the verge of screaming. But no. He raised his voice but continued to speak in pounding, perfectly coherent sentences. You can read it in the transcript for yourself.

"The law is the protector of human civilization. It is a wall against savagery and barbarism. Within the law is light; outside the law is blackness and chaos. Let the wall come down, and the powers of darkness rush in, and the darkness blinds us all and carries everything away that human beings have ever created to build civilization. Laws are made against the evils that lurk in the human breast, the foulest garden in the universe. And yet law permits every noble thing that human beings are capable of doing, for with the law's light, the darkness flees. Nothing noble can be done without the light the law casts on society, without the protection the law gives society from the people within who if left in the dark would sink into unending war and soon would devour themselves, for they would have destroyed everything else in creation."

He went on, his voice rising now but still deliberate and slow, his bald head bent over the scrawled notes he had made on a pad of paper.

"Above all these powers of darkness rises the light cast by virtuous womanhood. On our beautiful Christian women all the gentle virtues of civilization depend. Where would we be without our mothers? Where would we be without those nurturing women who paid the price of humiliation and pain to bring us into the world? Whose gentle hand would rock the cradle? Who but a mother could clean children who foul themselves? Whose soft voice would lull us to sleep at night? Whose kind figure would prepare our meals and wash our clothes and ply the needle and thread to sew up our garments when we have torn them at work or play? Whose tears would bathe our wounds? Whose wise counsel would restrain the bloody hand of men from carnage?"

Judge Yancy plunged on, delivering an oration that might have done credit to some nineteenth-century politician bawling the ideals of chivalry to an audience of men who had spent their lives reading every courtly romance ever written. Blackie Ledbetter said later on that if it had not been a courtroom, not been a murder trial, he might have burst out laughing. But he had been in Korea, cutting out chunks of human flesh from living bodies and sewing men back together when they had been torn apart by unchivalrous weapons. He came back sour on majorities. In his later life he would not have a television set in his house because he said it was too stark a reminder of how stupid most people were. He ruminated often that being a doctor, saving lives, might be a waste of time and even a mistake since most people spent their days and nights in worthless banality. In the courtroom, Judge Yancy's voice rose, putting so much force behind the words that they seemed to mean something deep and essential that people in the audience longed to believe.

Then he got down to the case at hand. "In this case, gentlemen of the jury, you will not decide merely the question of right and wrong between a husband and his wife and the man alleged to have been her importunate and adulterous lover. Only God knows whether they were adulterers. If they were, God will punish them, has punished them already, and will continue to punish them forever and ever in the burning fire that is never quenched and never cooled. If they were not adulterers, they will wear the crown of martyrdom.

"But this case is not about them and their relations. No, gentlemen, this case is an examination of that sturdy wall of law that keeps the darkest demons in the corrupt soul of the world at bay and allows us to be the civilized people we are here, in this courtroom, in this town, in this nation."

Judge Yancy glared down at Hugh Bedford. "I believe we have witnessed here a parody of the legal process. I have sat here listening to this testimony, looking the witnesses in the face, looking the accused in the eye, and I believe we all know who the guilty man is. I believe that you know that man killed those two human beings in cold blood, taking into his own filthy hands the sacred obligations given to judges and juries as though to priests of the Most High God. The blood of the young woman he killed cries silently out against him like the blood of Abel from the ground. You know his guilt. I know his guilt. And I charge you as good men and true to bring in a verdict that fits the violent and bloody deed that he has committed."

He glared down at the Kirby men, who looked back at him with their solemn and expressionless faces. "I suspect more than one man ought to be tried here, and I hope that the district attorney will do his duty to discover and bring to justice the accomplices to this heinous act that is here being remembered and judged. But now we have only one accused soul to try and condemn, and he stands under the matchless light of truth, and he cannot hide from it. I will not countenance any but one verdict in this case. It doesn't matter what he did in the war. It doesn't matter whether he ever told a lie in his life before this day. He lies by his silence. He is as guilty as any felon I have ever judged, any cold-blooded reptile I have ever looked in the eye, any killer I've ever sent to a just death in the electric chair. I cannot sit here and be silent when I feel his blood guilt in this room with us like the guilt of David when by his order Uriah the Hittite was killed."

Hugh Bedford struggled to his feet, his face blazing with triumph. "Your Honor, I demand that you declare a mistrial here and now. You cannot give such a charge to a jury. You cannot do the job that the law places in their hands alone."

"I can direct a jury to bring back a verdict of guilty if the facts in the case merit it, and in this case they do," Judge Yancy said.

"I want the record to show that you can direct a verdict of not guilty, but you cannot direct a verdict of guilty."

McNeil stood up. "Your Honor, please—"

"This court is adjourned until the jury brings back its verdict," Judge Yancy shouted, and with that he banged his gavel and stalked back to his chambers. Many thought that he knew he had overreached. All he could do was withdraw.

An appalled silence reigned. The jury sat stone-still. The bailiff, Ward Osborne, remembered himself finally to say, "All rise," but by then the judge had slammed the door behind him. Ward went over to the gate in the side of the jury box. He opened it and motioned with an almost frantic anxiety for them to get up and get out as though he feared that the judge might return to the courtroom with a gun and shoot them all down. Slowly, like a herd of animals, they followed him back to the jury room. And slowly, the crowd in the courtroom dissipated, murmuring and perplexed.

NOW THE town waited, not holding its breath but beguiling itself with earnest and ruminative talk that in its narcotic plenitude gave people the illusion of floating on time as though on the roll of a long and scarcely discernible wave at sea. Lunch came and went. A pimply-faced reporter from the afternoon newspaper in Knoxville called his editor from the telephone at the back of the Rexall drugstore. He spoke in a loud voice. No doubt now, he said. Judge Yancy had lost his head. Disgraced the bench. Should be removed. Any guilty verdict would be reversed on appeal. A new trial would come. Another judge. If the jury returned a verdict of not guilty, Hope Kirby would go free. It had been Hope Kirby's day.

But the hours slipped away, the afternoon passed, and the jury did not return. Talk droned on in the drugstores, on street corners in the cooling and fading light of dying October, and in the cafes where people drank cup after cup of coffee. In the courtroom itself some people sat, afraid to lose their places, and they talked while old photographs looked mutely down on them and the calm eyes of General Longstreet viewed the scene with authority.

Bailiff Osborne waddled out of the jury room a little after six in the evening. He created a murmur and stir of excitement that quickly died. He was on his way to fetch supper. People pelted him with questions. "I can't say nothing," he said, looking fatly important. He went to the Red Bud Cafe and into the kitchen at the back. He came out carrying a tray stacked high with sandwiches wrapped up in wax paper and covered with a towel. Grant Carmichael, bull-necked proprietor, chef, and headwaiter, followed with a pot of coffee, one of those big, shiny electric things that look like a keg. You see them at church suppers. He carried it with two hands. His son Sherman came after him with a restaurant-sized can of JFG coffee. Grant was huge; Sherman was as skinny as a reed, with black hair greased back over his narrow head and a reedy voice to match his appearance. He grinned to the left and the right. He was a cheerful soul. People crowded around them to get news. Grant said, "Nobody said a word while I was in the room." "I didn't hear nothing either," Sherman said, smiling at everybody.

The evening passed. Judge Yancy's chamber door stayed shut. The air in the courtroom freshened with the stirring of evening air, and people got up and shut windows. Eight o'clock came, then nine. Then ten. The clock in the courthouse tower struck the hours. Now and then a train passed. The locomotives rattled the courthouse windows. The horns were deep and mournful and carried for miles. A somnolence fell over Bourbonville. The cafes remained open. Some men had flasks and poured bourbon or moonshine into their coffee or else drank their coffee and poured the whiskey into the emptied cups.

At 10:40, Ward Osborne came almost furtively out of the jury room and went softly across to the judge's chambers and knocked timidly on the door. The door opened like a shot. Ward bowed his way inside and disappeared. The news spread through the wireless telegraph of voices, relayed from person to person in the square. A surge of spectators rolled back into the courtroom. The Kirby men appeared as though from nowhere and took their place in front. Their faces showed nothing. The regulator clock ticked above the door, brass pendulum reflecting dim light from the chandeliers. Reporters stood around the walls to get a jump ahead of the rest when the verdict was in. Ken McNeil came in, blandly nodding to people and smiling. Nobody smiled back at him.

The sheriff had been telephoned. He brought Hope Kirby over from the jail. Now they appeared, Hope Kirby handcuffed, the sheriff walking in front of him, a deputy behind him, and down they came to the defendant's table. Hugh Bedford followed the deputy. People thought, *Uh-oh*. Hugh Bedford's face was red. He had been drinking. The reporters brought out their notebooks. Ward Osborne went to the judge's chambers again and came out. "All rise," he said.

The spectators rumbled to their feet. Judge Yancy came in walking slowly, gathering his robe around him, his face set in a frown, looking at no one. Ward Osborne said, "You may be seated." People sat down. Ward Osborne went back into the jury room. In a while he returned, diffident in his authority. The jurymen followed him, shuffling, looking down, hangdog and weary. The few men wearing neckties had loosened them.

The foreman crept behind Ward Osborne. He was a skinny man named Lonnie Wyatt, not a stupid man. He had been a couple of years in the university to study agriculture, and he was a good farmer. He had served as a justice of the peace until he got tired of people showing up all hours of the night to be married. He went back to farming full-time, and he read the

Bible and went to church and otherwise minded his own business. Ward Osborne whispered, "Sit down." The jury sat.

Judge Yancy said, "Have you gentlemen reached a verdict?"

Wyatt stood up. He held a piece of paper, and his hand trembled slightly. The paper fluttered palely in the dull light. "We have, Your Honor." He had to clear his throat before he could get the sentence out.

"Will the defendant rise and face the jury?" the judge said. "The jury will rise." Hope Kirby stood up. Hugh Bedford stood unsteadily next to him. Hope was calm. He looked up at the judge. The judge did not meet his eyes. Hope looked back at the jury, his hands crossed in front of him.

"The defendant is charged on two counts of premeditated murder in the first degree," the judge said. "What is your verdict on count one?" Unblinking ferocity directed at Wyatt. Outside the sparse traffic of a late evening whispered in random gusts through Bourbonville. Wyatt cleared his throat, looked down at the paper in his hand, looked up.

"We find the defendant guilty, Your Honor."

There was an exhalation of breath, and it was an anticlimax when the jury foreman announced the verdict of guilty on the second count as well.

Judge Yancy looked coldly at Hope Kirby. "Will the defendant step forward." Hugh Bedford came around the table and stood with him. "Do you have anything to say before I pronounce sentence?"

Hope Kirby spoke out clear. "No, Your Honor, I don't." He looked the judge in the eye. Judge Yancy stared at him. Somebody said later you could have held a match up in the air between them, and it would have caught fire spontaneously. Then, like an old preacher who has said the wedding ceremony so many times that he knows it by heart, Judge Yancy rattled through the phrases that condemned Hope Philip Kirby to be conducted to the Tennessee State Prison in Nashville, there to have sentence of death executed upon him no later than January 1, 1954.

"Happy New Year," somebody whispered.

"*IT WAS* my fault," the sheriff said afterwards. "I should have given Charlie Alexander time. You know how it is when you start working a jigsaw puzzle—you fit one piece and then another one, and you can't stop yourself from seeing what it all looks like in the end. I was mad, too. Somebody made a fool of me, dragging me out to the Yellow Dog like that. But I ask myself, why didn't I just let it go?"

"Because you was the sheriff," somebody said.

"Yeah, I was the sheriff."

Hope Kirby had to be transported to Nashville next morning. The sheriff slept at the jail and got up at five and woke Hope up and loaded him into the sheriff's car. The sheriff drove. Hope sat in back behind the steel mesh screen. A Tennessee Highway Patrol car went in front, and another one came behind. "I didn't want the damned bastards," the sheriff said. "The governor sent them." The governor said he wanted to prevent a lynching. He also wanted to be president of the United States.

Nobody turned up to watch the little caravan depart. It was an hour before sunup, and people in Bourbonville were stirring awake and getting ready to go to work.

Deputy Luke Bright sat in the front seat with the sheriff. He smoked one cigarette after another, and he was as skinny as a bone. He took his .38 revolver out of his holster and put it on his lap. The sheriff said, "What the hell do you think you're doing?"

"Well, he might try to escape, and I'd be ready to shoot him."

"Put that goddamned thing up, you dumb jackass, before you shoot me in the balls. I might want to use my balls once or twice more before I die." Then the sheriff thought of Abby's longtime virginity, and he bit his tongue.

Luke Bright put his pistol back in the holster. He sulked. The two-lane highway stretched curving in front of their headlights in the twilight before dawn. Luke put his head back against the mesh screen and dozed. In a minute he was snoring.

"You'll get a new trial for sure, Hope," the sheriff said.

"Hit don't matter," Hope said.

"It matters a hell of a lot to me," the sheriff said. The late October sun rose red behind them, pouring down on fields where cattle grazed and flashing on rivers they crossed. They passed one decaying barn after another. Beer joints. Houses set back in fields. Filling stations. Small towns. Yellow school buses ferrying children to class. Red lights flashed back and forth across the backs of the buses when they stopped for children. The sheriff wanted to say that nobody was building new barns nowadays. Nobody was taking care of the barns already built. He started to talk about barns but gave up on it. Hope gazed silently out the window. The sheriff could see him in the rearview mirror.

When they got to Sparta, it was almost noon. Traffic was bad. Lots of trucks on the two-lane blacktop, and no place to pass on the hills when the trucks ground up the grades. The sheriff said, "Hope, you want to piss?"

"I reckon I could," Hope said.

The sheriff flashed his lights at the troopers and rolled down the window and stuck his arm out to show that he was stopping. They drew in at a Gulf station outside of town. A big woods on that side covered a hill alongside the highway and came down close to the back of the station. "He needs to piss," the sheriff said to the troopers who got out of their cars holding sawed-off shotguns ready to shoot. The sheriff thought about telling the highway patrolmen how stupid they looked with their shotguns. He thought better of it. You never could tell about a man with a gun, especially a highway patrolman. "I need to piss myself," he said.

"He ain't wearing cuffs," one of the troopers said in dull indignation. "You ain't supposed to transport a prisoner without cuffs."

"You transport your prisoners any damn way you want," the sheriff said. "But this here is my prisoner till we get to Nashville."

"You're going to let him go piss by hisself?" another trooper asked.

"You want to go aim his prick for him?" the sheriff said.

"Shit," the trooper said.

"I don't think he wants to do that," the sheriff said. "Hope, this state trooper thinks you might want to shit?"

"No, I don't want to do that," Hope said.

"Well, get in there and piss then."

Hope grinned and disappeared inside. The door to the toilet was on the side of the filling station towards the back.

"What if he gets in there and locks the door?" one of the troopers said.

"What's he going to do then?" the sheriff said. "Oh, I see what you mean. He might flush hisself and get away by pouring down the pipes and swimming down the river to the ocean."

"Shit," the highway patrolman said.

"You must be an educated man to know so many words," the sheriff said.

After a while Hope came out. The sheriff went in to take a piss. The room stank of strong soap and stale piss. He pushed his hat back in amazement. To one side a big window opened onto the woods in back—plenty big enough for a man to jump through. The sheriff stood there pissing and wondering why Hope had not made a run for it. "If he didn't come out after a while, I would of got wise to what he was doing, and I could have kept the highway patrol talking until he got clean away. Maybe they would of brought dogs and run him down. But hell, that man had lived two years in the mountains and jungles of the Philippines, and the Japs didn't catch him. Do you reckon the Tennessee Highway Patrol that couldn't catch clap in a whorehouse would have had a chance to run Hope Kirby down? But hell, everbody pissed, and we went on to Nashville."

At Nashville the sheriff drove up to the state prison, and a couple of guards came out, and they exchanged papers. The sheriff let Hope out of the car. One of the guards said, "You ought to have put cuffs on this man's wrists and manacles on his ankles."

The sheriff said, "Well, shithead, I didn't do it, did I?"

"Watch out who you're calling a shithead," the guard said.

"I always do," the sheriff said. He turned and put his hand out to Hope. Hope took it. "I'm sorry it's come to this, Hope. Good luck."

"Hit's all right, Sheriff," Hope said.

"You don't hold it against me, do you?"

"You was doing your job," Hope said.

"Hugh is sure he'll win on appeal," the sheriff said. "I sure hope it works out."

"Have a good trip back, Sheriff. And thanks for everthing. Thanks for them walks."

"I wish we could of walked all the way to Canada," the sheriff said.

The sheriff got back into his car. He felt like crying. It was a sudden, unexpected, and almost overpowering feeling. He fought it off. Luke Bright started to talk, but the sheriff told him to shut up. They stopped to piss at the same place outside Sparta. The sheriff stood at the dirty toilet with his prick in his hand looking out the open window and wondering why Hope hadn't made a break for it. The sheriff never saw Hope again.

ON THE day Hope Kirby was transported to state prison, Charles got up and drove to the university feeling glum and tired. Hope Kirby ran around and around in his head like a toy train imprisoned on its track. Charles began imagining the electric chair, thinking of himself marched to the chamber where an apparatus of wood, leather, and wire waited mute and without sentiment while officious men did their duty around him as they got ready to watch him die.

After Proust there was coffee. Charles was grateful to Tempe for putting him to bed and astonished with himself that he had spent the night under the same roof of a woman not his wife, and nothing happened except that they went to sleep. McKinley took him home the next afternoon, and all three of them could laugh at part of it.

Otherwise they found little to say for a long time. Tempe said, "Charles, I'm glad you told the truth. It never would have been the end of it if you hadn't."

"I was too tired to lie," Charles said.

"It's terrible to think of what happened. I've wondered and wondered if Abby knew her husband was killing her. Could she see him beyond the reflection of the windshield?" Tempe shook her head. "Maybe not. But we know Kelly Parmalee understood everything."

"Let's talk about something else," Charles said.

"Yes, of course," Tempe said. "I'm sorry. Forgive me. It's all because we have bodies, you know. Tell me something, McKinley. Don't you wish we all looked like Giacometti's people—those long, attenuated bodies?"

"Good God," McKinley said. Charles did not know who Giacometti was.

"Our bodies get so much in the way," Tempe said. "They give a false impression of who we are. If we all had the same unattractive bodies, we could concentrate on who we are instead of what we look like.

"That girl, the one with the bicycle," she said, turning to Charles. "She has done a Giacometti in reverse."

Charles lacked even the energy to smile. "I don't know what you're talking about," he said. "Rosy is fat and ugly."

"Oh Charles, you fool," Tempe said, not joking with him but genuinely impatient, even angry. "Rosy is big, but she is not ugly. My God! What do you think beauty is anyway? She has a beautiful face. It's a shame you can't see how beautiful it is. And she adores you. I'd hate to be the woman in love with you if that's how you talk about someone who adores you."

"I'm sorry. I spoke without thinking," Charles said. "I don't want to—nothing. I don't mean—" He stumbled badly and felt lost and helpless and foolish. He did not know what Tempe wanted.

"I feel sorry for her," he finally said impatiently. "Her mother's dead. She doesn't have many friends. She makes me nervous sometimes."

"I give up," Tempe said. "I think if we were all as thin as a Giacometti figure or as fat as Rosy, we'd have time to think about who we are, what we are, instead of what we looked like."

"And the cosmetics companies would go out of business," McKinley said with a short laugh. "Look, I saw Giacometti's work in Paris when I was there. I hated it. I want human beings to look human. Besides that, the bastard was Swiss. You know what Orson Welles said. The Swiss have had five hundred years of peace and democracy, and what have they given the world? The cuckoo clock."

He and Tempe argued. Charles sat like a rock, feeling himself cut off from that world where there was something called art and where people could talk about "attenuation" and "abstraction" and mean something by it. He had been to Philadelphia to spend a summer with his aunt Bess and his aunt Bert, and when they were not taking him to church or to Bible study groups he haunted the free museums, especially the Philadelphia Museum of Art, where he stood looking at paintings like a child looking through a wrought-iron fence at an ornamented garden where exotic flowers bloomed along pathways that he was not allowed to walk. He looked at crucifixions where Jesus did not look like Jesus and at the pictures of saints he had never heard of and could not understand and pictures of the Virgin Mary. Aunt Bert said with prim righteousness that these pictures demonstrated the depravity of Catholic superstition and that when Jesus came again, all these manifestations of idolatry would be consumed in the holy fire that would refine the dross from the world at the first trumpet of the Apocalypse. He tried to think of something that he had seen in the Philadelphia Museum of Art, but he thought that anything he said would only expose his ignorance, and this did not seem the place to deliver Aunt Bert's version of art criticism.

A little after noon, he drove back to Bourbonville through a day bright with autumn sunshine. The neighbor woman who usually came over and stayed with Guy during the day had telephoned in the morning that she was sick and could not come. Paul Alexander took Guy down to the Car Works, and Charles knew that Guy would take the portable phonograph with him, set it up in his father's office, and play hillbilly music all afternoon, beating time with his pencil in the air, bending up and down in rhythm to the music while his father saw people and talked on the telephone and worked at his desk. Paul Alexander was never ashamed of Guy. He introduced him as "my son" without apology or explanation, and he took him places where people might stare and murmur.

Charles stopped at his home and in the silent and empty house felt his mother's uncanny presence so that he felt tempted to call out to her as though she were in another room and might respond to him. Time and again Aunt Bess told the story of sitting out in the woods during her summer vacation at the farm in 1931, a few months after her mother, Charles's grandmother, had died. A clear, quiet voice spoke to her from a patch of mysterious sunshine and said, "You can see your mother if you turn around."

Her heart surged with joy, and she stood, but all at once she knew that she had heard the voice of the devil speak to her. The Bible, which, like all her sisters she knew by heart, leaped to her mind. No witches. No enchanters. No necromancers. Her joy turned to horror in the presence of the fiend she could not see, and she cried out, "Get thee behind me, Satan. Oh Jesus, save me." When she turned around, nothing was there. A miracle, she thought.

Aunt Bess lived amid miracle stories. The Old Testament God stood round about her, giving signs, answering prayers, taking His vengeance against blasphemers and others who in the many ways possible to sinful humankind did not show Him reverence. Her voice filled with awe when she spoke, and Charles could feel in her voice the tremor of divinity.

Aunt Bess. Even Eugenia Alexander tired of her love of the dramatic sometimes. Paul Alexander was amused by her and liked her. "If she had lived in the Middle Ages," he said, "she would have been a nun and a saint because she would have seen visions." Eugenia laughed when he said that. Aunt Bess the nun. It was a thought. She was unmarried. Eugenia, who adored their mother, said in a tone akin to reproach that her mother had been too critical of Bess, that no boyfriend Bess ever brought home seemed suitable, and that they had all been unkind to her. If Aunt Bess had lived in the Middle Ages, Charles thought, Mary would have blessed her. Angels would have spoken to her in dreams. The faithful would have made pilgrimages to touch her and to have her pray for them.

As he left the house, he heard the telephone ring. He started to go back. But he changed his mind and got into the '37 Ford and hurried to Bourbonville.

So it was that his friend David, tall and craggy and soft-voiced David Pleasant, came into the office a half hour afterwards when Charles was settling down at the desk. "I tried to call you," David said.

"What did you want?" Charles said. He supposed David wanted to say, "Just to tell you that I'm still your friend."

But David said, "Bob Saddler has killed himself."

Charles stood up at the desk. He did not say a word.

David leaned loosely over the counter, looking across at him with stricken blue eyes. "He took a whole bottle of sleeping pills. His mother found him this morning. He left a note. She won't tell anybody what was in it."

*H*UGH BEDFORD sat at the kitchen table the night of the verdict and listened to the courthouse clock strike midnight. Lloyd Brickman led a campaign to get the goddamned clock fixed. *The son of a bitch deserved his death. Stupid death. Fucking in a boat in the middle of the night. I'd sink the goddamned boat if I just sat in it.* For a moment he felt the bleakness rush over him. The bottle sat on the table in front of him, the empty glass beside it. *Don't get drunk now.* He had to write out an appeal. File it quickly. That could wait until tomorrow. He had to get a transcript from Jimmy Spenser, the court stenographer. Tonight he could have one drink. He pulled the stopper out of the bottle. It made a *plok* as it came out. He poured the amber bourbon into the glass and sipped. "Ahhhhh," he said.

I was a coward, but the worst of it is that Sperling Winrod is still alive. He imagined himself on trial, the stern faces of military judges all in a row behind a table the way courts-martial were conducted, the prosecutor in uniform. A small room. *Gentlemen, this man killed a colonel in the United States Army in time of war. It is not only murder; it is treason.* Sometimes Hugh dreamed of the firing squad, the blindfold, hearing the terse commands "Squad at the ready! Aim!" He supposed he would not hear the command "Fire!" The bullets would arrive before the sound of the shots. He would shit in his pants. He would not know it.

Sperling Winrod. It was a stupid name, one of those old pseudoaristocratic military names of men whose fathers had been in the army and their fathers before them, and the sons were brought up to believe that the military was their inheritance, spit and polish, brass and color. From birth they learned a posture, a bearing, an erect arrogance and look of command and a voice cut out of sheet steel. As hollow as an empty suit of armor. Colonel Winrod was a muscular little man, compact, with the erect bearing of a short man eternally trying to stretch himself. He spoke carefully when he was not giving orders, always trying to sound deliberative. He had no discernible accent. He had moved from military post to military post throughout his life, and he went to West Point. He was American. That was all you could say about Sperling Winrod. Not English. Not Australian. Clearly American. But still somehow nondescript.

I admired the bastard. Hugh scarcely remembered his own father. Nobody could admire him. Here in the army was ramrod-stiff Colonel Winrod who took an interest in him, promoted him to company commander in Sicily. *Captain Hugh Bedford.* He recalled with self-contempt his pride at his double silver bars. *Captain Bedford.* His highest rank in life. He knocked the hell out of the test they gave him to qualify for OCS, and Winrod commended him. "It says here you have an IQ of 149," Winrod said admiringly. "Well, let me tell you this, Bedford. You can be a damned smart man and a goddamned dumb officer. I think you've got what it takes to be a damned smart guy and a damned good officer, too."

"Yes SIR!" Hugh Bedford said.

Colonel Winrod's voice was sharp when it needed to be. You could hear it over the THUNK of mortar rounds falling, above the rattle of machine guns. Cold as the polar ice cap. He did not cuss much. He kept his profanity to use when he was surprised. That wasn't often. Officers serving under him thought he had a sixth sense about Germans, understood every devious way of theirs, moved one step ahead of them, and licked them in every battle. He took orders from above. Yet in the field with his regiment he seemed to be the supreme puppeteer of war, and when he gave an order, it was like a vision through a telescope of a landscape now infallibly known. He jerked the strings, and the enemy fell down. His men trusted him. *I trusted the asshole.*

Nothing warmed Winrod's chill. At Anzio some guys played softball back of the lines. Winrod hit a double, and he was on second base. A corporal named Ted Hicks hit a fly ball into the outfield, and a centerfielder named O'Brian ran in to catch it. Easy play. Except that just as O'Brian grabbed the ball, a Kraut sniper hit him smack in the back of the head with a bullet.

Hugh Bedford was next batter; he stood there holding a bat on his shoulder and saw it all, saw O'Brian's head explode outward in a gush of red blood and gray brains. O'Brian fell face down—still holding the ball in his death grip, eyes open.

The chaplain was umpiring behind the plate, an Italian-American named Pontano, Catholic. What did he do? He called Corporal Hicks out because O'Brian caught the ball. Father Pontano said that nothing in the rule book said an outfielder who caught a fly ball had to be alive at the end of the play. In the meantime Winrod tagged up at second and came all the way home because nobody thought to snatch the ball out of O'Brian's dead hand and throw to the plate. Some bazooka men and a BAR man went after the sniper, and all hell broke loose. Colonel Winrod stood at home plate asking Father Pontano for a call. The padre nodded and waved his hands and shouted, "Safe at home, and the Lord bless you!" Winrod laughed. It didn't matter if ten O'Brians were shot dead by snipers. What mattered was that Winrod scored.

And we scored. They could smell victory. He drained the tumbler and poured himself another. He luxuriated in the spread of alcoholic warmth through his body. Peace. He could contemplate Winrod from a distance.

Winrod peered through his field glasses at the Italian hill town north of Rome, red tile roofs peaceful in the sun. It was the last happy day of Hugh Bedford's life. Ahead of them the Gothic Line, Germans dug in before Bologna. Break the Gothic Line, and they were done. Hugh Bedford liked Italy. The olive groves. The hills. The palaces and the churches. Santa Croce in Florence. Machiavelli and Michelangelo buried under the same high roof, lying undisturbed there all these centuries, and near them an empty tomb waiting for Dante, who would never come. Not even the artillery could wake them up. He thought he would come home, maybe take up art history, teach in a university. One of the lieutenants in his unit, a guy named Miller from Boston, led Bedford around the churches in Rome and in Florence. "I was an assistant professor of art history at Harvard," Miller said. "I'll go back there after the war. My job is waiting for me. Maybe tenure after a few years."

Tenure meant you had a job for life.

"You just talk about pictures?" Hugh Bedford asked, like a man in a church asking if they worshipped something called God here.

"Yeah," Miller said. "Pictures and buildings and statues. There's more to it than you think, Captain." Miller laughed, not in condescension.

Hugh was amazed. It had never occurred to young Hugh Bedford growing up in Bourbonville that you could make a living looking at pictures and talking about them. Yes, he had been to the university. But he had not taken an art course. A good life, teaching in a university, reading books, smoking a pipe, speaking softly in a lecture hall while students bent respectfully over their desks taking notes, and he could cultivate good manners, live like a gentleman, as he had lived in the army. Students would not salute him. Not with their hands to their caps. Still, there were other kinds of salute. Respect. No one would remember his father or his mother. He would teach in New England or California and never let his mother come to visit him.

He planned it out with greater and greater assurance. The GI Bill. Congress had just passed it—the GI Bill of Rights. It made him think more about the future than he had thought before. Now he thought he would make something of himself, get out of Bourbonville with its dirty memories, flee from his angry mother and the nondescript company house that Paul Alexander enabled his mother to buy when his father had been shot to death by the National Guard during the strike. No gratitude from her for the house. "It's blood money," she howled. "He got us the house because he felt guilty for Will's death. Paul Alexander's cheap guilt can't bring Will back from the dead."

Hugh Bedford would not break with her, not add to her pain. No, he would not do anything disagreeable. He would go off to graduate school somewhere, leave her and Bourbonville behind. He had commanded men, seen men killed beside him, killed men himself, kept cool under fire. He had confidence, and now that the war was all nearly over, he thought he would survive. At the start he was sure he would die. Most soldiers felt that way. They saw portents of their deaths, imagined telegrams. "We regret to inform you that . . ."

Now, in the early spring of 1945 outside Bologna, after so much fighting, the war almost over, he thought beyond the moment to the mysterious condition called "peace." The Krauts knew they were licked. American armies were plunging across Germany. No sense getting killed for a lost cause. He read that logic into their retreat. But here they were drawing back slowly, and the Gothic Line was well fortified not far ahead of them. It was a beautiful April day, clear, dry, radiant, as if the light poured not from the sun but from the air itself, and the objects the air touched seemed to glow, and the hill town straddled the ridge and looked empty—no sign of life anywhere except in the spring-bursting land.

"I wonder where the people are." Colonel Winrod looked through his glasses and mused aloud. Sometimes as the Americans approached a town, people rushed out joyously to meet them. Hands waving for chocolate, chewing gum, cigarettes—the American Trinity. Pretty girls climbed up on tanks, kissed Yanks. The Americans ran their hands up under the girls' dresses, and the girls kissed them, squealed, and laughed. Men and women embraced the Yanks, bedecked them, pretending loudly that they had never lifted their fists over their heads shouting "DU-che, DU-che, DU-che, DU-che." They wanted to tell Americans about cousins, brothers, uncles, aunts in Chicago, New York, New Haven, Boston.

Not here. Not a sign of life. The spring sun poured down on houses suspended in light as though in amber. The town was on the flank of their advancing column.

"Captain Bedford. Take a detail and give that place a look. My orders are to get on to Perugia. But I don't want a pack of Krauts jumping on our flank while we're strung out on the road."

"Sir," Hugh said, "what if the place is lousy with Krauts?"

"We'll come and get you," Colonel Winrod said with a cold grin. "Just don't get your ass shot off while we're on the way. If we hear gunfire, we'll be with you in five minutes. If the town is clear, send up a flare. You can even liberate the wine cellars if you like."

"Yes sir."

"Enjoy yourself," Winrod said. He grinned. Captain Hugh Bedford saluted briskly, and Colonel Winrod tossed the salute back. Hugh went double-quick back to his guys and picked ten men. Ten of his best. He took Lieutenant Miller, the Harvard assistant professor of art history. Maybe there was a church there with a Caravaggio. Lieutenant Miller had explained Caravaggio to him. *I understand,* Hugh thought. *I could do that. We will drink wine. A reward. Maybe some women will be welcoming.* That would boost the morale of the men. Italian women could break out of the confinements of their upbringing. One night with the American hero. Forty years with some peasant. Given time, Captain Bedford would have ordered a consignment of condoms. No time. The men left behind grumbled. They could taste the wine they would not drink, the women they would not liberate. "You ought to take all of us, Captain. You never know what you're going to run into."

Hugh Bedford laughed. He set off, walking with Lieutenant Miller at the head of his little column of nine others, rifles at sling arms, the radio man with the radio strapped on his back, a corporal named Samson. Samson the strong. Antenna up. Behind them a couple of Shermans broke down in the road. Men were gathered around the tanks, cursing them. Hugh Bedford scarcely thought of the tanks.

I should have had a premonition. The uncanny stillness, the steady blazing April sun on sand-colored walls, the emptiness he felt rather than saw, no motion except their own lackadaisical line of men moving up towards the town through fields green with winter wheat, vineyards beginning to leaf, an olive grove, everything eerie because it was so natural in a world torn to hell by war. Not a soul to be seen anywhere.

A warning of emptiness.

Hugh Bedford relived the warning ten thousand times through countless bottles of whiskey. The scene played over and over in his mind, a mad newsreel endlessly turning. *I should have known.* But he felt no warning. Nothing. No premonition that a thunder shower was coming. Not the eyes on them as they drew near.

They entered the town through a narrow street, and cool shadows covered them. Overhead clouds began to congeal from nowhere. Nobody in sight. The little column halted. The emptiness of the narrow streets was oppressive. Maybe the people had hidden in cellars. Once they heard American voices, they would rush out in joy. Barrels of wine. Song. Embraces. Find the people, end the emptiness, lift the skirts of the women.

"All right. Two by two," he said. "Samson, you come with me." No calculation. He took the radio man. He started towards the church, thinking he might see a Caravaggio before Lieutenant Miller. Always something brightly white in a Caravaggio. The church sat in the square where a silence like the beginning of time pressed into sandstone houses and the rounded cobblestones in the street.

The first burst of fire caught Samson low down, not high enough to prevent him from screaming with pain, and the next burst killed him and spattered Hugh Bedford with his blood. All around the little town, stone streets exploded in gunfire and the whang of ricocheting bullets. Hugh ducked and ran. He carried a carbine. In his panic he flung it away. Machine guns roared behind him but not at him as he raced down a narrow, twisting street that became a tunnel of darkness against the sun. A door opened. A woman gestured violently. He plunged after her in unspeakable terror. He heard a shriek somewhere in the near distance, and he knew it was one of his men, trapped and killed like a cornered dog.

The house was narrow, dark, and cool. The woman whispered urgently in Italian, pointing upstairs. He raced up. She followed. At the top, on the third floor, an old and frail wooden stairwell led to a cramped attic under the tiled roof. She motioned him there, in a corner with boxes and trunks. With astonishing strength she pushed trunks aside and lifted a wide plank in the floor and gestured at him to slip under it. He lay facedown in a narrow, dusty space, so narrow he could scarcely breathe. Above him she replaced the planks and pushed the trunks and boxes back over them. He felt the panic of claustrophobia.

He waited. Time crept by. The gunfire went on. Where was Winrod? Hugh waited for the creaking sound of the caterpillars on the tanks. Nothing. Silence except for an occasional distant shout. Then a rumble overhead. Artillery! No, thunder. One of those sudden Italian storms, and rain hammered on the roof in a roar. Then a crash and shouting below. The Germans had broken into the house. Someone had seen him, betrayed him. The woman shouted angrily. A burst of a machine pistol, and her voice was cut off in mid-syllable. He knew she was dead.

Booted footsteps rushed up from below. Doors kicked open. Then, just below him men climbing the last stairway into the attic. He heard the hammering of hobnailed boots inches from his head and flecks of dust came down on his head. He knew he would die in this cramped and suffocating place. He gathered his will to cry out, reveal himself, win the game by not hiding anymore, dying swiftly. All in an instant. He heard and felt them moving trunks, opening them, strewing things about. Then he heard a ripping and splintering and a cry of pain and cursing and harsh laughter. Slowly with the concentration of voices and the laughter he understood that the spindly wooden stairway into the attic had given way under the weight of men. Some had fallen, were cursing. Others laughed.

He heard frustrated and impatient voices above him. His hunters were no longer fixed on him. Their attention was divided by the need to get back down now that the stairway had collapsed. In one final gesture of frustration, one of them fired a machine pistol and sprayed the attic with bullets. Someone shouted at him. He stopped. Anger now at the gunner. He had not fired into the floor. He would have hit the Germans below him.

So Hugh Bedford was spared. *Like Tom Sawyer,* he thought afterwards. The Germans were a tribe of Injun Joes. He found later that it was a house-by-house search. No one had seen him. They happened on his savior, and she protested, and they killed her as casually as they might have swatted a pesky fly. The Germans killed Italians at random by then; the Italians had overthrown the Duce, declared war against the Germans. Someone shouted an order. The Germans went out into the street and were gone.

They are in Germany now, selling Mercedes-Benz cars and getting rich. At night they sit in beer gardens and smoke and drink and laugh about the war, about tricking the Americans.

Where was Winrod? Troops were less than two miles away. Where was the armor? Artillery? Promises kept? He lay there for hours because he could not get out of his hiding place, could not move the stuff piled on top of the plank. Night came on still and empty except for the sound of water dripping and then another storm. Heavy rain set in for a while. He felt the night, heard the rain. Hours passed. He peed in his pants. He heard voices, Italian voices. They came into the house. He stank of piss and sweat, a suffocating stench. He called out, weeping. He heard steps, subdued voices, the grunting of men climbing up into the attic, things moved, and the plank was raised, and he saw a glimmer of a lantern in the dark. Sympathetic hands and strong arms hauled him out. He saw spectral faces in the dim light. The men were trying to explain. He sat on the floor weeping, trembling and shaking so that he thought his arms and legs and his head might fly off, that he might be reduced to disconnected parts, fleshly parts of a mannequin.

The bodies of his soldiers lay scattered through the town, all of them dead, bodies lying in blood and rain. Lieutenant Miller had been stood up against a wall with a couple of others and shot. This was an elite SS unit, accomplished in massacre. The tanks had blocked the road, an American said later. Preposterous, Hugh Bedford thought. Why didn't they drive around them? Wasn't that the point of tanks? They didn't need a road. Were there no tanks other than the ruptured ones? He never got the answers to those questions. Questions that arise from absurdity never have answers.

He tried to kill Winrod. When the colonel came into the hospital to visit, Hugh jumped out of bed and grabbed him by the neck with both hands. Five or six soldiers jumped on him and tore him away. He screamed every foul name he knew at Winrod and made up some more. It did no good. Hugh heard afterwards that Winrod couldn't talk for a week. *I wish I had killed the bastard.* He dreamed of killing him yet, making elaborate, fantastic plots in his head to accomplish the deed, kill him slowly, so he would know his assassin.

He escaped court-martial because Winrod did not care enough about him to want vengeance. Winrod was a good officer, and good officers are detached. He could sacrifice Hugh Bedford's men rather than risk more lives by sending in relief without armor and artillery support. So he said. Hugh was offered a medical discharge in lieu of court-martial, and he took it and went to law school on the GI Bill. He forgot art history. He did not believe in beauty anymore. He came back to Bourbonville because it was familiar. He did not want any more strange places. He no longer believed in himself. He no longer believed in anybody. He read a small item in a newspaper that Colonel Winrod was now superintendent of West Point. He was now General Winrod, a good friend of President Eisenhower.

In the dark, in his house, the company house that had been his mother's, he dreamed of the tiny space in the attic in Italy, Germans tramping above him, and in his dreams they dragged him down and threw him against a stone wall, and they were just about to shoot him when he jumped up in bed crying.

His only reward was insight. Hypocrisy and deceit ruled the world. The world was filled with Sperling Winrods. Bourbonville was filled with them. Ken McNeil, his religious cant, his bland face, his prim rectitude—the biggest hypocrite of all. And Kelly Parmalee. Hope Kirby had killed the man who was the symbol and incarnation of the worst hypocrisy of Bourbonville, the oily religious smarmy gregariousness of a man who spent his life acting a role to be accepted in a community where the only compelling desires anybody had were to fuck and make money and swim in the cesspool together like frogs. Hugh Bedford lived in Bourbonville so he could scorn them all, and he took the cases that affronted them. He took the case of Leonard Bulwer Millbank, who came to him with a federal indictment around his neck like a plump albatross. Hugh Bedford did his best. But when the jury came back and L. B. Millbank was told he had to go to prison a year and a day for tax evasion during the war, Hugh Bedford looked at him and said, "Well, you cocksucker, you deserve to be shot. So you ought to thank your lucky stars that you'll only be raped in the shower three or four times before those other convicts realize you're too skinny and old to be worth even a good piece of sodomy." He made sure that he had collected his fee and cashed the check before he made this commentary to L. B. Millbank, and he felt satisfied with his entire performance. Nor was it something that L. B. Millbank cared to repeat.

With Hope Kirby it was different. Here was a man. Hope Kirby would have moved a hundred men into that village, artillery or no artillery support. He would not have abandoned Hugh's men to death. Hugh Bedford wanted to save his life. *Maybe I can't do it. Maybe I'm not good enough.*

*B*OB SADDLER had to be buried. He belonged to the Tabernacle Baptist Church, but Reverend B. B. Hartpenny refused to do the service. "I'd have to say he was in hell," he said with a solemnity that was altogether sincere, explaining himself to his deacons whom he called together to consider the request from Bob's mother. "It would be like performing the marriage of people who have been divorced," he said, speaking in his most unctuous voice, the one proper to a preacher letting everyone know that he always did the right thing. "It wouldn't be marriage at all; it would not be a real funeral if I said words over Bob Saddler that his death had contradicted."

Charles Alexander went to see Mr. Finewood to ask if he would say something at Bob's graveside, give a prayer, read the Bible. With many apologies Mr. Finewood declined. His reasons were the same as Reverend Hartpenny's. "Charles, when you become a minister yourself, you will find yourself asked to do things you simply cannot as one of God's servants do. It is an unforgivable sin to commit suicide. It's the same as murder."

"But Bob was a saint," Charles said.

"Charles, only the redeemed of the Lord are saints. We do not know Bob's heart. Only God knows that. But we do know that the true saints of God do not renounce Him and kill themselves. God may have mercy on him, but that is not something we can know. We can only know the awful deed."

"So you won't do it?"

"I cannot do it, Charles." Mr. Finewood assured Charles that no true Christian minister could preach the funeral of a suicide. Mr. Finewood was large enough to make his pronouncements seem filled with authority, and he spoke in a tone that swept opposition aside like dust. "The best thing to do is to let the morticians have complete control and to get it all over with as soon as possible."

Charles absorbed this declaration mutely. Who was he to speak against such certainty? But all his certainties were dissolving, and with Mr. Finewood's adamantine refusal to bury Bob Saddler another little fragment of the structure of his faith fell in Charles's mind. He was nowhere near the attitude he would later assume when everything about his young religious life became a mystery that he could hide by telling funny stories. But something slipped away.

So what about Mr. Arceneaux? Mr. Arceneaux received him in the church study with Louise Renfrow crouching outside the door, but the conversation was quiet.

Charles began with an apology. "I want to tell you something. The day when you came to see me, the day after the murders."

"You did not take my advice," Arceneaux said with a hint of bitterness.

"Yes," Charles said, not sure how to proceed. "I just wanted to say that I didn't mean for our conversation to be spread all over town. I spoke to Mr. Finewood about it. I wanted his advice. I didn't mean for him to tell anybody else."

Arceneaux laughed. "And of course he burned up his shoes getting to Tommy Fieldston. Well, what's done is done."

"I'm very sorry it happened," Charles said.

"I am, too. I'm even sorrier you did not take my advice. Now you have to spend the rest of your life responsible for a man's life."

"He did kill them," Charles said.

"And is killing him going to bring them back?"

"No, of course not," Charles murmured.

"Let's not let it be a wall between us," Arceneaux said. "You have been through something that no one can give final advice on, not me, not Finewood, no one else. You did what you had to do."

A long and tense silence hung between them. Arceneaux waited for Charles to go on, knowing what had brought him there.

"Well, I'm here for something else," Charles said finally with a heavy sigh. "Mr. Hartpenny won't preach Bob Saddler's funeral. Mr. Finewood won't either. David Pleasant and I were Bob's best friends, I guess. We wonder if you would say a few words by his grave."

"You don't need me," Arceneaux said. "You can say the words yourself."

"But I'm not ordained."

"There's nothing in the law of any state that requires an ordained minister to preach a funeral."

Charles pondered this news, for it was news to him. "All right," he said morosely. "I can do it, but Bob deserves more than me. He was a true Christian. He was a saint."

"Yes, I know he was. He was one of those saints like Saint Francis of Assisi."

"We studied him in school," Charles said. "He gave away all his property."

Arceneaux laughed without humor. "Did you know he preached to the birds? I suppose he was crazy. Maybe all true saints are a little crazy. I think Bob was a saint."

"Yes, well, I suppose I could say something, but Bob needs to have somebody say that even though he killed himself, he is not a condemned sinner. I can't understand . . . I don't know why he did it."

"He may very well not have known why he did it himself. You will find in your own life that you may think of suicide sometime. What makes you do it or not do it may depend only on what instruments are at hand to do the deed. I wouldn't kill myself with a straight razor. But a bottle of sleeping pills . . . Who knows?"

They sat looking at each other, and Arceneaux thought of France.

"But will you do it? Say just a few words?"

"Of course I'll do it," Arceneaux said.

"Thank you," Charles said almost effusively. "Thank you."

He left Arceneaux's office feeling great relief and gratitude. "Mrs. Renfrow," Arceneaux said with cool efficiency as Charles still stood by. "I'm going to preach Bob Saddler's funeral on Friday at two o'clock. Put that in the calendar."

"I think a graveside service will be enough," Charles said. "I'm going to ask my father and his friends to play music. Is that all right?"

"Of course it's all right," Arceneaux said.

"But Mr. Arceneaux," Louise said in her gushy, informative, and all-wise voice. "Don't you know that Bob Saddler committed suicide? I don't know what the deacons will say if you preach his funeral."

"I hope they will not be such a pack of hypocrites that they object to a last mercy," Arceneaux said coldly.

"Some of them will be very upset," Louise said.

"Good," Arceneaux said. "Being upset is good for you once in a while. Clears out the juices."

*W*HEN he drove into the gate of the city cemetery at the eastern edge of the town on the day of the funeral, Arceneaux was astounded. Spread around the open grave where Glenn Snappit the undertaker and his brother had set up an awning was a great, quiet throng of people. Glenn said later that he estimated it at four hundred, wearing coats in the cool November air, silent and waiting. The first thing that Arceneaux noted was that they were black and white. He could not remember in his life ever having seen blacks and whites so close together in a crowd in the South.

The cemetery was crisscrossed by small roads, and Arceneaux pulled his white Jaguar quietly to a stop near the fringe of the crowd, and as he got out of the car, he heard the sound of music—guitars, a mandolin, and the sweet even notes of a violin. Arceneaux did not especially care for hillbilly music; it was not his tradition, and it seemed monotonous and sentimental to him and often lugubrious and silly. He had called at Jim Ed Ledbetter's home one afternoon when Jim Ed and Paul Alexander led their little family musical society in playing ballads and hymns, and he had seen the musicians and the crowd and poor, paralyzed Juliet Ledbetter swept up in the songs with an enthusiasm that he could enjoy in the fashion of someone who takes pleasure in the joy of others.

But he could not understand it. He was one to feel his heart surge at the "Liebestod," the great aria in the final act of *Tristan* or to feel a sedate thrill during the Triumphal March of *Aida,* and he could weep at Beethoven's Ninth and feel the peace of God in Beethoven's Sixth. Guitars, banjos, mandolins, and fiddles seemed to him thin and inadequate, and to fathom the power these instruments had on the people of Bourbon County (not those in First Baptist Church, of course) was to him almost a trivial mystery, like what he supposed might idly stir the curiosity of an anthropologist who in a primitive society noted the ecstasy into which some might fall while listening to the pounding of tom-toms.

But today was different from anything he had ever known in his life. The window on the driver's side was slightly open, and as he pulled to a halt, he heard the music begin and knew that his arrival had been a signal, so that he shut the door of his car almost reverently once he had stepped out. He heard what amounted to a fanfare, the last measures of a familiar hymn not in hillbilly style, not something that Arceneaux found either pretty or interesting. Then as the crowd spontaneously opened a way for him to walk towards the grave, men taking off their hats as he made

his way by, the crowd began to sing in slow, swelling power, and Arceneaux felt the earth move. Ridiculous, he thought. Ridiculous. But it moved
anyway.

Amazing Grace, how sweet the sound
That saved a wretch like me.
I once was lost, but now I'm found,
Was blind, but now I see.

Sitting on chairs around the grave were Jim Ed and his son, Blackie and
Paul, Paul Alexander and Stephen, mandolins and guitars, and then plump
Dr. Goldberg playing the violin, and on its straps above the open grave the
coffin, polished wood, the gift (as it turned out) of Glenn and his brother,
and Charles Alexander standing with his friend David at the head of the
grave, and Bob Saddler's mother sitting in a folding chair looking solemn
but not weeping. The girl Arceneaux had seen with Charles. And all over the
long slope of the cemetery, the singing. The singing.

Through many dangers, toils and cares,
I have already come.
'Twas grace that brought me safe thus far,
And grace will lead me home.

'Twas grace that taught my heart to fear,
And grace my fears relieved.
How precious did that grace appear,
The hour I first believed.

Glenn, careful and respectful, nodded to Arceneaux and guided him
with a light touch to a little wooden lectern by the grave, and Arceneaux put
his Bible down.

When we've been there, ten thousand years,
Bright shining as the sun,
We've no less days to sing God's praise
Than when we first begun.

The singing died away and across the long slant of the cemetery a silence
came back, and the crowd pushed closer. "I'm sorry I didn't think to bring a
mike and a speaker," Glenn whispered. "We didn't expect this crowd."

Arceneaux nodded. He opened his Bible.

O Lord, thou hast searched me, and known me.
Thou knowest my downsitting and mine uprising, thou understandest my thought
afar off.
Thou compassest my path and my lying down, and art acquainted with all
my ways.
For there is not a word in my tongue, but, lo, O Lord, thou knowest it altogether.
Thou hast beset me behind and before, and laid thine hand upon me.
Such knowledge is too wonderful for me; it is high, I cannot attain unto it.
Whither shall I go from thy spirit? or whither shall I flee from thy presence?
If I ascend up into heaven, thou art there: if I make my bed in hell, behold, thou
art there.
If I take the wings of the morning, and dwell in the uttermost parts of the sea;
Even there shall thy hand lead me, and thy right hand shall hold me.
If I say, Surely the darkness shall cover me; even the night shall be light about me.
Yea, the darkness hideth not from thee; but the night shineth as the day: the
darkness and the light are both alike to thee.

Arceneaux's voice was clear and strong, and it carried over this multitude in the still cold air so that, as someone said later, you could hear it at the very back as though it were coming almost from above you or behind you.

When he had closed the Bible, Arceneaux paused a moment. He had made no notes. He had not precisely known what he would say. Then he spoke:

"We are here to give back to God one of his saints. So many of us are here because Bob Saddler lived the Gospel. He visited the sick. He put food in the mouths of the hungry. He visited those in prison. He comforted the afflicted. He was one of those blessed who blessed others and never asked anything for himself except the pleasure of seeing us receive what he had to give.

"The verses I have read from the Psalms are filled with mystery. They do not tell us what we would like to know. They tell us that God knows us, our sitting down and our rising up, our thoughts from afar, all our words and all our deeds. But they do not tell us who or what God is. They do not tell us why the world is what it is. They do not tell us why there must be suffering, why there must be pain, grief, mystery, and death. They do not tell us why Bob, our friend and God's saint, did what he did.

"I know that we do not know the answers to any of the questions that we all ask as we stand here. Why do children sicken and die? Why do floods carry away the innocent? Why are tyrants able to rage and kill? Why does war destroy millions who have no desire to fight, no wish but to live at peace? Our Psalmist is clear. We do not know, and anyone who presumes to give an answer that claims to be God's word on the subject is a fool and a liar and worst of all must be desperately deceiving himself. We yearn for answers. So we make them up, and we say they come from God. But they do not come from God, and we remain in ignorance.

"Does even God have the answers?" Here Arceneaux paused a very long time. "My answer to that question," he said at last, "is that I do not know. How can we know? Has God spoken to us? Has He revealed Himself? He has not spoken to me. I do not think He has spoken to you. Why then is God silent? There may be no answer to that question. Or maybe the answer is simply that God does not care for our world. Is that blasphemy? You may say so. But who has not had the thought? Another Psalmist pleaded with God, 'Unto thee will I cry, O Lord my rock; be not silent to me; lest if thou be silent to me, I become like them that go down into the pit.' Did God speak to him? We do not really know. And Jesus cried on the cross, 'My God, my God, why hast thou forsaken me?' Was this a stage play? Was Jesus pretending the agony of loneliness in the universe? I do not think so.

"We hope for a God like the God of the Psalmist, for whom the night shines like the day and who is to be found with us in the uttermost parts of our despair and our ignorance. That is the best hope we can have, that if we make our bed in the grave God is there. If that hope is true—and we do not know that it is—our friend Bob Saddler is with God, and God is with him.

"We do know this, that we are here, that we grieve, that we have lost a friend who was not like us, not like anyone else we knew, tormented by forces that we did not know, departing from us in a way that fills us with sorrow and the regret that we did not see something, do something, that would have kept him with us. We are in grief now. Bob Saddler is at peace. That we know.

"Let us pray. God, receive back to yourself this friend whom you gave to us, and let him and us be at rest. Amen."

Dr. Goldberg put his violin to his chin then, and the pure, sweet notes of the instrument commanded the air itself, and for just a moment Arceneaux was caught up in a dreamlike state where the music seemed to dissolve all the physical reality, the white stones of the graveyard, the throng of people pressed silently together, the polished coffin, the hills and all, and he felt himself lifted almost into an ecstasy both timeless and all-encompassing. No one sang, but Arceneaux knew the words, and they seemed to float in the vibrating simplicity of the melodic line.

> *Joyful, joyful, we adore Thee,*
> *God of glory, Lord of love;*
> *Hearts unfold like flow'rs before Thee,*
> *Opening to the sun above . . .*

Beethoven in Bourbonville, Arceneaux thought. *And with guitars, a mandolin, banjos, and the divine violin of a Jewish doctor. How odd! Perhaps if Beethoven can exist in Bourbonville, God may exist everywhere.* The thought was almost hallucinatory. He felt on the verge of some enlightenment that eluded him, and the more he tried to grasp it, the more he seemed once again brought back to earth, and the hymn was over, and Arceneaux was shaking hands with people who moved forward in respectful silence to shake hands with him as if he had done something worth congratulation or celebration. Even Paul Alexander shook hands with him and thanked him!

"I will never forget this," Charles said.

"Thank you," David said.

"Thank you for asking me," Arceneaux said. Slowly, slowly the crowd dispersed, and Arceneaux hefted his Bible and went home.

I guess I'm really up shit's creek now, he thought, recalling an old expression one of his buddies in the OSS had used often. He felt exhilaration thrill through his body. He had done the right thing.

S*OMETIMES* at night Hope Kirby had nightmares. Once again he was on the Bataan death march, shuffling doggedly in the merciless sun with Jap guards leering and mocking and driving them, and if an American dropped from exhaustion, the Japs flung him onto his knees beside the road, and a grinning swordsman stood behind and with a mighty swipe and a shout, sliced the American's head off so that it went rolling in the dust and the body jumped and quivered and lay still with the blood pouring out the stump of a neck. Those Jap swords were so sharp that you could lay a hair on one, and the hair would fall in two, cut by its own weight against the razor edge. Hope Kirby became well acquainted with those swords later on in the rain forests of Luzon.

He woke up in his cell where a dim light glowed always in the ceiling, the ceiling and the walls painted a dark, institutional green, and by the light the guards in their regular passage along the corridors could pull the little slide back on the door to look in and assure themselves that he had not cheated the state by hanging himself.

He was glad for the light. He never liked to sleep in total darkness.

At the very end of the long march they came to the stockade where they were to be held, and at the very last John Sevier fell. A Jap soldier clubbed him in the head with a rifle butt while John Sevier struggled to regain his feet. Hope scooped him up, supposing they would both be killed. Other Americans milled around, making a frail human wall around them. It was the end of the march. Japs ran about, yelling orders, pushing and beating them like cattle, and Hope and his friends got John Sevier into the camp, and he lived. For days he lapsed into unconsciousness and drifted back, only to fall into a coma again. Hope nursed him and hid him in the confusion of settling down. He did everything he knew to do. John Sevier never spoke a word again. He sat or stood staring off into space. Tell him to do something, and he did it. He obeyed like a dog. That was all. Behind his clear blue eyes was vacancy.

When Hope escaped, he took John Sevier with him. That took him a couple of months. Hope could grow anything, and the Japs loved gardens. One of the Jap officers took Hope to be his gardener, and he took John Sevier along to help. They worked in big flower gardens, and nearby was the forest. Hope waited. Two guards with rifles watched over them without interest. One afternoon one guard turned his back on him, and Hope killed him with a pickaxe, took his rifle, killed the other one, and got away, hauling John Sevier into the woods. "Run, damn you!" Hope shouted. John Sevier ran. Hope thought, *Pappy would not like it if he heard me curse.*

Once in the mountains Hope was king. He knew mountains, knew how to live there. He picked up other Americans. They seemed to be waiting for him. No officers. He no longer trusted officers. He was in charge. He didn't want officers giving orders about things they did not understand. Hope Kirby understood mountains. He knew how to hit and run and hide and hit again. They went hunting Japs, and they killed Japs by the score.

The Filipinos sheltered them. The Japs were more cruel to the Filipinos than to the Americans, and the Filipinos took their revenge by sheltering Hope Kirby and his band and guiding them through the rain forest and the mountains. Up in one of their villages they came on Missionary. He had a name, but Hope called him Missionary. He was smart, an educated man who read books, and he could quote miles of poetry. Sometimes at night when it was safe, Hope asked Missionary to recite something, and Missionary did, and it was always beautiful even when Hope and some of the others could not understand all the words. They sat around a small fire with pickets posted to watch for Japs, and Missionary spoke in his deep, rumbling voice that was like music in the dark and Hope took a pleasure in the words that was like listening to Mammy read the Bible to him back in the sweet old days now gone.

Missionary went to school up in Massachusetts before he came to the Philippines. He could talk about Cambridge, how pretty everything was, a square where you could buy newspapers in languages from all over the world, and a subway you could take down into Boston, and a brick college behind a wrought-iron fence and brick walls and down the street another school, the one where he went and taught for a while, with buildings made of gray stone and green grass on the lawn and streetcars and people dressed up fine. He said you could sit down in a cafe in the square and drink coffee and read the newspapers for an hour if you wanted, and nobody told you to move on. You could go to concerts and plays and lectures where people who wrote books talked about things Hope had never dreamed about. Missionary talked about these things with a longing in his face that let you know he was seeing them all again while he spoke but that he knew they were far away in an inaccessible world to which he could never return. "Even if I live through all this and go back there, it can never be what it once was to me," he said. "I understand things now I didn't even think about then." Hope guessed that Missionary and Cambridge were a lot like Hope and the Smoky Mountains.

Missionary said he meant to spend his life reading books and writing one now and then. It was an education to hear him talk. When Hope found him hidden away in the mountain village, Missionary was still wearing clerical garb—a coal-black suit that used to have a white collar in front, but he had lost the collar. He was filthy, and his clothes were in tatters, and he didn't have much to say at first. He seemed dazed. The Filipino who led Hope into a hut where Missionary was sitting tapped himself on the side of the head as if to say, "This man is crazy," and when Hope introduced himself, Missionary sat staring at him and seemed hardly to understand what Hope was saying. Missionary was heavy, but he was not fat, and he had big hands. That was one of the first things Hope noticed about him—those huge hands.

He had run a school for Filipinos in Manila with nice young Americans teaching for him. Most Filipinos were Catholics, but Missionary said he was Episcopal, and it was almost the same thing except that the Episcopals had priests who got married. Only Missionary said he hadn't had time to get married yet because he was running his school. The American teachers were from fine homes and schools in America, and they were out in the Philippines doing good, and they were having a good time, too. Then the Japs came. They rounded up all the teachers, those nice young men and women, and Jap soldiers gang-raped the women. Then they made them all, men and women, dig a big trench and kneel down beside it. One by one the Japs chopped off their heads with those short, sharp Jap swords. While the raping and the killing went on, the Japs hooted and shouted, comrades cheering each other on. The Filipinos who saw it all told Missionary that the women were naked and crying and still trying to cover their bruised private parts when the Japs cut off their heads.

Missionary was not killed because he had been out in the hills looking after Filipino Christians scared because they heard the Japs were killing

Christians. Missionary thought he could protect the brown Filipinos because he had a white skin. He could not imagine that disciplined soldiers in a modern army would harm or even disrespect a clergyman. While Missionary was up in the hills, the Japs took Manila, and some of his brown Christians came up to tell him what had happened to his teachers. The Filipinos said he cried when they told him. That was the most unbelievable thing to Hope Kirby. Missionary crying. He was more accustomed to Missionary's laughter. But that was later.

Missionary said he wanted to join up with Hope. "I want to kill Japs," he said in his dull, dazed voice. Hope was skeptical. The wrong kind of man could get other men killed. Still, something about Missionary made Hope take him on. Something in his eyes. Even then Hope noticed those eyes. They fixed on you like nails. Missionary got rid of his black clothes and his collar and dressed like a Filipino. He even went barefoot most of the time. In a few weeks he had calluses on his feet like leather. Nothing seemed to hurt him. "Feet don't make as much noise as shoes," he said.

Before Missionary came along, Hope and his men killed Japs as they might have shot deer. They got word about Jap troops through the loyal Filipino grapevine, and they set up ambushes, and they killed Japs and then slipped back into the mountains where the Japs didn't dare follow them. If a Jap was wounded and not dead, Hope shot him in the head, quick and easy. He and his men killed prisoners the same way. They had no place to keep prisoners.

It began when they captured three Jap officers with those ugly little swords, ceremonial Samurai things, as deadly as any knife ever made. The Jap officers stood in a little knot with their hands behind their necks, knowing they were going to die and making the best of it, mute and rigidly at attention, prepared to show no emotion at all. Hope's men had a BAR, and Hope thought they would kill the Japs with that, but Missionary fingered one of the swords and said, "Let me try something."

He made a motion to one of the Jap officers. "Get down on your knees," he said. The Jap understood what was coming. He bowed and went to his knees, his body erect from the knees up. He shut his eyes and held himself in almighty dignity. Missionary hefted the sword, eyeing it carefully, testing its balance, and then with a mighty swoop he sliced the Jap's head off. The head went rolling, and the crimson blood spouted fountainlike out of the neck for a second, and the Jap's body quivered violently, fell over, kicked, and lay still. It happened so fast that the twenty-two of them, standing about in a watchful circle, jumped as though Missionary had shocked them all with an electric wire.

Missionary turned to the other two Japs who waited their turn. "That's what you did to my teachers. How does it feel to know that's what I will do to you?" Did the Japs understand? Hope did not know.

The Japs said nothing. They continued to stand at attention. The code of Bushido, Missionary said later. Samurai warriors face death without flinching. That's what bothered Missionary, made him mad. The Japs expected to die. They would not resist or cry out or offer one particle of fear, and they would not beg for mercy. "I want to make them afraid," Missionary said.

Hope stood by. John Sevier was just in front of him. John Sevier looked blankly on the scene as if he had no clue as to what was happening. Missionary stood in front of the other two Japs and spoke to them carefully. "You think nothing we do can make you afraid," he said. They said nothing. He nodded to the younger one, "Jerk his pants down." Two of Hope's men sprang forward, and in a moment they had jerked the pants of the Jap officer down to his knees. He stood there with his hairy prick exposed, and Missionary grabbed him by the testicles and in a moment had sliced away all his genitals. The Jap screamed.

"You see, they are not supermen," Missionary said. "Now the other one."

The Jap they had unmanned sank to his knees, holding the hole where his penis and his testicles had been. The other Jap tried to resist, but he had no chance. Hope's men swarmed over him and flung him to the ground, and held his legs, and Missionary did the operation with the expert stroke of a master surgeon.

"Now, let them go," Missionary said.

"I think we ought to kill them," Hope said.

"Let them go back and show their friends what's waiting for them," Missionary said. "We want them to suffer, Hope. You kill them quickly, and they don't suffer."

"They're going to hell, hain't they?" Hope said.

Missionary looked at him and grinned slyly. "Hope, what if there is no hell? We can't take chances."

That was the beginning. Next time Missionary did his operation on a Jap and did not turn him loose. Instead he staked him down on the ground spread-eagled and naked. "Let some bugs crawl into that hole, and you'll hear some screaming," Missionary said.

Hope's men thought Missionary was a genius at torment. It troubled Hope that so many of the men liked the lessons in torture that Missionary seemed eager to give them. They laughed and joked, and Missionary planned other things, and some of them gathered around him almost conspiratorially to whisper things that made them laugh harder. Some of the men were scared of Missionary pure and simple. Hope had no sympathy for the Japs. Or that is what he told himself when he looked at John Sevier and when he remembered the American heads in the bloody dust and the jeering of Jap soldiers who thought that prisoners were nothing but cockroaches.

Missionary said Jap soldiers were taught to believe they were gods. "When they act like gods, other people begin to think maybe they are invincible. Their reputation fights for them. It's all like the story of Attila the Hun. Whole cities would empty themselves at the sound of his name. But if I had had a few minutes to discuss things with one of Attila's soldiers, the reputation of his army would have been considerably diminished."

Was it his imagination, or did his band now begin trying to take prisoners rather than to kill every Jap it ambushed as quickly as possible? One afternoon up beyond Bosoboso on a rocky river, they hit a Jap patrol and killed all but four of them. One survivor was the officer in charge, a *choi*, first lieutenant, who kept firing until his pistol was out of ammunition. He was a dignified-looking man, about forty, Hope guessed, with an erect bearing and a calm face. He had been slightly wounded in one arm, and his sleeve was bloody, but he paid the wound no attention. He said something to the other three, and they gathered around him, holding their hands up and looking stolid and, Hope thought, proud.

Missionary held the BAR. He handed it to one of Hope's men and came up close to the Jap officer, a much smaller man. "Well, well, it looks as if we have a nice lieutenant here. Very nice. Very nice."

The Jap officer spoke up in a careful but fluent English. "I am a graduate of Columbia University, class of 1932," he said.

Missionary glowed. "Columbia! Well, now. I am a graduate of Harvard College, class of 1929. What a pleasure to meet you, sir. A real pleasure." And Missionary put out a hand and took the Jap's right hand and shook it warmly. It was the Jap's wounded arm, and Hope saw the man flinch slightly, but not much.

"I was at Harvard once. I love American football, and I went to Cambridge with friends once to see a game at Soldiers Field."

"I was probably there," Missionary said. "How interesting that fate has brought us together."

"It was very thrilling," the Jap said.

"So what did you study at Columbia?" Missionary said, his smile like the sun.

"I studied English literature," the Jap said. "I took course after course in Shakespeare and in Milton."

"Shakespeare and Milton," Missionary said, taking the air of a man delightfully surprised by an amazing discovery. "Two of my very favorite authors."

> *Ay, but to die, and go we know not where,*
> *To lie in cold obstruction and to rot,*
> *This sensible warm motion to become*
> *A kneaded clod, and the delighted spirit*
> *To bathe in fiery floods, or to reside*
> *In thrilling region of thick ribbed ice;*
> *To be imprisoned in the viewless winds*
> *And blown with restless violence round about*
> *The pendent world; or to be worse than most*
> *Of those that lawless and incertain thought*
> *Imagine howling—'tis too horrible!*
> *The weariest and most loathed worldly life*
> *That age, ache, penury, and imprisonment*
> *Can lay on nature is a paradise*
> *To what we fear of death.*

Missionary's performance was again a masterpiece. He spoke in almost a whisper but with such feeling that the air seemed to vibrate with it, and the Jap officer nodded soberly.

"Claudio in *Measure for Measure*," the Jap said. "No writer is better than Shakespeare on death."

"But," said Missionary, "death is easy to write about because we conceive it as a mysterious end of life and afterwards we do not know what we may expect."

"I do not believe Shakespeare expected anything after death," the Jap officer said thoughtfully.

"Exactly," Missionary said. "Death to him is but sleep. Endless night. I think of something that comes before death, something Shakespeare scarcely wrote about at all."

"Fear?" the Jap officer said.

"No, my dear colleague from Columbia. Pain. Shakespeare did not describe physical pain. It is very hard to describe. There are no metaphors for pain, you see. Pain is like itself, only it is not like anything else, and every pain is different."

The Jap looked at him. Missionary meditated, his hands folded across his chest. At his side in its sheath hung his Jap sword. "And how did you use your Columbia University education?"

"I taught English in Japan."

"You taught English, and the Jap army has you on patrol with common soldiers? It seems to me that you should be in intelligence, in something worthy of your education."

"I was opposed to the war," he said.

"A Jap opposed to the war," Missionary chortled. "But here you are leading a patrol trying to find us and kill us, and behold! We have found you and killed your men. You have not led them very well, Lieutenant. You should be ashamed of yourself. Your army should be ashamed of itself for not using you better." Missionary took out his sword and inspected its shining blade. "These swords are beautifully made," he said in a tone of admiration as if he had just noticed how beautifully made his sword was. "I was the principal of a school in Manila. Your men took all my young teachers and cut their heads off in a grave they forced my teachers to dig for themselves before they were executed. Oh yes, and they raped the women."

The Jap lieutenant lowered his eyes. Hope thought that in that moment he knew that he himself was going to die.

"I want you to tell your men what I have just told you," Missionary said.

The lieutenant looked up at him, knowing no apology was worth anything. For a moment he was silent. Then he spoke rapidly. The soldiers listened like bronze statues.

"Now let me tell you what I am going to do to you. Pretend that I am the doctor, and you are the patient. We are going to jerk your trousers down, and I am going to cut off your penis and your testicles. Unfortunately I do not have any anesthesia to deaden your pain, but we would not want such a womanish thing as anesthesia, would we? We have the code of Bushido to make us strong. Alas, I do not believe you can keep from screaming no matter what your code of Bushido tells you. When I have thrown your testicles and your penis away, I am going to turn you over, and I am going to run this nice sword into your anus, and I am going to run it up through your body trying to avoid your vital organs. It is an experiment. I want to see how much pain you can suffer before you go into shock and die. I shall be extremely careful not to kill you quickly." He turned to the rest of the band. "Gentlemen," he said, "will some of you pull the lieutenant's trousers down?" Three or four men leaped forward, and in a second the lieutenant was standing with his trousers around his ankles, and in another second he was flung on his back, and Missionary said, "Hold his arms and his legs. He will kick and squirm, and we don't want to ruin this."

That was when Hope moved. He seized the BAR out of the hands of the gape-mouthed American who held it, a man named Sloane. He pointed the

BAR at Missionary. "All right," he said, "that's enough. Get back, Missionary. All of you get back!"

Missionary looked at him coldly. "What's the matter, Hope? Are you getting squeamish?"

"Get back, Missionary. I'm warning you. If you don't get back, I'll kill you. And the rest of you, too. Who's in command here, you or me?"

"I think that's for the men to decide," Missionary said quietly. He looked around as though for assent, but nobody said anything.

"Are you going to get out of the way or hain't you?" Hope's voice was like steel.

Missionary got up, and the other men moved back. The lieutenant looked at Hope gratefully and started to pull up his trousers. That was when Hope opened up on him with the BAR, and after a quick burst that flung the lieutenant back open-mouthed and dead with his trousers down around his thighs, Hope turned the weapon on the other Jap soldiers and shot them dead before they understood what was happening. The Jap soldiers fell on the lieutenant, and Hope fired another burst into the pile to be sure they were all dead. The BAR held twenty rounds. He still had two rounds when he stopped firing. He knew to count.

"All right," he said, looking hard around at his men and at Missionary. "We hain't going to do no more cutting up of prisoners. We're going to kill them. You all understand that?"

It was as though he had waked them up. They looked around at each other, seeming a little sheepish, ashamed. Not Missionary! Missionary looked defiant. Maybe Missionary looked simply crazy. For just a minute Hope thought of turning the BAR on him, killing him the way you might kill a dog that you had petted only to have it bite you. Missionary may have seen the motion of Hope's eyes, a little flicker, a narrowing, something that said, "Death is easy; I have just killed four people; I can happily kill you, and you will not mess up the heads of my men any more." Whatever it was, Missionary gave way, and that was the end of it.

Except that it wasn't the end of it. "You don't understand, Hope," Missionary said sometimes, shaking his head as though he pitied Hope Kirby. "I see things you don't see." Sometimes Missionary said to the men in Hope's hearing, "We could have some fun with those Japs, but our lord and master wants us to kill them quick and sweet. Too bad. Too bad."

Hope understood the mockery. It didn't matter. After that they attended to killing Japs, and they did that quickly and well.

*D*ISASTER struck Joseph Ignazio's mall in early December. By November the grading had been hard. Somehow Ignazio had failed to understand that hills in Tennessee were underlaid by layers of rock. The bulldozers worked their way down to a layer of hard limestone, and there they were impotent to do more than scrape off a thin shaving of stone at every pass. The engineer shook his head. At least it isn't granite, he said hopefully, though it was very close to being marble.

The expanse of scraped earth tilted towards the north like an enormous tabletop left lying against something beneath it on one side. "I reckon we will have to dynamite the rock to break it up," the engineer said.

Ignazio retained his confidence in the ability of engineers to do anything. "Well, do it," he said.

So the engineer brought in a blasting crew from Knoxville. The members of the blasting crew wore yellow slickers and expressions of extreme importance and bristled with the confidence of men accustomed to letting nothing stand in their way. They drilled holes in the limestone and planted dynamite and called in the Tennessee Highway Patrol to block the traffic on Highway 70, and pressed the detonator, and the blast made a terrific show, very satisfying to everyone who gathered at a distance to watch. The sound of the explosion could be heard as a muffled boom in Bourbonville itself, five miles away, where it rattled windows. On the site it hurled shattered fragments of limestone high in the air, and these fell to earth with a heavy crashing and thumping that made all the spectators, safely backed off, feel that they had been awarded a fine show. Bulldozers quickly cleared Highway 70 of a few large rocks that had settled on the pavement, and traffic resumed.

The foreman of the blasting crew was already moving towards the area of broken rock to set more charges when he heard a different sound, much lower and seemingly much less significant than the sound of dynamite going off. It was a curious sound that grew louder but never seemed as threatening as in fact it was. It was the sound of water running.

Sound came before sight. Then sight came, a rushing of water foaming up amid the broken stones and rushing down the long incline in a broad sheet that swept across the highway and poured into a field on the southern side and found a channel in a small creek that, as a stunned Joseph Ignazio and an amused and amazed crowd watched, rose four feet. A foaming white stream rolled down this new course with the exuberance of a large dog let out of confinement to play.

The engineer was the calmest person in the crowd. He at least understood what he had done. "It's that spring on the other side of the hill," he said succinctly. "We've changed its course. It used to flow north. Now by damn it's flowing south."

"Well, stop it!" Joseph Ignazio said.

It took him about a half hour to understand that they had done something that could not be undone and a couple of days to learn the full extent of what they had accomplished. Two small houses built downstream alongside the brook were now washed into ruin by the raging torrent that had taken up new residence there. Highway 70 itself began to erode, and traffic backed up in both directions as cars and trucks slowed to make their careful way through ankle-deep water that extended more than fifty yards on the pavement. A great many people were angry. The lawsuits began to be filed about ten days later. But although those two small houses in the new course of the stream were reduced to wreckage, no one was killed or even injured.

It was a big story in the Knoxville newspapers—the first really big story that Joseph Ignazio had achieved in them. Despite all he had done to woo the press, he had succeeded in getting only a small and somewhat skeptical article in the Sunday edition of the *Morning Journal*. Now reporters and columnists from the morning and afternoon papers enjoyed themselves at the collapse of the crackpot ideas of the Yankee who had come south to show the rubes how to live and had ended in a ridiculous failure. Bourbonville came in for its own gibes. As one reporter on the afternoon paper wrote, "What will Bourbonville do next to entertain us? We have enjoyed for months the consequences of a double murder that was the climax of an adulterous love affair, the antics of a lunatic judge at the trial, and now the literal explosion of a madcap scheme to lure shoppers twenty miles out in the country—a forty-mile round trip—to buy merchandise they could buy in town. Maybe after Bourbonville has cleaned up after this strange thing called a 'mall,' the town can invite the Ringling Brothers Barnum and Bailey Circus to take up permanent residence."

Decades later, when Jane Whitaker sat on a bench in the indoor forest at Opryland in Nashville or when she went into any one of the tacky malls that by then ringed Knoxville, turning miles of fertile and once gentle farmland into parking lots and nondescript sheds that covered acres of ground, she looked back on Joseph Ignazio with a hopeless sense of a lost chance. He had seen it all like a prophet high on a mountaintop looking over into a land of promise that the god of fate refused to let him enter. Every time she saw a parking lot at a mall with row on row of cars parked by the thousand, she felt a hollowness in the universe.

In 1953, when her dreams and Joseph Ignazio's vision collapsed together in one tumultuous explosion of dynamite and water, she was simply stunned. In the end Joseph Ignazio escaped by declaring bankruptcy and fleeing back to New York, where, as far as Bourbonville was concerned, he disappeared. When he presented his accounts to the bankruptcy court in Tennessee, everything was meticulously in order. He had not diverted a cent to his own interest. He had conducted himself not only with scrupulous honesty but also with a frugality that no one could fault. He had failed. That was all the story.

Altogether he had put over two hundred thousand dollars into his venture—one hundred thousand from the First Bourbon County Bank and fifty thousand each from two smaller banks in Knoxville. The three banks were left with a large scraped expanse of land worth only a fraction of what they had invested in it, and when they had paid the considerable cost of diverting the stream back to its former course, they had lost together another eighty thousand dollars. And there were the lawsuits regarding the houses.

People were finally amused and a little happy. To most of them the mall had always been an inconceivable idea. Joseph Ignazio could talk about it avidly to civic groups and to individuals, but he had two flaws in speaking to such people. One was that he was sure the mall did not depend on locals. He was going to bring in people from afar to see his creation, and it would be a marvel like one of the seven wonders of the world that did not depend on those who lived in their shadows. The other was that he had a strong Yankee accent, and he talked continually about all he was going to change in East Tennessee. It was as if East Tennessee were some primitive place that had no enlightenment until he brought it from the North. Since Joseph Ignazio left town almost as soon as his dream collapsed, Jane Whitaker was left to bear the ridicule that was not always covert. That was very hard for her, harder than anyone could dream given the resolutely stony face she turned to the world.

She held her head up, appeared every Sunday morning at Central Methodist Church as punctually as a worker arriving at an assembly line, and she spoke with authoritative cheer to the minister at the door—the same voice that she used in dealing with her clients at the bank. She carried on with the manufactured assurance of someone sick with a terminal disease who resolves to act as if nothing has happened or as if nothing will happen.

She understood with fatal resignation that no more dreams would come and that she was trapped in Bourbonville forever.

IN DECEMBER, Arceneaux started going to Nashville to visit Hope Kirby. It was almost a six-hour drive. He got up at five in the morning and was in Nashville in time for lunch; then he went to the prison and visited with Hope Kirby. Then he came home.

Monday was the traditional preacher's holiday, and Arceneaux could do anything he wanted with it. He did not advertise his trips to see Hope. But it was not a secret that could be kept. It raised a buzz of gossip and speculation in the county. Arceneaux did not care.

His fantasies about the ministry were dying. He thought he would preach and do good deeds and never have sex again with a man and become a saint and justify his life. He met the only saint he had ever known, Bob Saddler, and he thought that Bob Saddler was crazy, but then sometimes he supposed that if Bob Saddler had lived, he might have received the stigmata. Whatever else he had done, Bob Saddler demonstrated that Arceneaux could never be a saint, that perhaps he did not want to be a saint.

Arceneaux did not seriously doubt the existence of God. He knew that many people did. Most of his comrades in the French Resistance were Communists. Most of them were militant atheists. Sometimes they had philosophical discussions, and he remembered how Jean-François ridiculed the Catholic Church. "Every nun is a whore for the priest, and if there is a convent in the town, the priest has a harem. And the pope! He is a Nazi, pure and simple." The tirades of Jean-François were almost amusing because they were so intense. In those days, in the midst of the war, in occupied France, Arceneaux never planned to become a preacher. He would have laughed at the idea. Nor did he have any thought of arguing with Jean-François or with anyone else. Arceneaux thought God could take care of Himself, and he prayed often, sometimes in long meditations when he lay awake at night on the ground or shut up in some supposedly safe house in a town where he could hear the hobnailed tread of German boots when patrols went marching by in the dark. Death to be seen by one of them, and he lay in his bed praying to God to keep him and his men safe, and when he prayed he felt that someone was there to listen, and that's about as far as Arceneaux's religion went.

But it was far enough. And after the "incident," as he called it euphemistically to himself, becoming a minister seemed the best way to hide what he was and redeem what he had done. Vomiting on Mrs. Beau de Vitry had made some action necessary, and Arceneaux thought that becoming a minister was as spectacular a repentance as he could muster. It would also be a way to hide himself from what he was. It would be a mistake to assume that Arceneaux willed himself into a life of hypocrisy and that he wanted to hide from other people. Oh yes, he was devoured with self-loathing when in his vivid imagination he saw himself exposed, blackmailed, made a public spectacle for being a queer. He imagined his father and mother, all their friends in New Orleans, humiliated beyond their ability to bear. The truth would kill his mother. No doubt. The thought filled him with an incendiary shame that reduced him to a speck, and in that speck he felt an infinity of horror. But he did not intend to become the sort of minister who preached on Sundays and frequented the toilets in bus terminals or, worse, made secret liaisons with other queers known to the sexually desperate network that rumor told him existed everywhere. No, Arceneaux would not practice sex at all, and in taking care of other people, he would hide from himself his perversion, and he would bear it. "There hath no temptation taken you but such as is common to man: but God is faithful, who will not suffer you to be tempted above that ye are able; but will with the temptation also make a way to escape, that ye may be able to bear it." Paul's advice to the Corinthians. They were tempted by the hundreds of sacred prostitutes who enticed the multitudes in Corinth. Paul warned against fornication, knowing the pains of fleshly desire. But God had a plan in all of it. Arceneaux pondered himself and thought that God had given him a special temptation so that in overcoming it he might become hardened and sharpened into being one of God's special tools. So he told himself, and perhaps the energy of his desire jumped a circuit in him and became an intense emotional commitment to what he said he believed.

But it wasn't working. He found that when he visited the sick he didn't like some of them very much. How could he like Mrs. Moore, who delighted in the multitude of her symptoms? When he went to visit her, she reproached him for not coming more often. "If you knew how much I'm suffering, you'd come to see me every day," she said. Somehow the thought of visiting Hazel Moore every day was as attractive as a daily trip to the dentist. Bob Saddler visited the sick and held little children in his arms and prayed over them with the fervor of a saint. But Arceneaux knew more and more that he himself was no saint.

He thought he might comfort the dying. But when he visited with the dying, he discovered that nearly all of them refused to admit they were dying and talked to him with weak enthusiasm about new medicines being developed or about a change in their habits that would cure them of heart disease or cancer. Even the dying preferred to talk about football or baseball rather than to enter upon philosophical and theological meditations about the end of life. Why not? Put off the thought as long as you can, and you won't have to face it.

When he went to see newborn babies, he discovered that he had no talent for adoring little children. He knew somewhat abstractly that he had been a baby himself once, but the knowledge did not give him much to say in the presence of a squalling infant. Truth to tell, he thought babies were rather ugly. When proud parents handed him a child to hold, he could not think of anything to say except, "Now *that's* a baby," as if he had expected a fish or a cat and was relieved to find instead an infant. The occasional sloppy wetness or worse in the baby's diaper was an additional burden that he bore bravely but without enthusiasm.

He found also that people seldom talked to him about serious things. Yes, young women of marriageable age came in to talk to him about their spiritual longings and discovered quickly that he was likely to dismiss them coldly, telling them that satisfaction of spiritual longings was likely to come with age. Sometimes they told him they wanted to be missionaries, only to hear that Arceneaux thought missionaries did more harm than good and that God would take care of today's heathen just as he had taken care of the ancient Greeks, Romans, and even Egyptians long before Christ had been born.

Otherwise preachers were set apart for trivia. His people wanted to talk about fishing; he did not like to fish. They expected him to be interested in football. He thought it was a brutal, stupid game. They resented his absence at the BCHS football games at Civitan Field on Friday nights in the fall. When he begged off, saying that it was a game he had never understood, some unmarried women offered to teach him the rules, rolling their eyes at him suggestively, and when he said he was too old to get interested in games, people supposed he was a snob.

He admitted his snobbery to himself and knew that in Bourbonville, snobbery was an affliction, as fatal to popularity as drunkenness or beating one's wife. He thought that when he told the church he would take no salary for his services, members of the congregation would be pleased with his generous spirit. The salary was paltry—four thousand dollars a year. Arceneaux made ten times that amount merely from the interest on his savings account in a New Orleans bank. In addition his father invested in his name thousands of dollars every year in stocks and bonds that had long since made Arceneaux a millionaire several times over. To collect a salary from the church would have been for him a nuisance, an accounting problem he did not need.

But instead of gratitude, he discovered in his congregation an envious curiosity about his money, where it had come from, how much he had. He tossed off their questions, irritated by them but unable to show his irritation because he was a minister. He did tell about the sugar plantation, in the way people speak of home, never making much of it other than to say how green it was sometimes and how torrential rains in Louisiana could be. He said he had an income from the plantation sufficient to his needs, sometimes trying to imply that he had financial problems just like the rest of them. But they could see from his beautiful suits and his fine shirts and shoes and from the white Jaguar that he had more money than any of them could ever dream of having, and they resented it.

"Preacher, you ought to let me sell you a Chevrolet," Paul Belks, the local Chevrolet dealer and a member of his church, told him sanctimoniously. "If you're going to be a preacher in Bourbonville, you ought to drive an American car." Paul Belks had a warm, ingratiating car dealer's voice, and he spoke about everything with such authority that people counted him one of Bourbonville's leading citizens. "I'm just trying to help you get along with people," Belks said, putting his arm around Arceneaux in the same way that he put his arm around members of the Civitan Club.

"But I love my Jag," Arceneaux said, almost plaintively. It was one of his great consolations. He despised American cars. He wanted to say to Paul Belks, "I'd no more drive a Chevrolet than I'd drive a tractor with a manure spreader hitched onto the back of it." He did not say such a thing. Instead he told a white lie. "My father gave me this car," Arceneaux said. "It would hurt his feelings if I drove anything else." The story was not entirely untrue. When he graduated from seminary, his father gave him a check for five thousand dollars. "Buy whatever you want," the elder Arceneaux said. "Waste the money." So Arceneaux bought a Jaguar.

Then Arceneaux discovered that people did not appreciate his sermons. People drew him aside, wanting to help the young minister, speaking confidentially, pleadingly, pained, but doing it for his own good, they said. They wanted him to be more enthusiastic, or maybe the word was "fervent." Maybe they wanted him to speak faster. He spoke slowly, deliberately, and (he imagined) thoughtfully, reflecting how much he had pondered the text he had chosen from the Bible, and he did not give fiery "altar calls" as Baptists called them, commanding the "unsaved" to march down to the front of the church and confess their sins and "accept Jesus Christ as your personal Savior."

Arceneaux thought such expressions were vulgar, and although he gave people a chance to join the church and even to make their professions of faith, he preached as if there were no emergency involved. He spoke with a dignified and genuine eloquence about things he had been thinking about, mostly in the life of Jesus. He thought that life was much more mysterious than members of his congregation thought it to be. Sometimes he startled them, as he did with his sermon on the shortest verse in the Bible, "Jesus wept." Why did Jesus weep, asked Arceneaux, if he knew that he would raise Lazarus from the dead in the next moment? Maybe he didn't know, Arceneaux said. He had emptied himself to be like us, and that meant that his knowledge about some things was as restricted as ours. The First Baptists found all this hard to fathom. Jesus is God, isn't he, and if he is God, he knows everything, right? It was not that easy, Arceneaux said, frustrating the First Baptists who believed that everything about their religion was easy, so much so that they wondered how other denominations could be so mistaken.

Understand that the First Baptists did not want a diet of ignorant hellfire-and-damnation preaching every Sunday. They didn't want ranting. They preferred their emotions cool rather than hot, although now and then they liked to raise the temperature to warm. They liked a poem or two in their sermons as long as the poems were done in rhyming verse and had a moral to them, but now and then they wanted enough fervor in the church service to recall that God was right there among them, keeping watch over them, and taking note when they did good things or committed sins. They were especially eager to hear condemnations of sins they did not commit, such as softness towards criminal behavior and the doctrine that all people had the right to a good life whether they worked for it or not. In the midst of Joseph McCarthy's war on communism, they adored sermons on the American Way and the godlessness of communism, which was akin to socialism. Arceneaux never preached any of these sermons. More and more frequently he preached about things they did not want to hear, such as the coming decision by the Supreme Court on whether school segregation was legal. When he did, many of his congregation said he should preach the gospel and leave all social issues alone.

It is in the nature of being a preacher that everyone who hears you must compare you to another preacher. In Bourbon County, there were many preachers to choose from. Over at the Tabernacle Baptist Church back in the spring the minister, B. B. Hartpenny, had a "football night" attended by the entire Bourbon County High School football team, and all the boys rededicated their lives to Jesus and vowed to go undefeated and untied and give all the credit to the Lord. The minister gathered all the young men around him, and they prayed, and they wept together, and at the end sang the school fight song. Arceneaux was secretly delighted when BCHS lost its first game to Oak Ridge 65–0. He almost wished he had attended. He heard that the defeat had been a sore test of faith to the boys on the team and that the Reverend B. B. Hartpenny had to weep some more with them.

Despite the mysterious ways of the Lord in allowing the Panthers to lose, nothing like that spiritual outpouring happened at First Baptist, and when Arceneaux invited a visiting preacher in for the fall revival, something expected at any Baptist church, he chose a former football star at Bourbon County High who had gone on to college and to seminary at Fort Worth, Texas, and who preached like a house afire. The congregation adored him, but people noted that Arceneaux sat on the platform looking exceedingly uncomfortable every night during the week. The truth was that he thought the young preacher was dumber than dirt, and he was embarrassed at the sermons and spent the week wishing he were somewhere else and longing for a drink.

Worst of all was Tommy Fieldston. Why did Tommy Fieldston have to come to First Baptist Church? Why didn't he go to Tabernacle Baptist? There Preacher B. B. Hartpenny stoked the fires of hell and lengthened them to eternity and told about the unending thirst and wept over the sinners within the sound of his voice who were going there and had the choir sing softly "Just as I Am" with every head in the congregation bowed and every eye closed and the preacher begged sinners to come forward and give their hearts to Jesus, and when the people who make public professions of sin and faith came down the aisle, Brother Hartpenny embraced them and wept over them.

Arceneaux did not weep in public, and he especially did not weep on demand. In all those ways he was drifting from his congregation, and he was reconsidering his life. Above all he was thinking that he had to save the lives of Charles Alexander and Hope Kirby. Charles Alexander was that boy in France. Hope Kirby was Lawrence Arceneaux.

If Hope Kirby deserves to die in the electric chair, so do I, he thought. He held next to his heart the secret that was to him more damning than his homosexuality. He had committed murder. All in the line of duty. Military necessity. Arceneaux knew better. It was murder pure and simple. No, those were the wrong terms. It was murder impure and very complicated.

A FEW days after Hope Kirby was transported to Nashville, Arceneaux saw Hugh Bedford sitting drunk in Bessie May Hancock's cafe.

Arceneaux was outraged. Maybe "furious" is a better word. He brooded about Hugh Bedford all afternoon, and after he had eaten his own solitary supper in his kitchen, he walked up through the deep November twilight to Hugh Bedford's little house across from the high school on B Street and knocked on the door. There was no answer. Arceneaux knocked harder, so hard that he used the side of his fist rather than his knuckles, and when there was still no answer, he tried the brass knob on the door, felt it turn, and walked inside the lightless house calling, "Hugh?" There was no answer. It was a chilly evening, not cold, but chilly. The house was unheated. He walked back through the darkened rooms repeating his call, louder and louder, but he got no response at all.

The kitchen door was shut, and there was no light on the other side. Arceneaux opened it, and he found Hugh Bedford—slumped in his chair, the upper part of his body spread across the kitchen table, his face lying in a pool of vomit. He was an obscure and sacklike lump of flesh in the semidark of the room.

"Damn!" the preacher said. He did not hesitate. He opened a closet and found a tin mop bucket with the mop standing in dirty water not thrown out since the last time Hugh's Negro servant had mopped for him. The water stank. Arceneaux took the mop out of the bucket, and with one mighty swoosh, he dumped the water on Hugh Bedford's head.

Hugh Bedford woke up angry.

Contrary to the clichés that abound, from Shakespeare's *Henry IV, Part 2* until now, rumors are sometimes true. It is not worth going into everything Arceneaux said and did the night he found Hugh Bedford drunk and poured a bucket of filthy mop water over his head. Hugh Bedford told the story himself later on, and even he may have been prone to exaggeration because, as it turned out, it was the moment that Hugh Bedford's life began to change in ways no one could have predicted.

Arceneaux did not stop with pouring the mop water on Hugh Bedford's head. He began opening closet doors, finding stashed bottles of booze, ripping out the stoppers, and pouring them down the sink. Hugh Bedford tried to stop him. He thought in the foggiest and most demented recesses of his intoxicated mind that stopping a preacher would not be a difficult matter. He went after Arceneaux with a roar of outrage, screaming curses at him, only to discover that in some way he could not understand he was lying flat on his back on the floor coming out of an unconscious state not caused by alcohol but instead by a blow across his ear delivered with the force of a sledgehammer that left him stunned and unable to stand. He woke up with the worst headache he had ever had in his life.

When he emerged from this second state of unknowing, he heard a terrific clatter that included the breaking of glass in the basement. He lay there on his back and began to weep. He knew he was listening to Arceneaux destroying all his whiskey, throwing some of the bottles against the wall. It was terribly distressing, not merely for the financial loss, the loss of his capital in booze, but for the more terrifying understanding that if Arceneaux kept on, there would be not a drop of whiskey in the house.

T HE GUARD spoke to him. "Hope, you got a visitor."

Hope looked up. "Is it Saturday?" he said. His father and his brothers came to see him on Saturday.

"Nah, it ain't Saturday," the guard said. "It's a preacher." If the prisoner was not deemed dangerous, the guards let preachers come in any time they wanted.

"Is it Mr. Arceneaux?" Hope said. He and Arceneaux had more to talk about than Hope had dreamed. Hope felt sorry for the preacher. Arceneaux could not forget some things. "We was in a war," Hope said. "You done what you thought was the right thing at the time. I did, too." Roy Kirby was grateful to Mr. Arceneaux. "That air man air the bestest preacher I've ever knowed in my life," Pappy said. Hope believed him. Hope did not tell his father everything Arceneaux said. He told Arceneaux, "You can't help being what you are, and I can't neither."

"No," the guard said. "It ain't Arceneaux. It's somebody else I ain't never seen before."

"What's his name?" Hope said. For a moment he felt a wave of terror. Maybe it was Abby's preacher. Hope didn't know what he would say to him.

"He didn't tell me his name," the guard said. "He ain't from around here, though. You can tell that by the way he talks."

Hope thought that maybe it was one of those evangelists who come to jails to save souls and go home to brag to their churches about them. He was about to refuse to see him when the guard said, "I'm surprised you know somebody like him. He's a Catholic priest. Are you a Catholic, Hope?"

"Nah, I hain't no Catholic," Hope said. "I don't know who he is, but I reckon hit won't hurt to find out."

"Be a little walk for you," the guard said. All the guards liked Hope. "We'll protect you from him if he gets mean."

They both laughed at the thought of a dangerous preacher. It was exercise, Hope thought. He got to walk around the prison yard once a day in the morning. All you could see from there was the sky and the gray stone walls. The men on death row walked while the others were eating breakfast. They each had two guards to walk with them, one guard on each side of a prisoner. The men on death row were not allowed to talk to each other. They were kept far apart. Hope did push-ups and knee bends in his cell, but he felt himself getting flabby.

The guard snapped the cuffs on and walked Hope down to the visiting room and led him to one of the steel cages where the men on death row sat when they had visitors, and Hope had the cuffs taken off his wrists as he was let in, and he sat down on a little stool in front of the steel-wire screen that separated him from the visitor. The guard locked the barred door behind him and stood there.

The man who sat opposite Hope was dressed up like a priest, long black robe, white collar turned around. He was going bald, and his hair was the color of gray iron. The receding hairline and the color of the hair fooled Hope for a minute. The last time they had seen each other, this man's hair had been black, and it had curled thickly down over his high, aristocratic forehead. They looked at each other. The priest said, "Hope Kirby, wherefore dost thou forget us forever and forsake us for so long a time?" He laughed. Hope laughed, too.

"Missionary!" he said.

"Bless you, my son," Missionary said in his booming voice.

"Missionary. My God," Hope said.

"I trust you are uttering a prayer and not profanity, my son," Missionary said. "You were never one to curse. I don't believe I ever heard you curse. You were a remarkable soldier."

"I'm glad to see you," Hope said.

"I have heard that you are in need of spiritual counsel, my son." Missionary continued to speak in his big voice. High above them the stone walls of the gloomy room, painted an institutional green, threw his voice back down on them. Missionary was the only visitor, and Hope was the only prisoner there. The guard who had brought Hope down drifted away from his position behind the cage to talk to another guard. Hope heard them speaking in low voices and laughing at a distance behind him.

"Well, I'm in some trouble, but my lawyer says we're going to get a new trial."

"A new trial! I knew it from what I read in the papers. Well, congratulations. The Lord God of armies has blessed you, my son. I shall express my thanks to him in my prayers." It was a big, formal voice. Hope remembered Missionary standing over a Jap soldier wounded in an ambush, and Missionary held a scalpel-sharp bayonet in both hands above the Jap's neck and said, "And now, my yellow son of a bitch, prepare to meet thy God. Slowly! Slowly!"

"How did you hear about me?" Hope said in a lower voice.

Missionary dropped his voice. "You have loyal friends, General." Missionary used to call Hope "General" because Hope hated officers. "Buck McGinty called me. You remember Buck? Billy Motrom called him."

"Sure, I remember Buck."

"He's in Lowell, Massachusetts, now," Missionary said. His voice had dropped still further.

"Is that where you are?" Hope said.

"It's near where I was. He said you'd killed your wife."

"I didn't want to do hit," Hope said.

"I know, my son," Missionary said. "I understand you. 'As in water, face answereth to face, so the heart of man to man.' "

"That's Bible, I reckon."

"You have not lost a speck of your intelligence," Missionary said with his strange laugh. "You had no choice. 'And the man that committeth adultery with another man's wife, even he that committeth adultery with his neighbor's wife, the adulterer and the adulteress shall surely be put to death.' You did God's will, my son."

Missionary's voice sounded like a rumble deep down in a house where graves were hidden. Hope squinted, trying to fix on a face through the steel mesh. Missionary's eyes were pale. He had a look that could make a strong man afraid. "Hit's done," Hope said softly.

"Yes, it is done," Missionary said.

"So what have you been doing with yourself? We lost touch," Hope said.

"I had the feeling you did not want to see me again," Missionary said. "I did not forget you, General. I have never forgotten those days. The freedom of them. I knew that you and I would work together again."

"We hain't got no more Japs to kill," Hope said uncomfortably.

"Yes, the war ended too soon. We should have killed millions more of them. Millions. I'm sorry we dropped the atom bombs, you know. We could have gone on killing them for years if we had not dropped those bombs."

"They would have killed us, too," Hope said.

"The price you pay," Missionary said. "The price you pay."

"Did you go back to preaching?" Hope said. The question sounded odd to him, but he could not think of anything else to say.

Missionary rolled his eyes sadly. "Yes, I went back to preaching, but Hope, I do not find people willing to listen." He displayed his hands in a helpless gesture. "I taught others to preach, but no more."

"Was you teaching in a school?"

Missionary laughed, throwing his head back. "What a clever question, Hope! You know that all teaching does not go on in schools. You know that the greatest teaching we ever did—and the greatest learning we ever did—was in the Philippines. Yes indeed, I learned things I never dreamed of teaching when I was confined to my school in Manila. But to answer your intelligent question, yes, I was teaching in a school, the Episcopal Theological School in Cambridge, Massachusetts."

"That sounds like a long way off," Hope said.

"Every place is equidistant from God," Missionary said piously. "He is a circle. His center is everywhere and his circumference nowhere."

"I reckon so," Hope said uncertainly.

"The school where I taught was directly across the street from Harvard. You remember, I went to college there."

"Well," Hope said after a short pause, "I'm glad you've come to see me, Missionary. You must of gone to a lot of trouble."

"Friendship, my son. Friendship. A friend loveth at all times, and there is a friend that sticketh closer than a brother. I'm sorry to see you in this state.

It's worse than the Philippines, isn't it? No chance to escape." He looked up at the high ceiling and turned his head from one side to another to survey the walls, and Hope knew he was calculating. Just what would it take to break out of here? "It does look hopeless, doesn't it?" he said in almost a whisper, a sudden expression of gloom.

"Well, hain't nobody come by to fetch me out to help in his garden," Hope said with a laugh.

"Maybe we could arrange that," Missionary said, his eyes lighting so that Hope thought, *He's crazy.* That same thought had zipped through Hope's mind many, many times in the Philippines. Now it didn't matter, he thought. Missionary was out there; Hope was in here.

"We could take a hostage," Missionary whispered, looking around. "I could bring in a gun under my robes. They barely searched me."

"Missionary, then what? Where would we go? We hain't got no place to hide."

"Ah me," said Missionary, his voice disconsolate. Then he brightened. "Tell me something—do you think you could still break a man's neck so fast he can't cry out?"

"I hain't tried that in a long time," Hope said.

"Yes, yes, you used a pistol this time, so I hear. Well, you never forget the art. It's like riding a bicycle or typing. Once you learn, you never forget."

"I hain't never rode a bicycle, and I hain't never typed," Hope said.

"Ah, General, always the literalist. That's why I loved you. That's why I obeyed you. A plain man who sees the world exactly as it is and acts. Pure act, that's what you are. No abstraction to you. None at all."

Hope grinned. He liked to hear Missionary talk. It was like being at a magic show that he and John Sevier had seen once in Colorado. You saw tricks you couldn't figure out, and you knew you were being hoodooed by somebody with quick hands, but you couldn't see how he did it, and that was the fun of the thing. That's how Missionary's talk was. Half the time Hope didn't know what he was talking about, but it was fun.

"Act," Missionary said. " 'All the world's a stage, and all the men and women merely players, they have their exits and their entrances, and one man in his time plays many parts.' "

"Is that in a book?" Hope said.

"It's in a play, my son. A play about acting."

"I seen a play once with John Sevier. Hit was out in the open in a little town on a summer night. I think hit was in Kansas when we was harvesting wheat. Hit was interesting how they knowed all their parts without reading from no book."

"You have not ridden a bicycle, and you have never used a typewriter," Missionary said. "But you have seen a play, and you have broken many a neck. Well, my friend, if you have the opportunity to do it again, it will all come back. The power, the memory, the skill lie hidden in your arms and fingers, asleep perhaps, but ready to waken when you call them to do their duty." He looked at his own hands and said almost in meditation, "I have not killed anybody since the Philippines. You have one on me, Hope. I have not killed a soul since the Philippines."

"Well, I wish I was in your shoes," Hope said.

"I admire you, my son," Missionary said. "I always did. You shot your wife and her lover. It would have been better to kill them with your bare hands."

"I couldn't of killed Abby with my hands," Hope said.

"Ah," Missionary said, "the pistol was more sanitary. Yes, I understand." He seemed to lose all his humor and to make the comment with the interested and almost scientific dispassion of a doctor describing the progress of a disease. "Tell me, Hope, do you ever wish you were back in the Philippines?"

The question was something only Missionary could ask. Hope recognized this unique quality of Missionary's mind. "Well, truth to tell," Hope said slowly, "I sometimes wish that. Once you been where we been, once you've seen what we've seen, done what we done, hit's hard to come back here. I just wish—" He did not know how to finish what he had started to say.

Missionary looked serious. "Not a day goes by that I don't think of what it was like out there. The freedom. When I was teaching in the Episcopal Theological School we had bells that rang to tell us when to go to class and when to get out of class, and I had a bell that rang to wake me up in the morning, and there was traffic, and you had to go to cocktail parties and to teas, and you had to listen to stupid people say stupid things while you leaned forward and nodded to them stupidly and tried to give the appearance that you thought they were walking wisdom incarnate. Sometimes I thought how sweet it would be to kill them, if for no other reason than to make the day interesting. Swarms of little people tie down the giants, General. It's a hard world for people like us."

Hope laughed. "I reckon hit's harder for me right now than hit is for you," he said.

"It is hard for me, too, my friend. I am called by God to preach truth, but pulpits are closed to me. It is not a world that cherishes truth. It is a world that loves sham, delusion, falsity, lies, romance. It is a world that confuses mercy with sentimentality. It is a world that lives for flashing lights and the belly and for the automobile and for the motion picture and now for this thing called television. Think of it, Hope. We did what we did so Americans can have two cars in every garage and television at night to keep themselves from remembering how dull they are, and movie actresses and queens to make them forget how ugly they are, and athletes to make them forget how fat they are, and steam irons and refrigerators on the installment plan and automatic washing machines to give them more leisure to worship all those hollow mannequins who are now their gods on the silver screen."

"You don't have to have them things if you don't want to. I never cared for television myself, but Abby loved hit."

"Then I don't blame you for killing her, Hope. Ah me, we are prisoners of people who count trivial things necessary to life. Why do you think you are in prison? You killed your wife and her adulterous sweetheart, and you had good reason. But the people who put you here imagine that you will kill them for no reason if they do not kill you. They do not want to die, because if they die they will not know how some episode on television will come out, and their children will have to finish paying the installments on the refrigerator."

"Oh, hit hain't that bad, Missionary." Hope laughed, partly because Missionary seemed so serious.

"Hope, you are so innocent sometimes that you disappoint me. No one wants to face truth. The world does not care for divine wrath or punishment for sinners, and do you know what the worst sin on earth is?"

Missionary did not wait for Hope to answer his question. He rushed on, answering it himself. "Not being free. Not doing what we are capable of doing because we hold ourselves in the shackles of what other people want us to be! We can all be supermen if we try; instead we live and die in a dullness that imprisons the supermen in chains more binding than this pitiful wire that keeps you and me from touching each other. We live in a world of positive thinking. I preach truth. But the world wants preachers who sound as if they were created by Norman Rockwell or Norman Vincent Peale. I preach the word of God and the world as they are. I am a different Norman, the Norman of the Vikings, the Norman who is the scourge of God."

"You always lose me when you talk like that, Missionary," Hope said.

Missionary laughed, and it was as though he had descended from clouds. "Ah yes, I know. You are brilliant, my son. Uneducated but brilliant. You lived on the edge like a dancer on a tightrope over Niagara Falls, and you never fell. The prospect of death in the next instant gave you a grace that I have never seen in another human being, and you danced away from it with a talent that was debonair. I could have done things with you if you had let me. I thought of so many things we could have done."

"I reckon you could of learnt me a lot," Hope said. "So did you quit teaching at the church school?"

"I was fired, Hope," Missionary whispered, lifting his hands in a gesture of helplessness and resignation again. "A prophet has no honor when he tells the truth. I taught the Bible. I taught young theological students the kind of God we worship, the kind of God who burns on the India-paper pages of Scripture, Hope, the Old and the New Testament, the God who inspired the Psalmist to say, 'Happy shall he be, that taketh and dasheth thy little ones against the stones.' And do you know what?"

"What?" Hope said. Missionary was beginning to make him feel creepy. Missionary could always do that.

"They could not bear it. My students, my colleagues—they could not bear what I had to tell them. The truth! They could not look God in the eye. Where are the martyrs? Where are the Crusaders? Gone, Hope. All gone."

"Maybe you should of kept quiet, Missionary," Hope said. "And let God take care of Hisself."

"No, Hope," Missionary whispered, his face close to the mesh screen. "God is pure will. Pure act. 'Tell them that I Am hath sent me unto you,' said God to Moses. I Am. That is the supreme name of God. I Am commands us to be his instruments, to have our being in Him, for apart from Him we Are Not. We must do what I Am commands, for we are part of his purpose."

Missionary's face was touching the mesh now, and he talked like a hissing hose on the airbrake of a train. His pale eyes seemed to flash sparks. Hope said sharply, "We don't have no war now, Missionary. You got to stop that stuff."

"We always have a war," Missionary whispered. "He is a fierce God, Hope. I could never persuade you how fierce He is. That was your flaw, Hope. Your only flaw. He is always at war against His enemies. I Am is a fierce God. We worshipped Him in the Philippines, and look what He did for us. Look at the Japs He let us kill."

"Missionary, them days is over."

"I tell you they are not, Hope. You worshipped that God of wrath in the Philippines. You proved to me that you are one of His own, smiting his enemies hip and thigh, but even you held back. You should have turned me loose on the Japs to do what I wanted to do to them, Hope. The Japs were the Amalekites. What does the Bible say: 'And Samuel hewed Agag in pieces before Yahweh in Gilgal.' We, you and I, we executed the judgment of God. We hewed the Japs in pieces before Yahweh in the Philippines. A new Scripture would have our deeds written in it, but you drew back, Hope."

"Missionary, I never looked at hit that way," Hope said. "I just wanted to kill Japs. I just wanted to get the war over and done with. I wanted to come home."

"That is the quality I love about you, my son," Missionary said. "Your will is instinctively in harmony with the will of the great I Am. You are unmoved by compulsion. You incarnate the pure act that is God, the image of original righteousness, my son, the image of God in us, in you. You know right and wrong without reasoning about it. When the Japs did us wrong, we did them justice, and justice was to kill them, but you resisted God's will to make them suffer more before they died."

"You might could say that," Hope said. Suddenly, like a revelation, he felt a flash of relief that he was on one side of the steel mesh and Missionary could not get to him. The thought made his skin crawl. He gave no sign.

Missionary looked earnestly at him. "Why didn't you kill the witness, Hope? That boy."

"He hadn't done nothing to me yet. I couldn't kill him."

"He is weak. I have seen him. He deserves to die."

"You seen him?"

"I walked through Bourbonville. Not in these robes, of course. I made myself inconspicuous. I wore a new straw hat with a broad red band. I looked like a tourist on his way to Florida. I drank a Coke in the Rexall. I saw Charles Alexander, Hope. I asked about the town, the people, its history. I did not speak to him, but I saw him. He is weak. He cries out to be killed. Why didn't you kill him?"

"I told you. Look, Missionary, he told the truth. Hit didn't work out. I couldn't help myself, and he couldn't help hisself. What is to be will be. Some folks can't tell a lie. He's one of them. I'm another one. Hit's all right."

Missionary's eyes flashed. "I'm glad I came to see you, my son. You need me."

"Missionary, I don't need nothing. I'm glad to see you. Honest I am, but there hain't nothing you can do. I want you to leave that boy alone. You hear?"

"Always the general, aren't you, Hope? Always giving me orders." He laughed.

Hope did not feel like laughing. "Please," Hope said. "Leave him alone. Just go away. Everthing's going to be all right. Maybe I'll spend a year in prison. That's less than we was in the Philippines, and we got through that. Lawyer's told all my family to leave the boy alone."

"Never trust a lawyer, Hope. Lawyers are liars. They are paid to lie. Lawyers equivocate. If there is anything I hate, it is equivocation. There is no honor in equivocation."

Missionary looked around. High up on the stone wall were tiny windows. They had steel bars over them, and the spaces between the bars were almost too narrow to put a hand through even if you could have climbed up there. "You know," he said softly, "I thought about getting the old squad together, trying to break you out of here."

"Break me out of here? You must be crazy, Missionary."

Missionary shook his head gloomily. "A fool for God's sake, Hope. I came to look the place over. This is a hard place. A hard place. Harder than anything we hit in the Philippines. But if you're as daring as we were, you can do more than you think. The world is made of cowards, Hope. You run at them and they run away. If we brought ten men in here and started shooting, we might pull it off." Missionary's bright eyes took on a hungry, wolfish look.

"You'd need a tank and some field artillery to bust out of here."

"Maybe that can be arranged," Missionary said, still looking as if he wondered where he might place the dynamite. "We were a team, General. A great team. Nobody could stop us."

"Hit was another time and another place," Hope said.

"How many Japs do you suppose we killed?"

"Lord, Missionary, I hain't got no idea. I never counted."

Missionary sighed. "It was so simple. It has not been so simple since."

"No, hit hain't."

"Now we have to leave it to God," Missionary said.

"That's what I say," Hope said. "What is to be will be."

"When Israel did what God commanded, He helped them. When Israel disobeyed, he let them be bound in captivity. We must do what God commands now."

"I never was no good at God talk," Hope said.

"No, that is my department," Missionary said with a laugh. He stood up, making the sign of the cross. "God bless you, my son. God bless you. I shall return. I shall lead you out of this place. Like Moses, destroying Pharaoh's army in the Red Sea."

Hope grinned. He thought Missionary was quoting MacArthur as a joke. Hope wanted to spit in MacArthur's face the day he pinned that little medal on him. But if he had done that, he would have been put in jail, and he would have been that much longer getting home, and who would have taken care of John Sevier? Hope accepted the decoration and wondered how many times during the day MacArthur changed his uniform. It was so clean you could have used it as a bandage.

Missionary did not smile. He stood there, all black except for the white collar, his shape cut up by the mesh screen so that he looked like something fuzzy in a nightmare, as scary as all the nightmares anybody had ever had.

"So long, Missionary," Hope said.

"You will hear from me soon," Missionary said.

Two guards led Hope back to his cell with the handcuffs on his wrists. "Never figured somebody like you would know a preacher like that," one of the guards said.

"Him and me was in the war together," Hope said.

"Sky pilot, was he?"

"Naw, fighter. You hain't never seed a fighter like him. Say, can you do me a favor?"

"Depends," the guard said.

"I'd like a Bible. Could you get me a Bible?"

"A Bible!" the guard said.

"You got ary one?"

"Sure, got a fresh one. Hadn't hardly been used. Belonged to a nigger that raped a white woman down Memphis way. He couldn't read, but he wanted a Bible. Held it in his hand till they strapped him in the chair. That was two weeks ago."

"Could I have hit?"

"Sure, 'lessen you mind that it belonged to a nigger."

"I don't mind," Hope said.

"He said he was innocent. That's what they all say."

"I kind of believed this one," the other guard said.

"Hell, you're getting soft," the first guard said.

"Could you bring hit to me?" Hope said.

"Sure, anything you want."

That's how Hope got his Bible.

ARCENEAUX typed up the legal brief Hugh Bedford wrote for the judge who would hear a motion for the postponement of the execution of Hope Philip Kirby.

"Goddamn," Hugh said. "You type like a machine gun. Are you sure you weren't a clerk-typist?"

"No, I wasn't a clerk-typist," Arceneaux said.

"Well, you could have been."

"I could have been a sugar planter," Arceneaux said. "But I'm not."

When Hugh Bedford drove up to Knoxville three weeks after the verdict in Bourbonville, Larry Arceneaux went with him. Arceneaux drove, and

Hugh Bedford sat beside him in the Jaguar morosely sober. They had almost nothing to say to each other. Hugh Bedford had not had a drink since the night Arceneaux broke into his house. "I could have you arrested for breaking and entering and for assault and battery," Hugh said, considerably aggrieved.

"If you'd look in the mirror, you'd discover you're a better man. Do you want to arrest me for making you a better man?"

They went to the chambers of the appeals court judge who had agreed to hear Hugh's motion. Ken McNeil was already there, sitting in a plush chair. When Hugh and Arceneaux came in, McNeil stood up and showed his bland grin the way a musk ox will flap its ears in the courtship ritual. Then he saw Arceneaux, and he frowned.

"Why is this man here?" McNeil said, pointing to Arceneaux.

"I'm not a lawyer," Arceneaux explained to the judge, a tall, slender man with a pleasant face and craggy eyebrows that made him look vaguely like the late Kenesaw Mountain Landis except that Judge Rayburn Quarrels had the kind of honesty that the revolting old hypocrite Judge Landis had only pretended to possess. "I know some things about the case, and I've come along in a secretarial capacity to Mr. Bedford here."

"He typed up the brief," Hugh said. "He's a great typist."

"This man is a preacher," Kenneth McNeil said. "His name is Lawrence Arceneaux. He's at First Baptist in Bourbonville. But I don't know why a preacher should be at a legal proceeding." He offered the stern version of himself, but it was hard for him to be convincing in that mode.

It must be said that the hatred he had for Hugh Bedford was now much more intense and single-minded than the contempt that had, before the trial, been Ken McNeil's only important feeling whenever he had to face Hugh in a trial or whenever Hugh's name came up in conversation. He wanted to see justice done, and now justice seemed overwhelmingly on the side of putting Hugh Bedford's latest client in the electric chair to demonstrate the power of the law and the power of the law's servant in the Fourth Circuit Court, District Attorney Kenneth McNeil.

Judge Quarrels eyed McNeil with a mild smile. "I don't see anything that restricts a counselor from having any kind of secretarial help that he might choose, Mr. District Attorney." The judge looked more keenly at Larry Arceneaux. "I don't think you're about to preach to us poor sinners, are you, Mr. Arceneaux?"

Arceneaux grinned. "No sir, I am not." Something in Arceneaux's voice made the judge look more keenly at him.

"Mr. Arceneaux, I think I may know you. Were you in the war?"

"He was a clerk-typist," McNeil said.

"I didn't ask you, Mr. McNeil," the judge said sharply.

Arceneaux looked uncomfortable. "I was in Paris at the end of the war," he said quietly. "I interrogated French collaborators. And then, in 1946, I was at Nuremberg. I met you then."

"My God, of course. You took the depositions from Jodl."

"And Goering," Arceneaux said, not without a trace of pride.

Judge Quarrels shook his head. "You were a captain. OSS."

"Yes sir."

"You did that mission in France at the invasion of Toulon. Blew up that tunnel."

"Yes sir."

The judge looked across the table, idly rubbing his hands together. "I have always regretted that Goering's cyanide pill kept him from the gallows. Oh well, the man was so fat he might have broken the scaffold." Judge Quarrels turned to the others. "This man was in the OSS, behind the lines in France for over a year. He's one of the bravest people you'll ever meet."

"The OSS," McNeil said. "I thought you were a clerk-typist. It's what everybody says." He seemed considerably let down.

"You shouldn't go by what everybody says, Ken," Hugh Bedford said with a big smile. "You ought to hear what everybody says about you."

"The captain knows German and French better than I know English," Judge Quarrels said.

The judge reminisced for a little while, his chin resting in a hand, thinking out loud about crimes fading in memory. Almost as an afterthought he said to Hugh, "And you were at Anzio and later on at the Gothic Line."

"Yes sir," Hugh said.

"You don't have to call me sir now, Counselor," Judge Quarrels said affably. "The war's over. You know, my son Michael was killed on the Rapido. He was twenty years old."

"I heard it was as bad there as it was anywhere in the war," Hugh said quietly.

"That's his picture." The judge pointed to a bookshelf where a photograph of a young man in a private's uniform smiled nonchalantly into the large room. Nobody said anything for a little while. They looked at the photograph.

The judge asked Hugh about Anzio, and Hugh told him a few things. "You had a run-in with Colonel Winrod later on," the judge said.

"General Winrod now, Your Honor," Hugh said. "Yes, I had a run-in with him. I tried to kill him."

The judge laughed. "So I heard. So I heard. You were almost court-martialed." They sat in a long silence, the judge holding his hands in front of his chest, rubbing them together in a mood of reflection. "You know, Mr. Bedford," Judge Quarrels said finally, "if Jesus Christ were to walk in here and tell me that I could believe Sperling Winrod if the general told me that a mile had 5,280 feet in it, I'd say, 'Jesus, give me that in writing and get it notarized, and I'll believe it.' " The judge burst into laughter at his own joke, and Hugh Bedford laughed, too, a laugh of relief and spontaneous pleasure mingled in one.

"And where did you serve in the war?" the judge asked McNeil, turning on him a suddenly cold eye that knew the answer to his question before it was answered. McNeil fumbled, turned red under his talcum powder.

"I couldn't pass the physical," McNeil said. "I wanted to serve, but they wouldn't take me."

"What's wrong with you? Flat feet? You look fit enough," the judge said.

"I have a skin disease," McNeil said. "It's called psoriasis. And flat feet. I have flat feet, too."

"Psoriasis! What does that do to disqualify you from military service?"

"It makes me itch," McNeil said. "I have to have salves and ointments or else I'll scratch until the blood flows."

"Did you ever itch in the army, Mr. Bedford?" Judge Quarrels asked.

"I remember not having a bath for six weeks during one stretch," Hugh said. "I scratched until the blood flowed." Neither the judge nor Hugh smiled.

"Did the itch keep you from fighting, Captain Bedford?"

"No sir, it didn't," Hugh said.

"Captain Arceneaux," the judge said. "Did you ever itch during the war?"

"In France I scratched sometimes until the blood flowed," Arceneaux said. He did not smile.

"What's the longest you've ever gone without a bath, Mr. District Attorney?" the judge asked, giving Ken McNeil a look that would have frozen rain to a wall.

"I bathe every . . . Your Honor, I don't see what my baths have to do with this case," McNeil said, looking blandly petulant. His soft face reddened.

"Of course it has nothing whatsoever to do with this case, Mr. District Attorney," Judge Quarrels said. "I was just curious. Now, Mr. Bedford. What is your motion?"

Hugh Bedford cleared his throat. "Your Honor," he said, "I think you can see by the transcript that I've had sent to you that we have had an outrageous miscarriage of justice in Bourbonville, and you can see that we have every right to expect a new trial in a different venue and under a different judge. Judge Yancy has set an atrociously quick date for execution. We need to have that set aside so we can file a motion for a new trial."

The transcript was lying on the judge's otherwise clean desk. He picked it up and riffled the pages. "I have never seen such a charge to a jury," Judge Quarrels said slowly, studying the transcript as though it might be the most troubling and marvelous legal document he had ever seen.

"I believe," Hugh Bedford said quietly, "that Judge Yancy allowed his passions to overflow. I might point out, Your Honor, that he is a very old man."

"He's an old fool," Judge Quarrels said. "He was an old fool when he was a young man. Some fools are born old."

"Your Honor," McNeil said with a hurt expression, "you are speaking of a fellow judge in the legal system of our great state of Tennessee."

Judge Quarrels eyed McNeil without changing his expression. "I believe that is so," he said.

McNeil sat there in his talcum powder and his immaculate suit and his indignant expression, knowing that he was licked when he began. "Your Honor," he said, "it's clear that Judge Yancy exceeded his commission. I grant that. But it's also true that Hope Kirby murdered his wife and a man in cold blood when there is no proof whatsoever that that man—a leading citizen of Bourbonville, I might add—and the woman murdered with him were doing anything that was in the least adulterous or in violation of any law in the state of Tennessee. If two people can be murdered for sitting together in a car at night, what are we coming to? Do you want Tennessee to become like New York?"

"So your view is that those two just happened to be sitting there talking about the weather at one o'clock in the morning," the judge said with an ironical smile.

"I don't know what they were talking about, Your Honor," McNeil said heatedly. "But we have a First Amendment to the Constitution. They might have been talking about forming a Communist Party in Bourbonville, and it still wouldn't have been enough to let them be murdered in cold blood."

"I hear that the condemned man's father is a tough old bird," the judge said, still in that cool, musing way. "Aren't you afraid he'll come after you, Mr. McNeil? He might take a shot at you some night."

"Your Honor, I have prosecuted many murderers in capital crimes. My great concern is justice, not my own safety. If I were concerned for my safety, I would have left Bourbon County a long time ago." But McNeil's eyes fluttered a bit.

"Indeed, indeed," the judge said in an indefinably mocking tone. "You know, Mr. McNeil, the record shows that hardly anybody who commits a crime of passion like this will commit another one. Why do you want this man dead?"

"I might point out, Your Honor," McNeil said, beginning to fume now, "Mr. Kirby stands convicted of having committed two murders within the space of about three minutes. I suppose you can take a chance if you want and give him another hour of freedom to see how many murders he can commit in that time. Maybe if the Olympic Games have an event in murder in 1956, we could enter Mr. Kirby." He did not laugh. He knew his motion was lost.

The judge's smile vanished. "Touché," he said. He pondered the papers on his desk. "I still believe that this charge to the jury is an outrage to the semblance of justice."

McNeil began to protest, saying some things he had said before. Judge Quarrels waved him to silence and picked up the packet of transcript. Now he threw it on his desk so that the pages scattered across the polished wood. "Mr. District Attorney, I'm tired of this conversation. We can't send a man to his death when there's been as much doubt about this case as there is. I'm going to grant a stay of execution until June. I'm also going to recommend a new trial for the defendant. Let's see. This is November. The appeals court ought to consider a motion for a new trial in March. Good day, Mr. McNeil." The judge nodded curtly. McNeil, red-faced and angry, stood up. Arceneaux and Hugh Bedford remained seated, looking up at McNeil with indifference. He looked round the chamber. Everything was mahogany paneling, and a rich crimson thread ran up the edges of the blue velour curtains drawn back at the tall windows.

"I am going to tell the press that I opposed your motion," McNeil said.

"You do that, Mr. District Attorney. And don't let the door hit you on your way out."

The judge did not rise. Ken McNeil glared at the judge for a moment, glared at Hugh Bedford, grimaced at Larry Arceneaux. Then he flung himself out of the room, closing the door hard behind him.

"Thank you, Your Honor," Hugh Bedford said. He started to get up, and Arceneaux rose with him.

"Oh, stay awhile, gentlemen," Judge Quarrels said. He opened his desk drawer and pulled out a bottle of Scotch.

"Captain, I suppose you don't drink now."

"No, not anymore," Arceneaux said.

"I seem to remember you drinking at Nuremberg."

"I had to quit," Arceneaux said.

"What about you, Mr. Bedford?" the judge said, finding a couple of small glasses in his desk drawer where the whiskey had been.

"He doesn't drink either," Arceneaux said quickly. "Not until this case is over."

"Well, well," the judge said.

"Have one yourself," Hugh said nervously. He looked hungrily at the bottle. He didn't drink Scotch, but any port in a storm.

"I will," the judge said. He poured himself a little whiskey and lifted the glass to them both. They nodded. He drank and put the bottle back in the drawer. "Imagine a man staying out of the war because his skin itches!" He looked at the photograph of his boy. Nobody said anything for a while. "I heard Winrod double-crossed you."

"He got all my men killed," Hugh said bitterly.

"You have to get a lot of your men killed if you're going to be appointed superintendent at West Point," the judge said. "I heard you went after him with your bare hands."

"Yes," Hugh said, looking down into his lap.

"That was your mistake," the judge said. "You should have used a bayonet. Or a shotgun." Outside, the hum of Knoxville came in through the shut windows. Arceneaux thought downtown Knoxville was the ugliest city he'd ever seen in his life.

"This witness," the judge said. "This, let's see, this Charles Alexander. How firm is he?"

Hugh shrugged. "I thought he was wishy-washy. On the stand he seemed to be talking in his sleep."

"Any chance he'll change his testimony in a new trial?"

"I don't think so," Arceneaux said.

"Too bad. Too bad," the judge said. "But it might not work anyway. Still, the case is outrageous." He looked into his empty glass for a moment as if he expected to find some secret of the future manifesting itself in the bottom. "Let's hope for the best," he said. Then, after a thoughtful pause, he said, "You know, if I'd found my wife like that, disgracing me in public, screwing some draft dodger, I'd have done the same thing your client did. Excuse me. I mean the same thing your client is alleged to have done."

"So would I," Hugh said. "Except that I'm not married."

"You need to lose a little weight, Counselor. None of my business, you understand. But you can't kill Winrod by chewing him to death. You'll just kill yourself."

"Sir!" Hugh said as though responding to an officer who had called for him on parade. They both laughed.

"Winrod will get his someday," the judge said in a sedate confidence. "Listen, now. One thing more. Don't let anything happen to that boy, that Charles Alexander, before the new trial. I don't want any accidents, you understand? No shots from the dark. No car wrecks. Even if Alexander doesn't change his testimony, your client's likely to get off with manslaughter, maybe even involuntary manslaughter. He may not get more than a year and a day. I'd bet my last bottle of Scotch he won't get more than five years. With time off for good behavior he'll be out in three. He's got a lot of life left."

"Don't worry," Hugh said. "The Kirby family trusts me on this one. Nothing will happen to the boy."

"What do you think, Reverend?" The judge looked at Arceneaux.

"I don't think anything will happen to the boy if the verdict is reversed. But if Hope should go to the chair—" He let the sentence hang in the air.

"If Hope goes to the chair, the boy is dead," Hugh said with finality.

"He won't go to the chair," the judge said, shaking his head and frowning as though Hugh had spoken an absurdity. "Not a chance." He stood, and Hugh and Arceneaux stood, too. The judge looked Hugh up and down. "Now seriously, soldier, you need to lose some of that weight."

"Yes sir," Hugh said. He started to salute but did not.

"And you keep him sober," the judge said to Arceneaux.

"Yes sir," Arceneaux said.

"And Captain Bedford?" the judge said.

"Yes sir," Hugh said.

"Buy yourself a new suit. You look like a bum. The war's over. Whatever happened, forget it."

"Yes sir," Hugh said.

*I*N *1953*, it was called falling in love. It was not a "long-term relationship," and those who fell in love did not expect ever to part. Yes, some people got divorces, but divorce remained slightly scandalous. Marriage was supposed to be for keeps, and the passions of romantic love were supposed to settle down into a less passionate but deeper affection that with the years created grandparents worthy to be written up in the *Reader's Digest* series "The Most Unforgettable Character I've Met."

Illusion compounded by delusion? Oh yes. But sometimes it was real. And even when it was not real, and a marriage became a commonplace partnership subject to bickering over money and who should use the car, and arguing over trivial things, the couple locked up in it usually did not give up hope that something more might come of it if the two of them lived a little longer together and waited for some epiphany, scarcely definable, that would draw them back together in the love that had arced between them in the magic moments of their beginnings.

All that made life frightening to Charles Alexander, who knew that Tempe Barker was falling in love with him and feared that he might be falling in love with her. In fact he was almost sure he was falling in love with her, and he did not want to fall in love with anybody. The blackness of the summer and fall, and then the winter, settled down on him like a blanket of lead. Bob Saddler's suicide was as if someone had knocked away the last support that held up the sky. He resented Mr. Finewood for not preaching the funeral. But then he admired Mr. Finewood for standing by the Bible. If the Bible was the Word of God, you had to respect its injunctions. But was the Bible the Word of God? If you asked the citizens of Bourbonville that question in a mass meeting, the shout of affirmation would have come back like a wild cheer with a touch of anger to it, for anyone deserved anger who even raised the question. For now Charles put the question on a shelf in his mind.

He went about in a comatose state, speaking to people sometimes with an exaggerated friendliness as though he had to shout at them to wake himself up. He worked in silence at routine tasks at the newspaper, performing like a machine, but often in the middle of talking to someone about the trivial matters that he wrote up to go into print, he forgot the questions he had asked and the answers he had been given, and he asked the same questions over again, and impatient secretaries of clubs or officeholders in the courthouse said, "Charles, you just asked me that."

Tempe and McKinley took him away from the Proust class three mornings a week and forced him to sit with them in the Ellis and Ernest to drink coffee, but he had nothing to say, and nothing they said to him could draw more than a yes or a no or sometimes only a blank stare. He was glad when the term was over at the end of the first week in December; Tennessee had three terms called "quarters" in the academic year, and the Christmas break was almost a month long.

He dreamed of his mother. She stood by his bed in the night, dressed all in black, and saying nothing. Yet in her profound silence she gave off a grief and a disappointment in him that filled space with a thickness which made him feel he was smothering so that he awakened and sat up in bed, and even in the cool air of his room he was in a terrible sweat that soaked his sheets, which stank and had to be washed before he could sleep in them again.

Guy in his sweet-tempered way sometimes came clumsily behind him and stroked Charles as though he were a big cat. "What's the matter with Charlie Boy?" Guy said in his growl of a voice. Charles shook him off impatiently, and then he had something else to make him feel that he had done the wrong thing.

Charles was grateful to his father for playing at Bob Saddler's funeral, and Paul Alexander was concerned about his second son. "I think you ought to go on a trip," he said. "I will gladly pay for your ticket if you want to go to Washington or maybe to New Orleans on the train. It would do you good to get away."

"I have money," Charles said. And he did. He lived frugally. He was saving for seminary. He had over fifteen hundred dollars in the bank. Years later when he looked back on these days as the greatest horror of his life, he knew that he had been sicker in the mind than he ever was before or afterwards. Paul Alexander knew something was wrong, but could not reach his son. Charles did not think of himself as ill. He thought of life as no longer having any content, and he wanted to be left alone. He did not think that he could do anything to help himself, and he did not want to talk to anyone. He did not want Tempe to love him, and he did not want to love her, because he wanted something out of life that she could not give him and that she thought was worthless.

Yet he loved her talk, her laughter, her scorn of everything, her brightness. He was silently jealous when she mentioned that she had gone out with this or that boy to a movie or a concert. She did not go to fraternity parties. Why? Charles supposed she was afraid she might get pregnant again. But she was not the girl of his dreams—the girl who would kneel with him in the morning to pray for the day ahead and kneel with him in the evening to thank God for the day gone by. She was not the person who would be rapt in his preaching and grow with him into saintly old age where all the doubts of this time would have been dissolved in the experience of a life. And she was not the girl in the collective dreams of Bourbonville's young people and the young people in *The Saturday Evening Post* or *Collier's* or any of the other magazines that brought a sweet world of love and roses into every living room.

Instead Tempe talked about art and other topics Charles knew nothing about. She did not go to church. She had a mocking tone when she questioned him about his beliefs. "Charles, I just want to know. I'm not a believer in God, Jesus, whatever. Oh, I think there was a Jesus, but I don't think he was the son of God, and I'm not sure what a Jesus who lived all those years ago has to tell us in 1953. But I want to know what you believe."

It was embarrassing, because when Charles set out to tell what he believed, it all sounded weak and ramshackle. "So what will God do with all the Jews and the pagans and the people in India?" Tempe demanded.

"He has his own purposes for them," Charles said.

"And the Jews Hitler burned up in the crematoriums. What purpose did God have for them?" Tempe asked.

The thought was more disturbing to Charles than he could have admitted, and he had no answer. "Oh leave him alone, Tempe," McKinley said. "You get on my nerves."

It was one of Tempe's qualities that he did not like—this insistence that she was right and her unwillingness to let an argument rest. Charles wanted things that he knew sounded absurd when he uttered them among ordinary people. He wanted to believe that God loved him, that the universe was all alight with benediction, and that death was not dust and ashes and eternal oblivion. If he walked into any classroom at the university or for that matter any cafe or restaurant in Bourbonville and said these words, he would draw blank, embarrassed looks, and people would look away from him not knowing what to say. He recognized the contradiction. Maybe it was simply that he was so weary that the contradiction could not be buried within his heart anymore. He was so tired most of the time that there was room for nothing in his mind but the blackness. His insomnia came back, and he lay for hours on some nights eyes open against the dark, sounds drifting from afar, but sleep as distant as Tyre and Sidon.

He kept going to church, sitting with Guy in the pew, Rosy always on the other side of him like some guardian child, silent and wary. That is where Tempe found him. She walked into the church on the Sunday after the university quarter ended. The congregation was standing, singing the first hymn, a Christmas carol. The church was well filled, the approach of the holiday season arousing in people the desire to stretch out the magic of the birth of a babe to save the world. Tempe came down an aisle looking for him, and when she found him, she pushed in between him and Rosy, giving Rosy a smile and a little hug so that Rosy beamed up at her and shared the hymnal, and they sang together.

Charles looked around at her without a word. People looked at them, an adventure going on before the eyes of a congregation. A love affair, people thought. She smiled at Charles. He smiled back in a weak and stupid grin. Not as pretty as Marlene, people thought.

Mr. Finewood preached on God's grace. He was emotional. He said that to receive grace from God in Jesus, we had to be willing to extend grace to others because of Jesus, to forgive them for their sins against us, to carry no ill will in our hearts against those who transgressed against us. Perhaps because Tempe was there and had never heard it before, he told one of his favorite stories, the story of the wife who ran away to Chicago with another man, leaving her husband heartbroken with their only child, a dear little boy. He told how the husband moved heaven and earth to find his wife, and how at last he came on her sick and weak in a rooming house of ill repute in the big city and forgave her and brought her back and restored her to health and never reproached her and lived with her still in North Carolina where he had been pastor. He wept in the telling of the story, and although the congregation had now heard it five or six times, people in the audience wept, too. The familiarity of the story, like the strains of an old hymn, gave it a power to some, and Charles himself had never heard it without wondering whether he could ever be capable of such forgiveness. The man who forgave such a wife had to be a saint. He was a mirror of God. Why could Mr. Finewood not have forgiven Bob Saddler? Why could he not have said even a few words over Bob's grave? These questions turned in Charles like a slow drill in his bones, but he had no energy to seek answers for them.

At the end Rosy took charge of introducing Tempe to everyone, present-ing her like some empress of India and delighting that such a person hugged her and greeted people with an easy grace that queens possess. Stephen came down from the piano and introduced himself and accepted with a laugh Tempe's pleased announcement that she could spot him and Charles as brothers from a mile away. Guy put out his hand. "This is my brother, too," Charles said—the first thing he said to her after her arrival.

Tempe took it all in stride, looking at Guy with surprise but also with compassion and taking his hand gently. "I'm very glad to meet you," she said softly.

"Charlie Boy goes to school," Guy said.

"I go to school with him," Tempe said.

"Is that so?" Guy said. He held one of his yellow wood pencils, beating his knuckles with it.

"Is your father here?" Tempe asked, looking around.

"No," Charles said. "He doesn't come to church."

"I'd like to meet him," she said.

They made their way outside, and Mr. Finewood exuded over her. "We're so glad to have you," he said. "Are you a Baptist?"

"I'm a Presbyterian," Tempe said in a cool tone. She did not smile at him.

"The main thing is this: are you a born-again Christian?" Mr. Finewood persisted.

"I've been born just once, and that was enough," she said. She smiled and strode briskly on, giving Mr. Finewood no chance to pursue his way into the secret regions of her spiritual life. This was obviously a great disappointment to him, and he made a mental note to speak to Charles about it.

"Goodbye," Rosy said tentatively.

"Goodbye, Rosy," Tempe said and hugged Rosy again. Rosy went away slowly, looking back.

"You should come down to the house," Stephen said. "Father always cooks lunch for us on Sunday. There would be plenty. I hope you like red rice."

Tempe looked at Charles. Charles did not say anything. "No," she said. "I couldn't do that. I have to get to Memphis. I'll have to drive all day long."

"You should stay overnight somewhere," Charles said.

"No, I'll be fine. Walk with me to my car, Charles."

It was a signal that Stephen picked up, and he took Guy away. Tempe had parked at the edge of the unpaved parking lot, and she led Charles there, and for a moment they stood uncomfortably together while she unlocked the door.

"Charles," she said, looking up at him with sadness and reproach. "This is not a life for you."

"Didn't you like the service? I thought Mr. Finewood preached a very good sermon," Charles said.

"Then you're more lost than I dreamed you were," Tempe said tartly. "I didn't believe any of it."

"You mean you think Mr. Finewood's lying."

"Of course he's lying. That story he told, the woman running off to Chicago. It sounds like something he read in a book of sentimental lies, the kind that's sold in religious bookstores."

The darkness settled more thickly on him. He could not speak. He had no thoughts.

"I wish I could kiss you goodbye," she said.

"Not here," he murmured.

She got into the car reluctantly. "Goodbye then," she said. "I suppose I should say Merry Christmas."

"Merry Christmas to you," Charles said. "And your family."

"I won't see all my family," she said sadly. She shut the door and started the engine, and without looking at him again she drove away. He was left looking after her in a parking lot where engines were starting and other cars were driving away. He had walked up through the woods to church. Now he set off back again, crossing the graveyard, looking for a moment at his mother's grave with its carefully carved stone. He felt more lonely than he had ever felt in his life.

*E*VERY hour Hugh Bedford craved a drink. But he did not take a drink, and the hangovers stopped. He pondered the irony of being glad he didn't have a hangover while he still yearned for a drink. He started walking down to the square from his house. He did not walk for the exercise. He walked to take his mind off booze. The trip was only about five blocks, but the first time he walked, he arrived at his office nearly dead. His heart raced like a train roaring across a trestle bridge above a canyon.

Arceneaux told him to stop smoking. It was not an order like the command to stop drinking. Arceneaux said, "You're going to kill yourself with those coffin nails." Before the war Hugh did not smoke. He was the Spartan, living the pure life to be stronger than anybody else in Bourbonville. He started smoking when he was discharged from the army. Arceneaux said, "Sitting in the same room with you is like inhaling cigarette smoke through your skin. You stink."

Hugh thought he'd try not smoking so much to see if he could get his wind back. He cut back to one pack a day, carefully rationed out. One cigarette an hour. He began listening for the courthouse clock to strike, and he got so shaky as he waited that he couldn't think. He decided he would quit smoking for the duration. He threw his cigarettes away—all in one grand gesture that he willed to make good. Sometimes now he got the shakes longing for nicotine and booze at the same time.

Arceneaux came down to see him every day. Hugh sat in his office going over and over the transcript of the trial looking for every chink in the case. He could recognize Arceneaux's step rising vigorously on the stairway. Arceneaux came in without knocking, something that irritated Hugh Bedford, but then when Arceneaux saw that Hugh was sober, the minister grinned. Hugh Bedford inevitably looked at him with a scowl. "What the fuck do you want?" Hugh said—or something similar.

"Just checking. Just checking." Arceneaux said. Hugh was secretly pleased at Arceneaux's approval, although he would have slit his own throat rather than admit this pleasure. It took Arceneaux several days to realize that Hugh had stopped smoking. "You're not smoking," Arceneaux said when he did realize it.

"What the fuck business is it of yours?" Hugh said.

"None at all," Arceneaux said. They studied the transcript together. They made notes. They argued. They sometimes agreed. They drank gallons of coffee.

Some people in town shook hands with Hugh and patted him on the back. "We're pulling for you, Hugh. I've always said Judge Yancy was crazy." The jurors who had brought in the verdict were hangdog and ashamed. If they had been able to sleep on it, they would have brought in a verdict of not guilty. They were tired and scared, and they were afraid to go against Judge Yancy's wishes. So people said. They still whispered about Abby. Six years a married virgin. What did that mean? Hugh Bedford was campaigning against Kenneth McNeil. On balance the town had shifted its feelings powerfully against McNeil, and like two buckets hanging on a pulley in a well, as one bucket rose, the other fell, and McNeil's popularity ebbed. Even his fellow Civitans were cool to him, and a cool Civitan was as unnatural as a Christmas tree with all its lights turned off.

Hugh even remembered what Judge Quarrels had said about a new suit. On a Saturday morning in December he drove his beaten-up old Hudson to Knoxville and parked on Cumberland Avenue and went to Miller's Department Store on Gay Street. He entered the men's department up on the fifth floor almost as if he were walking into a whorehouse in a Puritan town. It was an unfamiliar place. He didn't quite know what to ask for. One of the reasons he went to Knoxville was that he didn't want to walk into a clothing store in Bourbonville and make a fool of himself. Besides, the best clothing store in Bourbonville was the one now run by Sophia Parmalee. He did not think Sophia would want to measure him for a suit. A coffin maybe, but not a suit.

At Miller's he was waited on by an affable clerk who looked much more distinguished than the average seller of men's suits. He was tall and slender and wore rimless glasses, and he had a natural wave in his graying hair. "And what can I do for you today?" the clerk said.

"You ought to be able to look at my clothes and tell me what you can do for me," Hugh growled.

The clerk did not falter. "I suppose you need an entire new outfit then," he said. "I don't sell shoes, though. You have to get them in the shoe department."

Hugh Bedford had not thought about his shoes.

The men's department had a galaxy of full-length mirrors. Some were affixed to square columns that held up the ceiling, and some were in alcoves in sets of three so men trying on clothes could look at themselves at several angles. He saw himself in every direction, and he looked like a vagabond in every mirror, sometimes the effect multiplying itself. The clerk was dapper, wearing a suit that fitted exactly. Hugh Bedford felt suddenly ashamed. It was a different kind of shame. He had not thought about varieties of shame, but there it was—a new sentiment of disgust with himself. Maybe this was the shame that came on people when they were sober. Whatever it was, it pushed him, and he blurted out, "All right. I want the most expensive suit you have."

The clerk lost his smile. He looked solemn, almost embarrassed, and he spoke in a low voice whose tone begged Hugh to reconsider. "Sir, our most expensive suit costs two hundred and fifty dollars." The words fell in the large space of the men's department like a summons to a funeral of a victim of a meteorite dropped from outer space. The clerk went smoothly on. "Now we have some very, very nice suits for a hundred dollars."

"I'll take two of the two-hundred-and-fifty-dollar numbers," Hugh said with a scowl. "Bring them out here. Can you get them ready for me by this afternoon?"

"Well, I don't know, sir, but I'll try."

"I have to have them by this afternoon. I'm going to church tomorrow."

"Oh yes. Yes, well, we can manage that. And what faith are you, sir?"

"I don't have any faith myself," Hugh said. "But I'm going to a Baptist church. I reckon the place will fall down."

"Oh, I'm sure it won't do that. I go to the Presbyterian church myself, but I always say it doesn't matter what church you go to just as long as you go somewhere."

"I reckon that's so. We're all going to die."

The clerk did not lose his sunny smile. He had his tape measure out, measuring Hugh. "I like to see a man decide to move up in the world," he said. He was a school principal by profession, he said. He worked in the men's department at Miller's on Saturdays and weekday afternoons to supplement his income. He had two sons, he said. He was very proud of them. They were both Eagle Scouts, and now they were in the university.

This is a good man, Hugh Bedford thought. He wondered why he had not known more good men in his life. Lieutenant Miller had been a good man. Hugh looked at the clerk, listened to his banter, listened to the man's pride, and he thought of a guy working all week long in a school, and instead of going home after the last bell releasing the little urchins to diabolical pursuits, he came over here and sold men's suits. Instead of working in his garden on Saturdays, he came over to Miller's and worked all day long on his feet, serving slobs like Hugh Bedford. This was what Hugh Bedford thought about himself.

He chose a fine navy-blue pinstripe and another that was all navy-blue. He chose some nice neckties. "I like palm trees myself," the clerk said, all friendliness and even exuberance. "I've been to Florida several times, and I really like it down there because of the palm trees. We sometimes can afford to drive down to Miami during the week between Christmas and the New Year. We saw the Orange Bowl in 1947. What a disappointment that was! I don't understand why Bob Neyland always wanted his teams to punt on third down. Well, he did all right that year. Nothing like this year's team. Very disappointing."

He rattled on and on, and Hugh enjoyed it, liked hearing him, thought of how uncomplicated a life it was when you thought about it. Family and children. No memories of leading men to disaster and discovering for all time that he, Hugh Bedford, was at heart a coward. And maybe a knave, too.

The suits were large because Hugh had a forty-six-inch waist, and when the clerk put the tape measure around him and announced, almost under his breath, the size, Hugh said, "I remember when I went into the army, I had a thirty-inch waist."

"Well, we all put on a little weight as we get older," the clerk said. "Our tailor is very good. This suit will look like it was made for you when he gets through with it."

"But I'll still look like—" He started to say "shit," but something in the clerk's pleasant face deterred him. *Good God, I'm watching my language,* he thought, feeling a disgust in himself. What was happening to him? He wanted to please Arceneaux. Now did he want to please a clerk in a department store? Well, it was only for the duration, he thought. He could do anything for the duration. It was like war. He also bought ten white shirts. He paid for everything in cash. The clerk did not even raise his eyebrows. He counted out the six one-hundred-dollar bills into the cash register, figured the sales tax, and gave Hugh his change, and told him to come back at four-thirty.

He went down to the shoe department and bought a new pair of shoes. The clerk down there was dour and almost silent. "You ought to buy some new socks, too," the clerk said. "Your feet are sticking out the ends of these."

"Why, I didn't even notice," Hugh said. "I think those are my feet." He spoke in mock amazement.

The clerk didn't even smile. Hugh bought twenty pairs of nylon/wool socks that came almost all the way up to his thighs. "You don't need garters with these," the shoe clerk said. "They stay up by themselves."

"I need to come to town more often," Hugh said. He paid twenty-five dollars for a pair of cordovans. They had a beautiful shine.

"I'd go get a shoeshine first thing," the shoe clerk said. "That's what you do with a pair of new shoes."

"I seem to remember that," Hugh said. "I did have a pair of new shoes once. I think it was in the army. The first thing we did before we landed at Anzio was to shine our combat boots."

The clerk did not laugh. Hugh walked over to the cobbler's shop at Miller's. It fronted on a little alley that ran between the main store and the annex. The place smelled of leather and oil and wax, a very pleasant smell.

"These are fine shoes," the Negro shoeshine man said.

"They ought to be. I paid twenty-five bucks for them."

"Who-eee," the shoeshine man said. Hugh gave him a dollar tip.

While he waited for the tailor to do magic with the suits, Hugh Bedford went to a movie. The Tennessee Theatre on Gay Street was one of those big Moorish palaces built during the 1930s to make people think movies were art and that the people who came to see them were worshipping exotic gods. Hugh used to like movies. He had got out of the habit. He went to this one because he couldn't think of any other way to spend his time in the after-noon, and he thought that if he walked around town, he'd get tired and go into Comer's pool hall and get himself a beer, and then it would all be over. He wouldn't be able to drive home after he'd drunk ten beers. Even if he wasn't drunk, he'd have to stop to pee every mile, and it was twenty-six miles from the Knoxville courthouse, the center of town, to the Bourbonville courthouse. So he went to a movie.

He drove back home that evening with the smell of his new clothes and his new shoes filling the car. He felt content. The next morning he showed up at First Baptist Church in one of his new suits and with a new shirt and a new necktie and, of course, in his new cordovan shoes. He thought people were almost afraid when they greeted him. It was like one of those movies when something completely strange happens, like Dracula changing himself into a bat, and everybody in the dark audience gasps. Arceneaux stared at him from the pulpit for a moment, then ignored him. It was all very satisfying.

*W*HEN Charles looked up on a wintry Saturday afternoon before Christmas and saw the man in clerical garb, he assumed that a new Catholic priest had come to Bourbonville.

Only four Catholic families lived in Bourbonville. Once every three weeks Father Patrick McNamara drove down from Knoxville and performed a mass in the Nichols School Auditorium, using a portable altar. Father McNamara was white-haired and old, red-eyed and ruddy-faced, and about him hung a faint aura of old whiskey. He spoke with a brogue that was pure Dublin. Often he joked about being a missionary to Tennessee, but in fact that is what he was. He came into the newspaper at intervals to place the small announcement that mass would be held on the following Sunday morning, and he chatted with Charles in disjointed sentences that seemed to be musings half to himself. He spoke of his seminary, Maynooth, the young class of priests, over five hundred of them, scattered to the ends of the earth, and as lost to him as if they had been vivid old dreams whose reality was now suspect. He seemed tired and abstracted much of the time as if he had wrestled all night with an angel too much for him.

"I'll be leaving you soon," Father McNamara said dolefully to Charles in November. "The bishop is looking for someone to replace me. I'm going back to Ireland, back to my family. Most of them are gone. I'm almost alone." He heaved a large sigh and looked off into space as though into a desert of regrets.

"Will you live with them, with relatives?" Charles said.

"Oh gracious no," Father McNamara said. "My relatives are all strangers now. I'll live in a home for old priests. We will drink too much, and we will die."

Charles could think of nothing to say. Father McNamara looked at him with a penetrating, red-eyed ferocity. "That trial. You did the right thing," he said.

"Do you think so?" Charles said. Mention of the trial was like speaking of death in a cancer ward. It carried darkness with it. Weight and darkness.

"Yes. Yes. You told the truth," Father McNamara said. "I hear what people say. Even a priest hears some faint wind blowing out of the tumult and the shouting of the world sometimes. People say you should have lied, told that prosecutor that you could not identify the man you saw commit murder. But let me tell you, my son, you can make lying sound very moral, noble, like an obligation from God. But, my boy, the truth is the only force that is finally good."

His words were like a flame that suddenly leaped up to intense brightness from a guttering candle burning down. For a moment his voice did not tremble, and the slightly alcoholic slur that cradled his usual thoughts was replaced by a steely hardness that made every syllable distinct. He looked at Charles with watery blue eyes rimmed with red and peering out under shaggy white brows, and there was a power in his gaze that both startled Charles and made him grateful.

"That's what I thought," Charles said in a quiet tone. It seemed like a good thing to say at the moment. He believed that he had told the truth on the stand because he knew that Kenneth McNeil would beat the truth out of him if he lied. He could imagine himself losing complete control of his body, beginning to weep as he had wept before the sheriff, perhaps vomiting, becoming something squalid and humiliated. He lied to Father McNamara because the priest seemed to demand the lie or demand the moral view of things that the lie implied. But Charles knew better; he always knew better.

"Good," the priest said. "Don't worry about it anymore." The flame sank again, and he went away.

When Missionary walked into the office, wearing a sunny grin above his coal-black clerical suit and showing no sign of alcoholism, a big man but not fat, Charles assumed that Father McNamara had retired or even died.

"Do I have the pleasure of speaking to Charles Curry Alexander?" Missionary said. The purring voice had an edge of contrived joviality to it, but preachers were like that.

Charles stood up. "Yes," he said. "I am Charles Alexander. What can I do for you?" He spoke in a weary and irritated voice. Outside the world was gray and cold. He was alone in the office. The fan of an electric heater hummed on the floor.

"Ah, an abrupt greeting, born perhaps of fatigue from having to identify yourself to so many strangers. I hope not to be a stranger long. I hope to persuade you that I am your friend." Missionary put his hand out across the counter, and Charles took it. It was an extraordinary hand, huge and as hard as thick leather. "I'm Father Robert Pearson Winthrop," he said smoothly with a mirthless grin and with an accent Charles recognized vaguely as Northern.

"I'm sorry," Charles said. "I didn't mean to be rude."

"Ah, I have put you on the defensive," the priest said. "I have implied that you have been impolite, and like a true Southern gentleman, you immediately retreat because you fear the accusation of rudeness more than you fear the onset of a bore. I feel that way myself. There are so many interesting people in the world. Why do we spend so much time with bores? I think you must have many interesting things to say."

"Has something happened to Father McNamara?" Charles asked coldly.

"Most people change the subject when they find themselves enmeshed in an uncomfortable conversation," the priest said cheerfully. "I am happy to oblige. Father McNamara? I don't believe I know the gentleman. A priest perhaps?"

"Yes, a Catholic priest. I thought—"

"I suppose you mean a *Roman* Catholic priest," Missionary said. He smiled again, without mirth. From the first moment Charles knew there was nothing funny about this man.

"He is a Catholic priest," Charles said.

"I, too, am a Catholic priest, but I am of the Anglican communion," Missionary said.

"Well, I don't know much about priests."

"You should learn. You see, my fine young friend, the Catholic Church was one great body of the faithful until it was sundered by the Reformation. It was all because of the pope. Henry the Eighth, *Fidei Defensor*, Defender of the Faith, withdrew the allegiance of the Anglican branch of the Catholic Church from the papacy in Rome. He was wise. Wise. The papacy with its present, ridiculous claims to infallibility and sovereignty over the church is an aberration of history. The sacraments, however, remain even with the aberration. The heart of the faith is not the pope but the Eucharist. All over the world the body of Christ is broken again by priests as it was on the cross. All over the world the blood of Christ is shed on the altar by priests who administer this holy rite. Those priests are ordained. Ordination is a sacrament. The ordination of Anglican priests goes back to the Roman Communion, and that in turn goes back to Christ. Hands were laid on heads in a grand succession across the centuries. Our orders are equal to theirs. We go back to the Christ who is the fulfillment of God's wrath."

"God's—" Charles stopped, looking puzzled.

"You are surprised to hear me say that Christ is the fulfillment of God's wrath," the priest said, looking unbearably smug.

"Well, yes."

"God finds ways of expressing wrath against His creation. One might say God made the earth and human beings so He could have some outlet for His wrath. Is that not true?"

"No," Charles said.

"But look at the record. God can do anything He wants. God created the world, then destroyed it by a flood. That's in the Bible. Only Noah and his little family survived."

"Yes, but the world sinned," Charles said. He found himself parroting the things he had heard all his life in church, the things he had read in the Bible. There always had to be a purpose. Religion was cause and effect. He thought of arguments. It did not work.

"The world sinned." The priest threw out his hands in a gesture of impatience. "But who made the world? My dear boy, suppose you buy a car and drive it for two weeks, and the engine falls out on the highway. Would you blame the car or the manufacturer in Detroit?"

"It's not the same," Charles said.

"Oh no. One expects higher standards from Almighty God than one expects from a sleazy manufacturer in Detroit whose one aim in life is to make profits by selling the most cheaply made car he can produce for the highest price the stupid American buyer will accept."

"I don't think—" Charles could not complete the sentence.

"No, you do not think much. I can tell that. I am here to make you think. That is my calling, you see. To make people think. To make people understand."

"Look—" Charles began, but he had no chance.

"Here is my point," Missionary said. "Either we must assume that God bungled His creation and allowed it to slip out of His control. Or we must assume that God planned all along to let creation fall and punish it because it fulfilled His will. His will was to punish, to pour out wrath."

"I don't see that at all," Charles said.

"Do you believe the Bible?"

"Yes," Charles said.

"Every word?"

"Yes," Charles said. He knew he was lying.

"Ah me! I have more work to do than I imagined," the priest said. "I see the Bible as a collection of mirrors, hundreds of mirrors, perhaps thousands of them, all placed at angles between ourselves and God so that we see vague shapes seeming to contend with each other in an almost infinite regression. Am I making sense?"

"No," Charles said, but he was not sure.

"Well, let me say that in the various parts of the Bible we see dim and incomplete shapes moving, and we know that beyond those shapes is a reality, something that creates the reflections we see in such confusion. I think that reality is God. Don't you agree?"

"I—"

"Well, if you don't agree, let me continue for the sake of argument. You will surely agree that in the Bible God seems to take pleasure in destruction. Take the story of the Flood, for example. Now there is a mirror. I can scarcely stop thinking about Noah, that grandly comprehensive gentleman of an antique culture. All living things were destroyed except those that Noah and his family took onto the ark according to the command of God. There is the problem of the fish, but no matter. We will let the fish go."

"The fish?"

"Yes, the fish. Doesn't it seem unfair to you that the lions, the tigers, the poor sheep and the cattle, even the birds were all destroyed in the Flood—not to mention all the human beings—but it didn't make any difference to the fish? I would assume that some of them felt blessed by God once the floods had covered the land. They were able to feast on the corpses of men and beasts. How was it that the fish could be treated to a banquet while God was destroying all other life? But we will let the fish go. Let them swim away safely gorged on the corpses they devoured. That is not the point."

"What is the point?" Charles said.

"The point is that this story is a mirror held up to the way God works in the world, and we know that God can work in the world any way He wants. He is always busy. He can't stop moving. He can create it. He can destroy it. Right or wrong?"

"I suppose so."

"God calls people to Him; they come and fall away; He strikes them with His wrath. It is sport for Him, you see. That is why he sent Christ into the world, isn't it? To show them His wrath!"

"Christ came to show us God's love." Charles felt his voice squeak.

"We know that Christ came into the world to save sinners. But only if they believe. Is that not true?"

"Yes."

"Think how hard He made it for them to believe! Oh, I'm sure that you have never doubted, but others have, Charles. Many others have. Now, just imagine if we were required to believe that some felon electrocuted in that grim chair in Nashville, Tennessee, were the Son of God, and we had to believe in him or else be eternally damned? Don't you think God made it deliberately hard for His creation by making salvation depend on such an implausible story?"

"But Jesus rose from the dead," Charles said, feeling a little giddy now. He was locked in a battle that he did not fully understand and that he knew he was losing.

"How did that story come to us? No one of the four Gospels agrees with the other three. Read them for yourself. This woman or those women come to the tomb and find it empty and rush out and tell some men, and various apparitions of Jesus occur in improbable ways, and then He vanishes to men and women alike. The Book of Acts tells us that He ascended into heaven, but if you take a look at the Greek New Testament—by the way, do you know Greek?"

"No," Charles said.

"Ah, well, you should learn to read Greek, and you should read the Greek New Testament. In the oldest manuscripts of the Gospels, not a single one tells us that Jesus ascended into heaven. What do you think of that?"

"I don't know," Charles said.

"You don't know. Well, an honest answer. But let us take another angle on the problem, look into the mirror in another way. You do agree that if, oh, say Hope Philip Kirby were to be put to death in the electric chair and then were to rise again from the dead and to appear to a few women in Nashville, it would be very hard to imagine any large number of people who would believe such a preposterous story."

"It's not the same," Charles said.

The priest made a wry face. "You do see my point. God seems to delight in making life very difficult for human beings so that He can take pleasure in destroying them. Those who do not believe in Christ will burn in hell for eternity. Is that not what you believe?"

"It's what the Bible teaches," Charles said in a low voice.

"Exactly. Exactly. God seems to enjoy the prospect, doesn't He? And what about the Chinese?"

"The Chinese?"

"Yes, my dear boy, the Chinese. Millions and millions of Chinese are going to arrive before the great white throne of God and be told that they must be cast down to eternal hell because they do not believe in a Christ of whom they have never heard."

"They have missionaries," Charles said.

"I used to think that myself," the priest said. "Believe it or not, young man, I was once a missionary."

"So you gave people a chance to hear the Gospel," Charles said.

"Tut tut," the priest said. "You don't know what it's like to be a missionary. But we will let that pass. Take it as solemn truth, Charles. Millions of Chinese have never heard of Christ, not even from a missionary. But they will be condemned to hell forever and ever. Another mirror, you see. How God deals with the world."

Charles looked at him. The priest leaned slightly across the counter, taller than Charles, and Charles was six feet in his sock feet. The priest dropped his voice. "I am saying something very important, Charles. Very serious and very important. Do you know why I think God created the world?"

"No," Charles said.

"Boredom."

"Boredom?"

"Yes, boredom. Now I maintain that even God cannot evade Immanuel Kant. All things require time and space. Well, suppose that God is space. He must still live in time. Billions of years of time. Have you ever considered how long eternity is? What does God do with Himself? He can create angels, and He can provoke war in heaven and fling rebel angels down into a hell especially created for them. They are all His creatures. They do what He forces them to do, more obediently than a dog that we might train to sit or roll over on its back or fetch or do any of the other ridiculous things people command dogs to do."

"I—" Charles had no idea what to say. He knew only that he had to stop the rush of this man's words. The priest was not to be stopped.

"You see, God is in the mind of all His creatures, telling them exactly what they must do, even when they think they are acting on their own. He must have had a grand time manipulating some angels so that they believed they had the ability to overthrow their Creator. What would they have done with Him? They should have known there was nothing they could do with Him. Still, they revolted because that was God's way of amusing Himself in the loneliness of infinite space."

"Stop!" Charles cried. "Just stop."

"You want me to stop because you see how plausible it all is, don't you, Charles Curry Alexander! But you listen to me. God flung all the fallen angels into hell, and heaven had a great celebration, and God created more angels and beasts and heaven only knows what, and He enjoyed the praise of these creatures for several million years, perhaps several billion years, and

He was bored again. So He created earth, this planet, this place where we stand, transfixed by gravity. Oh, He didn't create it in the crudely mythological way that the Book of Genesis has it. The Book of Genesis is a mirror. We see God at work—creating human beings so they can imagine joy and life everlasting but then giving them sorrow and suffering and death instead. Now He has created millions, billions of human beings, and He gives them the world as a stage, and He watches, and He works His will to destroy them because He is a God of wrath."

"You are crazy. You are completely crazy, and I will not listen to this."

Suddenly the priest laughed. "I meant no offense," he said glibly. "I am trying to see what kind of young man you are."

"Well, I'm not crazy," Charles cried.

The priest shook his head dolefully. "Not crazy. Do you realize that being crazy is only a judgment of other human beings? Do you think the crazy man ever imagines that he is crazy? No, he imagines that all the others are crazy. And Charles—he may be right. The crazy man may be right."

"I have work to do," Charles said.

"Of course you do. Just as you had work to do on the night Hope Kirby killed those two adulterous people before your very eyes. Yes, work should lead to a better result. The world seems perverse, doesn't it, Charles? But it is the kind of world God wants. Believe me, Charles, there are only two kinds of people in this world—the kind God makes His instruments, and the kind He makes His objects of wrath, His victims."

"And you are God's instrument?"

"Yes. An instrument of His wrath. I tell the truth as it has been revealed to me. I see it like this. God has made a series of worlds, one after another, millions of them, and to each world He has given a different kind of suffering, a different kind of wrath." He lowered his voice. "I tell you what I think, Charles. I think that when God exhausts all His possibilities, He will die. He is the living God, you see, and to be a living God is to be in ceaseless activity, and now throughout the universe God is engaged in activity to make His creation suffer torments. When He runs out of torments, He will die. It's as simple as that."

Charles stared at him aghast. The man was clearly mad and perhaps dangerous. But he was something else, too. Something more terrible than Charles had ever imagined.

The priest looked up at the clock. "Oh dear," he said, looking hard then at his wristwatch, "I must really be going. I did not mean to stay so long."

Outside a cold December sun lay weak and fading in the streets, and traffic swished and hummed by the square in a desultory way. It was a slow Saturday afternoon, the light dying. People bundled up against the cold hurried by the plate-glass window of the newspaper office. They blew frosty breath in the icy air. Red and Myrtle were both out, Myrtle sick with the flu. Red was walking up and down the streets, trying to sell ads in the stores along Broadway and around the square, and trying to collect for ads he had already sold. Jane Whitaker demanded that all his arrears to the bank be paid by the first of the year. Red had dark bags under his eyes these days.

Missionary stood straight and tall, and his cornflower-blue eyes impaled Charles with a pitiless satisfaction. "I have much to do. But I will come back. I want to talk with you some more."

Charles could think of nothing to say. The priest smiled at him and put out a hand, and Charles took it awkwardly across the high counter. "Goodbye, Charles. You will find that I shall be one of the most influential people in your life, one of the most important people you will ever know. Who brought you into the world?"

"Brought me—"

"Who was the doctor who gave you birth?"

"Dr. Youngblood. He's dead."

"Dr. Youngblood. What a nice name. I'm sorry I did not know him. Well, Charles. You owe much to Dr. Youngblood. You will discover that you owe much to me, too. Goodbye, my boy. Goodbye until we meet again."

The priest smiled and went out the door and shut it gently. Behind him a cold breath of the December day rushed in and lingered when the door had been closed and the priest had gone away.

In a minute Red came in.

"What's wrong with you?" Red said. "You look pale. God, you look awful!"

"I've just had an unpleasant conversation."

"Who was it?"

"A priest, all in black. Didn't you see him?"

"I didn't see anybody," Red said.

The darkness around Charles grew thicker. He was left humiliated and vaguely afraid.

O_N THE Sunday morning before Christmas the following Friday, Mr. Finewood preached his Christmas sermon. Midway Baptist was crowded. In the evening there would be a Christmas pageant, as though, in repetition of these miraculous events, everything from that distant and exotic past would become part of the lives of the people who came to Midway Baptist Church and sought the unseen world and went regularly back into their own worlds believing they had seen it.

The Sunday-morning sermon was Mr. Finewood's chance to shine, and he did. Stephen sat up on the piano bench looking over the piano at the minister, and Stephen's face was completely calm, at peace with himself. Charles wished that he could be like Stephen in his beautiful simplicity. His brother had a cheerful openness about him that everybody liked. He spoke little, lived for his music, never showed a temper, and seemed to fight no battles with life. Charles felt himself full of lies and deceits, evasions, hypocrisy. He told the truth about Hope Kirby. He wished he had been able to lie. Lying was what he did best. Only he could not lie about Hope Kirby.

Holidays brought him—would always bring him—the recollection of other rooms and other voices that rose up in phalanx to confront him when he pondered the ceaseless movement of the days and the clicking of annual celebrations on the wheel of time.

He sat next to Guy, listening to Mr. Finewood, and he reflected that a year ago his mother was still alive, and Mr. Finewood was still coming to the hospital every day to pray for her to be cured. Later when she was moved home because she said she wanted to die in sight of her birdbath and her woods, Mr. Finewood came on his daily errand, and he prayed. But she had died anyway.

Mr. Finewood said he often thought Christ would return to earth on Christmas Day. "Nobody would be expecting him then. How could Christ ruin our holiday, keep us from opening our presents, make Santa Claus seem insignificant, by coming again and summoning us all to judgment? I can imagine millions of people at home opening presents, and all at once hearing, very softly at first, a sound they don't recognize because they have never heard it before, because it has not sounded since the beginning of the world.

"And then we will hear singing. Suddenly all around us will be the most beautiful choir we have ever heard. Oh yes, the damned souls will be plunged into hell all at once. They will leave us with a roar of pain, and if we could hear it, we should remember its agony and its heartbreak for all eternity. But my friends, I do not believe we will see them vanish from us. We all have people we love who will be damned, and I think that God will do for our souls what doctors do when they operate on the human body. I think the memory of the damned will be taken away from us. How could we be happy in heaven if a beloved wife or husband, a beloved son or daughter, a beloved father or mother is not with us? No, my friends, I think our minds will be filled with the sweetness of forgetfulness. I remember my own dear wife, when she lay dying, barely able to speak, she said, 'Clifford, I see my mother, but I don't see my father. I don't know where he is. But it doesn't matter. Everything is so sweet, and Mother is holding her arms out to me.' She said those words, holding my hand, and she drifted away into sleep, but she still gripped my hand until suddenly her fingers loosened, and I knew she was in heaven."

Mr. Finewood stopped and took a handkerchief from his pocket and wiped his eyes, and for a moment he could not continue. In the audience some people wept quietly. Not a soul spoke.

"At the last Christmas, when Jesus comes back to this earth and takes us to Himself, we will meet one another in the perfection of human being that God intended for Adam and Eve. Nothing in this sinful world will be present in heaven, my friends. The beloved mother we saw pale and thin and gasping in agony on her deathbed will be radiant with health with the bloom of youth eternally flowering on her cheeks. The retarded child will appear to us in heaven in all the manly strength of the youth he would have been had sin not come into the world. The prostitute who has been abused by men and who is diseased and hopeless and scorned except that God loves her, forgives her, and promises her eternal life in exchange for her faith, that prostitute will be a pure virgin in heaven, and she will be surrounded by choirs singing praises to the Almighty that will give her peace everlasting. The person who could never carry a tune in this life will sing in heaven in the soaring beauty of a magical voice. The blind will see; the deaf will hear; the lame will walk. We shall all mount up on eagles' wings. We shall walk and not be weary, we shall run and not be faint, and God will take us unto his blessed Self."

Mr. Finewood's voice rushed on in a mesmerizing flood, and as he listened, Charles felt something that was like a miracle. All the weights that had pressed on him seemed to dissolve. He felt light-headed, and his heart felt light, too, a lightness in all that he was that made him suddenly wonder if his body might be giving him a presentiment of the return of Christ when all bodies would lose the weight that tugged them down to gravity's pull towards the center of the earth. He would not have been terribly astonished had he begun to rise then, looking around to see the whole congregation transformed, a miracle happening to all of them and yet a miracle that caused no exclamations of joy and wonder because in the consciousness of everyone it seemed exactly right, completely fitting, something inevitable as dawn and so transforming that it was no more surprising than to waken from a deep and peaceful sleep and to see the eastern sun throwing its quiet light across meadows infinitely green and so wide that there was no place anywhere for the slightest doubts to hide.

That night after the Christmas pageant when Mr. Finewood had embraced him at the door, Charles walked back home by crossing the cemetery and by walking down through what his father proudly called the upper field. The field was planted in winter wheat, and even in December the tender shoots made the field pale green in the day. On this evening the moon was full, and the planet Jupiter stood close to it, and Orion marched high in the sky followed by the dogs, and Charles felt at complete peace with the world. He thought of what a good man Mr. Finewood was, how loyal he had been, and how in his simple but immaculate life he seemed to live exactly the kind of life that Jesus wanted his disciples to live. When Mr. Finewood's voice broke at the mention of his wife in the morning, the entire congregation was caught up suddenly and unexpectedly in a good man's grief and in his manliness at bearing it. Charles felt a warmth for him that was profound and comforting.

He looked up at the sky and recovered something of his childhood faith that had made the earth glow with the glory of God. There might be nothing out there, nothing but death and endless time. But then again Mr. Finewood spoke like a man who had seen over into another world and seen the glory. Charles could believe that because a man like him spoke so warmly and so eloquently, there must be something to his words. He was caught in a mysterious paradox that he recognized even as he walked and saw the shadow the full moon cast in the wheat. There might be nothing; but then there might be something; and whatever it was, he would be all right.

Y_{EARS} later he did not remember much about the week afterwards. The paper put out its Christmas edition on Wednesday. Red said they would not publish on Thursday since it was Christmas Eve, but he reminded everybody that they had to have something for the Monday after Christmas. They would also not publish on New Year's Eve. Monday's would be a thin paper.

When Wednesday's paper was on the streets, Charles drove home through the wintry dusk possessed with an idea. His father had decorated the house in his usual extravagant way. Guy believed fervently in Santa Claus. Paul Alexander made Christmas around the adventure of proving to Guy once again that Santa came through the night and descended through the chimney and left toys all over the living room before the fireplace. His father, afraid of heights, decorated a pine tree in the front yard by climbing up into it to string the lights.

"I'm going to take your advice," Charles said to his father. "I'm going to take a trip. Tomorrow. I want to leave tomorrow morning."

His father looked at him, startled. "But where are you going?"

"I don't know," Charles said. "Maybe towards the south. Maybe Florida. I'd like to see some warm weather." He looked desperately at his father's face. "I feel so sad," he said.

"It is our first Christmas without her," Paul Alexander murmured.

"Yes," Charles said.

"I understand. I think you should get away. Do you have enough money?"

"Oh yes. Yes, I have plenty of money. I don't spend much on anything."

"Yes, you are very frugal," Paul Alexander said. "Will you go in your car? You may take my car if you want. I can drive yours while you are gone."

"No, I want to take the Ford. I have a case of oil in the back. It ought to get me down there."

"You should buy yourself another car," Paul Alexander said quietly.

"I like this one," Charles said. Charles thought that to give it up would mean that Lloyd was finally dead.

They sat for a few moments in melancholy silence. Everything in Charles's mind felt sluggish. Thoughts came up like black bubbles in tar baking in the sun on a summer day. But they also came with an irresistible freedom, the restraints between father and second son broken away by the overpowering rush of events. "Tell me something," Charles said. "Why do you never go to church?"

They were sitting at the kitchen table, and outside the cold night air of December pressed against the house so that a ghost of itself seemed to penetrate the windows and hang in the room with them. Paul Alexander raised his eyes to look at his son.

"I do not believe there is a God," he said. He looked out, musing across the earth. "And if there is a God, I am angry with Him."

"Because of Mama?"

"My anger began a long time before Eugenia died," he said softly.

"But you play hymns with Jim Ed. I wanted to say—I—we all appreciated your playing at Bob's funeral."

"My uncle Stephanos killed himself. It was one of the most terrible things in my life."

"I didn't know," Charles said.

Paul Alexander shrugged slightly. "There is much you do not know. I should write it down."

"Yes," Charles said softly. "You should. So . . . it was your uncle's death."

"And the war. You cannot believe in God if you went through the war. Good people. Bad people. They all died in the same horrible ways. I was spared. I often wished I could have died with my friends." Abruptly and unexpectedly Paul Alexander choked up, and Charles thought he might cry. It was almost frightening to see the tears come to the eyes of this strangely reticent man, and Charles was embarrassed.

Paul Alexander quickly recovered himself. "I can't believe any of it," he said in a low voice. "The hymns? They come—the ones I like, at least—from the longings of people for good, for hope. They are the clamor of souls hoping for benevolence in the universe. It is the longing that I play for, not the God that the hymns address."

Years afterwards Charles looked back on that conversation, one of the few in his life he had with his father when all barriers between them seemed to be down. But now he was just very tired.

So he made his trip—not at first to Florida, but he did go there. Only later did he understand that his whimsical decision to take an unexpected trip had saved his life. Maybe it was the '37 Ford, he thought. Maybe Lloyd's spirit hung over the Ford, saving his life when Charles was in danger.

THE SHERIFF took the call Sunday morning, two days after Christmas. He was sitting in the jailhouse by himself, the cells all empty, his sock feet propped on the desk, reading the Sunday paper, drinking coffee, listening to music on the radio, happy not to be in church, when the telephone rang. He sheriff picked it up without taking his feet off the desk, and a strange exuberant voice said, "Hello there, Coondog. How are you this fine Sunday morning?"

The sheriff was taken aback, supposing it was some jolly soul who knew him, some old army buddy, voice grown unfamiliar by time, maybe an old comrade passing through town on his way to Florida who remembered, "Bourbonville! That's the place Sergeant Myers called home," and the sheriff said with an expectant laugh, "Yeah? Who is this?" He was ready to hear a name he knew, a whoop of laughter, and a question, "And how are you, you dirty-butt old son of a bitch?" and the sheriff was ready to laugh, too.

The voice did laugh, but in a silky and unpleasant trickle of sound. "Coondog, I regret that you and I don't know each other. We're going to get better acquainted. Believe me, we will. I'm sure we'll meet someday soon. I believe you will understand why I find it inopportune for us to meet this morning."

The sheriff was annoyed then. He felt himself mocked, and he knew that he didn't know anybody who talked like this. But then in his business lots of cranks called up and said annoying things, and he took another sip of his coffee before he answered again, letting the voice on the other side wait. "So what's your game, mister?" he said at last. "I ain't got all day to jaw with a horse's ass. I got coffee to drink."

The voice laughed. Genuine mirth this time. "Very good, Sheriff! Very good. You are uncommonly bright. It is a game. Yes, that's exactly what it is. A game, and I'm one of the best players around. You'll see. You're a player, too, now. You and I, and the Player upstairs. We two against you, Sheriff, and we will win the game. But I can tell that you will be a worthy opponent. Yes indeed."

"Look, asshole," the sheriff said. "You can go play with yourself for all I care. You can go fuck yourself on a doorknob."

The sheriff hung up. In an instant the telephone rang again. The sheriff didn't want to answer it, but you never could tell. Somebody might be drunk and pissing in front of a church, and the sheriff couldn't take a chance. He picked the telephone up and growled into it, "Hello."

"Sheriff," the voice said in an unctuous tone. "Forgive me for my levity. In fact I'm calling on a very serious matter. It's related to your dear friend and mine, Hope Philip Kirby. I'm calling to inquire if you have solved the mystery of the missing judge."

"Ain't no judge missing far as I know," the sheriff said. "Which judge you got in mind?"

The voice seemed to get upset, but the sheriff could tell the dismay was contrived. "Upon my soul, Sheriff, I gather you don't know that Judge Shirley Yancy has been missing since he was abducted from his home in Madisonville on Christmas night? I felt *sure* somebody would have told you before now. My, my. This is serious indeed. He may be dead by now."

The sheriff laughed. "Judge Yancy abducted! I ain't heard nothing about that. That's the first thing I got to say to you. The second thing is that if the old varmint is missing, it ain't none of my business, because he lives down in Madisonville, and if he's missing, it's up to Sheriff Carter of Monroe County to find him. The third thing is that I'm damned if I can think of anybody on earth who'd miss him if he was to get eat by a bear in the Tellico Woods."

The sheriff almost hung up again, but something about the disembodied voice got to him. The mention of Hope Kirby. What did that mean? It was like a snake sticking its head through a crack in the wall over your head in the night, and you looked up and saw a line of familiar and horrid black in an unfamiliar place against the darkness of the ceiling, and you might have ignored it, but it darted its head away, and you paid attention because you understood with abrupt discomfort that it was a viper. "Well, Coondog, I'm afraid I've ruined your Sabbath," the voice said, making a saccharine effort to sound mournful. "You see, Judge Yancy is in your territory now. I've buried him alive up in the back of the graveyard of the Martel Methodist Church."

The sheriff put his feet off the desk then. "You WHAT?" he shouted.

"I thought someone would have told you by now. I put an air pipe down in the box so he could breathe. I told him to keep calm and breathe deeply, and he'd be just fine. But the box where I put him is very small, and if he panicked, he may be dead. Heart, you know. You better go see. It isn't my responsibility anymore. It's yours. I hope you will spread the word that this is not the last that people will hear of the Hope Kirby case. Very badly done, Sheriff. Very badly done. Goodbye, Coondog. And Happy New Year." The telephone clicked.

The sheriff stood there for a minute. It sounded like the Yellow Dog Tavern call back in the summer. A trick of some sort. But why would anybody want to get him out of Bourbonville on a Sunday morning two days after Christmas? Besides, there was something about that voice, something . . . Afterward the sheriff said, "It was *evil*. That's what it was. *Evil*." He put on his hat and loaded his dogs in the car and drove out the old pike toward the Martel Church. He drove like a bat out of hell. The blacktop had deteriorated, and the car bounced along, throwing gravel up behind in a storm.

The meeting had started when the sheriff pulled up in front of the church, and he could hear the piano beating and the sprightly roar of the congregation singing something fast, the music coming through the shut windows of the little white churchhouse. The day was clear and chilly. Typical late December in Bourbon County. The grass in the graveyard was dead, and the gloomy red cedars threw fat shadows over the white markers. Martel had one of the oldest graveyards in the county. A few cars and some pickups were parked in the little gravel driveway that made a semicircle in front of the church on the side of the low hill where the church and its cemetery stood. He didn't try to find a parking place. He pulled up in the road and cut the engine and jumped out of the car and ran up into the graveyard with his dogs following him and starting to bay since they assumed he was on the hunt for something they could not yet smell. Up against the scraggly fence at the back of the graveyard he found a fresh grave, red earth heaped up, and sure enough a drainpipe stuck up out of the heap of dirt. The sheriff looked down into it and hollered, but he couldn't see anything, and he heard no sound. He had a flashlight in the car, but he did not go back for it. Instead he ran for the church and burst through the doors shouting, "Help, folks! I need your help right now." The dogs were howling and barking and jumping around behind him in the aisle of the church, and people leapt up and looked startled and angry. The preacher began yelling at the sheriff, and some of the men came out in the aisle looking ready to throw the sheriff out the door, and the women looked aghast, and some of the little kids started to cry. The sheriff shouted louder than anybody. "Men! I need your help. There's a man up there in your graveyard, and he's been buried alive. I think it's Judge Yancy. We got to get him out. Help me, please. Help me. Please God, help me."

It sank in. The sheriff yelled, waving with his hat. "Come on! Come on! Help me! Help me!"

They came pouring out, all of them in their Sunday best, old men and young men, fat men and thin men, and they raced up through the dead grass and the monument stones, the women and children following them, and they fell to digging at that cold, fresh dirt with their hands, getting in the way of each other, getting wet and filthy from the damp, clayey earth, and somebody came up with a couple of shovels they'd found in the church basement, and they took turns, and in pretty good time they hit the box and started scraping the dirt off the top of it. It was not a coffin. It was a new plywood freight box, long enough for a man, with a hole cut in the top of it for the drainpipe, and when they pulled the drainpipe out, they could see a face below it, eyes wide open, and the sheriff knew as soon as he looked that the man who owned the face was dead. They wrestled the lid off with the shovels.

Judge Yancy lay there with his clothes torn, the buttons of his shirt ripped out, eyes staring skyward. It was one of the worst sights the sheriff had ever seen, worse in its way than boys shot down in the snow at Malmédy in the Bulge, worse than Abby and Kelly. The judge's mouth gaped open. His false teeth had fallen out and lay on his neck, and in his frenzy he had scraped the teeth over his neck so that it seemed that he had bitten himself, and little streams of dried blood stained the skin under the self-inflicted wounds.

"He's alive! He's alive!" somebody hollered.

"No, he ain't," the sheriff said. They lifted him out. The rigor mortis had set in. He had died down there, died in that closed, cramped space. It was about the worst death the sheriff could imagine.

Blackie Ledbetter was not yet the county coroner. He would take the job in a year or two. The sheriff called him anyway. The sheriff didn't think it was a sight old Doc Bulkely could stomach. The telephone rang when Blackie was about to sit down to have Sunday dinner with his father and mother and his brother, Paul, and Paul's wife, Jenny, at the homeplace. Jim Ed rolled his eyes and went into the hallway to answer the telephone. He heard the aroused voice of the sheriff, got the story, and when he came back all the light had gone out of his face.

"It's for you," he told Blackie. "The sheriff. Something awful has happened."

The sheriff talked fast. Blackie had trouble understanding. He kept saying, "Slow down, Sheriff . . . What? . . . What?" Then he understood, and he excused himself from his mother's ceaselessly anguished and perplexed face and went out into the chilly December air and drove down to the clinic he shared with his brother, Paul, and waited for the sheriff to come in with the body.

A few minutes later Mr. Robinette, looking stuffy and professional, came in with his men bearing the body wrapped in a black rubber sheet. It was Judge Yancy. No mistaking the man. Blackie looked down at the frozen expression and felt the horror of it and thought with medical objectivity that death could surprise in infinite ways. The judge's eyes were shut. "I had to shut them," the sheriff said. "I couldn't stand that damned thing looking at me."

Blackie did not reproach him. "I need a real autopsy on this one, Blackie," the sheriff said with a sort of beseeching authority. "They's going to be hell to pay. Lord God! First Kelly Parmalee, and now this. The guy who called me, who said he did it, claimed to be doing it for Hope Kirby. But you can bet your life Hope didn't have nothing to do with this."

The judge had his necktie on. It was torn open, but the knot was still loosely fixed. The shirt had been ripped apart and was in tatters. Blackie studied the corpse a long time before he touched it. He supposed that in the narrow confines of a box placed underground, the judge had been driven mad by claustrophobia and had torn at his clothes in a smothering and uncontrollable frenzy. Later when Blackie saw the drainpipe—a good four inches in diameter—that had been his makeshift breathing tube, he decided that it was sufficient to have given him air and to have kept him alive if he could have remained calm. But a claustrophobe cannot remain calm in confinement. Judge Yancy fought the narrow confinement of the irresistible box and the unyielding earth piled above it. The more he struggled, the more uncontrolled his panic, and finally his heart burst with terror.

Blackie did the autopsy carefully. The judge's heart confirmed his first surmise. The aorta had burst.

"It was murder, Sheriff," Blackie said, reporting to the sheriff who came around in the middle of the afternoon. "About as horrible a murder as I have seen."

"I'm going to call Hugh Bedford," the sheriff said.

Hugh Bedford picked up the telephone instantly. The sheriff was surprised. "Hugh, is that you?"

"Who the hell do you think it is?"

"I don't know. It's Sunday. I thought—"

"You thought I might be drunk. Hell, Sheriff, I've been to church."

"Hugh, something awful has happened." And the sheriff told him. He also told him about the telephone call.

Hugh didn't hesitate. He got into his car and drove angrily south, towards the river. Before the narrow bridge over into Motlow, he turned right along the gravel road that led by Salem Church. A few cars remained in the parking lot while people visited, but church was over.

Hugh came to Roy Kirby's farm overlooking the brown sweep of the river. Roy lived with John Sevier in a small, neat house set back among trees. Hugh raced up the driveway and slammed the brakes on in front of the house and jumped out. Roy Kirby was already standing there, looking at Hugh with his stone-blue eyes in an expressionless face.

"Somebody has murdered Judge Yancy," Hugh gasped. "Buried the old fool alive at the Martel Church, and he's dead. The man who called Sheriff Myers claimed to be Hope's friend."

"Hit warn't me that done the deed," Roy Kirby said. "But I do not mislike the news you have brought me."

"You ought to mislike it, goddammit," Hugh growled. "It's going to make things a lot harder for your boy. Killing a judge. Lord God. You don't do that. Somebody called the sheriff this morning, told him where the body was, told the sheriff he had buried the judge alive to set Hope free." The more Hugh spoke, the more exasperated he became.

"I say if'n your judge hain't no good, hit is all right to kill him," Roy Kirby said, "but I did not do the deed. And none of mine done hit, neither." He stood there, a lean and tough little man dressed in clean overalls and a clean blue cotton work shirt faded out from many washings. "You look sick," he said. "You better come inside and set down a spell. Would you like some coffee?"

"I sure as hell would," Hugh Bedford said. He knew Roy Kirby was telling the truth. The percussions of his heart made his vision flicker. *I have not had a drink in a month,* he thought, *and I am still ready to die when I get excited.*

He managed to get the story out, and Roy Kirby sat in an old chair by the sheet-metal wood stove in the middle of the kitchen. Hugh sweated. John Sevier sat looking blank, his soft blue eyes fixed on Hugh Bedford as if the lawyer had been a rock or a post. Roy Kirby heard Hugh out, including the story about the telephone call to the sheriff, asking a question now and then, and at the end he looked at the lawyer with cold unfeeling. "Hit hain't the way I'd of done hit. If I'd kilt him, I'd of used a shotgun or a knife," he said. "I wouldn't of wasted no time digging a hole."

"Did Hope have a friend who might have done it?"

"Not as I know of. Anyways, hit hain't like Hope to do such like."

Hugh Bedford thought about it, all that dirt piled on top of him, and he remembered Italy, the German soldiers, the trunks piled on the narrow place under the floor where he hid, and afterwards when the Germans had left and the poor woman who had given him shelter lay dead in her foyer downstairs, he could not get the trunks off, and he thought he would die, but he did not die. *I would have died in that hole, with all that dirt piled on top of me. I would have died. Just like the judge. My heart would have burst.* He shuddered.

*A*RCENEAUX was in New Orleans that Sunday. He told his congregation that his mother and father were old, that he would like to spend Christmas with them, and therefore he would like to have one of his vacation Sundays the Sunday after Christmas. He flew to New Orleans on the Tuesday before the holiday, changing planes in Atlanta. The news that he would fly spread through town. Hardly anybody except some of the men who had been in the war had ever flown in an airplane. Air travel seemed unnatural and dangerous and wildly extravagant.

New Orleans was warm and rainy, and although the mosquitoes offered a surprise bite now and then, they were not the affliction they were in summer when a wind could bring them in swarms from the bayous. His father was noticeably older. They visited the plantation together and walked along the edges of the vast, groomed fields. "It is my fondest hope that I shall live to see an heir," his father said gravely. "I am in good health. The doctors thump me on the chest and tell me that for my age I am in remarkable health. Now, it may be that they mean that if I die on the stairway leaving their office they will say to your mother, 'Well, he was in remarkable health for his age. He got over here under his own power.' "

Arceneaux laughed. The air was mild. Good December weather in Louisiana. His father spoke with a thick Louisiana accent. When he came home from the war, Arceneaux found that his father and his mother sounded strange to him. He was strange to them. He never told them exactly what he had done. In World War I his father had been a captain of infantry. He had won a medal in the Meuse-Argonne campaign. "I know enough about war," the elder Arceneaux said. "You don't have to tell me about yours. It is not discourtesy I am giving you, and it is certainly not indifference. I give you privacy. If you do want to talk about your war, I will listen gladly."

Arceneaux never wanted to talk about his war.

"Karen de Vitry has a child. A son. A very healthy son."

Arceneaux could feel the unspoken longing in his father's voice.

"I never could have married her," he said. "It would have been like marriage to a mannequin."

"Perhaps, but in this society women are brought up to be like that. It is not her fault."

"No, but she is still like that," Arceneaux said.

His father sighed and was silent.

"I don't want to get married yet," he told his father patiently, sedately. "I am still uncertain about things."

"You are thinking of leaving this—you are thinking of leaving the ministry," the elder Arceneaux said.

Silence. His father smoked a cigar. An expensive cigar. Cuban. Its heavy fragrance drifted over the damp smell of the grass and floated in the direction of the great river. "I am thinking about it," Arceneaux said. "It is not what I expected."

His father spoke carefully. "I never thought it was the profession for you. I do not want to choose your profession for you, of course. No, no, no. You have your own life to live. But I thought it was a mistake when you decided to—to go to seminary. I did not think it suited you."

"I may have been wrong," Arceneaux said.

He loved his father. He knew the man's weaknesses, his pride in small accomplishments, whether his or his son's, his satisfaction with an aimless life, his great purpose being to see that the land was husbanded, that a meaningless and undistinguished tradition went grandly on with all its flags flying in the winds of time, that Arceneauxs kept being born, and that the land continued to be passed on, father to son, father to son. *And if I do not produce a son?* The thought came down on him like a blow from behind. He was thirty-three years old. His father was sixty-five. The land had been in the family for almost two hundred years. Arceneauxs had fought rattlesnakes, yellow fever, the market, and the great, mute, mighty, and implacable will of the river itself in its many moods, and the land lay stretched out in hundreds of green acres of accomplishment and pride, and it was all his by heritage and by responsibility. *And I am a pervert.*

Karen de Vitry Battersea (her name now) came to visit with her two-year-old son. The boy's nickname was "Bump." Karen talked like a flight attendant. But she and her child touched Arceneaux unexpectedly. It was nice to have a family, he thought, not to be alone in the middle of the night, to have a child to carry on one's name, to play with. Maybe more than anything else he thought it would be good to let himself sink into the expectations that other people had for him. What was he doing, losing himself in a little Tennessee town preaching to a provincial congregation of semi-educated people a gospel not to their taste?

He was beginning to see that his love of preaching was akin to building himself a house filled with mirrors where he could be happy with multiplications of himself. He preached God's love, God's forgiveness, God's mystery because he wanted to hear these things, and when he stood at the pulpit with the Bible open in front of him, he made himself a world where he was happy and almost serene.

He preached often about Jesus, the teachings with their parables, the sermons, the miracles. When he preached, the sound of his own words rolling through space seemed to propel him back into the mysterious past, mysterious because it was almost as if he could see that ancient time unrolling before his eyes, and yet he could not get to it, and he could not make others see what he felt was so near. His Jesus was not the epicene and haloed figure of Christmas and Easter cards. He was rather the mysterious God-man who revealed a perfect humanity. Follow that humanity and all would be well. We shall be like him, for we shall see him as he is.

He knew he did not communicate very well to his congregation. But maybe they would get the point after a while. Maybe they could see what he was talking about, and then . . . Well, what? Life would be better for them. Life would be better for him. Or could it ever be better?

YOU CAN thank Lieutenant McKinley, Colonel. The man is a surgeon with dynamite. The tunnel went down as if it had been stomped on by a giant.

And you didn't lose a man.

No sir. I don't think they even expected us. The tunnel was guarded by two fat old Germans. They were sitting in their guard shack drinking coffee. My Frenchmen killed them before they knew we were there. It was almost too easy.

Nothing is ever too easy, Captain Arceneaux. But frankly, if we'd known it would be this easy, I'd have said forget the fucking tunnel. Now we have to clean the goddamned thing out so we can supply troops up that way. You guys did such a good job on it that it's going to take us a couple of weeks to get the damned trains running again.

So many important things to do. Sweep the barbaric curse of Nazism out of the world forever. Make the world safe for democracy. The Four Freedoms. A just peace to all nations. Don't we get the clichés of our wars mixed up? Do we recycle them like rubber and tin cans?

I should tell about Mack. We got drunk together. We sang songs. We went to the opera. He told me he was going to give opera singing a shot when he got home. He had a beautiful voice when he sang.

Mack said, The boy didn't tell, did he? He kept his word. He thought he had been proven right. He said all along the boy would not tell, and the boy did not tell. I did not tell Mack that the boy did not tell because he was dead, because I killed him.

It all worked out, Mack said. Just the way I said it would. You know, we ought to go back south, look up Léon and Jean-François. And the boy, too.

I don't have any interest in that.

Come on, they loved you. You were their hero.

I was not anybody's hero.

I knew you were like me.

How could you tell? Was it the way I walked, the way I sat, the way I tossed my head when I spoke? I didn't do any of those things. Lord God, I saw men who kept their legs together when they sat down as if they were afraid some GI would look up their dresses, and I heard queers talk in mincing ways as if they were geldings just too, too happy to take your prick in their mouths and give you a blowjob if you would only scratch them behind the ears.

Hey, don't look so scared. I didn't mean you look like a fairy. No, just something. Maybe the way you looked at that kid that day. He was a sweet-looking piece of ass, wasn't he?

Yes he was.

The little son of a bitch probably likes girls.

Yes, he probably likes girls.

Kiss me. We have a lot to forget.

Yes, we have a lot to forget. Mack, when I go home, I'm not going to do this anymore.

You mean you're not going to fuck me in the United States?

No. Not you. Not anybody. I'm going to get married. I'm going to have children.

Oh, Christ! Well, we're not in the United States now. Not anymore. God, I love you. I really do love you. I'm going to go south. I'm going to look those people up.

Mack, it's over. It's all over. Don't be an ass. They don't want to see you.

Jesus, you don't have to get so mad about it. Hey, are you sick or something?

No, I'm not sick.

You look like you're about to vomit.

When I came home to New Orleans in the spring of '47, the air was just beginning to turn warm, and presently the suffocating New Orleans summer was on us. My father and mother met me at the train and drove me to our town house in the Garden District. The sidewalks blazed by day, and at night the fans in the ceiling stirred the air like wooden spoons stirring syrup, and the sheets had to be changed every day because you could wring the sweat out of them in the morning. The heat was broken by cloudbursts that roared on the roofs of the houses and in the live oaks and sent water rushing through the streets, and the storms went away as quickly as they came so that the heat rose with a silent roar from the pavement as though someone had opened the iron door to a furnace. A week after I came home, we went down to our country house on the plantation where it was cooler, and I sat in a lawn chair in my mother's flower garden for hours sipping gin over cracked ice, sinking peacefully into an alcoholic inertia, every thought wrapped up in a soft glow so that nothing bounced or made loud noises or got broken in my head.

I knew I had not killed the boy because I desired him. I knew that in war it was kill or be killed. The atom bombs on Hiroshima and Nagasaki. Thousands of children inciner-ated in an instant. Babies and their mothers. Teenagers innocent of the war. Thousands of others left scarred and maimed. In war people did terrible things, and in the catalogue of terrible things from my war, many people had committed worse offenses than mine. The jus-tification for the terrible things we did was that we got from them a better world than Hitler wanted.

I saw the camps and interrogated guards and ordinary German soldiers whose duty had been to direct doomed prisoners into the gas chambers with the orderly efficiency of policemen handling traffic in Berlin. German camp guards arrogantly serene in their assurance that they had done nothing wrong. They were soldiers, and soldiers obeyed orders. If we had not won the war, the camps would have held millions of the blank-eyed and skeletal prisoners we found when we liberated Theresienstadt, men and women and children scarcely more than living skeletons covered with loose skin, alive amid piles of reeking corpses, and we would have had camps in America, too, companies backed by Wall Street bidding to con-struct gas chambers and crematoria, and in every country the conqueror could have found men and women to be guards, arrogantly serene, assured that they did nothing wrong as long as they obeyed orders.

I sat in the garden under the live oaks, and I sipped gin over cracked ice and reflected that I had been on the side that kept such people from overrunning the world and that our victory had kept Americans from knowing how bad we could be, and that was a great good, wasn't it? A country cannot live without illusions, can it? I was a soldier, and I had obeyed orders, too. How was I different from the Germans? The answer was not clear. I had killed a boy, one boy. Yes, I had killed men, too, but I did not think of them. I thought of one boy.

Sometimes I thought of how the boy had laughed almost in embarrassment in that brief second just before I neatly broke his neck. I broke the boy's neck so expertly, so quickly that he had no sense at all that he would die or that he was dying, no fear, his last willed sound a laugh and then a brief, sharp pain perhaps, not prolonged enough to give him time to cry out, and it was over. He was over. He was a nothing, gone, only a memory to people who knew him. And that fading. I could not feel sorry for him because there was nothing to feel sorry for. He had no existence, no being. So I told myself. But why did I dream about him at night? Had I desired him? I had, but that is not why I killed him. It was not why I killed him.

THE SHERIFF called in Deputy Luke Bright and left him guarding the pit. He told Luke to keep people out of the graveyard on penalty of arrest, and he felt relieved when the young minister at Martel Methodist put on a heavy coat and said he'd help Luke keep watch.

In the afternoon the sheriff came back and worked his way through the crowd of curiosity-seekers, who had obeyed the command to keep away and congregated in the church parking lot, smoking cigarettes and chewing and talking and trying to make sense of things. He thought the killer would have come to the graveyard from the church side, and that he had gone carefully up beyond the hole where the judge had been found and where the packing crate still lay, its unpainted plywood top still leaning against the side. The killer had been clever. In the upper reaches of the graveyard, the land dipped sharply and rose again, and the hole had been precisely located so that the piled dirt was not visible from the parking lot or from the roads that passed not far from the church. The killer had made an effort to wipe the red dirt off his shoes, but the sheriff had the eye of a hunter and he found spots of earth on the grass, and when he had left the cemetery he crossed an over-grown field, seeing clearly where the dried sedge grass had been broken in the man's passage. In a grove of trees, he found the tracks of a car that ran down a dirt road to a gravel road which passed the church to the north and went off into the country. The car had turned right, leaving a muddy trail for a few yards.

The sheriff surmised that the man dug the grave sometime during the night of Christmas Eve and Christmas morning. So much for the holiest night of the year. Then he had kidnapped Judge Yancy, who lived alone in his house in Madisonville.

Sheriff Myers had already called Sheriff Carter in Monroe County. Now he went back to his own car and drove down to Madisonville. Sheriff Carter came out to greet him, and a reporter photographed the two of them shaking hands. The only person Sheriff Carter had allowed inside the judge's neat little house besides himself was a fingerprint man from Knoxville, who was finishing up when Sheriff Myers arrived. In the dining room were two cups on a small wooden table. One cup, half-filled with coffee, had the judge's fingerprints all over it. The other cup, empty, had been wiped clean. Somehow the killer got into the house, probably on Christmas night. Under what pretense?

Blackie Ledbetter drew blood from Judge Yancy's corpse and on Monday morning drove into Knoxville to the laboratory at one of the hospitals to test it. His suspicions were confirmed. The lab found traces of chloroform in the blood. In Blackie's view, that let out all the Kirby boys, including the old man. They were not the sort to use chloroform. Someone had overpowered the judge and put him out with the chloroform. Blackie calculated that the judge died sometime during the day after Christmas. He was probably alive twelve or fourteen hours, much of that time unconscious because of the chloroform. When the judge woke up, he was, as foretold, four feet underground with a drainpipe in front of his face and just enough room to lift his head no more than a couple of inches and to cross his arms over his chest.

Jim Ed said that Judge Yancy had been a colonel in the army during the First War—Jim Ed's war. He had been in the adjutant general's office, blessed with the job of reviewing sentences given to deserters. Blackie could imagine Judge Yancy's sour pleasure at ordering deserters to be shot. No one grieved for the old man. But the horror made Bourbon Countians speak of his death in hushed tones. They talked about it, imagined it happening to themselves, and choked with panic and fright and hopelessness. At night people half-asleep dreamed they were buried alive and sat up in bed flailing and gasping for breath.

Blackie told the sheriff about the chloroform as soon as he arrived back in Bourbonville. The sheriff told about the telephone call that told him where to find Judge Yancy. He told Blackie what the caller had said about Hope Kirby. Blackie shook his head. Blackie was the first person to suggest that it might have been one of Hope's friends from the war. That was Hugh Bedford's guess, too. That Monday he was already on his way to Nashville.

Blackie and the sheriff agreed that they had to tell the press some of what they knew. The reporters could help. The sheriff called Red Eason from the *Bourbon County News* and rounded up the reporters for the morning and afternoon papers in Knoxville who were already in town. They sat in the sheriff's office and took notes. The suspect in this death was a large man, strong enough to subdue Judge Yancy, knock him out with chloroform, stuff him into a box, and bury him alive. Digging the hole in the night must have been a job, and it had to have been done at night or it would have attracted attention, even in the Martel community, where the houses were far apart, separated by fields and woods. The sheriff told the reporters about the telephone call, but he did not tell them what the caller had said about Hope Kirby.

When he was left alone in his office, the sheriff made himself a pot of coffee and thought. Maybe he was on the wrong track. Lots and lots of people in Bourbon County had reason to hate Judge Yancy. And not only in Bourbon County. Judge Yancy's circuit ran through five counties, and he spread death through all of them. *Maybe,* the sheriff thought, *I don't know nothing at all. Suppose somebody hated Judge Yancy and thought this was a good time to kill him and put the blame on Hope.* In his gut the sheriff knew that Hope had had nothing to do with this killing. But if he had . . .

A GUARD brought Hope a newspaper on Monday morning. The story of Judge Yancy's murder was on the front page together with a photograph of the judge when he was a young lawyer at the Scopes Monkey Trial.

"I know hit warn't done by my pappy or by my brothers," Hope said, studying the paper carefully.

Monday afternoon Hugh Bedford arrived in the visitors' room. Hope went through the ritual of being shackled and led down the institutional-green corridors, grim in the glaring artificial light. When he walked into the little booth where he could look through the steel mesh into the larger room, Hugh Bedford was sitting there, looking like warmed-over hell. He had dark bags under his eyes.

"Lord God, this is a clammy place," Hugh said. He was sweating.

"The cells is all right," Hope said. "You ought to try one of them sometimes."

Hugh did not laugh. "Look, Hope, Something bad has happened. It may be real bad."

"You've come to tell me about Judge Yancy," Hope said.

"You know about it, then."

"Hit's in all the papers over here."

"Your father and your brothers say they didn't do it," Hugh said. He looked at the floor.

"Pappy always tells the truth," Hope said. "Besides that, him and John Sevier come over here on Christmas Day. They drove over in Pappy's pickup on Christmas Eve, and they didn't start back till late in the afternoon."

"Damn! Why in hell couldn't he have told me that he had an alibi?"

"I reckon you didn't ask him. Pappy don't tell you nothing 'lessen you ask him."

Hugh took a deep, pained breath. "And your brothers?"

"They all had Christmas with their families," Hope said. "Pappy was always a big'un for Christmas."

"Well, it's a bitch," Hugh said. He sat looking at the floor. "Judge Yancy had enough enemies to make a dozen men happy to kill him."

There was a silence.

"I know who done the deed," Hope said quietly.

"You know!" Hugh put his head in his hands. "Goddamn. I hope it wasn't a friend of yours."

"He says he is," Hope said. He told Hugh about Missionary. It took a long time.

"What can we do?" Hugh said at the end. "What the hell can we do? If it gets out—"

"You can't stop Missionary 'lessen you kill him," Hope said.

"Who's he going to go for next?"

"McNeil, I'd say. Maybe that boy."

"Charles Alexander."

Hugh made Hope tell the story all over again. He got a description of Missionary and wrote it down. It had taken him almost six hours to drive the nearly two hundred miles to Nashville from Bourbonville. By the time he finished with Hope, it was nearly four in the afternoon. He walked out into Nashville and felt the cold pushing at him, and he was so weary that he did not know if he could drive back to Bourbonville without passing out at the wheel.

He thought of how good a pull of bourbon would taste. His bones ached for drink. He put it out of his mind and got into the Hudson and started back home. He drove in a comatose state, now and then stopping for black coffee and feeling stiff everywhere in his body. Where was all this leading him? Arceneaux had gone off to New Orleans, and Hugh felt strangely alone. He didn't understand Arceneaux. He did not know why the minister wanted to save Hope Kirby's life. He also trusted Arceneaux. He hated to acknowledge that he trusted a preacher, but he trusted Arceneaux. Hugh disliked so many of the people who disliked Arceneaux that he had to trust the man.

Hugh did not get back to Bourbonville until nearly ten-thirty that night. The sheriff was sitting in his office drinking coffee.

"Don't you ever go home?" Hugh said.

"I'm thinking," the sheriff said.

"Can't you think at home?"

"Have you ever tried to think with a goddamned television set going full-blast in the house?"

"You got a pistol. Why don't you shoot the damned thing?"

"Hell, my wife would sue me for divorce, and my kids would tell the county welfare department that I beat them with a club."

The sheriff took a deep and exasperated breath.

"That pimply-faced reporter on the afternoon paper in Knoxville just called me up. He found out about the phone call, the demand that Hope Kirby be set free."

"Who the hell told him?"

"The man who kilt Judge Yancy."

"Is that what he said?"

"That's what he told the reporter. He was mad that I didn't let out that he'd killed Judge Yancy to make the state let Hope Kirby free. He said he was going to keep killing till the state come to its senses. I tell you it don't add up. Hope don't know nobody that talks like that man. He's from the North. Hell, it's crazy. Hope ain't crazy."

"He's from Massachusetts," Hugh said wearily. He sat down, and he told the sheriff about Missionary.

By the time he had finished telling the story, the clock on the courthouse tower had struck eleven and had gone on. The two men sat looking bleakly at each other. "You look like shit," the sheriff said.

"I feel a hell of a lot worse," Hugh said.

"If he kills again, who does he go for?" the sheriff said.

"I'd say Charles Alexander," Hugh said. "Maybe Ken McNeil. I won't cry if he goes after McNeil."

"Charlie Alexander has disappeared."

"Disappeared. What do you mean, 'disappeared'?"

"The day before Christmas he drove off somewhere. Didn't say where he was going. Nobody knows where he is."

"Not even his daddy?"

"His daddy said he mentioned going to Florida," the sheriff said. "Didn't say where."

"In that car?" Hugh said. "Jesus, he'd be lucky to get to Sweetwater."

"Ain't nothing wrong with that car if you keep putting oil in it," the sheriff said.

"I hope he is dead," Hugh Bedford said.

"I hope you don't mean that," the sheriff said coldly. "This ain't his fault."

"Who the hell is at fault, then?" Bedford said.

"Well, you might just consider the fact that Hope is the one who kilt them two. Hell, Hugh. What do you expect? If he wasn't doing his duty by that woman, why in hell shouldn't she find somebody else with a hard prick?"

"Sex isn't everything," Hugh said.

"It beats the rest of it," the sheriff said.

Hugh got up and drove himself home. Bourbonville slept in the cold night. He never locked the doors of his house. People did not lock doors in Bourbon County. He stepped inside and turned on the light. For just a moment he listened for some sound that might be from somebody else in the house. But the emptiness loomed at him. He sat down in the kitchen and thought that he deserved a drink. It would be a game. Surely Arceneaux could not have found all the booze in the house. Hugh was sly; he had hidden bourbon in places God would not have thought of looking. He would find a bottle and say to Arceneaux, "Gotcha!"

But he did not. Instead he put in a long-distance call. How many Arceneauxs could live there? You still had to go through one operator after another, first Knoxville, then Atlanta, finally New Orleans. A woman's voice, sprightly at this time of night. New Orleans was on Central time. An hour behind. "Lawrence Arceneaux," he said carefully. "Maybe his father's called something else."

"I have a Lawrence Arceneaux on St. Charles Avenue."

"Is that where rich people live?" Hugh said.

"Why yes, I guess you could say that."

"Could you get me the number?" Hugh said.

In a minute Arceneaux was on the line.

"Yes," he said, not in a friendly tone.

"Larry, this is Hugh. Sit down. I've got a story to tell you."

NEXT morning Arceneaux put in a call to the dean of the Episcopal Theological School in Cambridge, Massachusetts. He knew the dean would not be there. New England deans go south at Christmas, like birds. In 1953 they could get on a train in Boston in the morning, and thirty-six hours later step off in Fort Lauderdale. No one hung around a Boston school between Christmas and the New Year. He got a telephone switchboard operator. She was one of those cheerful women born to make the world marvel at how radiant they can be on a wintry day in an empty building where steam radiators hiss and pop in the hollow quiet of the holiday season.

No, she said in a voice of such assumed sorrow that she might have been commiserating with Arceneaux over the death of a pet dog, the dean was not available. He had taken a few days off. He would be back in the office on the following Tuesday. That would be January 5.

He told her he wanted to speak to the dean about one of his professors. He gave Missionary's name, Robert Pearson Winthrop. All the good cheer went out of her as if he had made an obscene proposition via long distance. Her voice turned icy. "Professor Winthrop is no longer a member of the faculty here," she said. Hers was now a voice of somebody one would not want to meet incarnate on a dark street at night.

"Why is he no longer there?" he said quickly. He knew she was on the point of hanging up. He rushed on. "You see, he's suspected of murder in Tennessee. We don't know where he is. We're afraid he's about to kill again, and it's important that we know something about him."

She sputtered. She started three different sentences before she finished the fourth one. "I will call the dean right away. He will want to speak with you. Please give me your telephone number." Her voice came over crisp and precise, a little too loud, even louder than voices were in those days when everybody shouted as if long distance were a complex of pipes running underground to the four corners of the world and you had to scream to be heard from Massachusetts. Arceneaux realized also that her voice quivered. She was afraid. Professor Winthrop terrified her.

He gave her his number. "I thought you said you were in Tennessee," she said.

"It's too complicated to explain," he said. "Just give this number to the dean." He waited. Not fifteen minutes passed before Dean Harvey M. Cowan rang him up. A person-to-person call. Dean Cowan came on, pronouncing Arceneaux's name with deanly precision and then his own, delivering every syllable as if Arceneaux might be about to introduce him at an important convention. Arceneaux expected him to add his earned and honorary degrees. He understood quickly that the dean was exercising all the self-control he could. It was hard for him. His voice sounded like compressed air slowly released from a tank. Arceneaux asked about Father Winthrop.

Dean Cowan enlarged on the name. "Father Robert Standish Pearson Winthrop," he said, speaking as if he wanted to be sure they were talking about the same man.

"I guess that's the one," Arceneaux said. "I don't believe you have an entire theological school filled with Winthrops. An old Massachusetts name, isn't it?"

"Old and very distinguished," the dean said with a touch of unguarded pride.

"Wasn't a Winthrop one of the Puritans who hanged Quakers and Baptists?" Arceneaux said.

"Those were unenlightened times," the dean replied uncomfortably. "I might say that John Winthrop was a Puritan unhappy with the moderation of the Anglican Church. Many of his descendants have recognized his errors and returned to the fold."

"Well, look," Arceneaux said, "I'm not blaming you because the original John Winthrop hanged some of my spiritual ancestors. I should tell you that I'm a Baptist, a Baptist minister in fact." Arceneaux threw in the last to make the dean more uncomfortable, and succeeded. Dean Cowan said, "I see," in the tone a family doctor would use if Arceneaux had told him he had contracted syphilis from a two-dollar whore and had given it to his wife and didn't know whether to tell her or not.

Arceneaux did not want to play games. He told the dean everything he knew about Missionary. That took awhile. He did not spare any details about the death of Judge Yancy. He was pleased to hear the dean gasp slightly on the other end. "We're trying to decide two things," Arceneaux said. "One is this: did Father Winthrop kill Judge Yancy? The other is whether he'll now go after somebody else connected with the trial."

The dean was silent. Arceneaux could imagine him feeling his winter vacation ruined, a tornado sweeping. He heard the hollow electronic sound of long-distance lines, and it struck him that the dean had not said where he was. Finally the dean spoke. "Everything I tell you must be in strictest confidence," he said in an unhappy voice.

"I have to tell the sheriff what I know," Arceneaux said. "We are talking about murder."

Very slowly and painfully the dean eked out his story. Father Winthrop was a graduate of Harvard, class of 1929, and then of the Episcopal Theological School. He had a doctorate in theology from Berkeley Divinity School in New Haven. He had gone to the Philippines filled with optimism and goodwill, intent on following Kipling's admonition to civilize the lesser breeds without the law. When the war came, he vanished. No word at all from him or about him. Not even a rumor. After MacArthur returned in 1944, people back in Cambridge learned of the fate of Father Winthrop's school. They assumed that he had died as a martyr with his teachers. "We even held a memorial service for him in the chapel," the dean said ruefully. Arceneaux surmised the dean's thoughts: *We would all have been much better off if Father Winthrop had died, reduced to honored martyrdom, recalled with a bronze plaque with a suitable inscription in some dark, leathery nook in the Episcopal Theological School.* Three weeks after the memorial service another flash came from the Philippines. Father Winthrop was alive. He had spent the previous three years as part of a guerrilla band in Luzon.

"We thought he'd served as a chaplain," the dean said with one of those ironical laughs you feel sorry for. ("I thought it was lumbago, but it turned out to be cancer.") "We supposed that out in the field before a battle, he set up a little portable altar and held the Eucharist for the troops. We had seen the wartime photographs, you know. Chaplains giving the Eucharist to troops about to invade Normandy. You remember them perhaps."

"I was already in France at the invasion," Arceneaux said. "I was in the OSS. A spy. I went behind the lines and killed people."

"Oh, yes, to be sure," the dean said, uncertain how to respond.

"MacArthur himself commended these guerrillas—and Father Winthrop. The priest couldn't get a medal; he wasn't a soldier. MacArthur gave him a citation for 'Keeping the Light of Christian Truth and Love Burning During a Period of Darkness and Barbarism.' MacArthur had a way with words. Father Winthrop had the citation framed. It hung in his office at the Episcopal Theological School.

"We wired our congratulations," the dean said. "We also offered him a job. We needed a theologian. We had so many young men coming back from the service, going into the priesthood, wanting to make the world a better place."

"Yes," Arceneaux said. "I know all about it."

"Perhaps I have described you," the dean said in a hopeful tone.

"Perhaps," Arceneaux said.

"Yes. Yes, well, he came back in the fall of 1945," the dean said with a sigh. "He was very popular, you know. Truly charismatic. Students filled his classes."

"How long did that last?" Arceneaux said.

"He left us only a year ago," the dean said after a short, tense pause.

"What happened?"

"Everything started splendidly," the dean said with difficulty, the kind of opening you might read in a Victorian ghost story where something unexpected, uncanny, and horrifying happens in the midst of serene perfection in a beautiful house in the country filled with unexplored rooms and malicious spirits.

The first difficulty was Father Winthrop's absorption in the almighty power of God. "God *is* almighty. We know that," the dean said, explaining something in the labored, desperate tone of a man who knows it's hopeless at the start. "But we mortals are *not* almighty, and when we try to understand God's omnipotence in our own terms, we are bound to fail. Part of our problem as human beings is that we strive to use our pitiful words and our inadequate reason to satisfy a vain curiosity, a curiosity vain just because it can *never* be satisfied, no matter how hard we try."

"Yes, of course," Arceneaux said impatiently. "This may surprise you, but I've read Augustine against Julian of Eclanum."

"Oh, you have?" the dean said, astonished and embarrassed.

"Get on with it," Arceneaux said impatiently. "I want to hear about Father Winthrop. He took Augustine and predestination and ran with him, and then what happened?"

"Ran with Augustine?" the dean said.

Arceneaux cursed himself. "It's just an expression," he said.

Another weary sigh of resignation on the other end of the long-distance line. The dean resumed, slowly, in pained recapitulant sentences dribbling through the wire in spastic iterations, a tone of morose injury. The world had not been fair to the dean. Yes, Father Winthrop was a devotee of Augustine. He taught Augustine's doctrine of the Church out of *The City of God*. Fine. Explanation of the calamity that befell the Eternal City when Alaric and the Visigoths sacked Rome in 410. Then God's plan for history, Creation, the Fall of man, the call of Abraham, God's casting away of Israel, His creation of a new Israel in the Christian Church, the triumph of the Church, its vision of the City of God in eternity. God ran the world; all would be well. All that was fine, the dean said. Father Winthrop taught for two or three years like a man who reincarnated Saint Augustine's intoxication with grace, taught the *Confessions*, taught Augustine's struggle to find certainty against death and the peace he found as the tool of an almighty God who held the destiny of mortals in His hands. "But then," said the dean in a voice almost suffocating, "other, more disturbing—more, how shall I say, more *eccentric*—ideas began to creep in."

The other ideas involved the backside of grace. Why did God save some from their sins and send them to paradise through no merit of their own and why did he inflict an everlasting fire on all the rest? "Father Winthrop took to reading aloud Augustine's descriptions of the torments of hell, the ones he wrote about in *The City of God*."

"The Argument against Origen," Arceneaux said.

"Yes. Yes indeed," the dean said. "I see you are a man of considerable learning."

"I try," Arceneaux said frantically. "Let's move on."

"Well, Father Winthrop kept asking questions we should not ask. He wrestled with God's way with the world, with predestination. It was like Jacob's wrestling with the Angel. You can only come away lame from such a contest. Father Winthrop became convinced that if God damned most of creation, He must take some pleasure in doing so. Why would God do something He didn't like to do?"

"Why indeed? Do you believe in predestination?" Arceneaux said.

The dean made a dry sound, a groan, and his weak laugh conveyed over the wire the despair of a lost soul. "I never thought about it very much," he said, making an effort to control himself. "Father Winthrop talked incessantly about it. Incessantly. Now I don't mean that he spoke in a fanatical tone. He wasn't like a ranting street preacher. He didn't rage at his students or his colleagues like Savonarola."

"I should hope not. No bonfire of the vanities in Cambridge."

"Oh dear no. But still—" The dean became almost incoherent at moments, but slowly a grim, almost humorous drama came across the distance. Father Winthrop: a gregarious, talkative, genial, and miraculously intelligent man who remembered everything he read and who could bring to almost any question of theology dizzying questions that left faculty and students uneasy and then anxious and afraid and, some of them, fanatically absorbed in Father Winthrop's ideas. "He terrified most of us," the dean said. "Always laughing, but he quoted Augustine from memory. From *memory*, mind you, in *Latin*, about the fires of hell."

By 1950 Father Winthrop had begun to talk about non-Christians as the Amalekites. He began to make comparisons with the conquest of the Holy Land by Joshua. Joshua slaughtered every human being in Jericho except a harlot and her children, and that harlot—Rehab—became an ancestor of Jesus. What do we make of such a genealogy? That God has a supreme sense of irony? Part of His irony was that He created other religions and gave them millions of worshippers so that they, like the Amalekites and the Canaanites, could be destroyed by true followers of the true God who thereby proved their own faith by not questioning anything God did, no matter how cruel. Anything was right because God did it, contradictions and all. God could tell people not to commit adultery, and He could make Rehab the harlot one of the ancestors of Jesus so even harlotry, fornication, adultery, and murder became part of His purposes. The dean told his tale with a voice almost breaking with frustration and unanswerable questions.

"He was fascinated with Elijah," the dean said in that desperate tone of frustration. "Elijah on Mount Carmel bringing down the fires of Yahweh on the water-soaked sacrifice he had collected. What did he do then? He killed with his own hands the three hundred priests of Baal. Father Winthrop claimed if we were serious about our faith, what we *said* we believed, we had to be willing to kill for it because it was God's will that only one true faith exist on the face of the earth."

Father Winthrop had arrived at this stage gradually and with a softly spoken, genial, but impeccable logic. His voice was so soft, his logic so plausible, that for a while members of the community did not understand what he was saying. The dean had given him the largest auditorium in the school, and still students overflowed it, sitting on the floor, standing around the walls, gathered at his feet when he spoke, all of them mesmerized. "And then last year, last *academic* year," the dean said in his desperately explanatory voice, "he began to speak of the boredom of God in eternity. Time. Kant."

"Boredom!" Arceneaux said.

"Yes, *boredom*. Imagine! He went back to Kant; he said that everything that happens in the universe requires time and space. Therefore if God exists, God, too, is subject to time and space, and all time is not present to Him as a single, glowing moment that embraces eternity. That was Augustine's God, you see. All time was present to Him. But now Father Winthrop said Augustine was wrong. The Christian God speaks and lives and therefore inhabits time like us."

Arceneaux began to follow this bizarre argument from a great distance. The dean plunged on. "He said God did all these cruel things. Well, I don't call them that. I'd never attribute cruelty to God. That would be blasphemous. Father Winthrop said they were cruel, and he said God did those things to *amuse* Himself."

The dean paused, overwhelmed by both the blasphemy and his inability to refute it.

"Please go on," Arceneaux said gently. Arceneaux pitied him, his collapsing world, his tidy rituals in ruins; dissolved were his triumphant Bach fugues, his oratorios from Handel, the haunting piety of evensong, his meditation in the sacred gloom of Gothic arches as twilight gently seeped a loving divinity into his soul and created sweetness beyond all words. Now he was confronted for the rest of his life by a God up to his knees in blood, treading the winepress of His wrath, and exulting in a creation that He could destroy with a hilarious and almighty sadism to deflect Himself from boredom.

"When he spoke of God's boredom, he began telling in detail what he had done as a guerrilla fighter in the Philippines. Horrible, horrible things! He told us that he had done them as the servant of the same God who had called Elijah to consume the priests of Baal, and Samuel to hew in pieces Agag of the Amalekites. He said he was sure the fire that consumed Elijah's sacrifice had been a nuclear blast and that the people of Hiroshima and Nagasaki had been incinerated by the same force and that God preserved them forever and ever in the sensation of burning at the peak of pain before their earthly bodies vanished into steam."

The dean ceased. Arceneaux waited. "Are you still there?" Arceneaux said.

"Yes," the voice said feebly.

"You fired him."

"Yes," the dean said. "Yes, you see, one of our students tried to kill a Chinese man in Chinatown. It was a nervous breakdown, of course. The student was crazy. Still, when he was arrested, he said he was doing it for the glory of God. Father Winthrop defended him! Can you imagine! We hushed up the influence of Father Winthrop on the attempted murder. We had to tell him he could not continue his duties. None of us could bear his influence anymore."

"How did he take it?"

"He laughed. He said God would judge us, that he himself might be God's tool to—to . . . Oh, I can't tell you what he said. He frightened us all."

Arceneaux did not force the dean to continue. He could feel in the tortured voice the unmitigated horror of a man who had come face-to-face with evil beyond all that a simple and innocent clergyman could imagine, even if he had preached against evil all his life.

"He said we were all the priests of Baal and that he was Elijah. He said we were servants of the Antichrist."

"Was he angry?"

"No," the dean said quietly. "He seemed happy, triumphant, as if he had supposed for years that we were damned and that he was now proven correct."

"And he left."

"Yes, he left," the dean said slowly and with great sorrow. Another long pause hung in the electronic hollowness of the telephone lines. "Something of him remains, you know. We're still demoralized. We can't get back on track. Many students have left. Several professors have resigned." Another painful pause. "I am resigning myself."

"Are you retiring?"

"I am entering an Anglican monastery. I'm going to begin a life of prayer and meditation. I'm going to try to recover my faith and my peace of mind."

The dean had no idea what had happened to Father Winthrop. Arceneaux told him. The conversation came to an end as an old man's climb up a mountain ends in fatigue beyond expression. The dean needed his vacation, and Arceneaux had spoiled it. The telephone clicked like a door shutting. Afterwards Arceneaux sat a long time thinking. It was a bright day, warm and promising. New Orleans was gearing up for the Sugar Bowl on Friday. West Virginia and somebody else, Arceneaux had heard. Georgia Tech? His father had tickets. Now Arceneaux would be relieved of the game and his parents and the de Vitry family and Karen and her ebullient husband and her adorable son and all the rest.

He flew back to Knoxville the next afternoon against the baffled and heartbroken protests of his father and mother. He changed planes in Atlanta, where he waited an hour for his connection to Knoxville, and picking up his car in the parking lot, he drove back to Bourbonville and found the town shut up against the dark. The streets were deserted, and his own house was empty and cold. He called Hugh Bedford.

"Hugh, I'm back."

"I'm glad," Hugh said. "Don't go outside wearing anything black. One of these crazy people will take you for Missionary and shoot you like a dog."

"Missionary," Arceneaux said. "Would you like a cup of tea?"

"I'd like a bottle of bourbon," Hugh said.

"I'd like a bottle of gin myself."

"I reckon I can drink tea without vomiting. Let me drive over there. I think people will recognize my car."

Arceneaux made tea. The two of them talked until deep in the night, turning things over and over in their minds. Where was Charles Alexander? The sheriff called his father every day, Hugh said. Today Charles had called from Florida. He said he'd been down there for a week. He'll be home by Sunday, he said. Why was he in Florida?

"I reckon he wanted to be warm," Hugh said.

Arceneaux pondered. Charles was not the sort to take vacations.

That night all the churches in town called off the New Year's Eve services by which they welcomed the new year with song and prayer.

*O*N NEW Year's Day 1954, Blackie Ledbetter sat in the kitchen with his mother and father, drinking coffee, looking out the windows, and seeing mindlessly the yard and the driveway of white stones that curved down through huge oak trees towards the highway that they could not see from where they sat. He pondered his mother without looking at her. What did she understand? What did he understand about her?

She had been married before she married their father. She never talked about this other man. Did she have children by him? No. She was not the kind of person to leave a child. But what had he been like? How had they got a divorce in an age when divorce was rare, scandalous, the kind of thing to ruin a woman's name forever? She had been so beautiful! Not glamorous like one of the movie stars but beautiful in a ruddy, healthy way, full of brightness and wit and an enjoyment of the world. Jim Ed sat silently at the table, smoking a cigarette, drinking coffee, sometimes coughing.

He's killing himself, Blackie thought in despair.

The telephone rang. Jim Ed reached over to the wall and took it off the hook. He spoke quickly into it, and his face changed. "Yes, he's here . . . Yes." He handed the telephone over. Blackie spoke into it.

"Blackie, we've got another one." It was the sheriff.

Blackie's heart sank. "Who is it?"

"Lonnie Wyatt," the sheriff said. "He went out to his barn to milk this morning. After a while his woman heard the cows bawling, but she didn't think nothing about it. Cows bawl all the time. But Lonnie didn't come back, and she went out to look for him." He stopped talking. Blackie could hear the horror in the silence over the thrumming wire.

"How did it happen?" he said.

The sheriff cleared his throat. "Whoever it was tied him up by the wrists and the ankles, just like you tie the carcass of a deer or a young beef. I figure Lonnie was alive while that was happening. He had tape over his mouth when we found him." The sheriff stopped again.

"Go on," Blackie said.

"He hung him up by his ankles to a beam in the barn and gutted him," the sheriff said. His voice was so low that Blackie almost automatically said, "Speak up, Sheriff," but then he recapitulated in his head the sounds that already hung in the earpiece of the telephone and understood them, and he did not want to hear them again.

"He was on the jury?"

"Yes, he was on the jury." The sheriff hesitated. "The killer, this Missionary guy, tacked a note on Lonnie's sleeve."

"What did it say?" Blackie said.

"The note says, 'This is the beginning. Let Hope Kirby go, or more will die.' "

The newspapers and the radio stations and television reporters snatched up the story. A priest was at large in Bourbon County killing people who had taken part in the trial that condemned Hope Kirby. The priest and Hope Kirby had known each other during the war.

A pall of terror hung over the county. People could imagine themselves not only buried alive in the confining space of a narrow box six feet underground, but hung up by the heels and gutted. *This is no dream; this is happening to me, now, to me. This is death.*

O_N *MONDAY* night, January 4, Charles Alexander arrived back home from his mysterious trip and learned about the murders. He did not have a radio in the '37 Ford, and the cheap motels where he stayed had no television. He had lived for more than a week as though in a chamber beneath the sea where no news from the earthly world could penetrate.

When he walked in the door, his father greeted him with calm relief. Paul Alexander told him what had happened, and Charles called Larry Arceneaux. "I need to see you," Charles said. "It's about the murders. Would you call the sheriff? I'll come to your house."

The sheriff came five minutes after Arceneaux called the jail. Arceneaux called Hugh Bedford, and Hugh was there in a minute, looking frazzled and angry. Another fifteen minutes, and Charles Alexander pulled up in front of the house in the '37 Ford. His father was with him. The cold swept down the empty streets. Every hardware store in town, including Tommy Fieldston's, was sold out of pistols, rifles, and shotguns. The emptiness of a town where fear assumed shape and weight pressed on all of them. The governor had sent in six highway patrol cars, each with two troopers. They drove around uselessly, stopping all cars with a male driver and no passengers, drawing their guns and frightening people.

Charles and the others sat down at the fire. Arceneaux poured coffee. Charles took a deep breath. "I saw the man you call Missionary. He came to the newspaper office before Christmas." Hugh Bedford looked at him in cold fury. Never in his life was Hugh able to forgive him.

Slowly and haltingly Charles told his story. His coffee got cold in his hands. The sheriff stood hulking by the fire, drinking his coffee silently, looking on with a frown of impatient concentration. Charles reached back to recall what Missionary had said about God. He spoke slowly, an archaeologist exploring a new find from old times. To the sheriff it was all words full of air with no substance. He never thought about theological matters. They had nothing to do with being sheriff. He couldn't understand why people quarreled about them. Above all at this moment on a wintry night he could not understand how anything Charles was saying was of any help in tracking down a lunatic killer whose peculiar form of lunacy was much less important than a thousand other details the sheriff would like to know about him.

"So," the sheriff said, "he said God was bored with eternity."

"Yes," Charles said quietly. "He said that if God was condemned to be Himself forever, he would run out of every possibility. At a certain moment in eternity, there was nothing left for God to do that He had not done before, and to amuse Himself He turned cruel and savage. After a while even the cruelty and the savagery would exhaust themselves, and God would dissolve into Himself and be nothing but a dot in time. He said that God by being cruel prolonged His life because He could only continue to have existence if He had something new to do. Now God was in the stage of His existence in which He had to create people to destroy them in new ways. He said there was a finite number of new possibilities and that in eternity, the billions of years that God existed, He could exhaust them all, and then when He had exhausted all the new things, He had either to begin again, or God would die."

"He said all that?" Arceneaux said sharply. "The dean at his school didn't tell me that."

Charles looked at him in a detached and sorrowing passivity. "That was the gist of it," he said.

"I see," Arceneaux said.

"Jesus Christ," the sheriff said. "I'm glad somebody in this room sees something."

"Shit," Hugh said, expelling a long, bewildered breath. "We have a madman on our hands."

Arceneaux sat pondering. You got started on this line of thought, and it ran away with you, he thought. It had run away with Charles. It made a sort of crazy sense—the uncreated God with no equals, no origin, no memory of divine childhood, alone in infinity with nothing around Him but His creatures, flattering spirits, a Satan made as though on a game board to amuse children and used for mock contests that God must always win, like a baseball pitcher victorious in every game so that His brilliant talents finally bored even Himself, and yet He must keep pitching through all eternity although the outcome had been decided from the fathomless creation of eternity itself.

There was God on a stage where at times He seems on the verge of defeat, allowing the pitifully hopeful underlings in the opposition, which He had also created, to load the bases in the last half of the ninth when God is ahead by one run and the heaviest hitter in the cosmos comes to bat, but with the celestial grandstand looking on, God works the count to 3–2 and strikes him out while His claque of angels cheer "Praise God!," led, doubtless, by a blond Billy Graham with a North Carolina accent waving not a black Bible but a red one. What sadness and loneliness God must feel at His own power. What tedium. For centuries, from the time of Gilgamesh, human beings had been troubled over the existence of evil and death. Arceneaux thought of Dostoyevsky's Grand Inquisitor in *The Brothers Karamazov*. Well, here was the solution. Evil existed because God was evil and loved to sport with men. Lear had it right.

"Look," the sheriff said impatiently, "I don't give a shit about all this God stuff. I want to know who this motherfucking priest is going to kill next."

"It's like he wants Hope dead," Hugh said.

Arceneaux had another idea. "He may believe that if he kills, God will come to his aid. He kills to prove his faith; God rouses Himself and makes war on all the wicked. He wouldn't be the first."

"And it might be just like he says," the sheriff said. "He might think that if he kills enough, the state will open the prison and let Hope go. What do you think, Mr. Alexander?"

"I think we may be dealing with a man who likes to kill, and he has brought God in to justify himself," Paul said.

The courthouse clock struck eleven. They counted the strokes in silence, listened to them die away in prolonged and lonely stillness, and Arceneaux yearned for the ringing to resume as if life itself had abruptly and unexpectedly ended with the final dissolving of bell notes in the dark, and he vainly awaited resurrection in the shape of a chime.

"And that's all," the sheriff said to Charles, bewildered and impetuous. "You just talked about the Bible. You didn't ask him about Hope Kirby? You didn't mention the murders? He didn't tell you he was going to kill people?"

"He said that Jesus was like Hope Kirby, a criminal put to death and rising from the dead. He said God liked to tease us. Who could believe such a man was the Son of God?"

"Shit," the sheriff said. "I'm sorry, Reverend." He looked impatiently towards Arceneaux.

"I've heard the word before," Arceneaux said.

"Where was you, Charles?" the sheriff said.

"I was in Florida," Charles said.

"What was you doing down there?"

"I wanted to get away from here."

"He had the engine of his car rebuilt in Florida," Paul Alexander said.

"Lord God," the sheriff said. "Why'd you want to put good money into that old rattletrap?"

"It was Lloyd's car," Charles said softly.

"Oh hell, Lloyd!" the sheriff said. "Well, I liked Lloyd, but he was a fool for women."

"He was a good man," Paul Alexander said softly. The others were surprised.

"Well," the sheriff said, "we got to figure out who he's going to go for next," the sheriff said. "I think he'll go for you, Charles. I think he'll try to kill you."

"And McNeil," Hugh Bedford said. "He'll go after McNeil."

They now had a description of Father Winthrop, but they did not have a picture of him. Arceneaux called the theological school again. Yes, a photographer came every year and took pictures of the graduating class, including a group picture with the professors. But Winthrop did not turn up in any of them. He told people he did not like to have his picture taken. He told people that the Bible commanded us not to have any graven images, and he said that he did not want people in the future to revere his image as though he had been a saint. "I don't want my students to remember what I looked like; I want them to remember what I taught them."

They went back into the files. Winthrop came to the school in 1933. He graduated in 1936. They thought his photograph would be on his application. But somebody had peeled it off. They found only the glue where the picture had been.

*C*HARLES no longer went to Midway Baptist Church. He said to Stephen, "You'll have to take Guy to church. I'm not going there anymore."

"Why?" Stephen said.

"I've decided I don't want to. I'm tired of being looked at like a freak in a sideshow."

"Everybody at the church is on your side."

"Have you taken a vote?"

"What's wrong with you anyway? Do you think anybody could say a word against you? Preacher Finewood would bring down fire and brimstone on their heads."

"I don't care. I'm not going."

"Shall I tell people you're sick?"

"All liars will be cast into the pit of hell," Charles said.

"Charles, I don't know why you're mad at me. I'm your brother."

"I'm not mad. I swear to God I'm not mad. I'm just tired. Sick and tired of this whole business. Sick of it."

"I understand," Stephen said.

But it was Guy who got sick. He had respiratory problems. Bad colds hit him, and you would think he was on the point of choking to death. Part of his condition, Dr. Youngblood said, and Blackie and Paul Ledbetter said the same after Dr. Youngblood died. Blackie thought he had a touch of asthma. Whatever it was, when it started, it was enough to make it seem that death had kicked down the doors and stood in the house with an expectant grin. Dr. Youngblood told Paul Alexander years before that Guy would not live long. "You'll be lucky if he lives to be twenty," Dr. Youngblood said in his grave and patient voice. Dr. Youngblood died just after the Second World War. Guy lived on, but Paul Alexander took his old friend's prediction as gospel. Every time Guy got sick, Paul thought it was the end for his beloved son. *I wonder if he would feel that way for us, for Stephen or me,* Charles thought.

On this night he got very sick, and Paul called the Ledbetter clinic. He got a nurse. "Bring him down," she said. "We'll put him in a croup tent. That's always helped before."

It always did help. Blackie called back before Paul Alexander could leave the house. The nurse had called him. "Come on down," he said. "I'll meet you at the clinic." He hesitated. "Listen, will Stephen be there with Charles?"

"Yes."

"I think it'd be good if I called the sheriff and told him to send a patrol car by, just in case."

"Yes, that will be fine."

Paul Alexander bundled his sick son up and drove him down to the clinic. The patrol car came by a little while afterwards, the sheriff himself driving. He got out and came inside, knocking briefly at the back door and entering without waiting for a summons. Jiggs went tearing to the door, barking ferociously. When she recognized the sheriff, she nuzzled up against him, and the sheriff scratched her behind the ears. She seemed rapt.

The sheriff stood facing Charles in the kitchen. They were uncomfortable. *The last time we saw each other here, I was crying like a child.* Jiggs went under the kitchen table and fell with a heavy thump into doggy rest. She lay there when Paul Alexander sat at the table reading.

"Your father said I might swing by," the sheriff said, pushing his hat back on his head and looking around. *He's trying to avoid looking me in the eye,* Charles thought.

"Why would he do that?"

"Well, because you're here alone."

"I'm not alone. Stephen's here."

Without asking permission the sheriff walked through the kitchen and peered into the dining room and beyond the wide opening to the living room.

"I don't see him," the sheriff said.

"He's upstairs in bed. He's got a cold, too. Dad didn't take him to the clinic."

"Well, I guess things are more serious for Guy than they are for Stephen."

Silence. The sheriff took off his hat.

"Can I look at the locks on your doors?"

Charles shrugged. "Help yourself."

The sheriff went around checking the locks. "You could break into this house with a can opener," he said.

"Let's hope whoever wants to break in doesn't have a can opener," Charles said.

The sheriff laughed. Then he stopped laughing. "Charles, you're in danger. There's a crazy man out here somewhere. He knows how to hide. Hell, he may be out there in the woods right now. He wants to kill you."

"Jiggs would bark if somebody were in the woods," Charles said.

"Has she barked tonight?"

"Once. Then she settled down."

"Listen," the sheriff said, drawing in a deep breath, "you keep these doors locked, and you stay inside. Draw the curtains in here." They were in the living room. "What are you going to do this evening?"

"I'm going to read a book," Charles said. *It will be quiet. Guy will not be here. The radio will not be blasting away from upstairs. Quiet. Peaceful.*

"You're not going out?"

"No."

"And you've got the dog."

"Yes, I have Jiggs."

"Okay," the sheriff said. "I'll have deputies come by every hour and check things out."

"You don't have to do that," Charles said.

Charles sat alone in the living room. He held a book. But his mind could not focus on it. *Everybody in the county thinks I'm a coward. Why not? I am a coward.*

The knock at the back door came softly, surreptitiously. Charles jumped in the chair as if he had been touched by an electric wire on the back of the neck. His heart raced. The large window in the dining room that looked out to the western woods had the curtain drawn. His mother had died in a hospital bed set next to that window. From it he could see the back door that led into the kitchen. The windows in the kitchen did not have curtains.

He drew the curtain gently. *He can shoot when he sees the motion.* His hands trembled. He used two fingers to part the curtain at the side, thinking that an assailant would expect him to part it in the middle. It was Rosy, standing there like a large shadow. She tapped again. He was shaking.

He went briskly to the door, thinking that if he walked briskly he would not be shaking when she saw him. "Rosy," he said in a tone of reproach. "What are you doing here?"

"I wanted to see you," she said.

"Come in. Come in," he said.

"We haven't seen you in such a long time."

No, they had not seen him in a while, and he thought he should tell her why.

"Sit down," he said, leading her into the curtained living room.

Rosy had tears in her eyes. "Daddy thinks you are about to change your story. What you saw that night. He thinks you are about to lie. He thinks you can't bear to face him when you're about to tell a lie. To face us."

"He worries that much about a lie?"

"He says that if you lie now, you will never be a preacher. He thinks something will be lost in God's plan for you. For all of us."

Charles very nearly laughed. It was all preposterous, he thought, and nothing added up to mean something he could get his hands on. He lied with a practiced sincerity.

"Rosy, I have stopped coming to church because nobody can look at me now and see just me. I'm like someone with a disease who has lost all his identity except the disease. I make people uncomfortable. And people make me uncomfortable because I know they are uncomfortable."

He went on. He managed gently to change the subject and to talk about her. She had a friend in school, another girl who had come from somewhere else, and the two of them resolved that they would be friends even if all the other girls in the school thought they were drips. He remembered that word: "drips." People thought Rosy was a drip. People thought her friend was a drip. The friend's name was Beatrice, and she had a lovely smile, and she and Rosy talked to each other about all the things they liked to do, and they went for walks together and ate lunch together, and Beatrice saw movies and told Rosy about them, and Rosy explained that her father would not let her see movies, but she thought it was all right to go to movies herself as long as people didn't see naked men and women who cursed and smoked cigarettes, and Beatrice said there were lots of movies like that.

On this evening Mr. Finewood, too, was sick with a cold, and he had gone to bed early. That was how Rosy slipped away. "I'd better take you home," Charles said.

"I can go by myself," she said. "I walked down through the woods."

"You shouldn't do that now," he said vaguely, thinking of Missionary.

"There's nothing to hurt me in the woods," she said. "I'm not afraid of the dark. I was not even afraid to walk down the edge of the graveyard."

"Well, let me walk you back."

"Oh, that would be nice, Charles. Very nice."

He thought afterwards that his sudden proposal was bravado. Somewhere out there in the dark, maybe near, maybe far, a murderer with a taste for torture waited for him. But Charles fought off the nightmare that welled up around him, and he discovered a calm that left him quietly surprised. He put on a jacket and helped Rosy on with her coat, and they went out together, letting Jiggs run before them happily.

The moon was down and the night was very dark, with a sprinkling of stars across a hazily clouded sky, and the forest was still with the wintry cold. The path, beaten hard with the footsteps of many years, led out the back door and across to the edge of the upper field and then up along the border of the woods, and at a large oak tree it bent into the deep shadow of the forest. Rosy reached out and felt for Charles's hand, and he held it, noting how warm it was in the chilly air.

"I've told Beatrice all about you," Rosy said. "I've told her what a friend you are to me, and she says I'm the luckiest girl in the world to have a friend like you."

"You should bring her by the newspaper office sometime," Charles said. When they spoke, he heard the detonations of their words in the vastness of the night.

Jiggs suddenly ran off into the dark. "Jiggs!" Charles called. They heard her race down the hill among the trees, and she was gone. They paused for a moment. Charles could feel the beating of Rosy's pulse in the hand he held. It was calm and slow.

They walked on, feeling their way easily along the path. The silence of the woods began to seem eerie to Charles.

"Beatrice eats too much," Rosy said. "I tell her sometimes that we both need to go on a diet. I guess you've never thought of going on a diet, have you, Charles? You're so thin. I wish Daddy would go on a diet. He's not as fat as he used to be. Mama used to say that Daddy was dangerous to all the furniture. He was sitting at the table one time and a chair broke under him. He didn't lean back or anything. The chair just broke, and he fell down. I'm afraid that might happen to Beatrice, but she laughs. That's what Daddy did when the chair broke. He laughed. Mama didn't think it was funny."

Charles wanted to ask Rosy about her mother. But he did not. It would be like opening a closet onto something terrible you didn't want to see. The path turned, and they turned with it, and they were out of the woods, and the graveyard was to their left. The familiar stones cropped out of the ground, dark shapes in the dark night. When he was a child the graveyard gave Charles a creepy feeling. He had long since lost it. He knew so many people in the graveyard now, people only names on stone. His mother was there, in the southeast corner. He could walk in the graveyard at night, and his mother would not harm him.

They walked around the sprawling church. People wondered why Mr. Finewood stayed at Midway Baptist. A couple of pulpit committees had appeared to hear him. You could always tell a pulpit committee—six or seven self-important strangers sitting in the back of the church together, swollen with the power they bore in their collective selves. No, he said. His work at Midway was not yet done.

At the driveway leading down to the parsonage, Charles paused. "Rosy, you shouldn't come out in the dark like this now. A man who means to harm is loose somewhere around here. He might hurt you."

"I have not done anything to hurt him," Rosy said. "But Daddy says he may try to hurt you."

"Your father told you that?"

"Yes. He's worried about you, Charles. He wishes you would come to see him. He's afraid you're angry with him for something."

"What makes him think that?"

"You don't come to see us anymore."

"I have some things to work out."

Rosy took both his hands. "Charles, keep telling the truth. No matter what happens. Keep telling the truth." Her voice was earnest. He thought it might be quavering.

"You think the truth is that important?"

"Charles, when you don't tell the truth, it's—" She could not finish. She flung his hands away and raced down the driveway to the house. He heard her footsteps diminish on the gravel and then the door open softly and close.

He considered going back down the road and walking to the highway and then down the hill to the drive that led up to his house. But he was troubled by the mystery of Jiggs. Where had the dog gone? It was unlike her to run away from him.

He made the transit around the front of the church, saw its tall columns looming darkly at him from the porch and the imprint of the steeple above him against the night sky. He turned down through the woods, and he heard the panting of his dog ahead of him, running towards him. Jiggs bounded against him, almost knocking him down. She was a substantial and joyful dog. Charles bent and scratched her behind the ears, and she rolled happily against him.

"Where were you?" he said.

He walked on into the woods and along the path, and he stopped. He stood for a moment in the shadow of an oak, and he listened. Had he heard something? He was not sure. His heart pounded, and the cold bit into his clothes and came up along his skin. He stood for a long time. Nothing, he decided. He walked on, carefully and softly.

He had then an eerie rush of feeling, something that came down his back like a chill and made him shudder. He felt a presence in the woods, something there besides himself. Something human. He stopped again and listened until he thought his ears must hurt from the effort. Nothing but the presentiment of something.

He walked on, and he *knew* that he was being followed, not knowledge in some auditory or visual confirmation of the warning some sixth sense sent coursing through his body, but still knowledge. He walked on carefully, taking a step, listening, taking a step again. Jiggs was at his heels. Would she attack anyone who attacked him? Or would she run away to save herself? He lacked the trust in dogs of those sentimental people who converted canines into some four-legged version of the human race. A dog was a dog.

At the marker tree at the edge of the upper field, he turned down towards the house, and he walked towards the lights gleaming from windows below. He veered away from the path, walking out in the field where, he knew, the wheat waited beneath the soil, not far from the month when it would sprout and offer a sheen of pale green to the wintry landscape. He wanted to leave space between himself and the woods if something leaped out of the dark there. But he came to the back door of the house unmolested, took his key and let himself and Jiggs inside, and realized how hard his heart was pounding and how frightened he was. But he had done it. He had, he thought, proved something to himself.

In only a few minutes the patrol car came grinding up the driveway, and two deputies got out and came to the back door and knocked. Charles assured them that all was well. He did not tell them that he had been out of the house.

*B*OURBON County passed through a crazy house of terror. Some people left town. Ken McNeil and his family felt the need for an extended vacation in New York City. The sheriff told Charles Alexander he ought to do the same thing. Charles refused.

Commonplace things became sinister. Was that sound in the dark the natural shrinking of wood after the heat of the day, or was it a footstep? Any solitary stranger stopping for coffee at Bessie May Hancock's cafe on his way north or south, supposing that Bourbonville was a pleasant little town, found himself scrutinized by unfriendly eyes. If he was a big man, somebody sat down beside him and asked what he was doing there. The question lacked any friendliness. The stranger left irate, sometimes followed out to his car where somebody else took his license-plate number. On farms men went in groups of twos and threes to do their chores, all armed with shotguns, all of them afraid. The sheriff said later that he never got an accurate count of cows shot to death or gravely wounded because somebody fired before he looked.

The sheriff and his deputies and the highway patrolmen and the local national guard searched the forests around Bourbonville. The sheriff knew how vast the surrounding forests were. Anyone flying low into the Knoxville airport at Alcoa across the river could have seen how even in 1954 settlement in East Tennessee seemed to be enclaves of town and field set amid forests with waves of ridge.

Not many people flew in 1954. Those who did looked on the forest as natural decoration and had no idea what it was to tramp through it, hear its noises and its quiet, and fear it. The big timber had been logged out years before. But nature replenishes herself with a tough and miraculous quickness, complete with dense patches of undergrowth, grapevine and honeysuckle thicket. The simpleminded notion that heavily armed men could find Missionary and snap him up like a rabbit in a trap thrust men into a land they thought they knew and discovered they did not. They found themselves baffled by its miles and miles of trees and its wintry silence and its windy and loquacious whispering so that they were reduced and awed and frightened. Their imaginations translated the inharmonious shout of a crow or the scamper of a squirrel in the high timber to premonitions of violent death or to the fantasy that these were the last sounds they would hear before a bullet smashed into their heads. Stony ridges gave way to almost impenetrable defiles, and ledges of great rock provided lairs where a man skilled at living in the woods could hide and observe pursuit and get away in plenty of time.

The bluffs along Fort Bourbon Lake and the river below the dam held caves in the limestone rock, and in one of them a guardsman found the remains of a fire, some empty food cans, and a note: "Give up. You won't catch me, and until Hope Kirby is free, I shall kill at my leisure." It was unsigned. It was in Missionary's handwriting. How did he travel? You got to the caves by precarious trails among broken rock where no car could go. The sheriff mused over all these things. Something was missing, he thought. But what?

There was a Tennessee Bureau of Investigation by this time, and some of its agents went to the prison in Nashville and quizzed Hope Kirby minutely about how his band had lived in the Philippines. Hope answered all their questions. He added his own commentary. "You hain't going to find him. He can be like a ghost when he wants to be. He can live on next to nothing, and he can move so quiet that if you put him down by a bear, the bear would seem to stomp through the woods."

Jane Whitaker was angry, more angry than ever. Her face seemed harder than it had been. In her thirties she began to look older. She avoided conversations except about mortgages, liens, cash disbursements, promissory notes, car loans, and late payments. The mall was dead, and rumors floated wildly about how much money she had caused the bank to lose.

On the telephone to someone thirty days in arrears on a note, she could sound ready to throw a family into the street and order into jail everybody involved in this insult to the bank, this cavalier dereliction of the most sacred obligation in human civilization—to pay one's honest debts. Her temper was like a volcanic fire blazing beneath a thin, hard crust. If anyone stepped on the crust, it broke.

She became an outlet for the town's fear and its anger at being afraid. People found reasons to mock her, sometimes to insult her. Some who did not owe her money struck up conversations about her when she passed by on the street, speaking loud enough for her to hear them. She stalked on like a tiger on the hunt, uninterested in snakes. Once somebody said, "I'd say Lloyd died just so he wouldn't have to marry the bitch." That brought her around, face as red as molten iron. She met an insolent grin, whirled, and walked on. It was enough. After that lots of people talked about Lloyd whenever she was near.

She appeared in the sheriff's office, her face red with fury and her mouth fixed in a tiger's hungry snarl. "I want to know why you're keeping a county patrol car up at the Alexander house every night."

"Because I know this crazy man called Missionary wants to kill Charles Alexander," the sheriff said.

"What about me? I'm living alone out in the country. Don't you think I'm in danger too? What the hell's going to stop that lunatic if he decides to come after me? Where's *my* patrol car?"

"There's no reason for him to kill you," the sheriff said. "You didn't have anything to do with this case."

"How the hell do you know? If you knew anything about him, you dumb son of a bitch, you'd catch him. He can rape me, cut me up in pieces, kill me, and who's to stop him?"

"Miss Whitaker," the sheriff said, holding on to his temper with the restraint towards women learned through the osmosis of living in the South. He took a deep, careful breath. "I am operating with a limited force. I don't control an army. The county National Guard is working with us now. That's eighty men. That still ain't enough to protect ever' soul in the county. Right now I've got to guess who's likely to be next on that man's list, and I feel damned sure it ain't you. I'm guessing that this Missionary feller is going after them men that was directly part of the trial. The jurors. Charlie Alexander. Ken McNeil, but he's left the county. I'll give you my advice. Buy yourself a 'thirty-two automatic and learn to use it. Get yourself a big dog."

This advice almost gave Jane Whitaker apoplexy. She called the sheriff every insulting name she knew. When she called him a coward, he felt like getting up and slapping her. Better still, he wished she'd been in the Ardennes so he could make her run out of a foxhole and race across the snow in front of a German machine gun.

"Let him try to rape the bitch," the sheriff thought. "He'd probably break his dick off."

To Charles Alexander on the public street, she yelled, "Are you such a coward that you can't take care of yourself? Don't you have some friends who can help you guard your place? Do you have to monopolize the whole sheriff's department?"

She unleashed these words in a tirade of questions exploding one after another and carrying their own answers of cowardice, humiliation, and self-ishness. Charles looked at her with an indifference so intense that she became only more angry, and he said not a word. The only satisfaction he gave himself was to stand with folded arms, staring at her as though she might have been a freak in the circus, until she had run down and with a mighty swirl of her body strode away.

Something happened in Bourbon County, and Jane could not see what it was. People were desperately afraid. But along with the fear came something else—some irrational sense of solidarity, of community, and people like Jane and others isolated themselves by becoming the center of their own universe. If Missionary did decide to kill her, not everyone supposed that it would be a bad thing. A few even said so. Many thought it, and the sheriff did not lose any friends by his refusal to send a patrol car to guard her house. Somebody yelled at her on the street, "Hey, Jane, if that Missionary feller tries to hurt you, just look at him. You'll turn him to stone." She walked on, every step pulsating with hatred.

The end of January came, and February started with occasional mild days surging with the hope that winter was over and done, hope quickly broken by cold fronts blowing over the land with a perverse and rowdy glee and bringing back gloomy presentiments of eternal cold. Life went on tense and guarded, but as the weeks passed and nothing happened, the litany of habit asserted itself in the way that people afflicted with a dire and painful disease will find their condition unreal when for a while the symptoms subside. A lunatic could not be predicted. Perhaps Missionary had taken his satisfaction by killing a couple of people, and he had gone away. Perhaps he had been moved by the appeal Hope Kirby made to him through the newspapers. "Missionary, please stop killing people. Come in. Give yourself up. I don't want anybody else killed." Hope told Hugh Bedford what to say, and Hugh wrote it in good English. People brought up on war movies with saccharine endings could believe that Missionary might read such an appeal and be converted and come in to surrender. Rise of sentimental music and Missionary throwing his gun away and walking in with his hands up, his eyes filled with tears as he thought about his mother. In fact nobody knew whether Missionary had a gun.

Then people woke up on Valentine's Day, a Sunday morning, and discovered that another juror had been murdered. For the males in the county this was the most horrible murder yet.

He was a scraggly farmer with no teeth, not even false teeth, six spindly kids, a tubercular wife, fifty acres of infertile land called Nubbin Ridge because when you planted corn there, only nubbins would grow on its shallow and rocky soil. His three-room clapboard house lacked electricity and running water. It sat lopsided on four piles of stones, one at each corner, so that flea-ridden hounds slept under the house in summer and permeated the rooms with the stink of unwashed dog, and in winter, when the dogs slept in the barn, the cold seeped up through the thin floor. He had a barn never whitewashed, the tin roof disintegrating in blotches of cancerous rust. He ran a bunch of undernourished pigs and cows. He had a tobacco allotment, a corn crib, a smokehouse, and a weed-choked front lawn littered with broken bottles and worn toys inherited from charity, and amid a pile of ashes an iron kettle for boiling clothes reposed obdurate and ugly, a throwback to a time when an iron kettle was sign and symbol of wealth in a world of primitively enduring frontiersmen.

His name was Zora Toulmin. How did a man get a name like Zora? Some whim of a drunken father, or was it an ancestral recollection from a heroic age? No one knew. The children in the household were testimony to a manly regularity in exercising one of the oldest biological pleasures. Otherwise his life seemed to be an unending round of baffled labor for pitiful reward. His wife coughed blood, and years before, when Dr. Youngblood examined her in Bourbonville one Saturday morning when she had managed to slip away from her husband, he said that she had TB, and she should go to a special clinic to be treated. He knew her husband would never permit her to leave home. Dr. Youngblood also suggested that she might use a jelly to kill her husband's sperm lest she conceive another tuberculosis-prone waif. When she slowly came to understand his elliptical words, she turned red. She did not stop having children. Each one seemed more frail than the last.

Toulmin lived obdurately confined within his rotting and tumbledown rail fences that were overgrown with honeysuckle and briars, and he toiled in resigned and mute industry at wrenching subsistence from his cursed fields. He had no time or energy for the rudimentary social life of church on Sunday or Saturdays in town. The second social act that anyone knew Toulmin had committed outside his own small bailiwick was to serve on the jury that had condemned Hope Kirby. The first public act was to venture to a nearby schoolhouse every four years to cast his vote for the Republican candidate for president of the United States. His name appeared on the voting rolls of the county and therefore had subjected him to jury duty.

The opposing lawyers questioned him, and he expressed complete ignorance of Kelly Parmalee, of Abby Kirby, of Hope Kirby, and the murders. "I don't get a newspaper because I can't read, and if I could I wouldn't waste money on no newspaper, and we don't have no radio." He was the ideal juror. He knew nothing about anything. He cared for nothing, and he came because the sheriff's deputies went to his farm and read him the summons to jury duty from a paper that to him seemed official and therefore threatening.

Thomas Rhodes, another juror, told Joe Marks that Toulmin had been for acquittal. The jury deliberated for such a long time because Toulmin had to be argued down. Toulmin had no respect for Judge Yancy. He said that if he caught his own wife fucking another man, he would kill her like a shoat. The reason was simple economics. "If she fucked another man and got a kid from him," Toulmin said, using the vulgar Anglo-Saxon word as unselfconsciously as he might have said "eat" or "see" or "smell," "I'd have to raise her bastard, and not know the little whelp ain't mine."

Rhodes, whose nickname was "Rocky," although it might have been "Dusty," spoke in fearful regret. He had persuaded Toulmin to change his mind. All the other jurors said so. They blamed Rhodes. The other jurors tremblingly washed their hands in public over Hope Kirby's conviction, loudly blamed Rhodes for swaying them all, spoke in frantic self-exculpation to the reporters, and claimed feverishly that they had wanted to vote for acquittal. Rhodes persuaded them otherwise. Rhodes was for justice!

The sheriff vomited when he found Toulmin. Blackie Ledbetter did not vomit, because he had seen at close quarters the infinity of ways the human body can be cut up or pounded to pieces by the impact of varied pieces of the physical universe. One of Toulmin's milch cows did not come in for the evening milking. She did not come in because she had been butchered at the back of his place. When Toulmin found her, the murderer found him. He was tied to a tree. His penis with its testicles—the entire external genital equipment—had been sliced off and forced into his mouth, and his mouth had been taped shut so he could not spit them out. Toulmin had choked to death on vomit and his own genitals. The killer had pinned a note on exqui-site paper to Toulmin's shirt. "Things will keep getting worse until Hope Kirby is set free." After that the terror that descended on Bourbon County was a plague that struck everybody down.

The governor sent in more state troopers, members of the highway patrol in their black-and-tan Fords, and he called out the National Guard from Harriman not far from Bourbonville. A hundred more men. What were they to do? They drove up and down the back roads of the county, two men to a car, one man carrying a shotgun, sometimes followed by cars filled with reporters as if the murderer would suddenly appear as a hitchhiker to flag down a highway patrol car and surrender.

At night, everything in Bourbonville shut down. Curfew was set at eight o'clock. National Guardsmen dressed in combat fatigues marched up and down the streets in parties of four, their carbines and M-1 rifles at the ready, witless with terror, ready to shoot any cat that moved.

Arceneaux watched them from his own house with cynical detachment. He thought of how he would set up ambushes to slaughter them, and he felt uneasy guilt at his pleasure in imagining it. The deacons of the First Baptist Church followed the lead of other churches in town, declaring to Arceneaux that for the duration of the emergency Sunday-night services should be can-celed and that the Wednesday-night prayer meetings should also be omitted. Even the most religious people were happy to stay at home.

Bourbonville became a ruined city, shut up like a besieged fortress. Fami-lies locked their doors and stacked heavy furniture in front of them. Men sat with shotguns loaded and waited in the dark and went to sleep and woke up shouting when they heard a noise. Families who still used a privy would not think of going out there in the dark, and the hardware stores sold out of slop jars, and some Bourbonvillians used milk pails to relieve themselves in the middle of the night.

Three days after Toulmin's murder, the sheriff got a call. "Sheriff, do you know who this is?"

The sheriff sat bolt upright. "Yes, you murdering, cowardly son of a bitch, I know who this is."

"Oh, Sheriff. Names. Names. Only words. They do not signify anything when you use them to insult people. 'Sticks and stones may break my bones . . .' You know the proverb."

"I don't know enough words to tell you what a low-down coward you are."

"Very good. Very good. I told you we were playing a game."

"You're crazy. Do you know you're crazy?"

"Craziness is in the eye of the beholder, Sheriff. People said the Apostle Paul was crazy. But look what he accomplished. I must say the game is not very interesting."

"So why don't you quit playing it?"

"Oh, Sheriff. I'm not someone to quit until I have clearly won. When Hope Kirby walks out of prison, I shall have won, and you and all those like you in the state will be humiliated. That is the end of my game. I am going to give you an advantage. You know, as in chess."

"I've never played chess," the sheriff said, furious with himself for being alone in the jail, furious for not thinking that Missionary would call, for not being set to trace the call like cops on radio and in the movies. "I don't care for dumb games like chess. It's a game for idiots."

"Yes, yes, you are a practical man," the silky voice said. "But I am a player. I ask you to think one thing, Sheriff. It will make the game more interesting. Think of the alphabet." The caller hung up. The sheriff heard the click.

The alphabet. Judge Yancy. Wyatt. Toulmin. The sheriff thought. The alphabet. He sat up. He was not stupid. He thought. If Missionary was moving backwards through the alphabet, the next juror on his list would be Rocky Rhodes.

Rhodes had three hundred and fifty acres of some pretty good land below Bourbonville on the south bank of the river, not far from the Monroe County line. He worked it well, and he had standing in the community, the sort of man people expected to take the lead because he expected to take the lead himself. He had an opinion about everything, and he delivered his thoughts with the certainty of a man who never doubted that he was superior to others because God had made him that way.

His hair had been coal-black when he was young, and when it turned, it became snow-white, almost a glowing white you might say, coarse and not needing any pomade to stay in place on his head. He seemed to have been ordained by God to look the part of the Southern gentleman even if he did not own thousands of acres of land. Still, in East Tennessee three hundred and fifty acres made a good lot of ground, and the combination of his land, his industry, and his way of carrying himself made most people in the county grant him the place of leadership that he considered his own. Sheriff Myers thought he was a horse's ass, but the sheriff found posterior equine resemblances in many of the higher sort in Bourbon County, and he did not express these opinions in ways that would lose him votes, which is to say that he did not express them at all.

Despite his secret contempt for Rocky Rhodes, the sheriff was disappointed at how the man dissolved in fear when the sheriff and Arceneaux went to his house and told him he was probably next on the list to be killed because his name began with an R. "My mother's maiden name was Anderson," Rocky Rhodes blurted out as though by speaking this meaningless detail he might guarantee himself immunity from death.

"We'll put a guard around the house, Mr. Rhodes," the sheriff said. "We'll do the best we can. But you ought to know what you're up against."

Rocky Rhodes trembled while he and the sheriff talked, trembled and his teeth chattered. His wife was a sharp-faced woman with a tongue to match. "Why haven't you caught him yet, Sheriff?" she asked in furious indignation. "It seems to me that you shouldn't rest until you have that lunatic in jail. What's the world coming to when a man can do things like that and the sheriff can't do anything but come and tell us that we're in danger?"

"Mrs. Rhodes, I've got fourteen men on your place right now. We've got enough guns to hold off all the Indians you ever seen in the movies. But this man was a guerrilla fighter in the war, ma'am. He knows how to kill and get away. We're doing the best we can, but you know what happened to those other men, and you need to be careful." Rocky Rhodes blanched. The sheriff went away. If Rocky Rhodes had been in the Ardennes, the sheriff could not have been more embarrassed by him.

He deputized men and set them to patrolling the Rhodes farm in threes and fours, armed with pump shotguns. He did not trust pistols in the hands of men as frightened as these men were. With a shotgun you could point it in the direction of your target and usually hit something even if you were scared shitless when you pulled the trigger. With a pistol most people couldn't hit a tree in the middle of a woods, and if they were scared shitless they might shoot their balls off. Night after night and day after day the men walked patrol like actors posing for movie cameras. Rocky Rhodes refused to come out of his house. Neighbors milked his cows and brought him food under guard by men with guns.

The sheriff drove around to the homes of the Kirby men. By some sure instinct he knew that none of them was sheltering Missionary. Still, he drove around to see them all in the same nervous exasperation with which a man who has lost his car keys will look time and again in the same drawer, opening it, closing it, looking somewhere else, coming to it yet again, opening it, looking, closing it, annoyed with himself for the futility of his actions.

The Kirby men welcomed him inside their homes with bashful indifference. They sat uncomfortably with their families. John Sevier was staying with Love, now and then drinking coffee silently but most of the time staring off into space like a dummy in a shop window. "Where's your daddy?" the sheriff asked Love.

Love turned red when somebody he didn't know well spoke to him. He turned red at the sheriff's question. "He didn't tell us."

"And you didn't ask him where he was going?"

"We hain't never asked Pappy questions," Love said.

"Can you tell me anything that might give me a clue?"

"He taken his cow over to Joye's," Love said.

Damn, the sheriff thought. But he didn't say anything.

He went by Roy Kirby's house, but Roy was never at home. Everything was neat and in order, the doors unlocked. Roy Kirby was from a culture that did not lock its doors, that could not lock its doors because it owned no locks, that would not lock its doors because shutting the house against somebody who might need to come in was inhospitable. The sheriff stepped inside, knowing he was there without a warrant. He also knew that if Roy Kirby found him there, the mountain man would say, "Have a seat, Sheriff. Cup of coffee?" No sign of him anywhere. Puzzling.

He put the same questions to all the Kirby men. He got the same answers. They had not seen their father in weeks. The Kirby boys told them their daddy had not hinted at where he was going or what he planned to do. The sheriff thought they were telling the truth.

"What if the two of them, that old man and Missionary, are in cahoots together?" the sheriff said doubtfully to Arceneaux.

"If they say they don't know where he is, they don't know where he is," Arceneaux said.

Hugh Bedford agreed.

"All right," the sheriff said. "I don't believe it neither. But tell me something. Either you boys ever been wrong about something you knowed to be right?"

"We're not wrong about this," Arceneaux said. Arceneaux could be irritating—that aristocratic bearing. *He's always been a boss,* the sheriff thought.

"Missionary and Roy Kirby are not the kind to work together," Hugh said.

"They's lots of folks that would say you two ain't the kind to work together," the sheriff said, pushing his hat back.

"We won't do it again," Hugh said with a grim laugh. "I don't think Preacher Arceneaux would take some of the cases I've taken."

"Christ took the part of one thief on the cross," Arceneaux said.

"That was because he didn't know a damned thing about him," Hugh said.

*O*N *THE* third Friday in March, Blackie Ledbetter woke up in his room at the top of the stairs to his father calling from the downstairs room where they'd moved his mother when she had the stroke. "Brian! Brian!"

Blackie was instantly awake, and in his underwear he went to the head of the stairs and called down. "Yes? What, Father? What?"

He heard a sob. "It's your mother." His father's voice broke in a fit of coughing. "I think—" Blackie hurried down the stairs and found him standing by the hospital bed where his mother lay. His father slept on an old, simple army cot next to her. In the night he tended to her.

Juliet breathed in a faint, shallow panting, eyes shut and pale mouth agape as if she had seen something startling in a dream. Jim Ed was weeping, not sobbing, but standing there with both big hands clasped on the steel railing of the hospital bed, looking at her, tears rolling down his craggy face. Blackie felt the pulse on the side of her neck. It was feathery and erratic. He lifted an eyelid with his thumb. The eye was rolled back in her head, and he knew she had had another stroke. He also knew that she was dying. He put his hand on his father's shoulder. He felt how thin it was. He bowed his head and shut his eyes and felt his own world dissolve as worlds will sometimes in the middle of the night when a man's juices are low and he is undefended against time and death. Jim Ed stood for a moment, looking down at his wife. Then he pulled himself away and went to the telephone in the hallway and called Paul Alexander.

"She loved both of us," he said to his bewildered son. "We both loved her."

Paul Alexander arrived in remarkable haste, racing his green 1950 Chevy dangerously up the curving driveway through the avenue of oaks that had guarded the house for more than a century. They could hear the gravel flying behind the car.

Paul Alexander came to the bedside, looked down at Juliet, saw the ultimate truth on her gaunt and unconscious face, and wept softly. Blackie was astonished. He had known Paul Alexander all his life, Paul Alexander a part of things, irrevocable as the courthouse or the depot or the car works or the steel rails and the sidings where the rust-colored boxcars and gondolas came—Paul Alexander quiet, unemotional, almost impassive, trailing behind him an impression forged by what people thought they knew of him, an impression shaped long ago in the fading collective memory of almost four decades before with his mysterious advent into Bourbonville and his settling here to become a fixture of the county.

Paul Alexander and Blackie's father stood side by side, Paul gripping Jim Ed's arm. Blackie had one of those occasional epiphanies that come randomly and always in startling surprise to children, the jarring revelation that parents inhabit a chamber of memory that the children find hermetically sealed against them. Within that chamber the parents are forever something mysteriously and utterly different from what the children know.

Stephen came shortly afterwards in his pickup truck, arriving even before Paul Ledbetter got there from his house on the lake. Stephen out of intuition or instinct or habit or for the more simple fact that his language was music brought his father's mandolin and his own guitar. A little later Charles came, bringing Guy, driving the '37 Ford. Guy shambled sleepily through the door, holding a yellow wood pencil in his hand, a black Bible that he could not read in the other, his eyes crossed and his round face bewildered with sleep and pensive as if some dark shade of impending death had penetrated even his murky sequence of thoughts. He looked into the bed and whispered, "Is she dead?" Stephen put an arm around him and led him away, whispering something, and Guy said in a loud and whining voice, "Quit telling me to be quiet." Stephen steered him into the kitchen and made him sit down, and they could hear Stephen's quiet voice calming him.

Charles came in weary and frustrated with Guy because Guy did not want to get out of bed. He sat down in the corner of the room where the body lay, his head back against the wall. He did not come much to the Ledbetter place nowadays. In childhood he had come obediently on Sunday afternoons during the seemingly interminable years when a kid obeys his parents and goes where they go because it is unthinkable that children be left alone, and besides, the parents are bigger than the child.

Blackie and Charles had nothing to say to each other. Blackie did not like Charles, had never liked him, never tried to hide his dislike, suspected that the boy's deafness to rhythm was feigned. How could anybody not understand rhythm? It was born in humankind with the heartbeat. Stubbornly and perversely Charles wanted to hurt Paul Alexander, Blackie thought. For years Paul Alexander persisted, hoping Charles would catch music by being infected with its delights. Nothing worked. In obstinate tantrums Charles pushed the mandolin away or else took it up and deliberately swept his fingers across the strings in discords and refused to learn.

When he was twelve or thirteen, he found other things to do on Sunday afternoons, and he rarely appeared at the Ledbetter house. Nobody begged him to come anymore. Then he was sixteen, old enough to have a driver's license, and sometimes he came alone to visit Juliet. She always had time for him.

They sat in the kitchen talking. They laughed. It was hard to laugh with Eugenia. She talked about serious things—the Antichrist, the Second Coming, the Millennium. Juliet joked with Eugenia. "I think you spend too much time thinking about what God is going to do," she said. "I'd rather think of all the beautiful things God has done now."

Charles brought Marlene down to meet her. Marlene was the proper Bible College Student. She gave her testimony. She said she thanked God every night for Charles and the Bible school and her parents and all the good things the Lord had given her. Marlene also praised the Lord for her voice, and when Juliet asked her to sing, she sang, and it was all very beautiful, and Charles was happy.

Afterwards Juliet told him she thought Marlene was beautiful and sang like an angel, but he should choose a girl who could talk about something other than "the Lord." Charles was crushed. How could anybody criticize his beloved? He was at that age. Juliet had the stroke before Marlene broke off with him. Juliet always said, "Give Charles time. He will be all right." He had had time, Blackie thought. He was still a stubborn ox. There he stood, looking solemnly at Juliet whose tortured breath came and went in gasps, and it was hard to see if he had any feeling on his face or not.

Paul Ledbetter did medical things to his mother as if Blackie had not done them already. He felt his mother's pulse, laying a hand gently against her neck. He lifted an eyelid and looked at the eye turned up in her skull as if she had no iris at all. He faced the others and shrugged helplessly, and his eyes filled with tears. In a little while Jim Ed picked up a guitar almost absentmindedly, the way someone will do spontaneously an act forged and tempered by long habit, and he ran his fingers along the strings and tightened them and sampled the frets. The notes drifted out into the silence, and as though conditioned by them Paul Alexander, Stephen, Paul Ledbetter, and Blackie himself took up their instruments, striking the strings randomly, quietly, until Jim Ed began to play softly an old ballad, and the music drifted harmoniously into the room, filling the quiet, and Guy came back in and stood before them beating time with his pencil as if he were the leader of the band. Juliet's breathing seemed to quieten. Maybe they imagined it.

Charles sat down in a chair and looked off into space, lifting his eyes to the tall painting done from a photograph of a Confederate soldier above the fireplace. Charles knew the young man's name. Samuel Beckwith. His young and solemn face had long been dust. He had lain in the Methodist graveyard by the river since 1870. On this morning before an early spring dawn, he seemed to be the sign of all that death took away. Charles had absorbed from Jim Ed and from Paul Alexander the recollection of the older Brian Ledbetter, Blackie's namesake, who remembered the man who was now only a portrait, remembered him in flesh and blood. His laughter filled a room, Brian Ledbetter said. Jim Ed had passed on the tale from his father of the youthful death of this stern-looking young man and of a son who disappeared and a wife who went mad. Charles visited his grave and wrote a story about him. Charles sat looking up at the portrait in profound and solemn meditation, and the music flowed on around him. Only a couple of dim lamps were on, and the people in the room seemed insubstantial. Only the blackness in his heart seemed to have weight. The room seemed filled with almost-visible ghosts. Bob Saddler seemed to be standing near him. So did his mother. Yet he knew that they were not there. He was very tired.

So they remained as the dawn came and a silver light poured over fields and woodland that were themselves at that pregnant moment when spring bursts across East Tennessee.

Around dawn the telephone rang. A neighbor had heard the cars in the night. Word spread as it does when death announces itself in a country community. Neighbors came in, and the room filled with quiet and watching people. Women brought food. Somebody made coffee, and the sacramental smell drifted heavily through the house. Charles sat apart, trying to hide by saying as little as he could. But people spoke to him. They wanted to know how he felt now. They wanted to know about Missionary. They wanted to know how he felt on the night when he saw Kelly Parmalee shot down in front of his face. And was he sure, absolutely sure, that the man he saw out there was Hope Kirby?

He put his head back against the wall and dozed, hearing the voices murmuring in the room but hearing them as though across a valley where the sounds became scrambled together by distance. He hoped that when people saw him with his eyes closed, they would let him sleep. But no such luck. This was a morning watch for death, and driven by their wish to hide from death, people saw Charles sitting there apparently asleep, and they put out rough hands, and they declared themselves sorry to wake Charles up, but they had to know the answer to a question that had been bothering them.

The endless conversation went rolling off again, and there was no help for it. He felt as though he were talking in his sleep, and even worse, he felt that he had no control over what he was saying. He was living with fatigue the way someone learns to live with a chronic disease. One farmer said, "Well, I thought that was the way it was," and Charles had no idea what they had been talking about.

In the middle of the long afternoon, Charles told Stephen, "I'm going out to sleep in my car. Maybe people won't bother me there."

It almost worked. He put the seats down in the back of the old station wagon and crawled in, wrapped in his jacket and so weary that it did not matter whether he was chilly or not. Within an hour he was wakened by a boisterous voice saying, "Charles, ain't you cold in there?" A banging on the window, opening the door. A friendly face with a cigarette stuck in it. A man out for a smoke and spotting the person whose conversation would get the largest attention when it was spoken of. Other friendly faces appeared, and soon there was a congregation of men, most of them smoking, and conversation about the murders began again, and somebody said, "Tell me this, Charles. Are you absolutely sure Hope Kirby is the man you saw that night with the gun that killed Kelly Parmalee?" Charles was so sleepy he wanted to put his face on the steering wheel and pass out. No chance.

He was struck by inspiration. "I just remembered. I've got to do an errand for my father. I have to get some things from our house." For a moment Charles thought it wasn't going to work. A couple of the crowd expressed a desire to keep Charles company back to his house, and one mentioned Missionary. He was firm. "No, I want to drive up by myself. Missionary doesn't know where I am."

At last he escaped. He did not go inside to say goodbye to Stephen and his father. At the moment his only thought was to get away from the crowd. He wanted to sleep, too. To do that he'd have to find a place to lie down—maybe somewhere to park the station wagon in the shade. He turned up the highway towards Bourbonville. He drove like an automaton, not thinking about where he was going. It was a little after four o'clock, and Bourbonville was locked in the quiet of a weekday afternoon, people scattered in knots on the sidewalks hunched a little against the coolness that came with the decline of the sun. As he passed the First Bourbon County Bank, Jane Whitaker came out carrying her purse. She recognized the '37 Ford and stood briefly, glaring at him. Charles had a notion to jerk the middle finger of his right hand up at her, but he lacked the energy even for an obscene gesture. She turned sharply and walked on, trying (he supposed) to show her contempt by a gesture rather than yelling at him.

The City Cemetery flew by on his right, and he thought of Bob Saddler. What would resurrection be like were such an improbable event to take place? While his mother lay dying, Mr. Finewood came regularly to visit, sitting by her bed, reading the Bible, praying with her, and talking in a voluble stream of bright hope. "I tell you what I think, Sister Alexander," Mr. Finewood said. "I think when you get to paradise, there will be a garden just like Eden. Yes, the heavenly city will have streets paved with gold, but there will also be a garden with paths and wooden benches, and a beautiful stream running through it, and nothing in the garden will hurt anything else.

"And one day you will be sitting on one of those benches taking your ease, and you will see a young man walking towards you with a shining face and the sweetest smile you will ever see except the smile of the Savior himself, and he will rush to hug you and kiss you, and you will be surprised. He will be so beautiful that you will want to know him, and something about him will set a chord ringing in your heart, and all of a sudden you will know who it is. It will be Guy, and he will be the person he would have been had God not chosen for his own secret purposes to make him as we all know him. He will say 'Mother' and you will say 'Son,' and he will sit down with you, and he will explain the reasons God made him the Guy we know here. Then you will know that this brief time of suffering on earth all had a purpose, and God will make it right to you in eternity."

Eugenia lay emaciated and faint on her bed, a smile of rapture on her face, and she said softly, "Yes. Yes."

Where could he go? He thought of Missionary in an abstract way. He thought afterwards that he had been so tired that he had lacked judgment. He would go home. That was the safest place. He would sit where his mother's presence hovered in the house still, and he would imagine that she could hear him speak when he said, "I have tried so hard, Mother. I've looked for Him everywhere, and I can't find Him." He felt like crying. But he thought that if he began to cry, he would never stop.

Perhaps his mother would say to him, "I will show you the way. Follow me, and you will never doubt again."

Charles went inside and locked the doors of the house. He felt a wave of anxiety followed by a long rolling wave of peace that left him sound asleep almost as soon as he stretched himself out on his bed.

AN HOUR or so after Charles slipped away, Paul Alexander said, "Where did Charles go?"

"He went to take a nap," someone said.

"I see," Paul Alexander said. He fell back into his moody meditations, a man distracted. The afternoon dwindled.

Stephen remembered his father's face, the pain, the stillness, and only much later on when he found the manuscript his father had left did he understand it. Then it all came back to him. Paul Alexander loved Juliet. Did he love her more than he loved Eugenia? Was his love for Juliet the way he managed to live with Eugenia? These questions were unanswered. Why could his father not have spoken the things that he wrote down? An enduring enigma with no solution, nothing but the mute, neat pages of a manuscript recording his life and secrets that Charles and Stephen had never imagined. As a mild spring twilight came on, Juliet died.

The undertaker was summoned. The black hearse arrived with darkness, Glenn and J. D. Snappit efficiently asking the family to retreat into the kitchen because, J. D. said, "it's awful hard to see a loved one go out the door in a bag." In the obedience of people who can think of nothing else to do at a moment, the family and Paul and Stephen went into the kitchen, and well-meaning neighbors comforted them with coffee and food, and sat with them while the undertakers did their work. And then Juliet was gone.

The crowd moved back into the living room then. Its emptiness seemed crushing. Weeping people embraced Jim Ed and his boys. Jim Ed looked at the empty bed and wept. "I always thought she'd get better," he said. Paul Alexander stood for a moment with his arm around Jim Ed's waist. A full dark lay over the earth, and clouds moved over the sky; the forecast was for rain. Stephen looked up at the clock on the wall of the kitchen. "Where is Charles?" he said.

Somebody said, "He said he was going up to your house to get something you wanted."

"Oh my God!" Paul Alexander said. "Call the house."

Stephen had the telephone off the hook before his father's sentence was finished. In a moment he heard Charles pick up the telephone on the other end. The brothers talked a moment, and Stephen hung up.

"He's all right," he said. "He's up there alone. He's been asleep. He was more than half asleep when I talked to him."

It came on them all at once. Stephen was out the door running to his pickup in a wink. Behind him Paul Alexander called the sheriff. Meanwhile Stephen raced up the highway and rolled through Bourbonville at nearly ninety miles an hour, hoping that a Tennessee Highway Patrol car would track him with sirens going and lights flashing. He cleared Bourbonville and raced with undiminished speed through the countryside, the dark land, the trees, the houses alight on hillsides hurtling by until he topped the low ridge above Dixie Lee Junction, saw the bright red sign of the Shell filling station glowing against the sky, slid the pickup between the water maples at the end of the Alexander driveway, and pointed it upward and to the side of the house where he saw a large Buick automobile sitting, and as he bore down on his brakes, barely stopping in time to avoid striking the Buick, he heard the shot. It reverberated in the dark.

"Oh no! No! No!" he said. He raced towards the back door on foot. In the dim reflected light of the ground before the kitchen door, he saw Charles standing next to a small man who held a gun. Stephen cried out, "Charles! Charles!" He saw his brother turn slowly to look at him, and only then did he see that at Charles's feet lay a hulking figure sprawled on his back with his arms flung out. It was a heavy man, gasping for breath, and beneath his body a dark pool of blood was spreading. Nearby, on her knees and sobbing uncontrollably, was a woman. "I told that hillbilly sheriff. I told him. I told him. I told him. But no. No. He said no one would harm me. Now look what's happened!"

The man was whispering, "I only did the will of God. I am His instrument. Now I go to meet Him. I am His instrument." The three men watched him die.

The woman was Jane Whitaker. The small man with the gun was Roy Kirby.

"You saved my life," Charles said in a daze to Roy Kirby.

"You go looking for Mr. Bear, you're going to walk all over the mountains," Roy Kirby said. "You wait for Mr. Bear to come to you, and you can get him."

When the sheriff arrived with his siren screaming, Jane Whitaker was sobbing in the Buick, and when she saw the sheriff, she began to curse him. "I told you I needed protection. I told you. I told you." The Buick had Virginia license plates. It had been stolen a couple of weeks before. The doors were open, and Jane sat on the passenger side of the front seat, her arms crossed on the dashboard and her head on her arms, and she sobbed as though her whole body might break in two.

"He came to my house with a gun," she said. "I heard a knock on the back door, and I opened it, and there he was with a pistol pointed at me. He ordered me into his car. I was terrified. He told me right away that he had killed Judge Yancy, that he had killed those other men, and now he said he wanted to kill Charles, and he said he would rape me and cut my head off if I didn't do what he said. I begged him. He did not rape me, but I thought—"

She spoke in half-sentences and in sobs, struggling so hard to get her breath that the men trying to soothe her and comfort her thought she might strangle with her own terror.

"He made me call out to Charles: 'Charles, all this is your fault. You have cursed us.' "

The sheriff had some blankets in the trunk of his car, and he wrapped them around Jane. She berated him, and he remained silent. A deputy took her down to the Ledbetter clinic, and somebody gave her an injection, and she went to sleep for the night.

"I'd say one thing," the sheriff observed. "Them two, that woman and Missionary, I'd say they was almost a match for each other. Why the hell did she open her back door before looking out to see who it was?!"

Missionary was lying on his back, his eyes shut and the smallest trace of blood oozing from the corner of his mouth. He was a large man, menacing even in death. His pistol was a few inches from his right hand. He had large hands. Alive and wrapped around your neck, they could strangle you in a minute.

The sheriff took out his camera and flashbulbs and photographed the body from different angles.

"What did you shoot him with?" the sheriff asked Roy Kirby in a matter-of-fact tone.

"I used a slug in my shotgun," Roy Kirby said softly.

"Single shot?" the sheriff said.

"Hit only takes one," Roy said.

"Lord God," the sheriff said. The sheriff turned the body over. The lead slug had spread out when it hit Missionary's back, and the hole it made was a little larger than a Ping-Pong ball.

"I sure wish I'd had you on my side in France when we was fighting the Germans, Mr. Kirby," the sheriff said.

"Some of my boys was there," Roy Kirby said.

"Have you been living out there in the woods?" the sheriff asked.

"I know how to get along in ary woods that is," Roy Kirby said.

"Several weeks then."

Roy Kirby bent down and scratched Jiggs behind the ears. "This here dog come up and kept me company some of the time. I don't much care for dogs, but this air a real good dog."

The sheriff took a deep breath.

Late that night Charles knocked on the door of Hugh Bedford. Hugh came to the door in his shirtsleeves. Arceneaux stood behind him, holding a cup of coffee. They had been sitting in the kitchen with a pile of typescript on the table between them, and they had heard nothing about Missionary's death. Charles told them what had happened. Hugh poured him some coffee.

"Mr. Kirby saved my life," Charles said. "I'm ready to change my story. I'll lie. I'll say I don't know who I saw out there that night."

Hugh Bedford glowered at him. "If you had told that story in the beginning, a lot of people who are dead would still be alive, you little son of a bitch."

"Hold it, Hugh. Hold it," Arceneaux said.

Charles lowered his head. "I'm sorry," he said. "I did try to lie. I couldn't."

"Too pure, I reckon," Hugh said.

"No," Charles said softly. "Not too pure."

"Come on, Hugh," Arceneaux said gently. "You take what you can get in this old world. Let's take what we have and go with it."

"It may be too late," Hugh said gloomily. He sighed. "At least that old man has forgiven you."

Arceneaux looked up. "Are you saying Roy Kirby has forgiven Charles?"

"Why the hell else would he have done what he did? My God, he must have camped out in that woods two or three weeks waiting for Missionary to show up."

"And you think he did it because he was smitten by conscience and decided that Charles here had done the right thing, and he sat out there and killed Missionary like some star in some bunkum Hollywood movie who's had a change of heart?"

Hugh sputtered. "Well, why the hell else would he have killed him?"

"So he could kill Charles himself, you fool," Arceneaux raged. "It's Roy Kirby's honor we're talking about. He wasn't about to let Missionary take that away from him."

Hugh took a deep breath and stared at the preacher. "Jesus fucking Christ," he said. "I reckon you're right."

"I know he is," Charles said, very softly. "I knew it the minute he came out of the dark holding that shotgun."

THE FIVE Kirby men went to Nashville every Sunday to see Hope. Roy Kirby milked his one cow at five-thirty, and by six M.L. was in the driveway driving his four-door 1948 Dodge with his brothers sleepily and silently sitting there, and they were on their way. Roy had to hire a neighbor boy to milk at five-thirty in the afternoon because there was no way in those days that anybody could drive from Bourbonville to Nashville and back in twelve hours. It was two-lane blacktop nearly all the way, and the big trucks pounding over the narrow Cumberland Mountain roads made fifteen miles an hour going uphill, and in their elephantine lines they blocked everything behind them. On a Sunday you could count on making the trip over in a little under six hours; coming back at night took longer.

When they went to Nashville a few days after Pappy shot Missionary dead, they said nothing at all. A soft rain fell, and the road was slick. M.L. was cautious and drove slowly. It was warm enough to lower the windows a little. The sweet smells of the Tennessee spring rushed by. The little towns along the way were in blossom, and the parking lots of country churches were filled with old cars. In the towns they heard church bells. Joye folded his arms and dozed after a while. John Sevier looked out the window with a blank and eager attentiveness. When the air rustled his thick black hair, the broken shape of his skull showed, the bones healed but the brain behind damaged beyond repair.

By a little after noon they were in Nashville, and M.L. drove to the prison on the homing beam of habit. Its gray walls rose before them, glistening in the soft rain, grim and ugly in the American conviction that those who broke the law deserved to be exiled from beauty as Adam and Eve had been exiled from Eden. They parked and entered the visitors' entrance, patiently enduring being frisked, questioned, and yelled at, being in a place that seemed to be a collecting vat for the poor and the miserable of the earth, the sick and the hopeless, the frightened and those beyond fright who had long ago given up even the fantasy of a good outcome and accepted instead the fate of moving from moment to moment as though walking a treadmill that clanked with slow and monotonous grinding under their feet.

Finally they were in the visitors' room in the death house, and Hope sat across from them in his convict stripes looking at them with an imperturbable serenity.

"Did you have a good trip?" Hope said.

"Hit was tolerable," Pappy said.

"Spring's coming on, I reckon," Hope said.

"Hit is that," Pappy said. "We come on through a good rain. The wheat is green. The trees is leafing out a right smart, and I reckon hay has been sown."

"Hit gets to be spring a lot sooner down here in this flatland than hit done up to home," Hope said. "I can smell hit in the air, but I can't see outside except when I exercise, and even then I only see four walls and the sky."

They sat in an uncomfortable silence. A large clock ticked high on the wall. Other visitors murmured with their prisoners. Somebody in a crowd of black people laughed, and the laughter trilled briefly and was gone. Most of the prisoners on death row were black.

"You kilt Missionary, I heard," Hope said finally.

"Hit were real easy," Pappy said. "He were proud."

"He was that," Hope said with a sudden laugh.

"And he were not patient," Pappy said.

"No, he wasn't that neither," Hope said. "Why did you kill him, Pappy?"

"I reckon you know."

"I'd like to hear you tell hit," Hope said.

"I hain't in the habit of telling why I do things," Pappy said.

"He would of kilt that boy. And the woman, so I hear."

"The boy at least," Pappy said.

"Pappy, Missionary wasn't no gentleman that wouldn't kill a woman. I seen him kill women. He was crazy. I knowed that back in the Philippines. Hit were what the Japs done to his schoolteachers. Hit turned his head."

"I heard the woman tell the sheriff he planned to nail the boy's hands and feet to the wall of his house and shoot him in the belly so he'd die slow," Pappy said.

"Just like Jesus," Hope said.

"Hit were because he is a preacher boy," Pappy said.

"And you saved his life."

"You might could say I done hit."

"I know why you done hit, Pappy."

Pappy didn't say anything.

"You done hit so you can kill him yourself."

"That air my business," Pappy said.

"Hit hain't your business," Hope said. "Hit's my business."

"You air talking to your pappy, boy. You remember that. You do not talk to your pappy like that. Your business and my business hain't the same. You recollect that."

"What air you going to do about hit, Pappy? Beat me with a strap?"

"I hain't never beat you with a strap in my life, but you hain't got no right to talk to your pappy like that."

"I am talking to you now like that because I am a man just like you air a man. I don't want you to kill that boy. Hit were an accident, him coming on me like that. Later on, he couldn't help hisself. Killing him won't do nobody no good. Hit hain't going to save my life."

"I hain't gonter kill him 'lessen Lawyer can't get you off with another trial. I give you my word on that."

"Pappy, I don't want Lawyer to get me off. Without Abby, I don't want to live."

"I never thought I'd hear such talk from a boy of mine."

"Well, you're hearing hit. I done what you told me to do, and hit were the wrong thing."

"She done you wrong. You sit there and tell me you'd let your woman do you wrong like that and not do nothing about hit. What happened to your honor, boy? Where'd hit go? Did hit run off like a rabbit in the woods?"

"I don't care nothing about honor no more, Pappy. We kilt Mr. Hamilton for honor, and where did hit get us? Hit put me and John Sevier on the run for I don't know how many years, and hit put us in the army, and hit put us in the Philippines when the Japs come, and look at him now."

"What air you trying to say to me, boy?" Pappy said. His voice trembled.

"I've thought and thought about hit, Pappy, the way everthing's tied up to everthing else. What we done to Mr. Hamilton is tied up to everthing that come later. If we'd taken his offer, taken that thirty-five hundert dollars, we'd of all come down to Bourbon County, and John Sevier and me would have had Mammy's last years, and we'd of gone to the war like Love and Joye, after the Japs got us into hit, and who knows what would of happened? I know this. John Sevier and me wouldn't have been in the Philippines when the Japs come. We wouldn't of been marched out along that road like thirsty dogs being clubbed by a bunch of little yellow apes. John Sevier wouldn't of been beat with a rifle butt by one of them apes, and maybe he'd be dead now from some German or some other Jap, but he wouldn't be sitting there not knowing who we air or what he is or what was yesterday or what will be tomorrow. That's what happened when we kilt Mr. Hamilton, Pappy."

"We done what we had to do," Pappy whispered.

"No, we didn't," Hope said. "Sure, we'd of give him a little victory. But what the hell, Pappy? What the hell? Look at you now. You got a better place than we had up in the mountains. All the boys 'cepting John Sevier is a lot better off than they was then. Look what honor got us. Why the hell did we do that?"

"Don't you cuss me, boy."

"I hain't cussing you, Pappy. I'm just saying I wisht we hadn't of kilt him. I wisht I hadn't never kilt nobody in my life. Like hit was, I seen things in the war I couldn't get over. And that warn't Abby's fault. I wisht I still slept in bed with her ever' night with her warm little body pulled up to me, and my arm around her, and I wisht she was still humming her little songs around the house, and I don't care what she'd of been doing with Kelly Parmalee. I couldn't do nothing for her. You made me think hit had to matter, Pappy, but hit didn't. Hit didn't matter nothing when you think about hit."

Pappy's face was as hard as granite, and he didn't say a word.

"I love you, Pappy," Hope sobbed. He caught himself, his head bowed, and for a moment they were all silent and shocked and embarrassed, and around them swept the faint murmur of others talking, melodious voices washing distantly against them like music heard from afar, laughter and sometimes a voice lifted in preacherly prayer and a choric sound of "Amen" spoken in sweet disharmony.

"I lived by my code," Pappy said. His voice was almost inaudible. "Hit don't matter where I am, I lived by the code of the hills."

Hope looked at him with tear-filled eyes. "We don't live in the hills no more. We live in the flatlands. If you got to live by the code of the hills, you go find you some hills, and you live in them by yourself, and you leave us alone. You go back to where we used to live and ask all them fat ladies driving over the Smoky Mountains in their automobiles if they is a code of the hills, and they will laugh. They hain't no code of the hills no more. Maybe in Virginia. Maybe down in Georgia. But there hain't none in Tennessee or North Carolina. You hain't got nothing over there but tourists in their automobiles and tourist courts where they can sleep at night. Hit's all gone. And if you can't get that into your head, you ought to get gone, too."

"I never could of dreamed a son of my own blood would talk to me like that," Pappy whispered.

"I don't want that boy kilt, Pappy. I don't want to live. That's what I'm trying to tell you. This hain't your business no more. Hit's mine, and I don't want nobody else kilt. If you got to pretend they's a code of the hills, you go off somewheres and build you a little cabin and clear you some ground and start hit all over again. But leave me alone. And leave that boy alone."

Pappy stared gravely through the bars at him, showing no emotion at all. Then in a weary gesture he stood up and looked around. "I figure hit's time to go home, boys," he said. He did not look back at Hope. Instead he walked back to the guard who stood discreetly twelve or fifteen feet behind them. "I reckon hit's time to go," he said to the guard.

"Is they going, too?" the guard said.

"Yep, they's going, too," Pappy said.

The other sons stared at Hope, silent and thunderstruck.

"Don't let him kill Charlie Alexander," Hope whispered. "You got families. You got to stop him."

"Oh Hope!" M.L. said in a passion.

The guard came to them. "Your daddy says you want to leave," he said.

The sons turned, looking back at Hope and then looking to where Pappy had gone, a small figure standing with his back turned to them at the steel door that would let him out. He did not turn his head.

"Goodbye, Hope . . . Goodbye . . . Goodbye," they whispered at him in a rush of anxiety. Then they fled, only John Sevier looking back now, baffled and anxiously curious but obeying the hissed, frightened command of Joye to come along.

*A*RCENEAUX preached to his congregation over a gulf fixed between them. Sometimes the auditorium seemed to have swollen and the audience receded from him so that he was tiny in a vast space, and his people in the distance, their intentions unknown.

If they knew about me, they would howl with outrage, and they would have the right. The boy! Not more than fourteen? Maybe fifteen.

The planes were late. Another half hour and I would have pulled back my men. Mission aborted.

Toulon. Summer 1944. I was twenty-four years old! What does a twenty-four-year-old queer know about anything? About himself?

The boy had blond hair, unusual in the South of France. *The sun shone on the blond hair. The most beautiful hair I had ever seen on a boy. When you come on blond hair down there, in that part of the world, it is a surprise.*

The British and Americans invaded France at Toulon three months after the invasion of Normandy. That's why Mack was dropped. Arceneaux and his comrades in the Resistance were to blow a railroad tunnel near a place called Le Cigalou. The Resistance was to blow bridges and tunnels on railroads into Toulon to keep the Germans from getting reinforcements, especially from northern Italy but also through Switzerland. The Swiss washed their hands of everything, let the Germans pass through unobstructed, did everything correctly. The Swiss code of honor: be correct and disciplined, don't take sides, go to church, forget about who's right and who's wrong, get rich, wind your cuckoo clocks, yodel now and then to clear the throat, don't cheat the tourists, and everything will be all right. Mack floated down as a demolitions expert, and with him came the explosives, and now they had to wait for the signal, tuning in the BBC every night at seven o'clock, listening for the sentence, repeated twice, "The washing has been taken in." Then they were to move fast.

We were sleepy that morning. What's a man to do after he's been all night waiting and worrying and finally watching black parachutes silently glide down the dark sky and discovering that his demolitions man is more than six feet tall and looked like, well, like Mack? We tracked the parachutes down and gathered up the crates. We brought them one by one to the side of a ridge called Barre de Cuers. We buried the chutes—one hell of a job in the rocky soil of the mountains in Provence. It was cool at night, but we sweated when we dug. By the time we were done, the eastern sky was pale, the stars burning out like candles, and as the mountains took shape in the early light, a German came over, flying low and slow. He was looking for us. When he droned away, we were not sure he hadn't seen us. We were worn out, and we stank, and it would be days before I could take a bath. Nothing to do now but wait for the signal or the Germans, whichever came first, and if the signal came first, we would blow the tunnel, and if the Germans came first, we would all die. I still had the cyanide pill. I meant to use it. Better than some other things.

It was a beautiful French dawn, a morning mist englobing the trees so that they soaked up light as a sponge will absorb water and seemed to swell, ghostlike and mysterious. The sun rose huge, red, and promising, the world so serene that Arceneaux dozed, daydreaming, thinking the war might be an illusion. *It was like being in the Boy Scouts on a camping trip, and the morning was so still and beautiful that somebody should have made coffee and beaten on a pan to wake us all up so we could drink the coffee, smell bacon cooking, and feel like men before we went back home and to school next day.*

They dozed. The heavy sun climbed slowly up the sky. It was to be a day of intense, Mediterranean heat, and the forested hills slept in a dreamy lassitude with light streaming down in shafts through breaks in the canopy of green that hid them from the prying sky, and by eleven, they felt sure the German plane had not seen them.

The boy was suddenly among them with a big, longhaired black dog, a friendly beast prancing about happy to see people, nuzzling them to be petted, and the crates of explosives were neatly arranged under the trees and covered with a green tarpaulin. The dog barked cheerfully and licked Jean-François in the face, and Mack pulled him off and scratched him behind the ears, and the dog tossed his head and tried to lick Mack in the face, and Mack laughed. Mack still had the blacking on his face. He looked like a Negro.

We were careless. Stupidly careless. My fault. I was in charge. We thought we could hear anybody coming in plenty of time. We could rig an ambush, or if there were too many—a German patrol or the blue-uniformed dog-soldiers of the Milice—we could buzz out of there, and if they had surrounded us, we would fight until we had to die.

"*Mon dieu!*" Jean-François jumped to his feet with his pistol, a man nearly forty, dirty, with black, unkempt hair. "Arnaud!" he said to the boy.

Arceneaux, stumbling to his feet, took his .45 pistol out of the holster he wore. *You hit a man with a .45 in the little finger and it will knock him down.* Wisdom of a sergeant from Arkansas in basic training. The army's hand cannon. Arceneaux held the pistol with the muzzle pointed at the ground and flipped off the safety.

"*Merde,*" Léon shouted, tearing his pistol out of his ragged trousers. The boy stood among them, frowning and startled at the guns waved in his face but looking to Jean-François with an air of confidence. He even smiled. To him this was a little joke, a masquerade in the woods.

Mack broke the tension. "*Il n'a pas un fusil,*" he said in his awful French.

Jean-François knocked the boy down with the back of his hand. "*Merde,*" he said.

"Hey!" Mack said, and seized Jean-François's arm. The boy did not resist or run. He fell, then sat up, rubbing his face, showing neither surprise nor injury where Jean-François had struck him. The dog cowered, long tail drooping, black eyes disconsolate, tongue back in his mouth and mouth shut. Léon pointed his pistol at the dog.

"No—no, someone will hear!" Mack shouted in French. "Good God!" He said the last phrase in English. Léon lowered the pistol and looked at Arceneaux.

"Take it easy," Mack said in English. "He's just a kid."

"Take it easy?" Arceneaux said. "Just a kid? My God—he can talk!"

"Il n'est que garçon," Mack said in his maddening French.

"Il est salaud!" Jean-François cried.

The boy sat on the forest floor, not speaking. He seemed to understand now that things were serious. The dog wore a brown leather collar with metal studs. Jean-François seized it, and the dog did not resist. The dog rolled his black eyes and looked at the men in canine beseeching.

"Who is he?" Arceneaux said.

"He is the son of the mayor of Monleon," Léon said.

"A *collaborateur*," Jean-François said.

"Shit," Arceneaux said.

"He is also my nephew," Jean-François said.

"Your nephew!" Arceneaux said.

"I cannot help who my sister married before the war," he said.

"Tie the dog up," Arceneaux said.

"What are you doing here, boy?" Jean-François said.

"I am hunting truffles. The dog can smell truffles," the boy said. "He smells them, and I dig them up."

"There are no truffles up here," Jean-François said.

"There are some; I have found them before," the boy said defiantly. He sat on the ground, eyes looking up, sullen but not in anxiety. When he saw his uncle, he thought that nothing could happen to him.

"If you move," Arceneaux said to the boy in an unemphatic French, "I will kill you." He pointed the pistol at the boy's head.

"Oh for Christ's sake," Mack said in English.

"I will not move," the boy said. He chuckled.

"Sir," Mack said in English, looking at Arceneaux with mock seriousness, "if I were you, I'd put that thing up. It might go off. And I know the kind of noise a .45 makes. It will be heard two miles away. Or pardon me, Sir. It will be heard three to four kilometers away."

"Shut up," Arceneaux said. "Come over here," he said to all of them.

They moved apart from the boy and spoke in low voices. "What are we going to do with him?" Arceneaux said.

"If we let him go, he will tell where we are," Léon said.

"We can keep him here until our comrades join us with the mules," Jean-François said.

"He will tell everyone that we plan to dynamite the railroad," Léon said.

"They know we will try to dynamite the railroad at the invasion," Jean-François said, spitting in Gallic contempt. "What difference does it make? We are predictable."

"They do not know *where* we are going to dynamite the railroad," Arceneaux said. "And they do not know the invasion will be at Toulon."

"They know we are somewhere around here now," Léon said. "The boy will tell them exactly where we are. They will chase us, and we will have German soldiers and the Milice all over us, and we will not blow up the tunnel, and finally, we will die."

"We can keep him with us," Mack said. "We can hold him prisoner until we get the signal and blow the tunnel."

"I know his parents. They will come looking for him by sunset," Jean-François said gloomily.

"Perhaps he will not tell," Arceneaux said slowly and doubtfully. "We can make him promise not to tell." The thing was beginning to take shape in his mind.

Jean-François laughed bitterly. "And what is a promise?"

"He is your nephew," Arceneaux said.

"We must kill him," Léon said.

"Don't be ridiculous," Mack said. "He is no more than fifteen years old."

"So?" Léon said. "When they shoot Jean-François and me, they will not say, 'Oh, this is the uncle of the boy; we cannot shoot him. And these are the nice American friends of the uncle of the boy; we cannot shoot them either.' You, my friends, they will shoot no matter what. American spies."

"It's a risk you take," Mack said.

"We can tie him up and leave him," Jean-François said. "He will not get loose until we have blown the railroad."

"We do not know when we are going to blow the railroad yet," Léon said. "We do not know when the invasion is coming. We do not have a signal. We cannot blow the railroad until we have a signal."

"People will start looking for him in a few hours," Arceneaux said, almost to himself. "What do you think, Jean-François? How many will search for him?"

"The family," Jean-François said with a grand shrug. "He has two brothers and a sister. Perhaps they do not know where he has gone. Perhaps his father will call on the Milice right away. Who can tell? Then . . ." He shrugged dramatically.

"Then we retreat," Mack said.

"And leave the tunnel intact," Arceneaux said.

Mack lifted his shoulders. He seemed to catch on quickly to French gestures. "It is one rail line," he said. "You cannot bring many supplies in with one rail line."

"We are not going to give up the operation," Arceneaux said.

"Then we hold him prisoner, take him with us, and take our chances," Mack said.

"The invasion may not come for three or four days," Léon said. "Perhaps not for a week."

The forest hummed with summer insects and rippled with birdsong, and the morning light slanted through the plane trees. It fell on the boy's blond hair. The boy was irrevocably and solidly *there*, skinny, blond, wearing blue short pants, sandals, a shirt to match, the French blue that seemed formulated by law and enforced by decree as more emblematic of the nation than the different blue in the tricolor flag.

"So, my sister will come and look for the boy, perhaps with soldiers because they know the invasion is coming, and they will find us," Jean-François said. He spoke slowly, in meditation, and looked at Arceneaux. Mack stood off to one side. Jean-François shifted his eyes in Mack's direction, a quick, mute gesture that only Arceneaux saw.

"Maybe not," Arceneaux said. "This is a big place. They may not find us."

"He found us," Jean-François said.

"He was not looking for us," Mack said.

"I think we must kill him," Léon murmured, looking sideways at the boy.

"Not on your life," Mack said threateningly in English, looking at Léon in a mixture of contempt, assertion, and astonishment and shaking his head violently.

Arceneaux listened to the argument and thought. They were speaking in low voices. The boy lay perhaps twenty feet away, stretched out on his stomach, his face on his arms. He slept, unperturbed, in the summer heat. The dog lay beside him, his muzzle on his paws, black eyes looking at the men, panting softly as dogs do when they are too warm.

"I don't want to have to face his mother after the war and tell her I consented to the death of her son," Jean-François said.

"We are not going to kill him," Mack said.

"He will not tell," Arceneaux said, acting a part now. "The invasion is going to happen soon. Maybe tomorrow. Suppose he tells. What will happen? Nothing. People come after us, and the invasion starts, and they run back again."

"That's right," Mack said. The two Americans looked at each other.

"While we run from the people who come after us, we do not blow the railroad, and the Germans pour down from Italy in floods," Léon said. "We will have failed. Maybe we will be shot by our own people." Léon was a Communist, used to discipline. *He does not understand,* Arceneaux thought. *Good. I am glad he does not understand. He makes the play better.*

The play was for Mack.

"He knows which side of the bread the butter's on," Mack said, translating the American phrase literally into bad French. The two Frenchmen looked at him as if he were mad.

"Butter! What does butter have to do with it?" Jean-François said in an impatient burst of annoyance.

"It's all right," Arceneaux said, soothing him. Jean-François and Arceneaux had an understanding.

"If people know we are here, the Germans will guard the railroad within the limits of where we can move from here to blow it up," Jean-François said. "And they will kill us."

"Merde," Léon said.

"One thing at a time," Mack said. The two Frenchmen looked at him. Mack was out of it.

Arceneaux sat on a boulder and thought. In his imagination, trainloads of Germans roared down the tracks in the night, and the invasion was pushed into the sea, and it was all his fault.

Then he thought that the Allies would have invincible air cover when they invaded, and with dive bombers they could destroy the trains and bomb the tracks. They didn't need to blow the tunnel. He knew that the theory was not as good as the practice. The bombs sometimes hit the railroads. Most of the time they did not. Damage to railroads from bombing was quickly repaired. Arceneaux remembered the orders: blow the tunnel. *In war soldiers obey orders. That's how wars are won. No soldier on the ground knows the plan completely. Always there is a plan.* Arceneaux did not know clearly how he fitted into the plan now. He had been there six weeks. He knew that if he did not do his part, another part of the plan might fail. *It was my responsibility. Mine. I had my orders.*

That is what soldiers were told when they were given responsibility like his.

The Roman soldiers had their orders when they hammered the nails into the hands and feet of Christ. They had their orders.

The boy slumbered peacefully. Not far from where Arceneaux sat, small blue flowers dotted the forest floor. It struck him that he did not know the names of flowers—not in France, not in America. He could tell a rose when he saw one. Once a buddy remarked about another blue flower, called it a hydrangea, and he remembered that his mother had flowers like it in her garden in New Orleans. Flowers were red or yellow or pink or blue or whatever, and they either smelled or they did not smell, and they grew in various seasons of the year, but he had never been a gardener, and he had never learned names of flowers. Sitting there on the rock that morning as the sun rose higher and grew hotter, he thought how much of life he had missed. *If I had been a normal man, I could have spent my time gathering information about things that interest me. I could have been interested in hundreds of things, thousands. I could have read books only to see how they came out. Instead I have spent my life tormented at being a queer.*

He would buy books about flowers after the war, he thought. He had faith that somebody had written at least one good book on every subject he wanted to learn. He knew there were books about flowers. Time inched by in the shadows of trees shortening. Soon the shadows would begin to lengthen. The boy raised his head. He had been asleep, and for a moment he did not know where he was. He sat up. "How long are you going to keep me here?" he said. He was not petulant, only curious.

"As long as it takes," Arceneaux said.

"You are Americans," the boy said, looking at Mack and Arceneaux.

"How can you tell?" Mack said, grinning that stupid grin of his.

The boy laughed. "Your accent. All Americans speak French with the same accent. But you speak French well. Even with the accent."

"Thanks," Mack said. "That is what six months in language school will do for you."

"I try to learn the English," the boy said, changing to a heavily accented English.

"I thought you would be studying German in school," Arceneaux said scornfully, in French.

The boy made a face and went back to French. "Who wants to learn German? Yes, we have to study it, but we want more to learn English."

"But if the Germans win the war, you will do well to learn German. It will be the language of power," Arceneaux said.

The boy shrugged. Arceneaux wondered if there might be a class in French first grade where boys learned to shrug. They all did it the same way—men and boys and sometimes the women. He could imagine the teacher standing in front of them, saying, "Today we will learn how to shrug," showing them how to lift their shoulders, make a contemptuous expression, then all of them practicing one by one, individually coached. "My father says they will win, but I do not think so now," the boy said.

"Do you want them to win?" Mack said.

"It is equal to me," the boy said. "Yes, I suppose I want them to win. My father wants them to win. If they do not win . . . ?" He made a cutting gesture with a hand across his throat. "My father is very frightened. He does not know what to do."

"They are going to lose," Arceneaux said.

"Then I suppose my father will be shot," the boy said, looking away, resigned or indifferent, Arceneaux could not tell which. He said nothing. He wanted to dislike the kid, to have some reason to hate him even. The boy drew his knees up and sat leaning forward with thin arms clasped around them.

"Are you with the Resistance?" he asked.

"Yes," Arceneaux said.

"Ah, then you are a spy," the boy said with an innocent smile as if he had just taken a bishop in chess without giving up anything. "You are not wearing a uniform. If you are found, you can be shot."

"You seem to know the Geneva Convention," Mack said.

"I have never been to Geneva," the boy said.

Mack opened his mouth and started to explain the Geneva Convention and gave it up. It was ridiculous to explain the Geneva Convention out here on the slopes of a mountain and to a boy. Arceneaux wished he smoked. Léon and Jean-François sat a little apart, smoking. Their tobacco smelled foul. The dog, hearing the boy talk, sat up and flopped his long, black tail on the ground and looked hopefully at the men. *He wants something to eat,* Arceneaux thought.

"When did you leave home, Arnaud?" Jean-François said.

"*Après le petit déjeuner, mon oncle.* Are you with the Resistance?"

"Yes," Jean-François said.

"Maman said she suspected you were," the boy said without interest.

"Why did your father not have me shot, then?" Jean-François said, annoyed.

"He does not have people shot. The police and the German soldiers have people shot," the boy said. He looked at the crates. "Do you have guns in the boxes?"

"Do not ask questions, boy," Léon said.

"No, not guns," Jean-François said.

"Then it must be dynamite," the boy said.

"A very smart little child," Léon said. "You should not be so smart. Smart children do not live long."

"Hush," Jean-François said. Arceneaux sat thinking. The day drifted past noon.

"Why did your mother let you come up here today?" Jean-François said.

"She is not at home. She has gone to see Grand'mère. She is sick."

"Sick? What is wrong with her?" Jean-François said. He seemed alarmed.

"No one knows. She is not well. That is all I know."

"So your maman does not know where you are?" Jean-François said.

"No," the boy said.

"So no one will be looking for you," Arceneaux said.

The boy shrugged again. He seemed indifferent, patient. Things would work out.

The men looked at each other. "I think I will walk the boy back towards his home," Arceneaux said.

Jean-François stood up hurriedly, moving so precipitately that he staggered and almost lost his balance. "No," he said.

Léon stood up, too. "I say yes," he said.

"You're going to let him go, just like that?" Mack said in English.

"It's the only thing we can do," Arceneaux said angrily, giving the impression not that he was angry at Mack for his ridiculous innocence but that he was angry with fate for sending them a child whom now Arceneaux had to release to return home to his parents with all the risks that involved.

"You will not tell anyone you have seen us," Mack said.

The boy shrugged again, the immemorial gesture. "No, I will not tell. It is no concern of mine. Me, I think the war is lost."

"You promise," Mack said. *"Tu promets."* He seemed so earnest, Mack in his terrible French, the accent like tin.

"I promise," the boy said with a grin. "I won't tell anyone. It will be my secret."

Jean-François looked wretched. "There must be some other way," he said.

"We have to trust him," Arceneaux said smoothly. "It's all we can do."

"It is good this way," Léon said. "Is not that so, Arnaud?"

The boy looked at him indifferently. "If you say so. I am hungry."

"Here, we have some food," Jean-François said. "We can eat together, and we can think. Perhaps we will get the signal. The invasion may be tonight. He could go with us."

"I should take him on now," Arceneaux said.

"No, we should eat," Jean-François said, rushing to his pack and taking out two loaves of bread. "I have some bread. Here, see. Some good bread."

"No, they should go on, now," Léon said. "Let the American take care of him."

"I am *hungry*," the boy protested.

"Let the boy eat. We cannot send him away hungry. Even those going to the guillotine are offered a last meal," Jean-François said. He made an effort to laugh.

Mack looked on in mild curiosity. Léon and Jean-François spoke with a Provençal accent, hard sometimes for him to understand.

"The guillotine," the boy said. "That is amusing." He laughed. Léon looked coldly at him. Jean-François stirred around, breaking chunks of bread off a stale loaf and handing it to the boy.

"Some wine," Jean-François said. "We should drink a little wine with our meal. I have a flask."

He brought out the flask. They ate and drank, breaking the bread and passing it around, taking turns with the flask, the boy sitting, the men standing. Mack was hungry. He had not eaten since he was dropped. He ate like a pig. Arceneaux's bread tasted like rope, but the wine was good.

"Are you ready to go?" Arceneaux said.

The boy looked up brightly. "Yes," he said.

"No," Jean-François said. His voice had a frantic edge to it.

"Yes," Léon said. "It is time to go. Take him on."

"Are you sure we can trust him?" Mack said to Arceneaux in English. "Perhaps we should wait until tonight." He looked worried.

"No, I will take him now," Arceneaux said.

"Why do you have to go at all?" Mack said. "He can find his own way back. He found his way up here."

"No, I want to be sure he goes back home. I don't want him hiding out in the woods and spying on us. I don't want him making his way right away to the Milice."

"Oh well," Mack said.

"Come along," Arceneaux said to the boy.

"You should wait until tomorrow," Jean-François said, raising his voice.

"Hush," Léon said.

Arceneaux started down the ridge through the forest, moving southeast. The boy walked along beside him.

"Keep the dog close to you," Arceneaux said. "Hold him by the rope."

"He does not like the rope," the boy said.

"Hold him by the rope," Arceneaux said sharply.

The boy obeyed, looking sulky. They walked in silence, descending steeply.

"Is the invasion going to be at Toulon?" the boy asked.

"You ask too many questions," Arceneaux said irritably. They moved quietly and had nothing to say to each other for a long time. But Arceneaux's mind burned. *I can force him. He cannot defend himself. He is beautiful, a virgin boy, and I am a virgin, and I could . . .* They descended. The sun came down in mottled brightness through the leafy trees. Arceneaux's heart pounded, and he thought his body trembled with desire and shame. He imagined the boy naked under his flimsy clothes. He thought of how easy the shorts would be to strip off. He was furious with himself. His hands trembled. The shame was like something sticky all over his body.

"There is a road across the river. It's just over there," the boy said after a while, pointing.

"We will not go to the road," Arceneaux said, turning away from the direction the boy had pointed. *I could feel my voice quaver. I wonder that the boy did not hear it. My heart must have been beating a hundred and fifty pulses a minute. Desire. Desire. Want. Need. Fear. Duty.*

"I suppose you do not wish to be seen," the boy said.

Arceneaux did not reply. He could not speak. They walked on. The boy followed thoughtlessly. They were in the shadow of the ridge now. The afternoon was moving on, and the sun was behind Pilon Saint-Clément. Arceneaux knew from his maps that was the name of the peak. It had been the checkpoint for the planes flying out of southern Italy with the explosives.

"Stop here," Arceneaux said. "Look down there. What is that?"

"Where?" the boy said. He looked, stepping in front of Arceneaux.

Arceneaux, mad with desire, put his forearm in front of the boy's Adam's apple. *"Eh bien!"* the boy said, laughing as if he had been goosed and perhaps in embarrassment because he felt Arceneaux's desire. Arceneaux broke his neck so quickly that the boy did not make another sound. He fell heavily and lay sprawled on his face, his mouth and eyes open as if in surprise. Arceneaux felt his neck to see if there might be a heartbeat. Nothing. *My erection went down then. Suddenly, as if I had murdered my own penis.* The dog looked puzzled.

"You're just a dumb animal," Arceneaux muttered to the dog in English. "So you can live." With that he took his knife and cut the dog free. The dog sniffed at the boy, smelled death the way dogs do, and flopped his ears back in perplexity. "If you follow me back up the mountain, I'll kill you," Arceneaux said to the dog, again in English. The dog sat, ears back, tongue lolling, and looked at Arceneaux quizzically. The dog sniffed again in puzzlement at the boy.

If I had not desired him so much, I would not have killed him. In him I killed my lust. That's the real story. Fuck the rest of it. That's the story.

*T*HE APPEALS court convened in Knoxville on a beautiful spring Wednesday. Hugh Bedford presented a brief thick with facts. He argued the stenographic text of Judge Yancy's charge to the jury and presented such evidence as he could about the old judge's infatuation with Abby. The safest way to fair judgment lay in another trial in another venue and of course now with another judge. Hugh laid heavy emphasis on Charles Alexander's changed testimony. The state's star witness, the boy responsible for the trial, the only witness for the prosecution, had now said he could not be sure who held the pistol to his forehead on the courthouse lawn that night. He had given the testimony he gave against Hope Kirby because he was sick during the trial in Bourbonville, and his mind was confused.

It was an impressive argument, and many of those who heard it thought that the simple reasonableness of Hugh's presentation would sway the three judges. Legal authorities who have reexamined the case in the renewal of interest in it during recent days have unanimously agreed that Hugh's arguments were convincing. A couple of national cable television networks have carried special presentations on the Hope Kirby case, and these have provided ample opportunity for moderns to scoff at the past and to have the added pleasure of boasting that such an outrageous miscarriage of justice could never happen outside the backward states of the old Confederacy.

The transcripts remain sterile. Missing is the lowering spirit of gloom and outrage that settled down over the Hope Kirby case when it came to appeal. Missionary's motives were never clear. There was a great and almost comfortable agreement that he had been crazy, and since his kind of craziness was rare—so far as Bourbon Countians knew—people could relax and think nothing so horrible would ever happen to the county again. Yet behind this odd effort to console themselves, Bourbon Countians had been pushed to the sharp edge of the worst terrors that they could imagine about what was possible to do to the human body. The human body could be subjected to the most hopeless and lonely kind of death, and in the deaths of those Missionary had killed none of the victims had any assurance that he would be avenged by the law. By his own quick death at the hands of Roy Kirby, Missionary seemed to have cheated a frightened populace out of its just revenge. It left a thousand unanswered questions doomed to no resolution and the frustration of a broken tooth from which the tongue cannot stay away.

Perhaps above all Missionary left people with a raw vision of how afraid they could be, about how unheroic they were. Many of them who had no reason to be an object of his vengeance had reacted with a panic that might have been explicable if they had been, like Rocky Rhodes, a member of the jury. But in retrospect they understood that they were nothing in Missionary's eyes, and they might have spent the whole crisis with unlocked doors, snugly sitting before their television sets, or in bed comfortably asleep. No one who had been to war had any such feelings, because they had recognized their own unheroic status time and again—though some more intensely than others. To all the others, life and who they were became something less worthy than they had pretended.

All this came to rest on Hope Kirby. Almost all sympathy for him evaporated from the county and the region. He and Hugh Bedford steadfastly said he had no connection with the murders Missionary had inflicted in such horrible ways. Yet there was a chain of circumstantial evidence that people standing in doorways or on street corners or sitting at meals recited to one another time and again. First was the working relationship Hope and Missionary had established during the war. Almost three years of guerrilla fighting could turn a man's head. The charitable agreed to that proposition. Folks believed the teamwork had resulted in friendship, because they knew the men could not have survived had they been at odds with each other. Even some of the veterans held to that view.

Then there was Missionary's visit to Hope in prison just before the killings began. Hope was the only witness to what had passed between them. To plain, honest people it seemed to add up to conspiracy in every direction. Did Missionary really think he could kill so many people that the state would release Hope Kirby? Well, that had been his claim. It sounded nutty, but who was to contradict this utterance from the horse's mouth? Altogether we must wonder if so much hostility was turned on Hope Kirby that even the antiseptic procedures of an appeals court in Tennessee in 1954 could not cleanse it all away. Justice may be blind, but she can hear the rustle of voices and even the thunder of newspaper editorials, which, in Knoxville at least, turned solidly against Hope and labeled him and Missionary as working hand in glove to bring terror on a community.

In the afternoon, when Ken McNeil's turn came, he spoke slowly and gravely, going over the case with methodical and lucid factuality. His case seemed more daunting as he went along. He spoke from his own brief and made much of the premeditation of the murders of Abby and Kelly Parmalee. This was no crime of passion, he said. This was a well-planned military operation, and he reserved the right, he said, to bring to the bar of justice those who had been accessories before the fact—those who had helped do the deed. With that he looked solemnly and with obvious threat towards the Kirby men, who sat squeezed in a row together in the front seats of the small audience that the appeals court allowed.

Yes, he conceded, Judge Yancy may have been a bit extreme in his charge to the jury. But he was a man of the deepest integrity horrified by the cold-bloodedness of the crime and outraged by the foolhardy and outrageous lies being told under oath in his court. And in fact the jury had brought in its verdict only after due deliberation. As for the claim that Judge Yancy had some degrading affection for the murdered woman, anyone who knew the judge and his deep sense of honor and honesty would know that these allegations were the worst kind of slander and lies. Several times during this part of his presentation McNeil spoke of the "martyred judge," careful not to bring into his remarks any more direct reference to the judge's murder.

As for Charles Alexander, McNeil read gravely from so many precedents that the effect was almost hypnotic. On and on they rolled out, all pointing in only one direction: a witness who changed his sworn testimony after a duly consummated trial was not to be believed. The earlier story, told under oath during the trial, was considered to be the truth. Changed testimony was likely to have been influenced by events or conversations that could not be known to the court but were in all likelihood unworthy of judicial consideration. The influence on Charles Alexander of Roy Kirby's act in saving his life was well known to all.

It was a hammering and precise summing-up, and it took up most of the afternoon. The judges announced at the end of the day that they would hand down a decision "in a few weeks." Hugh Bedford gravely reminded them that his client was facing an execution date in June. With that, the appeal was over.

*C*HARLES ALEXANDER finally told Tempe what he did on Sundays. He thought if he was honest with her, she would go away, not tempt him anymore, and leave him to reconstruct his private dreams of the kind of life he wanted. It was also one last forlorn test to see if he could still locate the living God in the universe.

Charles had a literal mind. There was no helping it. In those days if you told him that very probably Jesus did not raise Lazarus from the dead, Charles would have responded that if that miracle was a lie, the entire Bible was a lie, and there was no good in it or in any religion. Things are as they are for no reason at all, and if everything were different, there would be no reason for that either.

He would tell Tempe. She would be so disgusted with him that she would not want to see him anymore. He would start all over again. There had to be something to this Jesus business. It was monstrous to think that centuries of Christians had been wrong. He had now lied, and nobody in town took him seriously. "Charles, if you wanted to save him, the time was when it happened. But Lord God! Look what he's turned out to be." His great lie practiced and told in public turned out to be a benevolent little joke that no one took seriously. "I can't say who murdered Kelly Parmalee that night." McNeil laughed at him to his face and swore to him, "I'd file charges on you for perjury, but I've already got this case won. All you've done, young man, is make a fool of yourself."

It was McNeil without the bland smile and the innocuous cheeks. It was McNeil with a threat that Charles knew had a sting to it. Charles wanted a life where he could hide, someplace where the world would be simple again. He wanted Hope Kirby out of jail. He wanted never to see Hope Kirby again. He wanted to be free of the fear of Roy Kirby, a fear that haunted him despite all he could do to push it away. Roy Kirby said nothing to him; Charles scarcely saw him. People said, "Charles, I'd get out of town." Charles did not get out of town. One minute he thought that death would be simple and painless—even if Roy Kirby shot him. People were killed instantly by bullet wounds. It was not much different from going to sleep. You didn't wake up, but there was probably little pain—more like a finger prick in a doctor's office.

But he did not want to die that way. He wanted to die in glory, suddenly the sunset sky streaming around him and the sound of choirs and at long, long last the blessed assurance that it had all been true after all and that somehow God had worked it all out no matter how impossible it seemed. It was a completely confused time of his life when he wanted so many contradictory things that he could not settle on any of them but wanted them all at once. In the middle of himself was a hard rock of misery.

He had never asked Tempe out. Now she said to him, Let's go somewhere on Sundays. Since you don't go to Finewood's church anymore, you're free to spend time with me. April was sailing into May, and the air at noon was sometimes hot or else pleasantly mild and fragrant at night. On the farm the fragrance of the lilac bushes drifted across the spring evening on the slightest wind, and blue phlox poured across sloping ground in his mother's garden and pooled in the yard, and foxgloves with their delicate bell-shaped blossoms brightened the shade with pink and red. Here and there iris were beginning to bloom out, and the tulips were at the acme of their colors, some already beginning to drop their petals. Along roadsides violets and dandelions bloomed, and in orchards the apple trees spread a spray of white. Tempe's face glowed. "I'll even go in that rattletrap of yours. Especially now that it doesn't stink. Go to the mountains. Sit and talk. I can't let you ruin your life."

That was the fatal straw. He turned on her. "It's not ruining my life. You don't know everything," he said. She could not realize how important some things were to him. Or rather she did realize and mocked them all and took it on herself to save him from them. He owed her nothing, he thought. She dated other people. She told of going to a movie with a chemistry student and going to a baseball game with a law student and to a concert with a very nice boy from Etowah who thought he wanted to be a doctor. He imagined her in passionate embrace with these young men at the end of their evenings together, and he thought of how she would laugh if he told her that the girl he married had to be devoted to him alone. Wasn't that what marriage was? He was annoyed at his jealousy. She meant nothing to him, he told himself. Or rather he meant nothing to her. He was a piece of carpentry; she worked on him like a carpenter, and when she had turned him into exactly what she thought he ought to be, she would pass out of his life, and that would be that.

"No, I can't go with you anywhere on Sundays. I have another engagement every Sunday."

"What engagement?" She was puzzled and perhaps hurt at the tone in his voice.

"I go to church."

"You told me you'd stopped going to church."

"I stopped going to Midway Baptist."

"And Rosy. What has happened to Rosy?"

"She comes down to the house and talks to me. She tried to get me to come back for a while, but I told her I couldn't. Her feelings are hurt. But I think she understands."

"So where do you go to church?"

"I go to one church after another."

"What?" She was completely bewildered.

"Yes, are you ready to laugh at me now? Go ahead."

"I'm not going to laugh at you. I don't understand what you are talking about. I'm confused. "

"I'm looking for some church I can believe."

"Oh, Charles! Charles! You can't believe any of them."

"People all over the world worship God. Okay, they are not all Christians. But they worship. They build temples. Churches. Synagogues. They go on pilgrimages. They get down on their knees to pray. They stand up to pray. Sometimes they chant. You can't tell me that all those people, millions of people, thousands of years, are all deluded."

"Charles, they are. They are."

"No, I can't believe that."

"So, where have you been? What flavors have you tasted?" Her effort at humor fell flat to them both.

"I've been to the Episcopal church in Knoxville."

"Smells and bells," she said with a laugh.

"I've been to the Catholic church on Central Street in Knoxville."

"It looks like a mausoleum. A warehouse."

"I went, several Sundays this winter. I sat in the back, and I listened, and I watched. I talked to a priest. I knew a priest at that church. Father McNamara. He's gone back to Ireland to die, but I talked to another one. It's impressive."

"It's stocks and stones."

"What?"

"John Milton. The Catholic Church worships stocks and stones."

"It's almost two thousand years old, an unbroken tradition. It goes all the way back to the apostles, to Jesus himself."

"So you think Jesus worshipped his mother and told his disciples to set up images of himself so people could worship them, and Jesus gave out relics to worship, too."

"It's not worship. It's veneration. Offering respect."

"Oh bullshit, Charles. It's worship."

The scene remained painful and ridiculous in Charles's memory. His life was duplicitous from top to bottom. Religion had taught him not to reveal what he really thought about anything, and now when he began perhaps for the first time to tell someone—Tempe—what he was really thinking, what he had really done, he faltered before her outraged gaze that at first carried amazement, then scorn, then a growing incredulity that collapsed into the sort of concern that people show when they realize, almost in terror, that they are dealing with complete irrationality and that nothing they do can help. That was what he saw and remembered later with the regret that is like a pit in a cave so deep that to drop a pebble into it is to hear a dwindling clatter until finally there is no impact at the bottom but only a deep and suspended silence.

He argued so stubbornly about the Catholic Church that someone who did not know better might have thought he was about to join the Jesuits. Communion awed him. He told Tempe about seeing the congregation flock forward during communion to the altar to kneel and to receive the wafer on their tongues, and he pondered the question whether, if he went forward, the priest would turn him away, and if he did not, if he took the wafer and chewed it and swallowed it, would he feel God enter his body and his being and would he rise with assurance at last that yes, behind all this ritual and all this pomp and the grand swelling of the organ and the mystical invocation of God in Latin there was something, truly something that he could believe in because it was there, present, eternal, and radiant with hope. He scrutinized the people who went forward for the wafer to be placed on their tongues, searching for some sign of joy, delight, regeneration that might suffuse their faces, but he saw nothing like that. Perhaps for him, it would be different. Perhaps the wafer would feel like electricity in his mouth.

Or maybe God would strike him dead for his impertinence. He thought back on his first certainties after he had escaped Hope Kirby's pistol that night. W. T. Stace was wrong. God had a plan for everything, and God was present in every act, and now Hope Kirby had come close to killing him to let him, Charles Alexander, know that God had seen his lusts and his hypocrisy and his living lie and that God stood in the shadows ready to wreak vengeance on him, but in his solemn mystery had given him one more chance.

He told Tempe that much. "Even if I ended in hell, I could say that God ruled the world."

Tempe put both her hands on his and said, "Charles, that's crazy."

He spoke to the priest. He remembered a thick Irish accent and an offensive and truculent certainty. The Church was the Church. Most East Tennesseans, most Protestants, were a collection of blind fanatics who could not reason, because if they could reason, they would all be Catholics. "What do you think God was doing with His world until Luther came along? What kind of tricks was the Almighty playing while He waited for a sex-crazed monk to give his gospel to Christians?" The priest's voice was bitter and mocking. Luther was a beast. Protestantism was a joke, an aberration, a scandal whose origins were lust and disobedience, and in the end God would reveal himself in thunder and lightning and judgment, and Protestants would cry for the rocks and the mountains to fall on them and hide them. Charles sat listening with a subdued sense of inferiority and resentment. The priest came to a conclusion like a salesman closing the deal on a car. "I cannot tell you everything about the Church in an hour," he said, "but I can enroll you in a class for catechumens."

Charles was not sure what a catechumen was. Tempe laughed. "It's the catch of the day," she said. "It's like catching fish. You put your line out and catch a catechumen."

The priest was more serious. "We meet on Monday evenings for ten weeks, and at the end you will be able to join the holy communion of the Church. Let me get your name and add it to my list." He reached for a pad on his desk. It had several names written on it.

"It's all right," Charles said. "Let me think about it."

"I thought you had already thought about it," the priest said.

"It's hard for me. I'm still thinking."

"And what if you die before you have thought it out?"

"I'll have to take that chance, I guess."

Charles stood up and moved resolutely towards the door.

"You can take your chances with invincible ignorance," the priest said.

"Invincible ignorance?"

"That's the faith that God will forgive those invincibly ignorant of the true faith and take them at least into purgatory because they had no chance to hear the Gospel. That's the doctrine that may let a lot of Baptists in to the chance for salvation, but once they are there, they will discover that we have been right all along."

"I'll take my chances, then."

The priest did not find this comment amusing. "You may not qualify for it," the priest said. "You have been to see me, and I have outlined the truth of our faith. You may have committed the unpardonable sin if you turn away."

It was an unpleasant experience.

She bored in on him, angry. "You let an arrogant nobody intimidate you. The Catholics offer instant religion," she said. "Just add holy water."

He told her about going up into the mountains, to Sevierville, to Cosby, to Wears Valley, listening to churches and ignorant preachers. These he attended at night, thinking that the darkness would add to the effect he wanted. He wanted to hear people who *really* believed. It would be like see-ing a play when the actors became the parts they played, and the audience believed it too. To the end of the play, the final curtain; to death and the end of consciousness. He would believe as well, even if in the back of his mind reason told him he was deceiving himself. He was willing to deceive himself, to mesmerize himself back into belief. But it did not work. The preachers rained fire on their moaning and shouting congregations, and in the parking lots of their squalid little churches they shook hands and laughed, greeting Charles warmly but with a certain wariness once he had told them that yes, he was a Christian, and they drove away as if they had all had a good hot shower and now could go to bed. He tried to dress casually, but he was dressed better than any of them, and they wanted to enjoy each other, not him. He was in another world.

Years later, on the night after their father's funeral, Charles recounted the experience to Stephen, sitting at the table where their father had sat for so many years: "I saw them yelling against the universe, puny voices scream-ing in small churches where the congregations were as ignorant as the preachers, and it was like hypnotism. The preacher yelled, and they shouted and swayed in the seats and went into this frenzy, and I was in the middle of it, and it was like being ice in the middle of boiling water, and the ice wouldn't melt. I kept thinking that above them the sky was infinite, that it had taken a thousand years or ten thousand years or a million years for the light of some of the stars we see at night to reach the earth, that the stars may have vanished eons ago, and their light still poured through the sky like a balloon swelling outward from the point where the star had been, but in the center was now nothing, nothing at all. And where was there room for Jesus in all that? Where was there room for any of us?"

He told Tempe all his story, his disgust and his terror and his longing at the meeting where the congregation passed poisonous serpents from one to another. "Snake handling! Jesus Christ. Jesus fucking Christ."

"Yes, I did it. I was in Newport, at a little church where people were shouting out in their passionate frenzy to join God, to feel their sins and their mortality cleansed from their corruptible flesh and bone, and outside afterwards a little dried-up man drew me aside and told me I looked like a boy who wanted real faith. It was as if he looked right into my soul with those glittering eyes. I suppose he was crazy. But to me he seemed to have come from a spirit world, and the way he looked at me, I thought that he knew all about me, and I felt like Moses at the burning bush."

"If you want the real gospel," the man said, "come with me next Sunday night." Charles took the directions. He knew what it was to be. Nothing frightened him like snakes.

He drove above Newport one Sunday night, a narrow and rocky road up into the dark mountains far from the national park, to a primitive world. He found the little church, reposing in the spring twilight as in blunt and mute announcement that nothing here corresponded to anything familiar to shop windows and traffic lights and the glitter of moving lights on the illuminated marquees of movie houses. The church had a shingle roof and a squat little steeple, and trees behind it climbed to the top of the dark and crenellated mountains. The scant parking lot was like a junkyard of old cars and pickups, a crowd of them crammed in close together, and Charles got out of the '37 Ford, which for the first time since Charles had begun driving it seemed to find a fellowship of similar beings and to be unnoticeable amid them.

The little man waited for him. His name was Jephtha. "I knowed you'd come," Jephtha said.

"Well, I'm here," Charles said.

Jephtha pushed his way unhurriedly through the crowd, and people made silent way for him, and there was an air of quiet expectancy in the building, something electric in the air, and for a moment Charles thought, *This is it. This is it.* The congregation was mostly of men, many in bib overalls, many without teeth, their faces prematurely sunken into their mouths, men with amazingly similar blue eyes, and then there were women, dressed in simple print dresses, looking up with eager and glittering expectancy for the coming of God, the spirit. In a moment a large woman seated herself at a worn-looking upright piano, and she rolled her fingers up the keys and down and back again, and a couple of men playing guitars flanked her, tubercular-looking men with prominent Adam's apples, who began to roar out a gospel song, and the crowd fell into it, and the room was ablaze with motion and sound.

When they had finished, Jephtha walked to a simple pine pulpit and prayed, a long and vigorous prayer that was like teeth biting at the spinal cord of the universe so that the sound and rhythm of it seemed to rattle the windows and to shake the trees in the darkening world beyond. The congregation responded to him in a roaring cacophony, unrhythmic shouts of affirmation and appeals to Jesus, loving Lord of the Cosmos, not two thousand years dead but here in the room with them, teasing them to have faith in the God who could protect them from the serpent. From the back Charles heard a sound he had never heard before, someone shouting in what seemed to be a foreign language with a raw and guttural fluency that seemed at first to mock the idea of prayer. But then across the way someone else took up with a roar a similar and unharmonious discourse, incomprehensible syllables crashing together across the space filled with ecstasy, and Charles understood that for the first time in his life he was hearing someone speaking in tongues.

"I thought I had broken through the wall that divides the visible from the invisible," he told Tempe. "I thought that in a moment I would begin to speak in tongues, too, and that something would lay hold of me and shake me and that I would have all the proof I needed that God exists."

Tempe looked stupefied.

Another song when the sound of prayer and prophecy died away. Almost an hour had passed. While the congregation roared through its song, Jephtha and another three or four men brought in long boxes with walls of wire, and inside were the serpents.

Tempe cried out. "I hate snakes."

He could hear the rattlesnakes buzzing. The box tops were hinged, and while the crowd stamped and moaned and shouted, Jephtha went up to the men holding the biggest box, and he opened it up, and without any hesitation, without even a moment for thought, he reached in and took out a rattlesnake. It must have been six feet long.

Charles said to God, "Now is your chance to kill me." He whispered the words aloud, and they were lost in the tumult.

Jephtha handed the snake to someone. The other boxes were being opened. Hands lifted scaly reptiles aloft. The bodies of the serpents were all muscle, dry and glistening in the dim light. Charles kept his eyes on the big rattlesnake. It was a diamondback, not the kind of rattlesnake that flourished in Tennessee. This was the kind of rattlesnake that could kill you with one good bite.

"And you picked the thing up," Tempe said.

"Someone handed it to me, and I took it. He held it gently, and I took it gently. It didn't bite me. I let it crawl up my arm and across my back, and I could feel its scales gripping on the skin at my neck and moving along, and Jephtha shouted, 'Hallelujah! Hallelujah!' "

"Because you had the faith."

"Yes. He didn't know I was praying for the snake to bite me. He didn't know that I wanted to die. It would be God's punishment for all I'd done."

"Oh God, Charles. Oh God." Tempe put her face in her hands.

"Nothing happened. I passed the snake on, and nothing happened. I didn't get bitten, and I didn't get punished by God, and I didn't get faith like a lightning bolt coming from the outside. Nothing happened at all."

Tempe started to cry. "Charles, you're crazy. I thought I could help you. But you're crazy. You need help I can't give you."

ARCENEAUX preached his Easter sermon on segregation and the glory of heaven where all the peoples of the world would be gathered in one paradise, and the heavenly choir would have black faces and red faces and yellow faces. "Wouldn't it be a glorious mark of progress if we could throw aside our prejudices here on earth and live together as we will live together at the Resurrection? Wouldn't it be grand if we here in Bourbonville could look at a Negro man and see in him a Christian brother under the skin, someone we would be happy to eat with in a restaurant, someone whose children we would welcome to go to school with our children, someone whose injury would stir our compassion, someone whose griefs could make us weep?"

It was, Hugh Bedford decided, the most eloquent sermon Arceneaux had ever preached, and Arceneaux preached it with a fervor that was overflowing. *He really means it,* Hugh thought. *Or does he?* Most people in the congregation were not persuaded. Maybe he was only nervous. Hugh knew something about nerves. Eloquence flowed when you were afraid you were about to fail in court. Maybe that's the way sermons fell out.

Hugh sat in what had become his customary pew in the back and surveyed the auditorium, saw sullen, hard, and angry faces, women elegantly made up, men dressed politely and eager to demonstrate their devotion to the religion their fathers had always observed, but not to give allegiance now to some foreign heresy tarred with blackness. Oh, a few nodded approvingly, but not many. Hugh thought that Arceneaux had a talent for detonation. *There he stands, looking as meek as a lamb, ready to be taken out and crucified. Saint Arceneaux of Bourbonville. What possessed a man like that to become a preacher? Nobody in his goddamned seminary taught him to lick ass.*

Hugh enjoyed the spectacle with cynical humor, all those people in their finest spring clothes, the women decked out like fashion models in the department-store ads of the Sunday papers, the men in the gaudy neckties and bright blazers that they took not only to be stylish but to locate them firmly in a community of success and satisfaction. There they were, squirming and fidgeting and glowering at each other like a mob waiting to form. Tommy Fieldston down front looking around with his intense freckled face so red that he seemed on the point of apoplexy, his expression shouting, "SEE! SEE! Have you ever HEARD the like?"

Poor Arceneaux. Hugh imagined somebody shouting, "Lynch him!" With one accord, in his fantasy, the crowd surged forward; the women would lead the way with ululations of savage triumph, hands become claws raking the air before them, and they would tear Arceneaux to pieces and smear his blood all over their Easter finery until sometime in the afternoon civilization would fling its thin sheet over them all, and they would look at one another in astonishment and shame and slink away, fearing punishment, to where the men would have departed before them, and the church would be left in what Hugh supposed represented the most primitive and truest state of religion, the blood of the sacrifice reeking from the floor and the walls and the sacrifice itself in a state of such fragmentation that the species of animal it represented would be unknown except for a very skilled forensic pathologist. "It was a man, torn limb from limb. I've never seen anything like this before."

Nothing like that happened. The coldness of people leaving the church as Arceneaux put his hand out to them and grinned and spoke warmly in preacherly fashion was like the Easter snow that, Hugh's mother always said, killed the peach trees and ruined the flowers. Scarcely anyone greeted Hugh Bedford. The dislike most of them had for Arceneaux spread to him. He smiled mockingly at them, insisted rudely on shaking hands with some of the men and the women as if he had forgotten the Southern rule that a man never offered his hand to a woman unless she put out her hand first. Close to the surface was the dark and deeply riven suspicion that they all scorned him. They remembered his parents. He was a ball of shit on the floor, and they would ignore him, try surreptitiously to scrape him off, tremble with embarrassment that such an accident had happened to them—stepping in dog shit in the middle of church. He knew they scorned him, and he hated them for their scorn, and he resolved to be as rude to them as he could. He even slapped Mrs. Hazel Moore on the back and said, "How are you, old thing? I've never seen you looking better." It was almost enough to kill Mrs. Moore on the spot.

Afterwards Hugh walked around to Arceneaux's place, and they had lunch together. By now Arceneaux had become so unpopular among the generality of townspeople that even the parents of marriageable daughters had decided they wanted no girl of theirs to be joined to a man whose opinions were so dangerous. Next thing you knew, Arceneaux would be inviting Negroes from Bucktown to dinner with him, and some decent white woman would have to serve a stinking black buck dinner. And what if he wanted to kiss her goodnight? The eligible daughters had unanimously decided that they wanted nothing to do with him either, all of them having felt the polite chill that rose between him and them whenever they tried to have spiritual discussions with him. They had learned the wisdom of disdaining what they could not have.

Arceneaux cooked, calling up New Orleans. Hugh had never been to New Orleans. To him cooking was sissy stuff, something men shunned and women did because they were women. He thought there was something laughable about the care Arceneaux took in measuring things and making sauces and timing processes as exactly as he might have done an experiment in a college chemistry lab. Eating was man's work, and Hugh had to admit that the results were compelling. "It's too bad that we're a couple of drunks who can't have a bottle of fine Bordeaux, I should think a good Saint-Julien, with this lamb," Arceneaux said. Hugh said, defensively, "I never was one for wine except when we liberated some of the stuff in the war. I've always been a whiskey man myself."

"You are a barbarian then, aren't you?" Arceneaux said with a laugh that brought an instant retort from Hugh Bedford.

"Don't you call me any of those goddamned names," he said fiercely, putting down his knife and fork and glaring at Arceneaux momentarily as if he could kill him.

"Take it easy," Arceneaux said, not so much alarmed by Hugh's vehemence as annoyed that it should take away the pleasure of a meal he had worked hard to prepare. "I spent a lot of time on this food. Don't ruin it by picking a fight."

"You're leaving, and soon, aren't you?" Hugh said, resuming eating but still sullen. "You're running out on the town."

"Why do you say that?"

"That sermon about the niggers this morning. You don't give a shit about the niggers."

"I wish you would not use that word," Arceneaux said. "We never used it in my house."

"You never called them niggers? Or you never said 'shit'?"

"We never used either word, actually."

"Okay, I'm talking about niggers. Negroes. The colored. How many did you have in to sit with you at your table in New Orleans and eat a fancy meal like this?"

"We still never called them niggers."

"What difference does it make?" Hugh growled, digging experimentally into his *noisettes d'agneau* and chewing with thoughtful concentration, surprised that sheep could taste so good. "You treat them worse than we do, and now you're wanting the amalgamation of the races." He laughed. "Well, if your aim was to get your congregation mad at you so you can be a martyr, you did the trick. I thought Tommy Fieldston was going to have apoplexy."

"I was rather hoping he would," Arceneaux said.

"Let Negroes in church, and his wife will run away with one of them," Hugh said with a laugh. "Or one of them will buy the house next door to his. Or one of them will marry that pious little bitch of a daughter of his. That's what Tommy Fieldston thinks."

"He ought to be thinking about ways to sell Negroes his hardware," Arceneaux mused. "What do you think of the sauce?"

"You mean the gravy?"

"I mean the sauce."

"It's all right."

"I knew you'd say that."

"Then why did you ask me?" Hugh said grumpily. It was a damned good sauce. He would have to admit that—to himself, but not to Arceneaux.

"I meant what I said this morning," Arceneaux said.

"Have you been down to Bucktown? Have you talked to any of the Negroes down there?"

"No." Arceneaux felt uncomfortable, knowing Hugh was mocking him. "I don't know how to do it."

"I see your point. You drive down to Bucktown in that white Jaguar of yours and in one of your white suits, and I'd wear the white plantation hat, too, just to be sure they got the point, and you say, 'Here I am, black folks! Yo savior. Now you just tell me what you want, and I'll buy it for you.'"

"You make it sound ridiculous," Arceneaux said petulantly.

"No, I'm just trying to visualize the scene."

"We have to start somewhere. Every revolution begins with one shot. I preach sermons to white people, getting them ready. You use artillery to soften up a position before you send in the infantry. Maybe I'm an artillery man."

Hugh greeted this utterance with a long and derisive laugh. "Let me ask you something, soldier. How many times in the war did you see the artillery blast away until you didn't think anything could be left, and you sent the infantry forward and discovered that every shell hole had a Kraut with a machine gun in it firing directly at you?"

"I wasn't in the infantry," Arceneaux said.

"Well, I was," Hugh said. All at once Hugh had a huge and earnest desire to break down, tell Arceneaux about Sperling Winrod, about the village in the sun, about losing all his men. He suppressed it. But the desire was there. It came on him in a rush, like an attack of nausea, something he wanted to expel from his body while this odd duck of a preacher held his forehead and let him vomit. Arceneaux would understand. If anybody in the world could understand, somehow he knew it would be Arceneaux. But he made no confessions. Instead he said, "Do you know the only white man in this county the Negroes trust?"

"Bob Saddler, I guess."

"He's dead, Preacher. And he was crazy. They loved him, but they knew he was crazy. The live white man they trust is Paul Alexander."

"Why?"

"Haven't you heard the story? When he first came here, he got himself into a friendship with a black war veteran. I'm too young to have seen it, of course. But I know the story. The black guy was an uppity nigger. Drove a yellow car. Flew an airplane. That was the damnedest thing—flying nigger. Now *that's* uppity! They couldn't stand it. People say he was in the French air corps. I think that's right, too. He got ideas over there. Here, he didn't know his place. Paul Alexander gave him a job, and the nigger started talking revolution. Yep, just like you. Revolution here in dull old Bourbonville where a revolution would be if everybody started drinking RC Cola instead of Coke. He was lynched, and the KKK almost lynched Paul Alexander, too. An ugly spot in our pure little town's history that you don't hear about. Alexander's had a reputation for being a nigger lover ever since. But he's kept quiet. He comes to the Car Works, does his job, and he goes home. But he pays the niggers the same thing he pays the whites, and a couple of years ago he appointed a nigger a molder in the wheel foundry. Now do you know what that means?"

"I don't know what any of it means," Arceneaux said. "Molders. Wheel foundry. What are you talking about?"

"A nigger molder has to give orders to white molder's-helpers. That's what it means. Right here in Bourbonville."

"How does he get away with it?"

"Well, he's foreign for one thing, and he runs the biggest business in town for another, and best of all he doesn't want a damned thing from this town. He doesn't go to parties. He and his religious-fanatic wife never entertained people when she was alive, and I don't reckon he's going to start now that she's dead. He turned down an invitation to the Rotary Club. He goes home from the Car Works and tends to his garden and his idiot son. He's a hell of a musician, and he plays the mandolin. Roy Acuff wanted him to come onto the *Grand Ole Opry*, but Alexander laughed at him. He plays every Sunday with that son of a bitch Jim Ed Ledbetter and some other friends, including their children, except Charles, and that's all he wants out of life. So what can the town take away from him? Nothing. Oh, they could kill him. But he's not the kind of person to make people mad enough to kill him."

"This town is very complicated," Arceneaux said.

"The niggers name children after him, and he goes to their funerals and even their goddamned weddings. He and Ledbetter have even played music with some of those nigger guitar players and banjo pickers and singers. So if you want to get to know those folks down in Bucktown, get him to drive you down someday. But if you ask me, you don't want to know them, and they sure as hell don't want to know you."

"I do want to know them," Arceneaux said. "Look, we're standing on the edge of a revolution. It's going to decide which way the country goes for the next hundred years, maybe more. If the Supreme Court rules against segregation in the schools . . ." He left the rest of the sentence unexpressed. But Hugh finished it for him.

"We'll have riots all over the South, and the army will have to occupy Mississippi and Alabama and Georgia and South Carolina and Louisiana and hell, you name it. And you think you can do something to stop that, you, Reverend Lawrence Arceneaux? Let me tell you what will happen. Finally the good white people in the South will say, 'This is bad for business.' So they'll allow desegregation. Just enough to make the government happy. Oh, the ones who can afford to will pull their kids out of the public schools and send them to some goddamned private schools where they talk about Jesus all day long and make sure all the pictures of him are blond. In the end they'll hate each other all the more. You're talking bullshit, Preacher. Bullshit."

"You do what you can," Arceneaux said. "I do wish you'd stop calling them niggers."

"Oh, look at him," Hugh said, spilling his cynical laugh in the room as if he had thrown a glass against a brick wall. "He's gearing himself up to be a martyr. Another way of telling himself he's better than this bunch of rednecks he's tried to lead into the Promised Land. So they can fire him, and he can go back to Louisiana and run his sugar plantation and get richer and marry some Louisiana belle and feel superior for the rest of his life."

"I don't think I'll ever get married," Arceneaux said.

"I think I know the truth about you," Hugh said, giving Arceneaux a stab in the belly as though with a knife made of ice.

For just a moment Arceneaux felt terror, and he wondered if he turned pale. "What truth is that?" he said, coldly.

"Just what I say. All you want to do is make those good hypocritical folks at First Baptist mad as hell. You don't care about the Negroes. You don't care about the country. You want to make these hypocritical bastards mad."

"That's a lie," Arceneaux said.

"I see I've made you mad," Hugh said. He grinned sardonically at the preacher. "Truth does that, even to a preacher."

"And what's your truth?" Arceneaux said. "You've lost your case."

"I haven't lost it yet. I've appealed to the state supreme court."

"And if the state supreme court turns you down?"

"I'll go to the governor. It's my last hope. Hope's last hope."

"We've got to get him off."

"I'm damned if I can understand why you care so much about this case."

As it turned out, there was no hearing before the state supreme court. The court refused to hear the case, thereby affirming the decision of the appeals court in Knoxville. By then it was the first week of a glorious May.

L*ARRY ARCENEAUX* drove up to see Paul Alexander on a Saturday afternoon. He found him in the garden, patiently weeding rows of potatoes. Paul Alexander wore a floppy straw hat and baggy khakis and looked like a peasant. The bulldog came barking towards Arceneaux so that Paul became aware of his presence. He looked up at the preacher in surprise.

"Mr. Arceneaux," he said in his heavily accented voice. He did not smile. But his gaze was not hostile either. It bored into Arceneaux. Arceneaux thought, *He sees right through me. He knows I am a queer.*

"Mr. Alexander, I need your help. This time it's not about Charles."

"What is it, then?"

"It is about—about Negroes. The Supreme Court. Desegregation. What will happen in Bourbonville when—" He spluttered uselessly, beaten down by Paul Alexander's mildly curious gaze and eyes that held him in their grasp with unwavering strength. "Can we talk?"

Paul Alexander shrugged slightly and took off his straw hat. His hair was white now, and his mustache, too. He had a Roman nose and dark eyes.

"We can sit in the yard," Paul Alexander said. "Would you like something to drink?" The voice was mild. The gaze was mild, but it was also wary.

"I would like some water," Arceneaux said, and Paul Alexander walked inside and brought back a glass pitcher of water with ice cubes clinking against the sides. It was a warm day. From within came the sound of loud hillbilly music. Guy was playing records. The music grated on Arceneaux. Mournful bullshit, he thought. As music, it was nothing but noise. Guy played it at top volume. How could anybody live in the house with that sound? No wonder Charles studied in the newspaper office. But then Paul Alexander played it, too. These same ballads and older ones. Yes, much older ones. It seemed odd. Here was a man who ought to love Mozart and Beethoven, but he played a mandolin to sound like a pure hillbilly. They sat in chairs, the same chairs, it seemed, where Arceneaux had sat when he had come to see Charles to ask him to lie about Hope Kirby. The chairs were made of wood, shabby and weathered and badly in need of paint.

"What is your friend Mr. Bedford doing about the case?" Paul Alexander asked.

"He's got an appointment to see the governor next Friday. I'm going to drive over with him."

"The two of you have become good friends," Paul Alexander observed in a neutral voice.

"I suppose so," Arceneaux said guardedly. "We both want to get Hope Kirby out of the electric chair. After that, I suppose we will go our separate ways." He paused. Why not say what he thought? "And I want to save your son Charles's life."

"I thank you for that," Paul Alexander said softly. He paused. "You intend to return to Louisiana, I believe."

"Why do you think that?" Arceneaux said, wondering if the rumor might be out that yes, he planned to abandon the First Baptist Church and abandon the ministry and abandon Tennessee. Is that what he planned to do? He was not sure himself. He felt himself testing something.

"I think you are the kind of person who will go home again," Paul Alexander said. "You do not belong here. You have important things to do at home."

"Why do you think you belong here?" Arceneaux said, a little belligerently, feeling that he may have been insulted.

"I am not sure that I do. But this is where fate has put me. I have three sons and a farm and a job. I suppose that is as good a definition of fate as any."

"Fate. That sounds almost religious. No, maybe you're right. It's more philosophical. You're not religious, are you?"

Paul Alexander shrugged. "Why have you come to see me?" he asked, changing the subject bluntly.

"Mr. Alexander, the Supreme Court of the United States is going to rule on a segregation case any day now. I think it will rule that segregation according to race is contrary to the Constitution."

"Americans are very odd in that way," Paul Alexander said with a trace of a smile. "They require a Bible or a Constitution to tell them what is right and wrong. You have put black men in your armies since the Civil War and perhaps before that, and they die for a freedom they do not have. It is almost amusing except that it is also very sad and hypocritical and cruel."

Arceneaux was startled. He had not supposed that he could evoke so many words from Paul Alexander with so little effort.

"It's the way we do things," Arceneaux said. "I am as guilty as anyone for what we have done to the Negro. You grow up with a way of doing things, and there it is. You don't step back and consider. I've grown up that way. It's hard for me to change. But the Supreme Court is going to make us change. I think we have to prepare for it. We have to think."

"What do you propose?" Again the mild, untroubled gaze.

"Well, I've thought and thought and thought. Here's what I've come up with. An open discussion between Negroes and whites. The whites could tell why they're afraid of the Negroes, and the Negroes could tell why they're afraid of the whites, why there's such hostility between them, and they could tell what they want out of life, and I bet they would find that they want the same things. They don't know that, but it's the truth. At bottom Negroes and whites want the same things. They need to hear each other say that. It would build understanding, make people see each other as human beings. I know we can't have it in my church. My deacons wouldn't permit it. But we could have it in the Memorial Building."

Arceneaux's voice gathered force as he talked. He was a prophet with a message, and the more he considered it, the more reasonable and the more righteous it became. Even in Bourbonville reason and righteousness could prevail. What better place for this victory than the Memorial Building, erected to all the soldiers in Bourbon County who had given their lives for their country?

"What time of day do you intend to have this open discussion?" Paul Alexander said.

"Why not on a Saturday night? What's wrong with that?"

"One thing wrong with that is that Negroes are forbidden by law in Bourbonville to be within the city limits after six p.m. Everyone who participated in your panel would face immediate arrest."

"But surely that law could be suspended for one evening."

"I do not believe you understand how sacred Bourbonvillians believe the laws are about Negroes, especially those laws that ban the Negro from the town after six o'clock," Paul Alexander said with considerable irony.

"You are mocking me," Arceneaux said in an injured tone. "I thought you might be the one person in the county I could count on."

"I am pointing out the difficulties of the situation. The difficulties are not imaginary."

"Of course there are difficulties, Mr. Alexander. But we have to do something."

"The Supreme Court has not ruled yet."

"It will rule any day."

"Have you talked to any of the Negroes?"

"No. That's why I'm here. I'm told that—you seem to be the only person in the county the Negroes trust."

"Poor people," Paul Alexander said in a sudden mood of genuine compassion.

"I thought that if you went with me, you might introduce me, and we might talk to some people, see if they were interested. Get things rolling. That's always the hardest part—getting things rolling. I thought . . . maybe if you went with me, they would trust me."

"You propose to go in that white English car of yours?" The question carried its own answer. Arceneaux thought he had a right to his car. Nowhere in the Bible did anyone say it was against the will of God for a man to drive a white Jaguar. He drove it in triumph and in defiance. He was not the man to be pushed around. But he got the point.

"We can go in your Chevrolet if you want." It was beyond Arceneaux's understanding how the manager of the Bourbonville Car Works could be content with driving a two-door 1950 Chevrolet that did not even have a radio, but Paul Alexander had a reputation for frugality.

"I believe that would be best."

"You will do it, then?"

"I can drive you down to visit with the pastor of their church."

"They have just one church?"

"It is a small community when all is said and done. No more than a couple of hundred men and their families. Have you not even driven through it?"

"No," Arceneaux said.

Paul Alexander smiled. "Are you afraid they might harm you?"

"Of course not." Arceneaux was annoyed. He knew Paul Alexander was holding him at arm's length. "I just feel—out of place there."

"In that you are correct."

"Please help me. I'm trying to do something right. Don't mock me."

"We can go now," Paul Alexander said, rising quietly and going towards the house.

"Well, don't you think we ought to make an appointment?" Arceneaux called after him. He did not mean for things to move so fast. Perhaps this was more of Paul Alexander's mockery.

Paul did not answer him. He went inside, and Arceneaux heard him call Guy. The music abruptly ceased. The rush of springtime quiet that came in after it was a blessed relief. Guy came out, putting on a light coat despite the warm day. "Who is this?" Guy said, looking at Arceneaux and speaking in a harsh growl of a voice that Arceneaux could hardly understand.

"I'm Lawrence Arceneaux," Arceneaux said. Guy put out his hand, and Arceneaux took it. It was a soft, small hand. No grip to it at all. Guy was badly cross-eyed, and he was short, squat, and grotesque. *How can anyone love a creature like that?* Arceneaux thought, in spite of himself. Then he was ashamed because Paul Alexander loved his son, and every glance and gesture and touch revealed that love as though the two of them, father and son, were bathed in light.

"I had him put on his coat because people with his condition are subject to colds," Paul Alexander said, answering a question that Arceneaux had not asked. He led the way around to the back of the house to where his green Chevrolet sat in the open air. No garage. It hurt Arceneaux to see a car parked in the open. If a man cared enough to have a car, he ought to care enough to build a garage for it. Paul Alexander opened the door on the passenger side and bent the seat back forward and with infinite gentleness handed Guy into the rear seat.

"Where are we going, Paw?" Guy said.

"We are going to see some friends," Paul Alexander said, again with infinite gentleness.

"Are you going to play music?"

"Not today."

"Can I listen to the radio where we're going?"

"We'll see."

*P*AUL ALEXANDER drove in silence. The car was only four years old, but it had the worn smell of something left too long in the hot Tennessee sun and beginning to molder. They passed through Bourbonville, the streets filled with people disporting themselves in the May sunshine of a Saturday afternoon that had not yet turned into the heat of summer. What an ugly town it was, Arceneaux thought. Yes, the tree-covered square and the court-house had a certain dignity, and perhaps if the town were arranged like some towns in Mississippi and Louisiana with the main highway running into the middle of the square so that you saw a courthouse straightaway and perhaps a soldier's statue in memorial to the Civil War, the effect would have been better. But in Bourbonville, Highway 11 ran alongside the square so that when you drove through, the courthouse loomed up on the left, and you had to turn your head to see it, and if you were in a hurry you might miss it altogether, except that as you came into town you saw the clock rising above the canopy of trees. What presented itself on the drive in was a straight street, Broadway, with a row of brick stores and shops on each side and the three-story brick King Bourbon Hotel on the corner. Beyond the center of town, Broadway fell into seediness, fragile houses to the right and some feed and coal stores to the left and beyond the railroad the car works with the tall chimney rising near the steel foundry and the long, high shed of the wheel foundry, all of it industrial and ugly unless you had an aesthetic feeling for foundry buildings—which Arceneaux did not.

Then Broadway became Highway 11 again, passing a beer joint on the left and a shabby Baptist church on the right with a gravel parking lot; then the hedge on the left that the Rotarians had planted to hide Bucktown, and after a little distance the dirt road that plunged steeply down and crossed the railroad tracks and came up on a hilly settlement with unpaved streets and frame houses with porches and potted plants and a general air of woody decay. At the very top of a rise stood a church, whitewashed some time ago, but weathered badly except for a new corrugated tin roof that shone dully in the mild sunshine. *It must get hot as hell in there in summer,* Arceneaux thought. Paul Alexander pulled up before one of the houses, a small place, painted yellow, with a porch and a window on each side of a front door. A row of rocking chairs reposed on the porch.

"This is the home of Preacher Lewis," Paul Alexander said.

He got out of the car and went to the door and knocked. In a few min-utes a little black man with white hair and skin the color of walnut came to the door. He wore steel-rimmed glasses, and Arceneaux noted how his face lit up when he saw that Paul Alexander was his caller. The two exchanged words, and the little black man looked gravely towards him, and Arceneaux felt himself suddenly to be an intruder, unwelcome. Perhaps all this was foolish, he thought. If he wanted to leave Bourbonville, he should forget about justifying himself, going out with a bang. He should stand up before his congregation one day, tell his people that they and he knew that things had not worked out, and resign. But that would seem like retreat before Tommy Fieldston and the claque that Tommy had gathered around himself. It would add to the gossip that Louise Renfrow dispensed from her office where she watched him like a prison guard and commented on his comings and goings as if he owed her some explanation for everything that he did and everyone whom he saw. (She was mightily disapproving of his friendship with Hugh Bedford.) He realized it now more clearly than he had before; he wanted to leave with a cause, something that would be a town memory and something that might do some good. Martyrs seldom had their effect at the moment they died; that came afterwards when people put things in perspective, saw more clearly and with cooler appreciation what the passions of a moment had rendered invisible in smoke and fire.

The preacher came down to the car. "Come on up, brother, and sit a spell," Preacher Lewis said. "I've heard a lot about you." The voice was dry, almost toneless, impossible to read. Friendly or hostile or merely indifferent. Arceneaux couldn't tell.

Arceneaux got out of the car, hesitated a moment, saw that the preacher had not extended his hand, and then extended his. The hand he took was small and hard. He was surprised. Paul Alexander went to help Guy out of the backseat.

"How have you heard about me?"

"Oh, your preaching gets around. It don't get around like you think it might. Folks don't call us up and say, 'Hey, do you niggers know that they's a preacher at First Baptist saying you ought to go to school with us white folks?' Nah, it ain't like that. It's more like the man that runs the Rexall drugstore is saying to somebody getting a prescription that the goddamned preacher at the First Baptist Church that preaches above everbody's head has turned out to be a nigger lover and wants the amalgamation of the races. The Rexall man's got a black boy cleaning up the back of his store and throwing out old boxes and wastepaper baskets and bottles and suchlike, and the black boy ain't but fifteen or sixteen years old, but he's old enough to keep his mouth shut, and to the white man he might as well be a stick or a rock, but he's got ears, and he comes back home, and he says what he's heard, and pretty soon, you got lots of other folks that cleans up or does washing and ironing for the white folks, and they hear the same thing. So come on up and tell me about it."

By this time they were on the porch, and Preacher Lewis pointed out a rocking chair where Arceneaux was to sit. Paul Alexander helped Guy into another. Guy carried a funeral-parlor fan around with him everywhere he went, and he started fanning himself vigorously and rocking and looking out over the town with an air of mild curiosity, sometimes stretching his neck in a bizarre way and looking over at Arceneaux with an expression of uncrafty curiosity. Paul Alexander sat beside his son.

"Well, start telling me what it is you want," Preacher Lewis said, taking from his shirt pocket an old corncob pipe and charging it with tobacco. He lit his pipe, and the fragrance of the smoke clung around his head, and in spite of himself Arceneaux thought, *A right jolly old elf,* but Preacher Lewis did not look jolly. He looked skeptical, a man doing his best to be courteous but not sure at all that the courtesy was worth the trouble. Arceneaux felt himself at sea, not knowing how to begin and knowing, too, at the outset that his cause was lost. Still he had to try.

So it came out finally, in fits and starts and long, rambling sentences, spoken apologetically and then with the vigor of a prophet and then again with the pleading tone of a man begging to be believed. The mass meeting. The Memorial Building. Seats on the gym floor. A panel of blacks and whites on the stage at one end. A public-address system. They would begin with hymns. Blacks and whites sang the same hymns. Maybe they would call it a "rally." People talked a lot about rallies—enthusiastic crowds brought together by some kind of idealism for a cause, and what cause could be better than racial harmony and an end to hatred and a beginning of understanding on all sides? You had to start somewhere. Most people were reasonable when it came down to it. Most people were even kind and good. They stopped to help when they saw someone with a flat tire on the side of the road. They often did heroic things like pull unconscious travelers out of burning cars after a wreck. The rally would get things out in the open. Maybe some hateful things. It would be like lancing a boil. When it was all over, healing could take place. Arceneaux plunged on. He thought that he was talking faster and faster. He tried to slow down, sound reasonable. He was nervous, and his voice raced like his heart.

Preacher Lewis listened silently, puffing gently at his pipe, rocking with rhythmic back-and-forth motions that made the rockers knock on the plank floor of the porch. And finally Arceneaux was done. The more he had talked, the more he had convinced himself. The world was on the edge of chaos and violence. He had never seen a lynching, but he had heard the stories. Lynchings were as common in Louisiana and Mississippi and Arkansas as needles on a pine. He had felt the smoldering hatred of whites against blacks in the way that people living on the sides of Mount Etna among their green vineyards and picturesque villages feel the angry rumble of the pee-vish giant beneath their feet and see the plume of never-ceasing smoke scroll upward from the peak of the volcano. It's something you learn to live with, learn to accept in exchange for the fertile soil and the good life fate has allowed you, but the danger is always there, and sometimes the giant explodes, and the air is a blackness laced with fire and the destruction races down helter-skelter, sweeping all before it into fiery death. Any man with sense should want to ward off such a holocaust, and Arceneaux in his long, repetitive jumble of eloquence thought that he had proved his case to all rea-sonable men, especially to the two reasonable men who sat beside him on the porch of this pleasant house with the thick, rank smell of potted plants and something else, perhaps the fragrance of decaying wood, filling the spring air around him. "And so," he said weakly at the end, "what do you think?"

"You're through, are you?" Preacher Lewis asked.

"Yes, what do you think?"

"I think you ought to go back to your congregation and preach some more. It won't do much good. But it will make you feel better, and it won't get any of my young men killed."

"We're not talking about getting people killed," Arceneaux cried. "We're talking about peace and harmony and Christian brotherhood. A rally," he added feebly.

"We're talking about having a meeting in your nice white town where maybe fifty of my people will show up, most of them young men who work for Mr. Alexander here at the foundry. They're strong, hard young men. Lots of them was in the army in the war, and they have guns, and they know how to shoot, and they know how to kill people, and they will come because they have a chip on their shoulder as big as an oak tree.

"At this meeting of yours they're the people who will show up. They won't bring their kids, and they won't bring their wives because they know that maybe five hundred white people will show up, and those white people are going to be mad. The difference is that the white people will show how mad they are, and the black people won't—not at first. The white people will get up one by one, and they will tell how God intended the races to be sepa-rate, and they will say that putting black children and white children in school together will mean intermarriage, the amalgamation of the races. They will say that Negro people smell bad. They can't help it, of course, and they don't smell bad to each other, just like pigs don't smell bad to each other. They smell bad to white people, and you can't concentrate on your schoolwork if the child next to you in the classroom stinks. They're going to say that the Supreme Court has to be stopped, that if it's allowed to integrate the schools, the next step will be to let Negroes live anywhere they want to live, and everybody knows property values go down when a Negro family moves into the neighborhood. Somewhere along the way somebody is going to say that America was made by God for the white man, and Supreme Court or no Supreme Court, America will be changed over that person's dead body.

"What are my people going to be doing all this time? They're going to sit there getting madder and madder. They're mad now. Don't you think they're not. I tell you, if it wasn't for Paul Alexander, this town might have blown up years ago."

Arceneaux looked at the quietly sitting Paul Alexander with open-mouthed puzzlement. "What has Mr. Alexander done?"

"He's the boss of most of the black men down here in Huntsville. He's the man that pays a Negro worker and a white worker exactly the same wages for the same job. When the railroad tells the car works that demand is down and he has to lay off men for a while, he lays off blacks and whites with an even hand. He promotes black men when he sees they can move up— even if it means that sometimes black men have to tell white men what to do. He comes to our funerals. He comes to our weddings. My Negro men work and keep their mouths shut because they know he's fair to them, and we don't have such a bad life down here. Truth to tell, preacher, we don't want to mix with you folks. You kill us like we was snakes crossing the highway, and you speed up to run over us.

"But you get my men together with your mob in your public meeting, and I know what will happen. My young people will get mad, and they will talk, and they will tell you white folks in Bourbonville what they think of you and your religion and your preachers, and they may tell you they have guns now. You don't know what young men are going to say when they're mad and they get started talking."

"But how are we going to settle things if we don't talk?" Arceneaux asked. He felt angry and frustrated and scorned. This man was mocking his good intentions. But he recalled the building blocks with which the road to hell was traced, and he could see it all, just as Preacher Lewis described it— people yelling at each other, red and sweaty faces, and nothing good from it.

Preacher Lewis was not done. "We had a lynching in this town about thirty years ago. Mr. Alexander here was almost lynched with a black man." The preacher turned a venerable and almost worshipful face on the small white-haired man who sat next to him. "I still praise God that you wasn't killed."

Paul Alexander only smiled slightly. The preacher reached out and squeezed his hand and turned back to Arceneaux. "I don't want another lynching," he said. "Right now we've got young men with guns, but there are more of you with guns, and I don't want our little town burned up."

"Don't say 'more of you,'" Arceneaux said indignantly. "I'm not one of them. That's why I'm here."

"I reckon it is," Preacher Lewis said with a quiet irony that Arceneaux did not miss.

"You don't hear any talk about the lynching now. Hugh Bedford—he told me about it. It was the first I'd heard about it."

"It's not something you advertise in the chamber of commerce," Preacher Lewis said. "Folks forgets what they wants to forget."

"So we just give up. We let things take their course. What's going to happen?"

"Oh, white folks will do something stupid somewhere. In some big town where there are lots of black folks, Negro kids will start to the white schools, and a bunch of rednecks will try to stop them, and somebody will get killed, and the government will have to send in the army. Only this time it will be on television, and the army will have to be on the side of the Negroes, and Negro children and white children will go to school with each other here and there, but white people will still hate us and think we're itching to marry with them and they'll think we're dumb and tell us that to our faces, and we'll survive. Don't forget that. We'll survive. I'll tell you something else. We'll win our own battles in the end."

On the way back to Dixie Lee Junction, Arceneaux sat wretchedly in the passenger side of Paul Alexander's wretched little Chevrolet and mulled things over.

"I've never seen a man so hopeless," he blurted out to Paul Alexander.

"Hopeless? I thought he was full of hope," Paul Alexander said. "It is not your easy hope; it is a very hard hope. But it is hope."

They drove on in silence. "What about this?" Arceneaux said finally. "Do you think you could get Charles to interview me? I have an idea."

"You will have to talk to Charles yourself," Paul Alexander noted carefully. "He will not do something merely because I ask him to do it." The words were flat and unmournful. They settled in the car with the springtime air blowing in through the open windows. Paul Alexander looked straight ahead, and it occurred to Arceneaux to suppose that this man nourished memories and feelings that no one would ever know. He felt suddenly as though he sat next to a locked door and that behind it was mystery beyond anything he had experienced. Arceneaux believed that he had lied his way into the army, lied his way into seminary, lied his way into this misbegotten pastorate because he would not say to the world what he really was, a queer struggling to make his way in a world that viewed queers in much the same way that a housewife would react to a nest of vipers flourishing in a pillowcase in her linen closet. What did Paul Alexander hide by his silence? Or did he by his silence affirm that he had nothing to hide because he was completely indifferent to the world? Was it this indifference that made him promote blacks and pay them equal wages to whites, or was it virtue? Arceneaux did not know.

"I will talk to him," he said. The spring air carried a fragrance of flowers and growing things. *Maybe Bourbon County isn't so bad,* Arceneaux thought. "Are you interested in my idea?" he said to Paul Alexander.

"What is your idea?" Arceneaux understood that the question was not an answer to his.

"I can force the issue on the Baptist churches around here. The Salem Association meets in June. That's when all the Baptist churches in the county send representatives to hear sermons and talk about matters of common interest. I'm supposed to preach the associational sermon. I'm going to introduce a resolution. Let's see. I'll ask for something nobody can refuse. Support of the laws of the land. Christian brotherhood. Peace and goodwill to all people. Can't leave out the women."

"And you are not going to mention the Negroes?"

"Of course I'm going to mention the Negroes. I'll start with the Supreme Court decision. I'll have the resolution say that this is a time to put Christian principles and Christian love against our history. Don't worry. I'll make it a strong resolution, but it'll also be something that nobody can dispute and still claim to be a Christian."

"I would not have too much faith in that proposition if I were you, Mr. Arceneaux."

"Mr. Alexander, we have to do something. I'll prepare the ground. If Charles will interview me, the word will get to all the county that way, and every eye will be on what the association does. The Baptists can't stand in a spotlight like that and not do their duty."

"When is your association to meet?"

"Let's see. I've got it in my calendar here." Arceneaux reached into his jacket pocket and pulled out a slim black-leather-bound calendar. "Saturday, June 19," he said gleefully. "They will not forget this meeting."

"That is the day Hope Kirby is scheduled to be put to death," Paul Alexander said quietly.

Arceneaux stared at him and looked back down at his calendar. "My God," he said. "You're right. Lord God."

ARCENEAUX called Charles to arrange a meeting, and they had a tense conversation on the Monday afternoon following. Willy-nilly, the strings were drawn more tightly around Charles's destiny.

The burden of their conversation just after Hope Kirby shot his wife and Kelly Parmalee stood between them as they sat together in Arceneaux's book-lined living room and Charles looked around in awe and envy at shelf after shelf of handsome volumes in many languages rising from floor to ceiling. Arceneaux served him tea, the gesture being one of those slightly aristocratic acts that Arceneaux did naturally but that seemed odd to Bourbonvillians, especially since Arceneaux made a production of it with an English tea set that he said casually had come from London to his plantation in Louisiana in 1880.

They did not mention anything that had happened before. A door shut down between this moment and those past moments, and they exchanged meaningless and uncomfortable pleasantries, and Arceneaux explained what he planned to do at the Salem Association meeting. Charles leaned forward with interest and took out his narrow white notebook. They talked a very long time.

Arceneaux thought afterwards that he should have confessed everything to Charles. Not that he was a queer. He should have told Charles about the debt of honor he owed because of the French boy. How did anyone tell such a thing? "Oh yes, Charles, I want you to live because I murdered a boy a little younger than you are now, and he would be a man now if I had not killed him, and somehow I feel that I pay a debt back to the universe and redeem my own sins if I can keep you alive"? He knew he could not confess murder, especially a murder that he had decided was almost whimsical, driven by sexual desire that drove out of his mind the confusion he felt on the sunny and irrevocable day itself when he was afraid of the Nazis and afraid of the Milice and the blue-uniformed terrorists ready to torture and kill anybody in the Resistance and afraid above all of failing in his mission. He forgot his vanity, the quiet triumph he felt when his superior officers said, "Captain Arceneaux, if anybody can do this, you are the man." In Arceneaux's mind now, everything he had done was because of his homosexual desire, and he could not admit that he had committed murder on account of it or confess that he had murdered a child at all. It was a taboo he could not break without failing himself.

They talked about the Salem Baptist Association, and Arceneaux mused that it was like the general councils held in the early centuries of the Church when doctrine was confused, and emperors called the bishops together in the quaint belief that God might allow an individual to go astray but could not allow a group of devout Christians meeting in concert to seek his guidance to go away without it. The difference was that general councils went on with grand ceremonies and pomp and circumstance and ritual and processions and Latin or Greek proclamations from a pulpit and that sometimes emperors were present and took part in the debates. Imagine the President of the United States coming to Salem Baptist Association. Things were done on a lesser scale among the Baptists. But God was still God.

Charles knew almost nothing about councils of the Church and Eastern emperors and nothing at all about hypostatic union and three personae sharing one substance and Monophysites and Monothelites and all those strange combinations of Greek words that led people centuries before to slaughter each other with the bloodthirsty confidence that they killed for the pleasure of God.

Charles became enthusiastic about the idea, an enthusiasm that he did not show to Arceneaux except by the questions he asked and the furious way he scribbled his notes. Arceneaux's voice rolled on like a torrent, the voice convincing the speaker as it flowed through a channel that met no opposition. At the end, Charles flipped his notebook shut and looked at Arceneaux. "I wouldn't miss this for the world," he said.

"What do you mean?" Arceneaux said.

"I'll be there to cover the story. If they pull you out of the pulpit and beat you up, I will write about it." He smiled, but Arceneaux did not smile back.

"I thought you would rescue me," Arceneaux said, trying to smile.

"I would do that after I got my story," Charles said, but he did smile, and Arceneaux smiled, too. The smiles did not last long.

"Charles, that's June 19. Do you know what day that is?"

"It's the day Hope Kirby is set to be executed," Charles said, returning the minister's gaze steadily.

"Charles, you ought to get out of town. Take a trip. Hugh and I, we have an appointment with the governor on Friday. Maybe we can talk him into a pardon. But remember. Roy Kirby is still out there, and I think he will kill you if Hope goes to the chair. Don't you have relatives in Philadelphia?"

"I have a couple of aunts up there," he said.

"Go visit them. Stay for weeks. Philadelphia's a nice town despite W. C. Fields. It has a great art museum, and a beautiful park, and—"

"I'm not going anywhere," Charles said. "I'll stay right here. I've run too much already."

"It's no crime to run, Charles. Not when your life is in danger."

Charles shrugged. "I'm going to do what I will do," he said.

As it happened, the Monday Charles went to interview Arceneaux, the radio and the television news buzzed with the report that all nine justices of the Supreme Court had ruled that the separate-but-equal doctrine approved by that court in 1896 was unconstitutional, and the Knoxville afternoon paper arrived in Bourbonville with black headlines: RACIAL SEGREGATION UNCONSTITUTIONAL, SAYS COURT. The words took up two thick black lines of print.

Charles ran a story about Arceneaux in the Thursday paper. Some stirring quotations from Arceneaux about Christian brotherhood. Some antiseptic words about what blacks wanted. They didn't want to marry white women; they wanted to have a chance to get the same education white people had, to work the same jobs, to climb the ladder of success (Arceneaux was not above using a cliché now and then), and to give to their children the same opportunities white people wanted to give to their children. "We fought a war for democracy," Arceneaux said, and Charles quoted him. "But we cannot have democracy until all our people have the same opportunity, regardless of their color."

It was a long story, running a column all the way down the right side of the front page and passing on to another page inside. Suddenly everybody knew that the first response in town to the new decision would come from the Baptists. That in itself was amazing.

But maybe the most amazing thing about the paper that Thursday afternoon was that Red Eason contributed a story. It also ran on the front page— Red, who usually avoided controversy. Taking unpopular positions might cost the *Bourbon County News* advertising that the newspaper in its precarious financial condition could not afford. Maybe Arceneaux stirred Red up— although Red was a Methodist.

Red wrote an editorial urging calm and compliance and pointed out that so few Negroes lived in Bourbon County that even if the Bourbon County schools were forced to desegregate, it would not be a big thing. "Whatever the short-term effects of this decision," he wrote, "no one can doubt that it will eventually affect every school in the United States."

But in Bourbonville and the county most people did not react in panic or even in anger. Life had gone on so long in its customary ways that no one could quite fathom change, and change would not happen tomorrow. Whatever would happen would not happen today. It was a gorgeous May, and the town had receded from the headlines of the Knoxville newspapers and had settled back into its pleasant routines and expectations. For the moment, the world seemed suspended. Most people wanted the pleasant obscurity of their former days. Hope Kirby was in prison. The murders of the winter settled into everybody's heart, and more people locked their doors now than ever before in Bourbonville. They were suddenly aware that life was not regular and that absurd and terrible things could happen.

Tommy Fieldston was an exception. In the first place, Tommy Fieldston hated blacks more than anyone else in Bourbonville because he had worked with them in Toledo, and he had been enraged at their presumption and their lack of respect and on occasion their anger and their hard-eyed threats of violence. He was enraged that in the glass factory some blacks were promoted over him. He was enraged that blacks might move into his neighborhood and destroy all the investment he had in his house. From the day the decision of the Supreme Court was announced, Tommy Fieldston believed that Earl Warren had been infected by communism, and he was one of the first to sign a petition that summer that the Chief Justice of the United States Supreme Court be impeached. Soon a sign urging that impeachment would greet travelers driving out of the Knoxville airport.

He was even more enraged that Arceneaux should propose to bring a resolution to the Salem Baptist Association asking for acceptance of this monstrous decision. It was one more proof that Arceneaux was a modernist and probably a Communist, another sign that he had embraced the social gospel, and that therefore he had cast aside the true beliefs that Baptists had embraced from the time of Christ their founder to the present day. (Tommy was one of those who believed that Baptists had existed in hiding all during the Middle Ages and that they had never been Catholics.)

He drove up to see Clifford Finewood on the very evening the newspaper came out with Charles's story. Finewood was less emotional, but he saw the danger. Yes he did. Start preaching the social gospel, and you believed that people could improve themselves and their world without the grace of God. You stopped believing in original sin and grace and the power of God to save the sinner and the Resurrection, and then everything was lost. Man was a sinner, and his spiral was downward, and only Christ could relieve the corruption when he came again in glory.

They sat together and made plans. They would organize to be sure that Arceneaux's resolution went down in smoke. If they played the game correctly, they thought (not mentioning the word "game" in such serious circumstances), they would get rid of Arceneaux once and for all.

*T*HAT same Thursday, Arceneaux drove Hugh Bedford to Nashville in the white Jaguar for an appointment with the governor on Friday. They stayed the night in the Andrew Jackson Hotel. The prevailing color in the Andrew Jackson was brown, with brass rails and brass pilasters thrown in to relieve the monotony. Dirt was brown, and the suspicion could easily arise that the hotel had adopted its decor to reduce its cleaning bills. The hotel smelled musty, and the food was terrible. Arceneaux's room looked out towards the War Memorial Building. It was built with columns and was supposed to be Greek or Roman; it was hard to say which, but classical, no doubt about that. It had been built for the Tennesseans killed in the First World War. Those killed in World War II had been added. No sense building a new memorial for them when this one had so much space left in it.

He stood by the window and wondered if anybody remembered the name of a single Tennessean killed in that first war. If he himself had died in the second, he thought, his name would be on a memorial in New Orleans. His father and mother would be proud. A lot prouder than they would be to have him exposed as a queer. But they would be devastated too. The end of the line in a son dead in France. He stood at the window feeling lonely. What was life to be for him now? The sugar plantation? He loved the place, the sweep of the seasons across the land, the feeling that it was his land, his family's land, that in his brief and fragile life he had a part in a larger world that transcended time and gave him an identity. He was not one of those people who fascinated him on the streets of New Orleans by their appearance of living entirely in the moment, going to a job in a shop or a drugstore or one of the bars on Bourbon Street or merely sitting their days and nights on Jackson Square watching the world go by without any feeling of participation in it or any desire to be more than a listless human machine that went through one habit after another so that the habits added up to life with nothing left over. He had a life that was set apart, and it was rooted in land that had been in his family for generations.

Maybe he could manage marriage without being found out. He heard stories of people who lived together warmly for years without having sex, this after youthful passions that gave them children and quickly cooled. He would like to have a child—no, children, a house filled with children. He did not want to do with a woman what children required to be born. But he could manage. It was like the war. You could make yourself do anything when you had to.

The hotel room had a radio. Arceneaux tuned it to an all-night station and went to sleep listening to it and drifted into puzzled dreams with the bland music in the background. He sailed high over the land, adrift in clouds.

THE NEXT day Hugh Bedford and Arceneaux were shown into the governor's office promptly at ten. The governor had coal-black hair that he combed straight back and held in place with the greasy pomades used in those days. Wildroot Cream Oil. Vitalis, Vaseline. His hair always shone with the oil in it, and every hair was inevitably in place. He had a square, conventionally handsome face and thick, dark eyebrows and a mouth that in his campaign photographs seemed much stronger than it was in the flesh. He wore a dark blue suit with a conservative necktie, and a white handkerchief was neatly pointed in his jacket pocket. He looked very much as a governor ought to look, and he had the eager voice of the politician unwilling to let a single vote escape him.

The walls of his office were hung with photographs of himself with important politicians in the Democratic Party, or else of important men taken in elegant and solitary grandeur. All bore flowery autographs. The governor sat behind his desk with a slight smile, one hand to his cheek as though posing for the campaign poster he had used when he won the office in 1952. He allowed them to see him in the pose for a moment before he stood up and extended his hand.

"Gentlemen! Gentlemen!" he said. His words were slurred. "I've read so much about your case, Mr. Bedford," he said to Arceneaux.

"This is Mr. Bedford, Governor. I'm Lawrence Arceneaux. I'm the minister of First Baptist Church in Bourbonville. I'm a friend of Mr. Bedford's, and I've come to offer what help I can."

"Oh yes. Do forgive me, Reverend. Mr. Bedford. Good to see you, sir. Good to see you. Where are you from, Reverend? South Carolina? Mississippi?"

"Louisiana," Arceneaux said.

"I knew that accent didn't come from around here," the governor said.

There was a ritual and somewhat confused shaking of hands all around. The governor was in an expansive mood. His hands were softer than a woman's. He smelled strongly of men's cologne and faintly of whiskey. The governor directed them to chairs, and they all sat down.

Hugh Bedford spoke up. "You know why we're here, Governor. We want to appeal to you about Hope Kirby. I hope you've read my brief on the case."

"Indeed I have. Every word. Every word. Very sad case. Yes, very sad case. Your client's a war veteran, I believe."

"Yes, decorated by General MacArthur himself," Hugh Bedford said eagerly.

"I'm a veteran, you know. I never saw combat." He put on a mournful expression, and his voice dropped. "The sadness of my life. I think if you're going to be in a war, somebody ought to shoot at you. It didn't happen to me. I served in a supply ship during the whole thing. Never had a shot fired at me in anger."

"Governor, you didn't miss anything, I can tell you. We both can tell you."

"So you both saw combat? Well, well," the governor said, clearly impressed. "Were you a chaplain, Reverend?"

"I was in the OSS," Arceneaux said.

"The OSS. Well, well. You must be very smart. And from a good family. I've heard that Dulles didn't allow anybody in the OSS who wasn't from a good family."

"I don't know about that," Arceneaux said, trying to hide his distaste for this loquacious man.

"Well, I know," the governor said. "I doubt that he would have taken me. Not that my family is anything to be ashamed of. But we were not prominent. Not at least until I became governor."

"That would seem to be prominence enough, Governor," Hugh Bedford said in a desperate and clumsy effort at flattery.

"Oh, I don't know," the governor said a little sadly. His eyes brightened. "But a president of the United States. That might be family enough even for Allen Dulles."

"Are you going to run?" Arceneaux said, speaking before he thought.

The governor threw his hand up in an insincerely dismissive gesture. "Oh, it's too soon to tell. Too soon to say. Let's talk about your client, Counselor."

"Yes, let's talk about him," Hugh Bedford said. He held a neatly typed copy of his brief in his hand. "My client is caught in a web of circumstances, Governor. I must make you understand one essential detail."

"Ah, the essential detail," the governor said. "Let's get to the essential detail. I am sure that is very important, since it is essential. The key to everything else, isn't it? The essential detail." In a moment of hopeless anguish Arceneaux wondered suddenly if the governor was too drunk to understand what was going on. He remembered his own desperate efforts when drunk to hide it by speaking with elaborate precision. That is how the governor was speaking now, as if every word were of the greatest importance and had to be pronounced perfectly.

Hugh Bedford was having the same thought. He studied the governor carefully. "You have read my brief."

"Every word. A fascinating document. You are firmly convinced that there was no collusion between your client and the murderer, the man they call Missionary. A strange name, isn't it? Missionary. I never thought of missionaries being murderers."

"This man was a missionary in the Philippines before the war started," Hugh said. "He joined Hope Kirby's band of guerrillas, and he proved himself to be a sadistic killer. He was a killing machine. It's all in the brief. I think the war drove him crazy."

"You're speaking of the man named Missionary," the governor said. "Not Hope Kirby."

"Yes, Governor, I'm speaking of the man named Missionary. He was the sadistic killer."

"I just wanted to get that straight," the governor said.

Hugh Bedford took a deep breath and sent a look of troubled inquiry across to Arceneaux. Arceneaux shrugged almost imperceptibly. The governor sat back in his chair and assumed an expression of the utmost seriousness.

"So that is the essential detail," the governor said. "That Missionary and not Hope Kirby was the sadistic killer."

"No, Governor. Let me make the point. The essential detail is that Missionary and Hope Kirby were not friends. They were rivals. Hope had to keep Missionary in check all during the war, and Missionary resented it. Missionary wanted to be leader of the band."

"Now wait a minute," the governor said. "Are we talking about music now?"

"No, no, no," Hugh said. "We're talking about a guerrilla band, fighting the Japs in the jungles of the Philippines. We're talking about men who did not give in, who killed Japs all during the war, and Hope Kirby led them, and Hope Kirby was decorated by General MacArthur for his heroism. But Missionary wanted Hope's place. He wanted to be the leader. He was jealous."

"Jealousy is a very hard thing to bear," the governor said. "A jealous woman is one of the hardest things on earth."

"Listen to me, Governor. It's all in my brief, but I'm telling you the story. I'm talking about a jealous man. Jealousy is worse in a man than it is in a woman."

"I've read your brief. Every word. You can ask my secretary. Very interesting document."

"Thank you, Governor," Hugh said. "The essential detail is this."

"The essential detail," the governor said, mustering all his seriousness.

"Missionary and Hope had nothing to do with each other after the war. They didn't meet. They didn't talk on the telephone. They didn't write each other. When Hope landed in prison, Missionary heard about Hope's trouble, and he came to see him. They talked. But Missionary said nothing at all about killing people—about murdering Judge Yancy, those other jurors. Hope knew nothing about what Missionary planned to do until the killings started, and then he told me about it, and he talked to the authorities, and he cooperated in every way he could to bring Missionary to justice."

"So Missionary was arrested, was he?"

"No, Governor, he was shot to death while he was trying to murder the principal witness in the case, Charles Alexander. It's all in my brief."

"I've read every word of it," the governor said.

In deepening despair Hugh led the governor through the rest of the case. He became more intense, and the governor seemed to decide after a while that he was being badgered. He struck back.

"The fact remains that it seems pretty clear to me that your client murdered at least two people in cold blood," he said. "Two people. You can go to the electric chair in this state for killing only one person. You don't get a special rate for killing a half-dozen." The governor sat back and smiled weirdly, seemingly pleased with this mysterious bit of wit.

"Governor, the only witness to their deaths has said he could not be sure that Hope Kirby was the man he saw that night. It was a dark night."

"Oh, come now, Mr. Bradford. He did kill them. Let's admit that he killed them, and then we can talk."

"Governor, Hope Kirby has an alibi. The state now has no eyewitness to say he was on the scene."

"Oh yes, the eyewitness. The one who changed his story. The boy. What's his name?"

"Charles Alexander, Governor."

"Charles Alexander," the governor said, nodding as if he had known all along.

"Governor, Charles Alexander now says he cannot definitely say Hope Kirby was the man he saw out there that night, the man who killed Hope's wife and her lover."

"But look, Mr. Bradford. Let's be honest with each other. You and I know he killed the woman. His wife, wasn't it?"

"The dead woman was his wife," Hugh said.

"Too bad how marriages turn . . . Could you ever kill your wife, Mr. Bradford?"

"Bedford, Governor. My name is Bedford."

"Answer the question. Could you murder your wife?"

"I don't have a wife, Governor. I'm a—have never married."

"Is there something wrong with you, Mr. Bradford? Is that why you've never married? Well, you're among friends."

"Governor—"

"You, Mr. Lawrence. Are you married?"

"No, Governor. No, I'm not married, either, and there's nothing wrong with me. And my name is Lawrence Arceneaux, not Mr. Lawrence."

"Two bachelors! And the man, your client, Mr. Bradford. He never did it with his wife, did he? You know, that's the thing I remember most about this case. He never did it with his wife. Do you suppose he's queer?"

"Governor," Hugh Bedford said. "Please, we're here to beg you for a pardon for a war hero. Look, Governor, let's suppose he did—"

"It's amazing that a preacher saw combat in the war," the governor said suddenly, looking anew at Arceneaux. "I thought you all did what Billy Graham did. Preachers can stay out of the army, can't they? Billy stayed home and preached the Gospel while other boys were being shot at. I don't hold it against him. He's done great work. He's a friend of mine. I've sat on the platform during several of his crusades. A great honor."

"Governor, will you listen to me?" Hugh Bedford shouted at the governor.

The governor looked at him with slightly unfocused eyes. "No need to raise your voice, Mr. Bradford. Of course I will listen to you. What do you have to say?"

Hugh Bedford took a deep, exasperated breath. "I am trying to talk to you about a man's life. Are you such a drunk that you can't listen to me when I'm talking about a man's life?"

Arceneaux looked at him with amazement. He almost laughed. What else was there to do? The governor was their age. They were all still young. They had been through a war, and they had seen so much and done so much, and they were all still young, and Hugh Bedford and Larry Arceneaux were superior to this governor because they'd seen action during the war, and he had not. Arceneaux felt a sudden, impulsive thrill of joy. He was queer, and he was alive, and he was still young, and he had been brave in the war. He knew he had been brave. This man had never been brave.

"I am not drunk," the governor said sullenly.

"Goddammit, you are drunk," Hugh Bedford raged, jumping out of his chair. "Either you're drunk, or you are putting on an act to keep from having to listen to me and make a decision. I am talking about a war hero, a better man than you ever were, a better man than you'll ever be. I'm talking about a man who fought the Japs hand-to-hand in the Philippines for more than two years. He won a medal from General Douglas MacArthur himself. Suppose he did kill his wife. She was screwing another man right under his nose. And how do we know what he did with his wife in bed? We have the word of an old doctor who was probably confused. I'm saying that Hope Kirby might have been convicted of manslaughter. He might have had to serve five or ten years in prison. But he doesn't deserve to die in the electric chair because a buffoon of a judge was in love with the murdered woman and wanted his own revenge."

Hugh Bedford was standing over the governor shouting. The governor looked up at him bewildered and perhaps a little afraid. Arceneaux stood up to restrain Hugh.

"Sit down, Mr. Bradford," the governor said in a quiet voice.

Hugh Bedford sat down. Larry Arceneaux sat down, too.

"I'm doing the best I can," the governor said quietly. "I have a problem. I drink too much."

"I didn't mean to insult you," Hugh Bedford said quietly. "I drink too much myself. I mean, I have drunk too much in my time. I've not had anything to drink for a while."

"How did you do that? How did you quit?"

"I just quit," Hugh Bedford said. "I'm sorry. I didn't mean—"

"No, it's all right," the governor said quietly.

"It's a man's life, Governor. He's a hero. A true hero. You and I, we were not heroes."

"No, we were not heroes. I'm not a hero now. But I'm not a drunk either. I can quit this thing, you know. I can stop drinking. Any time I want."

"Sure," Hugh Bedford said. "But right now we're not talking about your drinking. We're talking about a real hero, somebody who did things we didn't do in the war, somebody who helped us whip the Japs and—somebody who did great things. You can save his life, Governor, and you know and I know that he will never kill anybody again."

"So you admit that he did kill them. That's what I'm waiting to hear. Don't give me this shit about Charles what's-his-name and the alibi and all the rest of it. Just tell me he killed them. Don't shit me, lawyer. Tell me he killed them." The governor stared gloomily across the desk at Hugh Bedford.

Hugh Bedford took a deep breath. He met the governor's gaze.

"Well?" the governor said.

"Governor—" Arceneaux said.

"I'm asking the condemned man's lawyer a question," the governor said; the slur in his words vanished as he spat them out. "I want to know what he thinks."

Hugh Bedford spoke softly. "I think he killed them, Governor. It was a crime of passion. She was humiliating him in front of his family, in front of the whole town. He killed her to save his honor—something you and I don't have."

"Speak for yourself, Mr. Bedford," the governor said, his voice hard.

"I think I can speak for both of us, Governor."

The governor stared at him and then shrugged. "Perhaps you can," he said in a soft voice.

He turned to Arceneaux. "What do you think, Reverend?"

"I don't think any good is served by putting a man to death when he will never commit murder again," Arceneaux said.

"It's not Christian, you're saying."

"It's not right to put this man to death," Arceneaux said. "No, it's not Christian."

"You don't believe in capital punishment, then?"

"I didn't say that."

"Can you think of something somebody would do that would deserve death?" The governor leaned across the desk and stared at him sharply, a soft man trying to intimidate.

Arceneaux returned the governor's gaze. "I was at Nuremberg, Governor. I interrogated prisoners. I talked to Goering, to Jodl, Ribbentrop. I could have pulled the trap on any of them. They all deserved to die. I'm sorry Goering escaped the noose by taking cyanide. We should have checked him better."

"You talked to them?" the governor said.

"I interrogated them."

"What were they like?"

"They were pathetic little nobodies, Governor. They were tiny men playing with big machines."

"I thought they might have had some—some kind of power."

"They didn't," Arceneaux said. "They had an army and a Gestapo and ambition. But they were Lilliputians."

"Lily what?" the governor said.

"Lilliputians," Arceneaux said. "Like in *Gulliver's Travels*."

"Oh yes, the cartoon movie," the governor said. He sat back and looked at them both. "Well, I see what you mean. Do you know why I wanted the truth, Mr. Bedford?"

"I suppose you have to make a decision based on it," Hugh said.

The governor laughed harshly. "Do you know how often you hear the truth in this place?" The governor swept his hand around.

"Not much, I guess," Hugh Bedford said

"About as often as you hear virgins sing hymns in a Japanese whorehouse. And you have told me the truth." He bent to his desk and pulled a drawer open and took out a bottle of bourbon. "Let's drink to truth," he said. He brought out three tumblers.

Hugh Bedford looked at the governor. He shook his head. "Governor, I'm off the sauce until this case is over, until you give my client a pardon. You give him a pardon, and we'll drink so much that the price of whiskey will go up five dollars a quart."

The governor did not get the joke at first. When he got it, he threw his head back and laughed. "Five dollars a quart!" he said. "Yes, we'll drink so much we'll raise the price of a bottle of whiskey five dollars a quart. Praise the Lord. What about you, Reverend? Do you want a drink?"

"I can't drink," Arceneaux said. "But suit yourself."

"Of course you can't drink. You're a preacher. I forgot." The governor poured a tumbler almost full of whiskey. The brown liquid caught the light like a transparent stone. The governor looked at it. "When I think sometimes that Jesus made water into wine when he could have made it into bourbon, well, I wonder what he was thinking about." He picked up the tumbler and tossed his head back and drank the way some people drink water when they are thirsty. His eyes watered, and he wiped them with the back of his hand.

"Gentlemen, I will tell you the truth. I'm in a truthful mood today. I want to be president of the United States."

Arceneaux and Hugh looked at each other. The governor could have been a doctor, holding an X-ray, looking apologetically across a desk at them, saying, "I'm sorry, but I have very bad news."

"To be president, you have to have the respect of people. You have to have a reputation. I have a plan. I'm going to take a vacation, go to Palm Springs or someplace like that, some discreet sanitarium, and I'm going to have a treatment. I'm going to dry out."

He looked at the bottle and looked at the tumbler, longingly. He took a couple of Kleenex from a box on his desk. Carefully he dried the tumbler, put the top back on the bottle, and returned tumblers and bottle to their drawer. He threw the Kleenex into a trash basket behind his desk.

"I'm going to stop drinking, and I'm smart enough to see that I need help to do it."

"I think that's a good idea, Governor," Arceneaux said.

"Yes, yes," the governor said vaguely. "Well, the point is . . ."

They waited.

"The point is what?" Hugh said finally.

"The point is simply this. In two years we're going to have the national convention of the Democratic Party. I'm angling to make the keynote speech."

They waited.

"I think that speech is going to make me the vice-presidential candidate for the party." He spoke these words with a rush, as though revealing a secret or making a confession. He waited. Hugh and Arceneaux could think of nothing to say.

"What do you think of that?" the governor said crossly, his expression changing abruptly, the way a drunk's face will change when he is able to hold on to only one thought at a time, that thought being the impression he is making on people.

"I think it's a very interesting idea," Arceneaux said. "Don't you think it's an interesting idea, Hugh?"

"Absolutely. One of the most interesting ideas I've ever heard. What then, Governor?"

The governor smiled. "The nominee will be Stevenson, of course. He's the darling of the liberals that run the party now. But he will lose. Nobody can beat Ike's grin. But I'll campaign hard, and I'll be in line for the presidential nomination for 1960. That's six years away, gentlemen. Six years. Not long." His smile widened to a triumphant grin.

They looked at him, not daring to look at each other.

"You think I'm dreaming," the governor said, his face going ugly again.

"No, no," Hugh said. "I think this is serious business. But the pardon, Governor. What about the pardon?" Hugh Bedford leaned forward and spoke in a beseeching tone. He told Arceneaux afterward that he felt like crying. "I just wanted to keep the stupid sot's mind on Hope. I felt like killing him, but I knew we couldn't get away with it. So I was ready to get down on my knees."

"You've told me the truth," the governor said magnanimously. "I've tried to tell you the truth, too. I'm going to look this thing over. I'm going to look at it from every angle. I'm going to see what I think is good for the state. Let me tell you this. I'm going to think about what's good for number one. I'm not going to lose the presidency because I do something stupid."

"Governor," Arceneaux said, "look at it this way. If you win the presidency, you will have to have the support of those liberals you're talking about, the ones in New York and California that control the Democratic Party. They don't like the electric chair. If you let a war hero die in the electric chair for a crime of passion, you'll look like just another yokel Southern governor not worth the trust of a Northern liberal. If you commute Hope Kirby's sentence, you can be a hero, Governor. The liberals who control the party now will look up to you, and you will have everything you want."

"Do you think so? Do you really think so?" The governor's dark eyes almost licked Arceneaux's face.

Arceneaux met the governor's gaze and spoke softly. "Yes, I think so."

"So do I," Hugh said.

Arceneaux said, "Governor, we're talking about both mercy and justice. What happened to Judge Yancy and the others was horrible, but Hope Kirby was not responsible for it. That man, the man called Missionary, he was crazy. Judge Yancy's death has as little to do with Hope Kirby as if the judge had been killed in a car wreck. The judge had a feeling for Abby Kirby. He—"

"Do you think that old man ever got into her britches?" the governor said.

Arceneaux shook his head in a distaste that the governor did not notice. "No, Governor, I don't. I don't think he wanted that kind of intimacy. I think he wanted—"

"What did he want if he didn't want to get into her britches?" the governor asked.

"I think he wanted to feel that somebody loved him," Arceneaux said.

The governor laughed out loud. "Who in the name of God could love that mean old bastard?"

"He *was* a mean old bastard, Governor," Hugh Bedford said. "And if he hadn't been killed, any appeals court in any state in the country would have granted Hope Kirby a new trial. If you commute his sentence, people's heads will cool down. They'll realize what a farce that trial was. You will be remembered in the history books for intelligence and mercy."

"Gentlemen, I want to be remembered in the history books as the president of the United States. I just might remind you that President Eisenhower got himself elected president because he killed millions of Germans. It's been a pleasure to see you. A real pleasure. I will think about it. I have another appointment right now. I must bid you good day. But I promise. I will think about it."

Hugh Bedford and Larry Arceneaux went out. The secretary at the governor's door looked up at them hopelessly. "How is he?" she said.

"I hate to tell you this," Hugh Bedford said in a stage whisper, looking back towards the shut mahogany door with an expression of mock alarm, "I believe the governor has been drinking something. I know that's a shock to you, but yes, I honestly believe the man is drunk. I think you'd better call a doctor."

"No, no," she said in alarm. "He's told me never to do that." She got up and rushed into the office, and Hugh Bedford looked at Larry Arceneaux.

"How can we kill him?" Hugh said.

"I could break his neck and make it look like a fall," Arceneaux said. He stared back towards the door.

Hugh Bedford looked at him. "You're serious, aren't you?"

"You're damned right I'm serious," Arceneaux said. "I've done it."

Hugh grabbed him by the arm. "Come on. I don't want you in the chair, too."

THE UNIVERSITY term ended in the fourth week in May. Proust ended with the term. Albertine was dead. Saint-Loup the homosexual was dead, and the class of five had become able to discuss literary homosexuality as if it were one of a number of human conditions, odd or perverse as the humor of whoever spoke might have it, but a condition to be mulled over and contemplated, if nothing else, in the same way that a doctor might discuss disease as one of the expressions of human life, objectively, dispassionately, and without embarrassment. Somehow the class ended in an expression of triumph, Dr. Stiefel beaming out at them with the pure pleasure of a man who had succeeded in conveying something he loved to students as if the conveying were all to intensify and perhaps to certify himself and his life.

McKinley was not present on the last day of class. It was a mysterious absence, as mysterious as his frequent silences had been in the classroom itself towards the end of the term. Sometimes Dr. Stiefel would turn a twinkling eye on him and say with a jocular voice, *"Eh bien, M. McKinley, vous n'avez pas d'opinion au sujet d'Albertine?"* McKinley smiled back and in his atrocious accent would make a response always on the mark and nearly always drawing from Dr. Stiefel a Gallic explosion of commentary and amplification of whatever it was that McKinley had said. Dr. Stiefel was clearly disappointed that McKinley was absent, inquired about him and drew blank negations from the other four in the class, especially from Charles and Tempe.

When it was all over, Tempe turned gravely to Charles and said, "Could we take a walk? I want to tell you some things."

From the time Charles had told her about visiting the snake-handling meeting, he had not spoken to her alone. By an unspoken and perhaps unthought agreement they had continued to drink coffee now and then, but always with McKinley, sometimes at Tempe's place, and sometimes they walked a couple of blocks from the university to a less-frequented drugstore near the Booth Theatre, and there they talked about the class and about this and that and scarcely ever about Charles and the world of Bourbonville, which had now grown quiet. One day McKinley observed that they had arrived at a time when nothing stayed in the news for very long. Television, radio, and even the newspapers had a ravenous appetite for new names and new places. "Once they are chewed up, they are spat out like old chewing gum, and they're lucky if they stick to somebody's shoe," Mack said.

"Oh Mack," Tempe said.

On this day, no Mack, his absence as striking as a missing front tooth. Charles and Tempe took a walk. Charles fell in beside her, and they went down the tree-covered hill where Ayres Hall stood with its towers amidst the leaves, and they came out onto Fifteenth Street. It passed the gigantic football stadium on the left, and after the stadium they took a short street called Yale and climbed silently up a slight rise of ground to a large, grass-covered circle with trees, surrounded on its perimeter by shabby Victorian houses built during an earlier heyday of Knoxville sometime after the Civil War but now used as rooming houses and slowly crumbling from neglect, for Knoxville's wealthy had shifted their interest to Kingston Pike where their brick mansions lined the broad avenue that led out of town towards Nashville and Chattanooga.

Tempe wore a white blouse with a little gold brooch pinned at the neck, and she wore a pleated skirt so that her slender form seemed fit for a fashion magazine that catered to college girls, something like *Seventeen*, perhaps. She wore white bobby socks and brown oxford shoes, and to look at her was to imagine that one was seeing one of the blessed of the earth. Her face today was solemn enough to dissipate any of those optimistic feelings, and she neither smiled nor spoke to Charles for a long time. But in the park she did take him by the arm, a hand gently clasped above his elbow, and she steered him across the circle and down a little street and out to the banks of the river where a crusted and weathered bench looked out towards the brown water.

"Let's sit here," she said.

Charles was caught in a confusion of emotions. He knew she had serious things to discuss, and he dreaded the conversation. But he also wanted with all his heart to do the right thing, to say the right thing, to hold himself in an attitude so that if a movie camera were turned on him and everything he said recorded and shown to an audience in a darkened room, he would emerge looking a little like Gary Cooper about to say goodbye to Ingrid Bergman. That, at least, was his analysis of himself in the rest of his life when he was given during occasional insomniac nights to raking through his past to discover, with shame, what kind of person he had been and why he had made so many mistakes.

Tempe released his arm, and they sat, looking out over the river scattered with houseboats where men and sometimes families eked out a living taking catfish from the dirty water. The idea of pollution had only barely begun to be noised about in those days. Some of the houseboats had bottles of whiskey tied under them by rope, and at night, so people said, anybody could come buy at a bootlegger's price, and if the police raided, the ropes could be easily cut and the evidence deposited on the muddy river bottom.

Along the banks on this side of the river stood a scattering of slum houses and ugly industrial land, including the inevitable sand and gravel works to be found along any river in almost any Southern city. Beyond the river a high, steep bluff arose, covered with vines and scrub brush of various sorts, ugly and confused except that they did offer a pattern of greenery that made the scene seem less sterile and desolate.

"This place could be so beautiful," Tempe said wistfully. "And it's not. Why can't Knoxville do something to make it beautiful?"

Charles laughed dryly. "Knoxville does not care for beauty," he said. "It cares only about money."

They sat in silence for a while. He knew she was shaping words to say to him. She had removed her hand from his arm when they sat down. Now she laid a hand on his arm again, running her fingers around his forearm. "Charles, I want to say something. I want to say several things, and I don't want to hurt your feelings. But what I have to say is painful. I think I have to say these things, or I'll spend the rest of my life wishing I had said them, and I don't think the chance will ever come again."

"Go ahead," he said, his voice not as steady as he wished it would be.

"The first thing I want to say is that I'm leaving school after this term, and I'm going away. I'm going to France. I've persuaded my father to let me go there for a year. He's worried that people will think I've gone off to have another illegitimate baby, but I've pointed out to him that hardly anybody knows I've had a baby. I've told him I have to get away because I'm in love, and the person I love doesn't love me and never will because he's too in love with himself. I'm talking about you, Charles."

First Charles was startled by her declaration. She dated other men. She made an effort to see him only after the Proust class. How could she be in love with him? Then he grew resentful. "I don't think that—" He was going to protest, to say that he did not think she was being fair, but she cut him off, squeezing his hand in a sort of fierce determination that was near to anger.

"Let me finish. I have a lot to say, and after that, you can talk."

He subsided. She gathered her forces again and continued. "When I met you, I saw how unspoiled you are. I thought you had no pretensions. You said funny things in the Balzac class. Everybody liked you. When the murders happened, you seemed so hurt, so vulnerable that I wanted to mother you and keep you safe from all those terrible things that were happening and you couldn't do anything about. I told McKinley we had to be your friends because you needed friends." She laid her hand on his arm. Her fingers were cool and smooth.

"When we talked, I discovered that I needed friends, too. I had never told anybody about my baby, about Florence Crittenden, about New Orleans. I didn't try to hide it. But nobody suspected anything, or at least nobody said anything to me about it. I guess that's natural. People don't go around saying, 'What's your name, and where are you from, and have you ever given birth to a child out of wedlock?' I kept it all locked up inside, and I brooded about my child and wondered what she was doing at this minute or at that and whether she was crying or laughing or sleeping and whether the people who adopted her really loved her. I wondered if they might get a divorce, and the woman who would keep the child might marry some man who didn't love children, maybe some drunk who would abuse my daughter. She has always been my daughter, you see. I know I'll never see her again, but wherever she is, she's my daughter. Sometimes I wonder if she might have died of some childhood disease, or died in her crib the way you hear about children dying. I couldn't put her out of my mind, and most of the time when I thought about her, it was with guilt and fear and all those fantasies of the bad things that might be happening to her. Sometimes I had fantasies of how happy she might be, laughing and cooing and learning to talk and to walk and say 'Mama' and 'Dada,' and then I was jealous of those people who had my baby, and I didn't have anything of her. Oh, it's a silly story. You can't have a story like this without it being silly." She gathered herself.

"It's not silly," Charles said, and as soon as he spoke he realized that the words came out sounding dutiful.

"Let me finish. You promised not to speak." Charles did not remember making such a promise, but he fell silent and sat staring at the river and feeling a sadness that was as black as night.

"You told me about your religion. I couldn't believe it. So backward, so ignorant, as if the nineteenth century never happened and Charles Darwin had never been born and Matthew Arnold had never lived. You say you believe the Bible is true in every word. So you must believe in witchcraft and slaughtering the enemies of God."

"I don't believe in those things."

"Let me finish." She raised her voice now in anger, and Charles thought she might be about to cry, and he thought that her crying would be the worst thing in the world that could happen to him. He fell back into his moody silence, and she plunged on, now removing her hand from his forearm and gesturing as though she were on the point of losing control.

"I thought, *I will be his friend, and he will get over this foolishness.* I thought I would save you. So I tried to be your friend, and that night, up in the mountains I felt so close to you because we were happy together, and I told you about my baby, and you held me and comforted me. Oh, you didn't kiss me, but I didn't expect you to do that. Maybe if you had kissed me I would have decided you were trying to take advantage of my grief. But you didn't kiss me, and I was glad.

"So then I thought that we had shared something, and with you things seemed to go from bad to worse—those awful murders and that lunatic, and you were almost killed again. Nobody has ever pointed a gun at me. I don't know what it would be like. I know I'd be frozen in terror if I were that close to death, and it happened to you twice, and you stayed so calm. Were you calm, or did something freeze up inside you so you couldn't express any emotions? I don't know. But I do know that I admired you so much for how you kept on living as though nothing had happened, and I wanted to help you, but I didn't want to push you into anything.

"You didn't want my help. I could tell that. You never called me up. You never asked me out. But I thought maybe you did want my friendship and couldn't tell me, and I kept offering you my friendship at least, and I thought maybe you would call sometime, and we would eat somewhere or go to a movie or just sit somewhere and talk. But you never called. And then it came to me. All at once I understood what was going on in your head. When I told you about my baby, you decided that I was not pure enough for you. You have this idea about yourself, that you're God's chosen man, and everything has to be perfect for you, and you have to marry a girl who is a virgin, and she can never have loved anybody but you, and she can never have made a mistake because the girl you marry has to be out of the *Saturday Evening Post* or maybe out of the *Boy Scout Handbook*. You don't think I'm good enough for you. You can't stop believing in your crazy God, not because the world loses all its meaning and we all die and that's the end of us. You can't stop believing or trying to believe because once you give up your God, you have to give up being God's chosen boy, the person God has ordained for great things. You become ordinary, and you may have to marry an ordinary girl who's made some mistakes. Or else you marry some stupid woman who will do anything you want and be somebody you dress and undress like a paper doll because you deceive her into thinking you're chosen by somebody, God or fate or I don't know what. You might make some dumb bitch believe she's chosen because you're chosen, two for the price of one. You believe in a God, or you want to believe in a God, who makes the world up just for you. You're the center of it, and nobody else counts.

"And I just wanted to tell you that I understand that now, and I think it's monstrous, and I won't bother you again. I can't save you. When I try to save you from all this craziness of yours, I realize that I lose myself in an abyss. I don't understand you, Charles. Well, I do and I don't. I don't care anymore. I'm dropping out of school after this term. I'm going away. Maybe I'll finish college somewhere else. Yes, you're graduating, and you wouldn't be around anyway, but I don't want to be around anything that even reminds me of you.

In Paris I'm going to forget you. So goodbye, Charles. No, I don't want to listen to you after all. I know you'd be telling me a lie, and I don't want to hear it. I'm leaving, and I don't want to see you again. You want to marry the Virgin Mary. I'm not the Virgin Mary. I never can be. I never could have been."

With that, she leaped up from the bench and raced away. Charles stood up, looking after her, tempted to chase her, to make her stop and listen to him, but she had struck a blow that left him breathless and empty. She had told him she loved him. He had not known. He saw her slender form disappear behind the houses that stood around Circle Park, and she was gone. He was left in the most brutal loneliness of his life. He sat back down on the bench they had shared. It was appallingly empty, and time was sweeping him along like the river below in its muddy channel. He sat until the afternoon began to fade into twilight. His brain felt full of glue, and he thought he could sit there until he died.

*T*HE GOVERNOR took his time. He began having press conferences, striving to look presidential. In 1954 reporters were silent about the wrestling matches governors and other politicians had with John Barleycorn. Besides, only four or five reporters showed up, and no television station, even in Nashville, considered the governor's press conferences worthy of broadcast. Even President Eisenhower's press conferences were not the extravaganzas that such affairs became later on. The governor wanted the reporters to ask him about his presidential plans so he could deny that he had any, always leaving a door open a crack for "future study of the situation." He was concerned for the country, he said, but he also looked forward to some time with his family, and he spoke with a martyr's sorrow about the price political leaders paid for their careers, the heavy responsibility, the continual demands of travel, and the lack of privacy.

Much to the governor's irritation, the handful of reporters who showed up at his press conferences wanted to know what he planned to do about Hope Kirby. They were shameless, these reporters. They wanted to know if the governor's decision would be influenced by the fall elections when the governor would have a Republican opponent. In Tennessee at that time, no one took a Republican candidate for governor seriously except perhaps the unfortunate candidate himself. Still, politics was an uncertain profession, and it had dangerous ups and downs. The governor professed righteous indignation at these queries. Anything he did was decided on principle, he said, somewhat vehemently, but not so vehemently that he seemed to be angry at any particular reporter.

Then, launching into the Hope Kirby case, he considered it in studious detail, repeating himself often but finally outlining its difficulties with enough accuracy to pass muster with the press. Yes, Judge Yancy's charge to the jury had been extreme, but a judge did have rights that included freedom to comment on the merits of a case, and the judge had seen clearly what the governor himself saw, that the evidence clearly stood against Hope Kirby. Relying on Ken McNeil's presentation to the appeals court, the governor commented on well-known precedents holding that the testimony of witnesses who changed their story should be weighed carefully but that the first story such witnesses told was always superior to the second. The second story, the governor said with something akin to the authority of a recording, was likely to have been influenced by various experiences after the trial and was therefore to be discounted. Charles Alexander had ample reason to feel gratitude to the Kirby family because Roy Kirby saved his life, and therefore the governor had ample reason to assume that the testimony Charles had given under oath at the trial had been his true and just account of what he had seen.

The question of the death penalty for such an offense must naturally arise, and here the governor always lost control of his own argument so that time and again reporters stopped writing and looked up at him in puzzlement. It seemed that the governor was saying that Hope Kirby ought to have a fair trial on every particular of his case. The governor's aim was that justice be done. He was for justice. The cornerstone of the American Republic was justice. Justice was the reason our revolutionary heroes had left their bloodstained footsteps in the snows at Valley Forge. Justice was necessary for Hope Kirby. But justice was also necessary for the state of Tennessee. A sitting judge had been murdered. True, Hope Kirby may have had nothing to do with that murder. But it seemed clear from the evidence that Hope Kirby had murdered his wife and Kelly Parmalee, who was not proven to be her lover. The case had many ins and outs. The relation of the priest called Missionary and Hope Kirby was mysterious. It needed to be probed more. Questions needed to be asked. Questions needed to be answered. It might be for a court of law to resolve the evident contradiction that the priest called Missionary had been a homicidal maniac and that he had also been a friend of Hope Kirby's and in evident conversation with him before he began his trail of carnage. That sounded suspicious to the governor. Yet there was such a thing as coincidence. The governor had experienced many coincidences in his own life. Once in the navy in World War II he had been stationed on a ship with a friend of his he had not seen from boyhood. That was a great coincidence, and it was just possible that some such coincidence had worked to bring Missionary to Hope Kirby in prison.

If the reporters were baffled at all this, Hugh Bedford walked the floor in a rage that he poured out to a moodily contemplative Larry Arceneaux. "He is stalling. He is drunk. He doesn't know what to do. In the end he will ask somebody else, and somebody else will tell him he can't afford to pardon a murderer."

Arceneaux had some ideas. Maybe they could get a veterans' organization to take up the cause. Fair trial. But such things took time, and it was already late May. Hugh got on the telephone and started calling people he knew in the American Legion, the Veterans of Foreign Wars, the Disabled American Veterans. A petition. He would circulate a petition. But the idea ground down to ineffectual wheel-spinning. So many veterans. Yes, a sense of brotherhood among them, but they could unite only for things like improving the GI Bill and giving medical benefits and increasing pensions for the disabled and benefits for widows and orphans. They could not unite on Hope Kirby, convicted felon, probably because by this time they could not understand the case, and maybe because it was already like a story that had been told, and there was nothing to do except shut the book, except that when they did that, they left Hope Kirby dead in the electric chair.

Hugh Bedford tried again to see the governor. But the doors were shut against him. He waited outside the governor's office in the Capitol Building. Through the open windows he could look out on Nashville and the green Cumberland River below. The governor came in escorted by Tennessee Highway Patrol officers, and they pushed Hugh back so that he was left to shout, "The pardon, Governor. It's the only justice." He was an attraction for the reporters. He spoke of the difference between life and death, the commuting of a sentence compared to the final decision of death that could never be undone.

By June the Republicans had the makings of a candidate for governor, and no other Republican rose on the scene to oppose him. He was a wealthy businessman from Nashville. His name was Robert Kenslow Jarrett. He had made his fortune through a chain of car dealerships throughout the Southeast, and he had translated his wealth into a horse farm not far from Nashville, a mansion not far from the Hermitage, which had been the Tennessee residence of General and then President Andrew Jackson, and he had a flair for public speaking attractive to reporters. He was also a steward in the Methodist Church, a teetotaler, and given to public displays of ritual humility that included tributes to teachers, preachers, parents, and others without whom he could not have attained the success he had managed in life.

Jarrett also sewed himself firmly to the coattails of Dwight D. Eisenhower. When he spoke, Eisenhower rose on his words to become the pure American saint, first in war, first in peace, and first in the hearts of his countrymen, and Jarrett was careful to wear the double-breasted suits and homburg hats that Eisenhower wore and that became the political uniform of wisdom, courage, and responsibility.

"When the Rosenbergs betrayed their country, Dwight David Eisenhower courageously stood against all the softhearted liberals and the softheaded one-worlders and the Communists and the pinkos that gather around communism the way maggots will gather on a dead horse. Dwight Eisenhower spoke the courage of his convictions, and the Rosenbergs burned in the electric chair and now burn in hell where they belong. It remains to be seen whether a Tennessee governor will have that sort of courage to put a man in the electric chair who not only betrayed his community by shooting to death his wife and a prominent businessman but who also almost certainly colluded with a homicidal maniac in putting to death a judge and two jurymen in the most horrible way that anyone can imagine."

When Jarrett got started on Hope Kirby, you would think that Hope had shot Abby Kirby and Kelly Parmalee to death while they were singing side by side in a church choir. Jarrett had a knack for getting his name in the newspapers. By early June, the newspapers made Hope Kirby a battleground, and reporters wrote excitedly that it was just possible that the election might turn on whether the governor pardoned Hope Kirby or let him die in the chair.

Hugh Bedford raged and fumed. Arceneaux listened to the rage and the fuming but already in his mind was resigned to Hope's death. Everything was falling together wrong. Things happened that way sometimes. First one thing and then another fell into place, haphazardly and fatally, and mere mortals could do nothing about it but follow their destiny to its grimy and bloody end. Military operations were always going bad because everything went wrong at the same time. In his operations with the OSS he had calculated everything he could think of that could make a plan fail, and he always imagined everything going wrong at once. Not for him the idea of so many novels and movies where only one minor detail, one singular piece of bad luck, could send the whole plan toppling into the abyss. No, in his imagination, everything went wrong at once, and there was no way out. That was how he felt now. Everything was going wrong, and though Hugh Bedford worked like a demon trying to redeem things, his efforts were like those of a man trying to lift a building off his back when the thing had fallen over on him. He was down there under the rubble thinking no, no, this thing cannot be happening to me; it is not time for me to die; I will survive; I will get out of this, and all the while the bricks and the stone and the steel were pressing him into jelly. Hugh had hope. But Arceneaux was resigned. His obsession now was to save Charles Alexander's life.

CHARLES ALEXANDER was not concerned with saving his own life. He graduated from college in the great ceremony that UT had, flash-bulbs going off everywhere, the moment being saved, victory at hand. His father and Stephen and Guy were all there in the balcony, and he felt his mother's absence like a dull pain in the gut. It was a hot day. He gazed out at the crowd packed into the Alumni Memorial Gymnasium, the graduates sitting in their wool robes on the playing floor listening to an interminable address by J. C. Penney, the chain-store magnate. The university invited rich businessmen and politicians to give commencement speeches in hopes that the businessmen would donate money and the politicians would appropriate money. Both these hopes were usually frustrated. J. C. Penney bragged about how he became rich. He had been virtuous. He didn't say, "I have been virtuous." But he named the virtues he had practiced, and this tottering old man wanted all these young men and women to be like him insofar as they could be. The women could rise only so far. Everybody knew that. They could be clerks in J. C. Penney's store, but in 1954 the duty of a woman was to get married, stay at home, raise children, and use the right soap in her washing machine.

Charles looked for Tempe in the crowd, but she was nowhere to be seen. She was not there, he decided. Why should she be? She was not graduating, and she had no family graduating. *She has me,* Charles thought. It was not enough to make her sit in the furnace that Alumni Memorial Gymnasium became under the mournfully virtuous oratory of J. C. Penney and then under the interminable business of passing out the diplomas one by one, the president handing the sheepskin to the degree candidate so the photographer down below the stage could snap the picture.

His father took them to the Regasopoulos Restaurant for lunch, and one of the two elderly Regasopoulos brothers came out to greet him, and they spoke Greek together. "This boy, he tell me he not Greek when he first come to Knoxville, but I know Greek when I see one," Mr. Regasopoulos said. He embraced Paul Alexander and shook him a little, the not entirely friendly gesture of an uncle who loved a nephew but was not pleased with him. Paul Alexander was embarrassed. Charles knew how much his father hated to admit that he was Greek, but he could not deny Mr. Regasopoulos. Why did they go there to eat? It was mysterious, but there they were. And Mr. Regasopoulos did not have one Greek item on his menu.

"I brought your mother to this restaurant when we first were courting," Paul Alexander said gravely, as if he had been recounting an event of great historic importance that deserved to be remembered with reverence. It was a good meal. Guy talked a lot, too loudly, Charles thought, and people turned to look at them, to see this slope-headed, cross-eyed boy and the brother who in his blue suit and red bow tie had so obviously graduated from the university that morning. Other graduates were in the room, and some of them made discreet pointing signs at Charles and murmured to their tables, and everybody at the tables looked at Charles, and Charles looked down at his plate.

Paul Alexander said, "When I first came here, there were pictures of the Acropolis and the Parthenon on the walls, and you could get a wonderful moussaka and baklava and other Greek dishes that I liked very much. I was so new, and I felt so foreign, and Greeks were looked down on, and I wanted to impress your mother and her sister Bert. Bert was very important because your mother loved her so much, and Bert was very much opposed to foreigners, and I think she was opposed to my courtship of Eugenia. So when the Regasopoulos brothers spoke to me afterwards, I pretended not to understand, and after that I was ashamed that I had denied who I was. Eventually I came in and confessed myself to them. That was after we were married. I think that if I had told Eugenia I was Greek before we were married, she would not have had anything to do with me."

It was a sudden and startling revelation. Charles and Stephen had seen their father and their mother together, and more particularly they had seen their father's devotion to her. It was a love so steady and so intense that they assumed it had no conditions and perhaps that it had no history. Only that bright June day in the air-conditioned precincts of Knoxville's only decent restaurant did Charles begin to weigh the possibility that his father had loved his mother much more than Eugenia had loved Paul Alexander.

In the cozy romantic world that Charles had constructed for himself, a husband and a wife loved each other devotedly and never had a thought that did not include the other one and spoke to each other in complete mutual understanding and had no secrets from each other. Now with Paul Alexander sitting waiting for his meal and clasping his hands together in warm pleasure as he looked around the room, Charles began to understand—it was only a beginning—that the marriage of his parents had been far more mysterious than anything he had dreamed of and that knowing that he was less loved than he loved had not deterred Paul Alexander from feeling that he had had a happy life, a blessed life, and that the goodness of that life had warmed to life here, in this restaurant or what had been this restaurant, only a while ago.

Later on, on the night of Paul Alexander's funeral in 1988, Stephen drew out the thick manuscript written in their father's small and elegant hand, the script of a European whose culture belonged more to the nineteenth century than to this one, and they turned through it in awe and regret. They sat reading different parts of it, and Charles read the account of that day when Bert, his mother, and Paul Alexander came into this place and the fear and the shame of their father. "Why didn't he share these things with us?" Charles said, his heart as forlorn as it had been on that morning when he graduated from college and for once a window seemed to open in their father's face, and the light from a more remote time came streaming in, and Paul Alexander sat there in rapture telling about his love for a woman now dead who had, her sons now knew for certain, never loved him as much as he loved her.

The moment passed like a radiance of sunlight between drifting clouds on a summer day, and Paul Alexander lapsed into chitchat about J. C. Penney's speech and the heat and how proud he was of Charles. Conventional things, and Guy talked loudly about his dislike of the salad because it had too many tomatoes in it, and the meal passed. Never once did they mention Hope Kirby.

Afterwards, when they walked out into the sunshine the day turned mournful, like a Sunday afternoon gone bad. Charles had driven up early in the '37 Ford. Now he had to take his robe back. Paul Alexander had brought the others in his 1950 Chevy. They said awkward goodbyes in the parking lot; they would see each other within hours. Charles was alone, driving back down Gay Street on an early summer afternoon, still spring by the calendar, but the heat waves rose miragelike off the asphalt, and people hurried from air-conditioned place to air-conditioned place except for the blind beggar who walked up and down rattling his tin cup and crying out that he was blind in a belligerent tone that blamed the universe and all sighted people for his condition.

The university was quiet. He turned down Fifteenth Street and passed the Ellis and Ernest drugstore on the corner, seeing that it was as empty as on a Sabbath, and parked in a vacant lot where honeysuckle vines grew in jungle profusion but where there was room to tuck a car. He got out with his robe and walked it over to the Memorial Gymnasium where his footsteps echoed in the almost empty building, and he turned his robe in to the forlorn kid whose duty it was to work the afternoon shift for latecomers like Charles. Then he went back to his car and drove to the Shelbourne Towers.

He went inside to the desk. Fans were stirring the air, but it was hot and sticky inside. The Shelbourne Towers was the last large apartment complex in Knoxville built without air conditioning. Even the new university dormitories that were to rise a few years later were to have air conditioning. The receptionist at the desk looked up at him. She looked uncomfortable, and her face was glazed with sweat. "Miss Barker," he said. "Is she in?"

"Miss Barker has left for Memphis," the receptionist said in a fatigued voice, studying Charles as she twirled a finger in her hair. He was an acceptable young man, she thought. She looked at him with more than usual interest.

"When did she leave?" Charles asked, nourishing for a moment the wild fantasy of chasing her down on the highway, but he supposed an almost new Buick could outrun a '37 Ford even with the engine in the Ford rebuilt.

"Three or four days ago," the receptionist said. "The moving van is coming later this week to move all her stuff out of her apartment. She said she wasn't coming back."

"I see," Charles said, trying to assume a nonchalant expression.

"Anything else I can help you with?" the receptionist said.

"No," Charles said, turning away. "No thanks. That's all I wanted."

So that was it. Tempe's departure had a finality to it that drove at Charles like nails in a coffin. No sense crying over spilt milk. What other forlorn proverbs could he summon to his aid? He felt crushed with loneliness and the desperate inertia of one who has not a friend in the world. But he did have friends. There was work to do at the newspaper. He would return to Bourbonville, fall into the routines of his job, and wipe away this graduation day that was like a Christmas when it was certain at last that Santa Claus had passed his house by.

He arrived at the newspaper office just as Jane Whitaker came storming out wearing the habitually angry look she had had for so many weeks now. "Well, how are you?" she growled at him as he came to the door, her voice seemingly making an effort to be more tender.

"I'm fine," he said. "I graduated from college this morning."

"Well, la-di-da," Jane said. "I never went to college, and it didn't hurt me."

"It didn't hurt me to go," Charles said.

Jane threw back her head and laughed, a harsh laugh. Charles thought, *Yes, it did hurt me. Why did I say it didn't?*

"It didn't hurt you," Jane said. "So what is it now? Seminary?"

"I suppose," Charles said. *No, no. It won't be seminary.*

"Give up that bullshit," Jane said. "You don't want to be a preacher. Join the army. Think about it a little. I can tell you one thing. You don't have a future here. I'm tired of covering Red's damned checks. I'm sick and tired of it."

"He's having a hard time," Charles said.

"Shit! I'm having a hard time. Don't think I'm not. He owes us money. If he couldn't pay us back, he shouldn't have borrowed the money."

"Lloyd borrowed the money," Charles said.

"Lloyd! When Lloyd drowned, this whole damned newspaper was like a ship with a hole in the bottom of it."

"It's not that," Charles said. "It's the equipment. It's all obsolete. We need a new press. We can't run photographs on this one. We can only run halftones. We could use an offset press. We could cover the paper with photographs if we had an offset press."

"So you want me to lend more money to Red to buy an offset press. Goddamn. You have the nerve. He's in debt to us up to his ears, and you want him to borrow more money."

She turned with another harsh laugh and threw herself down the street in an athletic stride. Charles stood looking after her, thinking.

When he went inside he found gloom everywhere. "I think she means it this time," Red said. "I've never seen her so mad."

"She must have lost a hundred thousand dollars to that wop from New York," Myrtle said. She was almost in tears.

"Charles, I can't pay you this week. I may not be able to pay you for the rest of the month," Red said. "I'm behind two months in the mortgage. I owe her two thousand dollars. I don't have two thousand dollars. You don't have to work if you don't want to. I understand."

Charles shook his head. "I've got some money laid back. Don't worry about it."

"I'll pay you when I can," Red said helplessly.

Charles almost said, "To hell with it." But he did not. Things were turning over in his mind.

Red cleared his throat. "Charles, it might be good for you to take off a little. You deserve a vacation. Hell, you've worked hard. The Knoxville paper says you graduated at the head of your class."

"I've got it right here," Myrtle said. "We're proud of you, Charles."

"Of course they wrote a story about you and your grades, and it gave them a chance to rehash the murders and—and all that."

Charles glanced at the story. It carried a picture of him—and a long recounting of everything, together with the date of Hope Kirby's impending execution. He did not read it. He tossed the paper back on Myrtle's desk and sat down at his own. Thank God there were piles of items from the stringers. A good week. He could type and edit them without having to think. He did not want to think about anything.

Red persisted. "Like I say, Charles. You might want to take some time off. Roy Kirby is still out there. I think he'll try to kill you if the state kills his boy. I don't know, you understand. But people are talking."

"I'm going to be here to cover the association meeting that Saturday," Charles said in a voice that almost choked. "This is where I belong. This is where I am going to be."

"Well," Red said with a sigh. "Suit yourself. I guess we'll still be in business then. We'll still be able to print your story. Yessir, if you live to write it, this goddamned paper will at least live long enough to print it." He shook his head woefully and grinned, and Charles burst into laughter. It was real laughter. Red had said something funny. It was very funny, and Red started to laugh, too, and Myrtle laughed, and soon they were all laughing, and life wasn't as bad as it had been.

*J*OYE was the one who called the brothers together and told them what they had to do. He was angry. He thought Charles Alexander deserved to die. He thought Roy Kirby had the right to kill him. But Joye had three children now and a good wife and a little house close to town, and he was afraid. He knew from talking to Hugh Bedford at the very beginning of this mess that Ken McNeil might come after all of them; they had all been accessories. If the jury did not believe him and condemned Hope despite Joye's fervent testimony that he and Hope had been together all night long, anybody could figure out what had happened—the threesome going out together in their boat, then slipping back to shore to drop Hope off, then, deeper in the night, coming back yet again to pick him up after he had done the deed. M.L., who drove Hope to town in his pickup, was the only one who had a chance of getting off clean. No witnesses to his deeds. Not yet. It didn't take a college professor or a lawyer or even a district attorney to figure all that out in a wink of the eye. The more Joye thought about it, the more he worried, and at three a.m. he was usually awake, listening to the noises a sleeping house makes, getting up to look at his children sound asleep in their beds, sometimes walking out into the yard and looking at the stars, and feeling something around his heart that was like iron shrinking.

Joye was the oldest now, in a manner of speaking. Hope was in prison, and John Sevier was wherever he was, dreaming away among the clouds. Hope said once that he wondered if John Sevier drifted in the stories he had memorized from Pappy in the days they lived in the mountains. Back then they all sat rapt and silent in the enchantment Pappy's stories created, lifted up to some place where their bodies seemed to lose all their weight, and they could float through the air as though they had been nothing but colors shaped in human form. Maybe John Sevier was up there in that soft and peaceful place and couldn't be bothered to return to them here where almost everything had hard edges, and everything took an effort, even speaking and listening to your brothers. One thing was certain. Not even Ken McNeil could charge John Sevier with murder.

So it was up to Joye. He gathered his brothers together. They had to talk. No women or children. Just the brothers. Before Hope killed Abby, the families used to get together almost every Sunday. The women cooked at one house or another. The men went outside with the children in warm weather and tried to do things fathers did with children. Pappy and John Sevier came over most Sundays. Once upon a time Hope tried to get Pappy to tell the old stories he told in the mountains, but he said, "Ah, I've forgot all them stories." They knew this was not true, but they also knew that Pappy's stories were about the mountains and about how his folks had gone there so they'd be left alone and not have to fight in any more wars, and they knew that Pappy couldn't talk about these things anymore. Abby's death put an end to these family gatherings—something else that was lost. So much was lost.

Something was lost inside the families, too. All the Kirby men could feel it, something between every husband and wife, something between fathers and children.

Abby was guilty. No doubt about that. M.L.'s sprightly young wife, Kay, the youngest of the lot and the most talkative, had seen the signs before any of them.

"Don't you think they's something different about Abby?" she said in a low voice, meant to convey mystery and perhaps humor and perhaps danger a couple of months before Abby died.

The other wives gave her puzzled looks. So far were they from imagining adultery. Cora, Joye's wife, said harshly, "What are you talking about?" in a tone that said, "You shouldn't be talking about it." Cora was large and cheerful and English. Joye met her in a USO in London. She could talk to anybody; so she talked to him, and she was pleased to come to America and pleased to settle in Bourbon County, and sometimes she could even make Roy Kirby smile because she teased him, and she was kind to John Sevier, sometimes stroking his head as if he were a baby and shaking her own large head in infinite sadness. Cora was close to Abby because they both liked to cook, and they swapped recipes and gave each other cookbooks when days came to exchange gifts. She had not noticed anything different about her.

"Well, she seems to pay so much attention to Hope here lately."

"Hope is her husband. She ought to pay attention to him."

"But she pays a lot more attention to him now than she used to."

"Maybe she's pregnant," Love's wife, Janice, said. She was also large, although now and then she went on a diet and got slender again and looked a lot prettier than the other two before slowly, slowly she started to swell up and get big again.

"She's got a glow to her," Kay said. "But it ain't because she's pregnant."

When they all knew why Abby had glowed, Kay said softly, "I knew it was something like that."

A coldness settled down in every household. The families stopped getting together. John Sevier and Pappy stayed out at their place, and the others left them alone. Pappy had taken on a lethal quality, something hard and unpleasant that the women had not seen before, but now they saw it every time they looked at him although no one could say exactly that his looks had changed.

In every home an icy silence descended that affected the children. The children old enough to go to school learned quickly how Abby and Kelly Parmalee had died. They bore tearfully the taunts of other children who called them hillbillies or asked which of the Kirby women would be the next to be shot dead. Since one of them had been shot, the Kirby children thought it natural to expect another one to die, and those old enough to understand woke up shrieking in the night from bad dreams. When Joye's six-year-old son, Roy, sat up in bed weeping and calling for his mother, Joye went to the child's bedroom to soothe him, saying, "Now, Roy, you hain't scared of a little bad dream, air ye? Come on now. Boys hain't suppose to cry."

Before he could finish the sentence, Cora swept in with a rush of bare feet and snatched the weeping boy out of her husband's arms and took him into her own, holding him close. "What do you mean, he's not supposed to cry? This boy's got a world to cry about—as if you didn't know." When she was angry, her English accent slashed like a razor. She whirled the child away and walked back and forth across the bedroom where their other child, Hope, sat up tense and afraid and silent.

In every Kirby household something like that went on, and quiet men who depended more than they had known on cheerful wives for life and consolation now found an icy curtain dropped around them so that wives and children receded deeper and deeper into the distance even while they were physically near. The husbands could not go with them.

So Joye's meeting. He summoned the brothers to the Methodist burying ground on the river below Bourbonville. The Methodist chapel there was long disused except for an occasional Sunday every year during warm weather when Methodists from all over the county and even beyond gathered for "homecoming and cleanup." They heard preaching and sang hymns, and they ate lunch from dishes spread on long tables under the trees, and then they cleaned up the graves, mowing the grass, cutting away bushes, and straightening up gravestones that tilted dangerously. Sometimes they planted flowers.

Here the Kirby boys gathered, sitting quietly at one of the tables, the three of them troubled and silent for a long time as if waiting for the right thoughts to form in the buzz and murmur of a day that was calendar spring and seasonal summer. They were alone.

Joye spoke first after he had waited to be assured that the others gave him permission. "This thing we done, we all done, this thing Pappy said we had to do." It was like a title to an address to follow. He let the words camp there in the shade for a few minutes so the other two brothers could get a good look at them. "Hit's near ruint our lives, and hit's got Hope heading for the electric chair." He said "ee-lectrick cheer." His brothers did not even nod.

"I hain't saying that Pappy was wrong for hisself. He lives by the code of the hills, and if all this had happened up in Sevier County, they wouldn't never of been no trial, and they wouldn't of been no crazy judge, and Hope wouldn't never have spent a day in jail and not no prison neither."

"They wouldn't of been no Charlie Alexander up there in Sevier County neither," M.L. said. Love nodded, and Joye slowly nodded, too, trying to wrestle with a lost world called Sevier County where no Charles Alexander existed and a man who set out to kill his wife and her lover would not have been forced to sneak around to do it. They would have had their tryst in the woods somewhere, and the avenging husband could have shot them down with a half-dozen witnesses standing about, and nobody would have seen a thing. *What is to be will be,* Joye thought.

"Well, we hain't in the hills no more, and we got a different kind of law down here, and that is the way hit is."

He paused to think while his brothers patiently waited. He took a deep breath. "The fact of the business is that Pappy was wrong for down here, and we didn't do what was right for us because they wasn't one of us man enough to stand up and tell him to his face that he was wrong."

There! The words were out, and they had the effect of a great renunciation. It was as though a creed that had been the chief sustaining force of a tribe was now overthrown. The creed called on them to obey, and they obeyed. Now Joye looked them in the eye and cast the creed to earth where it broke into a thousand pieces before their eyes. Why had they obeyed it for so long? They did not know. Now they knew they had to disobey.

"We should of told Abby to get out of town. Maybe we should of beat Kelly Parmalee within two inches of his life," Joye said.

"Maybe we should of told Mrs. Parmalee all about hit and brung her down to the courthouse square to see hit," M.L. said with a sly smile.

"Even that," Joye said. "That sure would of fixed his hash. Now, things hain't the same. Not at my house they hain't."

The mournful declaration was scarcely more than a murmur. They sat in silence again. Nothing was the same anywhere. Not at home. Not at work. Paul Alexander made his daily round through the car works, looking with benign and almost remote concentration into things. He spoke with his men, showing a remarkable memory for the details of their lives, demonstrating a familiarity they expected with the minutiae of casting wheels or steel or brass. He spoke to the Kirby men, too, but he did not inquire about Hope or their father, although from time to time he posed a neutral question about John Sevier. He never mentioned the trial or the execution date looming up on them. Nor did he ever speak of Charles.

Most other men on the job spoke to the brothers circumspectly. It was not unfriendliness. It was more the cautious attitude of men who recognized now that these brothers were capable of murder, and no one wanted to do anything to provoke them. The Kirby men had never been big talkers, never joked very much, but they laughed when other men joked, and they sat in on conversations like members of an audience at a play, enjoying the scene. They laughed when they were supposed to laugh. They nodded when they were supposed to nod. They looked solemn at the news of sickness or death. Now they were left out of the banter and the joking and the gossip, and at the half-hour break for lunch, no one opened a lunch pail and sat down with them to eat.

Things had changed.

Joye chewed on his thoughts. "If Hope dies, Pappy says he'll kill the Alexander boy."

The other brothers nodded.

"If he does, I reckon the whole bunch of us will end up in state's prison. McNeil will come after the lot of us. All he has to do is make a judge and jury think we helped Hope."

"He hain't got no witnesses," Love said. He had an anxious tremor in his voice.

"We didn't think he had witnesses for Hope," Joye said.

"We made sure we had lots of witnesses to see us go out at night and come back in the morning to the dock," Love said. They pondered this thought moodily.

"If we're in state's prison, our kids will grow up not knowing who we are. And what is our women going to tell them about us? They'll try to make them forget us, I reckon. I mean, you can see them doing that." Joye spoke solemnly. The way Cora talked to him now . . . She was afraid of him. He knew that if you were afraid of somebody, you didn't really love that person. How could you love somebody and be afraid? Were they all afraid of Pappy? And why shouldn't Cora be afraid of him?

The decision they reached was as silent as the mood that fell on them when Joye had spoken. They did not move immediately. They sat, their narrow Scotch-Irish faces set in contemplation and a kind of truculence as if they had all made a resolution against their father, a resolution they should not have had to make at all because anybody could see it. Spread before them, the gravestones of the old cemetery stood in the disordered places where those taken by grief in less crowded times had planted their dead because someone had randomly put a spade in the ground and said laconically, "This here's as good a place as any." Families lay buried in patches of graves, and the history of the county lay concealed here with its secrets and its forgotten dramas. The Kirby men were not interested in that history. They were interested in the present and the future of raising children and reconciling themselves with frightened and resentful wives.

"What time is hit?" M.L. said at last.

Joye yanked his watch out of his pocket and studied it laboriously. "Hit's twenty-three minutes past three o'clock," he said.

"He milks at five-thirty," Love said.

Slowly the three brothers got to their feet, looking not at one another but at anything else that would distract them from the task now before them. In moments Joye was in his pickup, and the engine spun to life. He had gone beyond the invisible line that marked the limits of where he might turn back. The other brothers, in obedient order of age, followed him, and the three trucks made a procession out the gravel road beneath the leaf-laden trees and emerged at Highway 11 south of Bourbonville where traffic on a Sunday afternoon moved in desultory patience because of the restrictions imposed by two lanes. At the gravel road that turned west off the highway before the river, they turned in and drove slowly past Salem Baptist Church and into the rolling green country where, a couple of miles beyond, Pappy's neat and trim house sat on a rise of ground above an immaculate field where wheat ripened.

Hit's better here than hit was in the mountains, Joye thought. Until this moment Joye had not allowed himself to finish the sentence that conveyed the thought. It would have seemed too much like betrayal. Perhaps there was a curse attached as if the thought contained an unpardonable blasphemy. But once it was expressed, collateral thoughts gushed out. Everything was better here. The fields were easier to plow and to plant and to harvest. The spring and the autumn lasted longer, and the few weeks of hot weather in summer were bearable—a lot better than the three or four weeks of sharp and bitter cold back in the mountains. They all had attic fans in their houses. In the worst of the summers they slept with a gush of cooling air rushing through the windows and up through the house cleansing heat away. They were closer to other people—or they had been until the murders. There were several hardware stores in Bourbonville where they could buy things ready-made. They had jobs with regular pay envelopes. Sometimes there were layoffs when the railroads slowed, but they passed quickly, and the regular money came back, and in the meantime the Kirby boys lived on good things their wives canned out of their gardens.

Their children went to school and did not depend on their mothers to teach them to read and to write and to cipher. Maybe that was not always a good thing. But most of the time it was. If Pappy had taken Mr. Hamilton's offer, they could have come down here years earlier—Joye's mind ran aground on his ruminations. He couldn't tell where they were likely to lead. He thought about Cora. He felt with a sharp pain the perhaps irrevocable loss of something he had not known was so precious.

"You were all in on it, weren't you?" Cora said last August when the deed was done. Her English accent, sharp and precise, carried a dismal authority. "You men, you were judge, jury, and hangmen, and if it had been any of the rest of us, you'd have all got yourselves together and killed that one, too."

"I never would have killed you," Joye stammered helplessly. He meant that she would never have been unfaithful to him. But then he thought of how monstrous it would have been to kill Cora. Horrible beyond any words.

"Oh, you wouldn't! But then that daft old man would have told you I had to die, and you'd have done exactly what Hope did to Abby. Now isn't that the truth?" Her eyes were filled with tears. She was angry and frightened, and worst of all she looked at him as if he were a stranger.

Pappy came around the corner of his house as they drove up. He looked the way he always did—lean and hard and brown as tanned leather and calm. Joye's mind shot back in time. This was how Pappy looked that morning when Mr. Hamilton drove up in that nice new Ford car of his.

And there was more. Pappy had never got over Mr. Hamilton. Being pushed out of the mountains, out of the house he had built, off the land he had cleared, had planted a poison in him and hardened his face and his heart and left his mouth tight with a bitterness that hardly ever left it. Pappy was glad to have grandchildren. All the boys could tell that. But he did not play with them, and they kept their distance from him, feeling not that he was unloving, perhaps, but that he was hard and bitter and maybe unlovely. Now he stood there, hard as he always was, his arms folded and waiting and ready, and Joye thought, *He knows why we've come.*

Joye felt almost drunk with the responsibility to speak for all of them. He exploded out of his pickup and came almost in a swagger to Pappy, who waited serenely and without a hint of surprise or even curiosity on his face.

"Pappy, me and the boys here have got to talk to you about something, and we want you to listen to us."

"I reckon I can listen. You want to sit on the porch, or you want to stand out here in the yard?"

The question took Joye by surprise. "Well, I reckon we can sit out on the porch."

It was a way of postponing things for a moment, and Joye gladly took it. But it quickly passed, and Pappy, bringing John Sevier out of the house, sat down in the porch swing suspended by chains from the ceiling, and John Sevier sat down beside him, and the swing creaked with their weight, and the other brothers drew chairs around in a semicircle to face him, and it was up to Joye again. He cleared his throat and looked about nervously.

"The first thing to say is this here," Joye said. "Hit don't look to us that Hope is going to get pardoned from the governor. If the governor hain't done nothing now, he hain't likely to do nothing."

"I figure that's right," Pappy said in a dull and subdued voice. "You can't never trust no politician."

Joye rushed on. "Hit hain't right. Hit's all wrong. We all know that. But the fact of the business is that hit looks bad."

"Hit looks bad," Pappy said, still in that dull monotone.

"We've been talking amongst ourselves, Pappy. Just as sure as Hope's going to die, we'uns is going to live. We got to live. We got kids to raise. We got wives to take care of. We got jobs. We got folks counting on us. You see what I'm saying?"

Roy Kirby looked at his third son with icy blue eyes. "I reckon I do."

"Well, good, Pappy. Good. Now, you say you're bound to kill Charlie Alexander if Hope dies in the chair. If you say you're bound to do something, well, I reckon we all know you'll find a way to do hit."

"I reckon I will for a fact." The voice was cold and steady.

"But don't you see, Pappy? If you do that, everthing goes bad for all the rest of us. District Attorney hain't going to stop. He's going to go after you. Then he'll come after us. All of us was part of killing Abby and her sweetheart. McNeil will come after all of us. Hain't no way around hit. He can put us in prison for years. Maybe the rest of our lives. And what's going to happen to our kids then? What's going to happen to our women?"

Joye ceased, his mouth stopped in frustration at something that seemed as obvious as a mountain. Pappy gave him an unwavering stare of contempt. "You mean to set there and tell me you think more of yourself, your kids, your women, than you think of your brother's honor, your good name as a brother? Hain't you got nothing left in your bones but yourself?"

"Pappy, what is honor? What'd we get out of killing Mr. Hamilton all them years ago? You tell me!"

"We kilt us a man that didn't respect us. Hit was the thing we had to do. You heard what he said to me. You was there. You ain't forgot, has you?"

"You kilt a man that didn't know us from a hole in the ground. We was nothing but a bunch of hillbillies to him. We lost Hope and John Sevier for years. You might could say you put Hope and John Sevier in the place where the Japs would do what they done to John Sevier. We got the police down on us and the threat of the army, and that FBI feller talked to us like we was stray dogs. Why didn't you kill *him*, Pappy? We had to move, and you had to sell your land to the gov'mint for thirty dollars the acre rather than the thirty-five that Hamilton offered us. That's what we got for killing him."

Joye had his own conviction now. He saw Cora and his kids, and he wondered if he could ever win Cora back. He was doing something he'd never done in his life. He was raising his voice to Pappy. Roy Kirby did not change expression, but the cold in his face was like a mountain of ice.

"You are not making your manners to your pappy," he said.

"Ah, Pappy," Joye said in desperation and sadness. "You hain't making your manners to our women, to our kids, to what we got here. The times is a-moving on, and life hain't what it used to be. Hope don't want you to kill Charles Alexander. You heard him say so hisself. Hit's his dying wish that you let the boy off. The kid done his bestest. When you kilt that Missionary feller, he changed his story to what hit should of been in the first place. Hit's like Sheriff Myers said. He tried to keep his promise to Hope, but he was so scairt and broke up. I was in the war, Pappy. You hain't never been in no war. I seen boys so scairt they messed in their pants, and they cried because they couldn't talk."

"Then they wasn't men," Pappy said.

Joye exploded then. "You don't know, Pappy! You don't know nothing! You hain't never had a .50-caliber machine gun sweeping the air an inch over your head. You hain't never seen a kid you're talking to one minute get his head blowed off the next second. You hain't never seen a man's leg blowed off his body so that all you can do is hold him while he cries and dies. You don't know nothing but them mountains, and they hain't like nothing else in this world. Men don't cry?! I've seen men cry, Pappy. I've seen brave men cry. And you don't know nothing."

He looked away from his father, unable to take in now the face of someone who had become almost hateful to him. He felt a terrible loneliness.

"I never thought I'd see the day when a son of mine talked to his pappy like that," Pappy said. "I'm waiting for you to tell me you're sorry."

Joye sat staring out over the sunny landscape to where the light glistened on the muddy river below. Joye's hopelessness put a shade on the day and gave a melancholy cast to the light. Pappy couldn't see the plain facts.

"Look, Pappy," Joye said. "Here's the facts of the business, and we all know hit. We air better off down here than we was up in the mountains. We got better houses than we had. You got better land. Hain't nobody to bother you 'lessen you go around killing folks. We all got good jobs. Our kids go to school."

The words fell with the force of a load of coal being dumped from a car on the railroad. For a moment there was a silence on the porch as deep as the silence at the opening of the seventh seal in Revelation. When Pappy spoke, it was like a machine straining to hold itself together without flying to pieces.

"What we had up in the mountains was ours, all ours, and I had made hit all. You was there. You know."

Love spoke up, his voice soft and sad. "We didn't even have no radio up in the mountains. We couldn't listen to no music."

"We went to church, and we had music ever Sunday. We had folks that could sing and play music." For one horrifying moment all three of the brothers thought Pappy might weep in anguish, and even John Sevier looked around at his father, sitting beside him on the almost motionless swing, and an expression verging on alarm swept across his placid face.

Joye could not accept contradiction in a matter where the stakes were so high and the unreason confronting him was so impenetrable.

"Look, they's lots of places in the mountains still where you can clear land and build you a cabin and start all over again, and they hain't nobody going to move the national park there and take your land. If you want to do that, we'll come help you. John Sevier can work, too. Hit will all be like hit was except that Love and M.L. and me won't be in no state's prison, and our kids won't be orphans. I'm saying this. You can't kill Charles Alexander. He may deserve to be kilt, but that hain't the point. The point is that if you kill him, you might as well kill us, too, because then we might as well be dead."

Joye paused for a moment, wondering if he dare go where his angry speech had led him. But he had gone too far to stop. "I'll tell you another thing, Pappy. If you set your mind to kill him, I will do everything I can to defend him against you. You air going to have to kill me if you kill him, and that's the truth of the business."

Love and M.L. gasped. They looked at each other amazed and shattered and afraid. The only moment like this one that they could remember in their lives was when Mr. Hamilton came driving up that day and told them that the government of Mr. Franklin Delano Roosevelt was going to take away their land.

Pappy sprang to his feet, and Joye stood up with his arm drawn back as if to ward off a blow. But Pappy did not strike him. He never struck one of his boys in his life. He said in a whisper, "You all get off this place. You get off right this minute."

That was his valedictory to Joye.

"*I WISH* you would not go to the church meeting Saturday," Paul Alexander said to his second son.

The two of them sat in the kitchen after supper. It was one of those long Tennessee twilights in June. The *Bourbon County News* was out with a long story that Charles had written about the coming meeting. Lines were being drawn. Clifford Finewood and Tommy Fieldston would present a conflicting motion, and they were going from church to church in the association to press their views. It was "improper," they said, for any group of Baptist churches to attempt to bind Baptists to any point of view. Baptists had no creeds. They were independent, and their churches were independent. God spoke to them individually—apparently giving very mixed messages. Any resolution that tried to enforce a social doctrine on them was a violation of who Baptists were. "Reverend Arceneaux is trying to bring papalism pure and simple to Tennessee, where it has no business being," Clifford Finewood said. "When Baptist churches begin meddling with race, they are forgetting the declaration of Jesus Christ himself that his kingdom was not of this world. It's not that we have anything against the Negro. It's a matter of Baptist principle."

"It seems to me that you are telling all the county that you will be at this meeting. Roy Kirby will know exactly where you will be all that day." Paul Alexander spoke in the quiet that followed his previous and unanswered remark. He was clearly anxious.

"Yes, I intend to be there."

"Even if the governor does not commute Hope Kirby's death sentence."

"I do not believe the governor will make any move."

Paul Alexander nodded in his grave and sometimes impenetrable way. "Politicians are a slimy breed of men, and it seems that the higher they climb, the more slimy they are."

"You do not usually seem so opinionated about things," Charles said.

"I do not usually speak of politicians."

They sat with the kitchen windows open on the mild June evening. Back in the upstairs part of his house where Guy had his room, the phonograph played hillbilly records, and Guy beat time with his pencil, bending up and down in the perfect rhythm that was one of the gifts of his condition. The sound came down to them faintly through shut doors.

Charles noticed his father's accent more tonight. He felt one of those waves of reality, as though he had been shaken out of the ordinary drift of things and saw reality as he had never seen it before. His father was foreign. The chances of dropping him in Bourbonville to spend his life were so slender that they could not be calculated. Everything is as it is for no reason at all, and if everything were different, there would be no reason for that either.

All this sped through Charles's head in a flash of electrons. He said, "It is something I have to do."

Paul Alexander sat motionless and made no effort to argue. They had not turned on the lights. Their forms were molded by the fading twilight, father and son, one short, the other tall, both slender, both still. Later when Charles thought back on this evening, he supposed that his father had argued unsuccessfully with him so many times that he lacked any hope of success in arguing with him again. Charles remembered how afraid he had been, how his decision to go to the association meeting was couched in that fear because he knew that yes, this would be the most rational place for Roy Kirby to kill him. He was tired of running; he was tired of fearing death. He had come to some conclusions.

Paul Alexander stood up and walked into the dining room. The door opening and closing let in a blast of increased music from upstairs. Ernest Tubb singing, "I'm a heartbroke soldier on Heartbreak Ridge . . ." Paul Alexander returned with a small pistol in his hand. Charles was startled. "What are you doing with that?" he said. Paul laid the weapon on the table, pulling out the magazine and snapping the slide back to show that the chamber was also empty.

"This is a Colt .32 automatic," he said. "I bought it this afternoon. Sheriff Myers also swore me in as a deputy sheriff of Bourbon County, here in this room. I tried firing the sheriff's .38 revolver, but it was too cumbersome for me, and the recoil is so great that I could not get a second shot off quickly with any reliability. With this .32 I hit a paint bucket eight times without missing." He assumed a look of boyish pride.

"But why?" Charles said.

Paul Alexander turned serious. "I will not stand by to let Roy Kirby kill you without making some feeble effort to defend you. When the governor announces his decision, the sheriff and a couple of his deputies are to stand by you every minute. If Roy Kirby tries to kill you, we will try to kill him first. We are all agreed that it is the only way."

Charles looked at his father as if he had never seen him before.

"And you have been practicing?"

"Much of the afternoon, out here in the backyard. The sheriff told me I was very good. He told me he would be happy to have me as a deputy full-time."

"I could not have imagined you with a gun."

"I was a soldier once upon a time." The voice was charged with sadness and memory.

Charles stared gape-mouthed at his father. There were so many things about the man that Charles did not know, and he would find most of them out when it was too late. They sat down, Paul Alexander at his habitual place at the small table covered with oilcloth where he would live alone with Guy when Stephen and Charles had moved out of the house and where he would write the manuscript that would tell his sons so many things they had never surmised and create in Charles the lost feeling that he had cheated them by not recounting these stories when he was alive. For a moment that evening Charles thought it might be possible to inquire about his father's past as easily as Blackie and Paul Ledbetter talked to their father, the easy companionship where the unimportant was like an ever-flowing stream where sometimes something important drifted by.

Paul Alexander closed the pistol and replaced the magazine in the butt. "At some moments in life, we cannot be passive," he said.

They sat, and in this strangely convivial mood Charles began to think of questions he might ask, but his father asked the first one.

"Tell me something," Paul Alexander said quietly. "In this story that you wrote—I almost felt that you were trying to make Tommy Fieldston and your friend Mr. Finewood look foolish."

"Do you think so?"

"The place where you asked them both if they thought Jesus would speak to a segregated audience. And you asked Mr. Fieldston if he thought the world had been created in seven days with all the fossils in the rocks."

Charles grinned and shrugged his shoulders slightly. "Well, I wrote down what they said. Mr. Finewood said of course Jesus would speak to a segregated audience if he spoke in the South because Jesus never changed customs, and Mr. Fieldston said that yes, God had created the world in seven days—well, six, since He rested on the seventh—but He put the fossils in the earth to test our faith."

Paul Alexander smiled, and his eyes crinkled. "That is sufficient, I suppose. And God doubtless got all the animals, including the insects, on the ark, and He killed a man for touching the Ark of the Covenant by accident."

"You know a lot about the Bible." Charles spoke with surprise. Night after night since Eugenia Alexander had died, he had seen his father reading alone at the kitchen table, locked in the thrall of books like a man who had procured the key to a magically walled garden where he could retreat amid fragrances and the colors of flowers and live a life isolated from the harsh and grinding disappointments of the real world. Cancer. The erosion of a beautiful body. Death. Loneliness. Decay. But Charles paid no special attention to what Paul Alexander read. He had not seen the Bible set up before him on the oilcloth-covered table, the Bible for Charles being always a black book printed on India paper and gilded with gold or at least with yellow on the edges and covered with thin and limber leather. Charles was startled in later years to find a Greek New Testament among his father's things and a heavy, buckram-bound Old Testament in Greek, too, the Septuagint.

As usual, under this surprise from his son, Paul Alexander was noncommittal. "As you know, I like to read all sorts of things." Paul Alexander hid and revealed himself continually, and he remained a mystery. He existed.

He smiled again, and the two sat contemplating each other, trying to preserve the moment of peace between them. Very cautiously, avoiding his son's eyes, Paul Alexander asked, "Have your own attitudes changed, about what you want to do in life? The tone of all your articles has been, well, different from something I felt in you earlier."

"Yes," Charles said softly, looking down towards the lower field and Highway 70 beyond, where a desultory traffic passed east and west. "I am not going to seminary. I have written the people in New Orleans that I will not come this fall. I am not going to be a minister."

For a long time a silence lay between them. Paul Alexander said at last, "Ah," an ejaculation that could not hide his pleasure.

The expression annoyed Charles. "So you feel that you have won?" he said coldly.

"No, I do not," his father said in a quick, sharp tone that carried defiance. "I feel that you have won. Your trophy is your life, snatched away from superstition and darkness."

"The life Mother lived," Charles said, meaning to hurt.

"Yes," Paul Alexander said with a tremendous sigh. "I would have saved her from it if I could have. I could not."

"Do you think that I will now be happy?" Charles asked in a hard voice. He thought that he would never be as happy as he had been with the sunlight of God streaming around him in the woods like a personal visitation from divinity itself, of feeling that he could speak a prayer to God while standing or walking or sitting and have God supremely there, a presence radiating Himself like a silent companion standing to one side.

Paul Alexander refused to seek compromise with his son. "I cannot tell you that. Your happiness depends on you and a million parts of chance. I know that at least you will be relieved of the misery of trying to believe absurdities that no intelligent person can believe. I suppose that all of us carry some burden of hypocrisy on our backs. At least you will be relieved from making hypocrisy your profession, a daily pretense."

"Do you think Lawrence Arceneaux lives in daily pretense?"

"There is something different about him. I do not understand him."

"There might have been something different about me."

"I think you are too sensible. Some people can pretend well. Your friend Bob Saddler was one of these. For you it is impossible."

"How do you know that?" Charles asked heatedly, knowing that this conversation should not be happening, not in this tone.

"You are my son." Paul Alexander's voice sounded harsh.

Charles thought his father demanded apology for all those years when Charles had carried the divine torch, the flaming conviction that he was destined to do some great work for the Lord. The new Billy Graham. The great preacher who would bring thousands to God, who would be the friend of statesmen and celebrities. Sometimes before the murders Charles himself walked into the pulpits where he was invited to preach, and he thought, *How privileged these people are to hear me! How much better I am than the regular minister. I have a gift, a divine gift. God has chosen me.*

He recognized the vanity, which he never admitted, and he thought that his father always saw every glittering sparkle of it and scorned it. Now the vanity was gone but with it something else, something dear and important, that had been like a lifeline suspending him over space in one of those photographs that made his heart stop when he saw them, men building skyscrapers in the 1920s and 1930s in New York, walking girders with the city far, far below as a smoky haze of buildings and fatal distance.

His father, he thought, scorning the son's vanity and hollow pretensions, now seemed to declare victory in a war: "I was right all along, right about everything, and I'm glad you have finally had the good sense to accept my point of view." Yet for Charles his new resolution represented defeat and loss and absence and loneliness in the universe, and he felt no victory over the decisions that had been forced upon him by facts he could not deny.

"I don't want to talk about it," Charles said. "I'm not going to seminary. I'm not going to be a preacher. I may join the army. I may go to graduate school." He stood up.

Paul Alexander looked at his son in alarm. "Are you going somewhere now?"

"I'm going out for a drive. I have to think."

"I would not go out now." His father's voice softened into faint alarm.

Charles assumed a weary tone. "Haven't you heard? Roy Kirby is a man of honor. He will not kill me until the governor has made up his mind about the pardon. I may live until Saturday."

He was angry with his father. The anger was unjust and he knew it, something complex and confused, but it was anger at the base like bile at the base of vomit. The gun-blue pistol lay on the red oilcloth of the table, emblem of his father's love, the willingness to kill for the sake of his son, and even as Charles drew himself up in righteousness, the solid mechanical perfection of the weapon rebuked him. He thought of his father shooting at a paint bucket. Yet he was also caught in one of those warps in human experience when he could not stop doing something that he knew was absurd and even cruel. He knew that he should relax, laugh, sit down, say something self-deprecating. "Oh Dad, I'm sorry. Yes, I have changed my feelings about God and preaching, and life, and I'll tell you all about it, and I'll start with the trip I made after Christmas."

He thought in the blazing flash of possibilities that rocked through his brain that yes, he and his father might for the first time in their lives have a real conversation, resolve some mysteries, speak honestly to each other, confess, narrate. But that thought was also frightening. How did a father and a son break those old habits that had regulated all their conduct towards each other for so many years? What new thing was likely to come in the place of those rituals of distance? He felt tongue-tied at the prospect, and in that state he backed away from his anger just a little, made a stumbling excuse, and went out to the '37 Ford feeling foolish and guilty and depressed. *I am about to lose my nerve,* he thought. He felt his father's eyes on him through the window as he drove away, the gravel cleanly popping and crunching under the tires of the station wagon. And he felt the darkened woods behind him and knew a gunman might lurk there, that danger might be established in the place where he had once met God in total assurance and prayer.

This was not an idle journey into the evening. Charles had a purpose. He knew where he was going, and he knew the craziness of it. His mind relished great, ceremonial moments, the forks in the road, the big decisions that, once made, made other decisions impossible. For such a long time in his life, "Pomp and Circumstance" played in the background of his mind, and he set off in stately march towards a high destiny. Perhaps his models were romantic conversion stories, piled on him fervently by his aunts and by his mother and by the preachers with their ceaseless torrents of miracle-filled tales depicting a world where God spoke in unmistakable tones that sounded like thunder sometimes and the still, small voice at other times and brought strong men to their knees with the everlasting knowledge that God was God. Paul on the road to Damascus. John Wesley in Aldersgate, his heart "strangely warmed." The infinite number of conversion stories he had heard in testimonials at churches when one after another sobbing Christian rose to recount the supreme moment when amidst doubt and fear he met God and was changed forever—although in the Christians whom Charles knew the changed life seemed strangely ordinary and even boring and perhaps smug.

Charles himself had such a moment when he was nine years old at a prophetic Bible camp called Ben Lippen over in North Carolina where he,

Stephen, and Aunt Bert went for a week. In the daytime, to the pleasure of the elders, careful teachers laboriously taught prophecy and the signs of the end time. At night there were evangelistic services designed to filter out any lost souls who might be present. One evening an attractive young man named Phil Saint sang one song after another while with colored chalk he drew a cross laid out as a bridge over an abyss with people moving on it, and he sang, "The Way of the Cross Leads Home." Phil Saint was said to be color-blind. So his painting seemed like a miracle. These services were addressed to the children and the adolescents who accompanied their parents to the camp because no one would have paid the fees and come without wanting to get a heartful of assurance that the end of the world was near and the skies were about to be rent in two. His mother talked to him about conversion, coming to that time in life when he could give his heart to Jesus. To Charles conversion was walking down to the front of the congregation assembled in an outdoor tabernacle with a roof but with no walls except the stone columns that held the roof up. The worst obstacle to conversion for him was not his sins or the desire to hold on to old vices. It was simple stage fright. So he gathered his strength and walked down the aisle and felt a tremendous relief that he had done such a thing, but whether the relief was the same as delight in God he did not know, although later when he gave his own testimony, as a young preacher boy was required to do now and then, he made the most of what had happened, and his conversion became God speaking to a child as though to the baby Samuel. But was it? No. Now he knew it was not.

He drove to the sprawling city cemetery on the east side of Bourbonville just before the lights began to introduce travelers to the town. His father had known the man who had the original idea for the cemetery, Jim Ed's half-brother. Charles started to write a story about him once, but he stopped. He would open too many graves with it. Caleb had killed the manager of the car works; he had been shot down by the National Guard. It was one of the stories that lay barely submerged in Bourbonville. Better to leave it there.

At one of the ever-open gates he turned the '37 Ford into one of the many unlighted graveled driveways that crisscrossed the grave sites, and driving straight ahead, headlights bouncing on the rough ground, he came over the railroad tracks and up the sloping hill into the newer part of the cemetery where Bob Saddler had been buried, and he came to Bob Saddler's grave on a rise of ground. A squared-off granite stone. Charles had contributed to buying it. He flipped the lights out on the car and turned off the engine and sat in the sudden silence. A mantle of spring darkness lay softly over the cemetery and Bob's grave was far enough from the highway so that the cars and trucks passed in a subdued quiet insulated by distance. In every direction the peacefulness of a mild June evening held the world in a spell, and for a moment he was caught up in the gentle fantasy that his world was a safe and unchanging place and that he could walk out of the graveyard and go to the place where the courthouse tower held its clock above the oaks and find Kelly Parmalee coming out of his store, and at the Rexall Bob Saddler would be trying to collect people to go to a revival somewhere in the country, and he thought that he could walk down to Abby's beauty shop tomorrow and tell her that he had decided that she would cut his hair from now on and hear her trademark laugh and perhaps laugh himself. "I swear, I don't know what I'm going to do with all you men. First Judge Yancy, then Kelly Parmalee, and now you, Charles Alexander."

He sat down on the grass beside Bob's grave. "Hello, Bob," he said softly. "It's Charlie Alexander, and I've come to visit, to tell you a few things." His voice sounded queer, and he knew that anyone passing along at this hour of the night would be frightened and then amused and then perhaps studiously alarmed to catch Charles Alexander speaking to the dead. But he went on. "I've come to tell you a few things. First is that I know now why you killed yourself. I know you are not in hell because you did it. I know you're not anywhere but here, and I know you can't hear me, but I want to talk to you anyway.

"You killed yourself because you woke up one night and looked into the emptiness of the universe. It was like looking into a hole a million miles down with nothing at the end of it, and in that great emptiness your soul shrank to the size of a grain of sand or something less, and the emptiness had weight, and it crushed you, and you reached for the bottle of sleeping pills. Oh, you tried, night after night. But you heard the silence, and you cried out to God in the dark, and you didn't hear anything, not even the echo of your own voice because no one was there. You did what you had to do, Bob. I wish you'd done something else. I wish you'd talked to me, because then we might have admitted the truth to each other, and you would have seen that you were not alone in the dark, that I was there, too, and that might have meant something. But you did something else, and I don't suppose there's anything wrong with dying when the reason for your life dies, too.

"I feel that way now. No, I'm not going to take a bottle of sleeping pills. That's not what I have to do. But the universe has gone silent for me, too. Death's out there waiting for all of us, sooner or later. Right now I'm living a stream of present moments, and every one of them skips away so fast that trying to hold on to it can make your head swim. Nobody can do it. By the time I speak a sentence, even a word, the beginning becomes the past, and memory lets us put the words and the sentences together, but memory lets us know that we can't know the present, the essence of life. We close our fingers on it, and it's gone.

"It's all so complicated, but then it isn't really complicated at all, is it? For all of us the present runs into our death sometime, and everything stops, and we're all like you, as inert as dust or rocks. We can't exist without that flying present. When it stops, there's nothing left of us, nothing, and we're at peace. You got exactly what you wanted from the sleeping pills. You got peace. The present stopped, and memory stopped, and you're as peaceful as the grass I'm sitting on. It's a blessed thought, isn't it? Peace.

"I can't think of any other way it could be. Mr. Finewood promised Mother that Dad would come to the Lord. He'd had a vision. I guess it was like the vision he had of Dora Hammond, cured of cancer in the middle of the night. He said Dad would be with her in heaven. He said that in heaven Guy would be the beautiful, normal man he would have been if he hadn't been retarded. But wouldn't he be a complete stranger then? And what would Dad be if he changed at the end of his life?

"Besides that, what would we do with bodies in heaven? The body is a machine that exists to keep itself going in time. We use our eyes and ears and arms and legs and taste and smell and touch to defend ourselves from things that can kill us. But nothing can kill us in heaven. In time we have to eat and drink, and we have to piss and shit like machines whose sole purpose is to keep going from one day to the next, and we reproduce ourselves and usually live long enough to get our children old enough to take care of themselves, and then something or somebody kills us, and that's the end of it. All earthbound.

"Why should we eat or drink anything in heaven? How could we shit or piss in heaven? Dirty up the place terribly. Maybe the sewer system in the new Jerusalem will smell like the Garden of Eden before the Fall. Like roses. Can you imagine the divine bathrooms in heaven? Millions of toilets. Maybe an individual one for each of us. But wait. There will be no shame in heaven. So maybe we will shit and piss as calmly as if we were shaking hands. In the Resurrection we will have bodies, but we won't have any use for them.

"Well, Paul says we will be raised as spiritual bodies. What does that mean? No shit or piss. But what about eyes and ears? Will we have the shape of bodies with eyes and ears and all that? But they won't have any substance? Is that what a spiritual body is? No sex. I guess you died a virgin, Bob. Like me. Well, maybe after all that semen I dumped into the toilet at the newspaper at night over Jane Whitaker's photographs, the only way that I'm a virgin is that I have not put my penis into a woman. We won't have any kind of sex in heaven. Jesus said no marriage or giving in marriage in heaven, and he's supposed to know what he was talking about. I guess you could think of the whole population of heaven being young, in the prime of life, and no marriage or giving in marriage might mean perpetual orgy. That would be nice. But I don't think that's what Jesus meant. I wonder if *he* died a virgin. All those women around him. And we don't know much of anything about his life in his teens and twenties. He was obviously attractive to women. But then, maybe there're no women in heaven. The Book of Revelation doesn't have any women in it. Maybe women are transformed into men when they enter the pearly gates. Or maybe women don't make it. Daughters of Eve. Wait, the Virgin Mary has to be there. She followed her son to the very end. Ah me, you see how complicated it is. You think about it just a little while, and none of it makes any sense.

"And what would people do in heaven? The Book of Revelation has the elders singing the praises of God forever and ever and ever. No coffee breaks or lunch or dinner for them. I suppose that's better than nonexistence. Well, if they sing, they have to be in time like ours. Time with the present darting by unless you have one note for eternity. But it's like Missionary said. After you've done that for a million or two million years, won't it get boring? Will we have any thoughts that are not like the thoughts of everybody else? No quest for truth in heaven because everybody has the truth already. Anybody with a different idea about the truth would be cast out, like Lucifer. I suppose that was Lucifer's trouble. One day he had a new thought. Why do we have to do what God tells us all the time? Well, now! Wham! That was rebellion, and down he went to hell or earth or somewhere. So in heaven everybody's thoughts have to be the same. It must be like living in Bourbonville with Tommy Fieldston in charge and no end to it. Oh yes, and everybody knows what everyone else is thinking all the time. I suppose we can read minds in heaven. Or maybe since we can't tell lies up there, we'll have to tell the truth all the time. What a strange business that will be! But then we'll have no vanity. Somebody might come up to me and say, 'Charles Alexander. You were willing to go on preaching so you could have an audience that admired you.' But is that what I wanted? Is it that simple? Was it that simple?

"Maybe heaven is nothing but an eternal present, and time will be no more, like the song says. We won't have any motion. We won't even have any thoughts because the briefest thoughts take time to think and represent motion. We might as well be dead because we won't be anything like what we are down here. How can that be anything like the eternal life that Mr. Finewood talks about? We will have everything we want, and so we won't be motivated to have anything else. I remember that from Psychology 211. Motivation is necessary for every conscious human act. Motion comes from motivation; so in all eternity there will be no motion. It will be all still. Like death.

"You see, it doesn't make any sense. So, Bob, I've given up. I don't believe any of the things we used to talk about. I guess I could go on to seminary and be a minister like Mr. Arceneaux and visit sick people and help out. Comfort them. Comfort them? By telling them lies? Believe in something that does not exist? Make them feel good several times a week when they come to church? The opiate of the people. No, I can't do that. A waste of time, and something dishonest about it. I wonder if Arceneaux is dishonest. No, he must believe in God, in something. He tells no miracle stories.

"There was a Jesus. I believe that. I don't think he was a charlatan. He came to preach to the poor, and he was poor himself, at least when we meet him. I can imagine him and his disciples having a great time wandering through the countryside and into cities where he preached and crowds gathered. I can imagine them feasting together under the shade of trees in warm weather when people who hungered for hope gathered around to get it from him. I can imagine them all, Jesus too, going off by the side of the road to piss or to shit and laughing as they did it, the way men do when they're together. It's all very simple. He gathered a crowd. Too large a crowd, and the people who ran the Temple and the Romans who ran the country ganged up to kill him because they thought that anybody who gathered crowds like his was dangerous. No mystery to that. Just the way people are.

"Still it was a shock, seeing a young man hung up on a cross with his shit running down the central bar and the flies swarming around and the heat. It must have been very hot because he died so soon. He might have hung there for two or three days. Instead he was dead by mid-afternoon. The Gospel writers get it all mixed up, one contradictory story after another, and Matthew said the dead came out of their tombs and walked around Jerusalem. If the dead did that, what was the point of his resurrection? They all agree he had a tomb. Well, suppose he did. Not a common burial pit with all the other felons killed that week or that month. Then what?

"One of the women, or several of the women, dreamed he came to her in her sleep. Just the way I dream that Mama speaks to me sometimes. But I wake up, and she's gone. Probably the women told others that they had dreamed about him, and he had said this or that, and that was enough to start some of the men off. Simon Peter was the most dogged of the bunch. He's the one who leads all the stories. He was like Preacher Finewood—always had a miracle story for the moment and a crowd of people like me eager to believe. Most of the other disciples dropped out, disappeared. Why? Because they couldn't accept the fairy tales of women. Simon soldiered on, and then came Paul, and everything changed, but Paul did not know Jesus and did not witness the Crucifixion. It was all a story to him. If you can tell a good story, you can make people believe anything.

"It happened all like that, Bob. You saw through it before I did. No, you admitted it before I did. You killed yourself. Now I'm waiting for somebody to kill me. It's the same thing. I'm not running away from death. It's out there. It's very close. What will be will be. I'm not afraid. I don't think I'm afraid. Maybe I am. Maybe I am. I wanted to tell you, Bob. I wanted to get it all out, so it will be clear in my own mind. And it is clear. It's as clear as anything has ever been. I can't pretend anymore. I can't run anymore."

ON WEDNESDAY evening M.L. Kirby heard a knock on his door. It was late, and he was puzzled while he went to see who was there. He expected Love or Joye. He was startled to see his father standing with John Sevier. John Sevier had a suitcase in his hand. He was wearing the jacket he wore to church at Salem Baptist. Roy Kirby wore a thin leather jacket despite the warmth of the evening.

Roy Kirby spoke out of the shadows of the porch. "M.L., you're the only one of the bunch I reckon I can trust now. Hit's up to you to take care of John Sevier. You and your brothers can work out what to do with him. But I don't want him put in no welfare home. You understand that?"

"Pappy, come in. What air you talking about?"

"I am going away," Roy Kirby said. "You hain't going to see me no more. I'm leaving John Sevier for you to take care of, and that's the long and the short of hit. Here's a piece of paper. Hit's been notarized. Hit gives my propity to all three of you in equal shares. I don't want John Sevier in no welfare home."

"Pappy, I hain't going to put John Sevier in no welfare home."

"You swear to me on your word of honor that you hain't never for no reason going to put him in no welfare home."

"Pappy—"

"You swear."

"I swear, Pappy. I swear."

"On your word of honor?"

"On my word of honor."

He turned abruptly and hugged John Sevier. "Goodbye, John Sevier. You be a good boy. I'll send for you some of these days. You wait and see. I won't leave you here."

Before M.L. could say another word, Pappy had turned back to his pickup, and in a moment he was gone. M.L. thought that Pappy whipped himself away so fast because he didn't want M.L. to see him cry.

M.L. went to the telephone and called Joye. He swallowed big, and quickly told what had happened. "He's give up," M.L. said. "Jest like you wanted him to do."

"Like we all wanted him to do," Joye said. Joye's voice had a hard bite to it.

"I didn't mean nothing, Joye. Sure, like we all wanted him to do." M.L. had no happiness in his voice. He seemed forlorn and bewildered.

"Where do you reckon he has gone?" Joye said. Joye didn't feel happy either. He wrestled with guilt and puzzlement.

"I reckon back to the mountains somewheres. I reckon maybe he's got kinfolks we don't know about. But he drove off looking like he was going away for good, Joye."

"Well," Joye said after a very long wait. "Hit's a good thing. I hate to see him with his feelings hurt, but sometime you got to stop. That's all they is to hit. Sometime you got to stop. You can't go on and on killing folks that has done you wrong. Hit hain't the way civilized folks live. Hit's why we got courts."

"I sure feel easier," M.L. said. But he did not. He did not like the way Joye was talking. Joye was scared. Not of his father. He was scared of civilization. M.L. knew it and was ashamed, but M.L. was scared of civilization too.

After a while Joye called Love. Then, thinking about everything, he called the sheriff. The sheriff was not so sure. "How do you know this ain't some way to make us all let our guard down?" he said. "That man can live in the woods for a year."

"He said he was going away, and I believe him," Joye said.

"But he didn't say where he was going."

"No, he didn't say that. He didn't stay long enough for M.L. to ask."

"Well, for the sake of you boys, I'm glad. I sure want Hope to get his pardon, but if he don't, ain't no sense in killing again. McNeil would be after all of you."

"That's what I figure," Joye said. He hated to admit so much to the sheriff. "And Hope's still got a chance."

Sure, the chance of an icicle in hell, the sheriff thought.

The sheriff called Paul Alexander. "Tell you the truth, Mr. Alexander, I think they's something fishy about all this. I don't reckon any of them Kirby boys would lie. But we wasn't there to hear the conversation. We couldn't look at Roy Kirby when he said what he said. Starting tonight, I'm going to come up there with Luke, and we're going to bring my dogs and keep an eye on things. We've already saw how he can hide out in the woods for a few weeks at a time."

"I believe that would be wise," Paul Alexander said. "But I don't think he can hide in these woods if we suspect he is there. My woods are not big enough."

"I'm going to drive around looking for that truck of his," the sheriff said. "If I find it parked somewheres in the county, I'll know sure as hell that he ain't left us."

"That would also be wise."

"And tell me this, Mr. Alexander. If he was going off somewheres, why did he leave John Sevier behind? He could of took him with him, don't you know?"

"It seems to me that way," Paul Alexander said.

"I don't like this one little bit," the sheriff said. The puzzlement of both men hung in the electric buzzing of the telephone line. Finally the sheriff said, "Well, Deputy, you might as well load up that pistol of yours. Something about this I don't like at all."

"I always thought the Kirby men were sensible people," Paul Alexander said. He spoke with immense relief. "Maybe it's as simple as that."

"I don't think so," the sheriff said. "Sensible people," the sheriff muttered when he hung up. "I've knowed a lot of sensible people that think the best thing they can do is go out and kill somebody."

*E*ARLY Friday afternoon, June 18, 1954, the governor announced that he would not grant a pardon to Hope Philip Kirby. He made a long, lugubrious pronouncement. You can read it in all the papers, preserved on microfilm now in libraries that young scholars spin through squeaking machines and in awkward positions read the miserable images on screens and take notes. This governor has not excited much historical interest since he came to an ignominious end while driving drunk years after he was out of office. So the story faded almost to invisibility until recent times when the Hope Kirby case flamed to attention again.

He called a few reporters into his office and read his statement, four or five pages long, answered some questions, allowed himself to be photographed, said there was nothing political about his decision, and disappeared. Hugh Bedford was in Nashville, lodged at the Andrew Jackson Hotel not more than a few hundred yards from the governor's office, but he was not summoned to hear the statement.

He got the news from Larry Arceneaux in Bourbonville who had heard it on the radio. By the time Hugh had thrown a coffee cup against the wall of his room and raced to the Capitol Building, cursing with every step, the governor had left his office, and no one could or would tell him where he had gone. His heart was pounding so fast that his eyesight blinked on and off and he thought he might be dying. Slowly he gathered his strength. Hugh Bedford gave a statement to reporters that he later regretted. He used a typewriter in one of the offices, ripped the statement out of the black machine, and handed it to reporters without even looking it over.

> The cowardly governor of this state is a mealy-mouthed coward who managed to avoid combat during World War II and who can now think of only two things—where his next bottle of booze will come from and how he can get himself elected President of the United States. A sentence of death for the crime for which Hope Kirby was convicted, a crime of passion if indeed he committed it at all, is outrageous. I ask judges in Tennessee to examine their law books and more important to examine their consciences to see if such a sentence has ever been imposed and to see if they find it in themselves now to impose it on a heroic veteran of the United States Army who holds a decoration from General Douglas MacArthur himself.

Hugh's statement appeared in boldface on the front page of the *Nashville Tennessean,* with the undignified reference to booze cut out. The two Knoxville papers quoted from it extensively. The *Chattanooga Times* published an editorial saying that Hugh was right. The *Times* editorial appeared on Saturday morning—the day Hope Kirby was scheduled to die.

The governor's long-winded blast was enough to make Hugh give up any hope for help from that quarter, and he set out to track down justices of the Tennessee Supreme Court, any one of whom could grant a stay of execution.

Charles Alexander was in the newspaper office when he heard. A young woman from the laundry next door came in breathless with the news and looked at Charles as if he were already dead. She had a crush on him. She gasped a little, bubbled out the story, and burst into tears. She had heard all the rumors. She now thought that the decision by the governor meant that Charles, too, was sentenced to death. Charles and Myrtle looked at her, his face stony, Myrtle's aghast. Myrtle lifted a hand to her face and looked at Charles. The young woman from the laundry turned and ran out the door crying. She was skinny and sallow and heartbroken.

"Charles," Myrtle said.

The sheriff was sitting in his patrol car in the parking lot of the Salem Baptist Church, looking down at the river, when he got a call on his radio from Luke Bright. "Sheriff," Luke said in a self-important voice. "He's going to burn. The governor just denied his pardon. It's on the radio. WNOX."

The sheriff turned on the radio to WNOX, but the bulletin was over. Lowell Blanchard announced that he was about to play Vaughn Monroe's recording of "Cool Water." The sheriff twirled the dial and got the station in Bourbonville. The station manager was giving the news to his part of the world. His name was Waldo Billingsley. He had a husky, artificial voice that he pitched as deep in his throat as he could, trying to sound like a big-league broadcaster. He had managed to stay out of the war, made money in the lumber business, and built himself a radio station where he liked to announce the news. The sheriff hated his guts. He turned the radio off.

He drove slowly down to the gravel road that ran by Salem Baptist Church and turned out towards Roy Kirby's farm a couple of miles away. "I planned to go over and, if he was back, arrest him for some damned thing," the sheriff said later on. "I figured I could keep him in jail for a couple of days and try to talk some sense into his head. Tell you what I worried about most: How was I going to tell Roy Kirby he was under arrest for disturbing the peace or public drunkenness or assault and battery and keep a straight face?"

The driveway to the farm was paved with milk-white gravel that shone in the sun. The sheriff remembered the place before Roy Kirby moved into it, before the war when the sheriff had been a boy not knowing what he would do with his life. It had been abandoned, the people who lived in it gone to California, somebody said. The fields were wild, but the house was in pretty good shape, and the barns were solid. Roy Kirby got to work on it with single-minded devotion. His boys knew he worked so hard to make himself forget what he had lost in the mountains. Everybody else who knew him in the county simply put him down for a hard worker and therefore a good citizen. No, he didn't go to church at Salem Baptist, and the various ministers who called on him received only one laconic and somewhat mysterious answer. "I don't go to church no more, and there hain't no use in talking to me about hit." Well, he was eccentric, people said. Nobody could complain about a neighbor who worked hard, kept his fence rows looking like weeded gardens, didn't drink, didn't smoke, and minded his own business. So what if he didn't go to church?

The fields looked as if they had been kept by a paid gardener. *He don't deserve what's happened to him*, the sheriff thought.

The sheriff did not expect to find Roy Kirby there, and he was right. Somewhat against his will, he knocked on the door, stood aside just in case Roy Kirby might shoot through it, then gathered his strength and pushed on the door, and it opened with graceful silence. He walked through the house.

It was empty and impeccably neat, but he did not find Roy Kirby. The beds were made, and everything in the kitchen was clean.

"I said to myself right then," the sheriff said, "if Roy Kirby had truly gone off, like he told his boys, why had he left everthing in place? Why didn't he sell some stuff? Why didn't he have an auction? If he was going somewheres else, he needed a nest egg. But then I thought to myself, This is Roy Kirby. He ain't like other folks. What he does is to his own account. You can't tell what he's going to do. But I wasn't at peace about it. No sir, I wasn't."

The one thing that made the sheriff feel that maybe Roy Kirby was really gone was that the pickup was gone, and all Roy's clothes. A man could go off without his stove and his refrigerator and his bed covers, but he couldn't go off without his clothes, and Roy Kirby's clothes were gone. So were John Sevier's. And where would you hide a pickup if you didn't have help? The sheriff had an intuition. Roy Kirby was not close enough to anybody in the county to ask a favor so obvious. "I'm going to hide my pickup on a country road. Will you follow me and let me hide hit and drive me back and not say nothing to nobody?" It was all contradictory.

The sheriff pondered these facts. A man going away would take his clothes with him. A man taking one son to live with another would take the clothes of the one to the other. But a man trying to keep his scent away from dogs would also be careful to remove the clothes he wore next to his body. As it was, the sheriff had not brought in bloodhounds. Duke and Ugly were good dogs, and he knew they would bite any son of a bitch who tried to do him harm unless said son of a bitch was shooting at him with a gun from a distance, at which point the best dog wasn't much damned good. Pickup gone. Clothes gone. Roy telling M.L. he was going away. Roy had a reputation for truthfulness. What did you make of it? One thing the sheriff decided right then. He called Luke Bright on the radio and told him to meet him up at the Alexanders' place. He was going to see to it that Charles Alexander wasn't killed, no matter what. There had been enough death in the county over the last year. Nobody could blame the sheriff for any of it. But he felt that these deaths had happened on his watch, and that did not make him feel good.

*H*UGH BEDFORD called Arceneaux. "I'm at the end of my rope," he said. "I can't believe this is happening. Any of it."

"Don't start drinking," Arceneaux said.

"What the motherfucking hell is there to do but drink?" Hugh Bedford said. He was almost sobbing.

"What are you trying to do?"

"I'm trying to get a judge to give a stay of execution. A judge on the Tennessee Supreme Court."

"What about the United States Supreme Court?" Arceneaux said.

"They're not going to look at a state murder case. Hell, what's one life to those bastards? They're trying to take care of a whole race of niggers. What do they care about one white man?"

"Goddammit, Hugh, I want you to stop talking like that. You don't make sense. Get going. Get to work."

"I made a preacher cuss," Hugh said, pleased with himself.

"I want to tell you just this one thing. If you stick your head in a bottle and don't do everything you can, I'll never be your friend again. I never want to see you again. And that goes for blaming the Negroes, too. The whole goddamned system from top to bottom, whether it's the Negroes or the whites. It's the people who have power who want to lord it over the ones who don't. That's it."

THE SHERIFF got an idea. He did not waste time. He drove first to the newspaper office in Bourbonville. Some people were milling about outside, digesting the news. The sheriff pushed his way through and went in the door. Charles sat at Lloyd's desk, viewing the scene with a faint smile of calm and perhaps sardonic amusement. Red Eason stood there with a shotgun held in his two hands. "Red, for Christ's sake put that goddamned thing up before you hurt somebody," the sheriff said.

"I aim to hurt Roy Kirby if he walks in that door," Red said.

"You think Roy Kirby's going to walk in here with that crowd of gawkers outside, Red? Jesus, in broad daylight?"

"If he does, I'll be ready for him."

"Shit," the sheriff said. He looked at Charles. " I've got a plan. Charles, I'm going to take you over to the jail and lock you up. We can guard the jail easily. Roy Kirby can't shoot through the walls, and as long as you stay away from the windows, you're okay. He ain't going to storm the jail single-handed, and I don't reckon he's got a grenade launcher to fire through the windows into a cell. That gives us a chance to find him and talk some sense into his head. Get up. Let's go. Come along."

The sheriff was so certain of the perfection of his scheme that he turned and started for the door, expecting Charles to follow him obediently like a dog on its way to be fed. The sheriff swung around in perplexity. Charles sat there.

"Get up! Come on. What's wrong with you?" The sheriff was sweating.

"I'm not going," Charles said. He took a deep, stubborn breath.

"What the hell do you mean, you're not going? This is serious business."

"I'm not going."

The sheriff looked at him. Red looked at him. Myrtle started to cry.

"I'm not going to go sit in a jail."

"Charles, it's a way to save your life. He may be out there right now coming after you."

"I'm not going to go sit in a jail."

The sheriff spoke softly. "Charles, it's a way to save his life, too. I don't think he cares anymore. I think Roy Kirby's the kind of man who will accept being killed himself just as long as he can kill you. If we can catch him, we can talk to him, talk some sense into his head."

"You said that before, about talking sense into his head. It's not going to work. He's going to do what he's going to do, and I'm going to do what I'm going to do. I'm going to go home." Charles got up.

"Charles, he's probably making for your house right now. That's where he expects you to be, and he'll kill you, and we'll probably kill him because we're going to be there, too."

"I'm not asking you to be there. I'm not asking anybody to help me."

"Well, I am high sheriff of Bourbon County, and I am not going to sit back and smoke cigarettes and drink beer while somebody murders you."

"I'm not going to the jail," Charles said, raising his voice now. "I have been pushed around by this thing until I'm sick of it. I walked out of here one night, and I walked into a murder. All I wanted to do that night was get in my car and drive home. I didn't ask to walk into a murder. I didn't ask for any of this. I've done the best I can, and I'm through trying to do things. Nothing has worked out, and I'm going home. If he kills me, it won't be any worse than what's been happening to me for months."

With that Charles got up from Lloyd's desk and picked up a satchel of papers and books and walked over to the door into the printing shop. In the print shop Jim Scott, the foreman, stood with a shotgun guarding the back door. The printers were at their work, but when Charles walked into the high-ceilinged space, they stopped and looked up at him. He walked through. Their eyes followed him. At the back door he stopped and shook hands with Jim Scott. "Thanks, Jim," he said.

The sheriff followed him into the print room and watched him go out the back door. Roy might be in town by now. But how? Maybe Charles had a deeper intuition. The sheriff's mother had believed that people on the verge of death, whether they died or not, had the gift of prophecy. But the sheriff never saw any evidence of it during the war. The boys who were sure they would come home alive and talked about it all the time were killed in about the same proportion as those who were sure every night they would die tomorrow. The war was all over the sheriff. It came on him now almost like the shakes, but he did not shiver. He felt the anticipation of combat as he had in Normandy and later in the Ardennes, a prickly feeling on the surface of his skin, like an electric field ready to discharge when out in the cedars and the snow he knew someone was waiting for him. "Shit!" he said. Charles disappeared through the door, and there was no shot.

The sheriff went back out to the patrol car. "What's happening?" somebody asked. The sheriff did not answer. He got in the patrol car, pulled away from the curb in a screech of rubber. He steered out of Bourbonville, heading out the four-lane extension of Broadway that became Highway 11, and ahead of him he saw the '37 Ford and noted the absence of a plume of blue smoke trailing behind it. *Why did the kid fix it up?* It had something to do with Lloyd, the sheriff knew. But it was crazy. Lloyd was dead. Money was money. The kid could have bought a good used car for all the money he had in that rattletrap with mechanical brakes.

*H*UGH BEDFORD drove to the prison in a state of profound melancholy. He knew the warden had a list of telephone numbers. Standard procedure. He also knew the warden would be at the prison the night before an execution. When he came in sight of the gray stone walls piled against the bright spring sky, he felt that the weight of the entire edifice lay piled on his chest. It was like losing a football game in the last second of play by one point, in a stadium where tens of thousands had gathered into one molten stream of incandescent spirit, as if their bodies had been dissolved in mystic communion and every atom of themselves had blended into the primal fire of the universe, and time ran out, and all the fire turned abruptly to cold and unyielding iron, and hope vanished as if it had never been. Football, hell. This was important.

Hugh Bedford, driving to the prison and looking down at the expensive warp and woof of his new gray suit, felt a rush of humiliation as if he had been propelled into the midst of an arena to be stripped naked and to have the ringmaster shout to the jeering mob as one article after another of clothing was removed from his body, the ringmaster calling out the thoughts Hugh Bedford had about himself as he put these things on: "He imagined he could save himself with his clothes." Hugh Bedford could hear above the tranquil spring sounds of a warm June day the tidal wave of mockery rolling toward him from all the tragic cosmos where the gods mocked the pretensions of mortals, and he felt as alone as he had ever felt in his life, a loneliness raised to such stony blackness above him that he remembered his hiding place in the fatal Italian house as something cozy, almost snug.

When he entered the prison he sent a request to see the warden. Then in morose and almost paralyzed sadness he presented himself to see his client. Hugh Bedford felt a finality like death. It was Hope Kirby's death. But it was something else, too. It was Death the grinning clown who finally picked up all human striving and ground it to powder in his skeletal hands. The guards spoke to him quietly, like mourners at a funeral of someone young and beautiful who had died by accident in the midst of celebration and festival. They were unable in words to convey the commiseration they felt but showed by their silent and respectful deference that they understood the horror of grief. The biggest change was that now Hugh Bedford was taken through steel-barred doors where the locks clicked behind him with a precise, fine metallic harmony that made them sound more like expensive watches than fasteners made to destroy even the random fantasy of escape. He was shown into a small, shabby room furnished with cheap institutional chairs and even a sofa, and in a moment Hope Kirby was led in, handcuffed and manacled, the guards quickly and almost apologetically removing the fetters, and one of them said, "Hope, can I bring you something to drink?"

"I would sure love some coffee with molasses," Hope said, grinning with diffident courtesy and appreciation at the guard who had asked the question.

"What about you, sir?" the guard said, looking at Hugh Bedford, who gazed at him blankly, not understanding the question at all, looking at this solemn man in a guard's uniform and hardly even seeing him so that the guard asked in a politely raised voice, "Mr. Bedford, would you like something to drink, too?" Hugh Bedford started. "No," he said. "No, I don't want anything."

The guard went away. Another guard stood by the door and tried to look indifferent. Hugh Bedford looked at Hope Kirby. *We are in the same room. But tomorrow sometime before six o'clock they will lead him away like a hog to the slaughter pen, and they will kill him. Now we are human beings, talking to each other, and tomorrow he will never talk again.*

"It's all right, Lawyer," Hope said.

"You've heard, then."

"About the governor? Yeah, I heard. The warden came and told me."

"I don't even know where the son of a bitch is now."

"Hit hain't your fault, Lawyer. Like I've told you, what is to be will be."

"Dammit, Hope, I don't believe that."

"Lawyer, I'd like you to do me one thing if you can."

"Anything, Hope. Anything."

"I'd like to be buried by Abby. Her and me—hit didn't work out, but hit warn't her fault, and maybe hit warn't mine. I was right proud of her."

Hugh Bedford felt himself abruptly on the verge of tears. He could not speak. It was not that he was ashamed to cry. It was that he didn't know what he would do after he got through crying. What came next when a grown man hadn't cried for so many years, and all of a sudden he wanted to cry?

"If I could be buried by her, and maybe if hit worked out so's we could talk, I might could explain hit all to her, and she might could forgive me, and then we could rest easy."

"Yes, Hope. I'll try. Yes, I'll—" Hugh Bedford could not go on.

"Hit was having to leave the mountains and the war and all the killing and stuff. I wish I could walk one more time in the mountains, up there where hit's so soft at night and so still, and you think you can feel the earth breathing like a baby asleep. Hit warn't Mr. Hamilton. Hit warn't his fault neither."

"Who was Mr. Hamilton?" Hugh Bedford spoke to have something to say, to change the subject, to recover himself.

"He was the gov'mint man that come to tell us we had to move off our place. We kilt him."

"You killed him."

"Yep, Pappy said we had to kill him, and we did. But hit warn't his fault. He was just doing what somebody else told him to do. When you think about hit, most folks is always doing what somebody else tells them to do. Pappy told me to kill Mr. Hamilton, and I drove the knife in him. Pappy told me I had to kill Abby, and I done hit. But I didn't want to. I loved Abby. I was proud of her."

"Hell, Hope, you had the right to kill a woman who was stepping out on you like that. It was bad luck to have Charlie Alexander walk up while you did it. You had the right, and if it'd been any other time, any other judge, any other county, all you would have got would have been five years for manslaughter. Maybe not even that. It was this time, this judge, this county."

"I want to be buried next to Abby, Lawyer. If you can do that for me . . ."

"We're not going to talk about dying yet, Hope Kirby. Not yet." Hugh Bedford stood up. The guard brought in coffee. It was good coffee. Hugh could smell how good it was, and on the wooden tray the guard carried stood a little jar of molasses. Hope Kirby looked up at the coffee and smiled at the guard.

"Just the way you like it, Hope," the guard said.

"Your pappy's gone off somewhere," Hugh said. "That's what he told M.L."

"The boys is coming tonight. They'll be here in the morning. They sent word that Pappy was gone."

"What do you think, Hope? Do you think he's really gone?"

"You never know about Pappy. I'd of had to be there to hear him tell hit. You got to listen to Pappy real careful. He don't tell no lies. But sometimes he can make you think he means one thing when he means another. I remember how he talked Mr. Hamilton into the smokehouse the day he kilt him. Hit was all as smooth as butter, but we boys knowed we was going to kill Mr. Hamilton, and if Mr. Hamilton had of listened, he might of knowed hit, too."

They talked about Pappy. It gave them a subject, something besides the death looming over them, something other than the whole miserable knotted net of circumstance that had led them here. They heard a boom of thunder, distant and yet loud, and the lights trembled. "Hit's going to rain," Hope said. "I hope the boys don't slip off the road."

"They'll be all right," Hugh said morosely.

"I reckon they will," Hope said. It was maddening, Hugh thought. The last end of the rope of life slipping rapidly through a hole, the loose end coming at them, death, and they couldn't think of anything important to say.

A guard came in. "Mr. Bedford, the warden will see you. He's got a list of telephone numbers for you."

"I'll be back, Hope. I'll sit with you through the night if you want. I'm going to call every supreme court justice in the state. I'm going to get a stay of execution."

"Good luck, Lawyer. You don't have to stay the night 'lessen you want to."

"I want to, Hope. I want to spend the night with the assurance that I've got more time. Just a little more time."

IT WAS almost a party when people thought about it later. The sheriff arrived. Then Luke Bright came in, carrying a shotgun and with a pistol strapped on his belt. Blackie Ledbetter and Jim Ed came in. Paul Ledbetter stayed at the clinic. "Somebody has to be ready if you bring in a man or two men with bullets in them," he said, ever the doctor. "I figure we have one doctor up there in the shape of Blackie, and then I'm down here with all the medical machinery." Blackie brought his black bag, the doctor's trademark. He did not carry a weapon.

Red Eason came in with his shotgun, and so did Jim Scott. They arrived in Red's old car, laughing a little sheepishly when they saw that others had come before them. Charles's heart warmed to see them. He shook hands with both of them gratefully. It was twilight by then, and the sheriff hustled them all inside. "No sense in making a target," he said gruffly. In a matter-of-fact way he swore them both in as deputy sheriffs. "I ain't putting no term to this," he said. "You guys want to make a little extra money, you can work for me as deputies anytime." They laughed in an embarrassed, companionable way. The sheriff thought that as much as Red needed money, it might be a good deal—Red letting Charles do the writing for the newspaper, and on weekends Red could pack a pistol and help keep the peace of the county. The county usually didn't need much peacekeeping. Sometimes that observation grabbed the sheriff like a hand out of the dark, shaking him. It was not normal in Bourbon County to have a house filled with men standing around with guns to keep another murder from happening. One thing that had appealed to the sheriff when he ran for the job after the war was that it promised a slow and peaceful life.

All three big American wars of the century were represented. Odd when you thought about it. A big crowd from World War II. Blackie Ledbetter from World War II and Korea. Paul Alexander, Jim Ed, and Willy Weaver from World War I. Yes, even Willy, blind since 1918, came in, driven by his wife. Willy was Jim Ed's nephew, in his fifties now, hale and talkative, the improbable watchman at the car works. He kept a pack of five big dogs. At night he found his way from checkpoint to checkpoint in the car works, turning his watchman's key in the clock of every one with the infallible expertise of a man who knew his floors by heart and by foot; and his big dogs, on the loose, kept up a howling cacophony of unmusical canine noise that would scare the daylights out of any thief they found and more than that would surround the thief barking and snapping if he resisted arrest. Several times through the years Willy had marched one poor wretch or another out through the car works to a telephone to call the sheriff to come charge the would-be thief for trying to steal coal or brass or God knows what from the huge sheds where the furnaces belched heat and made molten metal during the day.

Willy's wife drove him and the dogs up, the lot of them unloading in a tornado of barking and shouting and greeting. Her name was Miranda, and she took over the kitchen and set about to make coffee and sandwiches and commentary. "I tell you, I sure do miss your wife, Mr. Alexander. That Eugenia, she was the truest Christian woman I ever knowed in my life, and I knowed my mother-in-law, Willy's grandmaw, and there wasn't nothing wrong with that woman. Lordy, lordy, when she died, I thought the world would end. But your wife, Mr. Alexander. She had something quiet and peaceful about her, like she talked to God face-to-face every day. You could see her face glow, and it looked like a lamp, but she didn't even know it."

Willy brought his dogs for a purpose, to smell out anything that might be in the woods, and as the twilight thickened, Blackie Ledbetter took a powerful flashlight, one of those with five batteries, and went off with Willy through the woods, helping his cousin through the unfamiliar undergrowth while the dogs swept back and forth with an unremitting howling and barking, growling with a somewhat questioning tone because they could not figure out what they were looking for.

Blackie and Willy and the dogs checked the barn and the disused chickenhouse, relic of Paul Alexander's determination in the 1930s to be self-sufficient in food if the railroad went bust and he lost his job. The sheriff said time and again, "We do not want to kill him. We want to keep him from killing Charles, but we don't want to kill him."

The sheriff was the hero in all this, Blackie thought when he ruminated about these events years afterwards. Too bad he didn't live to see how it all ended, but nobody could have predicted how long it would take to see the end. Everybody thought it would end that night, and when it didn't end that night, they thought it would end the next day, and they could not understand that it would take over forty years for it all to come to a conclusion.

Blackie came to the Alexander house not to protect Charles but to be with his father, Jim Ed. He and Paul knew their father must have lung cancer. "What good would it be to X-ray him?" Paul said. "There's nothing we can do to help him now. Let's go on pretending it's just a cough."

"He knows," Blackie says.

"Of course he knows. But we can pretend anyway."

Yes, the world was like that, Blackie thought in his older brother's wisdom. We know all sorts of things, but we pretend that things are some other way. All life was like going to church. Why not? Who could bear reality? He could pretend that the spirit of his mother, Juliet, still lived in the old house out in the country, and when he woke in the night he could whisper to her, and she whispered back or so he imagined. She kept company with the spirit of the tall and slender Confederate soldier whose portrait stared solemnly out into the living room. She had always had a reserve about her, something not fully revealed. She never quite gave all of herself away to her husband or to her two children. She was warm, gentle, full of wit, and able to talk for hours in such a way that she drew others out but seldom spoke much about herself or about what she was thinking. She loved his father. Blackie knew that. Loved Jim Ed much more than Eugenia Alexander loved Paul Alexan-

der, and now both women, both mothers, were dead, both earlier than anyone would have supposed, dead before anyone thought they should die. Different kinds of love, Blackie thought.

He had been in love once or twice but not enough to overcome his doubts
about marriage. He had lost his virginity to a Frenchwoman in Paris after a
long night when they saw the sun rise on the Seine, a night filled with
romance and, he thought, promise. She said she could not take him home;
her parents would be there. He took her to a hotel, and he understood that
she knew more about sex than he did, and he discovered that sex was a very
much better thing than he had imagined it could be. He discovered also that
she expected him to pay her. She made her request almost timidly, as if
money had been some secondary but still necessary part of all this that he
had forgotten, just as a well-meaning man might enjoy a good meal in a
restaurant and become so engrossed in conversation with the waiter that he
rose as though from a family table and started to leave without paying his bill
so that when he was gently reminded, both waiter and guest might smooth
the matter over by hearty laughter at the absentmindedness of it all.

So the lithe young woman with whom he walked the summery streets of
Paris in 1945 all night long, telling her things, speaking of the miracle of survival in a hard war, loving in the romantic mood of boys far from home
falling in love with love as in the movies or the love stories written in books,
was a whore. The word seemed far too harsh for her gentleness. He paid
her. She laughed. She kissed him goodbye. In the clear morning light she
seemed a little older, a little more used than she had seemed in the com-
mending dark, and when she was gone, she was gone forever. He thought it
was all farcical once the surprise of being asked to pay had worn off—as it
quickly did. It was a story to tell people, a story to tell his mother since she
would have appreciated its ironies and its foolishness, but he could not bring
himself to speak to her about a subject that included sexual intimacy.
Beyond all that Blackie remembered the night sweetly, the girl's face, her
hunger for him or for the dollars he could put into her hand. She had to
make a living, he thought. She had survived the war, and she did not know
what she would do now, and she had to make a living. What had happened
to her?

The shades were drawn all over the downstairs of the house. When
Blackie and Willy and the dogs came back from patrolling the woods and the
barn, tension seemed to break. The conviction grew that Roy Kirby was not
out there. "I always had the feeling," Paul Alexander said, "that Mr. Kirby
was an honorable man and that he would not kill my son."

The sheriff remained skeptical, but he also remained silent. *So far, so good,*
he thought, ticking the hours off. Every hour was a small triumph. Charles

was alive that much longer. So was Roy Kirby. He did not agree with Paul Alexander at all, and things in the sheriff's mind were still unsettled. If Roy Kirby had done what he seemed to have done—gone off to make a new start somewhere, perhaps merely gone off to some wild spot in the mountains to be alone and recover himself—why not take John Sevier with him? John Sevier was like a pet dog. Why wouldn't he have gone with his father?

Meanwhile conversation went on in a desultory way. The men fell to talking about this or that in the self-deprecatory way that men tell some stories to keep themselves from thinking about the stories they don't tell. They brought back incidents—the cows the sheriff had seen lying stiff in death on their sides with legs swollen in the air—just beyond Saint-Lô. Red remembered the single wall left standing of a small church in an Italian village where everything had been shelled, and in this wall were two small windows glazed with stained glass, but the glass was not broken, and the villagers, emerging from the rubble, claimed loudly, fervently that a miracle had happened. One miracle amidst all the destruction.

Willy and Blackie patrolled with the dogs regularly but came in for coffee now and then, and Willy told how Jim Ed had come out under fire in the other war, the war of 1917–1918, and dragged him to safety after the shell burst that blinded Willy for life, and Jim Ed told him he made too much of it. Even Paul Alexander told a story of a fortune-teller, a madwoman, in the midst of a shattered Belgian village during the retreat of 1914, who read his hand and told him that he would cross the sea to marry a blond woman. Charles, sitting quietly in a corner, heard this tale as something utterly strange. He could not imagine his father a soldier; he could not imagine him going to a fortune-teller.

But Charles felt excluded from all this talk, ill at ease among these men there to protect him, and he had nothing to contribute, nothing to say about any of his adventures, because he had not had adventures. Adventures had happened to him. They were not adventures he cared to talk about. Everybody knew them, and if he had made the right choice at the right time Hope Kirby would not be awaiting death in the electric chair, and these men would not be sitting here armed and ready to kill Roy Kirby to keep Roy Kirby from killing Charles. He felt ashamed and responsible and sad and also trapped in his own existence where he had done nothing right. He imagined that the men in the house reproached him far more than they did, and he somehow could not make himself think that they were there because they felt bound to him somehow. No, they were bound to his father, he supposed, even Red Eason. He had to think about tomorrow. He had made a resolution—yes, another resolution. Would he keep it? Mr. Finewood would surely be here now had not a chill fallen between them. Charles had not been to

Midway Baptist Church in the whole of 1954, and now it was June, and Mr. Finewood had not tried to force a conversation between them. There were reasons.

About midnight he was overcome by a fatigue that pressed upon him like a sack of coal he could not carry anymore. He announced that he was going to bed.

His declaration sent a stir through the room, making the men and even Willy's wife look at him as if they had forgotten him altogether. "Where do you sleep?" the sheriff said quickly.

"In the room above this one," Charles said. "I'll be all right."

"Don't turn on the light up there," the sheriff said.

"All right," Charles said. "I'll be fine. Don't worry." Some of the men bid him goodnight, sitting. Some stood and watched him up the stairs. The shades drawn against the warm night made some of them sweat, and the smell of human flesh hung in the air.

He climbed the steps feeling more weary than he had ever felt in his life. The upstairs was dark, and as he walked into his room, he was seized by the terrific fantasy that Roy Kirby had slipped into the house sometime during the day and now hid in the big attic closet that ran to the back of Charles's bedroom, ready to leap out, to kill him. Who had been up there to check on things? No one, he thought, and for an instant he felt like crying out. But he subdued his fear. His life seemed to revolve around subduing fear these days and on this night in particular. Then he thought that he was so tired that life or death did not matter. Yes, that was it. Life or death mattered not at all.

He undressed in the dark and lay down on the small bunk bed that his father had bought from army surplus years before. For a long time he and Stephen had shared this room and had slept in the bunk bed, Charles on the bottom, Stephen on the top. The beds came apart. Then there was a shift, and Stephen moved downstairs to a smaller room at the bottom of the stairway, and Guy occupied the room next to Charles. Guy was not here tonight. Without explanation Paul Alexander took him to the neighbor woman who often looked after him during the day. Paul Alexander did not have to explain. He wanted to protect his child from flying bullets.

Below Charles in the living room the murmur of voices went on, broken occasionally by an outburst of laughter and a cry for attention so that someone else could tell a story. Charles reflected on the tendency of people to slide into normality whenever they could. Today is what is normal. Tomorrow somebody may be told that he has incurable cancer, and by tomorrow night that news will be normal. Bob Saddler is a presence about town, a face in the crowd, a voice recognizable, known by everyone, and Bob Saddler takes a bottle of sleeping pills, and he dies, and now it is normal to mention Bob

Saddler's name and to say with a tremble of pity, "Oh the poor man. He took a bottle of sleeping pills and died." These men had gathered in faithful friendship, and Willy's wife had come with them to defend Charles against the terror that flieth by night, and when all was said and done and Roy Kirby did not show up and Charles lived through the night and the following days, the night of storytelling and holding guns would pass into the collective memory of the county, and people who were not here would claim they had been, and people who had been here would toss it all off, feel a little foolish about it, but still tell the story with the air of men who had done their duty when they felt its call. That was how neighborhoods were—alive, organisms reacting to the vagaries of time and reshaping themselves to every change as if it had been expected all along so that there was nothing to become excited about; there was only the next task to be done. When the black death wiped out much of the population of Europe and left cities stinking with the rot of innumerable corpses or when the fiery stench of death lay over Hiroshima the survivors got to work cleaning up and restoring as much as they could of their old lives, and time went on. Yes, an individual might remember for the rest of his life that he had had a gun rammed into his forehead and that he had been as close to death as the infinitesimal twitch of a muscle on a trigger, but the assembly of the whole that constituted the community of continuation did not remember these things except as an abstraction to be set aside in favor of more worthwhile pursuits.

He dozed, for he awoke suddenly to thunder, lightning, and the crash of rain against the house, and he felt the spray of moisture blown through his window onto his face, and he got up and shut his window. When the lightning crashed, everything in view trembled with an electric blue. He lay there for a moment in the sudden cool, hearing the rain augment when the thunder had crashed outside, and then he slept again. He slept deeply, and he dreamed odd, convulsive dreams of action and confusion, but they were not unpleasant.

Willy and Blackie came up onto the front porch with their dogs. Somebody put a cup of coffee in Willy's hands, and he closed upon it gratefully. He shook his grizzled head and said, "I don't think he's out there. It feels empty. Long as I've been at this business, you can tell when somebody's about."

Paul Alexander said, "I do not see how he could be there."

"He's a good'un," Sheriff Myers said, shaking his large head. "If anybody can hide, he can do it. Still—" He let the sentence drop.

Everyone looked tired. The sheriff had red eyes. "He's bound to be somewhere else," the sheriff said. "He's waiting somewhere for Charles, just like he waited for that crazy preacher." The rain hammered on, and the lightning flashed.

"Maybe not," Jim Ed mused, smoking his twentieth cigarette of the night. "Maybe he's slipped away. Why shouldn't he make a new life for himself? He's lost his home. He's lost his family. Those boys of his have got an attack of civilization. He's not an old man. Why doesn't he go look for what he's lost, to see if he can find it again?"

Very slowly the dawn broke. Day would come late because of the storm. Willy's wife made more coffee. She had several pots going. The men were red-eyed and weary. Slowly the world outside became visible. They all looked out the windows now, raising the curtains. In every direction they saw the bleak and windblown sweeping of a soaked world with more rain falling, taking down with it the feelings of excitement and danger that had fueled the night. It was mysterious. The world had returned to normal, leaving all of them confused and feeling slightly foolish. Much ado about nothing, Blackie thought. In his fatigue he could not quite remember how the title fit except that it was a comedy. Why should he be here? He thought of his mother and Eugenia, two dear friends, dead together now. He hoped they were looking on this scene with mild humor. He didn't believe in such things, but he hoped. Why should he not entertain himself in foolish fantasy? Fantasies did not hurt. He looked across the room at Paul Alexander. The dark complexion. The thick mustache gone white now. The Roman nose. He felt his own nose. It was certainly not a Roman nose. He laughed.

"What's so funny?" the sheriff said.

"Nothing," Blackie said. "I was thinking of how different noses are on different people."

The sheriff gave him an odd look and did not laugh. It was only another oddity during the night. Too many oddities to worry about, and why should anybody be thinking of noses? Maybe Blackie had had a drink of something he had not shared.

*T*HE GUARDS woke Hope Kirby up early in the morning. They were solicitous, speaking to him gently as if he might be sick or perhaps as if he had suffered some grief and needed to be spoken to gently. They brought him a cup of coffee in a white mug, and it was hot, just the way he liked it. One of the guards brought in a little jar of molasses with a spoon in it. Hope smiled at him and thanked him, and the guard said it was no trouble at all.

Another guard brought in a plate of scrambled eggs and bacon along with biscuits and gravy. Hope was not hungry for the eggs and bacon, although he ate a few bites to make the guards feel good. He drank the coffee down happily, and one of the guards quickly brought him another cup.

The guard in charge hung his head a little and looked embarrassed. He said, "Hope, we got to bring in a barber." Hope didn't know what he meant at first. Then he understood, and he said, "Sure, anytime you want."

A skinny little black convict was waiting just outside. He had murdered another black man in a dice game, and he was serving a life sentence. He came gliding in with a white towel, a basin, and an electric clipper. He didn't have a comb or scissors or a razor like the barbers in town did. Hope looked at him, and the convict dropped his eyes. Hope said, "Just before he starts, would you gentlemen let me look in a mirror?"

One of the guards said, "Get him a mirror."

The black convict didn't say anything. He stood up straight and looked at the ceiling and clutched his clippers in his hand and let the white towel hang over his forearm. He looked like a man who had studied all his life how to look indifferent and bored.

"It's hot outside," one of the guards said.

"It rained all night," another guard said. "They say they'll be more thundershowers the rest of the day."

Nobody said anything to that. The guards looked embarrassed. In a minute the guard who had gone for the mirror came back with it. It was a large mirror in a wooden frame. Hope held the mirror and looked at himself.

Once, on the evening before his thirteenth birthday, he looked in the little scrap of mirror that his father used when he shaved. It hung over the metal basin in the kitchen, and Hope stretched himself and looked at it, and he thought, *This is the last day that I will be twelve.* He was going to be a teenager the next day, and it seemed like a big jump in life. He wanted to see himself one more time as he would never be again.

That was what he did now. He looked at himself in the mirror before the convict barber shaved his head. He could see all his face, and he could see that his hair was still rough and coarse and coal-black without any gray in it anywhere. It had grown out in prison, down over his ears, and he was almost amused at how strange he looked to himself, as if somebody he didn't know was looking at him, wanting to get better acquainted. His cheeks were fatter than they used to be, a lot fatter than when he was in the Philippines. His skin was rough, and he could not find the child he had been at age twelve-verging-on-thirteen.

The mountains were not outside either, and in the institutional brightness of his cell he thought of the mountains running up dark behind the cabin where they had lived under the starry sky, and he remembered when it had been so still on some nights that he thought if he listened hard enough he could hear a bird fly and a bug crawl. He ran a hand through his hair, felt how coarse it was. Missionary used to laugh at him and say he ought to use a lawnmower to cut his hair. He thought if he turned the mirror a little he might be able to see Missionary in the mirror, but he knew that was crazy.

"Whenever you're ready, Hope," one of the guards said, clearing his throat.

"I'm ready," Hope said.

A guard brought a wooden chair in, and Hope sat down, and the convict barber wrapped the towel around Hope's neck. Somebody brought in an electric cord from the corridor, and in a minute Hope felt the clippers against his neck and heard the *zzzzzzzz* of the blades, and he felt the hair falling off his head and he saw it tumbling down onto the white towel and onto the floor. He remembered his mama cutting his hair with a scissors, using a soup bowl that she put on the top of his head to shape what she did, and she was gentle and slow. The convict barber was not rough. Soon it was all done, and his hair was lying all over the floor, and the guard with the mirror asked Hope if he wanted to look at himself, and Hope said no. He didn't want to see himself when he didn't look like himself.

Somebody brought a broom and a dustpan in and began sweeping up his hair from off the floor.

*C*HARLES drove the '37 Ford. Stephen sat beside him holding a guitar. "I figure if Roy Kirby tries to shoot you, I'll play something off-key, and that'll throw his aim off," Stephen said.

Charles laughed. Stephen didn't say, "Why in hell are you doing this, Charles?" That would have seemed disloyal. Instead he said, "You got the windshield wipers fixed."

"I got everything fixed," Charles said.

"The old body's still rotting away," Stephen said. "You can't do anything about that."

"Maybe somebody will think of something before it's completely gone," Charles said. He was serious. "Somebody told me I might get some plastic that looks just like wood."

"But it won't be wood," Stephen said.

"Do you think Roy Kirby will be waiting for you down there, at the Salem Church?"

"He's bound to be soaking wet if he is."

"That won't make him less deadly, Charles."

"What is to be will be," Charles said.

"The sheriff says that's what Hope Kirby said."

"Everything is as it is for no reason at all, and if everything were different, there would be no reason for that either," Charles said.

"That's not Hope Kirby."

"It's the same thing."

Charles drove ahead through rain so heavy that the world beyond the windshield wipers was a blue of tumbling water. The lightning and the thunder had gone. This was a rain that meant to stay. It made streams in the road, and people drove slowly because they knew the asphalt could be slick. Beyond Bourbonville the two-lane highway rose and fell among the gentle hills and valleys. Soaked cows and horses stood lethargically in fields under the rain. Just before the iron bridge over the river, Charles turned right onto the unpaved road, and the tires crunched in the thin gravel surface. Two miles later he pulled into the parking lot of Salem Baptist Church, nosing the '37 Ford against the steep rise of ground that ascended to the Talliaferro tomb brooding in its grove of dark European poplars. The water streamed on the black roof and rolled down the pink Italian marble making dull coruscations of wet light.

Charles was already out of the car with his back turned to the tomb when the sheriff slid to a stop in his trailing patrol car and began screaming at Charles to get back into the Ford. In an instant Sheriff Myers was on the run up the slope, pumping a shell into the chamber of his pump shotgun. "Get down! Get down! He's in there. That's where he's hiding." Later he said it came on him as an apparition. Roy Kirby had come to the Talliaferro tomb in the night, slipped the great wheel to release the long bolt, and he was in there now waiting for his moment. The perfect lair. And no one had thought of it. Just when Charles got out of his car, Roy Kirby would push the door back and blast down at Charles at point-blank range, and the boy would be dead instantly. Sloshing mud and rain in every direction, the sheriff charged up the slope and laid hands on the wheel and wrenched it towards the shut position. It did not budge. He turned it back an inch or two, and it moved smoothly. Then he shut the lock to the full again. No doubt about it. The door was firmly shut, the steel bar set firmly in place in the steel striker fixed in the marble jamb. All of a sudden the sheriff felt foolish. The tomb guarded its air of exotic and perpetual tranquillity, speaking of timeless death in the perfect proportions of a Platonic ideal of mortality. Its stillness mocked the sheriff, mocked the whole wretched little spectacle about to unfold below them in the parking lot, and in the Salem Baptist Church later that morning. Rain poured off the roof and cascaded down on the sheriff. He might have been under a hose. He turned in morose resignation and with the feeling that he had been mocked by both humans and the elements, he came slogging down from the mausoleum ankle-deep in muck through the sticky red earth which he tried with annoyed futility to scrape off his boots on the gravel surface of the parking lot.

Other cars were pulling up. Even without Charles, there was to be excitement enough that day. People greeted each other warily, far from the exuberant backslapping and handshaking and preacherly warmth that made the usual Baptist congregation an affair to strike fire to gas. The rain dampened spirits further. It pummeled the roof and rocketed out of the drains and flooded down the slope to run in rivulets across the unpaved parking lot so that the women in particular had their moments of misery making their way in with the covered dishes that would serve for lunch. Salem Baptist was an ample church. There was a large refectory for eating downstairs and a kitchen adjoining it, but it was still a disappointment when you thought of a summer associational meeting inside rather than in the shaded protection of the great grove of oaks that sheltered the building and attested to the long time that it had been there. Baptists were not alone in their conviction that longevity was proof of the divinity the congregation worshipped, for how could God let things stand for so long a time were they not true? The contradictory signals of so many long-lived churches could be ignored, especially when Salem Baptist was the only church in view on this morning, its dignity and grace happily visible despite the cloudburst.

So people rushed in to escape the rain and to compete politely for choice seats. Afterwards many claimed they had got there early, but everyone agreed that the first to arrive that morning were Lawrence Arceneaux and Clifford Finewood. No one could affirm how the two ministers had greeted each other. They seem to have settled down in circumspect resolution not to speak or at least to do nothing more than to greet each other with the least courtesy required for the sake of appearances. Mr. Finewood sat as far as he could on the front pew to the left hand side of the pulpit, and Mr. Arceneaux sat as far as he could to the right. They were divided not only by the aisle that ran down the middle of the central section of the three grand divisions of the building but by a good forty feet of superchilled space. It was as if both warriors had come early to survey the ground before battle.

All this was seen at the time as nothing but a sign of mutual hostility, all to be expected, though deplored by eager spectactors who thought it was a shame, a terrible shame, that Baptists should fall out this way. Many who rushed to fill in the pews exclaimed silently to themselves that they were very glad to have arrived early enough to get such championship seats for the conflict that was sure to come, though even silently they did not express these feelings so bluntly. That is the definition of conscience sometimes—to repress in euphemisms uttered in silence some resistance to one's real emotions.

Of the two men Mr. Finewood seemed by far the more agitated. He shifted his corpulent body. He looked around. He opened his Bible and he closed it. He turned to look out the window. He tried to smile at people, but the smile collapsed almost as quickly as he tried to raise it on his face. It was ordinarily the custom of preachers to be among the last seated at any affair like this one. It was their habit to walk about greeting people with a pumping handshake and to call on all their talents for remembering names to speak personally to Brother Jones or Sister Smith and to recall some little detail like the birth of a baby or a recent death out of the Jones or Smith cavalcade of life that might indicate close and daily interest in these households. These were talents for survival, and Baptist preachers learned them in the instinctive way that bluejays learned to fly or that squirrels learned to leap from branch to branch without tumbling in an injurious or fatal spiraling to the ground far below. Today neither Preacher Arceneaux nor Preacher Finewood indulged himself in these gestures, and it was noted later on that although Preacher Arceneaux kept his eyes steadfastly averted from Preacher Finewood, Preacher Finewood could not keep his eyes from flicking in Arceneaux's direction, although he just as quickly snapped them back again as if the sight were painful. Later, people understood that Preacher Finewood had been afraid.

The church filled, all three great divisions of it, a down-to-earth, Baptist symbol of the Holy Trinity, not a blasphemous Catholic image of this blessed vision, and even the balcony that gave onto the central division was filled. Before the first hymn and the first prayer addressed God, the smell of damp clothes and bodies was noticeable and soon unpleasant. All the windows were opened as much as those nearby could bear the rain driven in on them by occasional gusts of wind. Men and women fanned themselves vigorously with funeral-home fans—the energy gained by the vigorous use of the fans generating far more heat than the cooling breeze that was desired. Yet it was something to do, and the Baptists did it, for it was their nature to act. No doubt it would be an uncomfortable meeting and a brutally hot, dank, and suffocating day. No one was likely to find any connection between one of the grand assemblies of the Catholic Church and this plainly dressed, even shabby, gathering of the Salem Baptist Association, although their rationale and their purpose were exactly the same.

It was like this. Three centuries or so after the Crucifixion of Christ, the Roman emperor Constantine the Great went shopping for a god and decided that Jesus was the greatest one around, even greater than the sun god Helios he had been worshipping. But who exactly was Jesus? You didn't have to worry about who the sun god was. There he stood up in the sky day after day, and you couldn't deny him. He was big and bright and hot and more or less regular, and he made the crops grow and sometimes did unpleasant things when he was displeased. But he had no advice to give on daily affairs, and in fact he was too regular to do anybody much good. Regular as a clock that had only one function—to tell time. Helios was otherwise silent—huge and silent. Constantine needed a god capable of a lot more activity than that, capable of helping him save the Roman Empire from splintering into a dozen or three dozen fragments. Jesus helped him win a great victory over a rival. That was practical. So he turned to Jesus, and he had hardly announced his conversion when one Arius of Alexandria in Egypt declared that Jesus was not completely divine. God created him as a son. No son could be as great as his father. Jesus himself acknowledged that he was inferior to his father. The great enemy of Arius was the bishop Athanasius. Athanasius declared that if Jesus was not completely divine, he had no power over death, and Christianity was not worth the parchment the Gospels were written on.

So what did Constantine do? He called a great council of the Church—bishops and other exalted officials from all over the eastern Mediterranean world showed up to hurl Scripture and philosophy at one another, and when all the anthems had been sung and the prayers raised and the emperor himself had looked on in semiliterate amazement, a vote was taken, and God was assumed to be in the vote. That's what you did when you couldn't make up your mind what God wanted: you called for a council, and your bishops came together, and they voted, and the ayes had it—inspiration from on high. God would not let a majority down.

But when Baptists did it, there was something amiss—the very appearance of the thing. You finally had to admit that Catholics and Episcopalians and even Presbyterians were simply a hell of a lot better at pulling off an extravaganza of processional majesty and incantation than Baptists were. Baptists were not to the manner born. This bedraggled and soaked congregation could go through all the pageantry it could muster, but it looked curiously nervous and uninspired as it gathered on this bleak morning, and finally the song leader of the day, a lean and lank man named Bud Piersall, rose and in a quartet-bass voice called on the congregation to sing a rousing round of "Faith Is the Victory."

It was a lilting Ira Sankey song, one of those rousing things popular with Dwight L. Moody evangelism, legendary among people who loved revivals and scored great evangelists the way some people put baseball players in a hall of fame.

> *Encamped along the hills of light, ye Christian soldiers rise,*
> *And press the battle ere the night shall veil the glowing skies;*

Against the foe in vales below, let all our strength be hurl'd;
aith is the victory, we know, that overcomes the world.

The congregation blasted away at industrial strength. Tommy Fieldston, standing down close to Preacher Finewood, roared out the words so that he could be heard above everybody else and so, Charles presumed, his faith could be seen to be the largest. He was also the most off-key. Stephen, playing the piano, looked down on the freckle-faced zealot from time to time with musical irritation, vexed because even he could not drown Tommy Fieldston out. Charles mused that many of the favorite hymns of Baptists had a militant edge. Christians were soldiers; their foes demons in human guise armed with guile and malice. Charles could imagine Tommy Fieldston with his bloody sword rising and falling on the necks and bodies of professors sitting at desks reading Charles Darwin and W. T. Stace, universities taken, fire crackling among the books, and smoke rising in piles above a sunny earth made safe for God. Faith is the victory.

Now Baptists did not have papalist corruptions such as bishops. Baptists had pastors and congregations, and it was an article of faith among them that all Baptists were equal in the eyes of God and that all congregations were independent of one another. No councils for them. No bishops. No synods. Not even presbyteries. But they did have associations. The word "association" did not seem to compel anything. It did not imply an overweening, almighty unity. Each congregation stood forth in its own purity as an entity that no group larger than itself could compel. Sacred independence. That was the Baptist way—just as Americans went to war in 1917 not as an "allied power" but as an "associated power," and the American army was not part of an "allied army," but was an American Expeditionary Force, the name intended to imply the right of the United States to do just what it did after 1919, to wash its hands of Europe, to take no responsibility for a larger world, and therefore to remain pure and uncorrupted in its splendid and puritanical isolation.

So the Baptists.

Every year in summer, churches in Bourbon County could send delegates to the Salem Baptist Association. Usually the delegates passed a few hard-worded resolutions against alcohol, dancing, evolution, atheistic communism, government aid for Catholic schools, and whatever the pope might have done lately, issues that raised no controversy and created no divisions. Two or three preachers delivered sermons in the course of the day, giving them an opportunity to show off to congregations not their own; a business meeting included a report by the "association missionary" who had done various good Christian deeds in the course of the year, such as financing athletic competitions for young men and women, all funded by meager contributions from the various churches; and part of the morning and afternoon was given over to discussing and voting on resolutions. Usually nothing to any of it that could raise the dander of anybody in the room.

But in 1954 there was a very large issue indeed—Arceneaux's demand that the association support the recent ruling of the United States Supreme Court on racial segregation in the schools. And there was yet another. Tommy Fieldston wanted not only to condemn Arceneaux's resolution but to raise one of his own—to condemn the Revised Standard Version of the Holy Bible, the infamous RSV, a "translation" put together by suspect scholars headquartered at Yale University Divinity School. This board of translators had been taken over long ago by liberals and modernists and unbelievers and now, very clearly, by Communists intent on eroding the strong biblical faith that made America the land of the free and the home of the brave. What was wrong with the RSV? Divine fanatics such as John R. Rice and Carl McIntyre and an army of crusaders like them could count the ways up to a dozen or two. But the great and critical verse was Isaiah 7:14. The King James Version—or the Saint James Version, as it was commonly called in Tennessee—was explicit: "Behold a virgin shall conceive and bear a child."

The RSV substituted "young woman" for "virgin" and therefore with one verbal blow destroyed the divinity of Christ, the authority of the Bible, and the salvation of the world. And as if to mock the sensibilities of loyal Americans and good Christians, the RSV appeared in a bright red cover—adopting for itself the red of communism that the RSV represented. "Why did they publish it in red?" Clifford Finewood said in a high pulpit whisper, conveying the awe that vast wickedness can inspire in the amazed hearts of the righteous. "I'll tell you why," he rumbled. "Because the people who translated this Bible were Reds theirselves, given over heart and soul to destroying the gospel of our Lord Jesus Christ from within." In Tennessee many congregations held public bonfires and cast the hateful volume into the flames, consigning it to the hell that awaited all those responsible for its nefarious subversions and all those who might be beguiled by its heresies. No one tried to tell them that red was the traditional theological color.

During the first hymn Rosy Finewood pushed her way into the pew beside Charles. The sheriff had begged him and persuaded him not to sit next to a window. So Charles sat on a pew at the end near the front, just behind Arceneaux, and Rosy squeezed in beside him, gripping his arm with her plump hand. She whispered to him cryptically. "Charles, it's like Daddy says. You must tell the truth. If you know the truth, you must tell it."

He looked down at her almost in alarm and with chagrin. What did she mean? Her round, pink face looked up at him with a plaintive desire and with an expression of urgency that he had never seen in her. He did not have time to think about it. Marlene Fieldston was there. She was home from the Bible college in Chattanooga, and she would sing. Charles looked at Marlene across the way, but she did not look at him. She stared straight ahead, a broad smile fixed on her face as though she knew that photographers were hidden in the church waiting to leap out and snap her picture at just the right angle. Charles regarded her with detachment, a curious lack of feeling. She had rejected him. The injury was still there but now as a scar rather than a wound, something that reminded him of an unpleasantness, an embarrassment, he could not bear to repeat or even to think much about. But he felt no desire for her. Without wishing it, he thought of Tempe, how lively she was, how ready to argue with him, how full of feeling that she hid successfully sometimes and then revealed with startling surprise. She was gone, too. She had rejected him, too, and for reasons far more damning than the lust that had so shocked Marlene. When he thought of Tempe, now in France—Paris, he supposed—his heart turned to ashes inside his chest.

Deputy Luke Bright stood at the back of the church, his pistol at his belt. He was scared. To one side of the choir a doorway led to the Sunday-school rooms tacked onto the back of the building, and there Sheriff Myers stood with a pump shotgun in his hands. Somebody said later it was a scene out of the old history books where men took their muskets to church to guard against hostile Indian attack during the service. Paul Alexander and Blackie were at the back door, Blackie unarmed, Paul with the pistol in his pocket.

The opening hymn concluded. A preacher got up to pray. People sat down with a great noise of bodies contacting with wood pews. Announcements came. The rain fell steadily and hard. The room was uncomfortable. Preacher Finewood sweated copiously. From time to time he wiped at his face and his neck with a handkerchief. Great half-circles of sweat darkened under his fleshy arms.

Marlene was introduced and praised for her Christian witness. She listened to the praise with a warm smile on her face, looking up with the polite attentiveness that marks the well-raised Southern girl. Charles did not look at her. He doodled in his notebook. Stephen sat on the piano bench. He refused to play an electric organ. Vulgar, he said. When Marlene stepped up onto the raised platform in the front of the church, Stephen looked up at her with the wordless affirmation that seems to be the universal signal of those who accompany singers. She nodded at him in the same language, and his fingers rolled expertly across the keys, and he frowned. The piano was ever so slightly out of tune, and with his perfect pitch, Stephen could hear it as a clash of intolerable noise even as he knew that most of the congregation probably did not know the difference. Marlene sang. Her voice filled the space. The tension relaxed. How could anything happen after a hymn like that?

THE KIRBY men got to Nashville too late on Friday night to gain entry to the prison. They were there early Saturday morning. The guards led them into a little room with benches and a couch. In a while Hope was led in, his wrists handcuffed. The guards solicitously released him. The brothers kissed one another. Hope kissed John Sevier.

"I wisht Pappy'd come to see me," Hope said.

"We've made him mad," Joye said morosely. "We've all let him down."

"Well, you're here, John Sevier," Hope said. "You and me has been through a lot, and here we air at the end, and I'm glad to see you."

John Sevier stared at him blankly. Hope reached out and ran his hands through John Sevier's hair. "You're in need of a haircut," Hope said. "I cut his hair in the Philippines with a pocket knife." John Sevier made a faint, moaning sound.

"I should of got hit done," M.L. said.

"Ah, hit's all right. Hain't much difference if you cut hair one day or the next. I always liked to keep our hair short so's the lice wouldn't get in there. I tell you. I don't know what good lice does in the world. Do you think he's really gone off?"

They all knew who "he" was. "You can't never tell about Pappy. We've drove around looking for his pickup, you know. Thinking he might of hid hit somewheres. But we can't find hit nowheres. I can't figure hit out." Joye spoke softly and deliberately.

"Hit don't seem like him," Hope said. "To run off like that."

"Maybe hit does," Joye said. "He can't bear to look at none of us because we've gone and let him down. We hain't men like he is. We're trying to save our necks and we hain't got no honor. He can't bear hit. Maybe that's the reason."

"Hit could be so," Hope said. "But you've done the right thing. I'm sorry I killed Abby. I don't want that boy kilt. Hit hain't his fault. What is to be will be, and we air what we air, and we can't help that."

"I reckon he's gone back up in the mountains somewheres," Love said hopefully. "Hit seems to me that that were always Pappy's life—the mountains. He hain't old. He hain't sixty yet, and he's strong and tough. Lord, he could of fought the war better than any of us."

"Hain't nobody that can fight a war good," Hope said. "I don't never think about the war if I can help it."

The others nodded in silent agreement.

"John Sevier, do you know who I am?" Hope said.

John Sevier smiled an idiot's smile.

"He does know me," Hope said.

"Course he knows you," M.L. said. "He knows you better than he knows any of us, better than he knows Pappy."

"Reckon what goes on in his head," Hope said.

Hope wondered what John Sevier remembered. Did he remember holding Mr. Hamilton while Hope killed him?

"You recollect how Pappy hoodooed that Hamilton feller the day we kilt him—the day I kilt him?"

The brothers nodded.

"I wonder if he's hoodooing us now."

"Hit might could be," Joye said uncomfortably. "I hope not. If he tries to kill that boy, the sheriff will kill him."

"That won't make no difference to Pappy," M.L. said. "You know how he is. He don't have us'ns to raise no more. He's lost all he worked for in the mountains. Hit don't matter to Pappy if'n he lives or dies."

"Where's Lawyer?" Joye asked.

"You know where. He's all in a work. Trying to find the governor," Hope said. "Trying to get a supreme court justice to postpone the execution."

"We got several hours," M.L. said.

A guard came in. "Hope, is they anything you'd like to eat?"

"Nah, I don't care for nothing."

"Anything you want, Hope." The guard looked foolishly eager to please. Hope felt sorry for him.

"I'd sure like some grapes," Hope said. "If hit wouldn't be too much trouble, I'd be much obliged. We had a lot of grapes in the army before the war. In the Philippines I used to think about grapes a lot. Hit'd come on me sometimes, a wish that I could eat some grapes."

"Grapes it is," the guard said with an expression of gratitude. He went out. Guards stood in the room with them trying to look as if they were not listening to anything that was said. But no one said much of anything. The brothers made fits and starts at conversation. The efforts died.

The guard came back with a big paper sack and gave it to Hope. "I went out and bought them myself," the guard said.

"I'll pay you for them," Joye said, going into his pocket.

"You won't do no such thing," the guard said.

"I don't want to be obliged," Joye said.

"Well, you got to be," the guard said. "I ain't going to take your money, and I ain't going to tell you what they cost."

"Thanks a lot," Hope said. "I sure do 'preciate what you fellers have done for me."

The guard looked away. For a moment Hope was afraid he would cry. The guard wore a pistol on his leg. Hope looked at Joye, saw his brother measuring the guard up. For a moment his eyes met Joye's, and as though they had spoken, they both recognized the futility of their thought.

The guards brought coffee again. The brothers drank coffee out of habit. When they drank coffee, they thought of childhood and home—their real home, the mountain place. When Pappy could go down to Gatlinburg and buy real coffee, they felt that they lived in luxury. They felt that real coffee on the table was a sign they had succeeded.

PEOPLE remembered the sermon of the morning. Larry Arceneaux preached it, standing before them all, humorless and stern. He looked imperial in the way of actors in movies about English colonials about to bring civilization to the natives. His tan pongee suit fitted him as if it had been manufactured by a professor of anatomy who had specialized in him. The auditorium smelled of fresh paint and bodies, and the rain blew the smell of fields and woods from outside in. The heat was mounting and the rain unslackening.

Mr. Arceneaux took as his text Romans 3:23: "For all have sinned and come short of the glory of God." Charles took notes in shorthand. The text was one of the old evangelical chestnuts. The ordinary ranting preacher took the text and sailed off into yowling castigation of the horrid sins of the human race, the fate of a fiery, eternal hell awaiting them, and if it worked, he might create agonies of remorse among people miserable with the blankness of life and the terror of time. The text could make people suppose that if they had not lusted or fornicated or lied or cheated or got drunk or danced or played cards or cussed, they could have soared beyond all the strange, invisible, and impermeable walls that confined them to a world where they were stuck in the ordinary. They could hear their sins denounced with divine authority, blamed on the devil, and knowing that there was reason for their failure, they could repent, and for a moment it would seem that the dry old self had been shucked off and that something new, soft, childlike had replaced it and was ready to flower into all that it had never been.

Arceneaux had never preached that way from the sturdy oak pulpit of First Baptist. When he spoke the familiar old words on this morning, you could almost feel a relief in the auditorium. Amid the tension of armed men, Arceneaux was not going to arouse anybody by one of his unexpected sermons.

The mood of relief lasted about five minutes. Arceneaux proclaimed in his dry, hard voice that we were all sinners, seeking the desires and the devices of our own hearts and not the will of God, seeing the world through the jaundiced tint of the selfish glasses we wore over our sin-diseased eyes and thoughtless souls. People settled down in gratitude, and then Arceneaux got to the point.

The point was the Negro.

Yes, he preached in the Salem Baptist Association about Negroes, about slavery, about the Ku Klux Klan, about segregated schools, segregated bathrooms, segregated buses, segregated trains. He preached about lynching. He called up the lynching in Bourbonville. He recalled his own great-grandfather riding hell-for-leather—he did not use that term—with some Louisiana cavalry unit in "the War." He told of how much he had revered the memory of that militant ancestor. But, he said, the ancestor was wrong—not only wrong but sinful for fighting for slavery. The South had been cursed for slavery, and now it was cursed by the residue of slavery—the blind, violent, merciless hatred of the Negro. The Civil War had been a trial by ordeal, he said. The Lord God gave the victory to the North. Still the South held on to its curse, in love with the demonic possession that had ruined Southern society. The nature of sin was to be in love with evil, as if evil were an addiction. Southerners were, he thundered, incapable of seeing the light because they willed to be blind.

His voice rolled with relentless and unmitigated fury across the bloody course of Southern history while his congregation sat incredulous and aghast. They were angry. He was angry. His anger was in part directed against himself, for he knew what he was doing. He had given up—given up on the ministry, given up on Bourbonville, given up on more things than he could count. Did he care about blacks? The Negro? The colored? Whatever you called them—did Arceneaux care? Well, yes he did. His intense righteousness was born of a little turn in the rudder of his mind. He began thinking about things he had not thought about much—blacks and whites, slavery, the black workers on the family plantation, and he felt right and wrong. He also felt the supreme pleasure of knowing he was right when he also knew that a great crowd of people he despised were wrong. He was not a fool about himself. He did not completely deceive himself.

This sermon was a parting shot, and he expected to offend people and to resign once they had rejected his resolution, and he knew the resolution would be rejected. That, at least, was the way that he began. But as he progressed something else happened to him, and he spoke in a rolling thunder of inspiration. Righteousness took over, fed on itself in his brain and in his heart. Arceneaux became all at once the prophet Amos striding down out of the hills to luxurious Israel to denounce the king of Bashan and the rich who sold the poor for a pair of shoes. Charles wrote furiously, but from time to time he had to look up to see how people were responding, the hostility, the almost unbearable constraints of ritual habit in listening to a sermon of a sort no one had ever preached at any church in the Salem Baptist Association. It was almost funny, Charles thought—the discomfort of incongruity, the astonishment, and the anger.

But then somebody said "Amen!" It was a male voice, lost somewhere in the crowd, loud and firm, and in a moment somebody else said "Amen," and some people were nodding, and the nodding people sought out or seemed to seek out the faces of those stern in disapproval to nod at *them* as if to show them that yes, they were agreeing with the preacher, and in a moment others took courage, for by the time Arceneaux finished he was preaching to a storm going on in the congregation, people riven and eager and angry, some shouting "Amen" and some looking about with furious wrath as though they could put a bullet through the head of anybody who dared to open the world to intermarriage and miscegenation and rape and the beast from the jungle.

With one final, great rhetorical sweep Arceneaux concluded and turned from the pulpit and walked back to his place in the pew in front of Charles and sat down, and the moderator of the association was congratulating him but at the same time looking at him with fear and astonishment as if Arceneaux had become suddenly an apparition, and the congregation settled down into a dazed and dead silence so that everybody could hear the ticking of the regulator clock hanging from the balcony in the back of the sanctuary, and outside the distant hollow ringing of a cowbell, deep and irregular, in some pasture not far away and the rain, now slackening at last though with the dark and ominous clouds still scudding above the treetops.

In that hiatus of sound it seemed that nobody could breathe. The world stood still, staring at Arceneaux. He sat in the pew with his head bowed, sweating furiously, feeling himself close to tears, suddenly understanding himself what he had done and wondering in the detached and distant way that his mind worked if this was how all the prophets had begun. Had they done something out of selfish anger, lashing out at people who had rejected them and refused to be led, and, lacking any other weapons but words against such people, had they struck them with the full fury of a message intended to be martyrdom? Then behold! A miracle happened. The people heard. Maybe this was the way it had been in the real life of Jesus—the young rabbi suddenly and monstrously enraged by the looting moneychangers in the Temple, overturning their tables, lashing at them, condemning them and expecting to die, but suddenly elevated by the crowd to become the Messiah—and as promptly crucified.

Mr. McPherson, the moderator, recovered before anyone else. He lunged to his feet and announced the hymn "Amazing Grace," and the congregation rose in staggered, unrhythmic shuffling, jolted out of its trance. Stephen Alexander's rolling harmonics tumbled sweetly across the piano, and people stumbled into the song, and in a moment the power of the music and the familiar words did their work. The hesitancy became force, and a multitude of voices blended into a single torrent of sound. Stephen's deft fingers found the notes in tune over the keyboard. The angry people sang their anger; the transformed people sang their transformation. Arceneaux sang, his head bowed, not knowing what he had wrought.

In the back, beneath the regulator clock, Luke Bright sang. Blackie Ledbetter, veteran of the Second War and of Korea, an agnostic unconcerned with religion, sang lustily, and swept his eyes over the choir loft where people crammed into the chairs sang like a chorus of titans. People looked at each other. Blackie was amused. It was as though this motley congregation was using the hymn as an interlude to measure foe against foe, to choose sides, and when the hymn finished, what would happen then? Blackie could imagine the congregation breaking into riot, deacons of one church slugging deacons of another, ministers beating each other with their Bibles, and when the flimsy India-paper Bibles fell apart under the blows, snatching up the green-bound copies of the *Broadman Hymnal* and belaboring each other to the death.

Blackie's eyes went on up to the baptistry, the water tank recessed in the wall at an elevation to allow the entire congregation to witness the sacrament when the new Christian was plunged beneath the water. Most of the Baptist churches in the country still baptized in the river or in creeks, but Salem Baptist had risen in the world and had brought the baptistry inside, and installed a hot-water tap so converts could be baptized in all the months of the year, even if ice crusted over the river. Very suddenly Blackie understood that Roy Kirby was up there, in the baptistry, that this was his hiding place. He saw a shadow above the tank, and he knew that Roy Kirby was there. He cried out in the midst of the hymn, "He's up there!"

Pandemonium broke out, and the hymn ceased in screams, and some people threw themselves on the floor, and some jumped out the windows. Luke Bright jerked out his big revolver and blasted away at the baptistry. The concussions of the shots roared in the room. People's ears rang with them. The .38-caliber bullets slugged the wall and penetrated to the cast-iron tank of the baptistry. In the midst of this uproar the sheriff came rushing up from the doorway to the Sunday-school rooms with his pump shotgun. "Put up them goddamned guns!" he yelled. "Goddammit, you're going to kill somebody. Stop shooting, you fuckheads!"

Someone said later on that he believed this was the first time those words had been spoken in the Salem Baptist Church, at least the first time they had been spoken altogether in sequence at the same time. The sheriff knew there was no one in the baptistry. He had quietly climbed the steps that led up from the rear and looked inside as soon as he had come into the church that morning.

It was a while before the service could be resumed.

*C*HARLES'S memories of what came next were surreal, a confusion where words ran together and colors changed and faces blurred and confusion reigned and no two people could ever tell the story in one way.

First of all, after the shooting and the consequent uproar in the church, with people diving under pews and men and women alike screaming and throwing themselves about in grossly indecent spasms of self-defense and terror, a wave of anger swept out of the mass and descended on Charles. People said such things as "If it had not been for you, none of this would have happened," and "What are you doing here anyway? Why after all the other bad you have done this county did you have to come here today and destroy our meeting?" and "If your mother were alive, she would be broken-hearted" and "If your daddy was the kind of man he ought to be, he'd give you a hiding that'd leave you eating off the mantelpiece for the next month." Charles, who had not moved during the pandemonium, bent his head over his slender reporter's notebook, folded his arms, and said not a word. But he was angry.

Then there was Mr. Finewood rising, commanding attention, and assuming the posture of a brave general about to lead his troops in a charge toward a dangerously fortified position of the enemy. "Please, please!" he cried in his great, booming voice. "Please, no one has been hurt. Settle down, all of you. Nobody has been hurt, and we have business to do, the Lord's business."

The words, thrown out over the congregation like the regular pounding of a large bell, reduced people to silence.

Outside the heavy rain had started again, and those who had fled that far came back looking sheepish and resumed their seats. It was a thoroughly irritated crowd. Then Mr. Finewood resumed, and this time he held up his big, black, limber-backed Bible and began his oration in defense of the Word of God. It was an eloquent statement in its way, and years afterwards, when Charles was much older than Clifford Finewood would ever become, he looked back on the moment with a bitter and profound nostalgia filled not with admiration but with sadness. Clifford Finewood on that rainy

morning was like some prophet out of the Middle Ages thrust by an accident of time into the blinding light of a world that to him was strange and
threatening and incomprehensible except that he was certain of one thing:
he had a message. He knew that his Bible was true. In the midst of a world
where no sacred presence spoke to human beings, Mr. Finewood held firmly
to the conviction that the presence was there and that it could be coaxed out
by those who believed or who said they believed, and then everything fell
into place, and there was a purpose for every random act that stirred across
the stage of human events.

The world of magazines, of movies, of newspapers, of people who
treated religion as weekend convention or not even that was not his world of
the Sacred Presence, and he would simply shut it out as if it did not exist.
Perhaps for him this commonplace world did not exist. It lay beyond a veil
much like the one said to separate the world of the invisible divine from
human events, except that on the other side of this veil in Mr. Finewood's
mind lay a world he did not want even to consider. In that world was no
room for a Sacred Presence, a Blessed Virgin, or a babe in a manger. In the
world Mr. Finewood refused to accept was no rabbi who opened the eyes of
the blind and made the lame to walk and raised the dead and made death
itself an illusion of darkness to be reduced to a pinhead of black against the
great, soft glowing of an eternal heaven echoing angels' songs and the thunderous praise of the victorious Lamb of God.

Mr. Finewood's world was the one Charles would always love. He would
look back on it in his great age with a nostalgia overpowering and melancholy. Christmas was a grand event in his household always, and no one
loved to sing Christmas carols more than Charles Alexander. But inside it
was all gone. Charles had shaken it off forever, or else that world had flitted
mockingly away while Charles raced after it in a desperate darkness.

Mr. Finewood had held on to that world, nourished it in his bosom, fed
on its illusions, and now behind all the foolish and ignorant verbiage that he
poured out on the Revised Standard Version, this man who knew no language but English, and that not surpassingly well, defended two thousand
years of sacred belief as best he could. It was spontaneous, out of order, but
everything was out of order on this rainy day, and Mr. Finewood rolled on.
"These are the same people who want to amalgamate the races, marry black
men to white women in the name of equality, but brothers and sisters, God
made whites and blacks equal in Christ. On this earth He put each of them
in their own place, and He meant for them to stay there and be blessed by
Him in their separate places, and we have sinned as white men in bringing
them where they do not belong."

On and on he went in a tirade that had terror beneath it. Charles felt the terror; he shared it.

Charles was never certain of his own mind that morning. He did not know if he intended to do what he did. Like Jacob he had wrestled with the dark angel, and he had come away lame from the battle. What was wrong with a child's belief in Santa Claus or in fairies? What could possibly be harmful in children on Christmas Eve struggling to stay awake to hear the first faint jingle of sleigh bells quivering across the frosty sky? What was wrong with people who believed that God cared for them and that He held the whole wide world in His hand? "If I die today," he thought, "it might be a good thing for everybody." Having shaped the thought precisely in his brain, he did not know if he believed it. He could only see its rationale.

But there was Mr. Finewood standing on that raised platform speaking with growing passion and holding his battered Bible aloft like a lamp before a rapt congregation, its worn black covers testifying to a life of devotion, and he began to speak of miracles—miracles he had seen, miracles God had done in this modern world, the greatest miracle of all that would come when any day now the trumpet of the Lord should sound, the skies be riven in twain, and Jesus and the angels and archangels would descend to judge the quick and the dead. And he began to speak about the lies told by the translators of "that abominable book they call the Revised Standard Version of the Bible."

It was then that Charles stood up, called out from the congregation, thought up in some rooftop of his mind, *I am doing this; I cannot believe that I am doing this,* and said in a loud voice, "I want to say something."

No one gave him permission. His gesture was so audacious that no one could have planned for it, and no one could command him to quit talking or declare him out of order. He spoke in a slow, measured voice, vibrating with intensity, his tone low and passionless, as if he had been hypnotized and now spoke in a trance. He was angry, but the anger did not show. People who remembered the day in a thousand diverse and unreconcilable opinions remembered how calm Charles was. Stephen suspected the anger and a rough, wild world of other emotions that contended with it. Stephen, sitting on the piano bench because there was no other place for him to sit, looked down on his brother and never forgot the scene—how unnatural Charles seemed, how unlike the brother Stephen had always known. Charles had been able to light a room by walking into it, smiling that smile that would have melted a glacier, and greeting everyone like an old friend, all as if he had been born for friendship and grace. That Charles had vanished, eaten away by these past months, and in his place stood a figure resigned, resolved, and almost robotic, measuring out every syllable slowly and with infinite care.

"I want to tell you about lies," he said in a high, sharp voice. A subdued but distinct sound of motion and murmuring in the church, bodies shifting so heads could turn to him. "I want to tell you about a trip I made at the end of December. I want to tell you where I was when Judge Yancy was murdered. Yes, I went to Florida. But I went somewhere else first, and my trip had nothing at all to do with the maniac we call Missionary."

Not a sound now in the church. Mr. Finewood stood in front. Then slowly he seemed to assume a great and resigned calm. Outside the rain fell softly now. Every eye burned at Charles.

"I drove to North Carolina," Charles said. "I went to Charlotte, North Carolina." Mr. Finewood stared at him and in one of those memorable gestures, he walked back to where Rosy sat and sat down beside her and put an arm around her. With his other hand, he reached to hold one of hers, leaving his huge Bible reposing in his lap.

"You see," Charles halted on, "I wanted with all my heart to believe in the God you all believe in—the God you all *say* you believe in. I couldn't do it. Yes, I confess before you all that I couldn't believe. I kept thinking it was all a lie, that every great pagan temple ever built, every cathedral that ever sent a spire towards heaven, every Baptist church like this one built for the glory of the Almighty could not have been constructed on imagination and deceit. I could not believe that the human race had been so deceived. It's monstrous to think that it's all a lie, isn't it?"

"Oh Charles!" The cry was from Marlene, sitting close up front, turning to look at Charles with an expression distraught and in agony. "Please stop. Please."

"No, let me go on," Charles said. He paused and looked around, an expression of indescribable anguish on his face, and for a moment Stephen thought he might break into tears, and wanted to go to him. But everyone in the church seemed rooted to the ground, and the throng looked on Charles in sullen and unwilling patience.

"But," Charles said, "some irresistible conviction told me that human beings as individuals are deceived every day. We live our lives in the folly of illusion, supposing that other people think well of us when they think we are fools. We may be like poor Kelly Parmalee and think our wrongs and sins are hidden when a whole town knows about them. We believe the word of vile politicians who play us like pipes, making us squeak their prating sounds after them. We believe the lies our friends tell us, and we believe the lies we tell about ourselves, lies that we tell simply by the way we talk and the way we look. So if individuals can be deceived and can happily deceive themselves, why can't the whole human race be deceived about religion?"

Silence.

"I could not get that doubt out of my mind. That fear. For it is a terrifying thought, that we may be deceived by religion and left alone in the world before time and space and death and darkness."

"Charles," Mr. Arceneaux said. Arceneaux was standing now, facing Charles. "This is not the place—"

"What better place?" Charles said, his voice quavering just a bit.

"Let him go on," someone cried vengefully from the audience. "He's showing his true colors at last." Arceneaux sat down painfully.

"I will go on," Charles said, his voice more firm now. "I could not get my doubts out of my mind. Yes, some of you will say I should have prayed to God to take them away. I did pray. Every night and every day I prayed. I got down on my knees by my bed, and I prayed. But nothing worked. Faith would not come. I prayed, and the sky was like steel, a steep vault placed over me, and I was under it, paralyzed with unbelief."

He turned slowly around and pointed to Mr. Finewood. "Then this man came to be the preacher at our church. Mr. Finewood. He came telling us about miracles. Dora Hammond cured of cancer by his prayers. A woman who came back to her husband when she had run away from him with a sailor and how the husband forgave her—because of prayer. The soldier in the Korean conflict who was hit in the chest by a Chinese bullet, but the bullet struck the Bible he carried there, and he opened the Bible to find the bullet, and it had stopped at the verse in the Psalms 'A thousand shall fall by thy side and ten thousand at thy right hand, but it shall not come nigh thee.' These were miracles, and they happened to people who went to that church of his in Charlotte, North Carolina, before he came to us.

"Nobody I knew had been in Charlotte, North Carolina. But I imagined what Valley View Baptist Church must be from all the wonders Mr. Finewood told us, miracles God did there. A marble cathedral, I thought. A tall spire reaching so high that your neck hurt when you bent back to look at it. All white and huge and glorious with a great organ and a choir of believers who sang like angels and maybe a light glowing over it at night and how God's presence was so warm that palm trees grew around it in winter."

He laughed a foolish laugh, and Stephen thought for just a moment that Charles might be on the verge of cracking up and he half raised himself from the piano seat.

But Charles recovered quickly. He took a deep breath, swallowed nervously, and went doggedly on. "Yes," he said, "I imagined all these things because I yearned to believe that Valley View Baptist Church in Charlotte,

North Carolina, was a place where miracles happened, and when miracles happen, no doubts or fears can rise, because who can doubt miracles? They are something you see. Something visible, and God uses them to reveal Himself. That's what Mr. Finewood told us happened at Valley View Baptist Church in Charlotte, North Carolina. Miracles happened week after week.

"Miracles didn't happen at Midway Baptist. Life went on the way it always had. I prayed for them—even the miracle that I would stop doubting that God exists. That would have been miracle enough—to have my heart strangely warmed, as John Wesley said. No miracles. I thought it was so unfair of God not to give me one tiny miracle to take away my anguish of soul. But I thought of Valley View Baptist Church in Charlotte, North Carolina. If I went there, I would meet people who told me that miracles happened."

Mr. Finewood sat with his head bowed. Rosy leaned against him, holding his hand.

"After Christmas," Charles said in his high, strained voice, "I drove over to Charlotte, North Carolina. I found the Valley View Baptist Church. It took some doing. It's not really in Charlotte. It's north of the city, surrounded by fields and a few farmhouses. And the parking lot is not paved. I don't know why that detail sticks in my head. But the first thing I noticed was that the parking lot was slick with yellow mud, and the church was shabby. Well, what of that! I thought that in the New Testament the church is made up of poor people and that God shows Himself always to the lowly and that He casts away the proud spirit, and it is harder for a rich man to enter heaven than for a camel to pass through the eye of a needle."

He laughed again—that nervous, high, strained laugh that seemed about to break into madness.

"Well, I went to a house," he said. "I met a woman named Dinwiddy. Clara Dinwiddy. I said I had heard so much about Valley View Church from Mr. Finewood that since I happened to be passing through Charlotte, I wanted to see it for myself. She was suspicious. But when I mentioned Mr. Finewood's name, she laughed. That's right. She laughed. Well, what would any of you do if somebody like me came to your door inquiring about a former minister whose wife had run away with a Bible salesman who stayed in their home while he went door to door in the neighborhood peddling Bibles?"

He paused at the flurry of whispering and muttering, people urgently inquiring of others, "What did he say?" "Did he say Finewood's wife ran away with somebody?" "A what?" "A *Bible* salesman?" "Is that what he said?"

"Yes," Charles said. "Mr. Finewood's wife deserted him, and he was crushed. That brings us to Dora Hammond. I think most of you have heard the story. If you have heard Mr. Finewood preach, you have heard it. Dora Hammond, dying of cancer in the hospital in Charlotte. Mr. Finewood heard the voice of God. He called everybody in the community to come to the church, and they stayed there praying all night long, and sometime after three in the morning, with people on their knees in the pews, Mr. Finewood stood up and said, 'I have the assurance that she will be all right.' Everybody went home. The very next day Mr. Hammond drove back to Valley View Baptist from the hospital at dawn to tell Mr. Finewood that exactly the moment that Mr. Finewood stood up and said Mrs. Hammond would be all right, she sat up in bed and said she felt better. When the doctors came to look at her, examine her, they could find no trace of the cancer. A real miracle, isn't it? Incontestable proof that God can answer prayers and that in our own time God can make Lazarus come forth by His almighty power."

He paused. The silence was like the weight of doom. Mr. Finewood held Rosy to him, and she buried her face in his shoulder. Arceneaux stood up again. He spoke sharply to Charles.

"Charles, this is enough. Stop it. Sit down." Charles stood there, his arms folded across his thin chest, staring back at Arceneaux. Arceneaux's face was red with anger.

"No, there is more to say," Charles said.

"But this is not the place to say it," Arceneaux said.

"Let him go on," somebody else said in a loud voice.

Charles did not wait to be encouraged.

"What happened was this. Dora Hammond died. Her husband came back to Valley View Baptist Church and stood up in the worship service and renounced God for letting his wife die so horribly. He said he would never believe in God again and that he would never believe in Mr. Finewood and that Mr. Finewood's wife was right to run away because he was a fat fool."

Charles lowered his head.

"So it was all a lie," he said. "Everything Mr. Finewood told us was a lie. The deacons of his church told him he should leave, find another pulpit. I suppose he drove around, looking for a vacant church, and he found ours, and he found my mother working out in her flower garden, and he told her that God had called him to our church, and so he came."

Charles looked around. "It's all a lie," he said in a strong voice. "Jesus. The resurrection from the dead. I don't know who Jesus was, but he wasn't the Son of God, and his bones rotted into the earth a long, long time ago. The people who told this story were like Mr. Finewood here. They were all liars. They wanted to believe, and they made up stories that they said they believed, and by the time they died, I'm sure they did believe them. But they lied to themselves. All of them. They lied to themselves."

He looked around for a moment, his eyes calm, almost placid, as if he had settled something finally within himself, and it was done.

The silence was awful. Outside the rain fell in a steady, unceasing washing of the earth. For a moment more, no one else moved. Then slowly and silently Mr. Finewood rose to his feet, gently nudging Rosy to rise with him, and the two of them went slowly back down the aisle between the pews and the wall and made for the door. They walked in a careful embrace as if each was conscious of the fragility and the uncertainty of the other. Mr. Finewood carried his big Bible under his arm. No one spoke. No one made a gesture. People turned to watch them go, and so they passed through the door into the pouring rain and went down the outside steps, and the people in the church heard car doors close and the grinding of a starter and an engine coming to life and a car departing, and Clifford Finewood and Rosy went away. Behind them Marlene began to cry. Her sobbing rose above the sound of the rain, and people began speaking to one another in a low and incredulous murmuring.

*A*RCENEAUX stood stock-still for a moment. He seemed to have forgotten where he was and perhaps who he was. He seemed like a man who had been cast into a spell that made him a statue. People in the congregation looked up at him almost in desperation as if he might have some key to unlocking the oppression and the astonishment that had settled over all of them, leaving them with no idea what to do next. Perhaps it was that expectation that he felt rise from all those heads that made Arceneaux do what he did next. He had not planned it. Not yet at least, although he supposed the moment would have come when he would have done something almost equally dramatic within the confines of the First Baptist Church in Bourbonville. Once long afterwards, when he sat on the Pacific coast in California and watched young men surfing in on the breakers, he supposed that at Salem Baptist Church that morning he had caught a wave and had to ride it in, and at the end of a thrilling ride, the surfer got off onto the beach.

Whatever it was, Arceneaux heard himself speaking before he had entirely willed to speak within his own brain. "I want to say something," he said. "I have something I must say."

His audience looked at him almost gratefully because as long as Arceneaux spoke, none of them had to do anything. They had to make no decisions about what to say or what to think. They did not have to walk out into that monotonously unvarying rain, and they did not have to tell the story or to have the story of what they had all witnessed told to them. They could sit for a while longer, winded and amazed, and let life flow over them. So Arceneaux spoke into a dead silence punctuated by Marlene's diminishing sobs. Sheriff Myers stood in the back of the church, cradling his pump shotgun in his arms, and outside two similarly armed men stood on the stairway that led down into the churchyard and to the parking lot behind. The sheriff looked at his shotgun and snapped on the safety catch and muttered on the futility and the incomprehensibility of all this.

"I came here this morning prepared to do battle," Arceneaux said, starting slowly. "I knew, as all of you knew, what Brother Finewood planned to do about the RSV and my resolution about the recent Supreme Court decision." He reached down to the pew where he had been sitting and picked up the book bound in its dark red buckram. He held it out so that its smooth sides shone dully in the light of a rainy day. "This was what the battle was to be about," Arceneaux continued after a brief and meditative pause. "Were the translators of this book evil men? Were they Communists? Were they trying to undermine the faith that all of us here have professed at one time or another? These were the questions I was prepared to argue with Brother Finewood."

A few people noticed that Arceneaux was calling Mr. Finewood "Brother Finewood" and that he had never used that familiar Baptist appellation for anyone before, least of all for his great rival.

"I was prepared to say that the translators of this book were doing their best to get as close to the original Bible as they could. Ladies and gentlemen, we don't know what that original Bible was. It was started centuries ago. Maybe the first stories began to be told as long as four thousand years ago, a length of time we can name with words and count with numbers, but one so long that we really can't conceive it. Many, many people wrote it, and as the centuries passed, many, many people put it all together.

"Let's suppose they were all inspired. Let's suppose that God dictated it all to them like a picture I saw once in a museum— an angel perched on the Gospel writer Matthew's shoulder and whispering in his ear while Matthew bent attentively, quill in hand, to write whatever the angel said. Well, if they were all inspired, they handed their works over to other human beings, human beings like all the rest of us, who made mistakes.

"I will suggest something to all of you. Take the King James Bible that Brother Finewood was prepared to defend this morning. Sit down at a table with a pen in hand and try to copy it word for word. Day after day after day, copy something out of the Bible. Copy some of the books we scarcely ever read. Leviticus, for example. Then after you've been at it for a month or two, make a comparison. Compare what you have copied with the King James Version. And you will find differences. Each of you, compare your copy with the copy of this person, of that person, of another person. And you will find something else. No two of you will have the same text."

He paused for a moment, and the silence that met him from staring eyes was as deep as the bottom of a lake.

"Thousands of people have copied those texts in the centuries that they have been in existence, and no two copies are exactly alike. The translators of the RSV were trying to do an honest job—trying to go back to the earliest copies, sort out the language, the Hebrew and the Greek and even the Latin, and they were trying to ask two questions: What is the oldest version of the text we have? What is the most plausible version we have? And I was prepared to talk about that process a long time.

"I was even prepared to challenge Brother Finewood to a contest. I was going to ask him to copy out the Book of Genesis, to take a week doing it if he wanted, and to hand his copy over to someone he trusted in this congregation—you, Tommy Fieldston—and have you check him for errors." (Charles noticed that Mr. Arceneax did not call Tommy Fieldston "Brother.") Arceneaux paused, looking down, looking for the next thing to say.

"But that would have been childish, and now Brother Finewood is gone, and Charles . . ." He shook his head in perplexity and looked towards Charles. "You discovered something that I had suspected all along. But I never would have gone over to North Carolina to prove it. I can't say that you were wrong to do it . . . but I never would have done it."

Arceneaux turned back to the silent throng. "But now I will say something else about this translation." Again he held the dark red Bible up and studied it as though he contemplated finding something in it that he had not seen before. "The translators of this book—and the translators of the Bible in whatever age and whatever place they have ever worked—have made a mistake. A profound mistake. The closer we get back to the roots of our faith, to Jesus who walked in Galilee and Judea and who was crucified under Pontius Pilate, the more baffling the story gets. It's like looking at a photograph in a newspaper. We hold the newspaper at arm's length, and we see a face or a scene. But if we bring the newspaper right up against our noses or put a magnifying glass on it, we don't see a picture at all. We see a confusion of dots, and the dots don't make sense. The closer we get, the less meaning we see."

He paused again, holding his audience in thrall.

"That's how it is with Jesus. We don't know anything about him except that he was crucified. All four Gospels agree on that. Now think about it a moment. It's something nobody would make up, not for the person who is claimed to be the savior of the world. For the rest of it we have stories, and the stories contradict each other."

"No they don't!" Tommy Fieldston shouted.

"Hush, Tommy," Arceneaux said gently. "You can have the floor when I am done."

Tommy Fieldston stood up, his face red with anger and all his freckles looking dark amid the crimson of his skin. "You don't have the right to be saying those things in a Baptist church."

"Tommy," Arceneaux said gently, "I am making a speech of resignation. Sit down, and you will never have to listen to me again."

"Let him go on!" someone shouted. Tommy Fieldston sat down slowly, as if his legs had been attached to hydraulic pumps slowly being released.

"Read the stories of the Resurrection. How do you put them all together? And what about the raising of Lazarus? What a wonderful story it is! How could three Gospels leave it out, and how could we have it only in the Gospel of John?"

He looked over at Charles again. "So Charles, you are right. One part of your story is right. The Gospels give us all these stories, and we can't sort them out to see what was true and what was made up, and some of them were made up. I don't doubt that. Some of them were made up, and passed along, and I'm quite sure that Jesus did not rise from the dead and that his body went back to the earth as ours will."

A murmur now swept through the church like a mighty wind, and for a moment it seemed that not only Tommy Fieldston but the whole congregation would rise to shout Arceneaux down. But he quelled them all by raising his voice and continuing, and no one could forgo the opportunity of hearing what he said because all of them felt themselves in one of those great moments when they were witnesses to events that would require them to tell the story for the rest of their lives.

"I have thought about these things for years. But they have not made me disbelieve in God, and Charles, there is where you are wrong. The fact that the stories can be told, that they have such a power over us, is a sign that they come from God. I don't know what God is doing in the world. But I do know that I feel His presence. I felt His presence in the war judging me because I committed murder. Oh yes, you can say that I killed in the line of duty, but I say it was murder, and I say that when I did it, I felt the judgment of God. But that God is also a God of forgiveness, a God of beauty, a God of love. And in all the religions of the world, that God works, but He or She or It has to work with what we are, and we can see what we are—poor, ignorant, vindictive, frightened beings who have the freedom to make of our world what we will make of it, and so we mess it up. We mess it up terribly, and we do it again. God has to work with that even in our religions."

Arceneaux paused again, standing there, holding incongruously that deep red Bible, looking at the congregation thoughtfully, almost as if he had forgotten them and had been lifted up into a realm of contemplation where he searched for his next thought. He came close to saying to them, "And furthermore I want to tell you that I am a queer, a homosexual, and I would bet that Jesus was a homosexual, too. He loved one of the disciples who lay against his bosom. The God that was in him loves me, as Jesus loved that disciple."

But although the words were at the front of his mouth, he did not say them. He thought of his mother and his father. Instead he finished in a quiet voice. "I thought I could preach here and make you see the God I believe in. But it turns out that I could not. I have failed. Is my failure your fault or mine? I suppose it is the fault of both of us—if it be fault. It may simply be that what I anticipated, what I thought could be done, cannot be done. Whatever it is, I am resigning effective today from my church. Since the church has never paid me a salary, I do not owe it any notice. I will send movers to clean out the parsonage and to move everything that is mine back to Louisiana. I have a sugar plantation down there. I'm more suited to running a plantation than I am to being pastor of a church.

"Now, I'm driving to Nashville. That's where my duty lies, in prison. I'm going to pray to that God I have just described to spare Hope Kirby's life. If He doesn't do that, I want to be close to him when he dies." Arceneaux turned back to Charles. "Charles, I think we ought to leave together. I feel certain that Roy Kirby will not do anything to you today. I think that's all over. But if we stay here, these good people may kill us."

Arceneaux laughed and made a beckoning gesture to Charles, and Charles came forward as though mesmerized. He held his reporter's notebook. "I have a story to write," he murmured.

"You can write it tomorrow in Nashville," Arceneaux said.

And so it was. At the door the sheriff looked around as Charles and Arceneaux came out the door and descended toward the white Jaguar.

"I don't know where Roy Kirby is," Arceneaux said to the sheriff. "But I don't think he will follow us to Nashville." The sheriff took no chances. He and his little armada went out to the white Jaguar, moving against the rain that put a torrential blur on the world.

Inside the Salem Baptist Church the congregation sat in stunned and ghastly quiet. Altogether it was a morning to remember.

*H*OPE KIRBY sat with his brothers trying to be attentive to them while they tried to find something to say to him. Neither effort was successful. Hope sat on the little couch in the visitor's room, and his brothers sat scattered around in straight chairs, or else they got up and wandered about, and since the room was small and there was no place to go, the afternoon slipped slowly, slowly away in a scattering of risings and sittings and extremely uncomfortable talk. Above all the futile efforts at conversation, Hope's mind went on turning memories over and over again and coming to no conclusion about them except a thick sadness that he could not dissipate in any way. He loved his brothers. But he discovered that their talking irritated him, and then he felt guilty for his irritation because he knew they loved him and meant well, and he loved them, too. He wanted to be alone with his thoughts.

He knew how it would turn out when old Miss Flitterby sent him a letter down at the car works and told him what was going on. She told him he could come and take a look if he wanted. He was struck first by the complete conviction that there was nothing to see and that this repugnant old crone— she must have been in her fifties—was lying to him and wanted to cause trouble. He thought that he would call her bluff, and maybe then he would scare her someway so she'd never do such a thing again to anybody else, and then he thought that he wanted to accept her invitation to look because very suddenly, like a man whose doctor has told him he has a fatal disease when the man has been feeling perfectly well, Hope Kirby knew that Miss Flitterby was telling him the truth.

So there he was one summer afternoon standing in her kitchen behind Abby's little triangle-shaped beauty shop on East Broadway, and he saw Kelly Parmalee enter the back door about five-thirty in the afternoon. He saw Abby let him in, and he saw her stick her head out and look this way and that. The street where Miss Flitterby lived was little more than an alley, and it had a couple of warehouses and not much else on it, and so it was quieter than might be expected. And there was Kelly Parmalee, and by Hope's watch it was thirty-eight minutes before he came out again, exiting through the little back door, looking both ways before he set out hastily up the dirty little street and passed out of sight.

It was something Hope had to take up with his pappy and his brothers. He knew right away what his father would tell him to do. And right away Hope did not want to do it. But what is to be will be. Miss Flitterby was extra-nice in a pushy way, and Hope did not like her, but he was polite, and she was a lady, and he thought she was trying to do him a favor.

"I just thought you ought to know," she said. She was a skinny woman with crooked teeth showing gaps here and there where she had lost some.

She reminded him of an old bear that had got too old to hunt, and he thought that if anyone ate her, presuming she was a bear, she'd be stringy and bony.

She said, "I have seen that scene again and again, and I thought I had to write you, Mr. Kirby. A false-hearted woman is one of the worst plagues on earth. A man like you deserves somebody who'd be faithful. It just made me so mad to see what I've seen. I hope you don't hold it against me. I just couldn't let her get away with it."

"No, ma'am. No, I don't hold anything against you."

He had gone to her place and seen what he came to see. Kelly Parmalee go inside and stay more than a half hour, and he thought of Abby taking off her dress and her white underclothes, and Kelly doing it to her, and she was helping him and liking it, and Kelly Parmalee could do it because he had never shot a woman in the stomach and seen blood and guts and shit pour out.

He stood there behind the thin white curtains, looking down at her beauty shop. It had been a little diner once, but the man with a mustache who ran it found he could not make a living there, and he sold it to Hope and Abby and moved on. It was paid for now. Abby's business was that good. Hope always admired Abby because she could make a woman's hair look beautiful even if the rest of the woman looked like the back end of a cow. Hope came twice to Miss Flitterby's, and twice he saw what he came to see.

Kelly Parmalee came out, and after a while Abby came out and went to her car. She carried the little red pocketbook Hope had bought her, the one made of real leather. It said "Genuine Calfskin" on it, and he had paid a lot for it because he liked to buy her pretty things. He bought it one day in Miller's in Knoxville when the air-conditioning was so strong it almost made him vomit. He thought that if he bought her pretty things, she wouldn't mind that he could not do it to her. She got into her Plymouth, and she drove away. It was a shock the first time; the second time Hope realized that Kelly Parmalee had something on him, and he had to do something about it. But what?

"I've got to be going, ma'am. Thank you."

"Well, I hated to write you that letter to the car works, Mr. Kirby. I sure did. I sent it there so she wouldn't see it. I hope you don't hold it against me now. Everybody knowed about it. Everybody in town. But they didn't have the willpower to tell you about it. Folks was talking about it, and I thought it was a shame you didn't know. I thought it was my bounden duty. My Christian duty. I hope you ain't mad at me. And I hear when you go fishing on Saturday nights, they meet each other in the square at one in the morning. There truly ought to be a law against suchlike. I hope I ain't done the wrong thing."

"Oh no, ma'am. No, ma'am, you done the right thing. They meet in the square, do they? On Saturday nights?"

"I ain't never seen them there myself, Mr. Kirby. I ain't going to tell you just what I hear. I'm here to tell you only what I've seen with my two very own eyes. But I do hear that when you and your brothers goes fishing, they go to his store, and they don't come out for hours and hours. It's a scandal, that's what it is."

"Yes, ma'am. Thank you, ma'am. I'll be leaving now."

I shouldn't of said nothing to Pappy about hit, Hope thought to himself. *What did hit matter to me? I had her most of the time and Mr. Parmalee could give her something that I couldn't give her. And I reckon she wanted hit more than she said she did, and why should I care?*

He knew why he cared. The talk. That was what he couldn't stand thinking about. *I could have moved away,* he thought. *I could have gone somewheres and changed my name and I could have been somebody else.*

He knew he could have done none of these things. And here he was.

A*T A LITTLE* after four-thirty in the afternoon Central Time, the time Nashville was on, Hugh Bedford finally reached the governor by telephone. He got through by a threat. "You tell the governor that I know about that woman of his in Knoxville, and if he does not call me back, I am going to go to the newspapers about it, and he will be in the headlines, and he will never be president of the United States."

It was a last desperate threat to a switchboard operator in the Capitol, and it worked. So there *was* a woman in Knoxville! Afterwards Hugh thought he had had a stroke of amazing and absurd luck. But then he supposed that the governor had women in many towns.

Hugh was in a room in the Andrew Jackson Hotel. The governor called him there. "What the hell are you talking about?" the governor asked.

"I'm talking about things I know that you don't want known."

"This is blackmail," the governor shouted into the telephone. His voice was slurred, and he was drunk. That much was clear.

"Are you with her now?" Hugh said.

"It's none of your goddamned business where I am!" the governor shouted. Hugh heard a woman's voice shushing him in the background.

"Billy Graham wouldn't like that, Governor." The governor had sat on the platform at several Billy Graham crusades in the South, including one in Chattanooga, and any time he was present, Billy Graham called on him to give his Christian testimony. The governor always spoke about "my sainted mother" when he gave his testimony, and he said, "I owe everything I am to her." His aides said privately among themselves that so far as they knew the governor's mother had not been a lush.

"Fuck Billy Graham," the governor said.

"I really wouldn't care to do that, Governor, but it's interesting to suppose that you think Billy Graham is a queer who goes around fucking men. Have you got any firsthand experience with that? Or maybe you don't experience such things with your hand."

"What?" the governor said. The man was truly deeply drunk. He recovered himself. "Billy Graham would suck my dick if it meant I'd go on the platform with him. That man doesn't get a hard-on around women. He gets a hard-on around power, and I'm power, you asshole."

Hugh Bedford took a deep breath. "Look, Governor, forget all that. I'm calling to beg you for Hope Kirby. Commute his sentence, Governor. It will get you good publicity all over the state, all over the country. It will show you as a man of mercy."

"His partner murdered a sitting judge and two jurymen. Do you think I can pardon a man responsible for such a thing?"

"Governor, give him a stay of execution. You can bring in all of Hope Kirby's old unit. You can talk to him. There was bad blood between the priest and Hope. The priest was crazy. We can get witnesses in here from that school where he taught in Massachusetts. We can get men from his guerrilla unit in the Philippines to testify. By the time they get through, you will know that Hope Kirby had nothing to do with Judge Yancy's murder. Please, Governor. Get on the telephone and call the warden of the penitentiary. Give Hope a stay of one month. That's all I'm asking."

"Shut up," the governor shouted.

"What?" Hugh said.

"I was talking to somebody else," the governor said. "Look, Mr. Bradford, I'll think about it. I really will think about it."

"You don't have time to think about it, Governor. It's getting on towards five o'clock."

"That's enough time!" the governor shouted. And he hung up.

On the slender thread of a drunken governor's promise to "think about it" hung all Hope Kirby's hope. Hugh sat looking at the dead telephone in his hand. Then he put it back on its cradle and went out. He had time to get to the prison.

He went downstairs and got his car out of the hotel garage and drove as quickly as he could to the penitentiary. Rain was coming down in an unwavering cloudburst. His windshield wipers sloshed ineffectually back and forth, and it was after five o'clock when he got to the prison. The process of admitting him to the death house took time. When he was brought into the little room where Hope's brothers were waiting with the condemned man, Hugh was once again astonished. Hope was standing up, shaking hands with Larry Arceneaux. Beside Larry Arceneaux stood Charles Alexander, and Hope had a hand on the boy's shoulder. The boy was crying, his head downcast. Nearby the warden stood, dressed in a gray suit and wearing a dark necktie. The warden looked uncomfortable and nervous. "You have five more minutes," he said to no one in particular. "Then we have to get started."

"Is there a telephone here?" Hugh Bedford shouted.

"Yes, and there's one in the room where the chair is," the warden said quietly.

"I just called the governor. He said he's thinking about a stay of execution."

"If he wants to get through to us, he can," the warden said.

*H*OPE *KIRBY* wanted it all to be over and done with. He and his brothers hugged and kissed each other, and the brothers cried. Charles Alexander was crying, too, saying over and over again, "I'm sorry. I'm sorry." Hope said to him, "Hit's all right. What is to be will be. I'm glad Pappy didn't kill you. But watch out for him, you hear? He'll do what he thinks he has to do."

"There's still a chance," Hugh Bedford said. "The governor can call." But Hope knew the governor would not call.

"You a preacher?" the warden said to Arceneaux.

Arceneaux hesitated.

"Yes, he's a preacher," Hugh said.

"You want to go with him, walk with him, have a prayer?"

Arceneaux stood there in a daze. He had decided that he was not a preacher anymore. But he had been ordained. First Baptist Church in New Orleans had ordained him. Could you ever take that away? "If it's what Hope wants," Arceneaux said, his voice almost a whisper.

Hope looked at Arceneaux. "I'd be much obliged. You've been a real friend, Preacher."

"Not good enough," Arceneaux said.

"You've been plenty good enough," Hope said. "I got a Bible here if you want to read out of hit, if'n the warden thinks we got time. Hit might make everbody feel a little better."

"We have time," the warden said.

Arceneaux took the Bible, a cheap King James Version. He opened it to Psalm 90. Everybody was standing. Arceneaux cleared his throat.

"Lord, thou hast been our dwelling place in all generations.
Before the mountains were brought forth, or ever thou hadst formed the earth and the
world, even from everlasting to everlasting, thou art God.
Thou turnest man to destruction; and sayest, Return, ye children of men.
For a thousand years in thy sight are but as yesterday when it is past, and as a watch in
the night . . ."

Arceneaux's voice rolled on, getting stronger and stronger, and Hope's mind carried off to the mountains where he had lived as a happy child and to Mammy and to Pappy and their green world of spring and the snow in winter, and he thought that, yes, the mountains deserved to be mentioned in the same psalm with God because they were all part of everlasting time and all filled with secrets that no man could answer, and he thought that perhaps in a spirit world where there was no flesh to get in the way he might drift in and out of all the mountain hollows and coves the way the mist rose off running water when the night had been cool and the sun rose. It would be nice, he thought, to float and dissipate like that mist and then at night to form again, coming and going like a man sleeping and waking and drifting endlessly, and Abby might drift, too, and she would forgive him and they would float together in the sunshine, scarcely visible to anyone who happened to see, and anyone who did see would not take account of what it was, and certainly would not see them.

He heard Arceneaux reading the Twenty-third Psalm, and he remembered when Mammy read it and how her voice rose as Arceneaux's did when she said, "Yea, though I walk through the valley of the shadow of death, I will fear no evil, for thou art with me." He thought of the valleys in the mountains, and he could almost hear the water singing down from the tops, the water jumping and splashing over the big rocks, making a sound like music if you listened to it long enough, and he thought with a high and inexpressible joy that he would never in his life have to kill anybody again.

He was taken with the thought of becoming mist, and he was only vaguely aware that now his brothers were leaving, hugging him and kissing him, and Charles Alexander was leaving, and Lawyer stood in front of him crying and cursing, and Hope heard himself trying to comfort Lawyer and to say that it was all right, and then everybody was gone but Preacher Arceneaux and the warden and some guards, and they were walking down a corridor, and they came through a door, and the chair was in the middle of a room, and off to one side some people were sitting, their faces obscured in the darkness because a bright light was shining down on the chair, and it made Hope blink.

He knew that the guards with great delicacy were strapping him into the chair with big leather bands, and the warden stood in front of him with tears running down his cheeks, and he said, "Hope Kirby, do you have any last words?" And Hope said, "I just want to thank all of you for being so nice to me."

The warden said something else, something formal and legal, and Hope paid no attention, and somebody put something on top of his shaved head, and then somebody dropped a hood down over his face, and he was thinking of the sunlight on Mount LeConte when it first fired the tops of the trees up there and how mighty the sun was and—

ARCENEAUX did not go back to Bourbonville. He sent a moving van to clear out his place and move him back to New Orleans. It took years for First Baptist Church to get over him, and even today you can start an argument among old-timers by mentioning his name, and you can get a dozen or two dozen versions of what happened that day at Salem Baptist Church when the Salem Baptist Association had its infamous meeting. For many in the county that long-ago association meeting is more vividly remembered and fictionalized than the story of Hope Kirby and his fate.

Hugh Bedford and Arceneaux seemed to shed Charles. Did he have enough money for a hotel? A ticket home next day? And so with those assurances they abandoned him. He did not want to be with them any more than they wanted to be with him. He knew somehow that they had forgiven him. But he found himself profoundly uncomfortable and depressed to be with them, and he bid them goodnight and went away. He left them standing together on a street corner saying so few words in parting that Charles could never remember what was said at all. He did not know that Arceneaux and Hugh Bedford spent the night first weeping in one another's arms and then sleeping fitfully in an embrace that was hopeless and sadder than either thought he could bear.

Charles felt miserable and empty. He could not sleep. He got up in the middle of the night when the streets were empty and dead, and he walked for miles. When morning came he saw the trucks from the two Nashville newspapers moving through the streets making deliveries, and he went into an all-night cafe and saw the headline on one of the papers:

HOPE KIRBY DIES IN ELECTRIC CHAIR

The reporter had been one of the witnesses. Charles read the first few lines and turned away. He ordered coffee, but he could not drink it. He went back to the hotel and fell across the bed and went to sleep. He had bad dreams, and when he awoke in the afternoon he called his father.

"I am very happy that you are all right," Paul Alexander said. Then after a pause he said, "No one has seen Roy Kirby. He has disappeared."

Paul Alexander had a theory about Roy Kirby. He held on to it until he died in 1988, and as the years passed he became more and more enamored with it.

"When it seemed as if the governor would turn down the pardon for Hope," Paul Alexander said, almost apologetically, "I went by night to see Roy Kirby. Jim Ed said he would go with me, but I told him no, that this was something I had to do for myself, one father pleading with another father for a son's life. I told him that I knew he had sworn to kill Charles, and I knew he thought it was an affair of honor for him. One son for another.

"I told him that a cycle of violence had to stop, that honor was one thing but that mercy was another. I told him I believed that Charles would suffer all his life for what he had done and that suffering was enough. I do not remember everything that I said. I do remember that I begged him to be merciful."

When Paul Alexander told this story, Charles always felt a resentment that, he told himself, was unjustified. His father seemed proud of himself, satisfied that two honorable and reasonable men had got together and made an agreement about sons. But how did anyone explain Roy Kirby's complete disappearance from the scene? Paul Alexander's theory was that rather than remain in Tennessee and be exposed to what he regarded as shame, Roy Kirby had gone away. "He did not commit suicide like Javert in *Les Misérables*," Paul Alexander said. "He simply went to another part of the country. I suspect he went back to the mountains, maybe up in Virginia, maybe down in Georgia. There are many mountains in the United States. He could have gone many places and started his life all over again."

The Kirby men kept their own counsel. No one dared ask them what had happened to their father because such a question would have seemed like prying. The truth was as simple as it seemed. The Kirby men did not know. John Sevier moved in with Joye and lived another twenty years and never said another word in his life. They talked about it, endlessly working out possibilities and rejecting them. Roy Kirby had left them with no information. To protect them, they supposed. They could not answer questions put to them by the police when they knew no answers. They could not be blamed for something they had no warning about beforehand.

Hope's body was brought back from Nashville and buried in the graveyard of the Red Bank Baptist Church in Richardson's Cove in the mountains, next to his mother. There's nothing on the gravestone except his name, the year he was born, and the year he died. A big crowd turned out for the funeral. The papers said over three hundred, and yes, the reporters came up from Knoxville. People who had known the Kirby family before the national park was imposed on the mountains appeared as though summoned by a mysterious telegraph. The crowd overflowed the church and stood around in the mild summer air, men hatless and coatless and very quiet. Solemn hand-shaking, murmurs of condolence, a quiet squeeze of a hand on a shoulder, unspoken and helpless anger at forces nobody could quite identify. Red Bank Baptist was outside the limits of the park, and some shook their heads and wished that Roy Kirby had chosen to settle there, in Richardson's Cove, where mountain men and women still coaxed and wrested a precarious living out of the land. But Roy Kirby was resolved to build something from nothing, and he had, and then it was taken away from him. That was the way life was. What is to be will be, said the preachers—there were five of them—who preached the funeral sermons. Larry Arceneaux was not among them.

Charles Alexander did not go to seminary. He tried to join the navy that summer, but a navy doctor discovered that he had an irregular heartbeat. Nobody had ever noticed it, least of all Charles. He went over to join the army, and the army doctor, without being told, detected an irregular heart-beat. "We don't want you leading a platoon against a bunch of gooks and have you drop dead on us," the army doctor said, shaking his head as though he had said something profound. Charles wanted to say that it seemed to him that anyone leading a platoon against gooks or some other enemy might very well drop dead from a bullet in the heart. But he did not bring the subject up. That was the end of his effort to hide himself in the military. For years doctors, as he told the story, took their stethoscopes out of the icebox and slapped them on his bare chest and turned very serious and began to listen carefully and ask him if anybody had ever detected his irregular heartbeat. He answered in the affirmative, and the doctors nodded and said that a heart could beat a long time irregularly, but he ought to have it checked neverthe-less. When he was in his fifties a doctor in Cambridge laughed and shook his head. "Hell, there's nothing wrong with your heart. So it's a little irregular. Who the hell cares? It sounds good and strong to me. We're not all stamped out by a divine cookie cutter, you know. Oddly enough, we're all different." And that was the end of concern about his heart.

So there he was in Bourbonville at the end of the summer of 1954, and he had to have something to do, and he knew he had to leave Bourbonville. It was not that people were still angry with him, although some were. Mostly people were relieved to get on with something in their lives that had nothing to do with Charles. It was simply that he was marked, and that all that any-body could see of him was the boy who had almost died at the hands of

Hope Kirby on a summer night, been given his life, and then betrayed his savior unto death. The name Judas was frequently applied to him in the stories people told. It was not spoken with great force. Sometimes it was even spoken with a laugh, and no one said anything like that to his face after that one day at the Salem church.

Such force as people mustered against him came from the association. People tried to repeat what Charles had said, and they got it all confused in their minds. Nobody who heard him that day seemed to realize what he was saying. They all believed in God. They could not believe that anyone did not share this belief, and even those who might occasionally claim not to believe in God were quickly told that deep in their hearts they did believe. By the time the tale wandered to its conclusion Charles had delivered some kind of revival discourse calling on the church people to live their religion. If they said they believed, they would clean up their lives. The questions that racked Charles almost to madness fell in the ears of his congregation into the clichés they were accustomed to hear in church, and so they dismissed them, all disarmed.

The story of what Charles did to Clifford Finewood seemed to fit his betrayal of Hope Kirby. But then Clifford Finewood did not die in the electric chair. Mr. Finewood had to leave, of course. He preached one final sermon the day after the association meeting. It was a tearful apology, and he made no accusations against Charles. He appeared before his congregation looking like a dog caught in the act of something, and then a moving truck came, and he and Rosy went away. Somebody said he had a loyal brother down in Alabama.

The day before the Finewoods departed, Rosy came down to see Charles. She appeared at the front door of the house in the twilight just after supper, and Charles had to speak to her. They sat out in the yard in the ridiculously weathered lawn chairs. Charles felt covered with shame. "Rosy—" he began with a stammer. But she stopped him.

"I came down to tell you that you did the right thing. You told the truth."

"I'm sorry for the part that hurt you. I thought about that."

"You've done me a world of good. Daddy had got caught up in a world of lies, and he couldn't escape. He begged me to forgive him. He got so sad sometimes thinking of how the world was that he wanted to make it turn out better. He said he didn't see what harm it did to make people happy with stories with happy endings. He said he knew Jesus had done miracles in other churches. He might have done them at Valley View.

"I was the only one who knew the truth, and when he told the first story, about Mrs. Hammond and the cancer, I sat there like a stone wondering what had gone wrong with a world where my father said things like that. He told me afterwards that he got carried away by the spirit, and he begged me not to say anything about it.

"Well, I liked one of the stories a lot, and he didn't have to beg me to be quiet about it. The one about my mother. I was a lot happier to believe she died young, loving me, than the truth, which was that she ran away with a Bible salesman to Chicago and didn't even leave me a note telling me good-bye. So Dad was sure right on that one."

She wiped her eyes on a sleeve, and Charles fumbled for a handkerchief he did not have. But she went doggedly on.

"It made him so happy to tell the stories. He said to me one time that sometimes he thought the world might be turned upside down and that if he thought about the stories enough, they might turn out to be true. Maybe they really happened and what we remembered was something else, a dream maybe, and we might go back over to Valley View Church and find Dora Hammond walking around healthy and happy as anybody. That's how far it went with him."

"Well, the congregation sure liked him," Charles said, feeling unsteady and foolish and awash in amazement at the whole scene—the story, the complete calm of the girl who told it, and her understanding of things beyond anything Charles had ever experienced.

"Yes, and he loved their love." She brightened. "But I'm happy to leave it. I never could believe it, you know. Even before Daddy started preaching those sermons where all the stories had happy endings, I didn't believe it. If God loved the world, why did my mother leave me? We're going to start a new life."

"What will you do, your father . . . ?"

"He has a brother who builds houses in Birmingham. They worked together before my father decided that God had called him to preach, but Daddy is a good carpenter."

"A carpenter!"

"Very appropriate," she laughed. "Just like Jesus, except that Jesus didn't get the chance to go back to the carpenter's trade."

Suddenly they both laughed. It was the image of Jesus giving up, going back to ordinary life. "Well, I enjoyed being King of the Jews for awhile, but the king business has its points and being a carpenter has its points," Charles said. They laughed insanely together.

They talked a long time, and the twilight covered over their talk and Rosy got up to leave. "Kiss me once before I go," she said timidly. Charles took her into his arms and kissed her warmly and dryly on the mouth. She clung to him and whispered, "I love you, Charles." Then she pulled away with a laugh. "No obligation intended." She went away swiftly, and he never saw her again.

No one understood why Charles had done what he had done, and Charles himself in the years that came afterwards looked back on that desperate post-Christmas journey with its seeking for truth as if it had all happened to somebody else. He thought of himself as a medieval man caught in hopelessness and anguish, embarking on the pilgrimage to Santiago like a barefoot pilgrim praying every step of the way that he would arrive at the mighty cathedral, be swept up in the thunderous adoration of throngs of the devout, see a magical glow around the head of the saint who presided over miracles. He had been reduced by then to knowing that he could never recover his faith either by willing it into his head or by the pretense that he had faith, a pretense that went along with his dogged resolve to get it back again. He knew that Paul not only had disbelieved in Christ but had raged against the new Christian sect and had persecuted it and put Christians to death. But then he had been struck by a vision on the road to Damascus, and God forced Himself into Paul's heart.

That was what he wanted, Charles thought—to find any proof at all that God worked in the world, that from time to time he stepped out from behind the veil of invisibility that hid his face and did something to show his presence and his power to those who sought him, however blinded they might be. No one could see God face-to-face and live. Charles knew that. Even Moses had to look on God's backside. But one could see God's mighty works, and God had done mighty works for Clifford Finewood in North Carolina.

Years and years afterwards when he stood in the great piazza before the cathedral of Santiago and looked up at its stone battlements and went inside and ritually embraced—while laughing—the head of the saint, he remarked to his wife that at least the pilgrims who made the long, long journey here had as a reward colossal size that one could very easily mistake for one of God's works. But when he arrived at the Valley View Baptist Church on the outskirts of Charlotte, North Carolina, he had found an ugly brick building with a white wooden spire set in a treeless lot behind a gravel parking area, and all of it testified to something almost tawdry and squalid. Then as he went around the neighborhood, telling people that he was a member of Mr. Finewood's present church and that he happened to be driving through Charlotte on his way to see an imaginary aunt on the seacoast of North Carolina, he discovered that all Mr. Finewood's miracle stories had been lies.

Not only had they been lies, but the members of his congregation had very little sympathy for him. Testimony of Gene Shoemaker, sole owner and operator of a crossroads general store and gas station a half mile from Valley View Baptist Church. Great talker, and Charles did not tell him that he, Charles, planned to enter the ministry. No, he put up a different front—the somewhat cynical tourist passing through wanting to check up on a man who told a lot of tall tales about things that had happened here. In short, Charles represented himself as what he was becoming.

"I mean, we could all tell," said Gene Shoemaker, sitting by the pot-bellied stove in his store, men from the neighborhood sitting around him, smoking, nodding, agreeing with him with a chorus of knowing grunts and smug smiles. "That slick young boy with the oily hair, living in that house, humping Finewood's wife right under his nose. She wasn't any beauty. I can tell you that. Poor Rosy took after her mother. Hell, I don't even know if Finewood was her real father. I mean, the wife—her name was Georgia—you could just look at her and know she'd been around the block a few times. She wasn't much to look at in the face. But she was bouncy, you know. Always had something to say. She was a fidget, you know. Always up and down, always moving. A woman like that is always aching to jerk her panties down, you know. She's always hot, and that was Georgia. She had a good-looking ass, and nice tits, too. Now, of course I never seen her with her clothes off, but a man can get a pretty good impression."

Nods and laughter.

"You know what they say about a woman with an ugly face and a nice ass. You throw a flag over the face and go for Old Glory."

Louder laughter.

"So you had this oily-haired Bible salesman living with them that summer, and Finewood would go to the hospital or come over to the church or go around visiting the sick, and I bet he wasn't more than a half-mile out of his driveway before that woman was leading the Bible salesman to a bed and throwing her clothes off like she was sowing wheat, and by God he sowed his seed. Hell, I bet he didn't sell fifty dollars' worth of Bibles the whole summer long."

"But the daughter? What did she do while—you know?"

"While the Bible salesman was fucking Georgia's lights out? Well, that was the sad part. Georgia would tell the daughter to go for a walk, go visit somebody. 'One of your little friends,' Georgia would say. Poor Rosy. She didn't have any little friends. So she'd go outside. Go for a walk. Go somewhere, off to the woods maybe or over to the church and sit on the steps. I reckon the kid didn't know quite what her mama and the Bible salesman was doing, but she knowed she didn't want to know. I always did figure that the one hurt the mostest by what they done was poor little Rosy."

"And then Mr. Finewood's wife—this Georgia person. She left?"

"I reckon she hoodooed that poor Bible salesman. Lord, she must have been ten years older than he was, but you know, a young man, having his first piece of pussy, he's likely to think it's forever. I reckon Georgia talked him into being in love with her. Anyway, they left. She left poor old Finewood a note pinned to her pillow, and she was gone. It like to have broke the man's heart."

AUGUST came again, and along with it a letter. Tempe's name and address: 122, rue de Grenelle, Paris. Nothing else. He was startled at how his heart lifted up at the meager sight of it. A resolution began to shape in his head. Go somewhere. Follow the example of Roy Kirby. Relieve the town and the county of having to think about Hope Kirby and everything else that had happened in this blindingly swift and tumultuous year. When people saw Charles, they had to think about things. When they read his byline in the paper, they had to think about things. When Charles called the presidents of the Rotary Club, the Civitan Club, the Clionian Club, the Lions Club to ask who was going to speak at their next meetings, and when he occasionally showed up to interview somebody who seemed especially interesting, people spoke to him guardedly, trying to keep themselves from asking him how he felt, whether he regretted anything, if he still feared Roy Kirby, if he would again have done everything the way he had done things.

Roy Kirby had disappeared. Paul Alexander carried about himself an aura of distinguished wisdom that persuaded people his version of events was the right one, even without argument. Roy Kirby had done the honorable thing, people decided. It began to make sense. Roy Kirby had understood that it would be wrong to kill Charles. A sin. When everything was said and done, Hope Kirby had started a train of events that brought the worst terror to Bourbon County that anybody had ever known. Maybe he should not have died in the electric chair. Arguments about his judicial death blew up now and then. But they were mild arguments. Nobody got angry in them. People were more likely to say, "Oh, maybe you're right." They said the same thing no matter what side they had argued. Hope was dead now, and his brothers had lives in the county, and they settled down to live them. At first they had seemed struck dumb by their father's disappearance. But as the days and then the weeks slipped away, they settled down to believing that yes, their father had left the county.

The sheriff pondered and doubted. But he could not arrive at a conclusion. The sheriff even got out with his dogs and tramped over all the land around Roy Kirby's farm. The rain that had fallen all that Saturday of Hope's execution had washed away any scent that the dogs might have picked up, but the sheriff thought he or they might pick up the smell of a rotting corpse. Shotguns were mean weapons. The sheriff didn't like them. You could bang the stock of just about any shotgun Roy Kirby was likely to have, and the thing would go off. Maybe it wouldn't happen with one of those high-class Brownings that big-time hunters used, but Joye and M.L. both said that their daddy owned a single-shot full-choke, twelve-gauge Iver Johnson, a deadly enough piece, one you could buy for maybe twelve, fifteen dollars in a Sears, Roebuck catalogue. Not a Browning or a Winchester.

Anybody could make a mistake with a shotgun, and if the shotgun was an Iver Johnson, even a skilled hunter could forget himself, and a twelve-gauge slug could make a hole in you big enough to pour water through. Maybe Roy Kirby had jumped over a fallen tree in the woods, and the gun went off. He would have hidden somewhere in the dark, back there in that great woods which from the air still spread surprisingly unmarred across Bourbon County's ridges. If he had moved in the dark, he could have stumbled just like anybody else, and the gun might have gone off, and that was the end of it. The sheriff remembered the Swanner boy, hunting rabbits on Thanksgiving morning and pulling a twelve-gauge through a fence, not doing more than banging the stock on the ground, and the gun went off, and lead shot went through the boy's gut as effectively as if he'd been machine-gunned. The other boy hunting with the Swanner kid called the sheriff in near hysteria, and the sheriff drove as close as he could to where they were and ran towards the screaming of the boy who wasn't hurt, and he took one look at the Swanner kid and knew he'd have a hard time talking to a couple of parents.

The sheriff ruminated over all these things, and he roamed the woods with Duke and Ugly, stopping often to sniff the air. But he found nothing.

At least Roy Kirby was gone, and people waited for Charles to go, too. Meanwhile Charles went on in the stolid and mechanical processes of life that had carried him along from the murders the year before. People marveled, not with admiration, that he seemed like a robot sometimes, showing no more feeling than a piece of metal. What he had said about Clifford Finewood at the association meeting was common property now. Preacher Finewood's departure confirmed it. Nobody had much of anything to say about it. But what Charles had said in addition, that nothing the Baptists believed was true, became more and more garbled. And people did not believe either that Charles Alexander had said what some reported he had said or that he meant it if he did say it.

Tommy Fieldston was glum and sullen, his business worse than ever and going down. Anybody who came into his hardware store got a lecture on Charles Alexander. Tommy was silent about Clifford Finewood. Oh, he had a conventional thing to say: "Judge not that ye be not judged." And he could sometimes add, "He did a lot of good." But he didn't want to talk about Clifford Finewood. He wanted to talk about Charles Alexander. He and Marlene joined in shock to put together a fairly accurate account of what Charles had said, and they repeated it to everybody, Tommy with outraged triumph and Marlene with a sorrow completely genuine and deeply felt. They could not succeed in evoking these feelings in any large number in others. So Tommy Fieldston became all the more outraged because people in Bourbon County were not outraged. He was coming to the conclusion that the county could not live up to his standards and that perhaps he should go into the deeper South to find true Christians—Mississippi or Alabama or Louisiana. Then he thought of Arceneaux, from Louisiana, and he rejected that state entirely. Well, then, South Carolina. Surely no place could be more Christian than South Carolina.

Now and then Charles ran into Marlene on the street. She looked at him briefly and sped by without speaking. He did not even turn around to see her disappear behind him. She became something strange in his mind. He remembered rationally that he had loved her, that he had been obsessed with her, but he could not re-create even a particle of the adoration he had felt for her. His lack of feeling for her was a surprise. In his careful, calculating, providential view of the world, she was exactly the woman God intended him to marry, and together they would have a great Christian ministry together and lead souls to Jesus, have lots of Christian children, and die in great old age in the sanctity of an accomplished purpose. Now when he thought of such things, it was as though he listened to a strange story told by a loquacious friend on the swaying deck of a ship in a distant harbor about someone Charles had never met, would never meet, and who served now only to beguile a long evening with the stars overhead and streamers of light washing in uncertain variation on the gently swelling and falling waves. Years later when on occasion he turned for amusement through the television channels that specialized in religion, he saw Marlene, heard her familiar voice, listened for a moment, and surfed on without regret or any other feeling except quiet astonishment.

Meanwhile out at Varner's Cross Roads the bulldozed hundred-acre plot intended to become a mall went back to nature in the quick and vital way that nature does these things. Throughout the summer tall grass grew up out of the red earth, and briars crept along the ground, and seedlings blown over from nearby maple trees took root by the dozen, unimpressive little twigs rising out of the earth by the end of the summer but enough to demonstrate that the mall was no more and that the expensive draining and grading had been for nothing.

Jane Whitaker held on to her job. She did it by blackmail. "You fire me, and I will tell this entire town what you've been doing to me for the last ten years. I'll stand up in church and give my testimony and ask God to forgive me, and I'll ask God to forgive you, and when you try to lie about it, the whole world can see the lie written on your face in letters a hundred feet tall and lighted up with neon."

It was bad enough for the bank to lose a hundred thousand dollars at a time when that was real money. But it would have been worse to have Jane Whitaker get religion in the way she threatened, and J. Pauley Oliver had enough sense to know he could never convince his wife that Jane was lying.

But having lost so much money, Jane was resolved to get it back, or at least to be sure that the bank did not lose any more money because of bad loans. Summer was a slack time for the newspaper. Flush times would not come again until the new-model cars with accompanying ads came out in September. By August Red was behind again, and Jane Whitaker seemed to concentrate all her anger in one little white-hot dot that she pointed at Red Eason as if he were made of lead and she determined to melt him down to type to be set in a press and pounded until all his identity wore off.

Early one afternoon she came raging into the office almost beside herself. "Goddammit, Red Eason, I'm tired of these bad checks. I'm so tired of them that I'm not even going to think about covering them." She threw them into the air and they flew like confetti before the blowing of the fan. Myrtle looked up from her desk, and Charles looked up from his, and Red looked like a criminal condemned at the dock to be hanged in public by the neck until he was dead. "And you know what? Everybody who took one of these checks has the right to put you in jail. I am sick of it."

Her rage went on unabated for a long time. A few people entered the office while her tirade went on. They quickly left again. The crew from the shop out back came in to see what was the matter, and when they saw that the matter was Jane Whitaker, they quickly fled again and went back to the job presses, whose clatter drowned out the noise Jane made and brought the printers the peace of ceaseless noise.

When Jane ran down, Red, doggedly holding his ground, looked at her with resignation and calm. "Jane, if I had an offset press, I could run more photographs. I could make the paper look a lot sharper."

"Why the hell are you telling me that? Do you think I give a precious goddamn if you have an offset press or if you draw every goddamned edition of your paper with a Crayola crayon?"

Again Red let her run down. "If you would lend me another ten thousand dollars, I could install the best press in a weekly newspaper in East Tennessee, and I could run lots of photographs and get lots more ads and have a design that would bring in more readers. This is the age of pictures. You can't give people just gray type anymore. They have to have pictures or they won't buy the paper."

Jane looked at Red with a shock so great that she might have had apoplexy on the spot. "You son of a bitch. You can't pay the mortgage you have, and you write six or seven bad checks a week that I have to cover for you, and you want to borrow more money."

"That's about the size of it," Red said. "I have to have some money before I can make more money. And the only person who can give money to me is you."

Jane's face turned an even more violent red. For a moment she had difficulty speaking. She seemed to jog some air back into her lungs by taking a furious little walk back and forth in front of the counter. "Before I give you another nickel, I will see you rot in hell. No more bad checks. If I cannot see you rot in hell, I can at least put you in jail."

With that she hurtled out the door, slamming it with such force that the glass rattled. Red looked around and lifted his hands in a gesture of helpless resignation. "Well, I suppose that's that. I guess we will have to close down."

"Oh, Red!" Myrtle cried. Her face was all in commotion, and she threw herself into Red's arms and hugged him while she wept wetly on his shoulder.

Charles sat looking on the scene and felt something more certain than any conviction he had had in a very long time. The rest of the afternoon passed mournfully. It was a Monday, and the paper had to be got out, but by press time at three all the print-shop men knew that this would be their last edition for a while. The knowledge did not lend itself to gaiety. The Miehle horizontal press, as though wishing to add to the spirit of the occasion, broke down, and Jim and Red managed to blacken their shirts and their trousers, not to mention their hands and their faces. The pressmen cursed the machine and life in general, and for a time all of them forgot that the paper stood in danger of closing and they of being laid off for at least another month until the ads for the new cars came in.

Finally the press was repaired, the paper was printed and folded, and the kids who came in to distribute the paper had their sacks filled, and off they went shouting and carousing. Red went back to his desk and fetched a bottle of whiskey out of a drawer and poured a tot for everyone into little glasses brought out of the same place, no two of them alike. Charles stood with the other men and, when Red looked at him somewhat interrogatively, picked up one of the glasses, and Red poured him more than a tot. Like most people who drink whiskey for the first time, Charles did not like it, but when it reached his stomach and began to warm him, he discovered that he could adjust to the taste in exchange for the effect. Myrtle said that of course she seldom drank anything stronger than beer but that since this was a sad occasion, a bit like a funeral, she said, she would have a little just to keep the men company. When Red in a pouring attitude offered the bottle for a second round, Charles took his turn along with the rest, and Myrtle did not bother to discuss her customarily abstemious habits.

The men and Myrtle found places to lean against or to seat themselves, and they talked, and Lloyd's name came up, and his life was reviewed, and Myrtle said that she thought Jane hated the newspaper because she and Lloyd had broken up, and Jim suggested that if only Red were not already happily married, he might have attached himself to Jane, and the paper would have a money supply that would be unlimited. Red shook his head at that remark in an attitude that suggested he would rather be tied to the back of a train and dragged over the tracks to New Orleans before he submitted to the fate of courting Jane Whitaker, and Myrtle remembered her as a girl and commented that Jane had spent so many years taking care of her ailing mother that she had missed out on real life. Red said that the word at the Civitan Club was that Old Man Oliver was furious with Jane for losing a hundred thousand dollars of the bank's money on that crackpot mall business. The upshot was that Jane was now so afraid of losing more money that anybody who wanted a mortgage to build a new house might as well go to Knoxville to get it because First Bourbon County Bank was not going to be lending money to anyone for a long time.

Red did not offer a third round, perhaps because the contents of the bottle had been so depleted that there would not be a tot for everyone, and one by one the men bestirred themselves and set out for their homes. Myrtle was one of the last to go. She planted a damp kiss on Red's cheek before she left, and she wept again as she went out the door. Red and Charles were left leaning on the counter, Charles feeling light-headed from the effects of the whiskey and, more than that, anticipating the rest of the evening, yes, anticipating it very much.

"Such a good bunch of guys," Red mused, half to himself. "And Myrtle, too. She's one of the guys. No more loyal soul in the world."

"Too bad she never married," Charles said.

"Oh, she marries every time she covers a wedding," Red said. "It's her wedding, or if it's not hers, she writes it up with her own in mind. You can tell sometimes when she doesn't think something is right. The Dickson boy getting married in a purple tuxedo. Myrtle thought that was tacky. Her groom would wear black."

"I'm sure he would," Charles said.

Red sighed. "I've had a great time here. If we shut down, I'm going to miss it."

"I don't think we will shut down," Charles said.

Red looked at him. "I thought you'd decided not to be a preacher."

Charles frowned in puzzlement. "What do you mean?"

"Well, you're making a prophecy." They laughed.

"It's just an intuition," Charles said. "I think she will lend you the money."

"For the press?" Now Red seemed uncomprehending.

"Yes, for the press."

"I was joking," Red said. "I wanted to make her madder. It was just something I thought of at the moment."

"But if we had a new press we *could* run more photographs, and we *could* put out a larger-sized paper, and we could do a lot more."

"Yes, and if I had wings I could fly home tonight rather than drive, and if I were rich, I could buy a Lincoln and have a chauffeur to drive me home and sit around all day on his ass in my Lincoln waiting to drive me wherever I ordered him to go."

They laughed again.

"How much would a new press cost?" Charles said. Red shrugged. "How the hell do I know. Ten, fifteen thousand dollars. You don't buy them by the dozen, I'll tell you that. I've got to go home. It's late."

It *was* late—almost seven o'clock.

"I'm going to hang around a little while," Charles said. "I'm going to let the whiskey wear off. I've never drunk whiskey before."

"Hell, we should have celebrated, then," Red said. He hesitated. "Charles, I'm glad you're not going to be a preacher. It didn't seem right some way, you joining up with that crowd of nincompoops."

"Arceneaux wasn't a nincompoop," Charles said.

"No, he wasn't. But he left it too. Lord God! I reckon that's the biggest scandal ever to hit First Baptist Church. Just walked out on them. That took some guts."

"Why?" Charles said. "He's rich. He can do anything he wants."

"He shouldn't have ever wanted to be a Baptist preacher," Red said. "I'm going home. Lock up when you leave. Say, I just heard something amazing. Hugh Bedford is leaving Bourbonville for good. He's moving to New Orleans."

New Orleans! The words fell in the room with a soft clatter. Red and Charles let them lie without further comment. New Orleans. Arceneaux was in New Orleans.

"It's a strange world," Red said. That was his final verdict on the matter. He went out the door and shut it behind him. Charles was left in the office alone.

*I*T *WAS* past eight-thirty when Charles left. He sat for a long time at Lloyd's desk, exactly where he had sat a year before in the wee hours of August 9. He pondered things, the whiskey seeming to make his thoughts roll smoothly through his mind so that no matter how bad the thought was, he did not reproach himself for it and indeed considered it, weighing its pros and its cons. When at last he did stand up, he was not sure that he had made any decisions. He did turn his key carefully in the lock, and he stood for a while in the twilight that was darkening into night, and he thought about the year just passed. Yes, a year ago to the day he had walked around the corner of the courthouse into Hope Kirby's pistol. The terror of that night swept over him briefly, like a spasm of fever, as if it might happen all over again. But the spasm left him, and he remained apathetic and tired.

The town was quiet. The last show at the Grand Theatre up on the square had already begun, and he could see Glenda Rowe sitting in the glass box office counting the money taken in during the day. A few people passed on the street and spoke guardedly to him, and he returned their greetings somewhat curtly. He no longer had it in him to greet people with an effusive smile, to inquire about their families, to make small talk about the weather or about football or a birth or a death. The courthouse loomed up in front of him, its clock tower illuminated and showing its great white eyes to the world. It really was a beautiful courthouse, Charles thought. Nothing could take that way.

Charles shifted a thick manila envelope under his arm. He did not want to get it sweaty.

He walked across the courthouse yard, taking the same track he had taken that night a year before, and the '37 Ford sat parked at a slant in the same place where it had been. He wondered if any atoms of Kelly Parmalee's blood might still be found under the grass growing where he had fallen, and he thought with a sense of bemusement that he could not be certain of the exact spot where Kelly had slumped to his knees and looked up beseechingly in the gloom as Hope Kirby put the pistol in the poor man's mouth. He supposed that Abby's beautiful body and Kelly's less attractive one were both in advanced states of decomposition now. Once he thought about writing a story about undertakers, and he interviewed Mr. Robinette. Mr. Robinette was flattered and took him around the mortuary and showed him the instruments and let him smell the embalming fluid to dispel the rumor that it stank, and he said very frankly that the best embalming fluid in the world wouldn't keep a corpse whole more than about six months. After that, decomposition inexorably set in. Mr. Robinette spoke with the tones of a doctor clinically describing an exotic disease. Charles decided not to write the story. He couldn't think of any way to make it upbeat. Red liked upbeat stories. Later Charles read Jessica Mitford's *The American Way of Death* and thought that he had missed an opportunity.

He went to the '37 Ford and opened the door on the driver's side and got in, placing the envelope carefully on the seat beside him. For a moment he sat with both hands on the steering wheel. He was sweating, and the wheel was slick to the touch, and he knew that his hands would be dirty when he had driven a little while. He sat thinking, then reached down and pushed the white starter button and heard the rebuilt engine roar smoothly to life. He eased the car out of the parking spot and went around the square and turned right on Broadway towards Dixie Lee Junction.

All the way out of town he told himself that he could go on home, leave Bourbonville, leave everything behind, get a new start somewhere, forget all this. But at the place where the road from the dam came into the highway, he turned right, and then he turned immediately left onto the narrow blacktop that led towards Martel. The smells of a humid summer night in the country drifted through the open windows. He drove slowly, thinking that just before Martel he could take the Muddy Creek Road and come back to Highway 11 and go on home. But he remembered his conversation with Red, his prophecy. He drove on. The railroad ran alongside the blacktop Martel road. He heard the horn of an approaching train and looked up to see the flashing light of the diesel electric engine on number 35 roaring towards him. The streamliner, called the Tennessean, an all-stainless-steel coach train that ran between New York and Memphis. The train roared by him, the railroad slightly elevated, and Charles had a fleeting glimpse of well-dressed people sitting in the diner looking out on the darkened land. He knew his headlights would be a flash of yellow in the night and then gone to these people forever, scarcely noted and forgotten in an instant. Tomorrow morning most of the passengers would get off in Memphis. At seven in the morning a northbound section of the Tennessean would call in Bourbonville and roll towards New York.

He drove up the driveway to Jane Whitaker's house through thick trees. Like the Alexander home at Dixie Lee Junction, the driveway led around to the back door so that if you went to the front door, you had to make an effort. Charles sat there wondering which door to take and thereby postponing things, and Jane opened the back door and looked out.

"Who's there?" she called.

"Charles Alexander," he called, getting out of the car.

"My invitation to you isn't good anymore," she said. "Get out of here."

"I'm not here to accept your invitation," he said. "I'm here on business. You'd better see me."

"That sounds like a threat," she said.

He came to the door. It was slightly raised, and he stood below her, and she looked down on him, one hip against the door, her arms still folded. She was wearing pants, called pedal pushers in those days, and a T-shirt, and Charles could see her nipples bulge in the T-shirt so that he knew she was not wearing a bra.

He held the manila envelope in one hand and raised it to make her look at it. "I'd like to show you something," he said.

She shrugged in bad humor. "I hope it's money," she said.

"I think it may be worth a lot of money," he said. He forced himself to meet her steady gaze with a steady gaze of his own.

"Christ! Come on in, preacher boy."

"I'm not a preacher boy anymore," Charles said.

"That's what I hear," Jane said. She turned from the door, her arms still folded, and went to her kitchen table. It was a nice kitchen, fixed up in a modern way. Charles had heard that Jane had remodeled the inside of her house so that it might have been built last month, and she had all the latest appliances. She even had a dishwasher, and next to it was a Bendix automatic clothes washer. Charles stared. All her life his mother had washed dishes with her own hands, and her washing machine was one of the old-fashioned kind that had wringers, and she carried the wet clothes out of the basement and hung them on a clothesline outside.

Jane sat down, keeping her arms folded under her breasts. She seemed to be unconcerned with her breasts. Charles tried not to look at them. She gave him a mocking look.

"Sit down, preacher boy."

Charles sat. He started to say to her once again that he was not a preacher boy, but he knew there was no use.

For a moment they sat without saying anything. Jane eyed him in her commanding bitterness and scorn. Outside the screened windows the noises of the forest went on, a monotonous roaring of insects singing away the night. Otherwise the silence was so profound that he could hear the splashing of Muddy Creek over its rocky bed in the shallow valley below them.

"I hope I didn't scare you," Charles said, falling back onto a habit of civility that he had tried to renounce.

"Why should *you* scare me?" Jane said, not disguising her contempt.

Charles faltered. "Well, after the priest—"

"Oh, him," Jane said, as if she had no more interest in the matter.

"Look," Charles said, plunging in and keeping his eyes on hers so he would not look at her breasts. "I'm here to talk to you about the newspaper, about Red."

Jane's face turned fierce. "I thought that sniveling bastard might have sent you out here for that very reason," she said, raising her voice and unfolding her arms. "You go back and tell that fire-headed son of a bitch that he can crawl out here on his hands and knees, and the answer is still no. The county doesn't need that shitbox of a newspaper. We could do with a throwaway advertising supplement. Do you think half the people in the county ever look at the thing?"

"We have a circulation of over three thousand homes," Charles said.

"Three thousand homes. How many homes do you think there are in the county, preacher boy?"

"I don't know," Charles said.

"We have thirteen thousand homes in this county. So you reach three thousand of them. Shit. If we had a throwaway shopper, we could put one on the doorstep of every house in the county, and we'd have something."

"The county's growing," Charles said. "Anybody can see that. We almost had a mall."

He was deliberately provocative, and he succeeded. Jane's face turned violently red again. "We almost had a mall. And what happened? A hillbilly murders his wife and a decent man who never did any harm, and the case makes the papers all over the state, and banks decide they won't lend us the money to give the mall a chance. You know what it was? It was like strangling a baby in its crib."

"I don't think it was that bad," Charles said, taken aback in spite of himself by the fury of her outburst.

"You don't think it was that bad! Of course you don't think it was that bad. It wasn't your baby."

"We wrote a lot of stories about the mall. We did our best to help."

"And you wrote that stupid sentimental story about tearing down a barn built in 1820. Listen, Charles, do you know where all the people are who built that goddamned barn in 1820?"

"You've already told me," Charles said. "They're all dead."

"You're goddamned right they're dead. And we're alive. We had a chance to lead the nation, to do something right here in Bourbon County that would go down in the history books. The first enclosed shopping mall that was a little city to itself. You wait and see. In twenty years they'll be all over creation. We had the chance to build one here that would have brought tourists in from five hundred miles away just to see it. And you had the sentimental gall to write a lot of shit about a barn built in 1820. You asshole. I'm tired of talking to you. I want you out of my house."

She stood up. Charles did not move. He looked at her with a calm that amazed him. "Sit down," he said. He was still holding the big manila envelope. He gestured with it.

She looked at it, and perhaps then something banged in her memory. She sat down slowly, staring at him, her mouth slightly open and her mood decidedly changed.

Charles opened the clasp on the envelope and turned back the fold and reached inside for the photographs. He had brought only photographs of Jane. He spread them across the table. She gasped and turned pale.

"I have not brought the negatives," he said.

"Lloyd . . ." Jane said, when she was finally able to speak. The single word came out like an obscenity or else like the most damning blasphemy ever spoken by a mortal. "That bastard! That bastard!" And she began to cry.

This was the worst part of it for Charles. He was of a generation of Southern males, perhaps the last generation, who could not bear to see a woman cry and who, if one cried in his presence, felt bound to soothe her and to stop her tears as though his maleness had elevated him to a paternal authority over the weaker sex. But he held firm in his purpose. Perhaps the whiskey helped. He now folded his arms over his chest and looked down at the photographs himself—Jane Whitaker in eight different positions that revealed every orifice and showed with unquestionable clarity that she enjoyed it all.

Jane sobbed in the choking and gasping lamentation of a woman doing her best not to cry but overcome by a rebellious body that would do what it had to do. "And to think that I loved the bastard!"

"He may have kept them because he loved you," Charles said in what he supposed later was an effort to sound like one of the grave actors who explain the motives of a disappeared character at the end of a movie. It was not a successful dramatic moment. Jane screamed at him, an incoherent cry of rage that made Charles look around in fright because he expected such a howl to bring neighbors rushing to her aid from miles around. She regained control of herself and spat out hateful words, the tears still streaming down her cheeks.

"Love me! You stupid little asshole. You think Lloyd loved anybody on earth but himself?! Lloyd cared for nobody. Nobody. He was like the North Pole; he thought the whole world revolved around him, and he was cold—as cold as any ice at the bottom of the Arctic Ocean."

Charles could not look at her. He sat with his arms folded, looking down at the photographs, and he waited.

"So what do you want?" Jane said after a very long time, controlling her voice now so that it came out as though the words were steel bars cut to measure.

This was it, Charles thought. "Red needs a loan to buy a new press. He needs a loan to float us to the end of the summer and to do some remodeling in the shop."

"And so he sent you to blackmail me."

"He doesn't know I'm here. And nobody has seen the pictures but me."

"How many times have you beat your meat over them, you little rat?"

Charles felt himself turn red, and he could not reply for a moment. Jane laughed cruelly. "So you found these damned things, and you've been beating your meat over them like a twelve-year-old. A fine preacher boy you are. Have you licked them?"

"No," Charles whispered.

"They're not very satisfying after a while, are they? I kept a photograph of Lloyd after he kicked me out. I used to look at it and masturbate and try to imagine that he was in me. After a while I realized it was no good, and I tore the photograph up and flushed it down the toilet."

"I'm the only one who has seen these pictures. But Red needs a loan."

Jane made a sudden motion, seizing the T-shirt she wore at the bottom and quickly stripping it off over her head. She sat there bare-breasted in front of him. "Have you ever seen a woman's real breasts before, you little rat?"

Charles looked away and shook his head.

"But you've felt them, I bet."

"Once," he whispered.

"Here, feel mine, preacher boy." She reached out and seized him by the wrists and pulled his hands towards her and clamped them over her breasts. They were firm and warm. He opened his fingers and felt her nipples in the palms of his hands.

"You've never fucked a woman!" Jane yelled at him.

"No," he said. "No." He wanted to say, "And I will not fuck you." But he was helpless.

"Come on then," she cried, and she jerked him up from the chair and pulled him like a rag doll into her living room and across a little hallway into her large bedroom and began tearing at his shirt. He heard the buttons go flying, and then she was jerking his T-shirt over his head and in a wild commingling of arms and legs and mouths and tongues and hands they were doing the act that evolutionary biology created for the propagation of the human race against all the enemies of procreation, including various carnivorous predators that could fall on the mating couple when they were so help-less before attack, and all the restraints laid on by religion and society because the passions released in fucking were so powerful that they were obviously dangerous, and the jealousies struck into green flame by the mag-nitude of this act were clearly sufficient to reduce humankind to a state of primitive nature where the life of man or woman was inevitably solitary, poor, nasty, brutish, and short.

And it was just at that moment that Charles had an irresistible desire to pee. His bladder seemed ready to burst. "I need to go to the bathroom," he gasped.

"You men! You get on the mark and have to pee first. You're all alike. It's over there."

She gestured indifferently towards a wall with two doors and lay lan-guidly naked back on the bed.

"So, my blackmailing friend, how much money does Red want to bor-row?"

"Thirty-five thousand dollars," Charles said.

"Thirty-five thousand dollars!" Jane was so startled that she sat up with a jerk in bed, aghast. He could see the shape of her breasts in the reflected light of stars and a rising moon. And then she screamed, "No! Not that door." It was a piercing and haunting cry that made Charles's skin crawl. He whirled to look at her. She was scrambling out of bed. But it was too late.

Hanging neatly inside on wooden coat hangers were two large black suits that for a moment Charles took to be some sort of costume, and then he saw the two stiff white collars wrapped around the necks of the coat hangers, and he realized that he was looking at the empty cassocks that had belonged to a large priest.

He stepped back in horror. Behind him Jane burst into a sobbing that she did not try to contain. He turned and stared at her. He was naked, and his mouth was agape, and he trembled so that he wondered if he could keep standing. But he thought that if he fainted, she would kill him.

"He loved me. The whole county was making fun of me, but he loved me. At night I sleep with his cassocks. I can still smell his body in them. No one else can smell it, but I can."

"You kept him here while he was killing those people?"

"They deserved to die! That horrid old judge. Those stupid jurors. They ruined everything. Everything."

"You tried to lure me outside my house. You knew he would kill me, and you called to me, and it was all pretense. He didn't force his way in here. You went with him willingly."

"You wrote about those old barns. You ruined my mall. You helped ruin everything." She held her arms out to him. "Come back. I'll make it all up to you."

Charles fled, gathering up his clothes on the run and racing barefoot for the '37 Ford. He had left the keys in the ignition. He drove away naked, racing the car up the narrow dirt road that led into the hills between Martel and the river where cedars stood thick and dark against the lightening summer sky. Pulling off onto an overgrown wagon track that might once have been used by loggers, he dressed himself, discarding the shirt that had been torn to shreds. "I will say I was hot," he said. "It's perfectly normal to drive around in a T-shirt."

Red got his new press. It was a beauty, and suddenly the circulation of the *Bourbon County News* jumped from three thousand to forty-five hundred. There was no more trouble with the mortgage. Charles did not even feel troubled in his conscience. What good would it do to put Jane Whitaker in jail where she belonged? Some good can come out of evil. And what better revenge than to force Jane Whitaker to raise the mortgage! As it turned out, the investment in Red Eason turned out to be the most successful one she made in 1954, for Red's sudden prosperity made him invest more in other new equipment, so that by 1960 the *News* won an award for the most thriving semiweekly or weekly paper in Tennessee. He never knew the circumstances that changed Jane Whitaker's mind.

Jane herself changed. She joined a Bible class and became one of its most devout members and so passed into being a respected lady of the community who proved that such things as quiet religious conversion was possible. She aged gracefully and softly and even with a sort of saintly air into old age, and so she was when the story of Hope Kirby burst again into the news in 1994.

Charles's life settled into relative simplicity. The first major move was to step down from the boat train at the Gare Saint-Lazare in Paris. He could see the top of Tempe's head. And then they looked at each other directly. The first thing she said to him was this: "I don't want any of our children to be called Chuckie. It's either got to be Charles or Cornbread."

"I like cornbread," he said.

*H*E HAD a good life, as it turned out. He became known and respected among archaeologists. His articles appeared in the right professional journals, sometimes mentioned in the *New York Times* and in *Time* magazine, and his excavations at Thebes were lauded as brilliant examples of modern scientific archaeology at its best. He did not become the writer that

Lloyd predicted he would become, for he never wrote a novel, and although he tried his hand at short stories sometimes in the spring digging season when he had worked all day long, he was usually too tired to concentrate on making up characters, and besides, he had reports to make and drawings to check. The annual expeditions always included a professional draftsman to make precise drawings of their findings, but Charles liked to do some of that work himself, and he came to be very good at freehand drawing.

Tempe said he was an artist at heart, and sometimes he sketched her and his sons, and now and then he sketched his colleagues and some of the Greek workers who labored on the site. The Greeks let him use prisoners from their jails. He found that they were excellent workers because if they failed him, he could send them back to the monotony of prison. Sometimes he sketched them and often gave them their likenesses, and they felt elevated and called him O Kalliteknis, the artist, and he was pleased.

He became fluent in Greek, although he always apologized for his grammar, but the Greeks said that did not matter. No Greek knew much about grammar, and the main thing was to understand. Paul Alexander came over now and then, bringing Guy with him, and they stayed for a month at a time, Paul observing the excavations with his profound silence and sometimes going off on excursions of his own, while at the same time reclaiming kinship with his surviving brother and sister and their spouses. They and their children revered him as a god.

Sometimes at night while the children were still young, Charles felt moments of the deepest contentment he had ever known in his life. He bought a stucco house in the town, and on many spring and summer evenings Charles sat late at one long table with his father, with Tempe, with his three sons and their two English tutors, and with a couple of his foremen, and once in a great while with Stephen, who came rarely to Greece and in fact went rarely anywhere but the farm where he stayed, and they drank retsina and a little ouzo and carried on conversations in three languages. Perhaps it was the warmth of the evenings or the seeming stillness that stopped time from moving, but Charles felt that all was right with his world, and Bourbonville and the county became as distant as blue mountains seen across a long and sweeping plain in Thessaly where all was strange and familiar at once.

Wherever he was he subscribed to the *Bourbon County News,* and now and then Red wrote a flattering story about him, something he had rewritten from some notice of what Charles was doing.

Yes, it was a good life, he thought, and it was good, too, when the family went back to Cambridge in the late summer and stayed there through the autumn while Charles lectured on archaeology—very wittily, his students said in the evaluations that they started keeping on teachers in the 1960s—and he worked hard in his office in the Peabody Museum to put together his reports from the spring and summer dig and to make sense out of the patches he had been able to excavate of Mycenaean Thebes. A very satisfying life. His sons grew up and did well in life, and best of all they laughed when he said funny things, and they were much adored, and they loved their parents in return. When his father died in 1988, and Stephen found the manuscript his father had so carefully written of his life, the two brothers, turning through the crisp white pages written in their father's fine hand, looked at each other with wry revelation. "He doesn't even mention us," Charles said.

"Well, it's not about us," Stephen said. "It's about those ghosts, you know."

"Do you think he really saw ghosts?"

Stephen shrugged. "If he says he saw them, I believe him."

The main thing they discovered was that their father knew how to keep secrets but also felt some strange compulsion to write them down. "He must have known that we would find it," Stephen said. "He doesn't mention us, but you know, he must have written it for us."

"Do you think Blackie is our brother, then?" Charles said. "Shouldn't we share it with him?"

"He looks a lot like Dad," Stephen said. "But no, we should not tell him." And they did not.

*T*HE FIRST break in the mystery of the disappearance of Roy Kirby came in the summer of 1987 when some boys swimming illegally in a rock quarry near the river dived deep and found a pickup truck standing on end at the bottom. The doors were open. A suitcase had lodged inside. An abandoned car at the bottom of a quarry was nothing new, but the boys knew cars and saw in their watery vision how perfectly preserved this model was, and they told the sheriff.

It was a new sheriff by then, but former sheriff Myers still spent some days of his retirement loafing around the jail swapping yarns with the new man. The pickup truck brought back Hope Kirby in a rush. Sensing publicity, the young sheriff, a Vietnam vet named Dick Crawley, had the truck hauled out of the quarry. The records left no doubt: this was Roy Kirby's truck. "I knowed he never left the county, but where did he go?" Sheriff Myers puzzled with his successor.

But there the matter rested. No one could answer that question. The mystery of Roy Kirby's disappearance remained, but it fell into the background, something that only his sons cared about, and they did not care about it in public. On the rare times when he came home to Bourbonville, Charles took a bouquet of flowers by night up to Hope Kirby's grave at the Red Bank Baptist Church. He stood there sometimes wondering if Hope's unquiet spirit might take human form out of the dark and strangle him there among these silent graves. But the graves remained silent, and the air remained empty of any human form except Charles, and after a few years, his rite of the bouquet became a ritual that always pulled up in him an almighty feeling but never left him afraid.

Then in the fall of 1994 the last surviving Talliaferro died in New York. Bourbon County had forgotten his existence. So had nearly everyone else in the world. He lived a reclusive life on the Upper East Side of New York City. He had made a lot of money, and he still had a lot of money even after three wives had claimed their part of his treasure. Even with three wives he died childless and with a will, and the will required his body—all expenses paid, of course—to be shipped back to Bourbonville and to be buried in a vault in the family tomb at the Salem Baptist Church.

So was the mystery of Roy Kirby finally solved.

The funeral was to be on a Saturday morning in October. The *Bourbon County News* ran a big story about the event. Red had long since retired, but one of the reporters—there were six reporters working for the paper now, and it was a big-time operation—went up to his house and interviewed him, and he recalled the Talliaferros and their tomb as best he could, which was pretty well, and he said he had supposed that no one else would ever be buried there. The editor of the paper, a zealous young man from Ohio who had now become more Southern than Senator Klaghorn, called on the county to turn out for the funeral since it would be a time to honor Bourbon County's past. Besides that, it was only decent and proper for people to be present to see an important personage like Luciano Talliaferro to his family's eternal resting place, given the melancholy circumstance that no member of the family could be present.

The mayor of Bourbonville, a shallow and somewhat ridiculous man with a whiny voice but an imperishable yearning for power and authority, decided that the occasion merited a patriotic speech about tradition, the Puritans, and all those devout people who had made America what it is. The pastor of the Salem Baptist Church, a thumping young graduate of the Criswell Baptist Seminary in Dallas, Texas, named Steven Greenleaf, decided that this funeral would be an excellent opportunity to proclaim the virtues of Italian Baptists who had bravely withstood the oppressions of the pope through many centuries.

Glenn and J. D. Snappit, Bourbonville's leading undertakers, viewed all this with a genial cynicism, knowing that if Luciano Talliaferro had been destined for a mere hole in the ground in one of the cemeteries in Bourbonville, they would have had to scratch around mightily to get a preacher to do the burial, and the crowd would have amounted to three people standing around a grave. As it was, the brothers, who now buried more people than any other undertaker in town, took great pride in their work. The body having arrived in a sealed coffin by train on Thursday morning, they drove down to Salem Baptist Church on Friday morning to be sure they could open the tomb and to be sure, too, that an empty vault remained inside large enough to receive the corpse in its coffin.

They found that the large brass ring in the door of the tomb was somewhat corroded, but it was solid brass after all, and one of them tried the wheel, striving to turn it counterclockwise, and when it resisted him, another grasped it with him, and the two of them gave a mighty wrench, and the wheel turned as smoothly as it probably had on the day it had been installed much more than a century before. The Snappit brothers assumed that the heavy marble door might be impossible for the two of them to move, and they were already discussing the prospect of getting some help from around the neighborhood to pull it open. But one gave the door a slight, experimental pull, and the brothers discovered that the long-vanished architect and builder of this startling edifice had done their work with astonishing art, and the door opened as if it had weighed only a few ounces.

Naturally enough the brothers looked straight ahead, into the depths of the tomb where the vaults lay in their rectangular ranks, and Glenn had already started to step inside, his eyes raised to what he thought looked like an empty place, when J.D. seized him by the arm and said, "Great God Almighty! Look here."

At their feet near the door lay a mummified corpse sprawled on its side. The skin had sunk dryly into the bones in the airless vault, but the clothes that the corpse wore were still remarkably intact. Next to the body at some little distance lay a shotgun as if it had been flung away, and as the undertakers studied the scene, one brother said, "Look. Whoever it was shot himself. You can see the bullet hole in the bottom of his jaw. And look here. The bullet came out the top. Look at that hole in the top of his skull."

Someone produced a pocket flashlight. He carefully stepped over the corpse and flashed the light around. He bent and picked up a shapeless chunk of metal. "It's a slug from a shotgun," he said. "He loaded the gun with a slug and he killed himself."

They looked at the door. "There's no handle on the inside," Glenn said, noting the obvious absence. "Somebody locked him in here. And he killed himself."

They carefully shut the tomb up again and drove back into town to the sheriff's office. The sheriff went back quickly with the brothers and looked the thing over. "God knows how long he's been in here," the sheriff said. He took some pictures and said they'd have to call a medical examiner before they moved it. But very carefully he went through the pockets of the corpse. In the front shirt pocket was a folded page from a newspaper, and when the sheriff spread it out on the ground outside he saw it was the front page of the *Knoxville Guardian* for Friday, June 18, 1954. The left-hand headline on the page announced that the governor had refused to grant Hope Philip Kirby a pardon.

"I've heard about that case," Sherriff Crawley said.

He closed up the tomb again, went back into town and roused the doctor who did medical examinations for the county, and drove out to the lake to talk with Coondog Myers. Coondog was in his eighties now, and he spent part of every day fishing from a pier down in front of his house. He was sitting down there more than half asleep under an umbrella with his line floating in the water when Sheriff Crawley came up, showing the respect a young man ought to show for someone old enough to have fought in the Ardennes. He told Coondog what the undertakers had found, and Coondog shook his head slowly.

"Goddamn," he said. "I'm dumb. I should have looked there. But that morning when we came down there with that posse, the first thing I did was check that tomb. I tried the door, and I could tell it was shut up tight."

Sheriff Crawley went down on his haunches and pushed his hat back on his head. "Well," he said. "I tell you what's clear as the nose on my face. Somebody locked him up in there and left him to die. Now I wonder who did that?"

"Jesus H. Christ," Coondog said. "I feel so dumb. He must have been still alive when I got to that parking lot that morning. He must have been. Jesus H. Christ."

"Whoever locked that door committed murder," Sheriff Crawley said.

"Jesus H. Christ," Coondog Myers said. "But whoever done that probably saved Charles Alexander's life. And more beside. McNeil would have gone after the whole Kirby family if the old man had carried out his plans. It all worked out."

"But he killed himself," Sheriff Crawley said.

"He couldn't call for help," Coondog said. "It was a point of honor."

SO BOURBON County had another sensation, a mummified corpse resurrecting the memories of an affair buried almost irrecoverably in the now sparse collective memory of a county where maybe half the population came from somewhere else and perhaps two-thirds of that half came from the North in search of mild winters and summers where the heat did not broil the life out of you. They shopped at the huge new Wal-Mart just outside of town and bought their meals at Burger King. Stephen telephoned Charles with the news, and Charles took the call standing in his kitchen, amazed and troubled and also foolish. Anyone should have thought of it, he said. And how long had Roy Kirby stayed in the dark hopelessness of that tomb before he decided he had to kill himself? Most important of all, who had locked him up in there to die, and who had left him there without telling anyone what he had done?

Roy Kirby's body was buried next to Hope's up at the Red Bank Baptist Church in Richardson's Cove. Several hundred people attended. It was the age of celebrity, and for a moment a corpse forty years dead was a celebrity. People wanted to be in on it. The TV cameras were there, and local TV "personalities" told the story breathlessly again and again, looking into the cameras as if they had uncovered a mystery that ranked up there with the resurrection of the dead. A couple of TV stations and several radio stations in Knoxville called Charles in Cambridge, but he refused to talk to any of them. Tempe answered the telephone and politely told people Charles was not available and hung up. Finally she took the telephone off the hook.

Stephen was there to be hounded, and he was good-natured about it, but he could not add anything to what people already knew. Joye Kirby had been reduced by age to a skinny and bent furnace of anger against Charles Alexander and against the world, and he swore with vehement and profane conviction that Hope had been with him and Love all night long on the night of the murders back in 1953 and that his brother had died an innocent man, and now his father was another victim of that miscarriage of justice. Joye raged when he faced the cameras, and his words came out so slurred that it was hard to understand him, but anybody could understand the anger, and naturally some people thought that a man wouldn't say such things with such conviction unless they were true.

But Love would not talk to anybody, and his daughter Pleasant came to the door and faced the cameras and said her father would not be making any statements. Love had become religious in his old age after his wife died. He went to the Pentecostal church and spoke in tongues when the spirit seized him, and he never talked about the case. John Sevier was dead. M.L.

shrugged off the cameras and the reporters, and although they followed him around his farm (he was long since retired) and did their best to make him talk about his father and his brother Hope, he preferred to talk about cows. He kept extolling the superiority of a Black Angus over a Hereford until the reporters got tired of this bovine preoccupation and went away, leaving M.L. grinning.

Charles did not come home again until the following summer. He slipped into Knoxville on a plane, rented a car, and drove out to the farm and stayed several days with Stephen and his wife. Their children were gone now, out in the world, doing well, and Stephen was doing good deeds for the neighborhood and still playing the piano when the occasion arose. They sat until deep in the night, time and again going over the whole case.

"I bet it was Arceneaux," Stephen said.

"Arceneaux! Why Arceneaux?"

"Just a hunch."

"That doesn't make any sense."

"Sure it does. He was there the morning we got to the church, already there sitting up front by himself with Finewood sitting across the aisle from him, and the two of them looking like they could freeze each other to death with a glance. Arceneaux got there early. He saw that the door to the Talliaferro tomb was open. He slipped around and went up and turned the wheel and locked it."

"You don't think Roy Kirby was so dumb as to leave the door cracked, do you?"

"How else was he going to hear when you came up?"

They argued awhile about the tomb, and there was only one way to settle the question. They drove down to Salem Baptist Church a little after daybreak. That was a time to avoid any visitors. The tomb was still drawing its crowd of rubberneckers, Stephen said. They came to look and take pictures. They were a nuisance.

It was the first time Charles had been there since the morning of the association meeting. Not far away they could hear the hum of traffic on I-75 crossing the big bridge across the wide river. A glut of filling stations and fireworks stands cluttered Highway 11, and the road out along the river to Salem Baptist had been paved with asphalt. Otherwise things looked remarkably the same, except that now the church had a signboard with an inspiring message in bright, blue lights across the top. THIS CHURCH BELIEVES EVERY WORD OF THE HOLY BIBLE. Well, that was not much of a change in spirit; the signboard was new, electrically illuminated and expensive, just like the sign out on Highway 11 that announced the church's presence to tourists passing by and yearning for a solid Baptist church where they could find God. The message atop the signboard was permanent. The changeable message set within the signboard itself was in white lights, like those that flash the scores in stadiums. DON'T CALL IT ABORTION, CALL IT MURDER.

It was a clear, sunny morning, and everything looked bright and hopeful. The two brothers went up the elevation to the tomb, and Charles tried the brass wheel on the door. It turned smoothly, and when it had turned all the way and they heard the steel bolt withdrawn from the marble jamb, the door remained in place, and anyone looking at it would have supposed it not only shut but locked. "The sheriff went up and tried the door that day," Charles said. "I remember. I turned around and watched him go up. He got his boots muddy."

"But he didn't try to open it," Stephen said.

"No, he gave it a pull and a turn, then turned it back again. It was locked."

"And Roy Kirby was inside, and he chose to die rather than speak up and tell the sheriff to turn the wheel and let him out."

"He wasn't the kind to call for help," Charles said. He pulled the door open. Talliaferro vaults stretched rank on rank beyond them into dimness. There must have been twenty of them. Charles stepped inside and looked around, his eyes adjusting. "You know something? This thing doesn't smell dank. It's dry in here. I bet all the bodies in those vaults are mummified, just like Roy Kirby's, and their clothes are as fresh as they were on the day they were buried."

"So in the great resurrection of the dead, they will all be well dressed," Stephen said. The brothers laughed.

"We still don't know who did it, who shut him in here," Charles said.

"It was Arceneaux. I know it was Arceneaux. He was in the OSS. He knew about such things."

"People in the OSS didn't go around locking Germans and collaborators in tombs," Charles said.

"I'm sure it was Arceneaux."

"He's probably dead by now," Charles said. "Otherwise we could ask him."

They shut the tomb and turned the brass wheel to lock it and went back to Stephen's house. They made coffee and sat moodily drinking it. And on a whim Stephen picked up the telephone and called New Orleans information. "Arceneaux," he said. "I'm looking for the number of a Lawrence Arceneaux."

The operator was gone for a moment, and then a computerized voice took over: "The number is . . ." Stephen wrote it down. "I'll be damned," he said. He handed it to Charles.

"It might be a son," Charles said doubtfully, looking down at the chit of paper.

"Call the number, damn it!" Stephen said.

Charles called the number. The telephone rang five times. "He's probably on a trip," Charles said. He realized as he spoke that he did not want to talk to Arceneaux; he did not want to relive those days. He was about to hang up when the phone was picked up on the other end.

"This is Lawrence Arceneaux," the voice said. It was an old man's voice, quavering a little.

"Is this the Larry Arceneaux who used to be pastor of the First Baptist Church in Bourbonville?"

A pause and breathing. "Who is this?" The voice was not friendly.

"Mr. Arceneaux, this is Charles Alexander."

Another long pause with breathing. "What do you want?"

And Charles had an inspiration. "I'm going to be in New Orleans for a few days. I wonder if I could come by to see you."

"I'm afraid I'm not well," Arceneaux said. "I have Parkinson's."

"I'm so sorry," Charles said. "Well, I wouldn't stay long. Could I stop by your place?"

A hesitation.

"Please," Charles said. "I would love to see you."

"All right," Arceneaux said after a long wait.

"Could I have your address?"

"My what?"

"Your address." Charles shouted into the telephone.

Arceneaux gave it to him. Charles hung up. "You're going to New Orleans?"

"Why not? It's a great town."

C*HARLES* had to change planes in Atlanta. The huge airport was crowded with men and women who should not have been wearing shorts but were. Americans were not pretty as a people, he thought. They had to be the fattest people in the world. The only fat people in Greece were occasional old women, and not many of them. In airports Americans had a smug look, as if they were proud of themselves for being able to fly and proud, too, that they knew their way around.

Charles flew enough to get himself upgraded to first class on the flight into New Orleans. He sat by a fat man in a Georgia Bulldogs T-shirt. "I tell you, I wouldn't sit back there in steerage for anything on earth," the Georgia Bulldog said. "You know, people don't shower enough, if you ask me. If you sit back there, you get all the sweat they haven't washed off. I take two show-ers a day. I'd be mortified if anybody was ever to smell my body odor."

Charles took out a book and began to read. The Georgia Bulldog seemed miffed. "You going to read?" he said.

"Yes, I have to finish this book," Charles said.

"Why?" the Georgia Bulldog said.

"Because I'm dying to know how it comes out."

"Is it a mystery?"

"No, not really."

The Georgia Bulldog leaned cumbersomely over and stared at what Charles was reading.

"My God, it's in a foreign language!" he said. "And I thought you was an American."

"Well, you never know, do you?" Charles said. He went on reading, hop-ing he had been sufficiently rude.

In New Orleans he called Arceneaux. Then he took a cab to a little hotel just off Canal Street in the French Quarter, checked in, and within fifteen minutes was in another cab on his way to Arceneaux's address. It was in the Garden District. Charles had not been in New Orleans often. A convention or two. Once he had taken a cab out to the New Orleans Baptist Theologi-cal Seminary to look at what his life had almost been. It was a dreary-looking place, located (as Tempe had said years before) in a pecan orchard. He thought about pissing on the front door of what looked like the main building, but he decided that an arrest by the police would be more trouble than being able to tell what he had done might be worth.

So he was in New Orleans again, and it was hot, and waves of humidity rolled across the still landscape, and the live oaks hung with moss. When he got out of the air-conditioned cab, the heat almost prostrated him. It was not like the summer heat in Greece. He climbed the steps to a nice-looking house with an ornate front door and a broad, roofed porch across the front. He rang and heard the bell chime in the interior of the house. A black maid came to the door. She was a pretty young woman dressed in black and white, the maid's costume you used to see in movies made in the 1930s.

"I'm Charles Alexander," Charles said.

The maid gave him a brilliant smile and put out her hand. "I'm LaToya," she said. Her fingers were smooth. "Larry is expecting you."

Charles thought that if anybody knew how to surprise, it was still Larry Arceneaux. LaToya led him into a large living room, elegantly furnished. The house was air-conditioned and pleasantly cool without being cold. She went out, and Charles was left standing for a moment, and then Larry Arce-neaux came in, pushing himself in a wheelchair. He still had a full head of hair, but it was now a brilliant white, and his body trembled and shook. Charles shook his hand.

"I'm sorry to see you like this," Charles said.

"Not half as sorry as I am, but you get used to it. I keep telling myself to enjoy today because it will be worse tomorrow, and Lord knows what it will be next week." He gestured toward a chair just as another man came in. Charles and the new arrival looked at each other. The man laughed sardonically, and Charles remembered that he had known somebody with a laugh like that, but he could not think where it had been.

"You remember Hugh Bedford," Arceneaux said.

"Hugh Bedford, of course. Yes, of course I remember you." Charles put out his hand. For just an instant he thought that perhaps Hugh wouldn't take it, and all those years rolled back, and Charles felt covered with shame. But then Hugh put out his hand and took Charles's and gave it a firm squeeze, perhaps intending to hurt him.

"I guess now we say it's been a long time, and you're looking wonderful, and all that shit," Hugh Bedford said.

"Well, it has been over forty years."

"That is a long time," Hugh said.

"And here we are, two old queers getting uglier by the day," Arceneaux said in a quavering voice with a jerking laugh. "Only they call us 'gay' now. Well, I felt a lot more gay when they used to call us queers, and sitting here in this wheelchair makes me feel a lot more queer than I did back in Bourbonville."

"Oh," Charles said.

LaToya came in pushing a cart with bottles and glasses and an ice bucket. "I thought you might like a little toddy, Charles," she said.

"Well, I would if you will join me," Charles said.

"Oh, we don't drink," Arceneaux said. "I've even forgotten what the stuff tastes like, and Hugh's not had a drink since we left Bourbonville."

"Well, maybe I'll have just a little one," Charles said. "Bourbon."

LaToya had the makings, lemon and sugar. She made him a toddy. Charles sat trying not to look startled, but he was surprised.

"You didn't know we were queers, did you?" Arceneaux said.

"I didn't think about it," Charles said.

"So, do you think about it now?"

"Look," Charles said, shaking his head impatiently. "I teach at Harvard."

"So that means you never think about queers," Hugh said. LaToya handed him a glass of orange juice. It had a straw in it, and Hugh held the straw tenderly to Arceneaux's lips. Arceneaux took the straw and drank in jerks.

"It means we have a lot of gays at Harvard. And in Boston. I've had three friends die of AIDS." He realized when he spoke that he sounded as if he were bragging.

"So you're tolerant," Hugh said.

"I don't care what people do with their private lives," Charles said. "It's none of my business."

"It's a very good thing you decided not to be a preacher," Arceneaux said, sighing. Hugh held the straw out to him again, and Arceneaux drank some more.

"Hugh takes care of me," Arceneaux said. "Who would have believed it? I always thought I'd have to take care of this big lug, and he has to take care of me, and I'm younger."

"I'm sorry you're not well," Charles said. "I really am."

"I am, too," Arceneaux said sadly. "I never expected this. I'm thankful I have Hugh."

"I never suspected," Charles said. "I mean, when you were in Bourbonville. I guess I was too naive to think about such things." He stumbled. "I'm glad it worked out for you. For you both."

"Well, it did," Arceneaux said. "It worked out better than I dreamed."

They were silent and reflective for a moment. Charles wondered that he did not hear the air-conditioning system running. It seemed completely quiet. Beyond the shuttered windows the sounds of the occasional traffic in the streets were muffled and distant. Charles cleared his throat.

"I came here for a reason," he said. And he told the story about Roy Kirby's body.

As he spoke, he knew that he had been right. Arceneaux was as surprised as anybody. "We don't keep up with people in Bourbonville," Hugh said. "For obvious reasons."

"And so many crazy things happen in New Orleans, it puts a screen around us," Arceneaux said, laughing wryly, his voice quavering but forcing the words out with long pauses between them. "You know. Like intercepting radar. A mummified body found forty years after its death in a tomb can't get through the tourists who get killed walking through our old graveyards above ground and the whores who get into knife fights in the Quarter and the mayor who goes to a funeral and steals the silver dollars off the eyes of the corpse."

Charles sighed. "I thought maybe you had done it," he said to Arceneaux. "I thought maybe you got there early and saw Mr. Kirby and shut him in."

"I wouldn't have left him in there to die," Arceneaux said.

Charles pondered this thought.

"Besides," Arceneaux said in his hesitant, wrenching voice. "I didn't get there first. Your friend Finewood and that daughter of his were there when I got there. The girl was asleep on a pew in the back of the church when I came in."

"Finewood." Charles felt a pang that was akin to terror.

"He looked bedraggled. Well, you remember how he looked. But then he always looked as if he'd slept in his clothes," Arceneaux said.

"Oh God, I hope it wasn't Finewood," Charles said.

Hugh shrugged. "You never know," he said.

"I wonder if it could have been one of the sons," Arceneaux said.

"His sons!" Charles said.

Hugh nodded gravely. "Hope didn't want you killed. He said that to his brothers, and I heard him say it to the old man. He said it several times. And he was serious about it. He didn't want the old man to kill you."

They sat in a wonder of thought, puzzling over the impossible.

"Which one of them?" Charles said.

"Well, it wasn't Joye, I can tell you that," Hugh said. "I think if Joye hadn't had a wife and kids by that time, he'd have killed you himself. He hated you."

"He still does, so my brother says," Charles said.

"He had a right, you know," Hugh said. There was nothing forgiving in Hugh Bedford's voice.

"Yes, I know," Charles said.

"So it could have been M.L. or Love," Arceneaux said.

"It was John Sevier," Hugh said.

"The loony?" Arceneaux said.

"The loony."

"But he couldn't talk. He was like a big mechanical doll," Arceneaux said, having more difficulty with his words as his excitement rose.

"What am I thinking of?" Hugh said. "It couldn't have been any of them, unless it was early Friday. They were all in Nashville by Friday night. I talked to them. And then with Hope at the prison, first thing Saturday morning."

They all paused at the thought of Hope and those long-ago events. Then, in the manner of people who hadn't seen one another in a long time, they picked up the threads of conversation.

Charles stayed for dinner. The three of them fell into a loquacious babble that seemed to be a balm against both the wounds of time and those older wounds that had bled so many years ago. LaToya brought out a bottle of Bordeaux, a 1961 Saint-Julien that was the best wine Charles had tasted in his life. Since neither of the men drank, Charles had almost a whole bottle to himself. The cook, a sturdy black woman of a certain age, came out and took a bow after Hugh summoned her. Arceneaux said her mother had been his mother's cook for years.

Arceneaux apologized because their adopted son was down on the plantation. "He loves it down there. Of course he's not really adopted. A couple of old queers like us can't adopt a child in Louisiana, but we raised him in our house, and he's the heir to all we own, including the plantation. So if my father's spirit is around somewhere, he ought to be happy."

They came back to the question of who could have sealed Roy Kirby in the tomb, as though to a garden that had to be cultivated again and again. By late in the evening when he had drunk brandy, and they had talked it through at least four times, adding details and variations, Charles was almost convinced they would never know.

It was unsatisfying. The last thing that Charles thought of before sleep swept over him was that it was all sad, a mystery that would never be revealed. He was the beneficiary of it. There could be no doubt about that. But life had no proportion to it. It unraveled. The patterns were lost. You were left finally with uncertainty. Everything is as it is for no reason at all, and if everything were different there would be no reason for that either.

CHARLES went back to Harvard. He would retire in 1998. He'd be sixty-five then. Students got younger and younger. Every time he looked in the mirror he felt how much older he was getting. Odd, he thought, that he was not as afraid of death as he had once been. He had a kind of immortality. All those monographs on Thebes. Nobody could dig in Thebes without mentioning the name of Charles Alexander. Sometimes Thebes depressed him. Too many modern buildings sitting on buried ruins of the ancient city. Charles sometimes found himself wishing for a good, clean earthquake—the kind that would not kill anybody but would shake everything down in Thebes and make the authorities build the city elsewhere. The problem of ancient builders: they selected too well. Time could bury a city, and the serially dwelling inhabitants had no reason to change the location. They kept smoothing out the ruins and building on top of them. If he had been born in the nineteenth century, he might have pulled enough money together to do what the French did at Delphi. They moved the whole village from off the ruins to another site. Then they dug up the ancient town, and the village of Delphi nearby became rich—at least by Greek standards. But you couldn't do that sort of thing anymore. The TV cameras would be on the spot, filming weeping villagers who would then raise the price beyond what any archaeological service could pay.

The digging season passed, and Charles worked hard, but at night he sat sipping at a little ouzo and sometimes smoking a cigar, and he thought about Bourbon County and the implacable dissatisfaction of not knowing who had intervened, not knowing who had killed Roy Kirby to save Charles's life. Very often he thought that he had not given enough back. He should have written a great novel or discovered an unplundered tomb filled with riches untouched for thirty-five hundred years. He should have entered politics, been elected president. He should at least have accepted one of the frequent invitations he had received in his younger days to become president of this or that college, and who knows? He might have reformed education in his time.

It was not that he wanted to be any of these other things. The only way he could measure the success or failure of his life was the feeling of satisfaction that came to him sometimes like the refreshment he felt from waking from a deep sleep after a day of wearing himself out with bending and unbending, the physical labor of the archaeologist done not with pick and shovel but with tweezers and whisk brooms and scrapers. He loved all that, and when he retired from teaching, he would keep doing it. He thought working crossword puzzles was a ridiculous waste of time, and he wondered that some people faithfully did the crossword in every day's edition of the *New York Times,* and he'd seen people on airplanes with crossword-puzzle books open on their laps, working one after another as they crossed the Atlantic. Why didn't they read a book and learn something they did not know?

Yet archaeology was a puzzle. You started putting pieces together, and a picture slowly came into focus, but with maddening gaps. So you kept looking and kept thinking, trying to arrive at some sense of completion, even if it took years, and then you looked at the calendar, and you discovered it had been just that—years since you started working on the puzzle you had started when you could deceive yourself into imagining that you had eternity to work. It was an irony, Charles thought. He had been racked by the fear of death when he was a young man, when Hope Kirby stood in front of him with the pistol cocked and death less than a second away. But he had never thought what it was like to be old, to be slower, to feel time running out even if you were healthy and alert. The math was implacable. When you got to be sixty, you had to get busy because time was short, short, short. And sixty-five? Lord God.

The end of the mystery came in a letter, thick, neatly written in longhand with a fountain pen and not a ballpoint and addressed from Alabama. It was from Rosy Finewood.

Dear Charles:

You will be surprised to hear from me after all these years, but
it's time to confess my sins to someone, and since you are most
involved in them, I confess to you, my beloved priest. You were so
good to me in Bourbon County that I have never forgotten it, and I
have reason to believe that before he died Daddy was grateful to you,
too, although he never said so. At the same time he never in his life
said a reproachful word against you.

To be brief and to say the most important things first. I locked
Roy Kirby in the tomb. I'm sorry he felt he had to kill himself, but I
understand it. He did himself and the rest of us a world of good.

I have thought often with a slight sense of wonder that I was a
murderer as a teenager. I put it in such harsh terms to make myself
aware and perhaps guilty for what I did. But the fact is that I have
never felt guilty at all about it. I teach Greek and Latin at a local and
very pretentious private school where once in a great while I can
hope a young Sophocles will come along. It is a pleasant fantasy, and
I am happy with it and happy to feel much of the time genuinely
loved by my students. I am sure you know that satisfaction.

I teach the Oedipus story—shocking down here in Alabama, but
since it's a classic, I get away with it. In the end the Eumenides must
take over, and violence must cease its malignant tracking from one
person to another, from one generation to another. I knew the town
gossip, that Roy Kirby ordered his son to kill poor Abby (she did my
hair for nothing) and her lover, and I knew he would kill you, and he
would die in the attempt and then others would die. I thought and
think that there was something mad about him. On our last day
together when you kissed me I knew Roy Kirby was locked away and
that you were safe, and I felt a happiness that I cannot describe. So I
shall go to my Maker with unrepented blood on my head. I will argue
my case looking Him directly in the eye, and I shall ask Him what
kind of God He is to make a world like this where so much good
comes to a bad end and the innocent or nearly innocent suffer such
horrors as they do. Some of us have to do what we can to make up
for His mistakes, and I killed Roy Kirby with a sense of triumph.
Well, I begin to sound like an Amazon or bloody Athena on the fields
of Troy. But I speak the truth about myself.

It happened like this, a complete accident as so many things are
in this world. Daddy still had friends at the old church in North Carolina. They did not communicate after his disgrace there, but they
were still friends, and one of them called the week before the associa-

tion met that Saturday. He said he had thought and thought about your visit, and he knew you meant no good by it. He pondered it all for months. Finally he decided to let Daddy know that you had been there and talked for a long time. Daddy knew right away that you would expose him, and he was conscience-stricken. He understood then why you had stopped coming to church. He knew somehow by intuition that you would not let the debate at the association go without telling his story because he saw how committed you were to the other side. He wondered whether he should take a chance and continue in the debate and pray that you would remain silent, or stand before the association and confess his lies and take the consequences.

It all turned on a whim. The night before the association met he woke me up about midnight and told me we were going down to Salem Church. He thought that if he spent the night in prayer, God would tell him what do. And that is what we did. You know these little country churches used to be unlocked all the time. He parked the car in a grove not far from the church because he said he didn't want some curious person like the sheriff to come nosing about and interrupt a sacred session. We went inside in the dark, and Daddy got down on his knees at the altar and prayed to God with all his heart.

I was a sleepy little girl hoping he would confess and release us from the bondage of his lies and let us go somewhere else and quit preaching and live normal lives. You will remember that a storm blew up that night. I always have loved watching a storm come. So I slipped out of the church and went over near the tomb and found a canopy of honeysuckle where I thought I would be dry if there wasn't much rain, and there I was when I heard Roy Kirby come slipping out of the woods and turn the wheel on that old mausoleum.

It all came on me in a minute. I knew that Mr. Kirby had gone inside the tomb and would stay there until morning to kill you. I waited until the first patter of rain began, and I knew what I had to do, and I did it. I pushed the door of the mausoleum shut as hard as I could, and I heard and felt him struggling against me from the other side. But I was stronger than he was, and I got the lock engaged, and that was all there was to it.

The rain began to pour down then, and I ran into the church. My father started praying out loud then, crying to God, and I was thankful his fervor had waited, and do you know what I did then? I curled up on the back pew and went sound asleep. Such a conscience I had!

When I woke up, Mr. Arceneaux was there, too. Funny how men so different could have the same whim. I suppose he had come to pray too. But there was no more praying aloud, and perhaps the spirit abandoned them both.

I follow your career through *Archaeology* magazine, and every time I see your name, I feel that I have helped add a measure of good to the world. Then I think that so many people saved your life along the way that I can take only partial credit. Hope Kirby, Roy Kirby, and I all had a hand in making you what you are, and I hope you believe as I do that mine was the most important hand of all. You and Tempe helped me endure the worst time of my life. Tempe exists only in my mind, and I still talk to her. You are flesh and blood, and I will always think of you with love and gratitude.

Yours ever,

Rosy Finewood

Charles could not speak when he had finished it. He gave it to Tempe, who wept. "She gave us everything," Tempe said.

"Do you know," Charles said, "I feel a relief I never dreamed of, a weight lifted that I took for granted so much that it was part of me. For years and years I expected Roy Kirby to come out of nowhere and kill me. I didn't creep about, but sometimes I thought, *It could happen.*"

"It's a strange story, and you lived it," Tempe said.

"It was all an affair of honor," Charles said.

"Then I am glad I am not an honorable woman," Tempe said. She laughed her wonderful laugh then, and they laughed together, and they wept together. It was finally all over.

A Note About the Author

RICHARD MARIUS was born and grew up on a farm in East Tennessee. He received his bachelor's degree from the University of Tennessee and his doctorate from Yale University. After teaching history at Gettysburg College and the University of Tennessee, he headed the Expository Writing Program at Harvard from 1978 to 1998.

An Affair of Honor is the third of a loose trilogy of novels set in fictional Bourbon County, Tennessee, the first two volumes being *The Coming of Rain* and *After the War*. He is also the author of a fourth novel, *Bound for the Promised Land;* two major biographies, *Thomas More* and *Martin Luther;* and a style book, *The Writer's Companion*. He edited a book of Civil War poetry and was the editor of several volumes in the Yale Edition of the *Complete Works of Thomas More*.

He died in 1999.

A Note on the Type

THIS BOOK was set in a type called Baskerville. The face itself is a facsimile reproduction of types cast from the molds made for John Baskerville (1706–1775) from his designs. Baskerville's original face was one of the forerunners of the type style known to printers as "modern face"—a "modern" of the period A.D. 1800.

Composed by Stratford Publishing Services,
Brattleboro, Vermont
Printed and bound by Quebecor Printing,
Martinsburg, West Virginia
Designed by Virginia Tan